CROWNS OF CRIMSON VOWS 1
LEGACY OF LIES & WINGS
T.M. CARUANA

Also by T.M. CARUANA

Midnight Wolf Curse Series

Dragon Assassin Academy Series

The Blood Bender Rebel Series

The Arakzeon City Series

Legacy of Lies and Wings, is a work of fiction. Names, characters, places and incidents either are the product of the author's imagination or are used fictitiously. Any resemblance to actual persons, living or dead, events, or locales is entirely coincidental.

First Printing: October 2025
KDP Publishing
ISBN: 9798299407419

ACKNOWLEDGMENTS

I owe thanks for this work to the countless authors whose works have inspired me and given me the strength to continue my career as I've been encouraged by every book I've ever read. Without the support from the author community and my family, this book wouldn't have been brought to life. I wrote this book with much persistence, late nights and too much coffee applying all my patience and stubborn belief that stories matter and are a great escape for many people.

I want to express my gratitude to my husband who has allowed me quiet moments in solitude to enable me to shape the ideas and put text to pages.

To all those readers who have always believed in me and expressed how much they have enjoyed stepping into my worlds, I can't thank you enough for making my dream come true.

DEDICATION

To those who fight for good and never give up.
May love, fantasy and magic be your sharpest weapon
and your strongest shield.

Die with honour,
or fight to survive another day!

Character List

White Wing Territory

Brandon Emille – King of the White Wing Territory
Miriam Emille – Queen of the White Wing Territory
Arnold Desry – King Emille's Counsellor and Lola's father
Lucka Pontus – King Emille's Counsellor
Wallan Denor – General of the Special Missions Unit
Lola Desry – General of the General Missions Unit
Harvey Coraly – Captain of the Special Missions Unit
Thomas La Roy – Captain of the General Missions Unit
Zayd Watson – Camp Leader of the Special Missions Unit
Collin Mewer – Camp Leader of the Special Missions Unit
Rhie Neville – Camp Leader of the Special Missions Unit
Seon Nar – Camp Leader of the General Missions Unit – Air Force
Terry Ward – Camp Leader of the General Missions Unit – Cavalry
Rella Tomason – Camp Leader of the General Missions Unit – Infantry
Emroyce Bengrey – Childhood friend to Angelica Coraly
Fern Bengrey – Emroyce Bengrey's younger sister
Robin Bengrey – Fern Bengrey's son
Valentina Karson – Childhood friend to Angelica Coraly
Zoe Hammerton – Angelica Coraly's best friend
Kate Pere - Childhood friend to Angelica Coraly
Mazdon Pere – Kate Pere's older brother
Brian La Roy – Captain Tomas La Roy's younger brother

Black Wing Territory

Ben Blackbone – King of the Black Wing Territory
Jonathan Murben – King Blackbone's bodyguard
Nick Nesso – Spymaster for King Blackbone
Valence Daffron – Commander of the Guards
Jason Davis – Sergeant at the Military Base
Duke Patrick Hartmore – Duke in the Banaly province
Duke Wallard Finningham – Duke in the Cathdear province
Nassara Finningham – Duke Wallard Finningham's daughter

BLACK WING TERRITORY
DORMONDAR
UPPLAND
LORD MALINGER'S MANOR
MILITARY BASE
DUKE FINNINGHAM'S MANOR
CATHDEAR
BLACK CASTLE
DUKE HARTMORE'S MANOR
BANALY
IRON FORGE
LORD GASTLING'S MANOR

WHITE WING TERRITORY
SPIRITS' TREK
ABARATH
PHARANIR
PANSERY
KABRY CITY
HARBOUR
BENSGUARD
SUMMER
COTTAGE
KATAGOON
CANDIR
DASHQAZ
GAITHBRY
EMENDROTH
EMENDIR

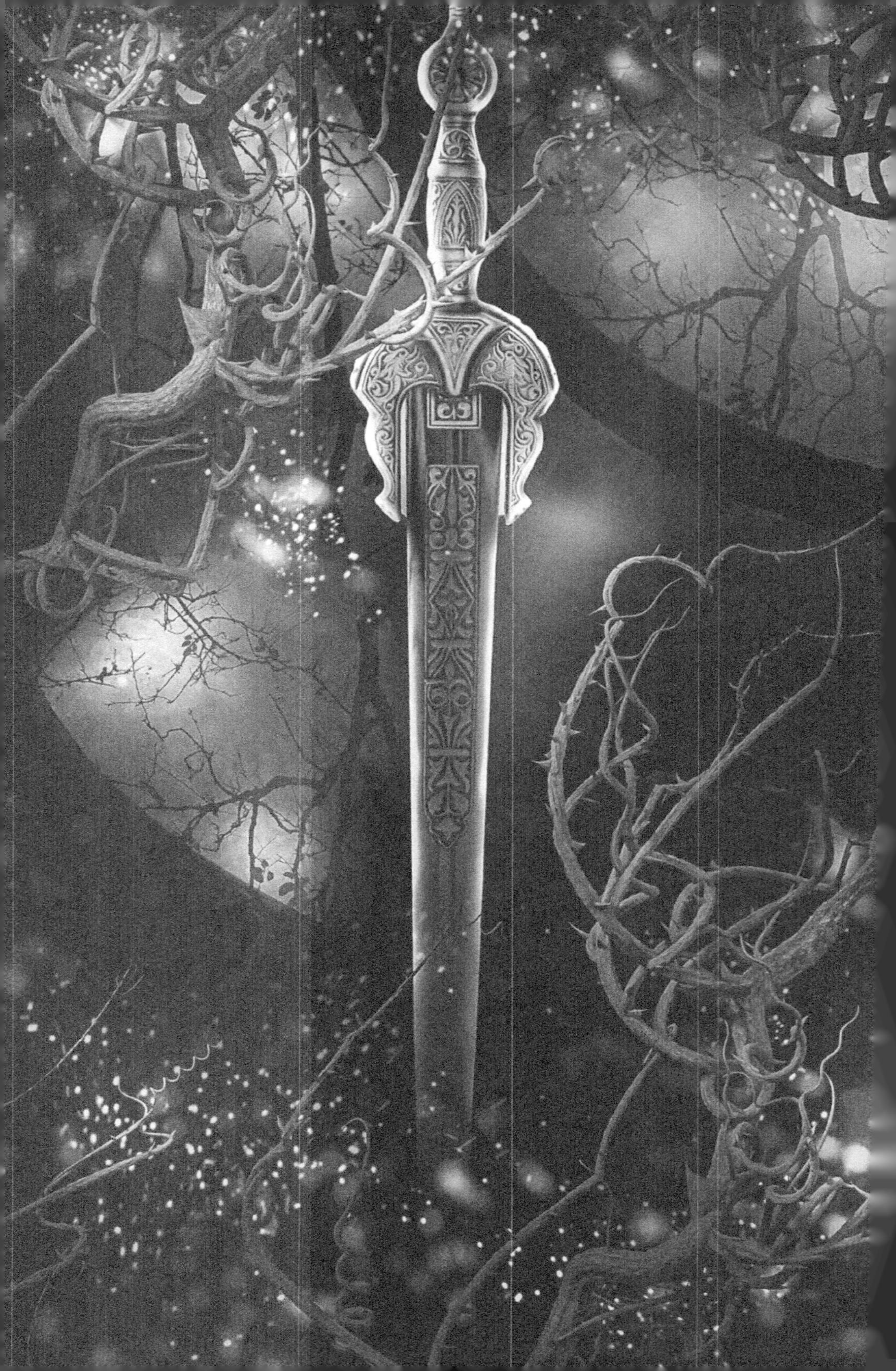

1

The Black Blade called to me. It fucking stole my soul – almost, enthralling me to come closer. Its magic caressed against my pale skin, a seductive pulse of raw power, stroking my cheeks like a forbidden lover. Inside its glass case, the sharp blade gleamed under the dim lights of the vault. The hilt, a masterpiece of braided black iron, hummed with the promise of destruction.

Finally, the sword was within my grasp. It had taken me two bloody years of undercover work in enemy territory to find it, and I swear I had thought it would be the end of me. *Still could be!* This was the boldest gamble I'd ever wagered with the Spirit of Death!

But I needed this blade. It was the only thing that could kill the enemy king for good.

I tightened the leather cord around my blue hair, tying it back in a swift, practised motion. I licked my lips. *Focus. Steady hands. No missteps*. My heart thundered, a war drum pounding in my chest. Slowly, I cracked open the case, careful not to trigger the military base's security system. If I tripped the magical trap, alarms would bring a horde of black-wing guards down on me before I could take my next breath.

Adrenaline pumped like a maelstrom in my chest. My fingers slid across the braided black hilt full of ancient runes, like I was possessed by its spiritual magic. This sword was said to have once belonged to the Spirit of Magic herself. Death by an ordinary black iron blade gave the chance for repentance, reincarnation, but not this one; this blade was dangerous. Lethal. It should also have been better guarded against intruders who used the vent to get inside this room.

Their mistake.

My victory.

The moment my fingers wrapped around the hilt, a sharp jolt of power shot up my arm, and an icy sensation quickly worked its way through my veins. I gasped as the magic coil around me like tight shackles.

I pulled the weapon off its stand.

And then…

Sirens screamed on all sides, the blue strobes in the room flashing like lightning trapped in a bottle. A door flung open behind me.

Damn it!

A furious guard stepped through the door from deeper within the supposedly most impenetrable military base of the Black Wing Territory. *Yeah well, they'll have to redesign the vent system if they want to claim that.*

Cold, grey eyes sparkled with anger and immediately locked on me like a hawk.

Spirits! He really did not look happy.

No time to waste.

I bolted.

I ran to the wall with the pried open vent. The Black Blade, crackling with untamed power, was already sheathed at my hip as I launched myself toward the vent. My boots grazed against the wall first, kicking off for momentum. Fingers latched onto the open grate, and I hauled myself up, twisting into the cramped space just as the guard grappled for my feet.

"Stop!"

Too late.

On my hands and knees, I crawled fast through the small space. But the guards were on my heels, making a racket in the space between the tin sheets through which their bodies would barely fit to crawl.

Hunted, my skin tingled with excitement as magic flared to life. I took the next left, not having a clue where either the right or left led me. Panic had jumbled my orientation.

Adrenaline burned through me, sending my heart into a wild gallop.

Another junction. Left, or right? No time to think.

I chose left.

Then I prayed; prayed it wouldn't lead me straight back into the belly of the beast.

Zoe had better have sent my backup squad!

A blade struck the wall near my feet. It sparked as iron hit tin, lighting up the tunnel with orange flares. Heart racing, I had one second to yank my boots to safety. The chase didn't allow for any hesitation. I had to make quick decisions and stay a turned corner ahead of death. Because this was a chase for life or death for all of us. Because they knew as well as I did that if I stole the blade on their watch, the black-wing king would kill them.

Moonlight beckoned at the end of the tunnel. I worked my palms and knees faster, my knees feeling the bite at each collision onto the tin sheets. I could almost taste freedom. My challenge was to get out of here before five…four…three…two…

Spirits no! Rods of iron closed in on me as I crawled forwards. My exit was blocked off. Iron grills buzzed with magic, just like the vent I had entered through. If the grills at my entry point had been warded, these would be too.

Desperation clawed at my chest. My fingers barely brushed the iron before a jolt of magic singed them like lightening. Pain seared my hand as if I had actually been struck.

I'm trapped.

I had no magic left in me to break the ward. I needed a new plan. The guards would catch up with me at any moment.

I yanked the Black Blade free. When my skin touched the iron hilt, its magic once more surged up my arm like a wildfire, exhilarating and dangerous. A quick jab secured the blade between the bars. I wrenched it sideways, my muscles screaming in protest. The gate didn't budge, but the bars groaned like a Spirit's complaint. Bent.

Not enough.

Bracing a foot against the wall for purchase, I twisted the blade harder, then kicked my boot against its flat side. The bars creaked…warped… bent. Just enough. Enough for me to squeeze through.

No time to hesitate. I shoved the sword back into its sheath, emptying my lungs of air, and forced myself through the tiny gap, my ribs scraping against the twisted bar.

Abruptly freed from iron claws, I lost control, and my balance shifted as I jolted forwards. The vent floor disappeared beneath my hands and knees and the world spun right round. For a split second everything was weightless as a blur of colours flashed before my eyes and air rushed past my ears.

I landed on my ass, shoulder deep in a pool of rainwater, the stench of mud potent enough to make pigs gag.

Bloody great!

Now I was wet!

How could I escape fast enough if I couldn't use my wings? *Curse the August showers!* Didn't the Spirits think I struggled enough as it was, giving me two sets of wings? Not one. Two…and they were bloody heavy to fly with, too. Now, the Spirits wanted to test my survival skills flying with them wet? Because whichever set of wings I'd choose to bring out of my back would get soaked in mud. That wasn't my only setback. When I stood up, my knee-high boots sank, the waterbed gripping my feet like claws pulling me under.

The sound from the guards pursuing me in the vent amplified. Who knew how many of them might crawl out like cockroaches that I'd have to fight, and they were coming closer. Fast. Father had honed my combat skills since I could walk, but clearly I had my limits, especially if I was outnumbered.

The mud tested my strength and fought my every step, so I forced my muscles harder to wade towards the bank and crawl up onto dry grass. My shadow reached it far before I did as the sun was set low in the dark-blue sky. I flexed out my onyx wings through the slit between my shoulder blades and my skin-tight, black jumpsuit. This uniform had no White Wing Territory emblem to show my rank or unit; not that undercover special mission agents had any badges like the soldiers did at the Bensguard Outpost. The leadership didn't want to risk our bodies being identified if we fell beyond enemy lines.

Stretching wide, I flapped my plumes, making the force of the wind swoosh beneath them.

"Stop! Or I'll throw my dagger straight into your fucking heart!" the guard shouted, almost bursting my eardrum.

Probably the entire Black Wing Territory heard him.

I halted instantly. I wouldn't make it alive to the pine trees that surrounded the camouflaged military compound.

And where is my fucking backup?

Zoe should have sent a squad to extract me by now. She was my best friend, so I couldn't kill her for failing me. But damn would I give her a bloody beating if she had forgotten. Or worse…made the judgement I didn't need the rescue!

With an irate shrug, I withdrew my wings through the freshly opened orifice, hissing at the agony as they nestled with my white wings inside my back. I raised my hands up. The heist was over, and as ordered by my big brother, Captain Harvey Coraly of the Bensguard Outpost, I was going to *semi-willingly* let the soldier take back the Black Blade from me. If I actually killed him and stole the blade, it would leave me with a very small window to kill the king. The king's death was planned to cause chaos in the Black Wing Territory. It might delay any further attacks on our people for years before they could appoint a new king and regroup their forces, as King Blackbone was the sole heir to the ancient royal line. If I failed to act fast, and King Blackbone would realise the sword was missing, he'd tighten security and search for the perpetrator at all costs. Apparently, that would make the war between the two nations really escalate. That's how Harvey had phrased it, anyway. My dear brother had made that very clear in his short briefing the day I left for my mission; kill the black-wing king with the Black Blade. Don't fail!

I rubbed the spot over my chest where Harvey had poked a hard finger that had left a soreness of phantom pain for days.

I turned around slowly, flashing the soldier a tired look, and craned to the side to glance at the vent, half expecting more guards to crawl out. Surely, this man who looked to be my age was too young to be a fully trained military officer, skilled enough to serve at this top-secret facility. He didn't even have facial hair to accompany his wavy blonde hair that looped around his ears. His skin had that sun-kissed warm glow of someone who spent his days outdoors. His posture was upright, with an air of authority, and even though his muscles were accentuated when he moved, he was lean enough that I could take him down without breaking sweat. *Probably.*

Having seen that I had black wings too, the guy obviously wouldn't consider the thought that I worked undercover for the white-wings in Black Wing Territory, but most noteworthy was the fact that the man's expression didn't change when he saw my face. All guards and servants of the king should know my face by now, anything less was an insult to my reputation.

He kept his tongue running over his lips to focus on my every move as I swayed my hips gently from left to right so as not to get too stuck in the mud.

Does he really not know who I am? My blue hair didn't give it away?

Had he never seen me around Black Castle?

I looked at his rank badges that revealed he was a sergeant in the Infantry Unit. Three vertical lines with a horizontal beneath sat on his shoulder, so he had completed his training. *Impressive.* Maybe he actually did know how to handle his palmed dagger, after all.

"Fine," I snapped. "You can have your blade back."

I tossed the Black Blade into the water, and the heavy weapon sank below the brown surface. The guy would go for it and I would whack him out. Problem was, he didn't. He continued to hold up his dagger, aiming it straight at me.

"Turn around and put your hands behind your back. If you make any attempt to reach for the dagger in your leg strap, I'll throw mine."

One foot after the other, I unstuck myself from the mud and slowly turned my back against him. "If you hurt me, you'll be in so much trouble that a week in the Demon King of the Underworld's dungeon will feel like paradise."

"You're threatening an officer of the law."

"No. I'm informing you of the facts, trying to spare you some pain."

Some pain. That was all I could do for him now. King Blackbone would go ballistic.

The sergeant closed in on my back, and I could hear him panting behind me, his rapid breaths not having settled from the chase. I contemplated knocking him out, but I guessed I could do with the ride back to the city. Icy water had seeped into my boots and folded over my feet like tight socks. My jumpsuit hung heavy, plastered to me like a second, soggy skin. I was cold, wet and cranky. So, quite frankly, I didn't fancy hiking all the way back to my apartment in the capital feeling like a drowned rat. The intel about me snatching the Black Blade from its case would reach the king's ear before I could get my arse over the border to White Wing Territory, so I had a better chance of staying alive if I continued as my undercover persona.

Pain flared across my skin as he snatched up my wrists and cuffed them behind my back.

"Ouch! Don't cuff them so tightly!" I shouted, looking over my shoulder.

He just shook his head at me, his hair bouncing in the light breeze. "Do you want to be tried before the court or the king?"

I chuckled softly. "The king."

"You have the right to remain silent. Anything you say–"

"I know my rights."

Harvey had recited them to me often enough as kids when he held me in a leg lock after I had annoyed him one too many times.

Their laws were roughly the same as ours.

The sergeant nudged my back with his dagger, guiding me towards the military base stables.

He circled a hand in the air beside him as we walked, and it created a circular swirl of blue essence in front of his face. A hearing portal. Exactly like Zoe's, magic.

He has magic? Okay, I'm starting to think this guy isn't so defenceless.

He spoke into the magic portal as if it was connected to another place where someone could hear him. "Murben, you can call off the search. I've secured the intruder and I'm on my way to the stables to take her to the king."

Murben is on duty at the military base?

What had the king's bodyguard done this time to piss off his king?

The alarm screaming through the hearing portal stopped, thank the Spirits, because I was about to go deaf.

"Well done, Sergeant Davis. I'll ride ahead to Black Castle and meet you there."

I opened my mouth about to say hello to Murben, but Sergeant Davis lowered his hand to close the portal. The magic abruptly vanished and I nearly choked on my breath.

I snapped my head to the side, staring the sergeant down. "Tell Murben to show his miserable face. I'd like a word with him."

He snorted and shoved the pommel of his dagger into my back. "Criminals don't get to make requests on how they want to be treated."

I blew aside a blue strand of hair that had fallen across my face. "Fine. Your funeral."

I looked over my shoulder once more when he didn't entertain my remark, neither did he shift his gaze to look at me. Yet, I was certain he was watching my every move and every twitch of my muscles in case I attempted to escape.

I noticed the Black Blade tucked into his belt and how muddy water had wetted his left sleeve up to his shoulder. When had he retrieved it without me noticing?

Oh, this guy is good.

"You look too cute to be a soldier. Where did you complete your training?"

His face was as hard as stone, honed with professionalism and duty. He didn't offer any reply as he stared at me.

"In the Banaly province in the south, or here in Cathdear at the king's training fort?"

Still nothing. He only narrowed his eyes for comfort as we walked facing the setting sun.

Fine. Don't talk then. See what happens when we meet Murben.

The path over the field stretched beyond the compound's grounds and the tallest buildings of the capital poked above the tree line in the distance. At the sight, my guilt tugged at my chest. What would happen to the sergeant if he brought me to the king and I'm in cuffs?

"One could say I know the king quite well. You may want to know that—"

"Save your negotiation for the king. You'll need it. I hear he's merciless."

I sighed. He was right, and I had too much heart to let this man suffer the king's wrath.

"If you'll let me explain."

"The next word that comes out of your mouth will be accompanied with a blade in your back." I felt a pinch from the tip of his dagger.

My heart pounded harder because I actually believed him. An unfortunate misunderstanding could be the death of me if I disobeyed. No matter if it was to save *him*. Considering my family's legacy, dying from being stabbed in the back would be ironic, but not the way I wanted to leave this world. With my honour being questioned when living, at least allow my death some dignity.

I pressed my lips into a line and remained silent, observing the woodland landscape on either side of me as we went past. The soldier led me towards the stables where a single horse waited, strapped to a carriage that resembled an iron box with a barred window on each side. Other soldiers busied around, seeming all worked up from the incident.

Sergeant Davis used his magic once more to create the sound portal. "Is the captor transport carriage for me, Denver?" he asked, pushing me towards the back doors.

"Hi Davis. Yes, Murben told me to prepare it for you. I have to saddle two more horses urgently, but I'll be right out to help you."

"No need. I've had a long day, and I want to get going, so I'll handle it myself."

Sergeant Davis opened the doors and gestured for me to get inside. I jumped in and turned to flash him a pitiful smile before he shut the doors. There was only a brief moment before the carriage started rocking along the country path. The iron was cold as I gripped the bars of a window and gazed out, savouring the countryside while I could. There was no telling when I would see it again. I guessed it depended on the king's mood.

This province was beautiful. Simple cottages nestled between the trees. The green leaves and the post-rain scent of grass had brought people out into their gardens. It reminded me of our family cottage by the lake where I spent my summers to escape the outpost in Bensguard and the busy city life fanning out from it. The city in Bensguard had densely populated areas with row upon row of concrete building blocks and jam-packed multi-lane cobbled streets between them. Here in the countryside, I felt free…even if I was a captive in chains. I preferred it to the crowded city parks and shopping streets where white-wings flew busily about, both at ground level and in the sky, and shoppers poured out of stores with overflowing bags under their arms.

But who knew if I would ever return to the White Wing Territory? It was on the other side of the butterfly-shaped floating island where the mountain ridges acted as a spine to divide us. Black-wings to the east and white-wings to the west. Along our borders, we had built outposts and fences to defend ourselves from attacks by the black-wings. At the Bensguard Outpost was where I had grown up and lived all my life, as my father had served there as the general. That was until the Battle of Bensguard when my mother had turned our lives upside-down.

The hurt from remembering my mother's betrayal was a distraction I couldn't afford right now. One wrong move might trigger the throw-happy dagger-soldier to make good on his threat to kill me.

Black Castle loomed into view at the far end of the city, with a moat surrounding it and a large lake wrapping around its back garden. The country road panned out into cobbled streets and my brain rattled along to every bump in the road. In the jumpy view out through the window, I saw the streets I had mapped for the last two years, and knew like the back of my hand, just in case I couldn't transport my physical maps to my brother at the end of my mission. Doubtlessly, my escape would need to be swift after killing the king.

The creaking hinges of the iron winged gates to the castle grounds let me know they were swinging open to let us through, and I waited for the carriage to park outside the rear entrance of Black Castle. The multi-pillared building poking the sky felt like a second home by now, having seen it for the first time two years ago. Its dark stone looked gloomy during the day and almost invisible at night. The fang-mouthed monstrous gargoyles, and the water that was coloured red before running along their spouts to resemble blood had once frightened me, but I barely noticed them anymore. The man ruling from inside of it did, though.

The carriage stopped and I almost lost my balance. Sergeant Davis opened the carriage door and snatched up the chain between my shackles to tug me outside. Murben came into view around the side of the carriage in his black leather uniform that was stuffed with blades. When he looked up, shock widened his eyes. There was no smile, no white teeth contrasting against his brown skin. Murben was a man of few words, but his presence was enough to make even the most seasoned warriors pay attention. His quiet demeanour and graceful presence made him seem like a figure out of a forgotten legend.

I flashed him a playful grin and chirped, "Hello Murben."

Because although Murben resembled a war veteran with scars, tattoos, deep dark-brown eyes and charcoal-black hair, to me he had always been a soft-hearted teddy bear. He was tall, towering over most people, and his muscles always bulged through any top he was wearing. He came from a tribe living in the mountains in the far north of the Dormondar province, where no intruders dared to visit. All black-wings feared him because of it, and because he was the king's bodyguard, enforcing the king's bidding.

Murben dropped his chiselled jaw now though and turned his gaze sharply to stare at the sergeant. "What sick joke is this?"

Yep, someone would be writhing in pain in a matter of moments. The question was, would it be Sergeant Davis?

Bodyguard Murben?

Or me?

2

"What?" Davis scoffed, dragging me forth by my shackles and lining up in front of Murben.

Murben gestured his hand at me, beating it in the air with rapid swipes. "Long, blue hair. Gorgeous, blue eyes. Stunning beyond words." He swatted Davis on the back of his head. "This is Angelica Stone. King Blackbone's…" Murben hesitated and looked at me. "What would you call your relationship?"

I shrugged my shoulders. "I'm his toy."

"Yes. Perhaps so." He stared back at the soldier. "I'm not escorting her to him cuffed."

"Shit!" Davis cussed, fear entering his eyes at the realisation of who I was.

Murben rested his hands on his hips. "I'm surprised she didn't beat you up and escape. She has trained with the best and you wouldn't land a punch on her."

Murben glanced quizzically at me. Accusing me of…something.

I smiled playfully, looked at the carriage and then back at him. "It was nice to get a ride back. You know I hate flying."

He scratched his chin. "I know it's not my place to say, but you could have warned Davis, knowing the king's temper."

Davis absently palmed his neck. "I didn't let her speak." His voice was spiced with regret. "Threatened her with my dagger."

Murben's eyes widened in disbelief, his face flushing with a mixture of anger and incredulity. "You did what?"

I stepped forward, and although amused, I kept my voice cold and steady. "He did." My words hung in the air between us like a verdict for a silent heartbeat.

Murben's fury erupted. "Bloody Underworld, Davis!" His finger jabbed toward my restrained hands. "And get those cuffs off her!"

Davis tossed the keys over to Murben, standing beside me. "Here!"

Murben dodged the keys, and they landed on the gravel. "I'm not getting my hands anywhere near those. And you'd better hurry to get the cuffs off. If King Blackbone sees as much as the tiniest scratch on her skin, you'll be happy if you walk away with only a few maimed fingers."

The man threw himself on the ground, scrabbling for the keys, and then rushed to me, shaking like a leaf in a thunderstorm to the point I thought his wolf head cuff links would fall out, as he did his best to remove the cuffs from my wrists quickly.

"I'm so sorry, my Queen," he stammered; fear marred his voice as if he stood face to face with his own ghost.

"Spirits no. I'm no queen." The horrible thought stuck in my mind.

No way will I marry the enemy king and be marked for life!

No one to date knew how to remove a mate mark once it labelled the skin at the side of your neck just above the collarbone. The Spirits' powers sealed that union for good. It was too sacred to fool around with during an undercover mission, even if it was to save our sky island from King Blackbone. Not even my brother would go so far as to force that into my undercover agent contract. Especially considering what our mother had put us through. Her twenty-eight-year long undercover act had felt so real that it had shocked me to my core five years ago when her true identity had been exposed, as her white-wing glamour had faltered, showing her black wings beneath. Harvey had been in the second year of the academy then and Mother and I had been watching Harvey and Zayd begin their navigation challenge. But instead of them starting a challenge, she had started a massacre, known since as the Battle of Bensguard.

But why am I so angry at hearing Davis call me his queen?

Was I getting too attached to King Blackbone? If I was, I'd have to abort my mission and that meant I would never see him again. A venom-stinging pain entered my heart. It wasn't as if I had a life back at the Bensguard Outpost amongst white-wings. After everyone found out my mother was a traitor, they had treated me and my brother as such, too, and we had to work twice as hard as the other soldiers to prove our loyalty.

With both a pair of black wings and white wings, I was fated to do this gig.

So do your job and fucking focus!

I rubbed my sore wrists as soon as Davis removed the sharp irons.

Please, let there be no scratches visible to the king's eye.

But unfortunately, the cuffs had left a faint reddish mark that wouldn't fool anyone.

Murben frowned as he saw the marks, too. We both knew what it meant for poor Davis.

Spirits! I felt ridden with guilt. *But I'd like to see them try to be a damned spy, tasked with mapping the Black Wing Territory so that the white-wings could disarm all their military operations, steal the Black Blade, kill the king, and at the same time, not harm an innocent in the process.*

Murben faced me, reflexively resting his hand on the hilt of his sword that hung from his belt. "So, Miss Stone, why were you 'visiting' the military base, anyway?"

I cleared my throat. "You know that blade collection I brag about and how much I love swords?"

"Yes. The one you speak of, which I have never seen because you refuse to let me in to secure your apartment, even when King Blackbone has ordered me to."

"Yeah, that one. Well, it doesn't have the Black Blade, does it?" I pointed for Davis's belt where it hung.

With the Black Blade I could kill a soul, and the magic the person possessed, sending them to the Underworld never to walk this world again, so I could understand why he was nervous about me having my eyes on it. The 'visit' had also given me the opportunity to inspect the facility. But I wasn't sure the blade collection story was a believable enough reason to appease Murben's suspicions.

"I wonder where you draw the line of your mischief, Miss Stone. If you aren't in trouble for spying on the top-secret military base, you could still get severely punished for stealing the only blade that could destroy the Spirit Heart."

Well fucking aware! But I'll rather not draw any lines and die undercover than going back home and having to enrol in the academy.

"Little old me? You can't believe I would be so foolish as to enter the Spirits' Trek, let alone hike to the end, which few have survived, purely to stab the heart?"

The Bensguard Outpost had a Special Missions Unit specifically for this purpose; to train cadets for three years in the academy and send one team of six members each year after graduation. No one had completed the trek, touched the heart and received three magical powers since my father had done it twenty-five years ago.

"I have no doubt you could do it if you put your mind to it. Your stubbornness would kill the tenacity of any demon. But as long as you don't stab the king's heart, your faith isn't in my hands. It's in the hands of the king's mercy."

Oh, but that is no fun, Murben. Stabbing the king is in my job description!

Although, I had been pushing the king's mercy too far lately.

"Hey guys," I called out casually. "Let's forget about today and go our separate ways. There is no need for anyone to get hurt."

But in the next moment, the courtyard swarmed with royal guards, leaving Murben with no control over the situation, and I didn't have the time to think of a foolproof alibi.

Commander Daffron was a striking figure of quiet strength. Standing over two metres tall, with broad shoulders and a lean frame, his every movement was that of someone who was as familiar with war as the back of his hand. His raven-black hair contrasted with his pale complexion and ended just above his strong jawline. His deep amber eyes looked me over, frowning at the sight of the mud on my soaked clothes. When he spoke, his voice was as steady as the calm confidence he exuded. "Miss Stone. Care to explain all this?"

His tone boded for no jokes and his wide stance emphasised that he wasn't about to be swayed by nonsense.

"Sergeant Davis has arrested me, so I guess I have the right to remain silent until I speak with the king."

It was the only way I could help Davis, hindering any gossip from spreading that would make it worse for him if the royal guards knew the full story.

Commander Daffron's frown deepened as he scrutinised me, a vein of effort to remain civil etched on his forehead, so I quickly pushed out my elbow in Davis's direction. "Shall we?"

Davis's pale skin bordered the same pink as my pet pig Flora and his grip on my arm was so slack I couldn't feel his touch.

"I'll escort them," Murben told Commander Daffron.

Commander Daffron didn't argue but still signalled for two of his guards to follow us. "The king is in the Counsel Chamber."

We walked down the corridor that was dimly lit by the torches in the sconces on the walls, the only sound being my rubber-soled boots squeaking on the stone floor. The other guards walked soundlessly, wearing leather soled military boots and black cotton uniforms with dark-blue details, with one or other medals sewn to their chest if they'd earned them.

The stone walls shielded by thick shadows came to an end and we crossed an external landing before we reached the Counsel Chamber's crimson double doors. I inhaled a full breath before I put a palm on each side and pushed them wide open, walking in first.

I choked for a second, seeing the regal form of the young king of only twenty-six years of age in his serene, thoughtful state behind the desk.

I liked him in this mood.

But I was about to ruin it.

"Ben!" I called out to get Benjamin's attention away from his enormous desk full of papers he burdened himself with instead of letting his advisors handle them.

His complexion had turned paler than the last time I saw him, probably from having spent too much time in this office and too long in the shadows.

Despite the enormous desk, his frame looked like a mountain behind it; his biceps as beefy as a bull's leg, his neck too chunky for a sword to hack through in one go. When his gorgeous ruby eyes looked up at me, my body reacted with the same crazy attraction as when I'd first laid eyes on him at the ball in this very castle nearly two years ago.

Idiot! He's a murderer and a tyrant! I rebuked myself.

His onyx hair lay in waves around his face and neck, tousled like he had just rolled out of bed, but I knew it was from enduring a hard day. Yet somehow it, *he*, looked perfect. I suppressed the rebellious fluttering in my stomach and batted my eyelashes at him apologetically. "I went to a restricted area. Stole a blade. Got caught. Here for my prosecution. What is your verdict?"

The black-wing king's face reddened to the colour of his eyes with anger, but he stayed silent as he inspected the guards tailing me.

"Miss Stone," he said, his dark hair bouncing as he rose from his seat, wild and untamed like him.

Slowly, with prowling steps, he rounded the desk. He flexed out his enormous black wings, folding their edges protectively around his arms that rested at his sides, as if to restrain them from strangling anyone.

I swallowed hard. He was massive, even taller than Murben; his body blocking out almost all natural light from the window behind the desk. Smoke, like the essence of death, followed him and faded at his edges as he moved. My nerves pricked, kicking alive my heart as it began pounding hard in my chest. His size and his authoritative presence made him almost impossible to ignore even if we had been in a large crowd but lethally worse when the confined room boxed me in between four walls, five guards and a king.

He used my first name or surname depending on how pleased he was with me; Angelica was the sweet purr he uttered when he admired me. Stone, he used when he thought I had a heart that was hard to crack. He pulled his fingers through his hair, clearly garnering patience before he spoke.

"How do you plead to these charges?"

I didn't hesitate, nor sugar-coat it. It would do me no good. "Guilty for the Underworld!"

There was no point denying it. The guiltier I seemed, the less pain Sergeant Davis would have to suffer. That was the best outcome I could achieve right now.

Ben grunted. My heart heated uncomfortably. He crossed his arms over his chest and leaned back against the desk, looking at me as if not knowing what to do with me.

He observed me with an intense stare, the same way a cat watched a rat before it was about to pounce, but I could never be sure when I should draw my daggers in defence. The stare lowered to size me up, but stopped abruptly, fixed on my wrists.

Dammit.

"Come to me," he called softly. It was like a sensual lure that drew me to him. He could be calling out my damned death sentence and I could still not turn away from him. *A damn curse he is!*

I made my way across the room with the confidence of someone who had never doubted herself a day in her life but realised my manicured fingers were trembling ever so slightly as I tucked a blue strand behind my ear. The gap between us vanished and I found myself cocooned by his wings inside his personal space. I felt like a tiny soon-to-be-eaten fly.

"King Blackbone, let's talk about this in private."

He didn't answer, going straight for my wrist, lifting it up with the calloused hands of a man who had worked hard his entire life, and pushed up the fabric of my black jumpsuit.

"What's this? This is new."

"Oh, I don't know. I squeezed through barbed wire, pressed myself along concrete walls and crawled through a vent. It could have happened at any point."

He gave a low grunt; a signature grunt I had never got used to, like an unpleasant hiccup rocking your chest. He brought up my other wrist and placed the fresh red lines side by side. "Looks like cuff marks to me." He looked over my shoulder. "Don't these look like cuff marks to you, Murben?"

Dammit.

Murben would never lie to his king, and he must have already disappointed Ben this week if he was serving at the military base instead of guarding his back.

Murben, standing in a military stance a distance behind me, craned his head, pretending to inspect it. It was futile though, as he knew the truth. "They do look like such."

I glanced at Davis, whose skin had taken on a green tint, ready to faint.

I quickly nestled my arms around Ben's neck and his wings seemed to reflexively close around me. It had taken me two years of balls, hunts and tournaments to get this far, and it was only last week that he had invited me to court to mingle amongst the nobles. I was still very much his toy, but I had privileges. I hoped they were enough now.

"Let's forget about this occasion." I pressed myself between his legs and gently ground myself at his groin, hoping no one else in the room would see it. I knew King Blackbone didn't appreciate public displays of affection, and we weren't at that level in our relationship where me grinding against him was appropriate.

We locked eye-contact, his red globes moving inside their sockets, seeming to ponder his next move. He frowned as he looked down at me; grinding his teeth, as if he had a hard time rejecting my offer. My heart burned with that fuzzy feeling again, knowing he accepted me in his own emotionally-deprived way.

Clearly having made up his mind, he pried my arms off him. "Who did this to Miss Stone?" he asked Murben.

I spun around to watch Davis's face. His knees buckled and hit the floor. He interlinked his fingers and held his praying hands up in front of him. "My king, I didn't know who she was. I swear it. I thought I was apprehending a thief stealing the Black Blade." He tugged the Black Blade out of his belt and tossed it in front of the king's feet. "I removed the cuffs as soon as I learned her identity. You have my sincerest apologies."

Ben grunted darkly this time. He approached the shivering man, who was kneeling on the floor; Ben's two metre frame towering over him. "A king is always under threat from those not content with his rule, and so is his lady friend, especially one as adventurous as Miss Stone. I don't want ignorance of her identity to be an excuse to harm her." Ben watched the guard in silence for a while. "Do you know how to paint, Sergeant?"

"Paint?" He cocked his head up, his shiny, grey eyes held a spark of confusion. "Not as well as I'd wish, my king."

Ben grunted in response. "Sever the thumb that was used to cuff Miss Stone, so that you can always remember its treachery in harming her. Paint her picture with your blood on a parchment and display it at the proclamation notice board outside the castle gates. If anyone else claims not to recognise her face, I'll execute you both, so make it your best resemblance of her."

Spirits! Execution for reddening my skin! I have committed far worse crimes, and he never punishes me. But one day my luck will run out.

Guilt hammered my chest more than fear did, as I pitied Davis. I wished I could put him in protective custody with the white-wings, but I couldn't risk revealing my double identity to the king.

Davis's eyes swam in their sockets before he fainted. Murben lifted him up onto his shoulder and headed for the door.

"And Murben," Ben called. "You're back on bodyguard duty. After I have had a word with Miss Stone, escort her to her apartment and guard her door until tomorrow. I want no more drama tonight. I have already had enough for one day, what with throwing Duke Hartmore out of the room earlier."

"Understood." Murben saluted and left.

I was alone with the black-wing king. I don't know why, but somehow that soothed me. In a million years, I couldn't believe he would harm me. But my life was a hefty price to pay if I was wrong. He retrieved the Black Blade from the floor and placed it on the desk on his way back to it. Then, he sank down to sit on the desk's ledge again, cupping my back with both hands, and pulling me closer.

His touch sent forbidden tingles up my spine. I palmed his rock-hard chest to support my balance. More unwanted heat coursed through me. Cussing inside my mind, I focused on steadying my aroused breathing.

"Miss Stone. You have a knack for mischief. What's it about this time? Why the Black Blade?" There was a hurt in his voice that bothered me.

To stab your arse when the time comes!

But if I confessed that, I was as good as dead. I had also truly started to doubt I could do it. The sadness I saw in his eyes pained me no end. A sadness that could derive from him having given that outcome a thought.

He can't know that is the reason I stole it.

"It's sharp. I wanted it for my sword collection."

That was one truth. It was the sharpest blade in the world; throughout all the three realms, I was sure of it.

His inky essence cascaded off him and crept around us like spirits of the dead coming to bring me to the Underworld. The hair on my skin bristled with a small dose of magical voltage as the black tendrils touched me. The pulsation of darkness from his soul rubbed over me like waves hitting shore. He possessed strong power, but what magic could he wield? No one in the White Wing Territory knew.

His eyes softened as he looked at me. "You know I could get you anything you want in the world save that sword. Pick another sword, or have the blacksmith forge you a new one. Or perhaps start using a smaller dagger better suited to your tiny body. They are more effective. But don't make more trouble for me."

I rolled my eyes and leaned sideways over his arm, caressing the Black Blade with my fingertip, tracing the sharp edge down towards the hilt.

"But I like swords."

My palm fitted perfectly around the shaft, and I brought it up and slowly dragged it across his wing and then his chest until I stopped it, poking its tip at his black shirt just above his heart. I hesitated. This was the hard part – to become a murderer, making my first and the most important kill of my life. My stomach knotted as I gazed at the black iron between us. I had one mission task. This was it.

The only thing I had to do was jab.

3

He breathed evenly, not flexing a single muscle other than a small twitch in his jaw. There was uncertainty in the way he looked at me, but there was also trust. If he only knew how much I wanted to stab him for having started countless wars against the white-wings, burying innocent families in ashes.

I pressed the tip harder to his shirt, damaging the fabric, determined to kill him. He didn't even flinch or look away from my eyes.

Dammit! Why is he so damn gorgeous?

My brother had relayed the message that under no circumstances should I attempt to kill the king unless I was certain my strike would end him.

If I killed him here, in his own Counsel Chamber, I wouldn't make it across the threshold before the guards apprehended me.

Awesome! I'm fine with letting him live.

There was a deep, dark part of me that wanted to keep him around for longer. A part of me I didn't dare examine too closely. Maybe I had inherited a traitorous quirk from my mother.

The Black Blade pulsed in my grip, its magic coiling like a hungry serpent, eager to strike. I didn't trust it. Didn't trust myself. If this magical sword had a will of its own, a heartbeat and a soul, I wasn't about to let it make decisions for me.

Spirits! I'm about to fuck this up.

I needed to complete my mission, but I just couldn't do it; couldn't kill him. Frustration burned through my veins with the echo of my failure, yet the hold this man had on me was too strong.

I exhaled with a low growl and leaned over his wing, chucking the blade onto the table. It clattered against the polished wood with a sharp, ringing finality.

My eyes locked onto the letter he'd been writing when I came in here. If I wasn't going to kill him, I could at least steal his secrets. The mere seconds only gave me enough time to read that it was made out to Duke Finningham and the first line, 'The northern army will get their backup', before Ben shuffled me around inside his wide frame to get me back close. I fumed with irritation as I really wanted to know why Ben had placed so much attention on the northern territory of Dormondar. It was the one province out of the three with the least inhabitants, so how could there be so much unrest there? My brother kept telling me information about the north was classified and above my pay grade.

Weirdos. I'd choose the warmer and lazier lifestyle in the south any day!

Ben tipped my chin up with a gentle knuckle that had a fresh bruise alike his others, a clear sign that his temper had gotten the better of him again. His warm breath hit my mouth. His gaze trailed from my lips up to my eyes and rested there for a few seconds as if he wanted to ask me to stay with him tonight.

I tensed. The king had vowed not to have anyone in his bed until he wed his bride. I had depended on him keeping that vow when I signed up for this undercover contract – if signing up was the same as my brother pushing a dismissal letter in my face, saying I was two years too young to start the academy. So, either I went undercover on a special mission, or I had to find a home elsewhere. It also seemed suspiciously convenient that, for some reason, I was the only one in the Bensguard Outpost who could pull out either black or white wings when it suited me.

As said, perfect for blending in, but a bitch when standing out and getting picked for suicide missions.

"Have dinner with me tonight." He bit each word out like a command disguised as a request, desperate not to be turned down but far too proud to beg.

My heart skipped. The damned thing had rejoiced over the attention. I could feel the weight behind those five words. They were heavier than they should have been between us. No one dared refuse him. Ever. Not without consequences. No one called him by his first name and walked away unscathed. But he let me. He *let me.* It had been a heart-throbbing gamble the first time, but now my rebellious streak rolled words off my tongue easily, and he knew it.

My mind reeled. I didn't want to get too close, not to *him.* I barely knew the black-wing king beyond his public face, and even that was carved from something foreign to me; part king, part executioner. Although, the artist had been a pro with the chisel. Ben had that psycho-gorgeous aura going on, and I couldn't decide whether it was sensual or right out lethally dangerous.

Ben wasn't a king who asked twice, so when he didn't receive an answer, he distanced himself by standing up and walking over to the window to look out, leaving me by the desk feeling cold as his body heat no longer warmed me. He tucked his wings tight against his frame, like he had put up a shield around his heart. That he even had them out must have meant that his previous meeting with Duke Hartmore had ended on unfriendly terms, as Ben rarely felt threatened enough to bring them out to show his superiority.

"Was that a request or an order, my king?"

He twisted his head in a sharp movement to look at me but then turned it away to keep staring out of the window. "It was an invitation," he growled, and there was regret in his words, as if the invitation had been withdrawn.

It had been over two years that I had been celibate for him, to ensure his spies wouldn't see me with anyone else, and my loins ached. But that wasn't the whole truth. I had left the White Wing Territory without as much as a goodbye to Zayd after our three-year relationship. He was my brother's best friend, and we had always known each other. That our affections had grown out of that friendship had felt natural. I hadn't known how to say farewell when my brother had pushed me into this mission. So, I hadn't. I had watched him from the sidelines as his lesson had dragged out on the practice field, but my nerves had got the better of me before his training had finished. So, I had left.

But why has the king invited me to dinner? That is next level shit I'm not ready for!

There was just so much I could take before I had to put a restraint-jacket on my heart not to fall for him. Utterly, madly fall for him. Crave him to my bones. I would, if I let it. There was something hiding inside the deepest darkest parts of me that was attractive to him, and it wasn't logical!

But if I got attached, and fell for the curse that was his charm, it would make it that much harder to kill him. I already pitied him for having lost both his parents, his mother in a battle ten years ago, and his father in a duel against the white-wing king three years later, leaving him to carry the burden of becoming a king at the age of nineteen.

"I feel I would be taking advantage of your vulnerability. You told me yourself that there had been too much drama today." I glanced over his papers quickly, hoping to see more information, but a thin layer of his magic essence diffused the sight of them.

I also needed to return home tonight to check if my partner in crime was back at the apartment alive. If Zoe wasn't there, I would have to venture back to the woods by the military base in search of her. Harvey had assigned her the mission to record the guard schedule and all entry and exit points of the military base, so that a battalion of white-wing soldiers could invade the facility to help me steal the Black Blade. But they had never showed up. Something must have gone wrong.

I pushed away from the desk and crossed the room to pick up the dagger Davis had used to threaten me with and had dropped on the floor when he knelt in front of the king. I had no empty sheaths, so I shoved the blade behind the leather strap to my leg holster. "If I used up all my time entertaining Your Majesty for dinner, when would I plan my mischiefs?"

He grunted, his lips tugging as if he was suppressing his amusement. "I don't want trouble, Miss Stone."

"What a boring way to live." I winked at him and left the Counsel Chamber with my heart pounding as I walked down the corridor, having walked out on the king without formally being dismissed.

But I passed the temptation test. That should earn me a frickin' medal!

Rounding the next corner, I ran into Murben, who turned on his heel and fell into step next to me. "You're not staying? Black Castle has plenty of guest rooms."

"Trying to make your job easier, Murben?"

"I'm tired, and I'd prefer to avoid chasing you around town tonight," he said, giving me a quick sideways glance. "Why don't you stay? The king would see it as bridging trust."

"Maybe it isn't his trust I want, but yours. You don't need to escort me home. Trust that I can make it on my own."

"But if you stayed in a guest room, I wouldn't have to do anything. I could station a junior soldier outside your door and sleep in my own bed."

"Or you could agree not to escort me home, and it would have the same outcome. Trust goes both ways, Murben. I won't tell the king."

He halted, pondering something as he looked mindlessly into the air. Awkwardly, we had stopped right beneath a huge portrait of Ben when he was about ten years old, wearing a hefty gold crown adorned with rubies.

"Okay. I don't believe anyone can kill you on the way back to your apartment. My friend's son has a fever, and I want to visit him tonight. We both go home, and you tell the king that it's none of his business if he asks you about when I left your home."

"Bodyguard Murben…" I leered at him. "I didn't know you had friends."

"That's none of your business. The kid is only seven years old and thin as a grasshopper. The fever has been hard on him. He might not survive the night, so I should visit the family, but I can't get leave from my duties."

"You've told Ben about this, and he refused your leave?"

"No. I didn't want to burden *King Blackbone* with more trouble. So, do we have a deal?"

"Sure. I'll tell the king you stayed at my door until the early morning hours before you returned to the castle. No problem."

"No. Don't lie to the king. He has magic. Simply repeat that it's none of his business."

I nodded and rushed forwards whereas Murben turned back. The corridors seemed endless until I finally reached the castle steps and descended them lightly on the pads of my feet. When I exited the enormous iron gates, I threw a glance over my shoulder to see a drawing with some resemblance of me, painted in blood and pinned to the notice board. I sighed. Poor thumbless Davis.

The guards at the gate saluted me, showing clearly skittish tendencies, probably fearing to make a misstep, causing the king to collect more thumbs.

I sprinted down an alleyway that would lead me to the town square. Evening had fallen and traders had begun closing their market stalls. But I could still discern some goods on display, and knew exactly which ones came from the three white-wing provinces and which were from the three black-wing provinces.

Closest to the mountain ridge, the landscape was barren, and the further towards the peripheries you travelled, the greener the floor of the island became. That meant that in the White Wing Territory: herbs, berries and water were from the Pharanir province in the Northeast; meat and milk came from the farmland in Katagoon; and silk and cotton woven fabric derived from Gaithbry in the south.

In return for these goods, the black-wings supplied spices from Banaly, the most southern province, as well as iron for our weapons. The spice trade I could understand, but why the king had agreed to supply their enemy with the material that the white-wings would use against them, baffled me. The organisation of extracting the iron from the mountain was an entire operation whereby all parties collaborated. A few brawls had rocked the relationship and agreements, so needless to say that the situation was more than a little tense.

I picked up some bread, cheese and olives on the way home, but was too eager to check on Zoe's status to do a larger shop. Heading for the suburb closer toward the White Wing Territory and after running for a good thirty minutes, my building came into view. Stone setting the ground floor foundation was supported by thick wooden beams to finish a second storey out of wood. That's where Zoe and I rented a two-bedroom apartment. I darted up the stairs, which ran up the outside of the building, jumping over the one rotten step that would be a death trap one day. The panic inside my chest intensified with each step until I reached the door and threw it open.

"Zoe!"

"I'm here, honey!" she shouted from deeper inside our home.

I buckled to my knees in the hallway, panting. "Thank the Spirit of Luck."

Zoe walked out of her room and put a sassy hand on her hip, and although she was petite, she carried herself with the confidence that made her seem two metres tall instead of her one metre sixty. "I wouldn't call it luck, honey, since I'm awesome. But yeah, thanks be to the nine Spirits. What happened to you?"

Her eyes were a piercing shade of grey and always seeming to know more than she let on. She had a brutality about her that made her stand out in a crowd. Her every movement was graceful, like an aerial dancer, but instead of using ribbons she had her blades. So delicate, yet there was something dangerous about her that implied she could easily hold her own in any situation.

"What happened to me?" I dropped my jaw at her question.

With a twitch of her hand, she flicked her towel dried purple hair behind her shoulders, so it was away from her heart-shaped face that was usually framed with wild waves that refused to be tamed. "Yeah, you're clearly irritated. What's wrong?"

Supporting my hands on my lap, I had to take a moment to reassemble my jaw from having dropped it. "We fucked up the mission and King Blackbone took back the Black Blade. Not a pleasant thing to report back to my brother."

Zoe snorted and both her hands were back on the hips of her black uniform, which neither featured the golden key emblem for the Bensguard Outpost on the collar, nor the rank or magic nominator on her shoulders. The same as mine.

"Who said anything about reporting it to the captain?"

"That's why I love you!" I chirped and straightened up.

She hugged the door frame to her room. "The longer we can stay here, the better. I don't want to go back to Bensguard."

Nor did I, but what the heck! "You aren't telling me you sabotaged the mission on purpose?"

She shrugged her shoulders with a bored look on her face.

I approached her slowly, flashing her my evil eye. "You knew I was inside the facility, right? I could have died. No one came to help me. And I swear, the sergeant who apprehended me, he had the same stubborn grey eyes as you!"

She put her palm across her heart to an accompanying sweet smile, the portrait of innocence. "I swear it by the Spirit of Family that I never for one second thought you were in any danger. The king has a thing for you."

"*A thing*, which can swiftly develop into my execution!"

"Oh, about that. Your father had his verdict yesterday and King Emille sentenced him to beheading in three days' time in the capital. Your brother is on his way there to be the one executing it. You know…like tradition.

The last honour."

It was as if someone grabbed my heart and squeezed it until it exploded like a fragile tomato. "You could have mentioned it with a bit more sensitivity. He is my father."

"Sorry. Just wanted to emphasise that the other side of the mountain ridge is no better than this one. Last week a unit in the Air Force Camp at Bensguard captured another black-wing soldier and they are training him for the Spirits' Trek. It was a young man. Nesso…something."

"That's just madness. Most people who have attempted to hike that stupid trek have died. No magic gift is worth the risk."

"You should remember that. I forbid you from going near that trek. Stay away from the academy and stay away from Nesso and the black-wing commander."

"The black-wing commander? They captured Commander Daffron?"

"Yep. Has King Blackbone introduced you to him?"

"Not officially, but our paths have crossed. Spirits, your intel must be so fresh. I saw him earlier today. I don't know him, but I have heard the rumours. Merciless. Muscly. Arrogant. The son of some late Duke. Too young to be a commander."

Zoe leaned her back against the wall. "He's thirty-five."

I gripped a leather strap from the side-table in the hallway and tied up my hair to get ready for a shower. "And do you feel like you could be commander material at that age?"

"That's not the same. I'm not a field officer from the Special Missions Unit like you, but an intel soldier from the General Operations Unit."

"Speaking of intel. I saw a map and a message on the king's desk. I think he's planning on attacking the Abarath Outpost in Pharanir. It'd make sense to invade the territory around the Spirits' Trek if he too wants to send a squad there to get magical powers. The war could shift in the favour of whichever territory gets there first." I put down the shopping bag on the grey upholstered sofa and zipped down the jumpsuit, wrestling my arms out on my way to the bathroom. On the way I tossed the leg straps with the two daggers, and the new one stolen from Sergeant Davis, on the sofa table.

Zoe followed me further into the living room area. "I say King Blackbone must be mad to even want to hike it. No one ever survives."

"My father did."

"Because he had a bloody strong team with the fathers of Emroyce and Fern Bengrey, Mazdon and Kate Pere, and Zayd Watson in it."

"True. Also true that the king is ambitious."

"Ambitious? I said mad. Because the Pharanir province has the trek, it's the most heavily guarded by the white-wings. So, if King Blackbone decides to take his army there, he knows he must use all his force to win."

"Yet, he hasn't. It makes little sense that he conducts these small and random attacks on the northern villages. Maybe King Blackbone doesn't want to jeopardise his trade agreements by starting a full-on war. If he wants to attempt the Spirits' Trek, he would do it on the sly with a small team."

"Well, I'm going to go and report *that* piece of information to Captain Coraly."

She disappeared through the door to her room, and I chased after her. "We don't even know if that is correct intel."

"I'd much rather report that though, and risk getting it wrong, than that you fucked up the mission and lost the Black Blade."

"I fucked up?" I dug my nails into the door frame to find patience but found little. "You didn't help!"

She sat and swivelled around on her office chair, diving into her intel work, her eyes darting between a missive and a map. There were letters and books filling her untidy workspace, which would give me a headache if I debated her methods any further. The shelf above her head was littered with small figurines of wolves, which were her favourite animal, some of them which I'd given her on her birthdays.

Not dwelling on the trust of our friendship, I went to my bedroom and undressed out of the muddied jumpsuit, took a quick shower, and changed into a pair of linen trousers and a tank top. All the while, I ate the bread, cheese and olives I had unpacked from the shopping bag until my stomach was settled. I brushed my hair, pulled it into a tight ponytail and headed for the bathroom to brush my teeth. Careful to count the seconds, I was halfway through brushing the upper teeth when I heard Zoe shouting.

"The squad did what?"

I rinsed my mouth and rushed into Zoe's room, seeing her reporting to the white-wings through a blue rotating hearing portal.

"What's wrong?"

Zoe swivelled around on her chair and looked me in the eye. "Camp Leader Ward," she called across the blue portal, "Agent Coraly is right here, honey. You're going to have to tell her. She's going to fucking kill you."

4

"Hi Angie." There was hesitation in his friendly greeting, like he was testing the taste of his own words.

"Don't 'Angie' me. What have you done, Ward?"

It was still strange, looking at a swirling blue portal as I spoke to him, not able to see him to read his expression. But I could imagine the twenty-three-year-old Camp Leader in charge of the Cavalry calm in the General Operations Camp Leaders' office. I'd known him face-to-face for two years before my mission commenced and a further two years through this bloody portal and he wouldn't be pacing the floor, no matter how bad the news was. He'd be sitting at one of the three desks under the enormous map that was pinned above them where recent activities were tracked.

"Just to be clear. Captain Coraly gave the order." His pitch rose slightly, as if waiting for confirmation or approval.

What fresh torment would my brother put me through now!

Normally, he was calm personified. He never pitched or darkened his tone of voice, like he could stand through a storm without flinching. Ward was often lost in thought about his family in the north, a burden that no one could truly understand. His long dark hair, unruly and slightly messy, framed a face that was sharp and angular.

Today was the first time I'd heard him sound concerned, but it wasn't as if I could reach into the portal and strangle him on the other side.

"To do what, Ward?"

"I was on patrol with a few guys when Watson came with Captain Coraly's order. We captured King Blackbone by the border, his bodyguard Murben and another guy with one bleeding thumb."

They did what? I wanted to swear and threaten to kill him, but nothing came out of my mouth. Shock numbed my brain. My brother had captured Ben, and he'd never free the black-wing king now. The two years of my life that I had spent on this undercover mission had been a waste. All my efforts at getting close to Ben had been in vain. My mission was ruined. My brother would have known this when he gave the order.

"Angie," he cleared his throat and waited a while. "Agent Coraly, are you there?"

"I'm going to fucking kill him."

"So, *we* are good, right?"

I didn't take the time to answer and rushed to my room to pack my duffel bag with my belongings, knowing I might not return. I laced my ankle-high boots and shoved my arms into a leather jacket.

What had Ben, Murben and Davis been doing close to the border this late at night? Ben had thought that Murben was guarding me, so had their venture out there anything to do with looking for me?

Oh Spirits, this is my fault.

Zoe's stout form blocked my route through the hallway towards the door like a starfish. "Where are you going? Remember how much you hate letting people into your life and how you love working undercover in the shadows where no one pays you any attention – where you can't get hurt or betrayed. You don't want to go back to the outpost. Having people around you, and having to trust them enough to cooperate, will make you miserable. They call you names. Remember that?"

I did remember. I wasn't looking forward to that part, but I had to get back to oversee what my brother would do to Ben. There was a part of me that didn't allow me to hide in the shadows this time.

"There is no point in me staying here. My mission has been a disaster."

I shook my head like a wet dog trying to rid myself of the agony of facing *home* again. But I had to go and stop Harvey from beheading Ben. Nor did I want any harm to come to Murben. He was supposed to visit his friend's ill child, not be taken captive in a white-wing outpost dungeon.

Shit! Shit! Shit!

I hugged Zoe tightly before pushing past her. "See you later!" I shouted to my best friend from the door as I left, which was more than Zayd got. Farewells really were my weakness.

The outskirts of the city were quiet. No turmoil gave away the secret the night hid; the horror that had fallen upon their king. My heart was throbbing. How could I get to Ben faster? My brother had probably planned to use Murben for the Spirits' Trek, but I wasn't sure what he would do to the enemy king. Would Harvey keep him around, considering what the black-wings had done to our family when sending mother as an undercover agent to infiltrate the Bensguard Outpost? If I knew my brother, Harvey would be quick to get his revenge, especially with his feelings running amok just returning from having to behead our very own Father.

Good. I should let him take our revenge on the black-wing king. But for some fucked-up reason, my blood boiled with fury when I thought about that evil tyrant getting hurt.

There was a single cavalry soldier heading my way down the cobbled street. *Perfect.* I could do with a horse. Quickly, I used the waterspout to climb onto the roof of a house aligned with the street and hid in the shadows of the night, waiting for the man to ride past.

A gust of wind made his dark-blue cloak billow backwards, but he slowly corrected it to lie neatly over his broad shoulders. *Crap, it's a castle guard.* He had ten years and twenty kilos on me, but I had adrenaline on my side, and a duffle bag so heavy it could have been packed with rocks. *Or so at least my brother would tell me.*

The moment the guard rode directly beneath me, I sprang from the ledge, wind whipping past my face as I dropped like a prancing cat from above. I landed hard on the horse's haunches, the impact jolting the animal and startling the rider. Before he could react, I drove my shoulder into his back and yanked him off balance. He let out a startled cry as he toppled sideways, crashing onto the cobblestones with a thud.

Without hesitation, I swung forward into the saddle, muscles tensing as I gripped the reins. The horse whickered and reared slightly beneath me, hooves scraping the ground, but I yanked it under control and spun it sharply around. My heels dug into its flanks, and we bolted, hoofbeats pounding like war drums against the cobblestones. The horse was fast and steady, clearly used to being in stressful situations and knowing to get the heck out of there. It practically flew through the city and across the fields like an arrow, and I bent low so as not to get caught in the wind.

When I looked over my shoulder and saw no sign of the capital behind me, I slowed to a canter, and as the horse tired, I allowed it to walk. I rocked on the charger's back to the sway of his walk for three hours, dozing off every now and then as I leaned over the saddle, thanking the Spirits he had not strayed from the set course when I woke up in the early morning as the sunlight shone straight onto my face.

A short distance away, I saw the tall fence running between the mountain walls that surrounded the Bensguard Outpost. *Home.* I had not seen it for two years and a pang of nostalgia set heavy on my chest. There were only a few moments between here and familiar ground, friends, my brother…and Zayd Watson. A chill ran down my arm even though it was clammy inside the thick leather and under the scrutiny of the summer heat.

A guard in each of the two watch towers on either side of the large iron gates glared down at me as I approached, pointing arrows my way momentarily before they recognised me, probably identifying me by my blue hair.

The guard in the right watch tower leaned over the railing of the waist-high balustrade. "Hello Agent Coraly. Are you supposed to be back already?" Brian La Roy shouted.

Brian was a cadet going into third year in the Special Missions Unit Academy after the summer; and the General Operations Unit Captain's younger brother. "I have not received a report from Captain Coraly."

Not sure why he bothered. He had grown up with me at the outpost, so he knew me well enough to expect my response. "If I told you, I'd have to kill you!"

"Still waiting to have that stand-off with you!"

"As long as you don't use your fire wielding!"

"Done deal!"

He didn't know I possessed magic. My brother had strictly forbidden me from telling anyone about our inherent powers, and the black-wing king wasn't the only one who could keep a secret about magical abilities.

I passed through as La Roy opened one side of the winged gates for me, making my way to the enormous military building, which I remembered as beige but was now a sun-bleached off-white. The left wing was for the Special Missions Unit and the right was for the General Operations Unit. The ground floor was for cadets and serving agents, the first floor was for workers and infirmary staff and the top was for the leaders. Each wing had two inner courtyards, and the main body of the building held the canteen, the sparring hall, the assembly hall, the infirmary hall and all the lecture rooms.

I quickly pounded every step of the stairs to get to the second floor and our family's apartment, which five years ago had been assigned to my father as a general but was now the residence of my brother as the captain. I wondered whether Harvey had kept my room the same as when I left it.

Outside the door, I lifted the strap of the duffle bag off my shoulder and let it rest on the floor before crouching low, searching through it to find my key. I stood up and bent over to shove it into the keyhole.

Hmm. It doesn't fit.

No matter how I turned it, it didn't slide into the slot. He must have changed the locks.

I knocked on the door and waited. No one opened it. The duffle bag went up onto my shoulder again and I made my way down the hallway to the Captain's Office. I hadn't seen my brother in two years, but there would be words to be said if I could catch him before he left for the capital. *Nothing like adding a little guilt trip before he had to behead our father for our mother's betrayal.*

Harvey should have launched a rescue mission to save Father and not follow King Emille's orders blindly. It wasn't Father's fault. It wasn't fair of King Emille to punish him – execute him – because there was a slight chance Father had been conspiring with Mother.

The walk over the green rubber mat that covered the floor between white painted walls was daunting, as I was closing in on a conflict with Harvey who would either act as my humble brother or as the strict captain of the Special Missions Unit. The corridor smelled of bleach, invoking childhood memories of my family living here and I couldn't count how many times I had walked these halls.

I passed the camp leader's office and reached the door sporting a large silver plaque stating, 'Captain's Office'. My nerves tingled, and I shook my arms and legs to relax them, readying myself to barge inside with the full force of my wrath. The door handle was cold in my hand. I breathed out, yanked open the door, and stormed inside.

The wrong blue eyes looked up from the ledgers on the desk and stared at me. A navy-blue camp leader uniform stiffened instead of a yellow captain's one. That wasn't my brother. What was Zayd doing in Harvey's office?

Fucking Spirits!!

I hadn't wanted to deal with him until later today. I had no idea what to say to him. My speech to him was supposed to be carefully thought out, but here we were.

It was strange to see him again. His appearance matched his rough, untameable character. His piercing sapphire eyes were often the first thing people noticed about him. At this moment, they looked tired though, revealing his exhaustion. There were dark circles under his eyes, a sign of sleepless nights from his emotional burdens.

He was speechless for a while, and I had definitely swallowed my tongue. I glanced around the room to avoid meeting his gaze, seeing the stacked boxes in the corner containing new study books, the wall-to-wall bookshelves filled with documents on how to run the outpost, the window towards the inner courtyard and the wall behind the desk hosting various paintings inside bulky golden frames. The walls were newly painted to cover the constant reoccurring mould, which my brother would have done himself as he liked things to look pristine.

"Agent Coraly, why have you left your mission in the Black Wing Territory without permission?" he growled through clenched teeth.

That's what he asks?

Two years after me walking out on him, that's what was on his mind?

It was weird to hear his voice again, like a smooth stroke of a brush that had once made me purr.

This was so awkward.

His expression didn't soften. He held his icy cold stare on me under his wide forehead, clear from his short auburn hair that was gelled straight upwards. He looked stronger than two years ago, but thinner, as if he hadn't eaten properly and worried too much. After his mother had left him with nothing but a letter in a basket on the military building's doorsteps, he didn't trust anyone. Not even me. Especially not me, considering I had done the same to him. My heart cramped. I had been despicable.

My body was twisting like a sponge, wringing out any last remains of self-composure. "Where is Harvey?"

"Ending someone's life, as I believe runs in the family," he muttered, not meaning my mission of killing the king, but referring to when I had left him without a goodbye. Then he focused back on the ledgers on the desk, avoiding looking at me.

Damn. Harvey had travelled to the capital, Emendir, already. *And Ouch! For the snide remark.* Although I deserved it.

"I'm glad Harvey didn't hear you say that." I raised my brows at him. He knew what I meant. Harvey held it together, a strong façade, but his heart was heavy with the assassinations of both our parents. None of them by his own choice.

My heart was definitely shrivelling up like a prune left out in the heat to dry. I couldn't stand his disdain. It was Zayd. My Zayd. The man I had known since I could remember and had loved since we were teenagers. I could have bet any money on him loving me no matter what. But he was pushing me away. Hurt. I had done that to him and had only myself to blame…and partly my brother. I started for the door but hesitated before exiting into the hallway.

"Did Harvey tell you he forced me to go on the mission to the Black Wing Territory?"

Something changed in his eyes. I knew him well enough to notice that my comment had captured his attention even when he did his bloody best to pretend I wasn't there.

"I'm sure your brother had his reasons," he muttered, casually writing something down in his ledger as if I was so unimportant he could afford to split his focus.

So cold. I would get nowhere with him in this mood. I had hurt him too deeply, and I had just ripped open the almost-healed wounds. He would need some time to digest my return.

"I came to the field to see you, Zayd, but you were in the middle of teaching second-year navigation training. I waited but my nerves…you know I'm no good at goodbyes. Especially not when it comes to you."

He turned a page of the ledger on the desk. "Zoe was with you in the Black Wing Territory. You could have communicated with me through a hearing portal anytime you wanted."

He was right, I could have. I hadn't known what to tell him. Leaving him was painful for me, too. But Harvey had sent me on a long-term mission with a high probability of death. He couldn't wait for someone who might never return. He had to move on.

He sighed and turned another page on his ledger. "I'm busy. I'm sure you can find someone else to report to."

What? Who? Zayd was the Deputy Captain for the Special Missions Unit when my brother was absent, and General Denor rarely visited the outpost. Thank the Spirit of Life for that, since he possessed mind bending magic, and could shape anyone's mind to become an entirely different person if he wanted to. There was no scarier person in this world. He had come to the Bensguard Outpost ten years ago and after having completed the academy he had been camp leader for a year before he was promoted to captain and the following year to a general when my father had been imprisoned. Although, he simultaneously held both positions as captain and general for a year until Harvey had graduated and had gone straight into the captain's role whilst Zayd had been promoted to camp leader.

So, Zayd was the next in line of command of those present at the outpost.

What would I do now? I didn't want to start a fight, as I was the one who had been an arsehole. He had those stern lines running across his face I recognised so well. If I pushed him right now, I'd just dig myself into an even bigger hole.

Unless...he's still...emotionally attached...

"As you wish. I'll leave and make my own arrangements to join the new class this year in the academy, so I get to hike the Spirits' Trek once I graduate. A few new magical abilities and be sent to fight the war in the north should do me good."

His head jerked up from the ledgers.

Yup, still watches out for me. Not pleased, though.

The lines in his face turned even harsher. "You're an undercover field agent. I can tell you now that such a request will be declined."

"Why would leadership decline it? My mission has hit a dead end. I attempted to steal the Black Blade and got caught." I wouldn't tell him I knew about King Blackbone being captured, as he might assign a guard to tail me, ensuring I didn't visit him in the dungeon. "It's the only way I'll be allowed to stay at the Bensguard Outpost."

Every person who had received inherited magic from their ancestors had to undertake three years in the academy and then serve a lifetime in the Special Missions Unit or be moved to serve in the General Operations Unit in either the Infantry, Cavalry or the Air Force Camp. Some were allocated to the Infirmary Unit, like Emroyce's little sister Fern. But no one, except the children, whose fathers went on the Spirits' Trek mission with my father, knew I had magic. So, technically, my brother could kick me out.

"You're too weak," he said straight to my face. "And you just told me you failed a simple extraction mission. When you fail walking through the Spirits' Trek, you die."

"So? Maybe I will die." I put my hand on my hip. "Not that you care."

He broke eye-contact, looked back down at his ledger and continued writing. "I do care." The deep frown lines etched into his forehead did not soften. "Harvey would be upset."

Fine. His pride is still hurt. I get it. But he was being an arse, which wasn't like Zayd.

"You know what? I think I'll find someone else to report to, after all. Might be easier to negotiate with someone who isn't so emotionally deprived." I left my brother's office, but I wasn't on my way to find a camp leader. I was set on finding Ben.

The dungeon cells were in the basement of this wing, so all I had to do was descend the same stairs to the ground level floor and then continue down underground. The lower I descended, the more the earthy and damp cellar smell intensified. I rushed my steps, and the dankness lay heavy on my chest by the time I arrived at basement level.

I peered around the door frame to the guard's office, and I saw the neck-long black hair of Camp Leader Terry Ward, as he was crouching down in front of the desk with his back towards me. He was tampering with a light crystal, probably using his amplifying magic to make the crystal strong enough to deter Ben's magic. The crystals were imbued with pure light magic that could deter any magic or evil spirit, but there weren't many crystals left in the world that held light. Hence, the academy tried to make Ward amplify their potency for as long as he could.

As he appeared occupied, I carefully extracted the big iron ring with the cell keys from a nail on the wall next to the door, making sure not to make a sound. I returned to the corridor, and I looked down the long hall with cells on either side, smothering the urge to call out for Ben.

They had added so many more cells since I was last here. This could take a while, as I searched between the bars on each in passing. My heart raced. I halted abruptly as I saw a beastly shape through the dim light. The sight made my composure come undone.

It was Ben.

5

Ben sat on a single bed, leaning against the far end wall. These newer cells rivalled the cadets' rooms on all levels, except that they didn't have windows or doors. The bed had a mattress and comfortable bedding. There was a shower cubicle and toilet in the corner with a shower curtain for privacy and there was a small table with one chair on the left side. On the wall above it, there was a shelf with some stacked books.

When Ben noticed me by the bars, he closed the book he was reading and tossed it onto the bed before getting up and sauntering towards me. My breath caught seeing the coloured patches of a beating on his face, a cracked lip, and a swelling under his right eye.

"Agent Coraly." His growl was guttural. "To what do I owe this visit?"

I swallowed and stepped backward as he reached the bars, but he was quick enough to snap up my wrist. He held it in an iron grip I couldn't even attempt to get out of, staring at me with so much hatred. My heart raced as I felt his grip hurt me more and more, and I tried my best to breathe through the fear that was like hot flames licking the inside of my belly. He finally relaxed and dropped my hand, resting his forearms on the iron rods running horizontally across the bars at stomach height.

"You know my real name," I whispered, not wanting Camp Leader Ward to hear us. "Who told you?"

He leered, staying unnervingly calm. "I knew it before you even stepped onto black-wing soil. I am a king. I have spies."

"Then why? Why keep me alive? Let me get close to…" I stopped talking.

Am I hurt? Have I confused the mission with genuine emotions?

I bit down on the inside of my cheek. Ben had betrayed me. Used me. I had utterly failed as a mission agent. Disappointment latched to my heart like a rake scraping the soil on sewing day, carving deep fissures into its wall. But the fact that his feelings for me weren't true hurt the most. Yet, I couldn't be angry with him, as I had betrayed him, too.

I craned around him to look for his bodyguard. "Where's Murben?"

He nodded sideways to indicate he was in the next cell along.

Ben kept glaring at me as if he could read my thoughts. Could he? I was fucked. Why was I even down here?

"You seem upset, Miss Stone," he crooned.

Stone? He wants passage into my heart.

I realised I had taken a cramping hold around the iron keys to the point they were digging into my flesh, so I loosened my grip, seeing the patterns indented into my skin.

I remembered why I was here.

The king couldn't stay captive. It would cause a valid reason for war in the minds of black-wings. My brother had made a mistake with his order to capture Ben; maybe Harvey wasn't thinking straight because of the focus on beheading our father.

I wanted to cry and when I cocked my head up, I saw Ben pucker his brows, casting shadows over his dark eyes. They were looking at me loaded with pity.

Get your shit together!

This man was dangerous, but I had to pluck up the courage to let him free.

I rolled my shoulders in my leather jacket, feeling the weight of my bag, and took a deep breath, letting it out slowly. "I'm going to come closer so I can unlock the gate."

He lifted his brows. "You're freeing us?"

Yeah, good question. One I can't really make sense of myself. It's the stupid, inexplicable attraction numbs my brain of logic.

I raised my chin, wanting to give the impression that I had thought this out even though I didn't know what the fuck I was doing. "Yes. Give me your word that you won't hurt me or anyone else on your way to your territory."

His tongue skimmed over his bottom lip as if he liked the taste of my fear, and he was still leaning across the iron bar as if he was in no rush. "Are you coming with us?"

I shook my head, and he must have immediately realised where my loyalties lay and that I had betrayed him.

He grunted in response. "Pity." He took a step back and crossed his arms over his chest. "I give you my word that I won't harm you."

I pinched the key to his cell between my fingers and snorted to myself. "Not that it matters. I'm as good as dead after I have signed the enrolment contract to join the training for the Spirits' Trek, anyway."

Before I could shove the key into the lock, Ben slammed his palm over the keyhole to cover it up.

"What?" His eyes, the colour of blood, glowed with anger, the eye-contact too intense to hold for long, so I stared at his hand.

"Hello? Anybody there?" Ward shouted from the door frame of the dungeon office.

Shit! Ben had shouted so loudly that Camp Leader Ward had heard him.

The sound of heels clicked on the stone floor.

I waved my hand in front of the bars. "Quickly," I hissed at Ben. "Remove your hand so I can unlock the gate before he arrives."

Ben hung his head, listening to the footsteps. There was no urgency twitching his muscles, no sign of fear for his life. He even took the time to grunt. "You aren't here to free me on official orders, are you?"

"Of course not. Don't be stupid."

He stared at me in silence, putting my nerves even more on edge as Ward came closer.

"Agent Coraly," Ben sighed. "I can see now why you need a lot of time planning this gravity of mischief."

I flashed him a sarcastic grin. "Remove. Your. Hand!" I barked in hisses.

"No. I think I'll stick around to watch the entertainment of your suicide plan. This *palace* far outranks the comfort in my castle. It almost inspires me to redecorate the dungeons in Black Castle."

"It will be the death of you too, if you don't let me help you. You know they'll use you for the Spirits' Trek at best. The cadets will kill you at worst."

No sign on his face showed he seemed bothered about that. "They can try."

The clicking of boots stopped behind my back and Ben's gaze lifted above my head where I knew Camp Leader Ward was standing before I had turned around.

"Agent Coraly, you're back already."

He wore a long, well-worn cloak of midnight-blue over his camp leader uniform, embroidered with intricate silver thread patterns along the hem. What made him truly unforgettable, though, was his teal-coloured eyes that shone through any dark spaces even when his tall frame moved through a crowd like a shadow. He had a glass vial hanging from a chain around his neck. The vial contained a swirling, silvery liquid that seemed to shift with an otherworldly glow. It was a rare amplifying elixir he used in conjunction with his magic. One that Ward had obtained at great cost, and one that he used sparingly.

Ward looked me over, noticed the keys in my hand and tapped the sword he was holding against them. "What are you doing?"

I swallowed. If Ward wasn't a friend, I was dead. No good would come from lying to him. "I had planned on freeing the king."

Ben tore his fingers through his hair. "Fuck, Angelica. Have you never considered lying just once in a while?"

Now, he had the decency to look nervous?

I looked at the camp leader who held outstanding achievements at the Bensguard Outpost. He had graduated last year and had already climbed in rank. Like most of the cadet descendants of the vigorous men who had completed the Spirits' Trek in the past, he had firm muscles set on a lean body. His biceps bulged under his uniform and his large hands were honed to hold a heavy sword.

"That's not my style, and there is no point. I know Ward, and I can't fool him." I held out the ring of keys towards him. "You can lock me in another cell while I await my punishment."

"I don't know." Ward shifted his weight from one long leg to the other and looked me up and down, as if he could judge whether I was still a friend or an enemy, by my clothes. "I'm pretty sure attempting to rescue an enemy king is considered treason and goes beyond the outpost's laws."

Ironic. My mother's genes come into play again. I couldn't help but snort, the sound bitter and hollow. "Traitor isn't a new label I have to live with after the white-wings found out about Mother's betrayal. Although, if you tell General Denor, I'm sure he'll be more than happy to add another chopping block next to my father's for tomorrow."

Ward scratched his head, his brow furrowed in thought. The dim light from the lanterns flickered across his face, partially hiding the turmoil in his eyes. "I guess my duty is to report it to your captain," he said, his voice tinged with reluctance. "What he does after that is up to him."

As he removed the keys from my hands, I wrapped my arms around myself, the chill of the stone walls seeping into my bones. "Thank you," I whispered, the words barely escaping my lips.

He nodded towards the corridor that led to the exit of the dungeon. "You should report to Camp Leader Watson."

"I tried," I admitted, my voice heavy with frustration. "Zayd made it clear that he didn't want to speak to me."

Ward sheathed his blade. "I don't blame him. Honestly, what you did to him was cruel. He really loves you, you know."

Ben's eyes darted up from the floor to glare at me; an intense stare that made my skin crawl.

Great. Now he knows exactly how he can hurt me.

I tried to ignore him and looked at Ward. "Yeah. I don't think Zayd appreciated my homecoming, or that I told him to sign me up for the academy."

Ward made a low whistle, his expression showing he had picked sides – and it wasn't mine. "You really swing hard blows at his broken heart. You know he had planned to propose to you at the Turning of the Year celebration the year you left. He showed me the ring and everything."

Ouch. Great, now my heart is hurting even worse.

Few nowadays dared to commit to the Spirits' mark of that sacred bond as the Spirits would be unforgiving if you broke the oath. Zayd had loved me so deeply he had been willing to pledge an oath to the Spirits that he would cherish me forever, and I had left him without a word.

I massaged my hand over my chest, struggling to draw a full breath in the dungeon's oppressive air. The walls, slick with age and dampness, seemed to close in around us. Shadows clung to the corners, and the faint echo of dripping water added to the suffocating need for better air. The space surrounding us had taken on a concealing hue that I suspected was from Ben's magic.

"Maybe it was for the best then, as we won't know if I'll survive the academy, especially second year's eighth challenge. My wings are too heavy to even carry *myself* very far, let alone a rope-bound teammate across that deep gorge."

"You're brave to join voluntarily without having magic."

Ben looked up and stared at Ward. "Talk her out of it." It was a king's command made with finality, but he was no king here, and Ward's calm wasn't something one would ruffle easily.

Ward nodded at Ben but kept his eyes on me. "He doesn't know you very well, does he?"

"Apparently not," Ben answered, and I could feel his eyes on the back of my neck.

I turned away, my arms instinctively wrapping around myself again, as if to ward off the chill that had nothing to do with the dungeon's temperature. "We shouldn't speak about the academy challenges in front of them," I told Ward. "We can't forget they're our enemy. I have not forgotten what side I am on."

Ward lowered his head to look me fully in the eye. "Do me the favour of not signing anything until your brother is back and you have discussed it with him."

I nodded, though my heart felt heavy. "I suppose I owe you as much," I muttered, lifting the strap of my duffle bag, its weight now making my shoulder scream.

"Now, make yourself scarce from the dungeon before anyone else finds you down here. Camp Leader Nar will arrive at any moment to relieve me. It's my turn this week to fly out on the morning patrols." Ward nodded, a glint of respect in his eyes.

"Seon Nar from General Ops Air Force Unit? She is still in service?" I asked, my curiosity piqued despite the heaviness in my chest.

"She's only forty and a heck of an air wielder. I think General Denor has his eyes on making her captain at the first wrong step your brother makes. They know each other, having grown up in the same small village in east Pharanir near the herb forest of Pansery."

"That group of peculiar people is tight," I mused aloud. "I don't envy my brother."

"I don't think anyone does," Ward agreed, his gaze distant. "But everyone respects him. He's a good man."

"Clearly, you don't have any brothers who kept you in leg locks for half your childhood." I replied with a wry smile, the tension in my shoulders easing slightly at the familiar banter.

Murben chuckled from the next cell over, and again it reminded me they were listening.

Ward's face turned grim as he heard Murben, but it relaxed once more as he looked back at me. "Actually, I have three brothers and two small sisters, who I have kept in leg locks for many hours. And parents who constantly want me to be stationed at Abarath Outpost closer to home instead of understanding the important work we do here at the academy."

Ben sneered this time, and we both scowled at him. But he kept a straight face, keeping his expression utterly bored.

"You know, there is another reason you might want to wait a year before you join the Special Missions Unit…or you could join the General Operations Unit instead. I'd be happy to take you in the Cavalry Unit."

Irritated, I pointed my finger sharply at him. "So, you're taking King Blackbone's advice to try and talk me out of it?" I folded my arms over my chest. "Let's hear your best argument."

In my peripheral view, I could see Ben's eyes switching between Ward and me, listening to the conversation.

Ward cringed and inhaled a deep breath. "This year, the first-year cadets fall under Camp Leader Zayd Watson's command. Your boyfriend would be your superior."

I rolled my head around my shoulders. "He isn't my boyfriend," I muttered, glancing at Ben to see his nostrils flare and his weight shift to his other leg. I turned back to Ward. "Who's doing second year? Collin Mewer or Rhie Neville?"

"Neville."

Fuck! If it had been Mewer, I could have asked him to take me into second year classes and skip first. But Neville was petrifying, literally. Her magic could petrify people, keeping them unconscious for hours with no recollection of what was happening in the world around them. She also hated black-wings as Abarath, her hometown, was the city and outpost most attacked, being so close to the border in the north.

I wouldn't be surprised if I was on the list of people who she wouldn't hesitate to use her magic on.

A chill ran up my arm just thinking about it. "I should get going," I muttered without admitting it had been a solid argument and headed for the stairs.

"Just remember that my unit is always an option, Agent Coraly," Ward shouted down the hall.

I reached ground level and went outside for air. I had a few hours, if not days, to kill before my brother returned, so I had to make a plan to keep myself busy. Maybe I'd practise archery. It was a while ago I'd held a bow and arrow, since the black-wing's practice fields didn't allow women on them. For tonight, I found myself under my favourite oak tree that no one wanted to fell, even though it was right on the side-line of the flight field next to a practice obstacle course.

This was the exact spot where I had stood two years ago when I had last seen Zayd before I had left. I had been dressed in the tight black jumpsuit and had the same duffle bag slung over my shoulder. It felt like all that weight was still on my shoulder. I lowered the duffle bag to the grass but felt no relief. I turned towards the tree, stroking my fingers over its rough bark, recognising every groove, having climbed this tree at least two dozen times every month during my childhood. Most of those times, I hadn't been alone. Zayd had climbed up and sat on the branch opposite mine.

I jumped to get a grip around the first branch and wrapped my leg around it to get up, stretching for the next branch and the next until I got to my spot. I scanned the empty field stretching out before me, which would be filled with arriving cadets in two weeks' time to settle in for the new year. Summers were always quiet at the outpost because the cadets and many workers went back home. Only a few workers, the sergeants in General Operations Unit and the leadership remained on the grounds.

It was peaceful. I leaned against the trunk and kept one knee up with the other leg dangling down. But a sudden scraping noise made me sit up straight. I held onto the trunk to twist my back around and saw Zayd climbing up. He was fast, reaching his branch opposite mine on the other side of the trunk in a heartbeat.

But all the nine Spirits knew I needed more than one heartbeat to figure out what to say to him.

6

It had never been as awkward sitting with him in this tree as it was at this very moment. I had no clue as to what to say. Where to start? It was Zayd. The man I had always loved. The man who had taken care of me at the Bensguard Outpost through thick and thin. He had bandaged my injuries, put plasters on my scrapes and kissed me better since as long as I could remember.

He had changed from his cotton uniform to the navy-blue flight leathers displaying his rank with one chevron on his right shoulder and our outpost emblem of a key at his collar. On his left shoulder were the three circles that showed the degree of skill that a person possessing magic could wield. One meant beginner, two meant adept and, having received three, it meant he was advanced at using his magic.

He had daggers strapped to his legs, two crossed swords in the baldric at his back, iron arm guards and bicep bracelets to protect him from the stroke of a sword. That was more gear than during a normal patrol run.

"Ward was quick to find you and snitch on me. Has he asked you to convince me to join his unit instead of enrolling in the academy?"

"Ward? No. I have not seen him today, but we're scheduled to fly out on patrol in a few minutes. I saw you from my window. I was expecting you to come here. Have you forgotten that I know you?" he said sorrowfully, as if he assumed I had.

I glanced at the window he meant. He was one of six camp leaders now and had been allocated an apartment one year before I left instead of the dorm room he had lived in when he was a cadet. His apartment windows overlooked the field, so it was no surprise that he had seen me in the tree, using his far-sight magic.

He looked up towards the second-floor windows following my gaze and then back at me. "I'm sorry about how I treated you earlier. I was in shock. Harvey never answered any questions when I asked about your mission. If you were happy? When you were coming home? If you were dead? It's been two years, and I've been told nothing. As the weeks and months passed, I flew deeper and deeper into the Black Wing Territory, hoping to spot you, and got severely injured a few times. I was close to abandoning the academy to search for you."

Spirits! He must have really suffered.

I swallowed the lump that had swelled in my throat. "Leadership would have executed you for desertion."

"Harvey reminded me enough times." He stared at me with his sky-blue eyes as if I was the Spirit of Love herself. "And finally, you're back." He released a deep breath as if he had been holding it the whole time. "I had hoped to get some warning, so I was prepared for what to say. It makes me happy to know that you wanted to come home at the first opportunity when your mission became redundant after we captured the black-wing king."

That wasn't the truth. I came back to free the king, but I would let him have his beliefs if they made him feel more at ease.

I dug my nails harder into the bark and looked up at the pink morning sky. "I wanted to have a word with Harvey, but the coward left before I got here."

Zayd leaned around the trunk to see me better and rested his forearm on his bent knee. "It's easy to blame Harvey. The Spirits know I gave him a hard time after he sent you away. For a long time, when we sparred, it wasn't friendly. But in all fairness, he has had his fair share of hardships."

"Well, he didn't have to go and do the 'honourable death' and behead his own father. That's just looking for heartache."

"He's purely doing it for you."

"For me? What the fuck! Why would you say that, Zayd?"

"King Emille is piling a lot of pressure on him, watching his every action. One wrong step, and leadership will remove him from the Bensguard Outpost. One traitorous sign and they will execute him. Ever since the Battle of Bensguard, people around here who were disloyal to your father keep muttering the word traitor behind Harvey's back and they beat him up if he strays too far into the shadows. He wants to show his loyalty by beheading your father so that you won't suffer the same label. He…" he said, gazing at me lovingly, "nor I," he continued but hesitated as if he wanted me never to doubt him, "can stand the thought of someone hurting you. Everything he does is to protect you."

"I needed my brother when my mother died and my father was thrown in the dungeon, and what did he do? He sent me away to the Black Wing Territory. How is that protecting me?"

"Perhaps he thought the Black Wing Territory was safer than it is here. Harvey and I had just started second year at the academy, and we were considered the strongest team, so everyone wanted to see us fail. We were a great team, but bloody near useless when we were both worried about you. Harvey couldn't be around to protect you all the time. He needed to focus on the challenges, or he could have got us both killed. And now you want to join the academy voluntarily when he got you out and into the undercover agency? More cadets die in the challenges now than they did five; and even two years ago. The soldier death count in General Ops is rising, too."

I puckered an eyebrow at him. "Is that supposed to scare me away from the enrolment ledgers?"

"I hope so. Please, don't enrol. The Spirits' Trek is a suicide mission. No one has survived the hike since our fathers did it. I beg you to reconsider. If not for you, then for me. I've watched my best friend in pain beyond what's humane and my friends die, but you…I don't think I can take it, watching you die."

I wanted to tell him not to watch then, but he would be my camp leader and would be forced to be there, right by my side as I died.

I couldn't look him in the eye, so I turned my head to look out over the field. "I have little choice."

"Stay with me in my apartment."

His plea struck at my heart. It was a scary thought to entangle myself in something so serious. I needed time to process what my new life would look like.

"Lovers are forbidden within the same unit in the academy." I stuck to the technical answer to recite the rule.

"You wouldn't be in the academy. You would be my housewife."

Spirits! What a horrible thought. What would I do? Knit all day and prepare dinner for when he came home? If he came home. He'd be fighting evil, and I'd do nothing to protect our territory? That was not how I had been raised.

"The cadets, workers or the generals would detect my magic and then I would have to do the training for the Spirits' Trek, anyway."

"Okay, so live in the city. I'll send you money and I can see you most weekends."

A knot formed in my stomach. Did I really want to resume our relationship from where we had left off? I wasn't the same person anymore. I had grown, having had to take care of myself inside enemy territory.

I shook my head. "No. I'm going to repair the damage to my family name even if it takes me my whole life to earn it back. Even if it kills me during the challenges. For Father. The Coraly name should not spell the word traitor in people's minds."

"You'd rather die than be with me?"

My chest heaved with a few sorrow-filled breaths. He couldn't think that was the truth. "I'd rather die than hurt you again." My focus swept across the field, seeking a change of topic, and found it in the obstacle course. "But I'm not planning on dying. I think I'll even outperform you."

Zayd followed my gaze. "At the obstacle course? You think you can beat my time on the obstacle course? You never could when we were growing up. You know I hold the all-time record as from last year?"

I didn't know that! But it didn't matter. The purpose of the challenge was to change the topic, and it had worked.

"What's your time?"

"Four minutes and thirty-seven seconds."

Spirits, that's impossible to beat.

The track went around in an oval and it contained eight obstacles, which Zayd had conquered in half a minute each. I glanced around at the obstacles; the six bars that you had to climb over and crawl under, the net wall, the monkey rings, the crawling under a long stretch of nets, the rope wall, the abseiling down the wall on the other side, the balance bar and finally the steppingstones.

I climbed down from the tree, and Zayd followed as I walked to the starting point. "I'll beat that easily," I teased, knowing there was no chance that could happen. "What's Harvey's time?"

Zayd crossed his arms over his chest, clearly amused with a wide grin on his face. "Four minutes forty-four seconds. Emroyce makes it in four minutes and forty-five seconds when not allowed to use his speed magic, so they keep challenging each other."

"Emroyce? He will start this year with me. He's my age."

"*If* you join."

"Whatever." I rolled my eyes at him. "Who else will I recognise?"

"You've already seen Ward. Valentina Karson is still alive, going into the second year. She is as terrifying as usual, shattering and putting bones back together, only using her mind. Her mother is still working at the infirmary with Fern and Camp Leader Mewer. Brian La Roy is starting third year."

"Yeah, I saw him at the guard post when I arrived. He must be doing well. He looked strong."

"He's a fire wielder like his brother, and speaking of fire wielders, you know who else will start first year?"

"Who?"

"Kate and Mazdon Pere."

"True. Kate is my age. At least when I join, I can try to protect her. She is so small and fragile."

"Not anymore. Small perhaps, but definitely not fragile. Nevertheless, your brother is going out of his mind worrying about her."

I kicked at the white paint marking the starting line. "Kate always had a special place in his heart after the summers at our lake cottage where he spent all his time helping her control her magic. And I believe it's more than just a friendly hand to a next-door neighbour. But wait." I stopped kicking at the grass and cocked my head up. "You also said Mazdon."

"He had been working in the Air Force Unit for a year after he graduated. But he has turned in his sergeant badge and re-enrolled in the academy to protect his sister."

"Madness."

Zayd took a step closer and swiped a strand of hair behind my ear that had torn from the ponytail and had been whipping in the breeze. "I would do it for you without hesitation. But I think I have a better chance of protecting you as your camp leader. *If* you join."

I stepped away from him and prepared myself at the start line of the obstacle course, shrugging out of my leather jacket, and jumping on the pads of my feet a few times to limber up. "And what is a respectable time for me to make it in? I can't remember."

"Well, four minutes and thirty-six seconds if you were going to beat me. But, to date, the record held by a woman is just under six minutes."

"Okay. Fine. Time me."

He looked me up and down. "You might want to change clothes first."

I pinched the fabric and held out my loose linen trousers at either side of my legs; a gust of wind immediately caught them, making them look like sails.

"If I beat your record in these, you'll have to fucking worship me."

His expression softened and two lines appeared between his sleek auburn brows. "I already do."

Again, pain seared inside me, and I prayed to the Spirit of Love that he would let it go and not torture me with those remarks for the rest of my life.

I glanced at the treeline behind the field. "We should hurry. The sun is rising, and I already have my clothes against me and don't need the light shining into my eyes, too."

Zayd flipped up his wrist to look at his watch with a small sigh. "It's seven forty exactly in a few seconds. How far does your magic reach now? No magic allowed."

"Don't worry. I won't be able to cheat," I replied truthfully.

"Good. I'll count you down. Are you ready?"

I nodded, staring at the first horizontal bar at chest height that I had to launch myself over. "Yes."

He held up a finger. "Hold it. Three…two…one…go!"

I sprinted towards the bar and braced my palms on top of it to fling my legs over, immediately smelling the dampness the last deluge had left in the wood. My feet felt the impact as I landed on the other side before launching myself underneath the next bar in the alternating pattern reaching lower and higher until it became almost impossible to crawl under or climb over. Twisting my hand on the last bar to roll my back over it, a chunk of wood tore loose, and a splinter lodged into my palm. A throbbing pain began pounding through my hand, but I kept going.

The net wall was the killer for building up acid in the muscles, and it was slacker than I remembered. My legs swung back and forth as I climbed at each new grip, and my arms quickly grew tired.

Stop moaning and fucking impress him!

If I got a bad time, he would make it more difficult for me to enrol in the academy, throwing concrete statistics into my face. This was my way of showing him I could cut it.

I climbed over the bar at the top and descended quickly, jumping to drop the last few metres, feeling the impact on my knees as I landed in a muddy puddle.

Darting for the monkey rings, I jumped up to grab the hoops and swung in a tactical momentum over to the other side. I had saved time on this obstacle, as it was my favourite when it didn't absolutely kill my hand, rubbing the splinter deeper into it. But next up was the rope wall, which was murderous under normal circumstances. Not that my ankle boots were particularly helpful either, as the military boots with the rubber soles gripped better.

The heels slipped on the wooden planks a few times and I slammed into the wall with my hipbone taking the worst of the collision, but I was determined to beat one record or another, so I kept going. Finally, I could curve my leg over the top and be on my way down, and the abseiling would be one of the easier challenges if it weren't for the boots. In the end, I just twisted the rope around my good hand and pinned my feet around it, sliding down. Not sure if that counted as cheating, but at least it brought me down.

I assessed the balance bar and hesitated. The rain had soaked it through, so it would be slippery like ice. I ripped off my boots and ran across it in my socks as I didn't want to fall on it and break a bone before first day formation.

Last up were the steppingstones, and I was panting heavily now. Glad I had removed my boots, I sped forwards, jumping across them without hesitation. The wooden poles sticking out of the ground would be too far apart to jump if I broke my momentum. After the last pole, I jumped across the finish line and almost fell as I stumbled into Camp Leader Collin Mewer.

"Wow, Agent Coraly, that was impressive. How did she do, Watson?"

I hadn't noticed that Mewer had arrived and had been watching. A black leather pouch hung from his belt, filled with strange charms, and he was always accompanied by the faint scent of herbs and smoke. His long blonde hair snaked over his shoulders as he looked down at me with serene, moss-green eyes that observed everything in this world with gentleness and kindness. He was wearing his navy-blue flight leathers with the same badges as Zayd, but he was responsible for the third year, although you could most often find him in the infirmary, which was lucky for me. Mewer was a healer, someone who lived by the rules of nature and understood the deep, silent bonds that connected all life. He was quiet and reserved, and his heart was always open to those in need. Without the help of his healing magic, my childhood would have been much more painful. I wasn't known to be a graceful child. Stubborn, that word I had heard a lot, though.

I turned to look at Zayd, his lips forming into a tight line and his head lolled, his giveaway that I recognised so well. "Six minutes and thirty-seven seconds," he raised a disappointed eyebrow.

Dammit! My pride plummeted to the Underworld.

"Although you did have to take your boots off and wore no combat leathers. I'm going to have to give you another chance at it before I pass judgement on this, but…" He clicked his tongue, shaking his head at me.

"Thank you. Next time, maybe I won't have a splinter in my palm. They should really get new equipment." I held my hand up to show him.

"Spirits, Coraly. That's a big one. Let me take that out for you," Mewer said, as he gripped my hand.

He wasn't just a skilled herbalist, his magic signet was healing, but I wasn't sure how he could cure a splinter. I watched intensely as he held his hand above mine. A soft golden glow the colour of his hair shone over my skin, and it was as if the splinter crawled out on its own like a worm seeking air above the ground during rain. When a centimetre of the splinter had withdrawn itself from my skin, Mewer pinched it with his fingertips and pulled it out.

"There," he said with a kind smile.

I rubbed my palm with my thumb. "And that's why you're my favourite camp leader!"

"Hey!" Zayd shouted at me.

"It's a title you have to earn," I said playfully as I kept massaging my hand.

"I'll fight for it," Zayd muttered.

"Against a healer? Please!" Mewer mocked.

The sun reached above the trees and Mewer turned to Zayd as if he had just remembered that they had patrol duty. "Ward and Neville are waiting for us by the gates. I thought it was best we warned Neville about Coraly being back, considering her hatred for the black-wings and all."

"Good point," Zayd answered. "It'll give me the chance to tell her that if she so much as looks at Angie with hatred, I'll fucking throw her into the isolation cell for a week."

"Only Captain Coraly can do that, unless you're acting deputy," Mewer remarked.

That was true. My brother wasn't only the captain of Special Missions Unit but the camp master of the entire outpost, having to oversee the schedules, the safety and the academic advancement of all cadets and sergeants. The camp master duty normally fell on one of the two captains and Captain Thomas La Roy hadn't wanted the position because he was too busy raising his brother, Brian.

"I don't think the captain will care if I put Neville there to cool off. She hasn't exactly been friendly to him, either." Zayd glanced at his wristwatch again, clearly anxious about the time but reluctant to leave. He took a step closer to me. "Where will you be when I get back?"

That thought seared my heart again. "I promise I won't leave you again without letting you know first."

"You won't ever say goodbye again, or the Spirits help me, I'll chain you to my hip." He rushed his question, knowing he had to go. "Where will I find you?"

"I don't know. Sleeping on a couch in the common room. My key didn't work to the apartment. Harvey must have changed the lock."

"Yes, his door has been smashed in a few times over the last two years."

What? Cadets have attacked our home? Attacked him when he was off duty?

Zayd reached into his pocket and held up a key. "Here, take mine. You can stay in my guest room until Harvey is back."

I accepted it. "And what will I do if you don't come back?"

Mewer swung his arm around Zayd's shoulder. "We'll only be out for the day, and I'll have him back at eight tonight. We're only conducting a perimeter sweep along the fence, not even entering Black Wing Territory, so you needn't worry."

I twisted my head to glare at him. "Mewer, you won't be my favourite camp leader anymore if you let anything happen to him."

Almost simultaneously, Mewer and Zayd flexed out their white wings that reached from above their heads to touch the grass. The sound of the wings snapping with their muscular force was glorious to hear. It was a sound I didn't have muscle enough to create when I brought mine out, and it infused me with a nostalgic feeling.

They sprinted across the field towards the mountain backdrop and Zayd glanced over his shoulder toward me before he launched himself up into the sky.

7

The shiny iron of the arrowhead glinted in the sunlight as I drew the bowstring back.

"It's so good to have you back, Angie," Emroyce remarked. He stared at me with the same incredulity now as when I had knocked on his dorm room and dragged him out to the field, not having even given him enough time to tuck his t-shirt into his hiking trousers. "At least I get some competition."

He flashed me his captivating smile that could both charm and disarm anyone. In the two years we had been apart, it seemed he had grown taller and beefier. His jaw was just as square with a soft dimple and covered with the faintest stubble, giving him a rugged edge. His brows still wiggled with playfulness and his hair that was darker than the night, had grown below his shoulder blades. However, beneath his outer confidence, there was a vulnerability brought on by the legacy of deep-rooted pain he didn't let show to many.

"Growing up together in this damned place, you'd think you'd get tired of losing to me," I retaliated, focusing on my arrow that wasn't aligned correctly as Emroyce had distracted me.

He barked a snort. "When did I ever lose to you? In what art?"

"Pick one and any day, Emroyce Bengrey. Although, let me just have one practice round in the sparring hall with Zayd to get up to speed. Undercover mission in a castle is luxury compared to the outpost life. Zayd will have to massage the knots out of my muscles from the obstacle course tonight."

I glanced at him and saw the biggest question mark on his face. "What?"

He looked nervously between me and the target board at the end of the field. The set of his shoulders tense, braced for a confrontation, but his dazzling smile belied just how much he had learned to hide behind a wall of cynicism. "You think it's wise to stay with Zayd? You know how he is.

He gets attached to things and doesn't like change, and you are…"

I lowered my bow to rest my arms and glared at him. "I'm what?"

His stance softened, the warmth in his amber eyes glimmering with a mix of humour and wisdom. "Unsettled. Like you have not found where you belong, and clearly it doesn't seem to be with him, is all I'm saying."

A vein of concern pulled at his forehead, clearly upset that I had hurt Zayd.

He was right about Zayd, though. He didn't like change. He was a man of routine and order, his apartment was amazingly clean and tidy with everything in its place, the way he always liked it.

"That man is no poor stitching. He can handle an ex-girlfriend staying in his apartment until I enrol and get my own room."

"Thank the Spirit of Life that you weren't the one stitching him up after you left. I've seen your needlework. I sat next to you in that class."

"Ouch!" I scoffed, closing one eye with the other focused on the target.

I took the shot and hit the bullseye right next to his arrow.

"Nice shot."

"Thank you."

"But can you do it from the air?" He flexed out his wings and launched himself up in the air, turning a lap around in a circle, before twirling in the air. A risky manoeuvre that could make him fall. Our wings normally didn't carry us that way, but he succeeded effortlessly and took the shot before he hit the ground.

He was a bit of a boaster with his speed magic, so challenging him in archery meant a level playing field, instead of in combat, where I wouldn't stand a chance. His moves and blocks were so fast, they were hard to follow with your eyes.

The arrowhead lodged on the line to the centre circle of the target board.

"Show-off! And you know I hate flying."

"Kind of have to practise that if you're going to make it through the academy and the Spirits' Trek."

"I wasn't expecting to make the cut for the Spirits' Trek. I know you'll win the most challenges during the three years and be the one choosing the other four members. And honestly, would you pick me for that team?"

"You've got the brains for it, and enough skill at doing mischief."

"Spirits! Thank you, Bengrey. That's the nicest compliment you've ever given me," I said sarcastically. But I knew he was grateful for all the times I'd helped him study for the exams with our private tutors when growing up.

"If you used your magic, you'd be powerful enough to beat me. I know you have powerful magic. I don't believe you didn't inherit anything from your father. We all had our father's magic passed down to us."

"How do you know I'm not using it right now?"

"Will you tell me what it is?"

"Nope. Classified. Above your pay grade. You'll have to speak with Harvey."

"Our camp master has been more than a little tense lately, so I will not be doing that. Seriously though, if you need me to help you practise flying, I'm more than happy to do it."

"Thank you. As payback for my study help, right? Not that it would be from the goodness of your heart."

"Of course. Don't take me for a softy." He retrieved another arrow from the quiver that leaned against the wooden bow rack.

"Don't worry, Bengrey. I won't tell anyone of your humble side and ruin your reputation."

"No one would believe you, anyway. And if someone is unsure, I'll just kill a few black-wings and dump them on their doorstep."

"Sure." I smiled, letting off another arrow, striking it between the other two.

"Impressive, but can you do it with one of these?" He brought out an arrow that he had kept in a separate pocket of the quiver and showed it to me.

"Black iron?" I gasped.

He inspected it like it was the greatest thing ever made. "Yes. To kill black-wings, who have magic." He held it out to me. "Give it a try."

I lifted it out of his hand. The arrowhead was pure onyx and the way he held the shaft made me realise it was heavier than a normal arrow with the balance closer towards the arrowhead. The thought of it lodged into Ben's heart tormented me to the deepest sinews of my scabrous heart. It would penetrate the black-wing king's breastplate easily, like it should. So why did that notion tear me apart? King Blackbone started wars. He needed to be killed.

Even the way the arrow fitted against the bowstring felt different when I anchored it, like it was only meant for a sinister purpose. When I let it fly, it dipped sooner than I was used to, and it didn't even hit the target board.

"I blame the bow." I looked pointedly at the length of the bow I had borrowed from Emroyce. "It's too long and too large for my hand."

I hadn't been able to get mine from the apartment. Not that it was the true reason why I had missed. I could use any bow. I just hadn't assessed the arrowhead's weight correctly.

Emroyce held in a laugh before he strode the length between us and the target board to retrieve the arrow. Once back, he quickly made a twirl-around and nocked the arrow, released, and hit the bullseye. *Show-off!*

When anchoring his next arrow, a gust of wind caught in his wings and blew him back a step just as he let go of the arrow. It missed the target board completely.

I returned the mocking laugh and raised my brows at him. "Lesson one in archery. Never have your wings out."

He smiled and withdrew them with a snap, and we carried on practising.

In the evening, I was so exhausted that I collapsed onto Zayd's guest bed with only a towel wrapped around me after a hot shower. When I woke up, it was morning, and I immediately wondered why Zayd hadn't woken me up when he had come home.

Is he back? Is he alive?

I pushed myself out of bed and sneaked across the living room to peer into his bedroom. Yes, he was there, lying in bed with the blanket pulled up to below his abs. His upper body firm as if carved out of rock. Normally, people looked serene when they slept, but Zayd seemed unsettled, his face set tightly, as if he was still worrying about things in life while he dreamt.

Seeing him half naked like this, I didn't know what to do when it came to us anymore. He was perfection. He was Zayd. But my gut instinct told me that going back to him wasn't the right decision. I needed air, so I took my Special Mission uniform out of my duffle bag, dressed quickly and left the apartment, darting down the steps towards the inner courtyard. It was crowded with people watching the new cadets arrive and no doubt trying to gauge who among them would prove to be the strongest.

The courtyard had windows and doors all around the sides leading to the various classrooms, the sparring hall, the canteen and the main doors to the front of the building. I made my way to a quiet corner where I could watch unobserved.

Passing by cadets, I received an elbow into my side, and even though it had barely touched me, its potency made me huff and bend over in pain.

"Mutt," called the cadet with wavy piss-coloured hair reaching his ears, and a large scar across his right cheek. Three circles of magic advancement dotted the shoulder of his uniform. His hazel eyes stared at me coldly, sending me the message that he didn't like traitors' daughters.

Only a few steps deeper into the courtyard, another cadet shuffled at my shoulder, hissing the word mutt behind a cigarette that was clenched between his lips. I hadn't expected to be popular, but neither had I foreseen being hated. Three tall men confronted me, blocking my path. One of them had a tidy combed side parting, a second was dressed in combat leather as if he had just got out of combat training, and the third had bright-red hair that was shaved down the sides of a square head. Their muscular builds made it impossible to pass. I turned around, but two more cadets had come closer and all five were now gathered in a ring around me.

I'm trapped.

My heart pounded like a war drum against my ribcage.

The man with the scar took a step forward and eyed me from head to toe, as if he wanted to identify what a traitor looked like. The malice in his eyes let me know that whatever he had planned next was going to hurt. He stroked his hand over the knife strapped to his leg, but as a shadow fell over us from behind my back, everyone moved backwards, hints of fear painting their faces.

After a short stare-off, they distanced themselves from me and made as if they were casually chatting amongst themselves. I slowly turned around, petrified of what I might see behind my back. Enormous, black wings, black combat leathers, and angry, ruby eyes towered over me.

King Ben Blackbone!

The weight of his focus clearly put me in the centre of his attention. His hard resolve amplified my desires for him. *Which I bloody didn't need.* A small grin added an appeal to his face I couldn't afford to look at for long.

What was he doing here? The camp leaders shouldn't have let him out for air from the dungeon already. Although, I was even more surprised that five muscular cadets had sidled away in his presence.

The way he kept staring at me without breaking eye-contact made my skin crawl. He was incensed with me, I got that. Was he annoyed he didn't have a sword to impale me with? Probably. I shivered but didn't look away. I wasn't bloody going to lose this damned staring contest, if that was what he was doing. So, like that, we stood for a while. Staring at each other.

"Captain Coraly is back," someone voiced from somewhere behind me. I couldn't help turning around then, seeing the group of brutish male cadets looking our way.

It didn't take me long to realise what that meant. Father's sentence had been carried out. Not even the fresh air in the courtyard could make it easier to breathe, as the sorrow gripped so tightly around my heart it made it hard for it to beat.

My father was dead. *Dead.*

I began to tremble and felt my eyes water. Shock sucked the strength out of my legs and my knees buckled from underneath me.

Ben gripped my throat and slammed me into the stone wall, his shadow essence wrapped like clammy hands around my limbs. Thorns from a climbing rosebush would have been in my back had Ben aimed a few centimetres more to the left. He folded his wings around me to hide my trembling body from view. I stared into those furious eyes that had deepened in colour. No doubt this was when he'd kill me as revenge for my betrayal. Adrenaline pumped furiously around my veins and the need to draw breath overpowered my grief. His gaze trailed down my tiny body, sizing up my weaknesses. But then his eyes softened with an emotion I couldn't interpret. His hand loosened from my throat but didn't let go entirely, and the pinch of his magic essence subsided from where his fingertips met my skin.

"It's suffocating to lose someone you love, but don't show the cadets in this courtyard any weakness. Compose yourself."

I leaned my head back against the wall, realising my life was caught between murderous cadets and a crazy enemy king.

"I'm a freak."

"Freak?" He tipped my chin up with his knuckle and looked in disagreement. "I thought they said mutt." He flashed me a quick grin that was there as quickly as it vanished.

I gripped his hand in an effort to pry it off me, but my strength was nothing against his muscles. "I didn't take you for a protector of mutts."

He cocked his head sideways as if he was trying to figure out what I was doing with my hands as I tried to free myself from his grip. "I don't protect. I kill when I want to see justice. Don't confuse the concepts."

"Sounds the same to me." I tried to kick him, but my leg was hardly long enough to reach him.

He sighed, my exertions to free myself clearly having irritated him. "Protection insinuates I care. I don't. I'm doing my duty as king to make society fair."

"You're all about fair? That's why you saved my life from those cadets?"

"Yes. Their nickname for you wasn't fair. The one I call you is more fitting, Stone. You're not what people say, but what you show them you are. You just need to strengthen your weaknesses. Your personality is already flawless."

"Yes. Like stone. Stop messing with me. I know you plan to kill me. I'm surprised they let you out of the dungeon."

He grunted. "Only for a short breather."

"They shouldn't keep you captive. They should execute you immediately."

He let out a dark chuckle. "I'm not a captive. I'm choosing to stay. Let's say I have a vested interest in your fate."

I couldn't help a smile shaping on my lips and I noticed his attention was drawn to my mouth.

"Are you composed?" he asked in a grave tone. "Here comes the warden." He removed his hand from my throat and let his wings fall off me before he flexed them into his back.

I caressed my throat. "Warden? I thought you said you weren't captive."

"I'm not." He nodded towards the door. "You are."

I turned to see Zayd approach with assertive steps and understood what Ben was insinuating.

"There you are," Zayd said, looking sharp in his navy-blue camp leader uniform and his gelled-up auburn hair. "I heard when you left the apartment. You always were out of bed early."

Shit. That didn't at all sound like the whole picture. But what would Ben believe? I looked up at him and he grunted at me; a tone laced with disapproval.

All Spirits be damned!

Zayd had done that on purpose, I was sure of it. His tone had been light-hearted, but his forehead was lined with irritation. His remark meant to tell Ben to fuck right off, having seen me held inside Ben's wings. I couldn't explain the situation to Ben without Zayd getting suspicious of my loyalty to King Emille; my king. Anything I'd say would also disrespect Zayd in front of all the cadets in the courtyard. Frankly, I couldn't find one reason I should provide Ben with an explanation, since my mission was finished, and I no longer needed a relationship with the black-wing king. He was my enemy.

"I needed some air, but I should've just opened a damned window." I meant to throw the comment in Ben's face but couldn't and instead aimed an accusatory look at the group of cadets who had threatened me earlier.

Ben clearly realised the hold he had on me and made an amused grunt.

Zayd wrapped an arm around my shoulder and pulled me away from Ben.

"Come. Harvey returned last night. We should go and speak with him."

He took my hand, and I recognised the grip, as my hand fit into his as it had done so many times before when our fingers had laced together during evening walks. I heard another grunt from behind my back, and this time it did not sound amused. By reflex, I pulled my hand away from Zayd's, regretting it the moment after when he turned his head to give me a sad, quizzical look. But I made it a point to carry on walking, falling into step next to him, fighting the urge to look at Ben over my shoulder.

"You should really lift the glamour on your blue hair and dress in standard uniform, so you don't stick out. The five men you glared angrily at are the most lethal out of all the first-year cadets. Especially Craig Malloopa from the Abarath Outpost, who has been in many battles with black-wings. His magic is a rank three grade. If he touches something, he learns all about it, so make sure he doesn't touch you. His teammate, Floyd

Gravelhorn, the one with the scar, has strength magic."

"I noticed. He made me buckle over with a soft shove."

"I'll get an ointment from the infirmary for you to treat the bruise that will probably swell and colour by the afternoon."

"You don't need to do that."

"Of course I do, and I want to."

There he was, the Zayd I was used to. Always taking care of me. I flashed him a smile and stared at the floor as we took the steps up to the leadership floor.

We arrived at the Captain's Office door, and Zayd knocked with one knuckle.

"Come in!" I heard my brother shout from the other side.

It made my stomach flutter to hear his voice. It brought back so many memories and so much pain. I hadn't heard his voice or seen him in two years, and I was torn between the feelings of being desperate to see him and never wanting to see him ever again.

He has killed both our parents. A man like that couldn't have a soul left.

Zayd appeared to have noticed my apprehension as he watched me with his comforting sky-blue eyes.

"Are you ready?"

I nodded and took a deep breath.

Zayd pulled down the handle and pushed open the door for me. There, my brother sat behind his desk, his blue eyes staring daggers at me in full captain mode that could cut through any lie. He had this intensity about him that could lock onto a person with a sharpness that made others fidget under his gaze. His rat-blonde hair fell back from a side-parting as he cocked his chin up, clearly attempting to hide the shame he felt. But I knew him, and I didn't think he was fooling Zayd, either. His broad shoulders and muscular frame spoke of years of hard labour, his forearms beneath his rolled-up sleeves were dotted with faint scars that were remnants of the many battles he had fought. He looked impeccable in his yellow uniform with the two chevrons under a star on his right shoulder, yet rough somehow. He'd not had it easy the last few days, I could tell from his extra straight posture he always put on when he was too tired to claim respect from purely his wits. I would have pitied him more if I wasn't so furious with him for ruining my mission and capturing King Blackbone.

I took another deep breath to hold the tears back with the words *Father is dead* playing on repeat in my head in a variety of tones. Harvey had beheaded him. How could anyone live through this and keep their sanity.

"Angie is back," Zayd told him.

"I can see that." His voice was so stale, I could almost hear it rasp at the back of his throat. "Without permission. She should have stayed in the

Black Wing Territory."

She, is standing right here! How dare he talk over my head?

"You blew my cover." Was the only thing I managed to bite back with.

"I believe you blew your own cover by coming back here."

"You made my mission redundant when you captured King Blackbone. Why would you do that to me? I had worked two years on that mission."

"It wasn't a straightforward decision to take, but ultimately, King Blackbone is strong and he's a good candidate to survive the Spirits' Trek," Harvey said with finality, as if the case was closed.

He was the type of person who commanded attention and received it effortlessly. But I was used to his ways, and I also had the Coraly blood. Few dared to approach him as they could feel the tension in the air he always carried around, like a spark just before an explosion. But I straightened against the pressure, ready to light a fucking match to set him off if I needed to get myself heard.

"And a good candidate to capture if you want to start a war."

"That is the risk."

"A risk? You're placing many civilians in danger just to prove your loyalty and gallantry to King Emille. And what does that mean for me? You seem to forfeit your family members' lives equally as easily as any civilian's."

Zayd shifted his weight nervously as Harvey's blue eyes glared straight into me, his brows took their normal position of looking perpetually serious even when he smiled.

"I'll find another mission that suits you, Agent Coraly."

"Don't bother. I'll enrol in the academy, and when I die, you'll have one less problem to worry about."

"I will decline your enrolment," he said firmly with an exasperated look on his face.

Zayd raised his brows when looking at me, as to say he'd told me so.

I snorted at the fact that my brother thought he could still win an argument that easily over me. "Since you made a poor decision, I have no other choice than to join. You're not kicking me out of the Bensguard Outpost. This is my home. You'll accept my application, or I'll tell General Denor about our inherent magic. After that, my fate isn't up to you, as my service will be mandatory. Your call, *Captain* Coraly."

Harvey gritted his teeth as he thought. "If you believe my job is so fucking easy, let me give you a taste of it. If you decide to enrol in the academy, then on the morning of the first formation, you'll be at the infirmary at ten o'clock and we will bind your soul to the black-wing king. He'll be your responsibility and teammate in the academy. He dies, you die!"

My chest flared up with intense heat, burning even. That was a twist of fate I had not expected.

8

My brother's office suddenly felt much smaller, as if the walls were closing in on me.

"Now, hold on, Harvey," Zayd interjected, walking forward until his thighs were flush to the desk. "Binding souls gravely violates privacy, and the black-wing king will be too strong for her."

Harvey leaned back in his chair. "I know. I'm barely able to keep him out of my thoughts. But it's better that he's in her head than mine, which is full of classified information."

I dropped my jaw. "You've bonded yourself to King Blackbone?"

Harvey's gaze shifted from Zayd to me. "Yes. To all the black-wings, so that they can't escape. It's the leaders' job to take turns doing it for the black-wings. How did you think we held them captive at the outpost whilst we trained them?"

I bit down on the inside of my cheek. "I hadn't given it any thought. Cadets and sergeants will target them as black-wings, and if any of them die…" I swallowed, understanding that my brother had worse pressures to deal with than I had imagined.

Harvey nodded as if he had won the argument. "I'll be the one responsible, and I'll die with them. Yes."

Zayd didn't back down, though. "Angie isn't trained to shield her mind. And it should be a voluntary decision."

My brother snorted and sprawled both his arms over the armrests. "I trust my little sister will drive him to madness, and not the other way around. She has a knack for mischief."

"So people tell me," I muttered, rolling my eyes, believing my brother wouldn't view me in any other way than the little girl who filled his boots to the brim with soil for saying I'd never grow taller than his longsword.

"It's too dangerous, Harvey," Zayd barked. "What if the king kidnaps her and keeps her locked in the dungeon in Black Castle?"

"She's an agent. She knows the risks. And she can't complain that I spoilt her mission, because once they're soul bound, she can carry on working on the king to extract secrets about the Black Wing Territory from his mind. With their souls bound, he'll die if she dies, which means he'll protect her with his life. And I don't have to worry about Angie doing anything reckless, like the time she thought she could jump from the boulder beyond the clearing without using her wings and not break an ankle."

"That was one time," I defended. "And I was ten years old."

Zayd ignored me. "But if he–"

I held up a hand to silence Zayd. "As my captain commands." I walked up to the desk and tapped my finger on the ledger in front of him. "I will succeed in my mission and when I do, you'll admit to me that I'm the stronger Coraly sibling. And you'll treat me with fucking respect!"

I barged out of his office, fury eating me alive, but at least this setup confirmed that Ben wouldn't be executed.

I heard the office door close behind me and someone jogging to catch up.

"Wait, Angie! Where are you going?" Zayd raked his fingers through his gelled spikes. "This all went so wrong. I'll bond with the king in your stead."

"You fucking won't. I can do this. I'll show my brother I'm not his baby sister stuck in his leg lock anymore."

"Why do you need to prove anything to him? Just start a new life and be happy and don't…" he paused, his eyes drifting off to a thought deep in his mind. "Don't die."

I sped up, knowing he wouldn't be my ally in this topic. "You don't understand how it is to have your family name dragged in the mud and labelled as traitorous. It wasn't any of our faults. It wasn't as if Father or any of us knew Mother was a black-wing spy."

"I know." He blocked my path and pulled me into his embrace, lacing his fingers through my hair.

I didn't struggle to get free. "You don't think I can do this? Survive. Complete the trek? You think I'm as weak and little as my brother does."

"No. If you want to do it to feel better about yourself, fine. But don't do it to prove a point to others."

I calmed and steadied my breathing, feeling every stroke of Zayd's hand through my hair as I stared at the green rubber floor beneath my feet.

"Thank you, Zayd. You're a good friend."

His movement through my hair stopped. "Friend?"

The word, the loaded question, made my heart stop. Why had I said that and made it all complicated? Now, he would demand an explanation as to where our relationship stood. I didn't know that answer.

"It's for the best, until I have survived graduation."

"And you think it'll be easier on me if I lose you as a friend than if you die as my girlfriend?"

There it was, him pushing me when I wasn't ready for it.

I realised we were fighting in public, but at least we were on the leadership's private housing floor so few, if any, would hear us, unless Mazdon had arrived and was listening in with his super hearing magic.

"Maybe you can make this easy on me? Do you think I like my situation? When I join, you'll be my camp leader, and leadership will lash us both if someone reported us having a romantic relationship. That's too much to think about when trying to survive for myself." I was near tears, but Zayd shushed me and resumed stroking my hair.

"Fine. I get it. I can wait. The important thing is that you live. And I'll still see you every day."

Why did that form a knot in my stomach?

Zayd pushed me at an arm's distance and looked me in the eye. "Have you ever been linked to anyone else's soul before?"

I shook my head.

He sucked a breath in between his teeth. "Right. We need to practise your mental block, or King Blackbone will swarm you with his thoughts and feelings, and steal yours."

"That sounds terrifying."

"It is. So, where should we do this?"

"In our tree?"

"No. We need white noise distractions."

"The canteen? I am hungry."

Zayd looked at his watch. "Yes. That's perfect." Side by side, we walked towards the canteen at the back wing of the building. "Mewer will be the one who does the soul binding."

"Mewer? But he's a healer."

"Yeah, soul binding is a kind of healing. It's to heal the souls together. It's not permanent. He can remove it, too."

I gnawed on my lip. "What's it like? Does it hurt?"

"No. You won't feel a thing when he does it, but if you get too far away from the black-wing king–"

"His name is Ben…or King Blackbone to you. He might kill you otherwise."

Zayd glared at me. "When you're far away from the *enemy king*, the humming sound in your ears will become uncomfortable. If you would go even further away from each other, a painful pressure builds up in your ears until you feel like fainting, and ultimately you die. The theory of it is that you become one soul. You'll share one mind, and all the emotions and bodily pain associated with it, hence if either of you die, the other one dies too. So, he'll be able to experience your sorrow and hear your thoughts unless you block them out."

Great! So, he'll get to know how badly I've always wanted to touch him naked and have him inside me. Absolutely fucking wonderful.

"But you can teach me how to block him out?"

We arrived at the canteen and grabbed a tray each.

"Yes, but it demands a lot of focus and the stronger the other person is, the harder it is to keep that mental shield up. Imagine you're standing behind a heavy iron shield, using all your strength to hold it up and at the same time he's ramming into it, trying to make you drop it."

"Sounds like I shouldn't even make the effort to bother and just invite him into my camp for tea." I took a step forward in the queue.

"No. You can do this." He put a red apple onto his tray, but not on mine as he knew I didn't like them and poured us both a glass of freshly pressed orange juice, placing one glass on my tray.

Admittedly, it was nice having someone around who knew me.

"Or," he drawled. "You can just threaten to cut his balls off if he enters your mind, like you did to me when we were thirteen and you wanted the last cinnamon bun at the summer solstice festival. Remember?"

I barked a laugh that turned some heads. "It worked. I got the bun and evidently made a lasting impression."

"You made a lasting impression, all right. In that long blue dress that matched your eyes and the dandelion flower wreath over your long blue hair. You were as beautiful as a sapphire gleaming in the sunlight."

I rolled my eyes at him, and we grabbed a pre-made cheese and ham sandwich each from the fridge and put it onto our trays before we sat down at a table by the windowed wall. There were already a few cadets eating and the white noise we had searched for filled the hall.

Cadet Malloopa and Cadet Gravelhorn; a team Emroyce had named the Angry Team saluted Zayd from a few tables down.

"Shit," I cussed under my breath. "Sitting with me is going to get you into so much trouble."

"Don't worry about me. If they try anything on me, I'll make their challenges harder. They know it."

That didn't settle my worries. They could kill him, and his threats would be empty, and the way they were staring at Zayd, clarified they wouldn't make it easy on him.

"How did Gravelhorn get that scar?" I wondered, assuming a threat on his life was met with violence rather that diplomacy.

"Black-wing," Zayd muttered and bit into his sandwich. "His family lives in Gaithbry beyond the Emendroth Outpost by the iron mines. A brawl broke out during one of the trades. Because of your connection to the black-wing king, he's going to come for you in the challenges." Zayd wiggled his eyebrows playfully. "Want to change your mind about joining yet?"

"Enemy king reading my soul, murderous beast who hates black-wings and tough flight challenges when I hate flying. Sounds like any Sunday to me."

He chuckled warmly and took another bite of his sandwich.

I looked around the canteen. "Are there any cadets joining this year who you know I can ally with?"

"Let me think." He drummed his fingers on the wooden table as he looked out through the window at the inner courtyard of the main building, where cadets cut through to take the fastest route to the sparring hall. They were all muscular men and women, wearing their black combat leathers with weapons strapped to every part of their body.

"You have Kate and Mazdon. There are twin men joining; Jeff and Giles Flinch, who I heard are kind. Although, I wouldn't advise you to really trust anyone. You have the black-wing teams. I doubt they'll try to kill you if you're bonded to their king, which I think is Harvey's point. There is Emroyce and his teammate, Cadet Gerard Kenyard."

"I didn't know Emroyce had picked a teammate. He didn't tell me. What is Kenyard's magic?"

"He is a beginner, but he can read intent from sounds. He can tell how you plan to react by listening to your voice."

"That's awesome, but kind of scary."

"Learn to keep your voice level when you speak to him. Then you've got the Hall family, a father and son duo. I can't remember their names, but the father worked in infantry until five years ago when he retired but is repeating the academy to protect his son. They are from the province of Pharanir but from the Abarnack village where they actually have enough honour to differentiate between traitors by behaviour and not the colour of their wings. Again, they could be potential allies but perhaps not. And our best bet is to befriend Klint Penya and Elinor Maruto. I have exchanged letters with Cadet Penya all last year and he's a good man. He has been excited to join the academy as his entire family descends from healers and he hopes to join the infirmary unit after graduation. He has teamed up with Cadet Maruto from his district in the Pharanir province, who has been dreading the arrival of tomorrow all year. Poor woman."

"What's her magic?"

"Water wielding. But we're getting off topic here. We only have two weeks to practise, so back to mind blocking."

Suddenly, we could hear voices shouting our names from behind our backs. I turned in my seat to see Emroyce, Brian and a woman I had not seen before with thick, walnut curls cascading down her back, looking incredibly sweet if it weren't for the three dozen sharp blades stuck into various places in her combat leathers.

They packed their trays with their lunch and came to sit at our table. Brian sat down next to me, and I friendlily shuffled my arm against his. He had a great smile, almost white hair that was wavy around his neck, and warm amber eyes just like his older brother, Captain Thomas La Roy. His shirt had three crosses over his right shoulder to show he had completed two years and would start his third, and the two circles on his left shoulder informed he wielded adept magic.

The La Roy brother's life had been a sad story. Captain La Roy's mother had been murdered on campus even though she was the wife of the general of the General Operations Unit and not a military woman herself. General La Roy had met Brian's mother after that, who then died during childbirth, and one year later he had died of a suspicious death classified as a hunting accident near the black-wing border. Captain La Roy had taken care of Brian himself ever since.

Brian gestured towards the woman beside him. "This is my teammate, Glenna Winters. I'm not sure if you ever met her before you left for the mission in the Black Wing Territory."

"Hello." I waved to her.

The woman had vacant eyes and stared forward at nothing in particular and she didn't move or acknowledge my voice.

"She won't respond because her corporal form isn't here. She can astral project and has tagged her ghost to follow me," Brian explained.

"That's so cool. Why is she tagging you? What is the *real her* doing?"

"Classified information," Brian scoffed.

"Classified mischief," Zayd muttered. "Don't get Camp Leader Mewer into trouble before the third year has even started."

Brian bit into his sandwich. "What are you guys up to today?"

Irritably, I tore off a chunk of my sandwich and popped it into my mouth. "My dear brother has assigned me to be soul bound to King Blackbone the day the term starts, so Zayd is teaching me how to block my mind."

Brian gasped and lost his words for a moment. "Shit! That's just fucked-up!"

"Yeah well. Family can be complicated."

"I feel you. Except for the mother traitor part. Brothers, hey?"

"Captains suck."

"Totally agree," Brian took another bite of his sandwich and pointed at me. "Don't enrol in the academy."

"Don't go there, Cadet La Roy," Zayd muttered. "She has made up her mind."

Everyone sighed in unison, as if they'd been told something that was set in stone.

"Guys, it's my decision."

"As if anyone could say anything to change your mind. Remember when we were ten and there was that fox that lived by the outlet of the forest sewer?" Emroyce reminded me as he tied his long onyx hair into a ponytail. His speed magic made the movement so quick, he finished before he completed his sentence.

"You said that only someone as fast as you could catch it. You said I couldn't catch it. Clearly, I could," I sneered.

"It took you five weeks. I thought you would sleep and die by the sewer just to prove a point."

I tapped a firm finger at the table. "I would have."

"I believe you." He swiped his hand in the air to illustrate his confidence. "No doubt at all."

Everyone laughed.

"Sure! Go ahead. Laugh at my expense. My life! Now, how do I bloody block my brain?"

"I wouldn't bother," Brian said. "Just reward him in the bedroom for every week he doesn't enter your mind. That's your best bet."

Zayd slammed his fist on the table and everyone around it startled, plus the entire canteen went dead silent. He calmed and scanned the cadets' faces. Everyone around the table watched him take a deep breath and circle his jaw.

"Just checking you're all alert," he called with a voice filling the canteen, and made a dismissive hand gesture. He lowered his head and stared angrily at Brian. "No, that's not a good plan."

My cheeks flushed with heat when an unbidden image of my mouth around Ben's cock flashed traitorously through my mind. I immediately blocked it out and cleared my throat. "How far does the mind-reading reach?"

Zayd drank from his orange juice and put the glass down slowly. "What do you mean?"

"I mean, is there a distance away from him where he can't read my mind because he's too far away?"

"Not entirely, but about three kilometres or so it starts becoming a whisper."

The reach where he could read my thoughts would cover the entire outpost premises, dammit. "Well, that ruins my plan B of locking myself into my room."

Everyone went quiet and stared at me.

"What?"

Zayd looked at Brian and then back at me. "Um, you're a team. Teams are put in the–"

"No, no, no. Absolutely no. Fuck no!"

I noticed Zayd's sandwich becoming more compressed inside his hand as we spoke about Ben and I sleeping in the same room. No wonder he had been against the idea.

"Will that make you reconsider joining then?" he asked.

My brother couldn't mean for me to share a room with the man when I had already agreed to share my damn soul!

I turned in my seat. "Brian, how do you and Winter share the space between you? Is there a drape or wall between you? Preferably a wall through which thoughts can't pass!"

He laughed. "I don't think that exists. I can't advise you on that, though, as I have never shared a dorm room. Thomas forces me to stay with him in the captain's apartment, so he can keep an eye on me. So, he says."

I sighed and flashed a sad expression at Brian. "My brother didn't offer me my own room back."

I grabbed my half-eaten sandwich and left my seat. "I need air."

I exited the building and climbed the oak tree, and it took longer than I had expected before Zayd joined me.

"What took you so long? We need to practise my block."

He pulled something from his pocket and held up two keys in front of me. He held up the one in his left hand higher. "I swung by the captain's office and got this. This key leads to the door of room twenty-five. The one in the corner with two windows. At least you can get in there first and chose which bed you want."

"Really? You're going to push this, aren't you?" I flashed him a glare that would have made my mother proud.

"Yep," he replied shamelessly.

"And the other key?"

He waved the key in his right hand that looked like the key I had left behind on his hallway side-table this morning. "Is to my apartment. But you can't have that one if you join the academy. Your choice."

"Nice try!" I snatched up the dorm room key from his left hand and shoved it into the pocket over my thigh.

He pocketed his own key and looked out over the field, and I wondered what he could see from over here with his far-sight. "And I will try again. There is still time to nag you. For now, let's practise. Clear your mind," he instructed, closing his eyes, inhaling a deep breath. "Think of nothing. Listen to the leaves in the wind."

I did as he instructed, and the scent of nature filled my nostrils.

"Focus on one sound. That is how you block King Blackbone out. Like hearing two sounds at the same time but only listening to one. Block the second sound out. Like when you're in deep thought and can't hear someone who is trying to talk to you."

"That's it?"

"Well, it might seem easily done for someone who never listens to anyone's advice."

I glowered at him, and he chuckled.

"Let's practise," he laughed. "You'll focus on a sound, and I'll try to speak to you, and you'll try to ignore me…like always." His smile was almost infectious, but I kept my stone face intact as I grimaced at him.

Another dig. Fine.

Not listening to people, I could do that.

A group of third-year cadets gathered at the obstacle course and one readied at the starting line, so I focused on him. His friend counted him down and he was off over the bars and onto the climbing net. He was fast, but all third-years were experts at that point, considering the weaker cadets had already either died, transferred to General ops, or had quit all together.

I suddenly felt Zayd shaking my shoulder from around the tree trunk. "Angie?"

"What?"

"You're a natural. I've been trying to speak to you for a minute and you held your attention on that race."

It hadn't been on purpose. I was relaxed around Zayd, so it hadn't been difficult for my mind to wander off. Question was, though, whether I could ignore Ben the same way.

9

It had been two intense weeks of getting back into the swing of things; seeing everyone, training shield-blocking with Zayd and celebrating his birthday last night. Zayd, who never drank alcohol, kept grinning at me because I probably still looked pale and rough from that party. He had dragged me out this morning to sit on the branch in our tree to watch the new cadets arrive. Like every year, we had gossiped over what we knew about them and who we believed would win the different challenges. He hadn't let me retreat into my dorm until after breakfast, seeming not to understand how inappropriate and dangerous it was for both of us to dine together when other cadets were watching.

I entered my new home and looked around one of the best rooms in the halls, as it had two windows, and because it was a corner rooms, it was bigger than the others. I knew I had Zayd to thank for it. The two single beds were placed below the windows, although there was only one desk and chair against the long wall next to a small kitchenette. The other door concealed a small bathroom, which was also a luxury as half of the dorm rooms only had a tiny toilet and the cadets had to take their showers and baths in the bath chambers at the basement level in the General Ops wing.

I pulled open the black Bensguard curtains, featuring the golden key emblem, and looked out of the window toward the archery station at the far end of the field. It was Monday and the start of term, and at eleven o'clock all cadets would join their first formation in the square at the outer courtyard in front of the building. But it was nine o'clock now, so it was an hour until I had to be in the infirmary to bind myself to Ben. A knot tightened in my stomach.

Spirits! Did I really want this? There was still time to walk away. Signing the ledgers meant leadership had the right to execute me for desertion if I changed my mind. A part of me didn't think the sound of being Zayd's housewife was so bad. But the General Coraly's daughter's gene wanted to prove this was my home, and I stood as good a chance as everyone else to become a fine soldier to protect the White Wing Territory.

I stared at the black beddings with the same key emblem as the curtains and a framed image by the door. It filled me with pride. This was my life! It was all that I had ever worked for. No one, not even the fucking black-wing king, could make me yield.

There was no point in stalling the inevitable, so I took a quick shower and got dressed in my uniform, adorned with one cross on my right shoulder but no circles on the left. No one knew what magic I possessed, and I kept denying I had any because it was voluntary to join the academy if you didn't have magic, although rarely anyone did. People with magic were forced to enrol. Saying that, all my fellow cadets probably suspected I had the same inherited magic as Harvey. A powerful magic too dangerous to be made public.

I braided my fringe in two strands on either side of my head and tied them back to get any distraction away from my face before applying makeup and lastly adding my favourite part to the dress code – my weapons. A dagger in either leg strap and a short-sword in a sheath at my side. To top it all off, I laced my heavy black boots tightly and shoved a small blade down its side.

I left my room and locked the door, sliding the key into my leg pocket, and nodded a greeting to a worker from central depot, who was busy collecting uniforms from his cart and stocking up the rooms. The corridor was full of new cadets, who were excited about first formation, and I was guessing second and third-year cadets were still in their beds trying to make the most of the few remaining minutes of summer break, not feeling as eager to start their challenges. Zayd was the camp leader teaching the formation class to the first-years, so he would be tailing my brother today, and taking over formation after Harvey's welcome speech.

It didn't take me long to arrive at the indoor entrance to the infirmary ward and I stopped to look around before I noticed the throng of people gathered around Ben, who was sitting on a bed with his wrists and ankles in thick, iron shackles. Everyone in the Special Missions Unit wore black uniforms unless you were a camp leader, captain or a general, but he was more handsome in it than anyone I've ever seen. His uniform had a crown emblem on his shoulder instead of a cross, but being an enemy, I guessed the academy had been told not to give him a royal purple uniform to show white-wings that he shouldn't hold the appropriate respect of a king.

I watched him and the crowd of people from behind the door frame, hesitant to bond with his soul. *Spirits only knew what I'll find in it.*

Perhaps also because seeing him took my breath away, or more accurately, stole it!

"Has Harvey had enough of me?" Ben asked Mewer as he supported a forearm on his lap to lean forwards. There were new bruises on his face, even though his hair had fallen over his face to hide most of his cheeks. "Is he scared of dying when I start the challenges?"

"You're getting a new soul host; a teammate," Mewer replied as kindly as he would to anyone no matter their status.

Mewer was dressed formally in his navy-blue uniform with a round camp leader emblem with a C in the centre sewn onto his right shoulder. In a few minutes, he had to begin the lessons for the third-year cadets, which were panic endurance exercises. They were different every year, as it had to be unexpected. I wondered what he had come up with this year.

Mewer slowly stirred an ointment in a bowl, just enough to keep its integrity intact whilst waiting for me to arrive. Valentina's mother, Healer Maid Karson, was standing next to him in her burgundy uniform with a droplet emblem on her right shoulder to show she was from the Infirmary Unit.

Ben crossed his ankles. "I thought you would team me up with Murben. This could be fun," he mocked, his voice deep and gravelly, making the joke sound like a threat.

"You might not find it that amusing when you see who it is. It's a mind twister, to say the least." Mewer handed the bowl to Healer Maid Karson, who scurried away to a young man on a bed three spaces down.

Ben frowned, staring at Mewer. "On the Captain's orders?"

It wasn't often Mewer crossed his arms in front of him, but he did now. "On the Captain's orders, to be sure. I'd never make the same call."

Ben didn't appear to be intimidated by Mewer and simply rolled his shoulders as if he was warming up his joints before a fight. "I'm surprised, as I almost broke the captain, and I'll break whoever you bond to me unless he's made of steel. I would have thought you valued your secrets in this territory more than that."

"Not a *him*," Mewer said, seeing me in the doorway and beckoned me forward. "Her."

I straightened and held in my stomach before realising there was no stomach to talk about and I could count my ribs with the mere sight of them, so I re-tucked my shirt into my trousers. Reluctantly, I approached, seeing the build-up of Ben's shadow essence wafting around his body and his red eyes flaring with intense anger. He got off the bed, and the shackles rattled. Mewer immediately had two daggers in hand, aiming for Ben's throat.

"No," Ben said, as if he had a choice. "I won't bond with her."

I stepped between Ben and Mewer's daggers. "Camp Leader Mewer, put them away. He won't hurt me." I said it with confidence but in earnest, I wasn't sure what horrible plan he had concocted for my death.

Mewer sheathed the blades with such care, he could have them up in a second again if needed. "You're not bonded yet."

"We won't ever be," Ben growled between gritted teeth.

I took a step closer to him so he had to lean back, or he couldn't make eye-contact, which was my plan. I wanted him to see the resolve in my gaze. "Why not? You're scared I'll die when we start the challenges? You think that because I'm a woman that I–"

There they were, his gorgeous eyes stared at mine, and as I looked into them, I barely remembered what I wanted to achieve here. *Fuck! I shouldn't be this close. He's shattering that resolve I demanded a second ago!*

His eyes didn't stray from mine for one heartbeat. "No! That's not it. Women don't belong on the battlefield. You're not joining the academy."

There, my resolve is back! How dare he say something so degrading to my face? *Arsehole!* My fists clenched as I composed my seething temper. "I already have," I lied.

The leather uniform was so tight around his muscles, it creaked as he tried to cross his arms over his chest but couldn't because of the short chain of his shackles. He grunted and looked to get increasingly agitated with each breath. More inky essence leaked out of him.

"Fine," I said, turning to Mewer. "Team me up with tiny Kate instead. I'm sure she'll be happy to be my partner."

"No!" Ben roared, just like I had expected. Or at least I had hoped that there was a small part of him that cared for me, and Spirits, I felt relieved that I had been right. If Ben didn't bond with me because he deemed me too weak, my brother would never look upon me and see more than a little girl. This had to happen.

I twisted my wrist to look at my watch as if I had somewhere else to be. "You're very indecisive today, King Blackbone. Make up your mind."

Ben inspected me carefully, and his full attention made my head spin a little. "Are you consenting fully to do this, or are you purely following the captain's orders?" Ben asked. "You're aware that I'll get full access to your soul?"

A raw and protective wave of power seemed to crash into my chest, stealing my breath for a moment.

"Just don't enter!" I wheezed out.

He grunted and scratched at his three-day stubble. "I thought so," he muttered, momentarily bringing his gaze to the floor before returning it to me again. "And you're aware that everyone in this place is targeting me? They all want me dead."

"And me, too. What a team we'll be."

He remained silent for a while, his eyes darting around inside their sockets as he was pondering the information.

Mewer sighed, flicking his long golden hair to his back. "I don't have all day. I still have lots of work to do in the illusion room that needs to be ready for next month. Not to mention all the healing work I'll have to do on second-years when they return from navigation practice. Agent Coraly, do you want me to explain anything about the bond and how it works before we proceed?"

"No. Camp Leader Watson has trained me."

Ben shifted his weight as if his entire body was itching every time I mentioned Zayd's name.

I held up my left palm in front of Ben and he observed it without a movement of his own, so I waited.

Slowly, he lifted both his shackled hands and used his right to lace his fingers with mine. I forgot to breathe. The sensual feel of his touch sent tingles to my stomach. Every thought that had frightened me dissipated, which was stupid, as he was the reason that my entire life was destroyed. He was my mortal enemy. Yet, his eyes on me calmed my heart every damned time. I trusted him. He wouldn't expose any part of me, and he wouldn't let me die.

Mewer put his hands around ours and shone with his golden healing light over them, focusing on his job with his eyes closed. Ben kept staring into my eyes the entire time and after a few minutes, Mewer removed his hands and glanced at us both in turn. "All good?"

I snatched my hand towards me and rubbed it with my other, but there had been no irritation caused on my skin, no pain. The only difference was a constant humming in my ears. I waited for Ben, expecting him to intrude on my mind, but my mind stayed silent.

Mewer brought out a key from his pocket and removed Ben's shackles, putting them on his infirmary station cart that was next to him, filled with jars with various contents and bandages.

"You have formation in fifteen minutes. Hurry along. We don't want to upset your brother any further, or only the Spirit of War knows what he'll put you through next."

"Thank you, Mewer."

"No, don't thank me for this. It's all on your brother."

I nodded and headed through the ward towards the front door of the building to line up in formation. I heard steps behind me as Ben followed closely through the corridor. Abruptly, he griped my arm and snatched me around, cornering me against the cream-coloured wall.

"Why did you enrol?" His eyes were so close to mine, staring straight into them as if to search for logic.

"That's none of your business. I told you I would, and you said you wanted to stay and watch the show. Guess what! You've got a front-row seat!"

His teeth clenched harder together. "I thought you would cower out. Do you even comprehend how dangerous this is?"

"I grew up here, remember? I have watched the challenges and witnessed people die all my life."

His grunt came out extremely frustrated, and he rubbed his face. "Just…just stay next to me at all times, okay?"

"Like what? Your pet mutt?"

"Like a Spirit I fucking worship, or however you like to twist this. But make sure you don't die."

I got his point. If I died, he died. He could be as almighty as he wished, but I was his weakest link from this moment on. If he had thought to relax with Murben through all the challenges until he was sent to get more magic at the end of the Spirits' Trek, his plans had been ironically twisted.

He gripped my arm once more, shaking me lightly until I focused on him. "Will you listen to me, or am I going to have to carry you around over my shoulder?"

The problem he had with me, contrary to any of his other subjects, was that I could hold his stare without budging. "Why don't you enter my mind and find the answer for yourself?" I spat, but then my breath hitched as he leaned in even closer, and I had no space to shrug back.

"I'll never enter your mind without your consent." His warm breath hit my mouth.

By reflex, I licked my lips as they turned dry. His glance lowered to watch them, and he swallowed as he waited for my reaction.

I stopped my breath at the peak of an intake. "Because you're too much of a gentleman to break a woman?"

He chuckled menacingly. "No. Because I can't break you." He leaned up, his contorted face relaxed. "Teammate." His lip curled at the corner, but the emotion never entered his eyes. He stared at me for a while and I felt so small under his scrutiny, like I was so insignificant he could easily crush me under his boot and scrape me off like dirt. "We should get outside and into formation before we're late. Deserters get lashed around here, I hear."

"Well, we need a way of keeping the soldiers at the outpost, or we wouldn't have any for the war."

Ben snorted. "I would just kill them. If they're that afraid of war, they're useless, and will get the brave ones killed."

"Guess you're just waiting for an opportunity to kill me then, after we're no longer bonded."

"No. You're the bravest soldier I know. Reckless and in need of a lot of training, but brave." He leaned in once more, this time so close our noses brushed with a feather-light touch. "Betray me again, and I'll reconsider my choices."

Something in my heart jerked with the pain of betrayal, a feeling I knew all too well. I nodded and ducked under his arm to hurry outside, trembling from our conversation. The man who had pressed me up against the wall was the same man who had severed Davis's thumb only two weeks ago. If I was wrong about him and his intentions, I could lose more than a thumb by crossing him. He knew I had already betrayed him once, and that had so far gone unpunished. *So far!*

Outside in the courtyard, the six camp leaders stood with wide spacing between themselves and with their backs against a small podium that the workers had rolled out for this occasion. Harvey and Captain La Roy were standing on it, watching the rows and columns of cadets in formation. For this occasion, Harvey had dressed in his orange Camp Master uniform, which was a rank above Captain La Roy. I had only seen him use this uniform during the summer breaks, on the day of first formation to highlight that he dealt with all the admin stuff, and on graduation day, but all other days, he wore the yellow uniform. Captain La Roy was wearing his yellow uniform with one chevron under a star, which shone in a gold tone as the rising sun set on them.

Both Captain La Roy's white hair and Harvey's brown side parting sailed on a soft breeze. They looked very different, but both stood with equal authority. Our family had no genes for growing tall, so Harvey's width was certainly more impressive than his height, whilst La Roy was taller and leaner. Harvey's gaze was harsh and assertive whilst La Roy's was calm and honourable, like someone you would want to follow no questions asked.

I carried on walking and glanced across the blue sky that sported no clouds above our heads. Today would be another scorching hot summer's day in September, and I had to remember to carry a water bottle with me or I would exhaust quickly.

I found my line in front of Zayd and headed down the row to queue up when someone suddenly shrieked and darted for me. I turned my head to see Kate.

"Kate!" I set off in a sprint towards her and we crashed with open arms around one another.

"You're alive!" she beamed. "Harvey told me about your mission."

Ben stopped behind my back, observing us with the unnerving keen eye of a bodyguard.

"Yes, and I guess I took my work home with me." I gestured for Ben. "This is King Blackbone."

Mazdon moved out of formation and closed in on his sister's back. They both looked like I remembered them; Kate with fiery red hair reaching to her stomach and Mazdon wearing his strawberry-blonde curls to his shoulders and both of them had the same shape to their faces with high cheekbones, small noses and rounded chins. They had big jade-coloured eyes and perfectly shaped eyebrows. The main difference between them was that Kate was tiny and Mazdon sized up to Zayd, which wasn't strange considering he was four years older than me and had served in the Air Force for a year. They focused a lot of their efforts on muscle training in that unit to be able to fly for longer than the average twenty minutes.

"Don't be a stranger, Mazdon." I hugged him, and heard Ben grunt behind my back.

Ben might believe I wasn't being careful, but I knew Mazdon and Kate would never hurt me. We had grown up at the outpost together and were also neighbours in the summer cottage, so we were very good friends.

I pointed my entire hand again at Ben. "King Blackbone. My teammate. There. Introductions made."

"Hm," Mazdon hummed. "An emotional backpack, that is." He sized up Ben from head to toe but finally decided to approach him and held out his hand. "I'm Mazdon."

Ben frowned, looking at Maz's hand as if it could poison him at a touch.

"What magic do you have?" he finally asked Mazdon.

"Nothing that will kill you from making a polite handshake."

Ben looked at me, standing so close his arm brushed against mine as he twisted.

"He has super good hearing. He traded his fire magic on the black market for it on a drunken night out on the town with my brother."

"Not regretted it since," Mazdon said, smiling.

Ben's gaze twitched up at Mazdon and he did the unfathomable act of shaking his hand like a civilised person. I carefully released the pent-up breath I had been holding.

"Cadets!" Harvey suddenly shouted to get everyone's attention to begin his speech.

"Let's speak more later," I told Kate and signalled that I had to get into formation.

Ben almost stepped in my footsteps before I had walked out of them, as I hurried to the end of the line of the first-year cadets in the Special Missions Unit. It wasn't as if we could get away with not being seen out of formation, considering Ben was easy to spot among the other cadets, being at least two heads taller than most of them, six years older, and a heck of a lot more muscular.

I realised I stood behind Gravelhorn, as he snorted the word 'mutt' before he turned to look forward again.

I felt Ben taking a step closer to my back, so that our bodies were flush against one another.

He didn't have to be that *protective.*

I looked forwards toward the podium to listen to my brother.

The academy grounds sprawled before us, evidencing the White Wing Territory's commitment to discipline and excellence. The towering stone walls of the Bensguard Outpost Academy loomed, their weathered surfaces etched with centuries of history. Above, the sky was grey, casting a sombre hue over the courtyard where cadets stood in neat formations. The ground beneath our boots was a mix of cobblestone and packed dirt, worn smooth by countless footsteps. The air smelled of damp earth from the recent rain and the faint aroma of burning wood from distant chimneys.

Captain Harvey's voice cut through the stillness, commanding attention. His figure stood resolute, framed by the imposing military building behind him. Beside him, Captain La Roy exuded an air of quiet authority.

"Welcome to the Bensguard Outpost Academy," Harvey began.

Amplified by Camp Leader Ward's magic, his voice could be heard to the last cadet in the formation line-up. "Captain La Roy," Harvey gestured for Thomas, "is captain for the General Operations Unit and I'm the Captain for the Special Missions Unit. We're here to help you when your Camp Leader is unavailable to do so. You're here to serve the White Wing Territory with your lives. I expect nothing less." His gaze swept over the gathered cadets, ensuring each of us felt the weight of his words.

Captain La Roy nodded, stepping forward. "As Captain for the General Operations Unit," he added, "my role is to oversee your tactical training and readiness." His voice was steady, resonating with the confidence of someone who had faced many trials.

Harvey continued, outlining the academy's rigorous curriculum. His words painted a vivid picture of the challenges ahead. The cobblestones beneath our feet seemed to tremble with the anticipation of the trials to come.

"There are ten distinct challenges you must complete during each of the three years throughout the ten months from September to June in order to graduate. The challenges for the first-year cadets are aimed to enhance your strengths, the second-year challenges are designed to improve your survival skills, and the third-year challenges have been tactically selected to harden your mental endurance," he declared. "The challenges mirror the dangers you will face in the woods hiking the Spirits' Trek. Fail, and you won't see the next year. Succeed, and you earn your place among the elite." The wind picked up slightly, carrying the faint sound of his steady breathing. "The strongest team, the team that has won most challenges, will chose the six candidates to join the hike to the Spirits' Trek after graduation and gets the chance to gain three magical abilities if you can touch the Spirit's Heart. *If* you survive."

The uncertainty of whether I would survive the next three years was a reminder of the academy's unforgiving nature. Unforgivable, perhaps even cruel, but it was my home and the pillar of my backbone. I looked at the building with admiration when many couldn't see what I saw. The stone walls of the academy seemed to tower higher, prouder, as Harvey's voice reverberated off them, emphasising the gravity of his words.

"Life here at the academy is simple. Follow the rules. Die with honour or survive to fight another day!"

Spirits, he's warm and compassionate today. I knew he loved the Bensguard Outpost's motto, but did he have to shout it out to the new cadets at first formation in that tone that suggested we'd all die?

I looked at Zayd, but he didn't have any particular expression on his face, so I turned back to watch my brother.

"I'm also the Camp Master on the premises and deal with your schedule, your supplies, your safety and I ensure that everyone follows our rules. We only have ten simple rules, so it'll be beyond me if they are too comprehensive for you to remember by heart, and follow. Just in case the new cadets haven't heard them, or the experienced cadets have forgotten, I'll state them to you. Memorise them!" He paused for a dramatic second before his voice came out even stronger. "One! There shall be no killing outside the monthly challenges. Two! Leadership quarters on the second floor are off limits to cadets unless solicited. Three! Leaving the Bensguard Outpost grounds without permission isn't allowed. You'll be retrieved and lashed for desertion. Four! Magic wielders must attend the academy and all challenges. Anyone finding out about magic wielders who aren't in the academy must report them. Five! There shall be no unapproved communication with family during the year. That, you can save for the summer breaks. Six! No unauthorised weapons, especially not those forged with black iron, are allowed to be brought into or be used at the academy. Seven! No one is allowed to impersonate a higher-ranking officer. Eight! It's prohibited to engage in intimate relations with fellow members of your own unit in the Bensguard Outpost."

Harvey spoke *that* rule louder than the previous, and his eyes fell to Zayd's back, as if he wanted to highlight our involvement. I'd had the impression over the years that he didn't like me having a relationship with his best friend and I had been wondering whether Harvey had sent me to the Black Wing Territory with the goal to separate us.

"Nine!" he shouted, lifting his gaze to everyone once more. "No assembling to conspire against the kingdom. And ten! A rule we had to add last year. Threatening infirmary or outpost workers is forbidden!" He looked at Captain La Roy. "You want to add anything, Captain La Roy!"

He nodded and looked up and at all the cadets. "As you know. No one survived last year's mission through the Spirits' Trek nor any of the missions over the last twenty-five years. So, my advice is that you work your damn hardest at surviving. Pray often to the Spirit of Luck. You're going to need it!"

"Couldn't have said it better myself!" Harvey agreed. "Your Camp Leader will take over from here."

Harvey finished and stepped down from the podium, giving the floor to the camp leaders, so Zayd took a deliberate step forward and stopped with a wide stance and his hands clasped behind his back. He looked handsome and strong in his navy-blue uniform, and he had shaved and gelled his hair up into his normal style.

"I'm Zayd Watson and I'll be your camp leader for the next three years. Any issues and concerns you have, you can come to me. Camp Leader Rhie Neville and Camp Leader Collin Mewer are also a part of the leadership for the Special Missions Unit and you can communicate with them when I'm absent conducting training classes to second-year and third-year cadets, or if I'm out on patrol myself. Any questions about that?"

A man with a swirling blue mark turning on his forehead stepped to the side of his line to look at Zayd. "Does the prohibition of romantic relationships apply to those in the leadership team as well, or can I sleep with Camp Leader Neville to get preferential treatment?"

What an absolute twat!

Both Zayd and I laughed at the same time to which Ben grunted from behind my back.

"Cadet Grim, I'm not even going to waste energy repeating rule six which applies to us all," Zayd replied. "Touch Camp Leader Neville at your own risk. I give you my permission to try." Zayd looked across the distance to where Neville was speaking to the second-year cadets. "Anyone who wants to keep their arms, I advise you not to touch Camp Leader Neville." He made a point of shouting so loudly that she could hear him and the lean woman with short cut golden hair responded with a sharp glare of hateful murky eyes and she hovered her hand above her sword hilt.

She was brutal despite her young age of twenty-four, having grown up with her mother being a waitress in a brothel in the city of Abarath. Therefore, Neville demanded a one hundred percent commitment because her father clearly hadn't, and it had hurt her. Being raised in a brothel, she detested anyone touching her, and if you did when she had a sword at hand; you risked losing an arm.

With two hundred cadets standing before him, Zayd moved across the front, walking from left to right to address all eight columns. "First challenge is about discipline and learning to arrive at a battlefield ready for anything in order to support your unit. In a real-life battle, it could be that you're called to the front and you need to get into the mind frame of fighting quickly, leaving whatever else you're doing behind. The challenge is to…" Zayd paused, seeming reluctant to tell us about the first and simplest challenge, and put his hands at his side, watching the ground as he finished walking to the end where I stood in the last column. He gave me a quick glance and pinched his lips between his teeth, taking a large breath. "The challenge is to listen to the siren of the outpost building and when you hear it chime once, you must get to your rooms and change into your combat leathers and come out here to line up in formation. Closer to the end of this month, the siren will ring twice. That will be the actual challenge test and the team that can line up first in full and correct gear wins."

As he explained the rules, I realised why Zayd disliked this simple challenge. He imagined me and Ben in our room changing clothes.

Well, that's just fucking great. No taking turns in the bathroom then if we want to be fast enough to win.

I noticed Zayd looking furious as he stared above my head. I turned around and saw a huge mocking grin on Ben's lips, deliberately provoking Zayd.

Zayd averted the eye-contact and carried on pacing across the front. "As I don't need to teach you how to dress. Feel free to use the sparring hall when it's free from classes. You also have access to the archery field, the obstacle course and the running path through the forest. The chapel, common rooms and the canteen are also always open. If you want to use horses, you must speak to the stable master to see when one is available, as Camp Leader Ward uses them often for the Cavalry Unit. You'll find your schedule on the notice board outside the Administration Office. Your next class is War Updates in the assembly hall tomorrow morning at nine o'clock. For those of you who are new to the Bensguard Outpost, I'm available now to show you around."

The man who stood behind Ben made it difficult to listen to Zayd's information as he kept hissing things to Ben. Irritated, I twitched and again tried to focus on what Zayd was saying.

A sharp move entered my peripheral view. I turned towards a cadet with long scarlet hair and piercing blue eyes, holding a dagger up, ready to stab me. The cadet rounded Ben's body, giving me little time to unsheathe my dagger from my leg strap. But Ben was faster, pulling the dagger from my other leg and slashing out with his arm, slicing a large cut across the cadet's throat.

For mere seconds, the man clasped at his bleeding throat and chipped for air, but only gurgled blood. His knees buckled slowly until they hit the cobblestone, and he tipped onto his side on the ground. Ben watched him die without a sign to indicate he might save the man or even feel remorse for what he had done – like he was made of stone rather than flesh. My heart pounded so hard I thought it would break my ribcage.

Harvey, who had stood watching Zayd from the side, saw what had happened and rushed towards us.

"What the fuck!" Harvey roared. "Do I have to reiterate rule one? No killing! Only during challenges!" He crouched down, probably by habit, to check for a pulse, but didn't bother getting his hands full of blood, as Ben had cut half the cadet's throat from his neck.

"Stay in formation!" Ben roared like a king on the battlefield at the four black-wings, who were ready to come to their king's aid before Ben resumed his eye-contact with Harvey and gestured with his hand towards the dead man. "He thought he could kill Cadet Coraly before I could kill him. That's a challenge. He lost." Ben had an utterly bored expression on his face as he defended his standpoint.

"Cadets, you're all dismissed so leadership can clean up this fucking mess," Harvey roared, his voice filling the entire courtyard.

It surprised me that Harvey hadn't threatened to punish Ben, but I guessed that if he did, he knew I had to share the punishment too. Or perhaps Harvey concluded Ben was right to apply self-defence, as I believed my brother couldn't care less about me.

Harvey looked at the dead cadet and turned to glare at me. "Still believe my job is easy? I bound you to him," he growled, pointing at Ben, "and you can't control him for one second. I have given you a taste of this life without having to sign the ledger, but now you must make up your mind. Enrol, or take Zayd's offer. I'm done trying to talk you out of it."

Ben snapped his head around to glare at me.

Shit! There went my lie.

Now he knew that I hadn't put my signature down yet, as I had told him.

Betrayal number two.

10

Ben scooped his arm around me, sweeping me behind him, severing the stern stares my brother pinned me with. Then, he took a threatening step closer to him.

The way I was shielded away was totally degrading. A lot of cadets were still around to see it. Didn't he think I could handle my own brother by myself?

Harvey straightened his knees and squared up with him. Fear began throbbing over my skin.

How dare my brother challenge Ben?

Not a minute had passed since he had witnessed what Ben had done to the man on the ground without having a speck of regret in his eyes.

But Harvey didn't look scared of him, and he didn't back down. "What in the bloody three realms will I tell his parents?" Harvey asked, gesturing for the corpse and the pool of blood seeping between the cobblestones. "I can't say that the black-wing king killed him because he couldn't stand still in formation."

Ben had his head cocked downwards to stare at Harvey. "I don't give a fuck about what you tell your people." Ben narrowed his eyes. "Wasn't that what you told me last year?" His growl had a low, levelled tone, sounding more lethal than when he bawled out in anger.

What? Harvey had spoken to Ben last year? About what?

Harvey shifted his weight and glanced unnervingly between the dead cadet and Ben. "Shit like this is exactly why I don't let you carry any weapons."

Leadership hadn't provided Ben any weapons of his own, as they didn't trust him among the white-wing cadets. He could only borrow them when needed. But he was still holding my dagger in his hand, and I was terrified of how swiftly I could be left with no living family members if Harvey pushed him further.

I took Ben's hand and laced my fingers with his. "Come," I told him softly. "I'll show you to *our* room."

Ben inhaled a large breath and relaxed, rolling his neck on his shoulders. He twisted his head to look at me and his expression turned playful, seeming to enjoy the thought of a joint bedroom. But he didn't say a word. Faster than a lightning strike, he sheathed my dagger in my leg strap, and I had to check to be certain I still had both my legs intact. I did. There was no blood drawn.

Ben headed for the building. I think he had forgotten that I had laced my fingers into his as we walked inside, but I was too worried he'd kill someone else to remove my hand from his.

We reached our door, and I could finally let go of his hand, as I had to fish up the key from my pocket and open the door. The room was still an empty shell. Bookshelves were without books. No one had fitted the bedding on his bed and the desk was free from stationery. Not sure If I could be bothered making the space more homely though, knowing there was a good chance I might be dead before the end of the month.

More than a little shy, I gestured for my bed. "I picked that bed and if you go near it, I'll slice you like a tomato."

The soft humming sound in my ears from our soul bond reminded me he didn't have to get near me to be intrusive. Yet, he hadn't overstepped so far.

Ben smiled at my remark but went to the wardrobe and opened every door and every drawer to search through them, pushing uniforms around and lifting boots up to look inside them.

"They are really not going to provide me with any weapons?"

I closed the door to the room and leaned against it. "Why did you have to kill the man who attacked me when I know you're capable of disarming a cadet without ending their life?"

Ben took out a uniform t-shirt that central depot workers had stacked in the wardrobe for him this morning. "Better that everyone believes I'm ruthless. It should be clear what happens if they attack you."

He grabbed the fabric at the back of his long-sleeved uniform shirt and pulled it off over his head, displaying his torso, and damn, if it didn't make me want to touch it. But I needed to keep my feelings to my damned self! Even if my clit throbbed with need. It had been two years since the last time I had been intimate with Zayd. Seeing Ben half naked wasn't ideal to keep my mind sane and not make a stupid mistake. I glanced at the tight skin over the rippled curves of his bulging muscles.

Nope! Definitely shouldn't look that way.

"You *are* ruthless," I coughed up, as he finally hid his body inside the t-shirt that had a crown on his right shoulder, reminding me who he was.

He was a fucking king! I couldn't forget. But he had no circles of magic ability on his left shoulder. Ben shrugged his shoulders as if it didn't matter. "People must stop thinking of you as a traitor."

"What does it matter to you? You think they'll stop trying to kill me? That isn't how this place works. The cadets will do anything to be chosen for the Spirits' Trek to get more magic, more power."

He came closer, and I wanted to back up, but the door pushed into my back. "No," he said in a low growl, bracing his hand on the door above my head. "Because I don't *want* them to think of you as a traitor. You don't deserve such malice."

With his body heat pushing up against me, licking at the edge of my clothes from my crotch to my neck, I couldn't do anything other than cock my head up to look into his intense eyes, realising that he meant what he had said.

"For next time, just so you know, I can defend myself. I *will* graduate."

"Yes, you will. Because I'm not going to let us die."

He was so close to me now that I could feel his breath on my face, and the depth with which he was observing me was unsettling…and hot.

"Oh! No way are you going to take credit for my achievements. If I fall, you'll not catch me. Whatever happens, you mustn't interfere, and if it is so, you must let me die. I need to prove to my brother that I'm a Coraly."

"That, you are. I swear, the Spirits must have put you in this realm just so you can antagonise me." He moved his lips close to mine, but without letting them touch, nearly stopping me from breathing. "Your brother said Watson made you an offer to get you out of the academy. What is the deal?"

My cheeks flushed and the heat in the narrow space of his frame became unbearable. "That he'd take care of me. To be his housewife."

Something dark flickered in his eyes. "Are you considering it?"

"No! I'm a warrior. I have causes to fight for and more things to do in life than to sit around gossiping with higher-ranking officers' wives."

His mouth veered right, and his lips snagged the top of my ear. "Good. What do you want to do next?" he whispered, a knot tightening in my gut from the tension. His lips dragged over my cheek back to hover just beyond the reach of my mouth.

Next? Was the king asking for permission to kiss me? He could just take what he wanted. *Right now.* The part of me who was sensible was gone, apparently. I wouldn't fight it if he ravished me. He was fucking hot, and it was tiresome fighting my attraction to him all the time. But even while debating whether or not it was a smart idea to lock this man between my legs, I was too proud to make the first move.

"What do *you* want to do next?" I challenged, hoping he would just press those soft-looking lips onto mine, part his mouth, and let his tongue enter my mouth. My heart raced uncontrollably and so did my breathing.

"I would like to see your moves."

Oh yeah! I have plenty of those. I'm no virgin like you in bed.

He picked up my blue ponytail from where it rested on my chest and curved the tip around his finger, yet I was missing his cocky smile. "The sparring hall should be free for us to have a combat session, so I can see what I have to work with."

Oh, bloody Underworlds! He was toying with me. My sanity quickly returned to me, and I shoved him away from me.

And there is the cocky grin! Yep, not missing it anymore.

"And one other thing." The cocky smile vanished instantly, and his fists were pumping the air at his sides, clearly fighting not to ball them completely. "Never lie to me again. I don't lie to you, so I expect you to tell me the truth or be quiet. But don't lie, and nobody will get hurt." His disappointment cut like a knife to my side. But what right had he to demand this of me? He was not *my* king.

I took a step closer to him this time, and he took half a step back, leaning out. His eyes softened insecurely.

"If you think you're a Spirit incarnate who can dictate what I can and can't do, let me tell you in fluent blasphemy, so that we are clear, I'm fucking unhurtable!"

That irritating, playful smile resumed on his lips. "That's not a word."

He wasn't genuinely meaning to correct my grammar, but was letting me know everyone could break.

I growled. Frustrated, I ripped open the door and set off towards the sparring hall. Sparring was a good idea right now. I could do with blowing off some steam.

When I entered the hall, I tore off my heavy soldier's boots and parked them next to everyone else's on the shoe rack before I walked over the stone flooring. After two years away from this place, I had forgotten how grand it felt to be inside this room, with its high vaulted ceilings with the enormous glass windows partly covered with the golden-coloured Bensguard Outpost drapes. I recalled the sound of cadets' punches and kicks echoing softly between the stone walls. I had missed my regular dark-blue mat in the corner of the forty odd four-by-four metre mats spaced out evenly in the hall. From the amount of times I had sparred on them with my father, Harvey and Zayd, I knew I could walk from corner to corner blindly without stepping off them. I also knew exactly how it felt to be flung across one and roll onto the stone beyond its edge.

On my way to the mat, I heard a familiar voice.

"I knew I would find you here."

My foul mood switched instantly. "Zoe!"

"Wait!" Ben called from behind my back.

But I ignored him and ran towards Zoe until we joined up in a tight embrace, making the many people in the hall look our way. We drew to the side towards the corner mat and Ben towered over us, staring me down.

"You can't just run away like that without securing your surroundings and identifying potential threats," he hissed at me.

I ignored his lecture. No one was going to kill me in here. Most people *actually* followed the academy rules.

"Zoe, this is King Blackbone. My teammate. King Blackbone, this is Agent Zoe Hammerton. My best friend. She worked on the mission with me in the Black Wing Territory, Intel Unit. And should have been the one organising my backup when I stole the Black Blade, so that I wouldn't have got caught."

In character, Zoe pinned her right hand on her waist and shot out a sassy hip. "Uh. Angie, honey. Confidential."

"It's okay. King Blackbone wants all the truths. Don't you?"

He grunted. "At least that explains it. It's not like you to get caught."

"Oh, Spirit of Love! I think that was a compliment," Zoe blurted out, as untactful as always, saying exactly what was on her mind even if it was commenting on the king's words. "That's so sweet, honey," she added, and I felt like sinking through the floor.

"I'll be damned," Ben mocked in a flat tone, as if his own act of kindness had surprised him.

But he turned his head so no one else had a view of his face and flashed me a mischievous smile.

I shook my head to clear the confusion of what that meant and faced Zoe. "Why are you back? Are you enrolling in the academy with me?"

"Fuck no! The challenges in the academy are some crazy shit I wouldn't go near."

"At least someone around here is intelligent," Ben muttered.

"Oh, the black-wing king compliments me, too. I like him already. Can I keep him? You already have a pet," Zoe chirped, observing him like she'd had him whipped and heeling already.

Oh, Spirits, this was so embarrassing. I can't believe Zoe had just called the king a pet. With regards to my pet pig, I hadn't visited Flora yet since my return. She used to live in the apartment with the family, but only the Spirit of Life knew what Harvey had done with her. I prayed she hadn't been made into a ham sandwich.

But mischief was mischief, so I leered at Ben. "Sure, have him if you want. But I warn you. He's like barbed wire; cold, hard and pricks when you get near."

Zoe aligned next to me, and we inspected him together. She inhaled and let out a long sigh. "In that case, perhaps it's more humane to release him in the wild."

Even though she had been joking, and I knew the soul bond would kill us if we separated too far apart. The thought of being forced apart soured my mind. I wanted him close to me. It was easier to breathe, and it felt like no one could hurt me as long as I had him in my sight. *Stupid attraction! How can I get rid of it?*

Telling myself that he was the reason my parents were dead, and my family name had a big fat 'traitor' stamp over it, didn't seem to help.

"I tried," I whispered. "But the damned thing stayed." We giggled and Ben held a 'will you girls stop talking about me' look on his face.

"Why do they need black-wings for the mission, anyway?" Zoe asked.

"The Spirits want us to collaborate. A peaceful world," I snorted. "The Spirits make the trek easier with the mix, and both kinds must be present when touching the Spirit's Heart for the magic gift to be received."

"And why even bother getting a gift? It's not as impressive as it's cracked up to be."

"Not sure why the black-wings do it," I said, and Ben rolled his eyes as I threw my interrogating stare at him. "But I guess the white-wings do it to get the gift, and to get a seat on the royal counsel table, which will bring wealth and honour to their families."

"Like goody-two-shoes, Watson." Zoe grunted in disgust. I knew she cared nothing for wealth or honour. She enjoyed being an undercover special mission agent and not engaging in the academy. Only a few people got the offer of becoming an agent, as I'd had. But which opportunity to live a cushy life I had just thrown away to earn myself a quick death in this shithole.

"Camp Leader Watson has a seat at King Emille's table?" Ben asked.

"Yes. His father completed the mission with my father, and Emroyce's father. But neither Emroyce nor I have a seat because my father is labelled a traitor and Emroyce's father attacked the king."

Ben's brows lowered. "Why did Erak Bengrey attack the king?"

Something suspicious grew inside me. How did Ben know Emroyce's father by first name?

"No one knows. No one is allowed to speak about it, and I'm not sure Emroyce and Fern want to, either, because King Emille executed their father on the spot," Zoe answered, as I had hesitated.

I inspected Ben's every expression as he listened to her.

"You do seem to sit on a lot of intel, Agent Hammerton. I'd like to get to know you better and pick your brain. What is your magic?"

"Oh, my! Are we at second base already? You tell me yours first and then I'll show you mine, honey."

I rolled my eyes unintentionally as I grabbed Zoe's arm and pulled her up onto the mat and further away from Ben. "What the heck, Zoe?"

She looked at me with raised brows. "You look irritated, honey." She suddenly gasped. "You like him." She paused for a second. "But what about Zayd?"

I cussed under my breath, because even though Mazdon was sparring at the other end of the room, I was sure he could hear Zoe with his super hearing.

"No. I don't like our *enemy king*. It's just…he *is* a king. Show respect."

Ben perused me onto the mat, and as he passed, he whispered into my ear. "Not just to me. You lie to your friends as well." He carried on walking before stopping, standing in the middle of the mat and beckoned me with a finger, looking smug with a wide smirk on his face.

I have clearly failed in making him believe I detest him.

I rolled up the sleeves of my shirt uniform, knowing I had to be tougher when playing with him. "Start praying to any of the Spirits that I don't hurt you."

"Hm," he pondered playfully. "Which one? You white-wings have so many. What is it now? Like seven?"

"Nine. We have more things to pray about than only one Spirit can handle."

"We've got two, actually. Spirit of the Living and Spirit of the World. Covers it all, really."

"Who will you pray to in death, then?"

"That's up to the demons."

"Demons," I snorted. I'd like to think I hadn't been evil enough in life to be sent to the Underworld in death – if it existed. Those creatures were mere myths to scare children not to stray too far into the woods at night so that they wouldn't get lost or be attacked by wild animals.

"So, can we spar two on one?" Zoe asked. "Or how many do you think we'll need to match your ruthlessness?" Zoe took out a leather cord from her pocket and tied her violet hair up in a bun.

The colour of her hair was vibrant, and it appeared as if she had dipped it in the same paint bucket as Valentina, who was sparring two mats down with Camp Leader Rhie Neville. Not that I complained about vibrant colours, as Mother had hired a friend to glamour mine in a sapphire blue when I was too young to remember it being any other colour.

I watched Valentina and Neville spar for a few seconds, and I could tell from her technique that Valentina had been raised at the Bensguard Outpost like me. She was good at combat, although only a second-year cadet. She looked so cute and innocent with her purple hair rounding her soft face, but that was just the packaging. Beneath it was a woman equally as scary as Neville. She could shatter and put together bones only with the use of her mind. Perhaps Valentina's ruthless streak was why Neville tolerated her more than most cadets.

I pointed at Neville. "Now, that's a woman for you, matching your ruthlessness single-handedly."

Neville had never petrified me with her magic, but those she had, said it was an otherworldly feeling of falling through a black void. Maybe the king needed some of that to become more humble.

Ben turned his head to look at where I was pointing. "By *both* Spirits, no," he huffed and leered at me in plain mockery. "I like to make love to a woman without worrying about having my cock chopped off."

Spirit of cursed Love, why did that make me feel a pang of intense jealousy? Hadn't I told myself enough times that the black-wing king was out of bounds?

"I guess you'll be forever a virgin, then." I leered back at him.

Ben turned his gaze towards Zoe. "So, you're adequate at combat, too?"

"She's the-"

"Adequate!" Zoe held out a finger towards me, silencing me as if Ben had hurled an insult at her and she wanted to defend herself. "I'm the Spirit of combat incarnate. No! I'm the Spirit of the Spirits, honey."

"And there's a lot of them," Ben mocked, throwing a quick glance at me before returning his focus toward Zoe.

"I beat Angie," Zoe said flatly.

I cringed. "Not always. I say we are tied."

She was good, but I moved faster than her. As our last mission to the Map Archives had proven, it was her short legs that made her slow when she needed to run for her life, especially from black-wing guards not too keen on us stealing the map with the location of the military base. She had a mean right hook, though, that could knock out just about anyone. Not three guards by herself, so that I had to turn around and help, almost earning an arrow in my shoulder, but in one-to-one combat.

"Okay." Ben seemed to stand down and made his way off the mat. "Ladies first. Let's see what you've got."

I balled my fist in front of my face and held them up in front of Zoe, like I had done many times before. Dancing around each other, I stepped into an angle where I saw Zayd and Camp Leader Rella Tomason walk into the gym. Zayd immediately saw me and approached with Tomason walking next to him, stopping at the edge of the mat a short distance away from Ben.

Tomason exchanged looks with Ben long enough to prick my temper, and now I couldn't concentrate for shit!

Tomason was gorgeous with a thin figure but curves in all the right places. Golden hair draped in locks over her back, and it spilled over her shoulders, framing her heart-shaped face and bright-blue eyes. Her unique beauty was striking in its simplicity, as if nature had taken extra care to perfect her features. Her skin was smooth and unblemished, with a touch of bronze that made her look like sculptured statue. What made me even more jealous was that at twenty-six years of age, the camp leader was the same age as Ben. They were alike, too. Her aura was that of a tense battle warrior, and one of the White Wing Territory's most lethal weapons, able to cloak herself to become invisible. I also suspected she reported everything that happened at Bensguard to her father who was the captain at the Candir Outpost. So, I didn't like her at all.

The way she stared at Ben, that dislike just boiled into hatred.

Before returning my focus back onto Zoe, her fist made impact with my cheek.

Fucking ouch!

I shook my head and held up my fists, making a move to ram into her in close combat and striking two fists at her abdomen. She blew out her breaths and backed up, hitting towards my chest, but I swiped her fist away with my forearm. There were four more quick attacks towards my torso. I blocked all of them, and as she took one second too long to think about what to do next, I kicked at her ribs. She stumbled backwards, and when she found her balance, she leered at me. She loved sparring with me when I didn't take it easy.

Two sprinting steps and then she was low on the mat, swiping out a leg at my knees. I fell to my arse but was close enough to wrestle over her, punching at her shoulders and face. She tumbled me right over and launched a few punches at me before we both broke up and got to our feet. A kicking frenzy began, and she planted a few hard ones over my ribs, and an especially hard one at my back.

Neither of us were here to have our spectators see us lose, and I could tell she was doing her best. But to my advantage, she was sticking out her tongue to concentrate, giving away her intentions as it swiped left and right over her lips.

"Take it easy, girls. It's just sparring," Zayd warned.

"They *are* just sparring." Ben remarked, insinuating that Zayd was holding back our progress.

Zayd had been facing the mat, but he turned towards Ben now. "I'm aware you're king of your own people, King Blackbone. But here, at the Bensguard Outpost, I'm their Camp Leader and I say they're being too rough. I don't want them getting hurt before Coraly starts the challenges."

Ben seemed to half ignore him and was more focused on watching us. "You're right. I'm not the boss of this place, or the academy would have been run a whole lot differently."

Tomason clearly tired of the cockfighting and left for another mat where she saw Glenna Winters, Brian's teammate. If Winters was truly there and it wasn't just her astral projection ghost. She too had grown up at the Candir Outpost, and they seemed on friendly terms, so they must have known each other from before.

Ben watched Tomason's figure as she left. Explosive anger erupted inside me. I used it in a blow with my fist against Zoe's side and she folded over, losing her breath. I shoved her onto the mat, and landing on her front, I grabbed her arm and bent it behind her back to where I knew her pain threshold made her wince.

Zoe tapped out, and before I had even let go of her arm, Ben stepped onto the mat and stared at me. "My turn." His voice bordered a satisfied purr that rose the hackles on my nape.

"Remember, you're bonded. You can't kill her without dying yourself," Zayd told him as Ben closed the gap between us and Zoe walked off to stand next to Zayd.

"There is a lot of pain one can suffer before death, though." Ben looked at me hungrily as he circled the mat.

"Coraly!" Zayd called. I shot my stare at him and was met with worried blue eyes. "Open the connection to the bond so that he'll feel your pain equally."

"I can do that?"

"Yes," he hissed, as if I hadn't paid attention to his lectures. "Your souls are as one."

"Have you planned to do that without my consent?" Ben growled, having rounded me to circle behind my back and appearing on my right side.

I observed him and shook my head. "No. We do things after agreed consent."

"Wise choice."

My nerves tightened all the way to curl my toes into the mat. Normally when I gazed into Ben's eyes, I saw someone who looked at me differently than everyone else, but I didn't see that same man in front of me at this moment. Vacant from recognition, he was lethal, and he sized me up as he padded around me barefoot, dressed in combat trousers and a tight t-shirt through which I could discern all his muscles.

"Any other rules or requests before we start?" he scowled impatiently.

"I'd prefer to keep my intestines where they are. On the inside. Other than that, go for it!"

It seemed a dark secret thrummed beneath his poised exterior, the corner of his mouth twitched as if holding back a retort. "I'll see what I can do."

With wavering resolve, I made a few quick punches to his torso. He deflected them with his arm, not seeming remotely threatened.

"I don't need the warm-up before I start, love. Do your best."

The way he called me 'love' brought chaos to my head, and I forcefully imagined that iron shield held up in front of me to block him out of my heart. I wanted to hate him so badly, but each time I looked at him, that damned mental shield faded, and I feared it would soon become translucent.

I aimed my next punch at his crotch. He caught my fist and held it. "That's foul play, Agent Coraly."

I growled and snatched my fist back, kicking twice at his side, which he let me strike without deflecting. He just looked at what I was doing, as if it was pathetic and didn't hurt at all. His arrogance was so damn annoying.

He was the black-wing king. It was naïve of me not to have expected that he'd be drop dead gorgeous, with battle skills matching the lord of the Underworld himself. If I had thought beating him would be as easy as fooling a low life couch potato with lesser ambitions than a carrot, I had only fooled myself.

As if it was his turn to attack, he barged forwards, and to defend myself, I jumped high on the mat to punch towards his face. He ducked sideways and caught my wrist in a firm grip, then he slammed the heel of his palm at my diaphragm, knocking me backwards. I flew across the mat, landing flat on my back. For a good while, I couldn't breathe, gasping for air as the world spun around me. Any thoughts I had about him liking me, heck, even tolerating me, died. He was obviously still sour about my betrayals and lies.

11

Zayd's head appeared in front of my face. Lines creased his forehead and panicked eyes looked into mine for answers. "Angie?" I felt two of his fingers at my pulse.

"Get off the fucking mat, Watson. I'm in the middle of a match," I cussed, angry with myself for having been so gullible.

Zayd sighed out a big breath, tearing his fingers through his stiff gelled-up hair. "Avoid his strikes rather than blocking them. Don't go for the hard targets. He's stronger than you."

"That's quite fucking obvious!"

"You heard her," Ben said from behind Zayd's back. "Get off the mat and stop babying her. She has been an agent for years and handled worse. Agent Coraly, get up!"

Agent Coraly? Not calling me Miss Stone, nor wanting to accept the term 'cadet'? That's interesting.

Zayd stood up. "Maybe since it's the start of term, you can go easy on her."

"Why? All your Spirits know a demon wouldn't They're stronger than me and would have ripped her arms right off if they caught her wrists."

Zayd flashed him an angry stare but moved to the edge of the mat.

"And apparently," Ben said, leering at me, as he approached, closing the gap between us, "she is unhurtable."

Ah, so he was proving a point to make me understand I couldn't be reckless.

I can break! Got it!

But his action only spurred me to be even more reckless. I launched a kick at his knee. He swiped his leg and kicked my foot away. I round-kicked, aiming higher. He caught my foot in his hand and shoved me backwards, the force sent me down on the mat. He turned to watch Zayd, so I quickly swiped my leg behind his knee, felling him to the mat. I climbed to straddle him, grabbing hold of his t-shirt with one fist and drawing my dagger with the other hand, pressing the blade against his throat.

He held his hands above his head. "Fine. I'll behave."

"Not so fun now, is it?"

"Oh, it has just been upgraded to fucking hilarious." He pushed my head down closer to his mouth, so he could whisper into my ear. "Especially if you saw Camp Leader Watson's expression when you climbed on top of me."

He rolled us over with a swift move, and I lost my grip on the dagger. He forced my face against the mat and braced a knee into my back, twisting my wrist at an unnatural angle.

I used my other hand to tap out before he would break it.

"My turn to play with the king, honey," Zoe beamed.

I was more than happy to walk off the mat, still finding it hard to breathe, and my wrist ached.

Ben stopped close to Zoe, advising her on a few techniques, and also that her tongue was a tell on her move so to keep it inside her mouth, which ruined my lifelong advantage over her.

I ignored them and placed myself a bit closer to Zayd than was normal between our ranks, but I didn't follow most outpost rules, and most people here knew our history.

"I need more practice. How is your tutoring schedule this year?" I asked him.

"My second month is free for sparring, so I can train you every morning after the war updates. Although, Mewer is working on a new feature with a mirrored room, so if his healing workload becomes too overwhelming for him, I might have to step in to teach his classes. But during the third month I must focus on the third-year cadets' battle tactic test. The sparring hall will be closed at the end of the month anyway for the Hunger Temptation challenge." He glanced around the hall at the other cadets. "I could always meet you out on the field in the evenings, but please, use some of your free time to make friends. Or at least, allies."

I nodded whilst looking around the hall and suddenly gasped. Zayd looked away from Ben and Zoe's match and tipped his head to look at me.

I pointed at the tenth mat to our right. "Spirits, look at that boy. He can't be older than sixteen. What is he doing here?"

"He's fifteen. Youngest that has ever enlisted. His name is Hans Oscarson, and his father is some hot-shot wine trader in the capital, who wants to impress King Emille. Cadet Oscarson will die from his father's expectations rather than the dangers here. I don't mind. He is a spoiled prankster. Good at climbing walls, though. His magic enables him to grip even on flat surfaces."

"And his teammate?"

"Fin Lerren. Also a spoiled brat from Gaithbry, where his father works in General Operations in the Air Force at the Emendroth Outpost. He has a breath that will make you faint."

"So, a normal man. Like you, first thing in the morning." I flashed him a cheeky grin.

"Really? You never complained about my kisses."

"No. I was joking. You were always a good kisser."

He put his arm around my waist and pulled me closer as he wiggled his brows.

And this is definitely too close between our ranks.

"I still am," he purred a sound of allure, a bait cast out to tempt me.

I heard the sound of a true strike and turned to see Ben's cheek had reddened. Clearly, Zoe had landed a hard punch with her lethal right hook. Had Ben dropped his focus on the match when seeing, and probably hearing, our last exchange?

Ben held out a hand in front of Zoe in his kingly way, as if to say it was enough.

I took a step away from Zayd and cleared my throat.

Zayd turned towards me with seriousness lacing his face. "Tomorrow, General Denor is visiting the Bensguard Outpost, and he's attending the war updates in the assembly hall. Try to sit far back and not draw his attention. You know what he can do with his mind bending, and since you have been close to the black-wing king, I think he'll be interested in prodding inside your head. And *he will not* ask for your consent."

As Ben was about to walk off the mat, Zayd strode deeper down into the room to watch Mazdon and Kate spar at the end of the hall. Zoe had also turned to watch other teams train with interest, but I was hungry and didn't feel like sparring anymore after I'd had the wind knocked out of me.

"Catch you later, Zoe!" I shouted and waved.

I donned my boots and crossed the hall to get to the open balcony doors to take the shortcut to the canteen via the inner courtyard.

"Can you stop sprinting away from me?" Ben scolded, catching up to me.

I didn't slow down. "We're bound by our souls, not stuck at the hip."

He fell into step with me, and for a while, he was quiet. "What's Zoe's magic?"

I followed the windowed wall on the inner courtyard of the main building, aiming for the balcony doors of the canteen a distance away. "That's the second time you ask. Why do you so desperately want to know? Should I set up a date between you or something? She isn't in your unit, so it's allowed."

He lifted a brow. "You're jealous?"

That was not true. It couldn't be. Not officially, anyway. "No. I'm being a helpful teammate."

He grunted casually in response. "You're getting back together with Watson again?"

Wow! I hadn't expected that straightforward question. "Is this some sort of team bonding exercise? I don't ask you about Tomason."

"Tomason? What about her?"

"I saw how you looked at her."

"And how did I look at her, exactly?"

"Like you wanted some white-wing arse."

He grunted again, a tick of his I was slowly growing used to, but this time it sounded as he had settled on something.

"Stop grunting at my opinions. You know nothing about me."

He grunted again.

That time he definitely mocked me on purpose!

I launched myself in front of him so he couldn't take another step. Then I stared straight into his eyes with all my fury, but the bastard responded by smirking at me.

"I think I know quite a lot about you," he said before I spoke, and he did it so fucking confidently. "When someone says you can't do something, you have to prove to them you can. When you're mad, you walk away. When you're *really* angry, you shove your face or black iron into your enemy's face. When you're sad or confused about life, you climb the oak tree by the field. When you're scared, you become too trusting. And you don't trust people because you don't want them to learn something about you that you don't like about yourself – when people get too close to your deep dark secrets. Your brother is the same on the last point. How many statements have I got right thus far?"

I didn't know how to respond to that besides dropping my jaw, and I didn't want to do that in front of him.

"You're silent when you're insecure," he added. "Do you want me to carry on?"

My breath caught. *How much of my soul had he been sifting through?*

I grunted back at him purposely before walking into the canteen.

"Oh, so you think you've got me figured out, too," he mocked, not being further than one step away. "This should be interesting. Go on."

We both grabbed a pre-prepared chicken bread roll from the fridge and a bottle of water.

"Okay. How about this?" I barked. "When someone tells you that you can't do something, you don't give a shit and do whatever you want. When you're mad, you cut off thumbs. When you're *really* angry, you simply kill them. When you're sad and confused about life…wait, you never are because you don't give a shit. When you're scared…wait, you're never scared because you never let people close enough to care about you…And you don't trust people. Period."

I guessed he hadn't expected that assessment because he stood staring at me in dead silence.

Still staring at me.

Well, this is awkward.

"When you're silent," I whispered, my heart in my throat, fearing I was crossing a line. "You're considering whether to kill the person in front of you who you hate most in the world because she has betrayed you and lied to you, but you know you can't only because you have been bound to her soul. So, there is nothing you can do about it except hurt her as much as you can." I swallowed hard. "How am I doing thus far?"

His smirk vanished. He looked heartbroken, but I was sure I had read that wrong. He opened his mouth to speak, but he didn't and closed it again. A second time, he tried, but no words came out of his mouth. He frowned and turned around, walking away.

"And you walk away when you can't admit you're wrong because you're the king, so you can't have flaws!" I shouted as he disappeared out through the balcony doors, having angrily discarded the empty tray on a nearby table.

Damn. Now I'm sad and confused about life, so I've got to climb that damned tree.

I crossed the inner courtyard and sauntered towards the main doors between the Administration Office and Infirmary Ward to get out the front. It didn't take long before I adjusted myself on the branch, slouching so I could watch the fluffy white clouds in the sky whilst eating my bread roll.

Not having been alone for long, I heard the scratching sound of someone climbing the bark, and wasn't sure I had the patience to deal with Zayd at the moment. I turned my head, but instead of auburn spikes and a navy-blue uniform, I saw wavy strawberry-blonde hair topping a toned body in a black uniform.

"Mazdon?"

Warmth and relief flooded me…and envy of Kate for having the kind of big brother I always wanted. Someone who cared for the entire emotional spectrum, not a person who only pushed me to train me not to break.

"Hello Angie. You've been back at the academy for a mere few weeks, and you have already stirred up bad tempered men quite a bit. Not that I had any doubts you'd turn this place upside down when you returned. You always had a knack for mischief." He made himself comfortable on Zayd's branch opposite from me.

"So people keep telling me."

His jade-coloured eyes looked at me with such kindness, I dared to relax back into my slouching position, from where I could still see him when I twisted my head.

He pulled one foot up onto the branch and braced his forearm on his knee. "Remember when you and Kate were ten years old, and you told her that if she stuck her fingers into the soil and poured water on them, she would grow taller?"

"Yeah." I laughed. "Harvey had told us we'd never grow taller than his long-sword."

"I still see her poke at the soil at times, stating she is purely gardening. And when she had received her fire wielding magic, you told her that if she blasted enough fire at a stone, it would turn into a diamond."

"Yeah." I laughed again, "But that was to encourage her to practise strengthening her magic."

"Yes. Very helpful. I think she's still doing that, too. Hope dies hard."

I smiled at the fond memories of the time we spent at the summer cottage when my family hadn't been broken, traitors…or dead.

But I doubted Mazdon had climbed the tree to talk to me about old memories.

"Why are you up here? Kate kicked your arse sparring and you needed a quiet moment for reflection?"

He pulled a leaf off a branch and fiddled with them in his hand. "I'm stepping in to give you some big brotherly advice. I doubt Harvey is the kind of guy who will provide life guidance."

"Damn right about that." When he didn't elaborate, I got curious. "So, what's your advice?"

"Zayd is a really nice guy–"

"Really! You're here to–"

"But!" he said sternly. "And I might play with fire here, and not my sister's kind. I think you're meant for something greater." He cringed as I glowered at him.

"Go on," I urged.

"You turn the black-wing king into an emotional wreck every time he comes near you."

"What?" I tensed and curled up to sit straight on the branch, staring at him.

"Every time he looks at you, I can hear his heart racing and when Zayd puts his arms around you, his heart races to the point I think it will fail at any moment and go into cardiac arrest."

My brows rose and there were so many emotions spinning around inside me.

"Just like your heart does when you look at him. You like him, too."

Mazdon's magic made me feel so vulnerable. I wrapped my arms around myself and stroked my hand over my shoulder.

Mazdon looked at me more intently. "Just like your brother's heart does when he looks at Kate. But none of you Coralys ever take what you want. What you deserve. You always fight to protect others and leave nothing to be earned for yourselves."

"You're saying it's a good idea for me to involve myself with the enemy king?"

"I can't make the choices for you. I'm only saying that you might want to listen to your heart once in a while."

"Thank you, Mazdon. That's good advice. But you didn't see Ben hit me today. I'm sure his racing heart is purely wrath and nothing romantic."

"I did see it. I saw he punched you at exactly the limit you can handle, making you look strong in front of the others whilst also making you understand the severity of your choice to join the academy. He's an intelligent man, Angie. Don't forget that there is a reason he's still the king of his territory and no one has overthrown him even when he started his reign being younger than any king in Skyberg's history."

"Am I missing something here? You're talking up a man who is the most unlikely match for me. Are you trying to get me killed?"

He laughed warmly and shook his head. "No, Angie. You're as much of a little sister to me as Kate. King Blackbone is a good man. You don't have the luxury of knowing all the secrets to his life, so I only wanted to level the playing field for the king if you ever had thoughts about resuming your relationship with Zayd."

"Why do you have the impression I would resume my relationship with Zayd?"

"For one, he's having a very awkward conversation with your brother in the Captain's Office right now."

"You can hear Harvey speaking to Zayd in his office? You must hear so much gossip. I wish I had your magic."

"Whenever you want. You can borrow it," he laughed.

"You know Harvey forbids me from using magic." I looked up towards the leadership floor as if I could see them through the window. "Would you tell me what they're speaking about?"

"Well," Mazdon scratched his head, "Zayd is asking your brother for his blessing to ask for your hand in marriage, but your brother isn't accepting until you have decided over signing the enrolment ledger. Oh, and not even then, he says. Zayd's heart is racing. With anger. He's panting, so I guess he's trying to stay calm. Harvey is saying that Zayd needs to find you and take you to him right this instance, as it's time for you to make your choice."

"I guess I only have a few more minutes of peace then."

Mazdon pinched his lips in a thin line and looked at me apologetically.

"Tell me other gossip. What is Ben doing?"

"Give me a moment to listen for him." Mazdon squeezed his eyes shut and his head tipped downwards in concentration. Suddenly, he looked up. "There he is. Okay, so he's sitting in the canteen with Murben, Commander Daffron, Nesso and Davis. They are talking about combat routines and the way a blade should be crafted to make it as sharp as possible."

"What else can you hear at the outpost?"

"Cadet Darling from the Party Girl Team, as Emroyce calls them…"

I shook my head at Emroyce's silly naming convention of the teams that he had adopted when we were young, but fair play to him, it made it easier to remember their teammates and what magic they possessed.

Mazdon seemed to focus on listening, as if she was further away than Ben was. "She's trying to seduce a poor bloke in third-year Cavalry Unit. She has sensual magic, so I guess she will succeed. Captain Thomas La Roy is scolding Brian for not working hard enough. Valentina is helping her mother in the infirmary, correcting bones on a man who has come back from a fall in the mountains during an attack and it sounds," his entire face cringed, and he clenched his teeth together, "unpleasant."

"What about Emroyce?"

"Cadet Bengrey… Uh, we won't have anymore time. Zayd is approaching and I want to make myself scarce before he gets here, or he'll know I've spoken to you."

I nodded. "Thank you."

"You're welcome."

He jumped down and jogged away.

Zayd barged over the grass and stopped beneath the tree crown. He was clenching his jaw tightly and he was balling his fists.

Yep, he looks tense and angry.

"Agent Coraly," he called out.

"Camp Leader Watson," I replied.

He signed frustratedly. "Can you please come with me? Captain Coraly wants you to decide whether or not you'll sign the ledger."

Zayd didn't want me to sign it, so that he could marry me. Ben didn't want me to sign it so that he could kill me for my betrayal, and if Ben didn't kill me the challenges might. But what did I want? Everything told me it was a smart choice not to sign, but if I didn't, I couldn't help with restoring our family name. Neither could I destroy it any further if I left. I felt so torn by an impossible decision. Deep down, my gut told me this was my destiny, my home. I was meant to complete the academy like all my ancestors before me.

I climbed down from the tree and followed in his step as he led me towards the building. We crossed paths with Camp Leader Tomason in the door, tailed by some of her third-year Infantry Unit cadets in their emerald uniforms with the three vertical lines on their shoulder. Suddenly, she dissipated, though, having cloaked herself in her magic, and it made me nervous. I brought my hands to the side of my legs, hovering them over my dagger hilts.

When nothing happened, I snorted at my paranoia and ascended the stairs to the second floor and took confident strides into my brother's office. That was until I entered and my confidence drained right out of me, seeing him seething with frustration behind his desk, clutching a pen between white knuckles.

Shit!

Show no weakness!

I walked right up to his desk, crossing my arms over my chest. "Where is that ledger so I can get this over and done with?"

12

The official ledger with all the cadets' signatures laid with a wide-open spread on Harvey's desk. He turned it around to face me and held out a pen.

"Please, don't do this," Zayd whispered behind my back, his finger stroked down the back of my arm. "Be my wife," his voice was so soft I wasn't sure Harvey could hear him. I ignored it.

I snatched the pen out of my brother's hand and searched for the next available space to sign my name, curving my signature neatly so that no one could mistake what name was printed on the page. The resigned sigh Zayd exhaled behind me cut into my guilt.

I tossed the pen onto the fold of the book. "There. Done."

"Welcome to the academy of the Special Missions Unit," Harvey muttered sarcastically, tidying away the ledger neatly in his drawer.

"By the way. What have you done with Flora?" I asked him.

"I arranged for a space in the stables for her."

That came as a surprise. "Not a ham sandwich, then?"

"You think very little of me, sister. I know you love that pig."

"Like I loved Mum and Dad but those you–"

Slaughtered.

He cut my voice off with a hard glare. My throat went dry. I inhaled. "Am I dismissed, Captain?"

"You're dismissed, Cadet Coraly," he growled.

Cadet. Not Agent. That was a downgrade, but I would remedy that when I graduated to sergeant. Perhaps I might become a camp leader one day or even replace General Denor. I had the magic for it.

Emroyce broke the tension between us, poking his head into the office. "Some guys are heading down to the obstacle course to challenge your record, Watson. Want to join us?" His glance through the room caught on me. "Angie, hello. You should come, too."

"More than happy to." I followed Emroyce towards the obstacle course. "Are they letting you compete yet?"

"No. They don't trust that I won't cheat, so I've become somewhat of the official timekeeper," he said, showcasing the golden pocket watch he held in his hand; a beautifully crafted family heirloom he was never without. "I heard you tried to beat the women's record in linen trousers and trendy boots. What was it? Seven minutes. Impressive." His tone was dripping with playful sarcasm.

I glowered at him. "I think I can make it under five minutes the next time I try."

"I bet you can't." He wiggled his raven-black eyebrows at me, knowing me so well.

Now I have to prove him wrong.

"I would like to see you do it with your speed magic, even if it won't count for the record books."

"My fastest is three minutes flat."

"Really? Wow!"

"And that day, I had a bad hair day."

I giggled and noticed his long black hair sleekly tucked into a tight ponytail.

Zayd jogged up behind us. "I can't believe you signed the ledgers," he muttered.

"You finally signed the ledgers?" Emroyce asked

"Yes, she signed the bloody ledgers!" Zayd barked.

"And that's a bad thing?" Two lines appeared between Emroyce's brows. "Man, of course, she should sign the ledgers. She belongs here."

"Thank you, Emroyce. Always so supportive," I chirped batting my eyelashes at him.

"I've got your back, Angie." Emroyce swung his arm around my shoulder as we walked.

"You better mean that for the challenges, too, Emroyce," Zayd warned. "As her camp leader, there is little I can do to help."

Emroyce flat out frowned at Zayd. "Of course, I mean it. Angie is important to us all."

We arrived at the obstacle course, and more cadets than I had expected to see here had gathered. Brian was on the monkey rings, swinging through them quickly.

"He's going to break your record," a man with long black hair and teal eyes told Zayd.

"Angie, this is Klint Penya, who I mentioned to you earlier as an ally. He's a healer from the province of Pharanir together with his teammate Elinor Maruto, who is a water wielder." Zayd pointed at a woman with the same style of dark hair as Penya with a slender body that she had squeezed into an extravagant teal dress instead of wearing a uniform.

Zayd was barely looking at them as he watched Brian crawling under the nets and jumping high up on the wall, grabbing the rope and starting to climb. Brian slid down the rope on the other side, the same as my technique of barely pushing off at the wall. It went quicker that way. Walking the balance bar, though, Brian swayed to one side, losing his balance for a mere second. But it would be enough to set him back. Zayd knew it too, and grinned. Brian was quick over the steppingstones and sprinted across the finish line.

"Four minutes and forty-six seconds," Penya called. "Fourth place after Emroyce, if his score counts. Third place in the official record book. Well done, mate."

Brian folded double and panted with his hands on his knees. His soft white hair wafted in the light breeze, being not quite long enough to be tied back. "If I hadn't had fucked-up on the balance bar, I think I could have beaten you, Watson," he said, panting.

"Dream on, Cadet," Zayd mocked.

"What time does your brother hold?" I asked Brian.

"Oh, Captain La Roy doesn't engage in these childish pursuits when there is a serious war just outside the fence that needs priority," Brian said, and it sounded as if he was quoting his brother's words.

"Who's next?" Emroyce called out, holding his golden pocket watch ready. "I'll take over the time-keeping." Everyone was too busy chatting to step forward. "Where is my teammate? Kenyard!" he shouted and held up a hand to get his attention, stabbing a thumb in the air towards the track. "You're up!"

"After Kenyard, I want to go," I told Emroyce, who nodded, so I started to warm up, jumping on my spot.

Gerard Kenyard walked up to the start line and Emroyce glared at him. "If you don't beat Cadet Coraly, I'm swapping partners."

"Great!" I smiled. "Then it's your turn to be bonded to the black-wing king."

I laughed seeing Emroyce's horrified expression, but it only lasted for one second before he grinned back at me and his almost black eyes seemed to look straight into my soul.

"Jokes on you, Angie," Kenyard said. "I can tell you don't want to swap partners."

Shit! This was the guy who could read intentions by listening to your voice. I looked up at Zayd, who looked back at me with a tightly clenched jaw and that stern camp leader stare.

"Get ready, Kenyard," Zayd growled.

Kenyard focused, leaning over the start line, prepared to give it his all. He tossed with his head, flicking the dark-blonde hair further backwards on the other side of his shaved skull.

"Three… Two… One… Go!" Emroyce counted him down and Kenyard was off.

He was adept at it like all the rest, but his weakness was climbing up the rope as his arms weren't as strong as the others'. He had been working hard on strengthening his biceps in the weights room, but some men are bony, and some are buff, and Kenyard would remain a frustrated shadow of his teammate; always a few steps behind.

"Four minutes and fifty-seven seconds!" Emroyce called out when Kenyard crossed the finish line.

"Oh! I think I could possibly beat that!" I shouted towards Kenyard, as I placed my foot just behind the start line and focused my eyes at the first of the six bars.

"No complaining about splinters," Ward, who was standing next to Mewer, said playfully.

"And this time I have proper soldier's boots. Count me down, Emroyce!"

"Three… Two… One… Go!" Emroyce shouted.

I could feel that I had already become stronger than the last time I attempted the course. The six bars were the easy part, but I also conquered the climbing net faster than normal. I gripped on the monkey rings easily now when they were dry. After the last of them, I threw myself down onto my front, pushing my elbows and knees on all fours under the crawling net and roused myself as I stood face to face with the rope wall. Climbing it, I roared out my efforts, acid building up in my biceps. I slid down the other side so fast, I truly thought the impact on the ground would fracture the same bone in my ankle as I had once broken in my childhood. I pushed through the throbbing pain, sprinting for the next obstacle. The balance bar had never been a problem for me as I was small, so the surface area was large compared to my boots. There were only the steppingstones left to conquer after that, but my legs were shaking with exhaustion.

Don't miss a step and you're home free!

I was ecstatic when I cleared the last step and raced in a flat-out pace across the finish line, tumbling to lie on my back on the grass. "How…" I panted, "did," I took a few more breaths, "I do?"

"Wow!" Emroyce bellowed. "Four minutes fifty-nine seconds. You beat the female record but not Kenyard's. Just off by two seconds. You were so close!" He pinched his fingers together until there was only a small gap between them as if to show how small the difference was.

"Kenyard has to increase the number of his weekly training sessions, or

I think you'll beat him next time, though," Zayd teased.

"No favouritism, Camp Leader!" Emroyce tittered. "Who's next?"

"I'll have a go. It was a while since I tested myself on the course," the navy-blue dressed Cavalry Unit Camp Leader said, stepping forward.

"I'll expect no slower than my time," I told Ward, and my tease almost died in all my panting, and the fact that I knew he'd finish closer to Brian's time than Kenyard's.

"I hope not to disappoint you, Cadet Coraly," Ward answered with an impish grin.

Emroyce counted down and started the time as Ward shot off towards the first six bars.

Still lying on the grass, I watched Ward fly through the course, setting a time just a second slower than my brother's and equal to Emroyce's at four minutes forty-five seconds.

After Ward had finished, I decided to turn in for the night. I got off the grass and pass by Zayd, reaching up to kiss his cheek; an old habit I shouldn't have done. "Good night."

He patted the hand I had pressed against his pectoral to keep myself balanced as I had tip-toed to reach his face.

"Good night, Angie."

I was glad he hadn't begged that I stay in his bed, but I guessed that offer was off the table ever since I had signed the ledger. My heart being too confused regarding how I felt about Zayd, I walked into the building before I could change my mind and broke a few more of my brother's rules.

It was only eight o'clock, but damned Spirits, I was tired from all the activities today. My feet dragged down the corridor, stopping by the canteen to grab two cold tuna pie slices. I ate them on the way to my room, licking my fingers before turning the key in the lock. As soon as I entered the room, I was flung around. My adrenaline kicked in and I was suddenly alert. The door closed, and Ben pressed me hard up against it with his hand against my throat. It wasn't a painful grip, but it held me in place.

He brought his face close to mine. "I always knew about your reckless streak. But, you realise that you have outdone yourself this time?"

Having gained more confidence after my conversation with Mazdon, I was just about able to control my fear of him. "You're letting your compliments just fly today. Fabulous."

He didn't let my charm-attempt fool him. "You signed the enrolment ledger."

"Was that what the punch at my diaphragm in the sparring hall was for? You were trying to scare me off!"

His nose almost skimmed mine. "It obviously didn't work. You're more reckless with your life than I am with mine." His breath stroked my mouth.

I looked up from his lips to his eyes. "Maybe you're just not as scary as you think you are."

He took a second to look at me…assessing. "I don't need to be scary. The demons are more than scary enough. They won't be merciful. They'll infect you by a mere touch. The fear will be all consuming. Maybe then, you'll respect danger."

"I'll worry about the demons when I have finished worrying whether you will kill me first."

He scoffed out through his nose. "It's not me you'll have to worry about, but every other fucking cadet at the Bensguard Outpost. They, or the nature of the challenges, will kill you way before I get the chance."

"You're upset." I searched for a glimmer of emotion in his eyes that I could use to push him over the edge. I wanted to see what he would do when his control slipped. A dangerous game that made my adrenaline throb beneath my skin. "You thought I wouldn't sign." I looked from one fury-filled eye to the other. "You thought you could be rid of me. That Camp Leader Mewer would unbind me from your soul, and you'd be free to kill me. You're angry because I robbed you of the challenge of killing me, knowing someone else will get to me first."

His eyes darted across my face, clearly unsure where to let them rest, and his jaw seemed to tighten with each breath. His body trembled with rage, and it was obvious that he was struggling to control his anger with the way his chest rose and fell in front of me. "Killing you is no challenge," he breathed slowly, lethally close to my neck. "I had *hoped* you wouldn't sign and go back to being an agent again. I *believed* you would enrol to prove your brother wrong, even if it tied you to this place until your death." The veins in his throat swelled and forked down his collar at the world *death.*

I bit down on my lip, so I wasn't tempted to bite his. "Well, that's too fucking bad."

His breaths grew deeper. Every time he inhaled, his pectorals pushed into my personal space, making my breath hitch and as he exhaled, I rushed a breath into my lungs trying not to faint. "You must talk to me about these things. Stop doing things behind my back."

"I'm not telling you shit. You're a king. You know how negotiations work. Sometimes you'll have to be the one to tell your truth before I'll tell mine. Focus on the challenges instead of me, as I guess us enemies will have to learn how to be a team if you want to survive."

His shoulders fell, and he sighed out his signature grunt. "It hurts me when you say we're enemies."

Oh? That was a development. He told me an honest feeling. *And why did that get my traitorous body to heat up like a summer sun?* I had to get away from this position or I'd soon lose my control, shove my fingers into his hair and do things he'd reject and that would kill me with embarrassment!

"I thought that's what you considered us. You said, 'When you're *really* angry, you shove a blade into your enemy's face'."

He raked his fingers through his onyx hair that he had let loose from his short ponytail and hang low enough to hide his ears. "Please, tell me that my poor use of vocabulary wasn't why you signed the ledger."

"No. I signed the ledger because this is my home. Everyone fights for their home, and I fight to protect my friends and family. I was actually on my way out to see one of my most loyal family members, but I just wanted to change first because I got sweaty on the obstacle course."

Again, he stared, assessing me. "May I come with you?"

The king wants to meet my pet pig?

"I don't know if I'm ready to introduce you to my family yet," I mocked.

"Please," he whispered.

I rolled my eyes at him. *He could say 'please'?* How could I say no to that? "Sure. Let me just have a quick shower and get changed first."

I found an opening to duck under his arm, quickly locking myself into the bathroom with a big sigh of relief that I hadn't done anything stupid so far. The hot water was amazing on my muscles, and I relaxed underneath the water pressure for a few extra minutes, soaping myself up twice after I had finished washing my hair. I turned the tap off and towel-dried my hair, letting it cascade over my back as I wrapped the towel around myself. Maybe next time I should have the foresight to bring my clothes into the bathroom with me as the next part of stepping out and in front of Ben in only a towel would be awkward.

I padded out on the wooden flooring and couldn't see Ben by his bed; relief flowed over me until someone knocked on our door and there was a waft of air over my naked skin. I twisted my head to see Ben opening the door, and behind it stood Zayd.

Shit!

You opened the door in front of Zayd when I'm only wrapped in a towel!

Ben turned his head and leered at me.

Had he heard my thoughts? No. He had promised not to intrude.

Zayd glared angrily at Ben, who looked even more amused at the situation because of it.

"Angie, I was going to let you know that I have some time now for sword practice. Do you want to meet me on the field?"

"Great! I'm just going to check on Flora and I'll see you there in thirty minutes."

Ben closed the door in Zayd's face, and I flashed him a tired look before I went to the wardrobe to find my clothes.

"Watson has met Flora?" he asked.

I snatched a shirt off a hanger. "Yes."

Stretching up onto my toes, I reached a pair of folded combat trousers.

"And what does Flora think of Watson?"

I halted with my clothes in my grip to think. What did the pig think of Zayd? Not much, really. She never paid him attention. She had bitten him once.

"That he should stop eating so many ham sandwiches," I said, and went into the bathroom and closed the door behind me to change, removing and re-applying my makeup and running a brush through my hair but leaving it loose over my back to dry.

"You look beautiful," Ben said, as I exited the bathroom, focused on retrieving my leg straps with my daggers and my sword that was leaning against the wall next to my bed.

I stopped in my step to stare at him. "In my uniform?"

Having glanced at him had made the intensity of the heat that was rising to my cheeks worse. Had he paid me a compliment…on my looks? *Probably a protocol of politeness.*

"In anything…or nothing."

Spirits! The words set my cheeks on fire. How in the bloody Underworld would I snuff that out now? "Well, the latter, you'll never see."

He grunted at that.

I passed Ben to get my boots, but again I stopped in my step and turned around to inspect him. His shirt looked less wrinkly than before I'd had my shower. "Have you changed your shirt?"

"Yes. I wanted to look presentable."

"I don't believe Flora cares, but *I* think you look nice." Nope, I hadn't been ready to say that. Heat exploded in my face once more and I had to avert from seeing his smirk to focus on my feet to make it cool down. I shoved my feet into my boots and laced them up. "Let's go," I called out, as I tossed an apple in my hand.

"You don't like apples," Ben said, nodding for it inside my hand.

This time, my heart burned. How did he know that?

"It's not for me," I said, leaving the room.

Who could have ever thought I would walk side by side with a king towards the stables to visit a pet pig? The thought amused me.

"You might want to roll up the cuffs of your sleeves."

The puzzled look on his face made this adventure all the more humorous.

He raised his brows. "Flora doesn't like men with long sleeves?"

"She does. That's why I advise you to roll them up, or she'll nibble on them."

Having walked down the lengths of the stable corridor, inhaling the smell of approximately a hundred horses, I stopped at the back where the academy held random smaller animals and glanced around the hay.

"Flora!" My heart burst with joy when she rushed towards me; her pot belly heaved as she ran, and her hooves kicked up the caked hay that was mixed with mud. "You remember me, girl."

"Flora is a pig?"

"Yes. Isn't she adorable?" I leaned down to scratch her behind the floppy ear the way I knew she liked it, and her little curling tail wagged high in the air. "Aren't you? Aren't you, girl?" I unsheathed my dagger at my leg and cut the apple into four slices. "Why? You don't like pigs?"

"Of course, I do. I like–"

"If you make any distasteful jokes about bacon, ham, or pork chops in front of her, I'll hurt you."

He held his hands up, as if to say he would never dare, before rolling up his sleeves and leaning with his forearms on the wooden fence.

I had forgotten how enormous this stable was with its high ceiling. A variety of tools hung from beams across the room that were used to care for the animals, living and dead. Multiple smaller windows lined the top edge of the walls, and the roof was a thin sheet of tin to hold out the rain, making the temperature in here equal to the outside.

Flora snorted the hay with her petite snout, ruffling it about and moving towards Ben as if he was made of sugar. He stretched down his hand to scratch her behind the ear the way I had done.

"Wow. She normally doesn't trust new people or get close to them like that. She still bites Zayd when he gets too close."

A playful smile curved his lips. "Don't insult Flora. She is obviously an excellent judge of character."

I rolled my eyes at him before luring Flora back, waving the apple near her snout. "Look what she can do." When she paid attention to the apple, I brought it a little closer to her mouth. "Flora. Sit." She did it on my first command and I was ecstatic that she hadn't forgotten.

"Neat trick. Can I try?" After I had handed him a piece of apple, Ben held it in front of my face. "Angelica. Sit."

I glared at him, crossing my arms over my chest.

He leaned his butt on the wooden fence and supported his hands on either side; apple forgotten. "What about; stay safely in your room at all times and don't meet with Watson? Or, come with me to the Black Wing Territory?"

"Ben! The apple is for Flora!"

He pushed off the fence and took a step closer to me, so I had to cock my head up not to have my face pressed up against his chest. His stares narrowing to focus straight into mine. "What about; kiss me?"

Yep, that got my heart pounding.

Warmth spread to my cheeks and slithered like a snake all the way down to my groin. I swallowed. A kiss? Why? To what end? Was this some trick to win my trust and betray me later as pay-back? Or was he scheming bigger than that and it had to do with getting to my captain brother's secrets? Was he trying to garner information about our military operations and resources? Why was he even still here when I had offered to free him?

"The apple is for Flora," I growled, not breaking eye-contact with those beautiful sunset tinted eyes.

Ben turned away from me and leaned down to Flora. "Sit." She obeyed. "Flora is clearly my favourite individual around here. Co-operative and reasonable."

"And too trusting," I glowered at him, and he responded with a soft chuckle.

Flora nibbled the apples from my hand as I gave her the last piece before heading out of the stables.

Zayd was already waiting for me on the field, making test swings in the air with his sword, almost imperceptible in his camp leader uniform in the dim evening light. When I walked across the grass, Ben stopped at the sideline and watched us with intense focus.

"Does he have to be here, watching us?" Zayd asked after I had drawn my sword and pointed it at him.

I twisted my head around to look at him. "He's not doing any harm. He's just standing there."

"He's watching me like he'll kill me if I take a wrong step."

I hit my blade over his. "I don't doubt he will."

He hit back at me, but I held my hilt firmly, and as he pushed at my blade, I swiped it over my head and circled under his arm, tapping my other hand at his back. "Had I held a dagger in my other hand, you'd be dead. It's not like you to lose focus."

He turned and struck a few consecutive blows. First low, then at my side, and lastly high. "It's not easy to focus with King Blackbone staring at me. Surely, he has somewhere else he could be."

Had Zayd thought he'd get some time with me alone out here and that was why he was sour?

"I don't mind having him around. He protects me."

His next hit was harder. "Don't get too attached to him, Angie."

"We're soul bound. We sort of are attached."

"You know what I mean. Why were you parading around your room naked?"

"I had a shower, and I had to get dressed. It's my room. What am I supposed to do?"

"Can't you dress in the bathroom?"

"I did after I had fetched my uniform."

"Oh. That's a relief." He danced around me and attempted a blow at my back that I parried, and then I launched myself into an attack, swinging and hacking at the height of his thigh. "Keep your elbow out a bit, but not too much, or you'll tire." I put my elbow out. "Yes, like that. And be careful placing too much weight into your strokes as you must be ready to jump back if there is a counterattack. Fight more on the pads of your feet and be light on your heel unless you need to block and push your opponent back, then you plant your heels firmly on the ground."

As I plotted to sneak around him, he put out his foot and I fell over it, landing on the grass, but I held my sword up immediately to guard myself. I noticed Ben twitch, as if he was ready to step in to defend me, but he remained in his position.

"See!" Zayd said, flinging an arm out towards Ben.

"Ignore him."

Zayd held out a hand to help me up. "Your swords skills are okay, but how are you doing with your wings now? If you need to flee a battle scene, how long does it take you to bring them out and be in the air?"

I inhaled the fresh air and pondered the question. "I don't know. Ten seconds, maybe."

"Ten seconds! No, that's too long. We'll have to practise that to get it down to a maximum of six seconds. You can come to my apartment tomorrow evening, and we can do some push-ups, and I can show you some other exercises you can do, so you can strengthen your back muscles."

Standing this close to me, his loving gazes fell on me like a moth to a flame. For a second, I thought he had forgotten where we were and the sight of me had taken him back to our past. He stroked his entire hand on the side of my head, nestling his fingers into my hair. "Maybe afterwards, we can have a glass of wine."

I cleared my throat and glanced at Ben. "Maybe we can do it in the sparring hall, and we shouldn't do this here."

Zayd clearly snapped out of his reminiscence and pulled his hand away from my hair, sheathing his sword in an angry rasp. His hands fell to his sides, fisting at the side of his legs. Agitation made him squirm on the spot as he looked between Ben and me. "Why? Because he's here? It's not like you two can ever become anything. He's a king, for goodness' sake! You know the traditions. He must marry a princess or some noble lady, and you're a simple traitor."

My sword-arm slacked along my leg, my chest twisted in agony until it was hard to breathe, and it grew more intense by the second. "I can't believe you said that." That was my worst nightmare, the word that cut me the deepest, and that it had come from Zayd, the word hurt a million times worse. Sorrow gripped over my heart, holding it secure in an iron cage.

"I didn't mean that I think so. But King Blackbone will."

"King Blackbone has never called me a traitor, nor has he ever treated me like one."

I sheathed my sword and turned around, wiping tears off my face with the back of my hand, as I rushed towards my room.

"Angie! I didn't mean it like that!" Zayd called.

He didn't pursue me. The thunderous steps behind me made me realise why. Ben was right behind me.

In my room, I went straight for my duffle bag to bring out a whetstone, but when I turned around to get my dagger, I slammed into Ben.

"You're upset," he grunted.

I tried to walk around him, but he kept himself in my way. "No shit!" It was extremely infuriating that he didn't move when I tried to shove him away, but my attempts were as if trying to push at a boulder.

"What reason do you have to be upset?" he demanded to know.

Why? What game is this?

His eyes followed mine wherever I looked, observing where I was placing my glances around the room. He took another step towards me and then another. I had to move backwards until he had me pressed up against the wall next to the wardrobe. "I challenge you. You won't dare tell me what is upsetting you."

Oh, I bloody dare. But that was his point. He knew he could get me to react if he told me I couldn't do something.

He stared at me hard. "That statement really makes your skin crawl, doesn't it?" He cupped his palm around the back of my neck and sensually dragged his thumb down my throat and then slid his hand down to my chest, expertly flicking two buttons open on my shirt with his fingers. "Holding in your defiance is eating you up." One finger strayed onto the swell of my breast. "What shall it be?" he asked slowly.

"It's nothing! I'm sorry I appeared weak. Okay!"

"This isn't weakness. It shows you still have some humanity left when everyone here wants to turn you into a rule-following weapon."

"Perhaps it would be for the best if I were a mindless weapon."

He grunted. "Your hurt twists like a knife in my chest and my control is slipping, so if you can't trust talking to me, I'll seek out Camp Leader Watson and I'll beat him until he tells me what he did to you."

"No! You can't fight a camp leader. Leadership will punish you with lashes. They'll punish us both as a team. Five lashes each."

He cocked my chin up and looked into my eyes. "If whatever he has said to you has upset you this much, I doubt he'll report it to your brother."

He clenched his teeth together as he waited for my response. But he was clearly too impatient to wait. He inhaled a deep breath and let it out slowly. "How many broken bones can Camp Leader Watson take before he's out of service?"

The intensity of his ruby eyes on me had me choking. Near suffocating, I needed more space than the small gap between us. I punched at his pectorals with my palms and shoved my shoulder into him. "Move! I won't tell you what he said to me!" My fists pumped at his abdomen harder and harder until he snatched up my wrists, shoved them behind my back and pushed me tightly into his embrace. He wrapped clamping arms around me to hold me up. I tried to fight it, but he held on firmly.

"Stop it!" I screamed.

When I realised fighting him was fruitless, I relaxed and leaned against his chest, supporting myself on him as I sobbed. Ben held me and said nothing, did nothing. Not even to wipe away my tears. After a while I managed to stop and stay silent.

"He called me…he *reminded* me I'm a traitor."

Ben tensed, his arms tightened around me. "I see." He was quiet for a while and his body trembled against mine. "Next time you speak with him, *you* can *remind him* that in the Black Wing Territory, you're not a traitor. I'll happily take you back there at any time he feels you're unworthy of him."

I snorted. "What place would I have among black-wings in your territory?"

He cocked his head down to look at me. "On the fucking throne!"

13

When I woke up, I was huddled in darkness, only able to make out feather-like patterns close to my face. I pushed my hands upwards at soft feathers, and when light penetrated the gaps, I realised Ben's black wings surrounded me.

What liberties did he think he could take with me to share my bed? Thankfully, I was still wearing my uniform and weapons, having collapsed into bed from last night's drama.

I pushed at his bare chest, shoving him back so he rolled and fell off the bed. His eyes snapped open. Still in attack mode, I pursued him over the bed frame and quickly slid down to straddle him. I drew my dagger from the leg strap and pressed it at his throat.

His hands latched around my wrist.

Threats were on my tongue but never left my mouth as my gaze wandered lower. His torso was uncovered and up close, and *my fucking Spirits* was it perfect. I licked my lips so my treacherous salivating mouth wouldn't drip drool onto him. In my state, I couldn't recall who of the Spirits I should pray to for mercy, so I begged all nine of them. Tanned skin, smooth and firm, sat like a second skin over *prominently bulging* muscles. Framed, straight in front of my eyes were shelves and ripples and curves hard as iron which rose and sank deliciously with his breaths.

I looked up and beyond our trapped hands where I was still clenching the dagger and aiming it for his throat but no longer applying pressure.

"Like what you see?" He had the most aggravating and gloating smirk on his face.

Before I could answer, something in my peripheral view made me look left. I dropped the dagger, gasping with my hands over my mouth. Three bodies lay on our dorm room floor. There was no blood or cuts on their bodies. They were just lying there, pale and lifeless.

"You're not going to like what you see if you look that way," he said playfully.

Ben was lying beneath me without trying to get free or seeming bothered, tucking his hands under his head, waiting for my reaction.

"Explain!" I demanded.

"You're a heavy sleeper."

I wasn't normally, but I had been especially tired last night. But that wasn't the point here, so I stared harder at him.

He easily tipped me off him as he rolled to his side, keeping his wings tucked along his body and propped an elbow on the floor to support his head on his hand. With his free hand, he pointed towards a smaller cadet with blonde hair and fair skin. Although, the paleness could have been because he was dead, which he clearly was with his right leg twisted in an unnatural angle. "He rushed in here first and said something about 'mutt' and thought he could get to your bed before I did. He was wrong. Hard to be fast with a broken leg. That guy," he said, pointing at the brown-haired man with a lot of weapons strapped to him, "he was actually quite decent with a blade. When the third one barged in, he was more set on killing me than you, clearly angry that I had killed his two friends. His words were more along the lines of 'enemy' and 'murderer' rather than 'mutt'."

Sitting on the floor next to Ben, I trembled at the scene he had described – a fight that had happened in this room whilst I'd slept.

Cadets attacked us in our room at night!

That was against the rules!

How would I be able to sleep?

"And you killed them all without a weapon? You could have used my blades."

His hand fitted naturally across my thigh when he had stopped pointing, as if there was where it belonged. "No need. I don't need weapons." He pulled up a victorious smile.

He must have used his magic. What was it? What had he done to them?

His hand twitched on my thigh, a subtle movement that sent a jolt of unwanted feelings through me. I turned to face him, my gaze hardening into a glare, but his words stopped me before I could spew my rebuke at him.

"I've been thinking about what you said earlier," he continued, his voice hesitant. "If we're to trust each other, I could also be the one initiating it." He shifted, leaning back against the bed, his eyes roaming toward the lifeless cadets sprawled across the floor. "My magic brings death to anything I touch with my hands."

His honesty hit hard like a sledgehammer against my chest, making it hard to breathe. He had told me something personal, something true and secret. My heart raced; each beat a drum drawing me into a war I didn't what to partake. Death magic. He had death magic. Magic that killed by a mere touch. How many times had I touched him? And I was still alive. The nature of his magic was otherworldly and more dangerous than I could ever have imagined.

I launched myself to saddle across his lap, and by instinct his wings folded protectively around my sides, protecting me inside a cocoon of onyx feathers. I pressed my hand to his mouth, desperate to stop the words from spilling out.

But it was too late.

His secret was out.

"No. Say nothing else. Mazdon can hear you."

"Mazdon?"

"Yes, remember I told you in formation that he has super hearing and hears everything that is going on around here. You also shouldn't have told me your magic if you're expecting me to reveal mine in return. I can't."

His eyes dimmed like a fire that was being snuffed out and were replaced by deep hollows hiding a wounded animal retracting into the shadows. "So much for initiating trust," he muttered, and the darkness of unspoken grief coating his eyes killed me. As he stood up, I rolled off him like sand, and he snapped his wings into his back.

"Ask me anything else," I pleaded. "I want us to trust each other, but I can't tell you about my magic." I had told myself enough times that keeping the secret was necessary, but the excuses felt thinner each time they passed my tongue.

"Why not?" His every glance felt like an accusation even when he couldn't have known whether or not I had magic.

My skin felt too tight, like who I had become wasn't the person I was meant to be, and my soul was trying to escape to find its true owner.

"I don't have any," I lied, as my parents had drilled into me to say.

It wasn't a matter of betrayal; it was kept a secret to secure my brother and my survival. Because my magic was inherited, Harvey had it, too. It wasn't my secret to share.

Ben crossed the room to the wardrobe and that's when I realised he was only wearing boxer shorts.

This will definitely distract me during this trust exercise.

Ben slid his arms into a black shirt and started buttoning it up. "Your brother is dancing on my last fucking nerve. He's holding you like a caged animal."

Had he listened to my thoughts again?

I stood up from the floor. "He's my brother."

"You deserve better." Angrily, he shoved the shirt down his cotton uniform trousers and fastened the button.

Unable to share my secrets with him burned my throat with the unspoken words and each time I swallowed them down, it scraped so sharply I was sure they left scars.

"Well, my life won't get better if anyone found out about my magic – that I don't have. The king wouldn't let me out of his sight."

I had rehearsed the truth in my mind a million times, but I never dared tell it to anyone. I had almost convinced myself my magic didn't matter, but every time I saw the look in the eyes of the people I hurt, the truth clawed its way back up my throat.

"Cryptic," Ben grunted. "So, I assume that the magic – you don't have – is powerful." He tightened his belt around his waist and sat on the chair to lace up his boots. "Does Watson know about your magic?" The question held a demand, as if Ben had the right to know that information.

I picked up my dagger, shoving it back into the leg strap. "That's irrelevant."

He continued with tying the laces on his other boot. "It was a simple yes, or no, question."

Obviously, that fact gnawed on him. "Zayd and I grew up together."

"Simple yes or no question," he repeated in a flat tone.

Although, observing his expression, he seemed to concoct vivid imaginations that his own demons were whispering into his ears, and my every hesitation was a clue.

"Yes. He knows."

For a moment it looked like his next words were trapped behind his clenched teeth. "Who else? I'm purely asking to ensure I can keep us alive." His tone stabbed like a knife between my ribs, weakening me until I feared I'd spill my guts out. I suspected the nature of my magic wouldn't faze him as much as the unknown did and at least the truth would put an end to this torment. "Emroyce and his sister Fern know I have magic, but not what it is. Mazdon and Kate know. They are all children of the team members who went to the Spirits' Trek with my father."

"The La Roy brothers?"

"No." I leaned my back against the wall and dared to relax as he wasn't as intimidating when sitting on a chair rather than towering over me.

"Zoe?"

I shook my head. "Definitely not Zoe. She has no filter."

"Who else went on the Spirits' Trek with your father?"

I was stunned to silence. I had never contemplated it. "I actually don't know." Father had only ever mentioned the five of them, but there would have been one other member to make the team of six that went.

The building siren went off.

"Oh, for fuck's sake!" Ben roared, who had just finished dressing in his cotton uniform.

I had completely forgotten about the first month's challenge. We had to get out to the front of the building and into formation in full gear.

Swiftly, I undid my trouser buttons and pulled them down without undoing the holster straps and before starting on the buttons on my shirt. When I had torn myself out of the shirt, I pushed up next to Ben to search for clean combat leathers in the wardrobe. He suddenly froze, staring at me. I quickly realised I had forgotten to be discreet in front of him and I was stupidly standing in only a black lace bra and knickers right next to him. In my peripheral view, I saw him bite down on his lower lip.

"Look the other way, or I'll gut your eyes out."

He grinned, and there was that challenged look in his eyes. "I'll take the risk."

I turned my head, and my stares shot like daggers at him. He didn't turn away but glanced over my form from head to toe.

"Ben!" I shouted, and snatched my combat leathers into my arms and made my way to my bed to change. After having done my buttons, I fetched my leg holsters but didn't waste time to strap them over my legs. I could buckle them when we were in formation.

I rushed out the door. "Ben?"

"Right behind you!"

We weren't the first ones outside, but we weren't the last out, either. We sprinted towards the last column and lined up after Mazdon.

"Hi Mazdon!" I greeted, securing my leg straps.

Mazdon put one hand to cover his ear and cringed in pain, giving me a look as to say that Ben's heart rate started pounding at ear-deafening heights the moment they had made eye-contact. He looked at Ben. "Kate and I grew up with Harvey and Angelica. So, she's practically like a little sister to me, too." He removed his hand from his ear as Ben shook the rage out of his eyes. "Cheers, that's better."

Had Ben been jealous of Mazdon?

Ben's attention swiftly turned towards the front. His eyes seemed to blacken with smoke swirling around his globes, and his mind became lost to a darkness in a place of chaos, as Zayd arrived.

"Ouch! There it starts again. Wrath rather than jealousy this time, though. That's new," Mazdon muttered and twitched his head as if he had water in his ear.

"Ignore him. Can't you listen to something else?" I whispered.

"With much difficulty, I assure you. And next time you spar with Watson close to my window at night, perhaps don't let Ben know. His insides made such a racket from his anger and jealousy that it was hard to wind down."

"We're bonded. There's not much I can do," I hissed at him. "Can you feel that humming sound of the bond in my ears, too?"

"No. That's in your mind. I can't hear your thoughts."

"That's a relief to hear. But if you're curious, I can tell you that they're on the lines of being annoyed with you."

He snorted and looked forward to check on Kate, who was standing in front of him. She twisted and gave me a small wave, and I waved back.

Suddenly, Ben tapped on my elbow and signalled for me to get Mazdon's attention.

"Who's that?" he asked, nodding for a woman with blonde hair and eyes that seemed to glow.

The woman was passing by behind Zayd's back with four guards who wore grey uniforms, signifying that they came from the Royal Guards of the Ivory Castle.

"That's Kristine Bostee from the Diva Team, as Emroyce calls them. She's a second-year cadet and probably on her way to practice for the navigation challenge."

"Why does she have royal guards assigned to her?"

"She's the only person known in Skyberg to possess the magic to energise light crystals."

"What's a light crystal?" I asked.

Mazdon looked at me in surprise. "A light crystal, when charged, repels demons or other heinous magic. Evil can't get within two metres of it. Like a safety shield."

"Oh, wow. So cool. I really want one of those."

"Does your magic have anything to do with your desire to obtain one?" Ben whispered into my ear.

I turned my head to glower at him. "I don't have any magic," I hissed, repeating myself like a broken record in case anyone was listening to our conversation.

"Doesn't matter," Mazdon said. "I doubt you can get your hands on one of them. The crystals are rare, and miners only find one every few years in the iron mines. And when the workers do find one, it goes straight to King Emille. I would recommend you don't speak with Kristine at all. That's her teammate walking five steps behind her." He pointed toward a man with short, blonde hair two sizes too large for his uniform, looking tenser than an angered badger, his fists clenched tightly at his sides as if ready to crush stones with his bare hands. "That's Cadet Tony Wix, son of Captain Wix of the Dashqaz Outpost. He and his mother can control the weather."

"I think you're being a bit *judgy* now. He looks to be a delight to befriend."

"Yeah," Kate scoffed. "Like hugging a hedgehog."

Mazdon sniggered. "Sure. But with him, you must pick a side. If you're friends with Tony, you're Dessen's enemy. They are rivalling third-year cadets and very territorial. Carl Dessen in Team Greedy is the son of the Torture Master at the Ivory Castle. Their family's magic is torture. So naturally, I do not befriend any of them. I refuse to pick a side. Deciding if to die by a lightning strike or by torture is something I'll try to avoid."

"Sounds like a normal Monday to me," I snorted.

"Be quiet in formation!" Zayd shouted, and Mazdon wiggled his finger in his ear, glaring at Ben, who was aiming hateful stares at Zayd. "Great effort, everyone! You're dismissed! Make your way to the assembly hall for war updates!"

Cadets poured into the building to get good seats in the assembly hall, and I stepped into line behind Mazdon. Reaching the front facade, I noticed Zayd was waiting for me.

"Angie, can I talk to you, please?"

I stopped, and so did Ben, but Mazdon waved for Kate to continue in with him. Most cadets wanted to secure good seats as far back as possible to stay out of the line of fire from the leaders.

"Zayd, what do you want?" I asked bitterly.

He came closer, invading my personal space, but I forgave him because I believed it was just out of habit. "General Denor arrived as planned yesterday, so he'll be at the assembly. Remember what I said about staying hidden. He already mentioned your name this morning at breakfast. I was glad you kept away from the canteen. You ate, though, didn't you? You're rested and strong?"

General Denor had lived at the outpost for six years before he became the general and sporadically visited the outpost after that, so I had run into him on several occasions, but I had never really talked to him as I was nine years younger and not of any interest to him. Now, he suddenly had his eyes on me? Why?

I rubbed my neck. "I totally forgot about breakfast. We had another issue to deal with." I twisted to gesture at Ben.

Ben's hateful stares didn't leave Zayd for one second as his chest brushed at my back. "The one, where I severed Zayd's head clean off his shoulders if you didn't forbid it?" Ben growled.

"No. Not that," I hissed at him and turned my back against him. "Three cadets attacked us in the dorm room last night. Well, I slept and woke up with three dead bodies on the floor. Ben handled it."

"Dammit, Angie! You should have come straight to me. That's against the rules. Have you at least told Harvey?"

"No, and he doesn't need to know it happened in my room. He thinks

I'm a burden already. Can you help clean it up, so no one finds out about it? Tell their parents they died in challenges or something?"

"Yes. I'll clean it up discretely. Don't worry."

"You have a spare key to all the dorms, don't you?"

Zayd nodded and seemed to do his utmost to remain calm even though I knew this information would have agitated him, because someone had broken the rules!

"Interesting," Ben grunted. "The men who entered our room seemed to have used a key to get in. There was no damage on the door."

I gasped and glared at Zayd, heat flaring up my neck, blooming into my face. "Did you order them to kill me?"

For a moment, we just stared at each other as if he needed a second for the words to sink in. "No!" Zayd lashed out, his bark honed with a sharp enough edge that it could cut. "You know me better than that. If you believe I called you a traitor, which I didn't, you just called me an assassin. So, can we forget about this and call it even?"

My hurt was too raw to dish out forgiveness. "I'll think about it."

Zayd stared right at me, like he wanted a deeper connection to find out what was now filling the gaping void where something irreplaceable had once been between us. "Angie. It's us. What happened to you in the Black Wing Territory?"

Ben stepped around me, shoving Zayd back. "I happened."

Zayd took a few steps backwards, holding his hand up in surrender. "Fine. You keep her safe."

"I'm planning on it. With my life. I believe that is what the white-wings have assigned me to do."

"Yes, but safety doesn't mean happiness, though, does it?" Zayd looked at me as if he shot me a message only meant for me to understand.

Zayd had to take another step backwards as Ben stepped towards him once more.

Ben's eyes darkened, a silent challenge resting at their depths. "No. That assignment I have given myself all on my own."

Zayd snorted. "Sure. Good luck. Angie never settles on anything. She always wants more. More mind games, changing environments, harder challenges, never settling down with anyone."

Ben clenched his muscles, and it was a warning, unyielding and unmistakable. "Maybe she has not found someone who is enough. Someone who is exactly what she wants."

"You think you know what she wants after only having known her for what, two years? I have known her all my life, and I have touched *every part* of her."

Incredibly fast, Ben chopped his hand around Zayd's throat, and held it so tightly, Zayd struggled to draw breaths.

I recalled Ben's magic, death by touch, and panicked. My pulse roared in my ears, drowning out every other sound surrounding us except the frantic pounding of my heart. My chest tightened like a vice, not allowing air down to my lungs. Everything in my life seemed to narrow to one single overwhelming moment where I could lose Zayd.

Before I opened my mouth to scream, I saw a hand stretch past me to gently rest onto Ben's shoulder.

"That's enough. Let's move inside. War updates are about to start," my brother ordered.

My gaze left the floor and glanced up and up and up at a yellow uniform, ocean-blue eyes and dark-blonde side-parting. Yes, thank the Spirits, my brother was here to stop this.

Ben let go of Zayd's throat and took a step closer to me.

Zayd breathed in and out slowly. "I'll be there in a while, Captain Coraly. I first need to dispose of three bodies in your sister's room. She was attacked last night."

I gasped, flashing Zayd a 'you fucking snitch!' stare.

"You seem to enjoy living on the edge, Camp Leader Watson," Ben warned, apparently knowing the language of my stares fluently.

"What?" Harvey glared at me with his usual look, as if I was only a little girl. The little girl he had carried to the healer in the village near our summer cottage because I had stacked three chairs on top of each other to reach sweets hidden in the top kitchen cupboard and broken my collarbone when the tower I built had toppled over.

I kicked at some gravel on the cobblestones. "It was nothing, really. King Blackbone handled it."

"Pack your things and move into the Coraly family apartment with me."

"Because you think you can protect her better than I can?" Ben asked, his voice thick with irritation. "Let me remind you that you're busy, and she's bound to me. I want to know where she is, and whether my life is about to end at any minute. I think that's fair."

"Fine," Harvey spat, forcing up a smile that was polite but far from genuine. "I'll make it Cadet Coraly's choice. Now, get your arses into the assembly hall!" He watched me leave with a sorrow-filled expression, as if he wanted to protect me from everything in this world but felt resigned knowing he had already failed.

A chill raised the hair on my arms when I saw General Denor on the assembly podium. For some reason, he was wearing an iron chest plate over his red general's uniform, displaying his rank on his right shoulder; a star between two horizontal chevrons. People gossiped that he had grown up in the wilderness with little human contact, and had only gained some social skills visiting Emendir. But he still had a cruel side at his core. He was probably as dark as he looked, with black hair sleeked back at the sides and a chunk of fringe curling over his forehead.

I continued up the steps of the staggered seating to find Kate holding empty seats at the back for us. Mazdon sat next to her, and I joined them with Ben to my left. Around the hall, I noticed how few second and third-year cadets remained intact in the Special Missions Unit. There were much fewer than other years, like Zayd had told me. The cadets here were only from the Special Missions Unit, though. The General Operations Unit would have their assembly after us.

Ben leaned over the side of my seat. "Your brother used his magic on me," he whispered into my ear. "It was unsettling."

My eyes went wide. Harvey couldn't have done, or Ben wouldn't be alive now.

I nodded over my right shoulder. "Remember that Mazdon hears anything you say."

"I doubt anything I have to say isn't already known to him. When Harvey placed his hand on my shoulder, my feelings went numb. I could feel absolutely nothing. No remorse, no anger, no happiness. Nothing. I was empty. I didn't like it. It pleases me that you didn't use that magic on me."

I fiddled with my fingers in my lap as I contemplated how much to tell him. "Then my brother has two kinds of magic, because I can't do that. Or maybe, but not without having…"

General Denor's beady black eyes scanned the room, so I slouched low.

"Not without having what?" Ben stared at me with intense curiosity.

"Never mind. I have no magic." I sighed. "Ask me anything else."

He grunted. "So, I know that's General Denor." Ben nodded at the general of the Special Missions Unit. "I have met his acquaintance before, but I don't like him. Do you know his background?"

I leaned closer to Ben as Harvey had begun to speak. "His father was a hunter in the wild who skinned animals with his bare hands to survive. He walked the Spirits' Trek without army training and that's why General Denor has his inherent magic to bend people's minds to insanity."

"In conclusion, his father was an all right guy, it's just the general who is a dick."

Mazdon scoffed out a laugh on my right.

"I'm glad the general hasn't got super hearing like you, Mazdon. And please, Ben, don't call the general a dick to his face."

"That sort of behaviour is beneath kings."

"You said General Denor's father was a good man. Did you know him?"

"Our paths crossed, so yes, I knew him. What I've heard, he died last month from a long-term illness. General Denor was granted leave to sit at his deathbed. After that, the general has become increasingly interested in you. Asking after you. Could you think of a reason why he's so keen on getting to know you?"

"Me? No clue. Maybe he wants to ask how I'm coping after my father died and exchange stories, and mourn together," I muttered sarcastically.

"I seriously doubt that."

Four outpost workers in white uniforms unrolled a massive map with the new updates for the year and two of the workers had to climb ladders so they could all collaborate to change the old map for the new and secure it to the wall behind the podium.

"Recent updates involve mostly the tense negotiation near the iron mines," Harvey began and kept updating the cadets for thirty minutes before he moved onto a raid the black-wings had carried out to destroy and burn a large farm estate in Pharanir near the Abarnack village.

I noticed Ben's hands clutch over the armrests and his jaw clenching tight, his mind lost in the dark pits of his own thoughts.

What was going through his mind? Had he sent the army there on purpose? Were they going rouge without his permission? Was my brother exaggerating the facts about the event? Knowing Ben, I couldn't imagine that he wanted to harm innocent farmers.

Zayd sneaked into the hall and stopped next to Mewer and Neville, searching the seats for me and when we made eye-contact, he nodded.

"Our room is clean and tidy again," I whispered to Ben.

Harvey finished the updates by reminding everyone of the academy rules, which I believed was courtesy of the recent assault on me, before he dismissed the assembly. We made our way down the steps to hurry out when my blood froze, hearing the general call my name.

"Give me permission to enter your mind," Ben stressed into my ear, as I changed course towards the podium rather than the doors.

"What? No!"

Ben wasn't more than a step behind me and keeping his hand pressed at the small of my back as we approached the general and my brother.

General Denor's pale lips stretched wide, and it was more of a threatening leer than a polite smile. "King Blackbone."

"General Denor."

"I'm surprised to see you. In here." The general turned towards Harvey, who immediately realised that the general wasn't happy about Ben listening into war updates.

"Well, yes. I hadn't put up any flags or markings on the map yet, as this was more of an introductory gathering rather than a war update." He turned to Ben. "But in the future, you shouldn't attend the war updates, for reasons which I believe need no explanation."

"Of course. We're more than happy to leave," Ben said, pushing at my back.

"Not so fast," General Denor called. "It was so long ago since I had the pleasure of seeing Cadet Coraly. How have you been?"

"I'm okay," I gritted my teeth.

Sure! Now he wanted to know how I was when he'd had no interest in me before I was an undercover agent in the Black Wing Territory. I turned around and pushed Ben to clear him from my path because he had stopped too close to my back, and I desperately wanted to get out.

"I have been asking after you, Cadet Coraly." The general had heightened his voice to emphasise he wasn't finished, and he hadn't dismissed me.

Fear coiled like a poisonous snake in the pit of my stomach. No one wanted to be the one getting the general's attention.

"I'm humbled," I bit back sarcastically, and faced him.

"How did your undercover mission go? I heard you failed to retrieve the Black Blade."

Ben's hand rested on my shoulder. "She did honourably. Few have been able to outsmart me."

That wasn't a protection of my life, but my honour. Ben didn't have to do that, and frankly, it made me look weak. But that was hard to focus on, as a sharp pain twisted inside my head. I pressed the heel of my palm on my temple. "Ouch!" White hot pain burned behind my eyes.

"Are you okay, Cadet Coraly?" Ben asked.

"Yes. I'm unhurtable."

The pain increased in intensity. It was as if too much blood expanded my skull, and the bone was about to burst at the seams.

"What secrets did you find?" The general's voice asked in my thoughts.

"Nothing," I whimpered.

"Give me something, so I'll have the right to execute King Blackbone. Confirm a war order given."

What? The general had nothing to accuse Ben of? Ben was our enemy and surely had done countless acts to be punished for. The fact that he was the black-wing king should be enough.

"You've got nothing?"

The pain twisted and my knees weakened. I bent low but didn't kneel on the floor.

"Permission," Ben hissed.

He wanted to enter my thoughts, too. No. Two voices in my head was already one too many.

"No."

I tried to push back. To get the general out of my head. Focusing on another sound, as Zayd had taught me. My defiance was met with an agony tenfold the volume before. My teeth chattered, so I clenched my jaw shut.

"How many soldiers does King Blackbone have?"

"I don't know. Captain Coraly intercepted my mission and captured King Blackbone just as I was making progress."

"Liar!"

My ears rang with a deafening crescendo, each pulse a hammer against my skull. Desperate, I pressed my palms to my ears, but the sound was inside me, relentless to the point I thought it would split my head right open. I whimpered, closing my eyes as the room spun and a tunnel vision threatened to consume me in its mouth. My cheeks flushed warm, and it was hard to focus on anything other than the pain. It hurt so much I wasn't sure whether he was going to push me over the limit and kill me.

"Let her go!" Ben's roar cut through the chaos, raw and commanding.

"You're a little traitor, just like your mother."

"I'm no traitor," I managed to rasp, my voice barely a whisper.

I attempted forcing his voice out of my head, and when that didn't work, I tried to settle on a thought in his mind, but he repelled me instantly.

There it was. My pain threshold. The pain was unbearable, a searing force that made me question if I could withstand it. If a soul could be sucked out of your being, this was how it would feel. I screamed and opened my eyes to aim all my hatred at him, certain he was about to cause my heart to stop. I buckled to my knees.

Then, horror struck deep into my soul.

It all was as if in slow-motion.

Ben stepped around me and punched General Denor square in his face, knocking him backwards with such force his feet flew off the ground and he landed on his side on the floor.

What the fuck had Ben done?

He was as good as dead now.

But there was no time to dwell. My body betrayed me, my legs giving way as the darkness claimed me. The last thing I felt was the cold stone floor beneath me. My body faltered as my brain was shutting down.

My world went black.

14

"Hello my blue-eyed warrior."

Red eyes. Black hair. Black uniform. A smile? Ben?

Why was Ben looking at me like he had worried I'd never open my eyes again?

Spirits. My head hurts.

My mouth is dry.

There is so damn much light in this room.

"Where am I?"

Ben was standing right next to my bed but still he shifted closer somehow, leaning over, his fists supporting his weight on the mattress. The weight of his worried gaze felt heavier than the residue of the injury I suffered. "In the infirmary," he said gently. "You have been here for the last seven days."

Seven days! What happened?

Oh yeah. General Denor messed with my head.

Ben put his palm over my forehead, like he was checking my temperature. "So, you thought tiny-little-you could take on the general all on your lonesome? If you allow me to enter your mind when I see it necessary, I can block him out for the both of us. Next time, please let me help you."

The thought made my body tense as a shudder ran down my spine. I let out a snarky laugh that did nothing to mask my fear. "I hope there won't be a next time. And how could you help by being in my mind, too? Two voices were enough to handle."

I pulled the white blanket higher on my chest, noting I was wearing a fresh white infirmary gown and not the leather combat uniform I had passed out in.

Ben shifted his weight from one leg to the other, but didn't move more than one step away from the bed. "I have more experience shielding against mind intrusion than you, and I could have blocked him from entering."

"You can do that?"

I corrected the pillow under my head. Ben's hand hovered near my arm, not quite grabbing onto the pillow to help me, but close enough that I knew he had wanted to. He lowered his hand and sat down in the chair next to the bed.

"I'm going to hate repeating Watson's words, but yes, we're linked as one soul. You mustn't have realised it because I've been blocking you out from the connection to me entirely."

"Because you have too many secrets. You're the black-wing king." It was as if I had to remind myself what was real and what wasn't.

"That part is true. I'm glad to hear nothing is wrong with your memory. But also because you haven't given your consent, as we agreed. Perhaps you can let me into your active thoughts."

"Active thoughts?"

He rubbed his hand over his face; annoyed and tired, as if he hadn't slept for days. "I really wished you'd have taken Camp Leader Mewer's advice to learn more about soul binding beforehand."

"It wasn't as if I had a choice, or much advance warning, to research the subject."

"And Watson did a poor job in briefing you."

"Please, don't start. Ouch! My head!" I squeezed my eyes together to let the spell of pain pass. "What are active thoughts?"

Ben's brows knitted together, his eyes scanning me with a mix of concern and frustration. "I'm not sure we should have this conversation now. You seem in pain. I should get Camp Leader Mewer."

"Tell me!" My voice came out clipped. Gone was my patience for him dancing around what he chose to disclose.

A flicker of hurt crossed his face before he quickly masked it with a mien of indifference, and a low grunt. "We have active and passive thoughts. The passive thoughts are your private innermost beliefs and impulse judgements that you don't want anyone to hear because you might not act on them, or you might evaluate them if given time, so that you alter your perceptions, or even dismiss them. Active thoughts are the ones you can throw at me because you have the intention to communicate them almost as if verbally. Like you did when you cussed me for opening the door in front of Camp Leader Watson when you were in only a towel."

I inhaled a sharp breath, my eyes opened wide. "I knew you had listened to that. I saw it in your eyes."

"I didn't listen. It's hard to block out everything, and you were shouting it at me."

"So, if I scream in my mind that you're a real arsehole, you can hear me?"

"Yes, if you scream it that loudly at me, I hear you. The same goes for emotions and physical pain…or desires," he added softly. "And just because you would let me speak into your mind, it doesn't mean I'll hear your thoughts. It simply means you hear my voice. You can still block yours. It doesn't work like an open door. More like the door is still closed and I'm shouting through it. Will you consent to me doing that?"

"Perhaps give me a taste of it first. Before I decide."

He nodded. "But not now. When you're well, we can practise that."

Fine. I could agree to that. I looked around the infirmary hall, glad to see there weren't too many injured cadets or sergeants in here. Fern was changing the bandage on a gruff man's arm two beds down and smiled at me when we made eye-contact. She was so alike Emroyce. Tall, with a bony facial structure, long black hair and the same warm amber eyes.

After a moment of silence, I realised Ben remained seated next to my bed after our conversation finished, as if he belonged there. He didn't have to be here. Our soul bonds reached far enough that he could move freely within the entire Bensguard Outpost premises. No one would harm me in here. Nobody I knew of, anyway. Definitely not more than General Denor already had.

My stupid heart warmed at Ben's loyalty and kindness. I wished I had never gone on that undercover mission to the Black Wing Territory. I wished I would have never met Ben. The attraction was so damn hard to beat. He made me into a traitor at his every touch, and the thought of him brought chaos to my brain. My blood ran amok with dark desires I didn't want; every glance at him a battle of my conscience. I wanted someone like him but who wasn't the enemy king; a genuine connection, not this pretend relationship because we were bound. For him to stay caring and loyal like this forever. But I could never have Ben, and if I couldn't block these feelings towards the one person I was supposed to despise, it would become my downfall. My heart was playing a dangerous game of striking a balance between pushing him away enough to deny any feelings and pulling him closer to secure its survival. Why couldn't my desires see reason? I could never trust him. I wanted to trust him, though. He had fucking punched the general to save me!

I glanced his way to discern any hint that he had heard what I had thought, but he was looking mindlessly around the room as if he had to wait out my illness for me to get better.

"You know. When I said, don't call the general a dick to his face, that also implied that you shouldn't punch him in the face. Punching a general in the face, is that not also beneath kings?"

The side of his lip curved, and he laced his fingers on his lap. "No, everyone understands the meaning of a punch in the face."

"Yeah. I think the general got it." I blew out my lips. "Dare I ask if he's still alive?"

"He's alive. Not by my choice. Your brother made a valid point that you would get into more trouble if I took another step towards the general."

My eyes traced the curve of his mouth, trying to understand even a fraction of what made them so irresistible. "You'll have to work on your temper," I said finally.

"I'll try, but it's hard to control myself not to kill those who're hurting you. Only punching him, that was me managing at least some sort of control. I wanted to kill him."

I believed him. He meant what he said and that was half of his appeal and danger. There was something about the way he carried himself, so effortlessly, that evidenced his greatness. Yet, I didn't think he knew how remarkable he was. "My brother won't give you an award for it."

"I don't care what Captain Coraly thinks. I care what you think. And you would have thought less of me if I had killed him. That, and the concern for your future safety, were the only arguments stopping me." Passion coloured his voice and it simply made it impossibly hard to look away from him.

"Killing seems to come easy to you. Perhaps lies and secrets, too." My chest tightened as I said it, my soul retracting into the shadows I only entered when vulnerable.

"Hold on!" He leaned forward in the chair and there was a new frown on his forehead. "That's double standards, considering what you did to me. And I don't enjoy killing, but some people make this world a worse place. Much worse place."

"I spied. I never killed anyone. Maybe it isn't right to take it upon yourself to decide who lives or dies."

He yanked his hand through his hair and exhaled through his nose, containing his patience behind clenched teeth. "You protect your family, members of which are who? Captain Coraly, sibling cadets Pere, sibling cadets Bengrey, Agent Hammerton, Cadet La Roy, Cadet Karson, Flora and, if we're generous, Camp Leader Watson? I'm a king. My family is every single person in my kingdom. So, unless you sit on a throne, don't talk to me about who I can and who I cannot kill. And some people, like General Denor, are walking a very thin line."

I was about to retaliate when Ben threw his hands up in exasperation and he growled because Zayd appeared in the doorway, walking straight towards my bed.

Zayd tucked his hand into mine and squeezed it gently. "Thank all the Spirits you're conscious."

Ben rose from the chair, clearly not wanting to be lower in height than

Zayd. "I don't think any of your Spirits favour her if they could allow this."

"We know there are more evil creatures in the world who we can blame for this rather than the Spirits," Zayd replied without placing much weight on Ben's outburst. "How are you feeling, Angie?"

"Before you two get into that," Ben interrupted. "Watson, can you guard her for a moment, so I can get something to eat and change my clothes?"

Zayd nodded and took the seat in the chair next to the bed when Ben left.

"What?" Zayd asked, as he saw me gawking at him.

My eyes blinked a few times in disbelief. "No angry threats? No telling him this was his fault? No exchange of hostility at all?"

Zayd stroked his hands over the armrests and crossed his feet by his ankles, pretending to look relaxed but not doing a good enough job to hide the unease crawling inside him. "Nah, he's all right."

My disbelief shot my brows sky-high. "What in all the Spirits' names happened during the seven days I was out? Am I in the same world? Pinch me, so I can know if I'm actually awake, and this isn't a super awkward dream."

Zayd sighed through his nose. "I did nothing when General Denor entered your mind. Ben punched him in the face. Broke his nose. Then he clasped his hand around the general's throat and threatened him to dare do that to you again. He risked his own life just to spare you from further pain. I could never be that brave. He has my respect. For seven days, it felt like my heart would stop, waiting for any word from Fern to tell me you'd live." He palmed his neck. "I've never been this messed up in my life. Gets you thinking of what is important."

He deliberately made eye-contact. Was he meaning me? There was an awkward silence between us when I didn't know how to respond. There were still many emotions between us that hadn't been repaired after I had broken them. There were so many issues between us. The Bensguard Outpost rules, for one!

I cleared my throat. "My lips are so dry."

Zayd stood from the chair and took a step to the side-table and grabbed the glass of water. "Here, let me help you." He shoved his arm under my shoulders and held me up, so I could sip from a straw. Even trying to sit up hurt. Every muscle throbbed and ached.

"How can everything hurt when it was only my mind General Denor was tampering with?"

Zayd's gaze lifted from watching my mouth and his blue eyes met mine. "Your mind connects to everything else. It's horrifying what he can do with his magic."

Mewer joined us by my bedside, hastily tying cord around his golden hair. He was wearing a brown coat stained with blood to protect his navy-blue camp leader uniform, as if he had to be in two places at once but had no time to change in-between.

I didn't know what I feared most; that his bloodstained state was because of the second-year cadets' reflexes challenge, or because of the third-year's poison challenge…or even worse, he'd been out on patrol by the border to the Black Wing Territory.

Mewer pressed the back of his fingers against my cheek before he palmed my forehead. "It's time for your treatment."

I couldn't see much with half his hand covering most of my eyes. "Treatment?"

When Mewer removed his hand, I saw Zayd peer at me having sat down on the chair again. "Mewer has been doing it three times a day. It's just an ointment and a massage."

"Massage?" Mewer said, amused, and gave me a polite smile that warmed his moss-green eyes even more with his kindness. "I pour my heart and soul into healing her mind."

Mewer prodded his finger into a white cream he had in a small tub and his golden ponytail fell to his chest as he leaned down to swipe the cream across both my temples. With two fingers on either side, he massaged so gently I wanted to purr.

Suddenly, there was a siren beaming one chime in my ears.

"Don't worry," Mewer said. "That isn't in your head. It's the training formation siren for first-year's challenge."

I tried to rise on my elbows, but Mewer pushed me back down. "Which you're excused from for the next two weeks."

"But I'm not," Zayd growled. "I really should be going." Zayd twitched in the chair, looking at the doors as if he hoped Ben would show to exchange guard.

"You go. I'll stay with her until King Blackbone returns," Mewer said.

Not long after Zayd had left, two black uniformed cadets with white and purple hair approached; Brian and Valentina. Brian came to the bedside with open arms whilst Valentina stood by the foot of the bed with her arms crossed and her brows folded low over her grey eyes as if she was beyond furious, but knowing her, it was how she glared at people when she was concerned.

"We heard you had woken up," Brian whispered. "We were really worried. General Denor shouldn't have pushed you that far. Even my brother said that."

I moaned and pushed myself higher in the bed. "Die with honour or survive to fight another day, right?" I punched my fist in the air with a theatrical salute. "You're just relieved I won't be on my feet for a few weeks to beat your record on the obstacle course," I joked, but then hissed in pain.

Brian looked at me with sympathy glazing his eyes. "Will you be able to compete in the first challenge? I mean. Me and Winter won last year, so not saying you'll beat that, but it would be good if the cadets saw you on your feet for the first challenge."

"I know. Unless Mewer straps me to the bed, I'll be there and I'll beat your record on that, too."

"You can try, although between you and me. Winter wasn't really there."

"Ah! You cheat!"

"You're allowed to use magic in the challenges. It's not cheating. Nothing in the fine print of the contract says you must be there in the flesh."

I laughed, but the sound turned into another moan from the agony twisting in my head.

"Cadet Coraly should avoid talking or thinking, and focus more on resting," Mewer said, as he screwed the lid on his tub and pocketed it in his brown robe.

Brian and Valentina nodded and left after uttering a 'speedy recovery' each.

Emroyce entered the infirmary halls a bit more rushed, and visiting me clearly wasn't on his agenda, as he headed for his sister with a toddler sitting on his forearm.

Spirits be damned, was that baby Robin? He had grown so much. He was only one year old when I had left. He would, of course, be three years old now. Robin was one of the Bensguard Outpost babies. Leadership had allowed Fern to stay at the outpost and keep him at the infirmary with the promise from Emroyce that he would help her raise him.

Fern's story twisted my heart even thinking about it today. It had been truly horrific. Fern had only gone into the Bensguard city to get a dress when a group of men had raped her in a backstreet. She had never given a description or pointed out the culprits, but I reckon it had been cadets from another outpost who had been at Bensguard for the First Year Ball event. Recognising their uniforms was probably why she hadn't seen the threat coming, or she'd have used her speed magic to escape.

"Kenyard will kill me for being late to formation," he told Fern playfully, and tickled Robin's stomach. Robin didn't want to let go of Emroyce, and kept a stubborn grip on his arm, shouting, "Uncle Emross! Play!"

Fern tore Robin off Emroyce and into a steady grip but pointed for me before they parted. Emroyce saw me and smiled. "I knew you would walk it off!" he called out before he ran outside to the front of the building, his speed making him a blurred line of light to my sensitive eyes.

Mewer smiled and carried on massaging the ointment he had applied to my temples, and I garnered strength from his hands as he worked.

Ben returned and with a shadow-like move sat down on the chair in silence as we waited for Mewer to finish and leave us alone.

I turned my head on the pillow, seeing Ben's hair was towel dried, smelling of flowers, and he wore a clean and ironed uniform. "You don't have to stay here to guard me all the time."

A smile the blend of dubious and playful curved on his perfect lips. "Don't see it as guarding *you*. I'm guarding my own life. Anyone could attack you here in the open. There are no guards or locks on any of the doors."

A part of me understood his reasoning but there was a deeper part of me that detested his suffering. "It can't be comfortable sitting in that chair all day and night."

The new smile he pulled was even more soul-haunting. "You could stay in your own bed in our room."

Oh, Spirits, I was melting. How could I get rid of all this heat between us? My breath shuddered. "I couldn't expect you to take care of me there. The healers do all sorts of things to patients here, ointments, massages to my temples and bringing food three times a day."

Yep, definitely should not imagine him treating me and having his hands all over me.

Why in the Underworld did he lick his lips and lean forward in his chair?

"I wouldn't mind doing it," his voice was deep. Hungry. Seductive.

My cheeks burned. I'd blame the summer heat. It was hot in here. That I would struggle to keep my desires at bay wasn't the only thing wrong with that picture. "You're a king."

He relaxed against the backrest, his shoulder slumped just slightly, and his smile faltered. "I'm also a man."

A pang of hurt for him stung in my chest. Of course, there was more to him than only being a king. He didn't need to point that out to me. I was crazy about that part of Ben who wasn't the king. Every part of my body ached for his closeness. It was the enemy king part of him that stood in my way.

Annoyingly, I couldn't bare seeing the dimming light of his disappointment in his eyes. "You're going to have to clear it with Camp Leader Mewer to see if he wants to dismiss me yet."

Ben instantly glanced around the room until he spotted Mewer standing by Fern and took aim, walking over to him.

Ben's stare was made of iron will as he looked at Mewer. "I'm taking Cadet Coraly to our room," he said sternly, and it was clearly not a request.

That's one way of doing it.

Ben returned to my side after a brief chat with the healer. "Camp Leader

Mewer says it's okay."

You threatened Mewer to say it is okay! Threatened a worker at the outpost!

Another Bensguard Outpost rule broken!

I sat up, testing my body and the probability of getting out of bed on my own.

"I'll take you, though." Ben scooped me up into his arms with ease and I wondered if my body wasn't as heavy as my damned soul, which clearly had conflicting feelings on whether I loved being in my enemy's arms or felt highly degraded by being treated as an inferior.

"No, I must walk. I can't look weak. We haven't even completed the first challenge yet and I'm being carried."

"You don't have any shoes on."

"Get my leathers from the drawer and my boots, and I'll walk!" I flicked my fingers in the air, gesturing at them by the side-table.

"Nope!" His gaze lingered on me, daring me to argue.

I would have argued it if I had found my words before he stormed off with me bobbing in his arms all the way to our room in only my damned infirmary gown. He put me down on my bed and sat down by my feet. "Take off your infirmary gown."

Uh? Say what now? Yeah, no, that wasn't going to happen. Only the Spirits knew what fresh chaos would obliterate my mind and completely slay my restrain of touching him if I got naked.

He tipped his head sideways when I didn't obey, massaging my foot gently. "You're looking at me as if I would stop my charade of being nice to you at any minute and cut your feet off."

His voice was hiding amusement behind a controlled smirk, alluring yet dangerous. That unreadable expression of his only made it worse. Or better. I couldn't decide. The more I couldn't read him, the more I wanted to. He was a riddle I couldn't solve, and somehow that made the threat of him even more seductive.

"Are you?" I asked, my voice quieter than I had intended, almost breathless, like I was daring him.

I saw a single raised brow and a slight tilt of his head. "Was that a genuine question?"

From one second to the next, the space between us felt too small and too charged, like a single wrong word might ignite a lethal feud.

"There is a lot of pain one can endure before death. You told me so yourself. I'll survive without my feet, but I'm quite fond of them."

"I only said that because I wanted Camp Leader Watson to stop you from enrolling. But I obviously drove you straight to the damn book. It didn't help when Watson told you not to sign because as a result you proved him wrong and bloody signed. So that plan backfired."

"Well, it was pointless to try to threaten me or beg me not to sign the ledger in the first place."

"I discovered that. And for the record, I'm a king, I don't beg. I order people. That's what I've always done. But you, you don't take my orders. Neither begging nor threatening you gets me what I want, so I'll have to find another way around my problems."

He stayed quiet, looking at me as if he was evaluating how I would react next.

"I don't think I'll like what you're thinking," I muttered.

"Nope. You won't." His onyx hair bounced around his head as he shook his head. "Not if you thought me carrying you here was undignified."

He stood up and stripped as he went to the chair to fold his shirt over the backrest.

I gasped, seeing his back. I was ripped open in ten places. The frayed flesh clearly caused by the iron tipped whip rather than the leather one. My heart clenched so brutally with unbearable agony as my eyes tracing the deep, raw wounds carved into him. Each cruel lash mark, swollen and streaked with blood, felt like a wound torn open in my own soul.

"The general already punished you. There are more than five–" I gasped. "You took my lashes."

The iron-tipped whip hadn't only torn through his flesh; it had shattered something inside me. I felt helpless, drowning in sorrow, rage, and guilt. Guilt, that I could do nothing, that I hadn't been the one to bear what should have been my own suffering.

He looked up as he balanced on one foot, taking his boot off. "Of course. Don't worry. Captain Coraly went easy on me."

A sob caught in my throat, imagining the brutal force of each strike, the searing pain he must have endured. "My brother did this to you?"

He steadied himself on bare feet after having removed his socks. "Would you rather General Denor or Camp Leader Watson had done it?"

I guess not.

His trousers came off next, and only wearing boxer shorts, he knelt at my bedside and pushed his arms underneath me. He yanked me up as he stood with me once more flopping inside his frame.

"What are you doing?" I shrieked, clinging to him instinctively as his arms scooped me up. My hands flew around his neck, gripping tight as he lifted me like I weighed nothing.

His expression didn't shift, but his voice carried that familiar blend of maddening calm and restrained amusement. "Camp Leader Mewer's condition for bringing you back was that I ensure you wash. You've been in bed for seven days." He glanced down at my infirmary gown. "You refused to change into your underwear, so…looks like we're doing this your way."

"You could've *told* me that before discharging me!" I hissed, heat rushing to my face. "Put me down! I can shower myself!"

"Nope," he said without hesitation, his grip unyielding as he strode forward. "You're not supposed to stand yet. Technically, you're not even supposed to be *talking*. That would've been a nice bonus if you ever actually listened to medical advice."

His tone was infuriatingly dry, but the way he held me; secure, firm, as if he'd never drop me, sent a strange flutter through my chest. My indignation battled with the awareness of how close we were and the warmth of his body against mine.

"I have no issues listening to advice," I muttered.

He looked down at me like that was the biggest lie in history. "You *don't* when it's about *your* own safety."

As I had a cramping hold around his neck, he let go of me with his right arm to reach the tap to turn on the shower. "Last chance to undress?"

"You wouldn't dare wet me!"

"I guess that is a no to the undressing part."

He walked straight into the little cubicle with me in his arms, my feet sweeping across the wall. The water cascaded over us both. It was warm and soothing; admittedly what I had needed. The water streamed around his bulging pectorals to create a pool in the curve of my stomach. I swallowed as my need to touch him all over peaked. That tight skin. Those perfect shapes. Firm body. I looked up beyond the side of my shoulder were mountainous biceps framed me in his arms. Continuing my gawking higher, I found his comforting red eyes. He looked at me like something precious and beautiful. His touch, as he stroked water over my head, rushed heat to the wrong places inside me.

He grunted. "Keep you shield up," he reminded me.

Fuck! He had felt that through our bond. "This is so undignified," I muttered, as my hair sleeked against my head.

"I'm sorry. It'll get worse."

"Worse?"

He cleared his throat as if he tried to steel his own emotions. "I'm going to have to add soap."

"No," I moaned a long note.

There was no point telling him he wouldn't dare, because frankly, he did, and he would. But two could play this game of making the situation mutually insufferable.

"Oh, no." He tensed. "I don't like that specific twinkle in your eye. You thought up some mischief, didn't you?"

"No. Not at all. I thought I should be an obedient subject."

He was shaking his head by reflex. "I really don't like the sound of that."

"Put me down to sit on the floor and help me out of my gown before adding soap. That's what you wanted, wasn't it?"

"Yes," he stretched out the little word with much confusion. He lowered to one knee and gently placed me on the shower floor.

"Now. Undo the gown buttons."

He glanced at the buttons running along the entire front of the white fabric that was soaked through, plastered to every curve of my body. "You can undo your own buttons."

"Oh, but no. You said that Camp Leader Mewer had instructed I shouldn't move or even speak. You said you'd take care of me. Undo the buttons!"

He frowned and glowered at them as if they were poisonous before he put down his second knee on the floor next to my thigh and got closer with his hands. Reluctantly, he pinched the first button with nimble fingertips and undid it.

Deeply, he stared into my eyes after the first button had left my gown open to reveal some cleavage. He swallowed hard and breathed shallowly, seeming not to notice the water falling over us except for the occasional drop riveting down between my breasts.

"It wasn't difficult. You really can do that yourself," he grunted.

"Next button!"

He undid the next one, and the next, all the way down to the last one. He finished and pulled the sides apart, revealing my breasts hidden in a lace bra, naked stomach and lace knickers. He suddenly started releasing his breaths through his mouth, as if he found it hard to control himself.

Had I won? I don't know. There was still the feeling that I was deprived of something I wanted, too. My desire was to dip my hand inside his boxer shorts and grab a hold around his hardened cock I wanted to stroke his chest and push my hands over his shoulders, nestling my hands into his onyx hair. My breath shuddered involuntarily.

I looked at my shoulder as I rolled it back, showing him that he needed to take the gown fully off. But I didn't speak, or my own restraint would break. I'd be damned if this wasn't one of the challenges I would win in this Spirits forsaken place.

His chest trembled as he slowly pushed the fabric off my shoulders simultaneously using both his hands. This close, I could make out the blood vessel pulsing at his neck.

After I had bent my arms out of my gown, I supported my hands on the floor at my sides, craned my back and lifted off the floor so he could slide the fabric from beneath me. His mouth landed on the curve of my neck and as I uttered a soft moan, it formed a cloud in front of my face in the steamed-up room. He stiffened, and slowly pulled his head further away, breathing through his nose and out his mouth. Once he had tossed it to one side, he leaned backwards. The way he stared at my body made me feel desired, like a woman and not a traitor, so I let him gawk. Obviously, that was a mistake, as it did nothing to pacify my own urges.

With my chest clenched tight and all my muscles braced, I gave a daring nod towards the soap before I leaned my head back against the wall and leered at him. "Now, the soap," I whispered sensually.

He choked out half a laugh, but it sounded agonising. He got the soap bottle from the corner of the cubicle and squeezed a blob into his hand before stroking it over my shoulder.

Yes, he could start there, but I expected him to do it all over.

When my shoulders and upper chest were super clean, he hesitated.

I chased his wavering glances until they steadied on our eye-contact. I took my time to curl up a victorious smile. "I need to be clean everywhere."

He inhaled a large tremoring breath before he did my legs, slowly pushing his hand along their entire length. "I'll look away when you do your private areas."

"I'll do it myself, but you're not allowed to look away. This is your punishment for not telling me you agreed to this before you brought me back here."

I put soap in my hand and rubbed it onto my breasts beneath my bra before I pushed one hand down my black lace knickers, closing my eyes when I saw him grow harder inside his boxer shorts. I expelled soft moans to tease him even further as I washed myself.

"This is a cruel punishment," he grunted.

That made me remember the whip wounds on his back. "The water must be too hot. How is your back?"

"It stings a little, but it's not the biggest of my problems considering what you're putting me through."

I waved with my hand towards the shower, gesturing for him to turn it off. "We're done. Get us out."

The heat I had felt, dissipated instantly, which I was glad for, even though it had felt as if someone had stolen a moment I had wanted never to end.

Ben shut off the water, wrapped a towel around me, and carried me to the bed. He grunted darkly. "That wasn't so bad. I made it. You can trust me to take care of you and I even controlled myself not to touch you inappropriately."

He said it as if it had been *his* achievement that I had showered. I responded by ordering him to hand me a new uniform so I could dress. He held a shirt and trousers out to me, and I snatched them from his grip.

"What's wrong?" he asked, his voice low, searching.

I folded my arms, pulse tightening. "You're pushing me to trust you. That's not something you can demand. It needs its own time."

His jaw tensed. "I've given you no reason not to trust me. Not *personally*. But you look at me like I'm already guilty of all the crimes in the world. Like the title stamped on my name is all I'll ever be to you. I'm normally used to carry that burden. I've done it my entire life. But I never expected to be judged that way by someone like you."

My laugh was bitter. "Someone like me? You mean a *traitor*?"

"No!" he snapped, running a hand roughly through his hair, his control beginning to crack. "Someone intelligent. Someone who sees beyond politics and rumours. Someone who thinks for herself instead of clinging to whispers like they're truths." His eyes locked onto mine, the fire in them barely restrained. "So, tell me. What in the Underworld is your problem with me?"

"My problem is that magic reflects who you are and the Spirits gift them according to what you need. That begs the question. Why do you have death magic?"

With one grip over the backrest, he lifted and turned the desk chair around to face me and sank down onto it, supporting his elbows on his knees as he rubbed his face with his hands. "I don't know. As I told you earlier, I don't enjoy killing. I kill those who deserve it."

"Like me."

"What? No! Even if we weren't bonded. I promise you. I don't want to kill you."

"You wanted to kill me. The first day when you got imprisoned here, you grabbed my hand through the bars. That's why you gripped my wrist, wasn't it?"

15

He stilled, not seeming to breathe. "I did," he answered finally. "It was foolish. I knew you were a spy, but a part of me didn't want to believe you were loyal to the white-wing army. I thought I had changed your mind. When you made your choice to come back here, I wanted to kill you for the hurt it caused me. Controlling my magic wasn't easy, yet I couldn't harm you. I already cared too much for you." He inhaled a deep breath to calm an uproar inside his chest. "Then you insisted on binding your soul to mine, becoming a part of me. That action confused me because you made the decision to become more intimate."

I turned around to put on a new bra and slid my arms into my shirt. I did the buttons up not looking at him as I muttered, "My brother forced me to bond with you."

He grunted behind my back. "I hope we have moved on from that and have established our own relationship without your brother's commands affecting it."

I rose slowly, the towel clutched around my hips as I turned away to get changed. My fingers trembled slightly as I reached for my knickers. "I *want* to trust you. But trust doesn't come easy. Not after what my mother did."

"I know," he said quietly, but there was a bite to the words. "You only trust the wounded and the helpless ones. You like tending to things that can't hurt you. But the person who wants to protect you the most? You shut him out."

I didn't answer. I pulled up my trousers in silence, tucking in my shirt with more force than necessary.

"But I'll be patient," he went on, voice tightening. "We can take small steps. Nothing personal. Just enough to work as a team. To survive graduation. Maybe… maybe start with your magic. Tell me about it."

I shook my head. "I have none."

A pause. He inhaled through his nose. "Still sticking to that lie, then?"

His tone sharpened, frustration creeping into the supposed patience he claimed he had. "You still don't trust me with that secret?"

"Maybe with time," I said softly, buttoning the collar of my shirt. "Maybe then it'll be different."

"I want you to trust me *now*," he snapped, stepping closer. The heat of his presence pushed against my back like a current. "Spirit, this is so damn frustrating. I want to make you see that you can trust me – force it, if I must." He bit back the last part too late, already said, already out.

His voice dropped to a rough whisper. "Am I going to be just another one of those people Watson says will never be enough for you? Always chasing a version of you that keeps slipping away? You always want something else… someone more."

If he only knew how much I wanted him, prayed that he was the person he claimed he was. That person would be more than enough.

"I don't know." My heart found it hard to deny him my trust, hearing him almost beg me for it. There was nothing more I wanted than to give in to the attraction I was fighting with all my being. Spirits, I wanted him naked in bed this very moment. But not only was he a man who could be a wolf dressed in sheepskin, if I allowed us to get romantically involved it'd tear down the walls that kept me from worrying about him all the time. How would I be able to focus on my tasks while not knowing if he was in danger? My situation would become unbearable as a cadet at the Bensguard Outpost. Relationships within the same unit were forbidden. We would get punished. Him worse than me. I couldn't imagine that my brother or higher leadership would accept me falling in love with the black-wing king. But damn, I wanted to let go of every restraint I had clamped down on my heart.

"But I know exactly how it is," he grunted in that low, lethal voice. "You're someone fearless when it comes to your body, pushing yourself to the limit, but when it comes to your heart, you're a coward, boxing those emotions up so protectively, not even a sledgehammer could break the shield you keep around them."

"I'm the daughter of a traitor. How can you believe I can ever trust anyone?"

He let out a bitter humourless laugh. "I really regret that now."

I picked up my daggers from the floor and put them in their normal places when they weren't on duty strapped to my thighs; one under my pillow and the other on the bedside table. "Regret what?"

He shook his head at himself. "I need to get some silence. I'm heading out." He went to the wardrobe and got out a clean shirt and when he changed his wet boxer shorts, I glimpsed the bottom of his arse below its hem.

Damn, those are firm!

I sank down onto the bed and tipped my head to view from a lower angle. "Regret what, Ben? Tell me."

"It's nothing." He yanked on his trousers angrily and shoved his feet into his boots.

"This is what I'm talking about. How can you expect me to trust you when you don't share your secrets?"

"There are many dark secrets. If I told you all of them at once, you wouldn't judge me fairly. It's like a poisonous mushroom. If I held it up to you, what would you do?"

"I don't know. Not eat it."

"Exactly. You would stamp on it. Destroy it so no one else would eat it and die. But what you didn't know was that if you cut it, prepared it and cooked it the right way, it would be safe and the best damn thing you'd eaten in your life."

"That's a simple excuse to fool those who can't work it out themselves. I think you know what trust is in theory, but to actually give it, that's a different matter."

"Like telling you about my magic and trusting you to keep it a secret?"

"If that secret got out, it doesn't destroy you. I mean to trust someone fully with things that make you vulnerable. Someone to share your thoughts and beliefs. Someone who you'd let share your life and your bed. You can't even do that, having vowed off women."

The movements with which he tied his laces were sharp. "It's not a vow. It's not like I have made promises to the Spirits. I haven't actually said I would swear off a lover at all. It's people drawing conclusions. But I have a reason for that."

"What reason do you have to abstain from women? You can take contraceptive tablets or bind yourself with magic if you're afraid of producing bastards."

Ben looked at me and appeared to make careful judgments about whether to tell me more. "I had concerns."

"Oh. Okay." He didn't seem to have any issues getting it up when we were in the shower.

"Not that type of concerns." He gave me a look like I had insulted him. "My magic flared up when I was twelve and for a long time, I couldn't control it."

"So, you weren't a merciless child as rumours state?"

"No. My father believed a lucrative kingdom was achieved by ruling his subjects through fear. What better tactic than to make people think I was ruthless than telling them the truth that I couldn't control my magic. You can't even comprehend how it feels to kill someone you like accidentally because you touched them for too long," his breath hitched, barely noticeably, but enough to reveal the guilt he held at the core of his heart. "My magic is harder to manage during spurts of increased emotions. Already at foreplay, the magic flares out of control, and I fear I'd kill a woman during the act."

Silence filled the room, and a faint crease formed between his brows, searching for reassurance.

A chill ran down my arm. He had just told me something personal that made him vulnerable; his heart exposed. Something he wouldn't have told me if his goal was to betray me. Unless he planned to kill me soon and his secret would die with me.

"You exist, so your father must have managed it."

He braced his forearms on his knees, his head hanging slightly from his shoulders. "My father didn't have any magic."

"So, how do you have it?"

He looked up, levelling a reprimanding stare at me. "Oh no. One secret at a time. You said a king could start negotiating, and I have told you two secrets with none in return."

"You want to know about my lovers?"

"Spirits no! Especially not if they're as poor choices as Camp Leader Watson. How was it to grow up with your father as a general?"

"Pretty much like growing up with a big brother as a captain. The missions they give to…good try," I spat at him.

He was nearing the topic of the secrets the Bensguard Outpost held. The only outpost in the White Wing Territory with a Special Missions Unit and an academy training programme for cadets with magic strong enough to defeat him.

Was it a coincidence he had ended up here?

That he had decided to stay even when I tried to free him?

He was trying to gain my trust to draw out classified information. Leadership had forbidden Ben to attend war updates, so now he needed me to fill him in. Jokes on him, as Harvey never told me anything more than he told the other cadets.

He looked so hurt I wanted to kiss him, but my anger wiped that desire clear off. Being his teammate was tearing me apart. He was so sexy and powerful and perfect. But he was the black-wing king, and Mazdon had already warned me of his intelligence.

In a sharp move, I twisted to lie down with my front facing the wall, turning my back against him, and closed my eyes.

"Don't tell me anymore of your secrets. I don't want to owe you anything. We can't be…anything. We're enemies, forced to be teammates. That's all." I wouldn't be a foolish little girl that Harvey believed I was and put my heart on the line, only to have it snuffed out by his deceit.

"I need air. A lot of it," Ben grunted.

"Because you're angry and not in control of your emotions? You're worried you'll kill me, and you'll die, too?"

"No. Because your cruel words are killing me."

The door opened and closed and the humming in my ear grew louder the further away from me he went.

I collapsed back onto the pillow with a frustrated groan, the sigh that escaped me sharp enough to puncture my lungs. I stared blankly at the ceiling, counting cracks I'd already memorised. The silence was smothering me. I *had* to fill the day with something, anything, or I was going to lose my mind.

I pulled a book from the wardrobe and forced myself to read, turning page after page without absorbing a single word. The characters were hollow, their problems distant and utterly small compared to my own. I abandoned the book, threw down a few games of solitaire; won some, lost others, didn't care. Then I ended up right where I'd started, shifting restlessly in the bed, my skin prickling like it didn't fit right on my body. My eyes roamed the room for the hundredth time, dissecting every dull object like it might suddenly come to life.

All the while, my fingers tapped a rhythm on the blanket, some ridiculous song lodged in my brain, looping like torture. The stillness clawed at me. My thoughts churned, loud and relentless. If this was how the next few days were going to be, I'd rather be dead. And why the *fuck* couldn't I stop thinking about Ben?

It was like he'd stitched himself into my thoughts. Every quiet moment opened the door to him. His face. His voice. The space he'd left behind felt louder than everything else in the room. The hours stretched on, quiet and shapeless.

At least I felt safer here than in the infirmary, but the solitude was unbearable. He'd been gone all morning. I told myself I didn't care. I lied. The moment I heard the key turn in the lock, a spark of hope flickered to life too fast, too needy. But it snuffed out just as quickly when I realised the hum in my ear didn't fade. It wasn't him.

Zayd poked his head through the door, eyebrows lifted. "Are you decent?"

I stared at him like he'd interrupted my own funeral that I hadn't invited anyone to.

"Yes," I drawled.

He entered and came to the bed, holding a bread roll and a glass of milk in his hands. "Ben said I should take lunch to you because you might think he'd poison you. He clearly can't poison you because he would die himself, so what is going on? Are you two fighting?"

I side-glanced at him. "Standing up for your new best friend?"

"He has my respect for punching the general, but I never said I'd bury the hatchet. I still detest him. No doubt, I'd probably attempt killing him if Harvey hadn't bonded him to you. If you two are fighting, that makes a good day for me, unless the fight jeopardises your concentration to survive challenges. Do you remember what the next challenge is?"

"The snakes."

He straightened slightly, rolling his shoulders. "Yes. Highly poisonous snakes."

"If they bite me, I'll bite back," I spat, flashing a too wide smirk.

He exhaled, resigned, shaking his head at me as if I should take things more seriously. "Yes, but even when using your magic, the poison will kill you."

"I'll avoid their teeth then," I replied, pretending to be completely unbothered, crossing one shin over the other.

"That's an excellent strategy." His smirk widened as if I had just thought of the most brilliant plan, but underneath his humour was a kernel of concern. He knew me too well. He knew I'd find a way to make the situation more dangerous than it was already.

I propped the pillow up on the wall and sat up against it, biting into the bread roll while Zayd put the glass of milk on the bedside table, tugged up his navy-blue trousers and sat down on the mattress.

My fingers traced the edge of the blanket, and absent-mindedly I glanced at the door. Ben's disappointment was harder to accept than my curfew. "Have you spoken to Harvey any? He hasn't come to see me."

Zayd palmed his neck as if he was accountable for my brother's behaviour. "King Emille and General Denor are putting a lot of pressure on him, wanting results. Since King Blackbone interfered with General Denor's mind bending on you before he had even started, he's saying King Blackbone seems too protective of you. Someone that protective of an enemy spy must be trying to cover up secrets. They want to separate you, but Harvey refuses to agree. He doesn't even tell me why."

"Ben told me he fought off General Denor's magic to save us, but he never said he did it from the moment it had started."

"He weakened it so you wouldn't feel the extent of the pain, even when it didn't threaten your life. He didn't need to do that. It made it worse. Your brother wants to keep away from you so that the other cadets don't think you get special treatment, and I guess he's satisfied that King Blackbone can protect you."

"I almost died."

"But you didn't."

"Harvey couldn't have known that, and he could have visited me in the infirmary to see that I was alive and ask how I felt."

"And let the entire outpost know he cares about you, giving the cadets ideas how they can harm you to get to him? Better people think you don't get along."

"We don't get along!"

Zayd leaned back on his elbow. "I have approached Christopher Charney. He's a second-year cadet, in a team Emroyce has named the Scare Tactic Team. I know it doesn't instil confidence, and his father is a soldier at the infantry at Emendroth, so not sure how reliable that makes him. However, he has magic that can block other's if he's within five metres. I asked him if he could help protect you next time General Denor is visiting. He said he would think about it."

"Thank you, but you can't go around letting people know I need protecting. If the cadets believe I'm not a good ally for the Spirits' Trek, I'm a weak link in the academy and cadets will be keen to dispose of me. Everyone is desperate to show their strength by killing others around here."

Zayd nervously fiddled with his fingers in front of his chest. "I didn't mean to make you look–" The siren went off and Zayd hung his head. "I have to go. Eat and rest!" he shouted as he pushed off the bed and left.

I had just finished my sandwich when Zoe came to visit me.

"Since everyone is out on formation training, I thought you'd be alone," my best friend chirped, holding up playing cards. "How are you feeling, honey?"

"Confused and stupid for returning to the White Wing Territory. We had it so good being agents and partners in crime at our cosy little apartment across the border."

Zoe dealt out the cards between us. "Maybe you'll end up back there. I already told Ben you two should disappear back to Black Castle. You're tied to each other, not to this place."

I gasped. "Zoe! Wow! First of all. First name basis? Secondly, he's a king and probably using me."

"Nah! He's so totally into you, honey. He stayed by your side all the time when you were unconscious, apart from when he got too exhausted and had his minions guard you, for crying out loud."

"Zoe," I crooned, playing another card. "I think you're more gullible than I am. General Denor forbade him from attending the war updates, so you'll see, now he'll change his mood towards us, as he must find another way to extract information. I thought he'd approach you, actually."

"Is the humming from the soul bond so loud in your ear that you don't hear me?" Zoe asked, her voice dripped with dry humour. "It's not kindness. It's not a crush. He. Loves. You."

"He. Is. A. King! He can't love me! There are laws against that!"

Zoe scoffed out her lips. "Kings can do whatever they want, honey."

"He did ask if he could have a kiss." My lips curled at the edges when I thought of our moment in the stables.

Zoe gasped. "I knew it. You've kissed."

"No! I ignored him. He's a king, Zoe. I'm better off with–"

"Better off with who? Watson? No, honey. I'm aware I haven't known you for as long as the Bengreys or the Peres, but when I arrived here four years ago because that arsehole I worked for in the tavern in Emendroth snitched on me having powers, what did I tell you? I said you're meant for greater things than Zayd. The Spirits have given you powers so strong you won't even tell me what they are. You and a king make sense."

"I have no magic," I muttered and placed a card on top of hers in the pile between us, realising I was about to lose.

"Bullshit. You must have inherited something from your father and unless you have given it away, you deem it too scary to share with the world."

I didn't answer her and moaned as I lost the game. We played a few more rounds before I was too tired to focus on another turn and she left me to rest.

16

Several days passed, my body no longer felt like a complete stranger. The dull headache, reminding me of what I had gone through, was tolerable. The throbbing agony reverberating through my muscles was numbed to a point my limbs obeyed me perfectly. My confidence sparked to life as I could fill my lungs to keep steady breaths.

Mewer had insisted I stay in bed for another three days, saying it'd help ensure my reflection looked as composed as my reputation demanded. But by the end of just twenty-four hours, I was climbing the walls with boredom. The confinement gnawed at me, turning the room into a cage dressed in protective intentions.

Ben had only used the room to sleep, rarely saying much, though I knew he was never far away. The soft, constant hum in my ears told me that much. His presence lingering like a low-frequency tether I couldn't shake. It was both a comfort and an irritation, a reminder that he was near but not *with* me.

The only human contact worth anything came from Zoe, who visited after the academy schedule ended each day. She brought noise, warmth, and laughter, pulling me out of my own head. We played cards until we knew each other's tells by heart, then turned our attention to dagger throwing, sharpening our aim on a sketch I'd made of General Denor, now proudly pinned above the desk with several blades protruding from his smug, pencilled face.

But I'd had enough rest, and I needed to spar to pacify my overactivity. I showered and got dressed in my combat leathers, so I could allow training to get rough, and strapped my daggers to my thighs.

I twirled out into the corridor, the cold air biting against my skin as I locked the door behind me. Then I nearly leapt out of it when a shadow moved just at my side.

Ben rose slowly from where he'd been sitting on the floor, his eyes unreadable in the dim light. "What are you doing out of bed…and why in the Underworld are you dressed in combat leathers?" he asked like I had broken curfew.

My hand flew to my chest. "Spirits, Ben! You scared the life out of me!" I pocketed my key. "Have you been lurking just outside our door every day?"

"I've been guarding your door." His voice was low, clipped. "Why do you care?"

"Our door," I corrected sharply, but the words felt empty when we were fighting. "I've been losing my mind in there."

"I didn't think you wanted the company of your enemy."

Yep. That cut deep. I see what he means now when he says the word 'enemy' hurt.

The hit landed before I could brace for it. His tone was flat, but it carried a blade. I swallowed hard. I could feel something undeniable splinter inside me. My insides crumbled and sifted away the bullshit I had been holding onto. The lies I'd told myself began to fall apart, one by one, exposing the truth we'd both been avoiding. We couldn't keep walking this tightrope of pride and denial, pretending we weren't already falling.

And Spirits help us, I was falling hard.

Why was I circling around a pool of suppressed emotions I inevitably had to cross? It was a losing battle with equal losses of sanity on either side. He looked so unravelled, as if my words had genuinely affected him. It was as if he was at war with himself; a battle between desire and restraint that left him hollow-eyed. Or maybe the shadows under his eyes weren't from stress, but from sleepless nights, his stubborn devotion to me keeping him from his most basic needs. It made my chest tighten.

I couldn't do this.

I couldn't keep resisting him. Not when he refused to give me space to breathe, to think. Not when *he* kept dragging the attraction between us back into the light, again and again.

Two strokes of the siren sounded. But it was only the twenty-fifth of September and that made it the earliest I had ever known the challenge to take place. Normally, I could hear the double siren going off on my birthday, as Leadership waited for the penultimate or last day of September. *Thirtieth of September. My Birthday. I hate that day.*

That the challenge had also been on my birthday five years ago was why the white-wings had stood a chance against my mother's attack in the Battle of Bensguard. Most cadets and soldiers had already dressed in their combat leathers and were already brandishing their weapons.

Which is his fault. Ben was ultimately the man behind the attack and the one ruining any love I should have for my birthday.

Irritated, I glared at Ben. "Two chimes. The real challenge." I looked down at my body. "I'm already dressed in my gear." Fumbling, I took out the key from my pocket again and opened the door. "Hurry, and we might win this."

I watched him from the gap of the door, as he rushed inside and changed into his combat leathers, my eyes drawn to the angry flesh on his back that were still raw from the lashes. Guilt twisted my gut. He shouldn't have taken my punishment. When he turned around, my heart did a double take. He looked lethal with the tight leather strapped across his muscles. He tightened the last leg holster around his thigh, even though they didn't hold any weapons.

"Run! I'll catch up!" he shouted, clearly surprised that I had waited for him.

I didn't. "We're a team. We arrive together."

He grinned, and pushed me out of the door, sprinting just one step behind me. I took the corners of the corridor snugly, having played in them growing up I could navigate them with my eyes closed without a misstep.

At the front of the building, a small group had already gathered, so we hadn't been first. *Damn!*

At the front of the formation stood Cadets Chelsea Starly and Betty Darse; the Agility Team. They were fast and could bend their bodies in ways that had me wondering whether they had all their bones and joints intact. They were both ruthless, as expected of those from the province of Pharanir, with long black hair and tanned skin. Although, Betty normally hid her face in white makeup to look like a corpse. I wasn't sure why. It could have something to do with the northern cultures. It wasn't surprising that they had come out as winners, as magic use was allowed in the challenges, and Cadet Darse could slow time. Only slightly, so it looked like someone was moving in slow-motion, but it would be enough for them to get a head start. *Cheats!*

Both women were also favoured for the flight challenges. Hardly surprising, considering Darse's parents owned a Flight Practice Academy near Abarath, and Cadet Starly's parents just so happened to help run it. I also knew they prided themselves on wielding a sword in each hand, yet I didn't see a single sword on them, just the daggers strapped to their thighs. No arm straps, no baldric, no sign of their usual gear. Clearly, they hadn't bothered to suit up properly. But of course, Zayd wouldn't mark them down for that. As long as they had *something* sharp within reach, the rules would bend just enough in their favour.

When everyone had arrived and lined up in formation, Zayd paraded to look at the cadets after having thoroughly inspected the Agility Team. I felt Ben's combat leathers stroking against my back as Zayd walked past us, clearly having taken a step closer. Zayd returned to the front and spread his legs wide and crossed his arms over his chest.

"Well done, cadets! You weren't the slowest year to have completed this challenge!"

I rolled my eyes. What a compliment. But formally-dressed Camp Leader Watson wasn't the same kind man as the relaxed tracksuit-wearing friend I knew him to be.

"And congratulations to Cadet Starly and Cadet Darse for winning the challenge. They will enjoy their prize of a private session in the bath chambers." He finished with dismissing us and applauding, to which all cadets joined in.

Ben stalked off towards the field without a word.

"Where are you going?" I shouted.

"I'm giving you space, and I have things to do."

Things to do? What things? And I never said I wanted space from him.

Why did him having other things to do than focus on me, not sit right with me? He had guarded me day and night when I had been unconscious in the infirmary. He had sat on the floor outside our door! It was like I needed him next to me. A dangerous addiction.

Whether Ben did what he did out of genuine care or just to wring national secrets from me, I couldn't say for certain. But either way, he'd done enough. Enough to earn a debt I couldn't ignore, no matter how conflicted I felt. Maybe part of me also wanted to make a statement, something territorial and a little irrational, because the sight of him talking with Tomason at the edge of the field had lit a fire in my gut I hadn't expected. It was petty, maybe even possessive. Ben wasn't mine...but Spirits help me, I didn't want him being *anyone else's* either.

On my way back from formation, I detoured to the infirmary and asked Mewer for a tub of wound-healing ointment. Something strong, meant for raw skin and bruised muscle. I told myself it was just a practical gesture, a small repayment. That was a lie.

Ben caught me off guard when I returned to our room. I hadn't expected to find him already back when I opened the door. Like a frozen statue, he stared out the window, as if waiting for something or someone.

Without thinking, I pointed towards his bed. "Lie down," I said sharply, my voice cold, firm. Not a request.

He turned, eyes narrowing slightly, surprised by my tone. "Where did you go? I looked for you."

"Infirmary," I replied, already stepping toward him. "Take your shirt off and lie down. Front down."

His brow furrowed. "Infirmary? Are you not well?"

My fingers tightened around the tub in my hand. I could feel the pressure of what I wasn't saying pushing against my ribs. The words just wouldn't come out. *You're the one who's hurt. And yet you're the one who keeps caring for me.*

His eyes stayed locked on mine for a beat too long. The barrier I had put up between us felt fragile like paper that could fall apart with a single word, or worse, even the softest mental caress.

"I'm unhurtable. Bed!" I hissed to steel myself from crumbling.

There was a soft smile pulling at his mouth as he slowly undid his shirt buttons and shrugged his shoulders out before folding the fabric across the desk chair, his muscles moving like waves on a calm ocean when he moved. The panther-like movements looked lethal as he walked towards me where I waited by the foot of his bed.

He dropped a knee to the mattress and stretched out to lie on his front with no objections. The deep cuts between torn flesh, too close to his wing-slits, made me repulsed by my brother.

"What's going on?" he asked, brow creasing as he turned his head to look at me as I straddled over his thighs.

The ointment was cool against my fingers as I dipped them in the tub. "It's my turn to take care of you."

He pushed himself up on his forearms, muscles shifting under skin marred by fading bruises, healing wounds and old scars. "No one has to take care of me. I'm the kin–"

"By all the nine Spirits, Ben!" I snapped. "Lie down and let me do this, or I *swear* I'll wrestle you down onto that bed myself. And trust me, it won't be a pleasant treatment with your face mashed into the mattress."

He smirked, eyes glinting with that infuriating challenging charm. "I don't know. Sounds fun."

I slapped his shoulder, half playful, half exasperated. I didn't have the strength to argue anymore, no willpower to fight the attraction. Even offering to do this felt like peeling back a layer of armour I hadn't meant to shed. My voice softened, almost crumbling. "Just let me do this. Please. I'm…lowering my pride here. Don't make me regret it."

My heart was thudding hard in my chest. The vulnerability laid out in a feast in the open for him to devour.

For once, he didn't push back. His arms slid beneath the pillow, and he eased himself flat onto the mattress with only a quiet breath in reply.

I hovered over him and scooped out a slab of ointment. It was thick, clinging to my fingers. As I smoothed it gently across the raw, bruised skin of his back, he sucked in a sharp breath through his teeth.

"Sorry! Does it sting?" I asked quickly, hand hovering.

"No," he murmured, voice muffled by the pillow. "It was just cold."

"Oh," I breathed, my fingers pausing for a second. The silence between us deepened, not from strife but from a quiet comfort.

Carefully, I continued to spread the cream over the ten viscous marks running from the top of his neck to his lower back. Cuts, which weren't cleaved cleanly but frayed at the edges where the metal whip has struck him. The skin was an angry red tone and hot. Ben was breathing shallowly, clearly observant on my every touch.

"Thank you for saving my life," I whispered.

He held his breath in for a moment. "You're welcome."

I clenched my teeth as my fingers touched a particularly deep area. "But maybe next time you should stay out of white-wing politics and let me–"

"Out of the question," he barked before I'd finished. "I'll follow my gut instinct when I deem it necessary for our survival."

It wasn't for his survival, though, was it? He had stepped in way before then to oppose General Denor.

I swept some cream down his side onto a patch of irritated skin, blue and swollen. My heart was in my throat, throbbing with the tension. I inhaled. "Was that all it was? An act to secure your own survival?"

Ben sat up and turned around so fast, I still had cream on my fingers as I toppled over.

Why had I asked him that? It was foolish and naïve. I didn't want to hear him say he cared for me. I couldn't trust anything he had to say to me. Still, for some fucked-up reason, I needed to hear it.

He looked deep into my eyes, his gaze intense, searching, like he was trying to read something buried beneath the surface of my soul. Then his expression shifted. Something akin foreboding passed through it, and his brows drew together in a tight, conflicted frown.

"You're not ready for that conversation yet," he said quietly.

My own frown rose to meet his like a shield drawn in challenge, as if we were preparing for battle, not with weapons, but with words. The air between us crackled, our faces close, too close that I couldn't fit my shield between us. Still, I wouldn't retreat. The war had been set in motion, and there was only winning or losing.

"Oh? Because if you aren't a king, you're too stupid to understand?" I snapped, the words sharp as a blade.

"No," he growled, the word ripped from deep in his chest. His jaw clenched, and the warrior in him broke loose. "Because if I told you that I've fallen so recklessly, completely in love with you that I've lost all sense of the man I used to be, you wouldn't believe me."

His voice was raw now, ragged with feeling to the point I no longer knew what side of our war he was on. "Every noble woman I've ever met bored me to tears. They were all performances, rehearsed and empty. But you…*you* make me feel like Ben. Not the king. Just *me*. You challenge me, defy me, make every damn day feel like something I want to wake up for.

And still, if I told you that there is no way I'm leaving the White Wing Territory without you, because I need to be by your side or my heart will stop beating, that it beats just because yours does, you'd tell me that I'm manipulating you. You'd say that I'm purely trying to win your trust to get access to the magic I know you're hiding."

He leaned closer. Not threatening, never that, but powerful, confident. But underneath the façade I saw more of what he was. I saw vulnerability, as if each honest word cost him a part of his kingdom, of himself. "I won't lie to you. I *won't*. But I also won't say those things again until you trust me enough to hear them. However long that takes…I'll wait. I'll fight for it. I'll prove it, again and again."

A grin tugged at the corner of his mouth, laced with warmth and defiance. "Since punching General Denor wasn't proof enough."

I stared at him, heart pounding, a thousand thoughts making words tangled in my throat.

"You make it sound so easy," I whispered, though nothing about this, nothing about *him,* felt easy at all.

"Easy? If you don't think I know that there are more people in this world who disapprove of a relationship between us than there are those who accept it, I can tell you I'm well fucking aware. Dammit, the person whose opinion matters most in the world to me, will kill me if she finds out. And the hardest part is when you're in my bed. I'm maintaining the best control I can not to ravish you, fearing both that I could kill you and that I could scare you away. You would show me a kindness if you could decide whether to stay in it, or to keep out of it."

My insides tightened. Was he asking me to stay in his bed? He had never had a woman in his bed, and I didn't think he'd invite one without careful consideration.

I felt my indecision and panic start to shatter, like a thin layer of ice that could crack at any moment. I couldn't hear more of this, or my shield would split.

I scraped the cream on my fingers off against the edge of the tub and put it down on the desk when heading for the bathroom to wash my hands. I had no clue what to answer. It was unacceptable to stay in his bed, but I'd be damned if I rejected his offer. What if it never came around again?

Why the heck did I care so much about my brother's opinions and who were our enemies, when I couldn't care less if the world burned as long as I could keep Ben for myself? My panic inflated even further, tearing at my seams. The conflict between who I wanted to be, and who I was, did it's best to split me right down the middle.

I had been on my way out to spar before the first challenge, and now, I really needed it. The iron rod was in my wardrobe, so I grabbed it and stomped towards the door.

"Iron rod. Angry stomps. Murder blazing in your eyes," Ben said from where he lounged on the bed, one brow arched. "You're heading to the sparring hall, aren't you? And you're not planning to go easy."

There was something in his tone; half observation, half accusation. It snagged under my skin like a thorn. I was a cadet. This was what we did. We trained. We fought. We learned to wield every weapon thrown into our hands. Swords were for grace, for form, barely tapping steel. But a rod? That was a different language entirely. With a rod, you could beat the shit out of each other, bruise flesh, crack ribs, vent rage, without the mess of blood. As Ben had pointed out; there was a lot of pain one could endure before death. So yeah, this was my life now; swing, hit, survive.

"I'm going to see if I can spar with Gravelhorn," I lied.

Ben knew my arch enemy, who despised black-wings, would love the opportunity to beat me lifeless with his strength magic.

That'll piss Ben off.

He could stew in it the same way he made me suffer as he pressured me to get closer.

He had been right – I wasn't ready.

17

I hated waking up to this day; the day Mother had brought me to life twenty-one years ago, and a day she had ruined for me exactly five years ago when she had initiated the Battle of Bensguard. Camp Leader Nar had Mother called out as a traitor but not before she killed about three dozen people. Harvey had then hunted her down and killed her by the border near Abarath.

Happy fucking twenty-first birthday, Angie!

Ben was still asleep, so I got dressed in a black tracksuit and tiptoed outside. Might as well start the day keeping my mind occupied with the obstacle course. Time after time, I pushed myself to do better, cussing at the rope wall as it killed my arms more and more each time I climbed it. None of the times did I beat my own record, either. I blamed my grumpy mood. In anger, I kicked at a rock jutting from the grass but swore as it hurt my toes through the boot.

A bolt of lightning tore the sky and lit up the vast field. A deluge poured down from the sky like the clouds were emptying bucketfuls of an endless supply of water. It was pissing it down on me, soaking me through and through. This was really a shit day. I cocked my head upwards and let the rain hit my face.

"Spirit of Family! Give me a sign. Tell me what to do! Am I on the right path?" I screamed.

No one answered. There was no sign, and I was as lost today, as I was five years ago. I dragged my feet into the stable and leaned over the wooden fence. "Flora!" I waited, but she didn't show, and I couldn't see her among the hay bales. "Flora! Come here, girl." There was no movement or sound.

I jumped over the beam with a racing heart and searched the area. She was gone. Was this some cruel revenge by any of the cadets who thought me a traitor? Probably Gravelhorn. He had looked at me with eyes promising death during our first encounter at the inner courtyard, and he would have probably done it there and then, too, if Ben wouldn't have come to my rescue. Now, he was going after me by slaughtering my pig?

On this day of all days! I'd kill him if he had hurt her. If my brother punished me for it, so be it.

To kill him, I needed my daggers. My feet had never hammered the courtyard so hard. Ben woke up as I rummaged through the wardrobe for my combat leathers and grabbed my daggers.

"What's going on? Classes for the second challenge don't start until tomorrow," he croaked sleepily from the bed, hugging his pillow harder and stretching out his legs.

"I'm going to kill Gravelhorn." I felt truly feral, as I pushed the blades into the leg holsters.

Ben tossed the blanket off himself and was only in black boxer shorts again. That damned six-pack caught my attention-although it was more like a twelve-pack. "Why? What has he done? He's much larger than you and you're angry." He rubbed the sleep out of his eyes.

"I'm sure he's the one who has killed Flora."

"Stop!" He shouted, as I darted for the door.

I twisted in the open doorway, not planning on being convinced to stay with the amount of revenge burning in my chest.

"I moved Flora," he said.

My brows rose. "What?"

Ben swung his legs off the bed and sat up with his feet flatly planted on the floor. "When you were unconscious in the infirmary, I gave the order for Murben to care for Flora. She lives with him and Davis in room sixteen."

I planted my hands on my hips and stared at him in disbelief. "You assigned *Murben*, the royal bodyguard, to protect my *pig*?"

Ben didn't even flinch. "Yes, she's important to you. Family. With the trade supplies from the farmers in the west being less regular, I thought someone might get...hungry."

I blinked. "Murben. The massive, terrifying, break-bones-for-breakfast king's bodyguard, is walking around the grounds... *babysitting my pig?*"

"Yes," he replied, calmly, eyes never leaving mine. The stare was tense and focused, like he was ready to tackle me to the ground if I so much as *thought* about charging off to fight Gravelhorn.

I threw my hands up. "Brilliant. Shall I add Murben to the ever-growing list of people who want to kill me?"

Ben's mouth twitched. "Don't worry. I think he's become rather fond of her."

"You *can't* just assign elite royal guards to *babysit my pets*," I snapped.

He lolled his head lazily around his shoulders, not a trace of apology in sight. "I can. I'm the king."

I groaned and pinched the bridge of my nose, turning to close the door before this conversation got anymore surreal. But just as it was about to latch, a foot wedged into the gap.

Zayd pushed the door open and leaned into view, eyes wide and assessing, clearly seeing the both of us tense with defiance and determination in our faces.

"Hi," he said, voice small and filled with awkward hesitance, like someone about to walk into a battlefield.

I could tell from the way he was looking at me that this visit had to do with my birthday, but he also knew I'd cut his tongue out if he said the two merry words 'Happy Birthday'. But just in case he had forgotten, I stared at him in a threat.

"I thought maybe I could take you to a restaurant tonight. Not our favourite one, as I think that one might be too far away from him and the soul bond." He glowered at Ben, who still sat in his boxer shorts on his bed. "There is a new place. Andros' Rose. It's supposed to be good."

Ben got off the bed, his muscles tense. "She isn't going."

My jaw almost dropped. What right did he have to forbid me from going? He knew that if he challenged me this way, I'd do the opposite, so what was his plan? Did he want me to go? Never mind. Ben didn't know the history of this day. I had to get away from the Bensguard Outpost.

I brought my attention back to Zayd. "That would be lovely. What's the dress code?"

Ben got off the bed to put his enormous hand on my shoulder. "Angelica has black wings. I'm her king. I say she isn't going with you. She shouldn't miss the remembrance bonfire tonight."

Zayd stared at the hand Ben had on my shoulder as if he considered cutting it off.

"Angie hates to remember this day. It hurts her. I always take her out and away from the outpost. Though, she does like to watch the bonfire, so we'll be back before then." He had told Ben the information like he wanted to remind him who of the two of them knew me the best, before he glanced at me with a softer sapphire gleam. "A black dress should be fine. My schedule is full of duties all day that I can't get away from, but I'll pick you up at eight?"

"Eight," I confirmed before he left down the corridor and I closed the door to face a furious king.

His voice dropped to a low growl; each word laced spoken in a tone darker than concern. "So, you're dating Watson?"

I stiffened, my pulse quickening. "It's not a date," I snapped, though the words felt hollow even as they left my mouth. "He's distracting me from a past I don't want to remember."

His gaze hardened, eyes narrowing with a mix of suspicion and possessiveness. "Good. Then you don't mind if I tag along, so I can protect you."

I recoiled slightly, the tension between us attacking me with burning intensity. "Zayd can protect me just fine." I made every effort to relax and shake off the threat that didn't exist. I plastered a smile on my lips as I chirped. "See it as your day off."

His lips curled into a tight, humourless smile in return. "I don't want a day off from you. And I don't want you to go out on a date with him."

"It's not a date!" I repeated, more forcefully this time.

"I don't believe Watson knows that. He wants you back."

I froze, the blood draining from my face. "Technically, we never broke up."

He blinked a few times for the information to sink in. Then his expression shifted to something way beyond anger. "What!"

"Well, I left him without saying goodbye and kind of showed up again with no warning two years later."

"Holy fuck! That's cruel, even for you." He ran a hand through his hair, pacing the floor like a caged animal. His movements showed he was mightily agitated. Finally, he stopped in front of the wardrobe, yanking it open and pulling out his clothes with a force that made the hangers rattle. "And dammit, Angelica, put your damn shield up so you don't pass your emotions for him over to me."

I opened my mouth to respond, but he was already tying on his trainers, his back facing me. It took seconds before he stood and walked towards the door.

"Where are you going?"

"My control is slipping," he muttered, his voice tight. "I'm going for a run."

"It's raining."

He grunted, not looking at me. "Maybe I'll visit Flora. As you said. She's very loyal."

He slammed the door as he left, making my heart jump. If he was faking feelings for me, he was bloody good at it.

After having waited for as long as I thought it'd take for the corridor to be clear of him, I went to knock on Zoe's door. She knew better than to say, 'Happy Birthday', too. But she gave me a plaited leather bracelet that she had made for me. We spent the day together sparring and eating, and then sparring some more until every moment of this diabolical day was coming to a close.

I returned to my room to get ready for the restaurant and prayed to the

Spirit of Luck that Ben wouldn't be there.

But he was.

The Spirits had let me down once more.

He was sitting on the chair by the desk, intensely focused on sharpening my sword with my whetstone.

Ben didn't say a word to me when I entered, so I countered with the same courtesy whilst showering, doing my makeup and putting on a black dress that had a discrete glittery fabric and a slit on the left leg all the way up to my thigh. I had put up my hair, displaying the long diamond earrings at the side of my neck which Zayd had given me on my seventeenth birthday, matching a wide diamond band strapped tightly around my throat.

"It's not a date. Your uniform is black. Wear that," Ben muttered lowly.

"I assure you, going out with Zayd and remembering this day hurts me more than you."

Ben grunted darkly. "I seriously doubt that."

"The day your mother is called out as a traitor and ruins your life, come back and we can compare miseries."

"My mother is dead. She died on the battlefield, stabbed by a… She died fighting."

His mother had died on the battlefield? Ben had said that women didn't belong on the battlefield. Now, that comment made sense. It wasn't because he thought women couldn't fight as well as men or were weaker, he wanted to protect them. My heart almost shattered for him.

"I'm sorry. I guess we all have days we'd rather not remember. Let me get through this one, and I'll be less grumpy tomorrow. Promise." There was no mirror in the room except for the small one over the washbasin in the bathroom, so I couldn't see my full figure. "It's a nice restaurant in the city." I turned around to face him. "How do I look?"

He looked up and tensed, seeming to have stopped breathing. His eyes traced my body and lingered on it as if he was committing every detail to memory. His jaw tightened and there was a spark of wrath in his ruby eyes. "Spirits give me strengths." He rubbed his entire face with one hand. "Awful. Change to your uniform."

"Oh," I felt my spirit sink and looked down, but couldn't see anything wrong with it. Maybe it wasn't fancy enough? He was a king, so he would have seen more exquisite gowns.

He let out a guttural grunt, like he was fuming because someone was about to take what was his away from him. He ran a hand through his hair before flinging it toward me in exasperation. "Beautiful," he breathed, his voice submissive, like it had been dragged out of him against his will. "You look…*stunning*." His eyes clung to me, devouring every detail, and whatever composure he'd tried to summon was balancing on a tightrope.

"It's the arm you'll be on that's the wrong one," he added bitterly.

I gave a half-hearted laugh, trying to shake off the heat crawling up my spine. "You should have asked me out first," I teased, feigning lightness.

I hadn't expected him to make plans for us, not given it any thought…so why was there a sadness lingering in my chest?

He stood abruptly, the scrape of the chair against the floor jarring. In two strides, he was towering over me, forcing me to tilt my head back to meet his gaze. His expression was guarded, but seething underneath layers of real jealousy. "I didn't realise this was a *first come, first served* situation."

"It wasn't," I murmured, caught between his nearness and my own traitorous pulse. "But if you had asked…I would've chosen you."

His jaw clenched. One hand lifted to the back of my dress, fingertips grazing the fabric near my shoulder blade. The touch was casual in theory, but his fingers twitched, restless, like he was barely containing his desire beneath the surface. He didn't seem to notice what it was doing to me, how it set fire to every nerve-ending in my body.

"I did ask you to have dinner with me a month ago. You made excuses."

I tipped my head, glaring at him. "That was different. My agenda wasn't to eat, it was to kill you."

"Well, you're not killing me today, so I'll ask now. Have dinner with me tonight?" His voice was a fine line between an invitation and a command. He leaned in until our lips hovered achingly close, only a whisper apart. *Too close.* Yet. Somehow. Not close enough.

I placed both hands on Ben's chest and gave him a firm push, forcing him a step back. "It's a little late for that, don't you think? I'm already dressed. Unless Zayd happens to break a leg in the next ten minutes, I'm going."

His expression twisted into something darkly playful. "Oh, that can be arranged."

I shot him a sharp glare. "Behave."

Turning away before he could say something worse, I snatched up my little black handbag and struggled to snap it shut after wedging in a few essentials: my room key, a few silver coins, and my small dagger. The dagger especially refused to settle, but I wasn't going anywhere without it. Not tonight. I had to make the damn thing shut, as I couldn't remove the coins either. Zayd usually covered the cost of our meals, at least he had when we were dating, but I couldn't count on those assumptions anymore. Not with the tug of war that was going on between us as he wanted us together and I tried to keep him at the same distance as all my other friends. Problem was, the boundaries between us were still vague.

When the punctual knock came, I opened the door to find Zayd standing tall, one hand in his pocket, the other braised on the door frame.

Ben stiffened at my side, and I felt the shift in him instantly, like a drawn bowstring straining to snap.

For a moment, I thought a fight might erupt then and there – no words necessary to rile each other. Zayd's casual greeting met with Ben's silent, bristling tension. Every word Zayd spoke seemed to spark a reaction from Ben, each syllable like a challenge Ben wanted to crush.

But Zayd was prepared. Instead of his standard navy-blue ceremonial uniform, the formal attire for off-duty leaders, he wore a tailored black suit; a clear break from the rigid identity of the camp. No medals. No insignia. Just clean lines, subtle elegance, and a fresh shave. Even from a step behind me, I could catch the scent of his cologne, musky and sensual, almost daring. And judging by Ben's flaring nostrils, *he* had caught it too.

Zayd offered me his arm, and we left together, leaving Ben behind. Oddly, it felt as if I was leaving a piece of me at home. The further away into the city we walked, the louder the humming in my ears became, and once we were seated in the restaurant, the humming even overpowered the chatter of the other guests.

The restaurant was a fancy place with many chandeliers hanging off the ceiling and their prisms reflected light in the tall nine-pane windows that run along the side viewing the street. Thick, red curtains with a golden hem draped across half of them and matched the red carpet and gold decor in the enormous room.

The waiter handed us the menus, and Zayd's effort at trying to impress me was reflected in the fancy ingredients and the extortionate prices.

The waiter poured our wine and took our orders, and when he left, I raised my glass to Zayd.

"Thank you for taking me out. To you!" I clinked the glass with his and brought it to my mouth to sip.

"To us," he said, and drank.

Reflexively, I paused the glass on my lips, wanting to say something gentle to object to that, but my ears screamed, so I lost focus and drank instead.

"Have you arrived at the restaurant safely?" Ben asked.

I pulled wine into my air pipe and coughed. Zayd frowned, looking worriedly at me.

"I'm okay." I tapped my chest gently. "Wine got into the wrong pipe."

"I have not given you consent to speak in my mind! And now isn't a good time."

"Can you not always argue? Are. You. Safe?"

"I am, and I was perfectly happy, but now I'm pissed off. You promised me you wouldn't enter my mind without consent!"

"You're on a date with Watson and definitely didn't get my consent."

"What's wrong, Angie?" Zayd asked. "Are you thinking about King

Blackbone?"

No, not thinking of him. He's inside my fucking mind!

"I can date whoever I want! Stay out of my mind!"

"You said it wasn't a date."

"Must you always argue with me. Stay out of my head during my non-date!"

His voice in my ears ceased, but the humming remained as distracting as before. "My teammate is a handful. But I can handle him."

"I hope so. King Blackbone isn't good for you. He has many secrets."

"If you know he has many secrets, you must know them too."

"I do. If you work hard enough, and show Harvey you want it, you could become a Camp Leader and be privy to those secrets. I think Counsellor Arnold Desry is retiring soon and King Emille has his eyes on Mewer."

"Collin Mewer?"

Zayd spun the wine glass by its foot on the table. "Yes. He's a great healer. If he had been at any other outpost than at the Bensguard Outpost, you'd be dead for what General Denor did to you. I'm glad King Blackbone stayed true to his word and didn't share King Emille's secrets with you. General Denor was checking how much you knew, and your life would have become a whole lot more complicated."

"Well, King Blackbone hasn't told me anything. No one tells me anything."

"Probably for the best. I don't think you'll enjoy joining leadership."

"Why not?"

"Because I have to follow the orders passed on by King Emille and if I had known then what I know now, I would have rather joined the Air Force after I graduated than having joined leadership."

"You're a strong flyer. You would have done well in the Air Force."

"Thank you. But let us talk about other things than those involving the outpost."

The waiter stopped at our table, placing our food plates in front of us. We had ordered the same dish and gawked at the beautiful presentation. Mint sauce was drizzled over lamb chops, stacked on top of a fine layer of sweetcorn mash, and to top it all off there were edible flowers in soft pink and violet colours.

"You enjoy baking. Have you kept it up?" Zayd asked. "I remember you making a mean peanut butter cake."

The meal had blown my mind right off topic, so it took me a while to realise Zayd was asking about my hobbies. A pang of hurt settled in my chest when I thought about the peanut butter cake I hadn't eaten in so long.

"That wasn't me. It was Mother's, and she probably stuffed it with herbs that made Father talk. I don't want to speak about her. Not today."

"That's okay. How about the obstacle course? What time have you recorded?"

"I was at it this morning, trying to beat your time, but I couldn't even do better than my personal record."

He swallowed his mouthful and pinned his eyes on me. "It was raining this morning."

"I know. Didn't care."

A slow, knowing smile tugged at his lips as he watched me. "You're in a foul mood today. Well, I had expected that. Let me roll up my sleeves."

He pulled something small out of his pocket. "Hold out your hand."

All the blood in my body rushed to my head. My heart pounded, fearing it would be that engagement ring Ward had told me about. Had Harvey finally given Zayd his blessing?

I made a silent prayer to all the nine Spirits that it wasn't the case. Reluctantly, I closed my eyes and held my hand up, and he placed the item there, which indeed fitted into my palm. My fingers trembled as I held it and I fought to swallow a wave of panic that twisted its way up from my stomach to my throat. I didn't even know how I could get away with rejecting a proposal without hurting him, and hurting him gravely a second time terrified me more than anything else I could think of.

18

I opened my eyes to look at the item. The red paper box with a thin golden ribbon made me gasp with excitement as I recognised it. "You didn't?"

"Yes, I went to the best chocolate shop in the capital to get you your favourite."

"When were you in Emendir?"

"The king summoned a counsel when you were unconscious."

"What if I hadn't survived?"

He folded his forearms on the table and leaned over as if he was going to tell me a secret. "I was sure that if I held it under your nose, it would bring you back."

I laughed, and it made him laugh. "Thank you. I'll save it to eat at the bonfire later."

"Good choice. I heard it is going to be a big spectacle this year. Captain La Roy has spent a lot of his time tutoring Kate fire wielding one-to-one, to your brother's frustration. Harvey won't break the outpost rules to court Kate as long she is in his unit, but he knows Captain La Roy has no such restrictions."

"She'll be better off with Captain La Roy. He's kind," I said, pinching my lips over the fork to pull off some sweetcorn mash.

Zayd stared at my fork and talked slowly. "And boring and uncharacteristic and too righteous."

"You think that because you're used to my mischief." A soft moan escaped me as I savoured the delicious flavours of the food. It was a long time since I'd had a meal this good.

"I love your mischief."

My cheeks blushed in a way I didn't agree with. At no stage of this evening did I want to lead Zayd on to believe there would be something between us again. Maybe going on this *non-date* was a bad idea. It was especially obvious when I looked around the room. A man in a black suit stood in the corner by the window, playing softly on a violin. There was still some daylight outside, but the moon showed, and luminescence glowed upon the violin player's face, as if he had chosen that spot purposely. Each table was decorated with a red rose and a thick candle on white linen tablecloths over red velvet that reached the floor, and I could only see couples dining. Spirits, this was a romantic place.

"How is your sparring going with Zoe?" he asked, bringing my attention back to our table.

"With everything that has been going on, I have had little time for sparring, but I'm glad she's staying at the Bensguard Outpost, so I can see her more often."

"What things have been going on?"

I paused my next bite, confused how he could ask that. "I don't know…having my two-year mission ruined…being unconscious for seven days, being soul bound to the enemy king. How is your Sunday going?"

"Of course. Those things. I didn't mean to offend you. I'm glad you consider King Blackbone an enemy, though. He hasn't been able to charm the wits out of you. You always were a clever girl."

That comment didn't sit right with me. He *had* charmed the wits out of me. I was just too proud and stubborn to face the truth. It would also mean I was the traitor everyone accused me of being. I didn't want to be branded a traitor knowing my father had dedicated his entire life to the Bensguard Outpost. What of his life's work would I pass down in our legacy?

"Enough about me. What about you? How is it to be a camp leader this year? How have the other classes been? Tell me about your two last years at the academy. It hurt me that I missed them. I should have been there for you."

Zayd talked for an hour uninterruptedly and I nodded and smiled, but inside me, my anxiety for the dangers of the challenges that the cadets had to go through grew inside my gut. It would be my turn to try my best to survive them soon.

As the darkness had settled outside, I had finished my meal, and I felt so full that I couldn't take another bite.

Zayd stopped talking and looked at his watch. "We should get back, so we don't miss the bonfire." He paid for the meal without hesitation and when I offered that I could pay my own share, he flashed me a hard glare saying there was no way in this world he'd let me pay.

On the walk home, I noticed Zayd's attempts to walk close enough to hold my hand, but I distanced myself every time and cursed myself for believing that this had been a good idea. Falling into old ways had felt so natural; a lure to trap me in a life I didn't want to get stuck in once more.

"Thank you for tonight," I said when we had reached the academy grounds and saw the throng of people.

Everyone was gathered around a clearing in the forest across from the field, where a sky-high pile of firewood was about to be set on fire. "It's probably best if we don't show up together. You're my camp leader, after all. If they believe we have resumed our relationship, we might get lashed."

His smile vanished, but it wasn't because he feared getting lashed. I knew him better than that. He would take the punishment if it secured what he wanted. What pained him was the fact that what he wanted wasn't the same thing as what I wanted.

"If that's the only thing that stands in our way, I can put in for a transfer to the General Operations Unit."

That made my heart really bleed. He had worked so hard to become a camp leader and was willing to throw it all away for me.

"Zayd, I could never allow that to happen. If there is an us in the future, it can wait until I graduate."

He nodded and kissed my hand before stalking across the field to get inside the building, probably swinging by his apartment to change into his camp leader uniform.

It took me a while to cross the vast field to reach the campfire area. I sat down at the far back on a thick tree truck that had been fashioned into a bench. Mazdon turned around and waved at me from a few rows ahead. How did he know I had arrived? Could he hear every person's heart as if they had a specific signature beat? I waved back and smiled at him, nodding at Kate who was standing in her combat leathers next to Captain La Roy beside the bonfire pile. He stretched with pride and looked forward.

They would need to light the bonfire soon, considering no one could see much and would struggle getting back to the military building. Along with the darkness, the chilly air had arrived as well, but I'd be fine in my thin dress once the fire roared to life.

A large jacket draped across my shoulders the moment before I thought to return to my room to change into something warmer.

Ben sat down next to me. "How was your non-date?"

I folded the black leather jacket around me and felt his warmth still on it. Not wanting to admit to him that the meal had been nice, and as he had told me he'd rather I stayed quiet than lie, I didn't answer. Ben wore a tight black t-shirt that hugged his biceps and green hiking trousers, looking casual. His hair was windswept and damp from a recent shower. And Spirits, did he smell nice of flowers, which wasn't his normal scent.

With the fire wielders' show illuminating the night, I unpacked the chocolate globe Zayd had given me. A display of flames lashed up into the air to light the bonfire to the sounds of awes and applause. The large flames that caught onto the firewood crackled and shot flares around. Even when I was far back, I felt the heat of the fire on my skin. Captain La Roy, Brian and Kate stood near the bonfire but none of them seemed bothered by the extreme heat as they made the flames dance higher and higher towards the sky in orange and yellow against the dark void and dotted stars above.

I held the chocolate between my fingers, its smooth surface catching the shifting light of the flames. I inspected it like it was a precious light crystal, noting the subtle aroma of cocoa that teased my taste buds. This wasn't just any chocolate. It was a rare indulgence I wouldn't typically allow myself.

"Zayd gave me this," I murmured. "My favourite chocolate from a shop in the capital."

Ben's response was a low grunt. "Your favourite chocolate? I hope that doesn't make my gift underwhelming."

He reached into his pocket and produced a small velvet box, its deep navy-blue hue blending in with the surrounding darkness. The box was elegant, its texture luxurious. He extended it toward me, his gesture tender. "Happy birthday."

I took the box from his hands, my fingers brushing against his for a fleeting second. The warmth of his touch lingered, sending a ripple of desire through my chest. I glanced at the box that was small enough to fit inside my palm, then back at him, my heart swelling with gratitude and an affectionate throb that somehow connected us.

I gawked, not at the gift, but at him. "You didn't need to rush out to get me a gift."

Ben put his hands flat against the bench to his sides, slightly rocking back and forth in his seat. "As always, it hurts when you're surprised that I can be kind and caring. Of course, I'd get you a gift. I knew it was your birthday. It took me more than a few days to source your gift. It wasn't that easy to come by."

I slotted the chocolate ball back into the red box to savour later, as Ben's gift had piqued my curiosity. I opened it carefully, wondering what a king gave a teammate as a present – a gift that had taken days to get hold of.

The moment I had lifted the lid off and saw the item, my eyes shot wide open. "Oh, my fucking nine Spirits! That isn't? That's not what I think it is?"

"It is. It's not very big, and it isn't charged, but it's what I could source for now."

It was hard to take my eyes off the light crystal inside the box. I had never dreamt I would own one. This must have cost him a fortune. More than a fortune. "I can't accept this. It's too much."

"I had wanted to do something more special for you today, but you chose to go out with Camp Leader Watson."

Fury of red ribbons flashed before my eyes. "I didn't choose him. I didn't choose any of this. Not one single part of my life did I choose to be this way. Zayd and I share many memories. I can't just clear them from my life."

"I'm not asking you to forget them. Only that you make your standpoint clear to him. We have history, too. Remember when you poked the Black Blade at my heart and almost vanquished my soul? That was fun."

I glowered at him. "That isn't history. That was only six weeks ago, and I prefer not to remember that incident."

He cleared his throat regally. "Fine. Remember when you knocked out five of my guards with what you claimed were your 'bare hands' because one of them had groped your arse in the Crossbow Tavern?"

I pulled the flaps of his leather jacket tighter around myself to lock my body heat inside. "That was self-defence!"

I hadn't even known I'd done it before the bodies lay unconscious around me. Zoe had got me drunk and it had all happened so fast and in a blur.

He shrugged. "I'm not saying I disagreed with the punishment you handed them. Just reminiscing about our past."

"How did you know that by the way? You weren't there."

"Does it only count if I was there? Okay," he said, clearly pondering other occasions. "And none of your mischievous visits to my office, either? What about the spring ball? You dressed in that deep blue gown, a silver tiara in your hair that was up in a ponytail and curled over your back. And you danced twice with Duke Hartmore."

Images of that night flashed in my mind, and I recalled the golden-haired duke with that sleazy look in his eyes, as if I was made of chocolate. "That doesn't count, either. You didn't ask me for a dance."

"I danced past you. Smelt your perfume. I was close enough."

"I might give you that one at a push."

"I hope so. That ball created a nightmare for me. Ever since, Duke Hartmore has wanted me to hand you over to him. You intrigued him, so he has kept his eyes on you."

"Was that why he had been in your office that time Davis caught me with the Black Blade?"

"Yes. Tedious bastard. Just like Watson. But I guess I have myself to blame for the non-date as forbidding it clearly drove you straight into his arms. I was stupid. But when you flash me those blue eyes, my mind blanks and I find it hard to determine the best cause of action."

I rocked sideways, nudging my shoulder against his. "You know…you're quite charming when you want to be. It's beyond me why you're known to be a very different person when you're in the Black Wing

Territory." There was a hint of playfulness in my tone, and I could see that he had heard it.

"I know. I have to be. There, it's me who decides who lives or dies, in order to keep the balance between good and evil for the betterment of my people."

"Would you kill me to save one of your subjects?"

He hesitated.

"I thought so," I muttered and looked down at the light crystal in the velvet box before I closed the lid again.

Even though I loved seeing the flames of the bonfire licking the sky; as if I could imagine the entire world going up in flames, I had lost the will to watch it.

I rose from the bench and left Ben with a self-scolding look on his face, and he didn't follow me as I crossed the field to get to the front of the military building. I removed my high-heels and climbed my tree, settling on my branch and tore the chocolate ball out of the red box, biting off half and savouring it in my mouth, almost feeling my tense nerves relax along each vertebra of my spine. But too soon, the sound of scratching bark alerted me that I'd not get my respite. Ben swung up in one second to sit next to me, supporting his hand on the trunk just above my head.

Now who was the tedious bastard?

Normally, guests in this tree sat on Zayd's branch but Ben had intruded on mine, giving me very little wiggle room. The bark was rough beneath me, and the leaves of the branches rustled uneasily in the breeze, as if they too resented the stranger. I shifted uncomfortably, trying to find a more stable position, but the branch creaked ominously under our combined weight. Ben, clearly sensing my discomfort, ignored it and shifted closer, his presence overwhelming in the confined space. His knee brushed against mine, and I flinched, the closeness stirring a cocktail of emotions I wasn't ready to drink.

"I apologise. Please forgive me. I don't want to make this day worse for you than it already is, and I can't help but feeling some responsibility for having to make it better."

His voice was so gentle, his words so incredibly sincere that it made the walls I had put up finally crumble. I crossed my arms to build a physical wall instead and turned my gaze downward, focusing on the ground far below, trying to steady my racing heart. "You can't possibly understand me. How it is to live a life among those who call you a traitor. Feeling like you're worth nothing."

Ben was silent for a moment, his gaze fixed on me with an intensity that made my skin prickle. "No, I can't," he admitted quietly. "Do you want me to kill them?"

"No!" The absurdity of his suggestion caught me off guard, and despite myself, I laughed. "Please, just…leave *my* branch."

He sighed, his eyes never leaving mine. "You'll not forgive me?"

No, it wasn't that. He was too damned close, and I had no strength left to fight, to keep my shield up. This stupid attraction made little sense. I didn't want to keep my hands off him. I wanted him to ravish me and make me feel like a desired woman.

My breathing had sped up and was trembling, ventilating out of my mouth. I tried to stop my growing needs by shoving the second half of the chocolate ball into my mouth, but the orgasmically good taste of the chocolate only intensified my lust level and my clit throbbed with need for him.

Ben observed me with inspecting eyes and his glance fell to my lips.

Spirits, I can't take this anymore.

"Why do you care?" I snapped, tipping my head, the back of it scraping at the bark.

Ben put his forearm on the trunk above my head and leaned closer and closer. "Have I ever acted as if I don't care about you?"

"Of course you care about me," I breathed, as words would be too loud between us. Then I found my snarl. "How can I forget? You don't want to die." My defiance only brought our faces even closer to each other's.

He didn't pull back, not one bit. "I thought I had proven my emotions to you but let me be blatantly clear." He pressed his lips against mine, kissing me softly at first but the passion spiralled, making our lips part and tongues touch.

I pulled my head sideways, gasping for breaths and hanging onto consciousness so as not to faint. "This is forbidden. What about the lashes? What about my brother's threats?"

"I'm king. I don't ask for permission, but for forgiveness."

Heat pooled between us as he ignited the urges at my core, and I gripped the fabric of his shirt before hesitation could steal the moment. My hands travelled upwards until I tugged at the roots of his onyx hair, pulling him towards me, our lips crashing at the impact. He held his forearm steady on the trunk above my head and curled his other arm around my back to get our bodies to connect. The way he ravished my mouth made it clear how much he wanted this, too. With starving hunger, he pushed his tongue beyond my lips where he was met with delicious chocolate, my tongue and ardent desire. His movements were raw, feral as he claimed me as his. My body pressed against his like a second skin, my entire front was aware of him; his minty smell, his dark moans, and his warm possessive touch.

Suddenly, Ben ripped my hands away from his neck and pulled away from me. He panted a few times, looking apologetic. "Without doubt, that was the best chocolate I've ever had."

I settled back against the trunk and stilled my racing pulse. "You just wanted to taste my chocolate?" I felt vulnerable. "Why did you stop? You fear someone can see us?"

"Stop caring about what the people who believe you're worthless are thinking. I didn't stop, I'm…refraining. Firstly, you're sad and that makes you too trusting. You wouldn't want this to carry on any further if you weren't emotional. Secondly, I want to make sure I'm in control of my own emotions. They got too overpowering, and I feared I'd hurt you."

"You'd never hurt me." I searched his eyes for a disagreement but found none. "Because we're bonded," I teased.

His smile didn't show.

"What's wrong?" I asked.

"It's so typical of me to fall in love with the one woman, who is so protected by people who'd kill me to keep her away from me."

"At least it isn't as bad as suffering from an insane attraction to the king of the enemy."

We snorted at the irony in unison.

Ben took my hand and stroked his thumb over it. "I know I can't kiss you, embrace you or even hold your hand in public, but know that my mind is occupied with you in my every thought. I'm still fully intent on showing you I'm an honest man. Abstaining from your kiss and that chocolate when you're vulnerable is my way of proving it."

"If you simply proved it by letting me into your passive thoughts, then we could get on with the sex part."

"Fuck, I'd like to get to that part." He was shaking his head. "But I can't. I have too many secrets that I keep in my head for your own protection. Some things need to be put right before you discover them. Maybe you'll never be able to forgive me for some things you learn, but maybe you'd hate me a little less."

"So, first sign of having to do some real trusting, and you fail." I turned to climb down, but he grabbed my arm.

"I will let you in. Just give me a bit more time. It's a big ask. Are you so keen on letting me in to listen to your most private thoughts?"

"Is this a trick to garner white-wing secrets?"

"I knew it was your birthday. I smuggled a light crystal inside the premises. Don't you think I have my own resources to retrieve information other than from a cadet who hasn't been in the White Wing Territory for two years and clearly doesn't know any secrets worth fucking this up for?" He gestured between us with his free hand before he let go of his grip on my arm.

He had a point. If he wanted intel, he could have seduced someone in leadership, or even Zoe. Everyone at this place knew more secrets than I did. "I don't have any secrets. None that I keep from you."

"Okay, so perhaps not secrets, but you might not want to share your thoughts about how you feel about Watson with me. And you want to conceal the true nature of your magic."

"Nice try. I have no magic. My father gave all of it away before I was born," I lied.

"When I met with your father, he still had his magic, and you were very much alive."

"What?" I straightened, instantly intrigued. "You met my father?"

"See. Many secrets."

Damn! I wanted to know that particular secret, but I could tell he wasn't about to speak of it. I gritted my teeth. *Angelica, remember that he's your enemy!* I rebuked myself.

19

When I woke up in the morning, I instantly felt my muscles aching with a relentless burn that had started to feel like a companion by now. My arms felt heavy and my legs sluggish with the simplest movement requiring more effort than it should. The sparring session with Zoe last night had been satisfactory after my argument with Ben, although too rough. Fighting with iron rods wasn't a great idea when Ben's secrets frustrated me after leaving the tree with unresolved issues between us. It left a lot of bruises. I hadn't told Zoe about the kiss with Ben, but I had danced really close to the subject. She had probably already worked it out, though. She knew me well enough.

My legs throbbed as I swung them over the edge of the bed to sit up, and rolling my shoulders, I felt a tight soreness that spread down my back, forcing a wince out of me.

Ben wasn't in his bed, and he had left it made neatly enough one could bounce a coin on it. I leaned over my bedside table to see the time on my watch and moaned as it was only thirty minutes until I had to be in the Zoology Classroom. Spirits, today we were going to play with venomous snakes. It made me wonder what other women my age did on a normal Monday. Surely not gamble with the Spirit of Death.

I got ready for class and my stupid insides wanted to sing when I crossed paths with Ben in the corridor. But I kept my face level, watching the other cadets file into the classroom.

"You didn't come home until I was asleep last night, and you left this morning before I awoke. I could only tell you had been there because the shower was wet. Are you avoiding me because of…" I quieted immediately when I saw Mazdon passing the doorway but looked at Ben with a stare demanding an answer. Had he hated the kiss? Why had I kissed him? It had been stupid. Weak.

"I was training Davis out on the field. He has some trouble holding weapons because of his severed thumb."

"The one *you* severed," I reminded him.

"Yes." There was no regret in the small word. "Hence, it's fair I put in the time helping him."

"If that's the reason you avoid me, it's okay. I wanted to be sure I hadn't overstepped a line that made you uncomfortable."

"You're concerned about my comfort?" He grinned at me, and closed the gap between us, doing what he loved most; cornering me against the wall. He smelt so damned good; of leather and our flower-scented soap that I had thought he'd be too proud to use, but he wore it as if no fragrance in the world could diminish his manliness. The intake of *him* set off the heat inside me that coiled around my heart.

The gleam from his ruby eyes bore into me. "I explained that we shouldn't be seen intimate in public, but trust me, that is for your benefit, not mine. Say the word and I'll be all over you." His voice was a seductive purr into my ear and my brain went numb, making it impossible to decide whether to push him away or throw my arms around his neck.

"If you two are quite done!" A sharp tone lashed the space between the classroom and us.

A tremor always ran down my spine at seeing Camp Leader Rhie Neville, who was tutoring this challenge because of her ability to petrify anything living. She had that look in her ghostly, grey eyes that if you fucked with her, she'd ensure you'd suffered for it.

"Yes, Camp Leader Neville!" I answered with discipline, as my father had required of me each time he needed my attention.

Calling a higher ranked officer by their first name was frowned upon in the military, but calling Neville by her first name was out of the question.

We followed her into the classroom where there were five standing workstations that fitted ten cadets each. At the far left side there was a podium on one raised step where the Camp Leaders desk stood, free from the rest. Neville leaned back against it, looking annoyed as always with lowered blonde brows below short cut hair. She was wearing her navy-blue combat leathers as she did at all times, not seeming to bother with her cotton uniform. Two daggers were at her thighs, a further two under her arms sheathed at the holsters around her shoulders, and I spotted a handle sticking out of her right boot.

Mazdon beckoned me to join their table where I saw Kate, Emroyce, Kenyard, Maruto and Penya. Joining them were also Cadets Aros Dixon and Tom Toran, the team Emroyce referred to as the Underdog Team because they were not as brawny as the rest of the year with their strength being attributed to their brains rather than their muscles. They were of no significant backgrounds, with Dixon's family coming from a long line of silk farmers in Eastern Gaithbry and Toran's father being a clock maker in the capital.

At least everyone seemed alert. We had been fortunate to have this lesson in the morning before the other three groups. The disadvantage was that Gravelhorn and his teammate Malloopa were also in this group. They were on the workstation closer to the front, together with the Agility Team, the Prank Team, the Fistfight Boys Team and the Backstabbers Team. Not a wonderful combination of dangerous allies to share a group with, since I very much desired to live and walk out of this class when it finished.

"Okay. Shut up!" Neville shouted and she turned to dip her hands into the terrarium on the desk behind her back.

Without first petrifying one of the deadliest snakes in the Katagoon province, Camp Leader Neville pinched a grip around the snake's mouth before it had a chance to bite her. In a one-handed hold, she paraded the bright-yellow, metre-long, muscle in front of the class.

I shrugged, withdrawing a step as she passed by me, my back pressing up against Ben.

Ben leaned in and tipped his head closer to my ear. "What? It's not like you to fear anything. I know you to be fearless…unhurtable."

"You don't know me as well as you think," I hissed under my breath.

"I know you dared to put the Black Blade against the black-wing king's heart. A snake should be child's play for you."

Neville pinned angry eyes into mine, demanding silence, clearly having heard us whisper.

"This is how you hold the snake. Any other way and you're dead. Got it?" Her glower crossed over all the fifty cadets in one sweep. "I've got enough antidote for five screw-ups." She pointed at five glass cylinders in a stand on the camp leader's desk. "I won't hand them out like you're children, praising you for good behaviour. It's first come, first served. If you're screw-up number six, you better sprint for the infirmary and pray Camp Leader Mewer is there. Don't die in the classroom and make it my mess to clean up."

She pressed herself in between Ben and me, staring at me bitterly before she retrieved a glass cup with a thick edge from the case on our workstation.

"Look carefully, because I'll only show this once." She held up the glass cup and the snake so everyone could see her demonstration. "You push the snake's mouth against the edge and then you loosen your grip slightly to let the snake extend its fangs and bite over the glass. Then you push its snout down, holding right under its eyes, so you get as much poison draining into the cup as possible. When you're done, put the snakes back carefully into their terrariums. I want them unharmed. I like them much better than any of you." A low rumble of laughter went around the classroom. "Focus when you label the snake's breed on the sticker because the poison goes to the third-year cadets' second challenge, and if you get it wrong, they might die from drinking the wrong antidote."

Mazdon shifted nervously, tucking strawberry-blonde hair behind his ear and looked at Kate and me. "Last time I did that challenge, we didn't have to drink anything," he muttered, probably bitter that this time around, it would be even harder to keep the both of us alive.

Neville's arm swept out, still with the poor snake around it, gesturing for the sides of the classroom where hip-high cupboards lined the walls with terrariums atop. "There are twenty-five terrariums with a snake in each, so you work with your teammate."

"There are twenty-six," I corrected, counting them again to be sure.

She pointed toward the terrarium that was bigger than the others. "If you're so stupid to put your hand into that one, you don't deserve a vial of antidote. I call him Terence, and he's a ridge-back desert snake. Fast. Aggressive. And always ready to bite."

"Like Camp Leader Neville's dating profile," Emroyce coughed under his breath.

I chuckled softly but stopped instantly when Neville glared at him.

"Terence's venom works through your blood with instant effect. You'd be dead before you could blink."

The yellow snake Neville was holding went back into its terrarium before she returned to her desk and jumped up to sit on top of the worktop. "Don't feel you have to extract venom during your first lesson. This is practice for the challenge at the end of the month. It's better you're alive then than show courage today. You may start. May the Spirit of Luck be with you!"

I looked around the room at all the different coloured snakes resting peacefully in their homes, probably not wanting to be bothered by cadets. "I think I'm going to team up with Emroyce on this one," I joked, and flashed a smile at Ben, who seemed utterly unafraid.

It wasn't a complete joke, though, as I would have swapped partners in a heartbeat if I could, considering Emroyce's magic was speed. If Ben used death-magic on the snakes, I bet Neville would chop his hands off or plainly kill him and deal with leadership's wrath later.

Ben tipped his head down to look at me darkly. "So little faith in me."

Emroyce, Kenyard and I grouped in the corner around two terrariums, watching thick brown snakes slide against the side in each of them. They were gorgeous with a black pattern on their backs, and the one I was closest to was more than a metre long, circling a few branches, stones and leaves in its habitat.

"Have you guys all volunteered me to go first?" Emroyce asked, his eyes following the snake's movements.

"I'm not sticking my hand in there," Kenyard scoffed, raising his already high eyebrows and twitching his head to make the floppy hair on his unshaven side snatch backwards.

Emroyce's ebony hair fell to his front as he looked down into the terrarium and pinched one of the sticks propped up along one side and poked the snake with it. The aggressive viper turned around so fast I had little time to react before it had hooked its fangs around the bark.

I swallowed. Was I supposed to grip a snake like that during the challenge? Worse thought was that in here, they were in captivity, but along the Spirits' Trek, they would be wild.

"Are you sure you're faster than the snake?" I asked Emroyce in a whisper, so the other cadets wouldn't hear me.

"Yeah, I'll be fine. Wouldn't hurt if Camp Leader Neville could petrify it a little."

"She won't. Not even for you," I told him. "You should trick the snake to bite into the twig again, and at that moment go for its jaw."

"I guess that is as good a plan as any. Here we go."

He held his elbows out so his arms could move quickly before he lowered both his hands down into the terrarium, holding the stick in his left hand and ready to pinch the snake with his right.

"King Blackbone!" Neville shouted out in the classroom, causing us all to turn around. "I specifically said, not that one!"

My heart stopped when I saw Ben holding a grip over Terence's mouth and petting its head as if it was a tame puppy.

"Ouch! Shit!" Emroyce hissed behind my back, so I turned around, seeing him inspecting two bloodied prick holes on his forearm. "I got distracted," he moaned.

The snake had bitten him! "Quickly! The antidote!" I pointed at the vials on the Camp Leader's desk.

He rushed between the four workstations, but Gravelhorn intercepted him before he reached the front.

"Let me help you." Gravelhorn brought his palm out flat on the desk and swiped the entire stand to the floor. The glass vials shattered on impact and the liquid inside them spilled out.

"You twat!" I yelled at Gravelhorn, as I reached the front and hooked a grip around Emroyce's sleeve.

I wouldn't let Emroyce die, but I didn't have magic that could help him, either. I swept my gaze around the room. Who was here? What magic could I work with? Death magic. Strength. Speed. Turning iron into gold. Size changing. Knowledge absorbing. Pattern learning. Extreme focus. Wall-climbing grip. Faint breath. Emotion manipulation. Time slowing. Reading intent from voices.

I panicked. There was nothing useful.

Penya could heal, but he wasn't very good at it, which showed with the sole circle on his left shoulder on his black uniform. Maruto had water wielding and…Maruto!

"Maruto! Can you bend the antidote off the floor and back into a glass?" Maruto also only had one circle of magic strength on her uniform, so I wasn't hopeful.

Maruto shook her head. "Maybe I could, but there are glass shards mixed in with it and I wouldn't be able to separate those from the liquid and then you need the know the dosage not to give Emroyce too much or too little."

Shit! That was a good point.

"Cadet Gravelhorn!" Neville shouted, as she realised all that had happened. "I'll beat the shit out of you later. Everyone! You're dismissed! I need to find Camp Leader Mewer. Cadet Bengrey Go lie down on a bed in the infirmary and have Healer Maid Bengrey tend to you. Don't use any speed magic, it'll quicken the process of the venom circling in your blood."

My heart pounded like a drum in my chest. What if Mewer wasn't at the outpost? He could be anywhere. Without forming a plan with the others, I darted out of the classroom. I didn't need to take it slow and Emroyce meant too much to me to hesitate. Turning the corner, I saw Zayd in the doorway to the admissions office.

"Where is Camp Leader Mewer?" I shouted at him.

He tensed and stepped out into the corridor. "Cadet Coraly, what's going on?"

"Cadet Bengrey has been bitten by a snake, and Cadet Gravelhorn destroyed all the antidote vials on purpose before he could drink one."

Zayd turned fast and aligned with me as we jogged forwards. "Mewer isn't in the infirmary. He's holding a class in the new Optical Illusion room on the basement level of the east wing."

We sprinted past infirmary and down the corridor until we reached the steps and descended them rapidly.

"How long has it been since he was bitten?"

"Not long. A few minutes. But with his metabolism, I worry he won't get the same mercy of time as us others."

"I can take it from here, Angie. You shouldn't watch in case it goes badly."

"You cannot protect me from everything, Zayd. I'm not your housewife," I snapped, but regretted it. I wasn't angry with him. I was just scared I'd lose my friend.

"I didn't mean…" He closed his mouth, and continued running until we reached Mewer, who was standing in front of a large glass window that viewed into a room that was lit up with a red light.

"Camp Leader Mewer!" I screamed, my voice ragged and high-pitched. "Cadet Bengrey has been bitten by a snake." That was all I had to say before Mewer bolted for the stairs and was out of sight.

Then…silence.

The echo of his footsteps faded, and the reality of what had just happened slammed into my chest like a battering ram. I stood rooted to the spot, arms limp at my sides, the stillness pressing in around me. The edges of the corridor seemed to warp, as if they too were folding double by the panic. I gasped, but it was like trying to breathe through a straw. My chest wouldn't rise. My throat closed. My heart galloped, wild and out of control. My knees buckled, and I crumpled to the ground with my back against the cold stone wall, like I might drop straight through it.

My fingers clawed into my scalp as I buried them in my hair, tugging at the roots as if that pain could distract from the bigger one spiralling inside me. Tears threatened, burning behind my eyes, but I bit them back. No. Not here. Not now. Not Emroyce.

Zayd was there, silent but present, watching me as if to assess whether I was going to fall apart. I hadn't even noticed him approaching, as he crouched beside me, slowly, like he was afraid that sudden movement might shatter me completely.

His voice broke through the fog, quiet but firm. "Are you okay?"

I couldn't answer, not yet. My mouth opened, but only a broken exhale came out. The question dangled in the air, unanswered, as I fought to pull myself back from the edge.

I rubbed my hands down my face. "Yeah…no… What if Emroyce dies?"

"He won't," Zayd said, shaking his head as if the gesture would make his answer more convincing. "He's strong."

I didn't want to cast blame…but…Ben had been stupid. I twisted my head with a tired look at Zayd. "Ben petted Terence."

He snorted. "Fool."

"Yeah." I cocked my head back against the stone wall. "All of this is a fool's game."

The bright yellow door beside the large window opened and Valentina walked out cussing, pulling large shards of glass out of her arm. "I should shatter Camp Leader Mewer's bones for this!" Then she saw Zayd and glared at him as if he was in on making her suffer. "Really? Glass shooting out from the walls? One shard was close to cutting my throat." She pushed her purple hair away from her throat as if to show Zayd where the throat was located on the body, as I saw no mark or blood on it.

"Let him heal Emroyce first," I moaned. "Then, by all means, break his bones."

"What happened to Emroyce?" Her eyes showed genuine worry. Not surprising since she was one of the children who grew up with us at the outpost. She knew Emroyce as well as I did.

"Snake bite. You can shatter Cadet Gravelhorn's bones whenever you please, though. He destroyed the antidotes."

"Oh, I will," Valentina said darkly, as if she had just been waiting for an opportunity to use her magic.

Her teammate, Andress Treylieh, walked out behind her, his black uniform shredded in various places as if he had been in a fight with a lion. He was a peculiar man from the Pharanir province where he had grown up in a herb garden. His magic enabled him to persuade people to his will, but he hardly spoke. It was probably so that he wouldn't unintentionally give anyone an instruction to carry out. He didn't even moan at the pain he must be feeling from his fresh wounds. His eyes told a lot though, and right now he seemed upset at what had happened to Emroyce.

"I should go and see if I can help my mother at the infirmary," Valentina muttered. "I know she has been working day and night on the run-up to this challenge to produce enough antivenom. I'm sure I can find her hidden stash if leadership becomes stingy with the handouts."

"Thank you, Valentina," I said, watching her and Cadet Treylieh leave.

Mindlessly, I sank onto the cold stone floor, my legs folding beneath me like they no longer belonged to me. The chilly basement air seeped through my clothes, numbing my skin, but I barely noticed. My mind was screaming at me to move. To get up! To go to the infirmary. But I couldn't make my body obey. The thought of finding out if Emroyce was dead gripped me like a vice. What if he hadn't made it? Losing Emroyce would break me completely?

I wrapped my arms around myself, holding tight, as if I could keep everything from unravelling. I just…couldn't face it. Not yet. Not if it meant seeing a lifeless body where *he* should be.

Zayd turned his head my way. "Were there many cadets in the classroom? You couldn't help Emroyce with your magic?"

I shook my head.

He stood up and held out a hand to me. "I'll walk you back to your room, unless you want to spar to get your mind off things. I have some free time until the last lesson this afternoon."

"What do you teach that late?"

"I have a few third-year cadets, who wanted some private combat tutoring. There are only about fifty cadets left alive from the original two hundred who started out in their year. The remaining cadets must step it up if we're to have enough living bodies to send to the Spirits' Trek after their graduation."

I shuddered at the thought. Only fifty had survived out of two hundred. "I think I'll be taking that offer of a sparring lesson."

20

Zayd rolled up his sleeves as we stepped into the sparring hall, revealing forearms corded with muscle and dusted with faint scars, which were proof of his experience, not vanity. The sharp scent of sweat and polished steel filled the air, clashing with the low thrum of tension that always lived in this place.

Every mat was occupied. First-year cadets, fresh from Neville's gruesome snake lesson, crowded the floor. Third-years loomed nearby, arms folded, waiting for us first-years to finish brewing the toxic concoction they were expected to drink during their challenge. Meanwhile, the second-years were locked in the Optical Illusion room, eating glass from the sound of Valentina's description.

Zayd marched up to the weapons rack and tore two iron rods free with a sharp clatter. He turned and held one out to me.

I stared at the metal in his hand.

Not the iron rod again.

My fingers closed around it, anyway. Of course they did.

I glanced around the room to see if I could find an available mat or notice which team seemed almost done. Murben and Commander Daffron trained on my regular mat in the corner, but they moved off the mat when Zayd and I approached. It made me sick that they thought they had to move for me and Zayd. They weren't worth less than us and why shouldn't they spar? They had to survive this shithole and the Spirits' Trek the same as me.

"Hello Murben," I offered him a sweet smile. It was the least I could do since he was babysitting Flora.

"Good morning, Cadet Coraly," he said as formally as always when addressing me or someone important to Ben. His gaze swept by Zayd and then around the hall. "And what have you done with King Blackbone?"

Good question. Where was Ben? I had left him when rushing off to find Mewer.

"I haven't had the time to dig a grave and bury him yet, I assure you," I joked. "He's around somewhere."

Murben sized up Zayd with hostile dark-brown eyes. "May I offer to take Cadet Coraly off your hands and spar with her? I'm sure you have more important duties to undertake."

Murben was a good sport and highly skilled at combat, so I would be happy to spar with him, but I got the feeling his offer wasn't about me but to help Ben get Zayd off me.

To make matters worse, Zayd circled an arm around my back and rested his palm on my hip. "Sparring with Cadet Coraly is a pleasure I indulge myself. It's no trouble if that's what the black-wings consider training her to be."

Zayd was obviously not referring to them as much as to Ben, and their exchange made me wish I had sought Zoe to spar with.

"Time spent with my future queen…sorry, Cadet Coraly is always an honour," Murben said simply, but there was a clear undertone of a threat in his voice.

Murben had chosen his words carefully and on purpose, as I knew he'd never mistake anyone's formal title.

Zayd's grip around my hip tightened, and he stood tensely beside me as Murben and Commander Daffron passed us to lean against the wall, watching us from a short distance away.

By this point, I wasn't paying any attention to them as I laid eyes on Cadet Kristine Bostee. Her four royal guards pressed up against the wall, watching her as she sparred with her teammate Tony Wix, the weather wielder. How in this world did they end up as a team? Except for Ben, I would say Cadet Wix was the most muscled man at the Bensguard Outpost. It wasn't for nothing that people gave him a wide berth when he walked past in the corridor. He was sparring without a t-shirt, so I noticed something on his back that I had not seen before. His spine seemed deformed, bulging out just by the lip of flesh at the wing opening.

Zayd was on the mat, so I took my boots off and walked up to him. "What's wrong with Cadet Wix's back?"

"Nothing. His skin is pushed out because he has such large wings that they don't fit comfortably inside his back. Now, focus on me."

"Yes, yes, but what would I have to do to get Cadet Bostee's attention? Does she have a hobby or habit of being somewhere alone at any time?"

"What? Why are you asking? You have plenty of friends. She isn't someone who would have time for friendships. King Emille has strict instructions for her education and will snatch her up as soon as she graduates."

I grunted, realising I sounded much like Ben.

"Oh, no," Zayd muttered, lowering his arm. "That was too easy. You didn't argue. What mischief are you planning this time?"

I brought my light crystal from the side pocket of my uniform trousers to show him. "Look what Ben gave me for my birthday."

Zayd's blue eyes widened into pure shock.

"Okay. Not the expression I like to see on your face," I admitted.

As if mentioning Ben's name was a summon, he strode into the sparring hall, and with a discontent expression on his face, he closed in on the mat.

Zayd turned to see him approaching. "You can't give her that." He turned back to face me. "Oh, please, Angie. Do not use that for… Don't approach Bostee. Your magic… Don't do what I think you plan to do."

"Oh, but I will," I crooned.

"You can't tell Cadet Coraly what not to do. She does the precise opposite!" Ben lectured Zayd as if Zayd hadn't known me his entire life. "What about your magic?" Ben asked me. "I really think I ought to know what your magic is. For both of our safety." He looked at the light crystal as if he realised that he had been foolish to provide such a magical tool without knowing more about my power.

"I don't have any magic," I reiterated in a monotone voice, as I had been told to do since my inherited magic activated when I was ten years old.

I had promised father not to tell anyone and after he was sent to the dungeons to wait for his fate for five years, Harvey had persistently reminded me to keep that promise.

Now, more than ever, did I need to keep it a secret, as I felt the two black-wings' eyes prowling by the wall.

"She doesn't have any magic," Zayd emphasised, and it was clearly a standpoint to remind Ben that Zayd knew.

Ben pranced on me, grabbing the wrist to the hand in which I held the crystal. "What are you planning on doing with the crystal?"

I snatched my arm back, pocketed the crystal again, and held both my hands on the iron rod. "I want to ask Cadet Bostee to charge it for me."

"And then?" Zayd asked rhetorically, pushing me into trouble with Ben.

I cocked my chin up and kept my lips sealed tight.

Ben leaned closer, casting a shadow over me, and his stare was intense. Insecure, I wanted to back up, but if I lost all my fights with him, I was screwed. So, I held the line.

"And then? What?" Ben pressed, wanting to know, and I noticed his eyes twitched towards the black-wings by the wall before they settled back on me.

I stayed silent, not losing this stare-off.

Zayd took a step closer, seeming like the third wheel at this point. "What will you do with the magic once the crystal is charged, Cadet Coraly?" Zayd obviously knew, but he wanted me to say it out loud. He knew I couldn't. But if I didn't, I would push Ben further away from me. Zayd had realised that, too.

Swiftly, I knelt and swiped the iron rod at the back of Ben's knees, but he was in no mood for games, and with his muscle strength, he wasn't even near buckling. I pushed off the mat and backed away, keeping the rod in front of me in a fighting stance. "In this place, you earn information," I challenged.

Ben snatched Zayd's iron rod away from him and strode towards me.

Shit! With that look in his eyes, this could hurt.

My brain had forgotten for an instant who he was and how he could so easily sever a thumb, a head…a life.

Think! If he didn't want to hurt me, where would he strike?

I blocked my side and heard the metal clang. I had guessed correctly. So, we were still playing. Good. I leered at him, literally seeing his aggravation grow thick in his expression. Pushing him back, I swung the iron rod in a display around myself to show him it wasn't my first time with this weapon. He clearly didn't mean to smile, and it vanished as quickly as it had settled on his lips.

"Zayd, you might want to step off the mat. This may get ugly," I warned.

Zayd glowered at me in an unspoken warning before he sighed and took a few steps backwards to find the stone floor, crossing his arms over his chest as he watched us.

I swung at Ben's chest, and he gripped the rod with one hand and tugged it out of mine.

"One point to me," he growled, as he tossed it onto the mat in front of himself.

Did he not think I knew that was a trick? He wanted me to go for the rod so he could whack at my side.

I circled him, homing in on my weapon and planning a swift roll across the mat. Certainly, he wouldn't attack me if he didn't have a clean shot in the fear of hitting my head or any other vital part. I faked a move to hit at his rod and his arms twitched, but instead I swerved around him, planning to snatch his hand away from the rod and bend it behind his back in an armlock. But when I tugged at his arm, the beastly muscles on his arm didn't give way one bit. In one move, he circled his arm around my waist and swiped my legs from beneath me before lowering me to the mat. He pressed his palm over my chest to pin me to my back with an incredible force that made it impossible to get away.

"Two points to me," he growled. He lowered his head closer to mine to make a point that I was in over my head if I thought this was a match for him. "How many points do I need to earn information about you?"

"Maybe this isn't at all the way you earn my information," I whispered teasingly.

His expression changed from serious to quizzical.

"Maybe those points are counted in kisses," I whispered and smiled, inconspicuously stroking my palm along his trousers over his cock.

"And who of us would feel it most awkward if I kissed you right now in front of Camp Leader Watson? Not to mention the black-wings and forty mats full of cadets."

I stiffened and removed my hand from his cock. *"I told you to stay out of my head."*

"Ah, so you're going to be cherry picking the moments you feel vulnerable enough to want a kiss?"

I glared at him, feeling I had lost this battle, too.

"Keep your damn shield up, Miss Stone! Imagine the iron and raise it in front of your face!"

I tapped the mat to yield, which I normally never did. He looked worried, but he lifted his hand to let me go. Quickly, I rolled away and used the momentum to stand, walking for my boots. With an angry tug, I brought them with me without first putting them on and left the hall.

I swung by the canteen to grab a pre-made salad and a water bottle to take to my room as I didn't want to eat in here, knowing Ben normally met up with the other four black-wings for lunch, ensuring that they wouldn't miss a meal. I also believed it was during lunch they kept Ben updated with any information they'd garnered spying.

But I had been naïve if I had thought I would eat it in peace and quiet, as Ben entered the room moments after me. I tried to ignore him while he paced the floor, and I started picking at my salad with a wooden fork that hardly pricked through the tomatoes.

I'll be better off using my dagger eating this salad.

When I thought Ben would keep quiet, he started huffing harder, glowering my way every so often. Instead of sitting on the bed's soft mattress it felt like I was sitting on a bed of nails.

I finished a sip of water, putting the bottle down on the bedside table. "What is it?"

He stopped pacing, resting his hands on the backrest of the chair. "When you speak about me with other people around, especially in front of black-wings, please remember that I am a king."

"How can I forget? You keep reminding me. You want me to bow or curtsy?"

"No!" he hollered, and I could tell my remark had frustrated him. "I didn't want to be king, but the alternative at the time of my coronation was worse. Believe me, you don't want Duke Finningham to sit on the throne. I do it to protect the white-wings. So, you could display some sort of token of respect. Do you know where I have been all day? I helped Bengrey to the infirmary when he was bitten and took care of him until Mewer arrived. I stayed until I was sure he'd survive. Do you know why?" He didn't let me speak as he ranted on. "Because I thought it was important to you. And when I went to find you, where were you? Playing with Watson, having run straight back into his arms at the first sign of trouble."

"You took care of Emroyce?" My heart throbbed with gratitude. He had stayed with my friend when I couldn't.

"Yes, so maybe you can repay me by saying *please*. Or answer my questions. Dammit, just agreeing with me once in a while would be progress. You've got black wings, so technically, I'm your king."

I shrugged back and almost tipped the salad out into my bed at his comment.

What? Doesn't Ben know I have both sets of wings? Had I never told him I have white wings, too? Does he think I only *have black wings?* No wonder he had hoped that I would convert to his side.

He raked his fingers through his onyx hair that had grown a bit long compared to how he normally kept it. "I know that's not what you like to hear when your brother was the one sibling born with white wings, but–"

"Wait!" I held up a finger and almost caught my nose with the wooden fork I had in my hand. "What is the score of us telling each other secrets? You've told me two, and I have given you none, is that right?"

"I'm not keeping scores, Angelica! That's not the point! Sharing. Trusting. Those are the objectives."

Be it so, but this information I could give him. Most people at the Bensguard Outpost already knew. I put my lunch on the bedside table.

"Just to be clear. If I have black wings, I must obey you, but if I have white wings, you'll refrain from giving me any orders?"

His confused mien was amusing to watch. I slowly unbuttoned my shirt, as it didn't have the slit in the back like the flight uniforms.

He observed my small circling movements as I undid each button and sensually tugged the fabric off each shoulder. It was as if each touch mesmerised him, making him wait keenly to ogle at my naked skin.

"Ben?"

"Um," he grunted, as if brought out of an enthral, and his eyes moved up to look into mine, having lost track of what we were talking about.

I stood from the bed and removed my shirt entirely, pushing my chest out, hoping that seeing my breasts would weaken his resolve. "Do we have a deal?"

He frowned, his eyes twitching, wanting to dip lower but he kept the eye-contact. "But you don't have white wings. I have seen them. They are black."

A slow, cunning smile curled on my lips, and I drank in the silence that followed to set the tension for my final point to win this argument. "Are you sure?"

I twitched my back to snap them out. The two sets of wings caught in one another, so I fought to bring out the chosen pair. I jutted my side out as my left wing caught in another bone of the black wing, but then the familiar rasp of pain shot through my flesh as they popped out.

Ben gaped as he silently watched them, lost for words, it seemed. "So, this is your magic? You're a chameleon? You can change their colour?"

I savoured the moment, watching his frustration flicker across his face. "No. Your guess isn't even close. They can't change colour." My voice was dripping with smug amusement, revelling in my victory.

It wasn't that I wanted to gloat, but I had to demand respect so he would at least treat me as his equal when we were on White Wing Territory.

His hold on the backrest tightened until his knuckles turned white. "But I saw them. They were black before."

"Nope." I caressed the feathers of my wing like it was a lover. "These have always been white." Then the smirk settled over my mouth again. "These are black." I twitched out my back once more and forced my muscles to bend the second pair out.

Ben stumbled backwards, grabbing in the air to steady himself but found nothing and dropped down on his bed. "You've got two sets of wings, both white and black."

"Correct."

I had never seen his face this long, shocked as if he had been slapped across his face. His breath caught mid-exhale as he spat out, "That's not normal."

A pang of hurt stung inside me. I knew I was abnormal. My two pairs of wings had nothing to do with my magic. I was born with this deformity. Until now no one had said anything about them that made me feel ashamed. I snatched them both back inside me with embarrassing difficulty and picked my shirt up from my bed to put it on. The finger movements this time were snappy and irate.

He pushed off the bed and raced to my side, putting his hand over mine as I was about to do the last button.

"That came out wrong," he muttered. "I only meant that you having two pairs of wings must have a greater meaning than the trivial everyday matters. What I should have said was that they are extraordinary."

I rolled my eyes at him. "You're not privileged to change your reaction to first impressions, not even being a king."

"My first impression wasn't what I said. It was what I thought." He narrowed his eyes at me when I craned my head forward to listen more intently. "And now you wish you had consented to listening to my thoughts."

Really? He was going to play that card? Two could play that game. "If you tell me what your initial thoughts were, I will consent."

He scanned my facial expression in silence for two heartbeats. "Are you sure? You'll agree to me speaking into your mind and you can speak into mine, if I tell you? Maybe you want time to think about that. My thoughts weren't that elaborate."

I was sure, and truly tired of keeping my distance from him. I held my hand out to shake on it. "Deal?"

He shook my hand, yet he spoke to me out loud. "I was gripped with fear."

"Fear?"

"I saw you struggling to bring them out. It took way too long. In a battle and with the need to take off quickly, that could bring upon your death. Two sets will be heavy for your little body to carry, and they'll weigh you down. You won't be able to fly as long before you need rest, and you probably can't ascend at a forty-five degree angle. They will put you in danger when journeying through the Spirits' Trek."

Of course, he had instantly realised those things. That's why he had held his position from a young age and was still the king.

My jaw tightened and I forced myself to stand straighter, putting on a mask of determination. "I'm fine. Zayd is giving me extra lessons."

Ben's fists curled at his sides. "From now on, I'm taking over your coaching. This is too important to get wrong. Let's go."

"Now? No. I must visit the infirmary to see that Emroyce is okay."

"You'd rather spend time on someone who may or may not be dead any coming day, than making sure that you survive in the future?"

I nodded. "Without a doubt. Maybe after dinner."

"Six o'clock. The far end of the field. Don't be late."

I nodded and turned on my heel to leave the room, heading for the infirmary, and found the bed Emroyce was lying on. I looked at one of the fiercest fighters I have ever known and saw a broken spirit within him. His legs were lying flat out in the bed with a thin blanket covering him up to his waist where a white infirmary gown began. His face looked grim, with his long black hair draping like curtains at the sides of his cheeks, showing more shadowed hollows above his cheekbones than I had ever seen on him before.

I leaned in with my thighs against the bed frame. "How are you feeling?"

"Fantastic." He stared up at the ceiling.

I looked around to verify that we were alone and none of the healers were around. His sister was a distance away in the hall, but I doubted she could hear us.

I glanced at the bandage covering the bite. "Does it hurt?"

"Nothing can hurt me."

"What a true soldier," I mocked. "Can we speak as friends now? You don't need to act all brave in front of me. When will you be up on your feet again?"

He sighed, avoiding eye-contact. "Mewer has given me this tonic made from elder leaves, barley, walnuts, onions, salt and honey to draw the toxin out, and if I have to drink much more of it, I'll be sick. Even the smell of it makes me gag. No good does it do me, either. Mewer said he didn't get to me in time. I'll have reduced magic abilities because of the nerve damage. But I'm fine. Fern is working on my discharge paperwork, but…" he muttered, eyes glossing over. "I'll always be…less me."

"Aw, Emroyce, I'm so sorry. But hey, you're so amazing, even without magic."

"Yeah, fucking awesome!" The confidence didn't reach his eyes.

"They might let you compete on the obstacle course," I said gently, trying to give him some encouragement.

"Silver lining," he muttered, but I could have forgotten how to breathe, watching his misery.

The warm glow in his amber eyes was gone. The happy, carefree soldier I had always known had been defeated by his own body…by a snake, because Neville had shouted at Ben and distracted him. If Ben would have never touched the snake he was told not to play with, none of this would have happened. Hopefully, time would make him realise how proficient he was the way he had been born, and without magic. Anger grew in the pit of my stomach at seeing him so deflated. He was stronger than this. If he couldn't see it, I'd make him see it.

"Stop moping and get to your damn feet, Emroyce! Self-pity isn't a good colour on you. You haven't even been outside to test your strength. Maybe it isn't that bad."

He chuckled. "Glad to see you keep your fighting spirit about you. You haven't changed one bit."

"Oh, I have! I've become even more stubborn living in the Black Wing Territory, knowing I had to be, in order to survive. Right now, is no different for you. You'll graduate at the top of our class, and you'll hike through the Spirits' Trek just like your father did and gain three more magical abilities. You'll have one too many and will have to choose which one to get rid of. The magic isn't who you are. It's a gift you can receive and give away. To be fast, isn't who you are. You're a Bengrey. A legacy of solid warriors."

"Wow, Angie. They should employ you as the herald that rouses the troops before the battle. Damn, you can get the dead to feel alive."

"Good! Now, get your dumb-arse off the bed and dress in your uniform. We'll go out to the obstacle course and test your speed."

"Cadet Coraly!" my brother called across the threshold.

I turned to face him. "Yes, Captain!"

"Come to my office immediately. I have an urgent mission for you. You too, Cadet Bengrey."

Harvey left me gawking at the empty doorway, having left as quickly as he had arrived, hurling out his orders.

"This isn't right," I stammered to Emroyce. "He can't ask you to go out on a mission when you haven't recovered yet."

"What happened to your sharp tongue, Cadet Coraly? Wasn't it you who roused me a minute ago to get off my dumb arse?"

"Yes, to test yourself on the obstacle course, not to go on patrol."

Emroyce swung his legs over the edge of the bed with a grin that suggested mischief rather than concern. "We're just first-year cadets. I doubt it'll be dangerous. Not even your brother is that cruel."

I snorted, not so sure. "Fingers crossed," I muttered, walking over to the side-table. The drawer creaked open with a familiar scrape of wood, and I pulled out a folded clean uniform, the fabric still smelling faintly of detergent. I tossed the clothes over to him without looking. "Let's see how fast you can get dressed."

There was a sudden rush of air behind me, a soft swoosh lifted a few strands of my hair, and I knew he'd activated his speed magic again. I started counting under my breath.

One… two… three… four–

"Ready!" he called.

I turned and gave him a short nod, noting with concealed admiration how not a thread on him was out of place. "Five seconds. Impressive," I said flatly, not to inflate his ego too much.

He winked, cocky and effortlessly charming, before turning to exchange a few quiet words with his sister. I didn't hear them. My mind was already moving ahead, nerves fluttering like restless wings in my chest.

We stepped into the hallway, boots thudding softly against the stone floor, our shadows dancing alongside us in the low morning light. The academy felt too quiet, the kind of quiet that precedes a storm. Something in the air had shifted.

When we reached the Captain's Office, the door yawned open, the scent of burnt parchment and sweat wafting out like a warning. We entered slowly.

Inside, Mazdon, Kate, and Zayd were already gathered in a tense huddle in front of Harvey's desk. No one spoke. Zayd's arms were crossed tightly across his chest, jaw clenched. Mazdon looked up, his eyes glinted with something I couldn't place. Suspicion? Worry?

Harvey stood behind the desk like a stone pillar, his fingers steepled beneath his chin.

When we were all gathered and he had our attention, Harvey finally spoke, his voice low and cold, like the crack of ice splitting.

"I'm sending you out on patrol to the boarder."

The room dropped ten degrees. Emroyce stiffened beside me.

That was beyond the area of a normal routine patrol and too advanced for first-years if enemy activity had been spotted. The mission specification was very odd.

The silence was charged with…a palpable dread…something was wrong.

Very wrong.

21

The assignment was simple. Patrol the mountains to the Southwest near the border with the Black Wing Territory. Spies had been spotted and Harvey wanted to know whether it seemed they'd attack, or whether they were plotting some other plan. We were told not to engage with them. Harvey ordered Zayd to use his far-sight and Mazdon his hearing, but I wasn't sure what use Emroyce, Kate or I were on this mission. Perhaps it was solely for their protection.

We rode on horses the first two-hour stretch, and when we reached the mountain, we calculated the distance and angle before we set off flying upwards.

"You're late. Where are you?" Ben roared in my head. *"My ears are humming hard."*

Shit! I had forgotten about our coaching session.

"Captain Coraly sent me on a mission."

"Why didn't you tell me?"

"It was so sudden and urgent. I can't really focus on you now, or I'll fall."

"Fall? Where are you?"

"I'm flying and you aren't allowed to come."

"Who is with you?"

"If I say, Zayd, will you freak out?"

"Are you two alone?"

"No. Mazdon, Kate and Emroyce are also here."

He grunted the grunt I though meant he didn't like it but he found it acceptable. *"Those are the only people who know about your magic."*

"Don't read into this. I'm safe. It's just a spy patrol mission. Leave me to it, or I'll plummet to my death."

The humming in my ears from our bond became more agonising the further away from him I flew, but at least he had gone silent.

The mountain east of a narrow passage that we were going to patrol rose majestically straight ahead. With its twin on the other side of the pass, they looked like two natural guard towers with the mountain ridge serving as a divide running along the border. I ascended to land together with the others, but a small miscalculation made me set foot on an outcrop twenty metres from the top. The wall didn't have a steep incline, so it was an easy climb to make it to the top platform. Kate joined me, but the men still had the strength to land atop the ridge. I didn't curse at my failure because I was just so happy that Emroyce had managed the flight perfectly. Maybe he would realise that he was worthy of being called an excellent soldier despite his reduced speed magic.

"I was just about to practise my magic with Captain La Roy," Kate muttered. "Harvey could have chosen any of the camp leaders or third-year cadets to do this patrol. This doesn't make sense, and if he doesn't explain it to me when we get back, I'll pry it out of his mouth and lungs."

I smiled at her as she angrily stomped the narrow, pebbled path next to me that couldn't host more than two people abreast. She looked ready for a fight, her fire-red hair secured in a sleek ponytail pulled tight to her head and she wore multiple daggers strapped in holsters around body parts I didn't even know one could arm.

"He'll like that," I said with a leer.

She twitched in her step, glaring at me lethally with her jade eye and two deep lines between her brows. "What the heck is that supposed to mean?"

I dropped my smile, my own wrinkles tightened between my brows. "You do know that he has always had a thing for you. I wouldn't put it past him to send us on this wild goose chase just to get you away from Captain La Roy."

"Then I'll break his arm as well."

"For loving you?"

"Yes!" The spark of anger in those jade eyes showed me just how annoyed she was at the information. "Men!" she cussed. "I have loved your brother for years. Since I was thirteen, and he helped me gain control of my magic. Throughout the years, I batted my eyelashes, wanting him to look my way. I dressed in the thinnest materials, hoping he would touch me. But he saw me as nothing more than Mazdon's baby sister. And what? Because another man pays me attention, he decides to mess with me? For how long have you known?"

I bit the side of my lip, wondering whether my brother would punish me for telling her. "Since you were thirteen," I said, cringing.

She splayed her hands in the air as if to say, 'and you couldn't have told me'. "My brother?"

"Yep. Mazdon knows, too."

"Great!" She cocked her head up towards the top. "I'll deal with you later, brother," she said without increasing the strength in her voice, knowing Mazdon would hear her. "And why has no one told me? What has kept Harvey away?"

The path got narrower, so I waited for her to walk ahead of me. "His legacy. His guilt. I don't know. Maybe his ambition to become captain and knowing you would at one time become his cadet. Who knows what he's thinking? He could be waiting it out until you join another unit after graduation and then he has free rein to court you."

"That is still years away!" she moaned. "And what? He thinks he can practise on other women whilst he waits and then I should accept him when he comes knocking?"

"As far as I'm aware, I have never seen him dating anyone else."

She massaged her hand over her chest as if she was touched by learning that he was holding out for her. But I couldn't say more, as I had only made guesswork of what my brother was thinking, or what he was intending to do about their relationship in the future. Not that I needed to. Kate was that sort of person who wouldn't shy away from confronting him about it herself. So, my work was done.

We reached the top where the men had huddled themselves behind a boulder and were spying out over the field below belonging to the Black Wing Territory. Zayd was particularly tense, his eyes focusing far away. Two hours passed, and this stake-out was becoming boring. There hadn't been the slightest sighting of any people at all. What source had told Harvey that there were black-wings spying here?

The humming in my ears started crackling, and I had noticed the sound happened right before Ben was about to speak in my mind.

"The Royal Counsellor, Arnold Desry, is at the outpost. That's probably why your brother has sent you away with anyone who you might have confided in and who know of your magic. For some reason, Captain Coraly doesn't want Counsellor Desry to talk to you again."

"Again? I have never been in the same room as Counsellor Desry."

"Interesting."

"What is interesting?"

"Counsellor Desry's magic is to see the greatness in your soul and seeing your death. Why would your brother not want you to meet him?"

"Harvey probably doesn't want to find out when I die."

Ben's grunt drawled as if he wasn't convinced.

"Captain Coraly has locked me in the dungeon. I had forgotten how cosy this cell was."

I continued walking in Kate's footsteps but slowed to fall behind. *"Why would he do that? None of this makes any sense."*

"It makes perfect sense. The captain isn't confident you wouldn't have confessed things

to me or that I read your mind. As a result, he doesn't want me talking to the Counsellor, either. He's concerned I could strike deals with the Counsellor that benefited me greatly but put your brother on his knees."

"With what information?"

"Secrets."

I sighed. *"You wouldn't do that to me, would you?"*

"I'm hurt that you had to ask. Be careful out there."

The crackling stopped. He had left my mind. Arms wrapped tightly around myself, I keep my cracking heart together, as his words echoed in my mind with his disappointment. *I'm hurt that you had to ask.* I hated leaving the words hanging in the air. My chest ached, feeling hollow without his presence to fill it with…his part of our soul that made it feel complete. I waited, with a lump in my throat and held on to the tiniest hope that he would talk to me again. But he didn't and that hollow in my chest seemed to grow bigger.

Loose stones littered the ridge like a broken path. One wrong step and I'd be nursing a shattered ankle. I moved carefully, making my way through the debris, my eyes fixed on the solitary navy-blue uniform that stood out among the sea of cadets in black.

"Camp Leader Watson," I said, my voice formal and steady as I came to a stop beside him. We were on a mission, after all. Protocol mattered.

But the moment the words left my mouth, the others turned to look at me, confused. Their eyes silently asked the same question: *What are you doing?* Among friends, ranks were usually left at the door. We didn't stand on ceremony when the threat wasn't breathing down our necks.

Zayd slowly turned to face me, brows raised in disbelief. His lips quirked with a mix of confusion and mild mockery. "*Camp Leader Watson?*" he repeated, scoffing. "Seriously?"

Kate jammed an elbow into my side. "What is going on between you two?"

"Ben," Mazdon whispered towards his sister before he looked at Zayd. "Angie addressed you correctly."

"Thank you, Maz," I chirped.

"No, she didn't," Zayd growled. "By now it should be, Babe, Fiancé, or my warrior, if it wasn't for the monster she keeps in her room."

I gasped and gawked at him, lost for words for a moment.

He raked his fingers through his gelled-up hair and focused his blue eyes on me. "You used to call me 'my warrior'. Especially when we made love. Does, 'harder my warrior' or 'faster my warrior' ring any bells?"

"Spirits! Zayd! Too private, don't you think?" With a sweeping arm through the air, I gestured for him that we had an audience.

"I hope King Blackbone betrays you to show his true colours soon enough, so we can get back to being warriors and leave this nonsense behind."

My eyes watered, stinging fiercely as the tears wanted their release. Anxiety I recognised from my past when first called a traitor gripped like an iron gauntlet over my heart. *I can't breathe.* My mouth went dry, and I had to open the top button of my uniform, but it did little to help my breathing.

Mazdon had obviously heard the signs of my panic and rushed to envelop his arms around me. "Calm, Angie. Steady."

"Should I punch Zayd in the face?" Emroyce asked.

I shook my head, although it would have served him right. But I didn't want Emroyce to get involved in the quarrel between Zayd and me.

Zayd had taken it as no more than background noise as he stood with the unshakable confidence of a man who saw no fault in his actions. "What have I done wrong? She's the one out of line."

In my peripheral view, I could see Mazdon shake his head in a rebuke towards Zayd.

Still holding onto Mazdon, so as not to buckle to my knees, I twisted my head towards Zayd. "I have done nothing wrong. Leaving the White Wing Territory was Harvey's order. Sharing a room and being teammates with King Blackbone were also Harvey's orders!"

"As if you haven't liked it. Tell yourself what you want, Angie, but you have feelings for our enemy king. Tell me I'm wrong."

I had to switch to breathe through my mouth and felt such relief when my ears started crackling.

"Captain Coraly has let me out of the dungeon and told me to call you home. The Counsellor has left the outpost."

"Okay. Thank you."

"Your voice is shaking. Why?" Ben's voice was harsh and demanding.

"I'm okay."

"Perhaps in the eyes of those who don't care about you." I felt his range building in my gut. Fast. *"Are you hurt? In danger?"*

"No. Zayd is being a prick."

"Tell him to stop or I'll kill him."

"Ben!" I scolded. *"See you in two hours."*

I threw up the mental shield to shut any further comments out of my head.

"Ben says Harvey has called us home."

"Oh, what great timing of our noble king to come to your rescue. So adorable that you speak in each other's minds now. So, not soul bound then, but rather soulmates," Zayd hissed. "How do we know the order is from Harvey and not from King Blackbone, wanting to lure us away from scouting his men?"

With the back of my hand, I dried the tears that had dampened my skin and inhaled a large breath, releasing it slowly. Purely to piss Zayd off, I flicked my black wings out along my body and ran towards the cliff edge and jumped out, sailing on the wind to get off this mountain.

My heart stung, and I wondered if this was how it would feel to be bitten by Terence and have your blood filled with venom. Wingbeats pushed the air next to me like a second heartbeat as Mazdon caught up with me. Emroyce flew a few metres behind with Kate, and lastly, Zayd sulked. When we landed and approached the horses, Zayd grumbled to himself, as if he tried to find words to talk to me, maybe to utter an apology, but I paid him no attention. I wasn't even sure I cared to hear an apology. The atmosphere was more than tense between us, riding in silence all the way back to the Bensguard Outpost.

We arrived home in the early morning, and I was exhausted and still angry with Zayd. He didn't get another chance to apologise as Ben stood by the stable doors with a shoulder leaning against the wall and angry glares that he cast at him. My heart warmed. It was endearing to know that he had come here to meet me, and goodness knew how long he had patiently waited here for my return.

The stable master and Brian were ready to tend to the horses and when I had handed mine over, Ben pushed off the wall and ensured Zayd couldn't get near me, keeping his wings ready to wrap around me if need be. My friends headed for the military building and Ben's head snapped away from watching me to search through them.

"Wait, Cadet Bengrey. A word," Ben said, and his voice wasn't like the one he used when talking to other cadets.

The tone of his voice was sombre to the point it made my skin crawl. What did Ben want with Emroyce? I looked up to see his eyes sorrow-filled, and when he noticed I was looking at him, he wrapped one wing around my back.

When the others had walked through the building doors, Emroyce squared up with Ben. "You wanted a word…Ben," he said, and my heart almost burst out of my chest with love for my friend. He had called him Ben. Not Enemy. Not black-wing king. Not filth.

Ben's back rolled up to a stretch as if he rode on the wave of joy I felt.

"Better I am bearer of bad news than your friends."

"Any friend of Angie's is a friend of mine," he interrupted.

Ben nodded his thanks. "I'm afraid I must inform you of a tragedy. It may come as a shock, and I urge you to keep calm and seek those you can confide in before you do anything reckless."

My nerves stung under my skin. What had happened whilst we were gone? What had Counsellor Desry done?

"I appreciate your warning and concerns," Emroyce said. "I have already lost half of my magic today, so I doubt it could be worse."

Ben bit his lip as if he knew it would be worse. I leaned in closer to him, placing all my attention into what he would tell. My heart pounded. If a king with such brutal upbringing as Ben hesitated to tell the news, it would be bad.

"When Counsellor Desry couldn't garner information from Captain Coraly about Cadet Coraly's nature, he went to the next best person. When your sister said she knew nothing and wouldn't speak, he resorted to the unforgivable method of using your nephew's mind. A small body like that… It rendered him dumb after he had finished. I'm truly sorry. Leadership had locked me in the dungeon, so I couldn't interfere, or I would have."

"What!" Emroyce roared and twisted on his heel, darting towards the infirmary.

I couldn't hold myself together anymore. Tears streamed down my cheeks. Ben wrapped both his wings around me to seal me from anyone's view and I curled my fingers around the fabric of his shirt to hold on. Ben left me to grieve a long while in silence, keeping me cocooned to his chest.

My lungs hiccupped between my breaths. "Fern must be so upset."

"Any mother would be distraught if their child's mind was destroyed like Robin's. Any uncle would want to sever Counsellor Desry's head from his shoulders."

"He can't!" I sobbed. "His father lashed out at the king, and they killed him for it. King Emille wouldn't hesitate to kill the entire Bengrey family if it happened again."

"I'm aware. It was probably Counsellor Desry's intention. We must ensure we keep an eye on Bengrey and provide any support he needs."

"Thank you."

"Don't thank me. I did nothing. I was locked up," he growled.

"Yes, but you care for my friends."

"Of course." He lifted one wing so he could peer inside to see me. "Can you walk, or do you need me to carry you to our room?" His offer was filled with warmth and compassion, devoid of any intention to insult me.

I let go of his shirt. "I'll walk."

Cadets moved about in the corridors between their dorm rooms and the common rooms, but I walked past them without registering who I passed, or what they were talking about. I almost crashed into a cart from the central depot that stood in the middle of the corridor. Everything was a blur. Poor Robin. How could a powerful man abuse a three-year-old that way? Ruin his mind and life forever.

We entered our room and Ben's warm hands immediately slid up either side of my cheeks, gently pressing his lips to mine. It was exactly what I needed. My mind to be obliterated by passion and pleasure. Not feeling the grief and hardship of the real world. I wanted Ben to sweep me into a world where everything was bliss, and he must've been doing something to calm my emotions through our bond because it was working.

Hungry for much, much more, I pressed myself against him, slipping my tongue into his mouth and tasting every bit of it, nibbling on his lips. I curved my arms around his neck like they had latched on forever and would never let go. He groaned my name, as if he was confirming this was real, but there was also a hint of warning.

He couldn't get my shirt off fast enough. One hard rip and all my buttons snapped and pinged against items around the room as they shot in all directions. Ben savagely kissed down my neck, elevating my lust and satisfying it in the same breath. I gave way with my arms around his neck for him to ravage the swell of my breasts. He kissed my entire body as if searching for the piece of me that would satisfy him but could not find it.

In a rough lift, he swooped me up to sit on his waist as he carried me to my bed and laid us down. I tipped my head down to see him kiss and nip my skin. Never had I seen his eyes so wild and famished. I closed my eyes to feel every kiss, every touch, every pump of my blood as my arousal intensified. Ben's kisses trailed upwards once more, devouring my lips and mouth as if he had found the woman that he had been looking for all his life. His tongue pushed into my mouth at the same time as his fingers slid below the line of my trousers.

Black smoke billowed from his hands, and he pulled away and snatched out his hand from my trousers like he had been scolded. He rested his forehead on my shoulder, panting with his eyes closed.

"I can't lose control. That was too close." He seemed to be angry with himself. Hating who he was, even.

"It's okay. We got further than last time. Progress." Although, it didn't truly feel like a triumph. It felt like frustration was going to burn me alive.

I took a few deep breaths, playing with his black hair around my fingers.

He tipped to his side and curved one wing around me, so I wouldn't fall out of bed. His finger started lazily tracing the clammy skin over my stomach and around my navel. "If this is all it can be, will it be enough?"

He looked so vulnerable when he put those red eyes on mine. Clearly, he couldn't shake the fear that he wasn't enough. He worried I'd see that he wasn't flawless, falling short of the man he believed I deserved. Doubt ate away at a confident king who had armies and power at his disposal to conquer anything but me. But maybe this was exactly what kings looked like when they were stripped away from everything and living in an enemy camp.

What could I answer a man who had opened himself up to such exposure when behind it all lay so many secrets and barriers that pulled us apart?

"I guess that depends on what secrets you keep," I finally answered.

He nodded, and his sigh was so large, I was glad he held a wing around me or his chest would probably have pushed me out of bed. "What is not good enough, though, is your ability to fly. You scared me senseless when you said you were at risk of falling from the sky just because you lost focus when talking to me. To get the strength up in your wing muscles is important. You can't postpone practising. We should get some time in tomorrow morning before classes."

"Tomorrow morning, I have war updates, so we'll need to get up early. Sure you don't want to sleep in, since you can't join war updates? Combat lesson isn't until eleven."

"I'll wake you up at six and that leaves us thirty minutes to get ready and an hour and a half to practise before war updates. Don't even get me started thinking about combat. Camp Leader Watson teaches that, and I have a good urge to break his neck."

"Feel free to use your magic and end it quickly," I said bitterly, not really meaning it, and Ben knew it but seemed amused, nonetheless.

"So…" He traced his finger over my bottom lip. "You two had a fight, uh?"

I bit gently at his finger before turning my head away. "I don't want to talk about it."

He chased my cheek with his palm, turning me back to make eye-contact. "Oh, come on. This is a feast for me."

"Your favourite pudding is my misery?"

"No." He could barely contain his grin, and I could almost feel the sheer thrill of his victory buzzing under his skin. "This is only the starter, and it's Camp Leader Watson's misery I'm savouring. My pudding is his misery when we marry."

He was revelling in this a bit too much and I wanted to wipe that self-satisfied smug right off his face. "That's a bit premature, isn't it?"

He bit back a chuckle. "If you don't tell me the gossip, I'll extract it from your mind myself."

"Don't you dare," I warned, but I feared he was seriously enjoying this.

"Oh, I dare." The gleam in his eyes was unmistakable like he had stolen my mischievous spark. "I can't pass up on this amusement. Let's practise your mental shields. Keep me out, or I'll find out why you're angry with Camp Leader Watson."

"Ben!" I told him sternly, staring straight into his eyes. "I don't want to play games right now."

Ben gave one silent nod and kept circling his finger over my chest, but his eyes had turned vacant as he brooded over something. His face showed various expressions: frowning, pinching his lips and squeezing his face together as if he recalled something painful. His focus returned, and he moved his finger to my lips, where he also held his gaze.

"Angelica…" he said, but hesitated, and I waited because I gathered that he was about to say something that wasn't easy for him.

Inhaling a large breath, he let it out slowly, tracing his finger over the skin around my cheekbones. He moved his hip and tilted his torso to align himself to see my face better. He bit his lip. I found his nervousness adorable and kept observing him. His heart pounded so hard I noticed his skin moving slightly with each beat. Another deep breath. Finally, his ruby eyes dared meet mine as he looked at me.

He wet his lips. "Angelica Coraly, I have fallen in love with you," he whispered, the words seeming irrevocable.

22

Waking up with a smile on my face was rare nowadays, but I had fallen asleep to the words of the black-wing king telling me he loved me.

My smile faded.

I hadn't been brave enough to return those words and it gnawed on me like someone was digging out pieces of my heart with a shovel to leave a large hole. It was those damned secrets that blocked the 'love' word from leaving my lips.

Ben was still lying beside me the way he had fallen asleep, fully clothed in his uniform. I had mine on too, save the buttons on my shirt. I twisted my wrist to see my watch showing five fifty in the morning. Trapped under Ben's arm and wing, I watched him sleep; a serene portrait when the weight of the world wasn't on his shoulders.

This was a sight I could live with waking up to every morning: soft breathing, three-day stubble, large pectoral bobbing my hand up and down as it rested on one side of his chest. Beautiful. Not able to refuse the urge, I stretched up and kissed gently at his full lips. They pulled into a wide smile immediately and the enormous body began moving, arms coiling around me, and as if I weighed nothing, as he pulled me towards him. He didn't open his eyes, as he stole more kisses.

"Is it morning already?"

With my palm still on his chest, I gave it a tap. "Yep. Five fifty-two."

"I have changed my mind. I'm going to keep you with me in bed until eleven."

His arms tightened around me, trapping me to his torso, so I rested my head on his chest, hearing his heart beat. "Nice try, coach, but I don't believe you for one second. You're more than keen on dragging me out on the field to test my wings."

"Wanting, and needing for your own safety, are two different matters. I *want* to stay in bed." He kissed the top of my head. "You can hit the shower first whilst I stretch and wake up and since you're half undressed already." He slowly pushed his hand underneath my bra to cup my breast, gauging my reaction.

I moaned out a small sound through my nose, and that made him stop and retract his hand to rest at his side. Unfortunately for him, his cock had already given him away, growing hard against my abdomen.

"No need to take turns. We could both go."

"You said the shower was too small to fit us both."

"That was when your ego was tenfold what it is now."

He grunted, his expression reverting to that of an unyielding king. "The answer is still no. Imagine the restraint on my death magic necessary when seeing…touching you naked in the shower." He shuddered and loosened his grip around me.

"So, you were bluffing before, when you wanted to join me?"

"No. Then, I wanted to do it for fun. Now, I can't do that because I care if you live or die."

So, I guess he won't spoil me often by saying those three lovely words. Fine.

After I had tugged his wing free from under me to the sound of his impish chuckling, I climbed out of bed. Really? You want to play?

"You know when you took the Black Blade away from me?"

He tensed. "Yes."

"That wasn't very nice." I lost the shirt and undid my bra from my back, slowly sliding the straps down my arms and dropped it suggestively onto the floor.

His eyes went wide at seeing my naked breasts.

Then I undid the button to my trousers and pulled them down slowly, kicking the creased fabric off my feet before stretching my hands above my head to tie up my hair in a messy bun in just my black lace knickers.

He was staring – hard.

His eyes punctuated heat where they roved across my skin.

I sashayed towards the bathroom.

Ben turned onto his back, staring at the ceiling. "You're going to kill me. Or someone else. This isn't good for my control."

"Maybe next time, you'll let me keep my toys."

He grunted darkly, spoiling the mood. "I told you. You can have anything you want, except that blade."

"That's precisely why I want that blade."

"What is beyond me is how you failed to steal it and allow yourself to get caught by Sergeant Davis if your magic is so powerful that it can't be spoken of."

He was fishing for information again and I couldn't be certain to what end, so I pinned my lips into a thin line and shook my head, showing him that I wasn't budging.

Like a ball of feathers, he rolled out of bed, and the overwhelming power that always radiated from him slammed against me. He snatched away his wings, and passed me to go to the wardrobe, tearing a wrinkle-free shirt off a hanger. "I'll meet you out on the field after your shower," he murmured, buttoning the shirt as he went over to the desk, quickly rummaging around the drawers, and picking up a pen and paper. "I'll shower when I get back."

Shamelessly, I paused in the bathroom doorway to watch his muscular torso disappear behind the buttons, and smirked at him when turning around, seeing me gawking. He kissed my forehead as he passed by to get to the door, and then he left without looking back.

As I was getting ready, I couldn't help thinking about how much Ben had sacrificed for me in being here. He had said he had stayed because he found it intriguing to see how I would survive, but the way he acted around me didn't support his claim. He protected me at every turn and told me his secrets bit by bit. Yet, I had given him nothing in return. There were no logical reasons I could imagine for which he would betray me once he had gotten the information he had come here to get. But a king staying here purely because he cared for me was also an absurd thought. Wasn't it? He was risking his life during every second in which he stayed by my side. There were people at the outpost strong enough to end him and plenty who would do it purely to get rid of me. A mutt. A mutt and a king. I snorted.

"If you ever call yourself a mutt again, I'll take you over my knee."

My thoughts had been borderline passive, so I was ready to scold him for having listened to them, but instead, I relaxed and smiled. *"Promise?"*

I only heard a grunt echoing through my mind.

"Mutt, mutt, mutt, mutt, mutt, mutt!" I shouted.

"Angelica, you're full of mischief. Dare to come out here?"

"On my way!"

I buckled the last leg strap around my thigh and shoved the blades in before taking quick steps out to the far end of the field by the archery area, waving at Cadet Ashton Hall, who was already out training with his teammate; who also was his father. Hall nodded once in acknowledgment. His veteran infantry father, who still looked sour, having returned for a repeat of the academy from his retirement, swatted the back of his head. Then he pointed at the target board. Hall anchored another arrow, drew the bowstring back, and put his cheek to rest on his thumb before letting it fly. I paused in my step to watch it hit the bullseye and then carried on walking to meet Ben at the other corner of the field.

From a distance away, I noticed he was talking to someone, but there was no one in sight. Tomason! She had cloaked herself whilst talking to him. My blood boiled. Jealousy burned inside me.

When I reached his side, he had stopped moving his lips and smiled at me.

I pinned my hand to my hip, not letting his smiles disarm me. "Do you talk to yourself often?"

His eyes widened a fraction before masking his intentions. "I get the best answers that way." His gaze was searching for an escape from my interrogation, looking across the field to shift the focus away from him.

I grimaced at him, and he walked around me to scan the wing-slits at my back.

Wasn't he going to tell me what he had been talking to Tomason about? Surely, he couldn't believe I had bought his excuse and hadn't worked out she had been around him?

When he pushed his fingers through the large slit in the back of the flight uniform, and I felt the heat of his warm hands touching my skin, all that was forgotten and I purred like a kitten.

"The skin flap on your back isn't larger than average," he muttered to himself. "Today, I thought we could start by timing how long it takes to bring them out. We'll record it," he said, holding up the pen and paper he had taken from the desk drawer. "And your aim is to get faster every time." He twisted his wrist up to look at his watch. "Ready…go."

Oh. Okay. I wasn't ready. Emroyce normally counted me down from three when we did the obstacle course. I twisted my back and turned my wings with the muscles inside my back, uncurling the wing sets from one another before I finally flicked the white wings out.

His eyes flicked to his watch, his face set in a grim frown. "Twelve seconds," he grunted. "That's a bloody nightmare."

"Well, I wasn't exactly ready."

He jotted the time down on the paper nonetheless, and then pushed the pen behind his ear, as he tugged one wing towards him for a closer inspection.

"These wings aren't white. They have an undertone of shimmery silver, or gold. My eyes can't make up their mind. I have never heard of anyone with two sets of wings."

I stared at them myself and realised I hadn't noticed before that they were actually not completely white. "I always thought it was because of my parents being from two different territories."

"No. I know some of my subjects have had children with white-wings and they never got two sets. It's either one or the other colour. Never two pairs."

"Lucky me," I muttered.

"So, you get two pairs of wings and demons have none."

"Are you saying that you've considered whether I was a demon?"

"No. Purely stating facts." He let go of my wing and retrieved the pen from behind his ear. "Again."

I tucked the wings inside my back and stared at him to start the timer.

"Ready. Go!"

I hadn't twinned the wings together in my back for comfort this time, so I was much faster at bringing the white plumes back out.

Still, Ben grunted discontentedly. "Nine seconds." He jotted it down. "For us to survive, you must at least half that time. Aim for five seconds."

I threw my hands in the air at the absurd expectation. "That's impossible."

He watched me carefully before he asked, "Even if you used your magic?"

I thought about it, but there was no way Harvey would let me practise that or show anyone I had magic. "I have no magic," I muttered, lifting my gaze to the rising sun, it's rays visible from behind the mountain ridge.

"Interesting," he grunted. "Again."

I snapped my wings back in. "You speak. Let me see how fast you can do it."

Without hesitating, he brought out his massive wings. It took him three seconds, maybe four. Spirits! I swallowed. "Time me again."

He had the audacity to smirk. Bastard! But he didn't say a word to tease me, and snapped them back inside his back, turning his wrist up. "Ready. Go!"

A few more times, I managed it in nine seconds, then I did get it down to eight and seven before I was exhausted.

"That was good progress. We have time for just a few more. Next time we can move onto take-offs. Before I dismiss you to the war updates," Ben said, tilting his head with that infuriating calm of his, "I'm just curious, how long does it take you to switch from white wings to black?"

I opened my mouth. "That takes–"

"Ready. Go!"

"Shit!" I hissed. *Bastard.*

My body tensed as I retracted the white wings, the tendons tightening like cords drawn too fast. I felt the membrane slide and twist beneath my skin, muscles shuddering as I tried to shift the black wings into place. One got stuck, snagged awkwardly against the last fold of the white wing that hadn't fully retracted. Pain flared under my shoulder blade, but I gritted my teeth and forced it through.

By the time I straightened, wings fully changed, my heart was racing, and not just from the strain. I looked at Ben, breath sharp and uneven.

He raised his brows, clearly unimpressed. "Fifteen seconds, if I'm being *generous*," he muttered, raking his fingers nervously through his hair. "Can you at least tell which colour you changed to last? Which wing-pair will come out the fastest the next time you need them?"

I narrowed my eyes. "Of course."

He exhaled, clearly relieved. "Well…at least there's some good news. I can't believe no one at this outpost trained you to get quicker. What were you and Camp Leader Watson doing?" He slammed his eyes shut and bit his teeth together. "Actually, don't answer that." He sighed and his eyes glinted with fury like rubies in the light once he opened them again. "How many people know about your wings?"

"I don't know. It hasn't really been a secret. I would say everyone, but thinking about it, I never bring them both out as it tips me backwards with the weight."

He looked at the watch again. "We'll keep practising another time. You must get to war updates, or you'll be late. Off you go."

Why was he so eager to send me away? Had he not finished speaking with Tomason? Was she close by? Had she been here, observing me? That thought that people could be standing around without me knowing felt creepy.

I squared up with him and he looked down at me tensely. I retrieved his hand from his side and stroked my fingers over it gently. "Thank you."

He was still looking at me tensely as if waiting for me to bite. "Those two words are a luxury commodity I don't get often." He smiled. Genuinely smiled. "You're welcome."

That was sad. He did so much for others, but no one ever thanked him for it. Didn't he have anyone close to him who could tell him how appreciated he was? Maybe that's what Tomason did.

I dropped his hand and turned around, jogging to the assembly hall, and found a seat next to Kate, Mazdon and Zoe. None of the four black-wings were here, nor was Emroyce.

"Where is Emroyce?" I asked Mazdon.

"He's still consoling Fern, helping her with Robin. He has threatened a few times to go to the capital to kill King Emille and Counsellor Desry, so I'm keeping my ears on him. If I hear he straps on weapons, we must intervene."

I nodded my agreement as Camp Leader Seon Nar stepped up on the podium in a perfectly ironed navy-blue uniform and polished black boots. Her inky hair laid in waves across her shoulders, swaying in the light air magic she wielded around herself. Because she was the leader of the Air Force Unit, she frequently held war updates, having the most recent information.

I saw little of Mewer as he had both the second month challenge for the third-year cadets and the colossal amount of healing to deal with. Tomason wasn't there, either. Go figure. She was probably out on the field, talking to Ben. A sour acid turned my stomach. Camp Leader Ward and Camp Leader Neville were out on patrol, but Zayd stood at one side of the podium watching the cadets. Teaching combat wasn't until the fifth month of challenges, but he coached during the free sessions in the sparring hall, which were straight after lunch.

"This morning, scouts on patrol reported that the black-wings advanced into Pharanir and are planning on invading Pansery," Camp Leader Nar called out to get everyone's attention and to quieten down.

She seemed unsettled by the news, which wasn't strange since it was where she had grown up and her family still resided there. It was also where General Denor had his family home, so I couldn't imagine he would sit by and not try to push back the attack.

She pointed to the map and along the path the black-wings had most likely taken to get into our territories. "I'll take a battalion of the Air Force soldiers and leave for Pansery this afternoon. I hope to be back for the fourth month's challenge that I teach the first-years, but if not, I have instructed Camp Leader Neville to cover for me. If you have any friends or family within the Air Force who are joining me, I advise you to let there be nothing unspoken between you."

"Can volunteers join the battles, or get leave to go home to family in Pansery?" Cadet Elinor Maruto asked, sitting at the edge of her seat.

She was from Pharanir as well, but from the outskirts and closer to the mountains, but she could have friends in the Pansery area.

"That isn't a war strategy question," Camp Leader Nar shouted, not that I had imagined her to be soft and cuddly. This war advancement had really got her edgy. "And no! You're a first-year, Cadet Maruto, and not trained sufficiently for war. You'll be in the way of the Air Force's work." She glanced across the crowd and waited. "No other questions? So, the black-wing's intention is crystal clear to you all? Ask me questions to show me you can evaluate a war situation."

"Why attack Pansery? It's a small village without a stronghold to protect it. It'll be hard to keep it. Why not take Abarath Outpost?"

"That's a good question, and I agree it's a stupid strategy by the black-wings," she said, searching the audience and stopping her gaze at me.

Was she pissed off with me? I didn't attack them. I guessed that was what I got for being the black-wing king's teammate. She might as well shout 'mutt' across the entire hall.

"There is no logic in their advance. No riches. No locational advantage. It's not near enough to the Spirits' Trek. Nothing. Savages! Remember that when you get into one-to-one combat with them. The only thing I can think of is that they didn't have the size of army required to attack Abarath Outpost and went around it, believing we wouldn't detect them crossing into our territory. And now we'll come to them and kill them."

She talked non-stop for the remaining two hours until lunch, her voice tight with concern as she laid out the escalating situation in the coal and iron mines. Trade raids had disrupted supply lines, cutting off weapons transports to the White Wing Territory. Tensions were flaring. Even the joint teams, those rare groups made up of both territories working near the iron mines, had turned on each other after someone reportedly spotted light crystals. What began as cooperation had quickly spiralled into chaos.

When she had finished, everyone left their seats and headed out into the corridor. In the doorway, Camp Leader Nar rushed out, squeezing past me and Kate, and shoved her shoulder into Ben, who had been waiting for me outside the assembly hall. Strangely, her shove knocked him back a few steps and must have taken him by surprise, as he normally didn't budge.

"Call your armies out of Pansery, or by the nine Spirits, I'll kill you!" Nar shouted into his face and her rage released her magic; the air around them storming and pulling their hair around their faces. The icy air bouncing between the walls made a chill run down my spine. Even though her stare was so vicious it could pierce a soul, he simply grinned as if he wasn't responsible for her hardships.

"Nah," he said with a shrug that was uncharacteristic for him.

Ben normally grabbed for the throat as that was how he extended his magic, but a…Nah? How could Ben not care more than that?

Nar took a controlled breath and stormed past him, and it was as if the air was sucked out of the corridor to follow her.

I joined his side. "Nah? What in the Underworld, Ben?"

He sensually gripped around my waist. "That's old news. Do you know where they'll attack next?"

Was that a challenge? "No. Are you going to tell me?" I tried to cross my arms over my chest, but he was too close for me to get my arms between us. It wasn't like him to invite me into his personal space in public places. He always worried we would get caught and I would be lashed. He hadn't even grunted.

I shook my head. Maybe he was under a lot of pressure. "I need lunch."

He grabbed my hand as I was trying to leave and he swung me around, pressing me up against the wall. The red eyes that closed in on me were somehow foreign. I didn't recognise the soul behind them as belonging to Ben. I couldn't see the man I knew. The warmth and softness he looked at me with was gone. Where was the unspoken connection that was always there between us? It had been replaced by the cold and unfamiliar distance of a stranger.

He flicked, not gently caressed – *flicked!* – a strand of my hair back. "I prefer to head to our room and have wild sex."

Wild sex? Now I knew he was out of his damned mind. Had he planned that Mazdon would be listening and tell Zayd to wind him up? Something was definitely off with him.

"Ben! You know that is too dangerous."

"What is?" The calm tone of his voice was confusing; too soft and mismatched with the feral expression in his eyes.

"Sex!"

"What?" It sounded as if he was choking on something, but I couldn't see him chewing on anything. "*We have talked about that, Angelica. I thought you understood. If you're not satisfied–"*

"You're the one suggesting it. Although those kisses are… Not here. Stop."

At least his grunt was in my mind now. *"What are you talking about? Where are you?"*

"Oh, who's the funny one? Who are you imagining is in front of you right now? Tomason?"

His grunt was longer and angrier than normal. *"Angelica! Tell me where you are this instance?"*

I stiffened. *"You're having your hands all over me just outside the assembly door."*

"I'm in the canteen with Murben, Commander Daffron, Nesso and Davis. I'm on my way."

I shoved my hands over the chest of the imposter, who was trying to smother me in kisses. I pushed him away from me so easily, I knew for certain he wasn't my Ben. "Get the fuck off me! Ben could teach you a thing or two about kissing." I wiped my mouth with the back of my hand. "Ew."

Imposter Ben smirked and his skin started turning paler, his eyes lightening into a blue colour and his black hair changing to golden. Lastly, his body shrunk to be little more than my own size.

I should have known. Theo Grim from the Backstabber Team. His magic could shift him to look like any other man.

"Don't flatter yourself," he spat. "Your kisses weren't great, either. Relax. I meant no harm. I just wanted to check if King Blackbone had told you anything about the next attacks. Although, if you would have taken me to bed, I wouldn't have objected." Then the bastard winked at me; a bastard who didn't realise how close he was from death.

I crossed my arms over my chest now that I could. "No offence taken. But you may want to run. Run far away, and hide. Hide well."

"What?" He looked puzzled.

"King Blackbone doesn't like other men touching his toys. Well, you can ask him about it yourself if you're brave enough to stay." I looked at my watch, although I didn't need to. "He will be here in five…four…three–"

His breath seemed to have caught in his throat at the realisation, like a punch to his gut before the blow had even landed. "No. This had nothing to do with him."

I cocked my head, pitying him. "Didn't really think this plan through, did you?"

The colour drained from his face. "I'm sorry," he said, as if he thought for a split second that maybe the apology would save him.

"You made Camp Leader Nar believe he didn't care about the attack on her village. Two…one…" I pointed a finger down the corridor in the direction of the canteen and, sure enough, Ben rounded the corner.

'Run,' I mouthed.

I had to hand it to him. Cadet Grim was a fast sprinter.

"Ben!" I shouted a while before he reached me to ensure I would get his attention, and hopefully make him stay with me, rather than take up chase on Cadet Grim.

Ben didn't seem intent on stopping, so I shouted again and caught his hand in his speed past me.

"Ben! Stay!"

Breathing out like an angry bull at full pelt, he stopped and glared at me. He couldn't be angry with me. I didn't make out with the other Ben on purpose. I should get a freaking medal for figuring out that he was an imposter so quickly.

"Are you unharmed?" He looked me over.

"I'm unhurtable. It was a prank." Although, later I'd have to inform Ben to speak with Nar about the attack on Pansery. At least, try to appease her anger.

He grunted. "A prank? You consider the violation of my woman a prank?"

My brows reflexively raised. "Your woman?"

"Aren't you?" There was no room for jokes in his tone. Blinded with rage, he saw only black and white, and in this instance, the white-wing had to be eliminated.

I swallowed. What was the best approach to deal with Ben when he was in this mood? He was a protector, but above all, he was a provider, and his main priority was my health. "I'm so hungry. Shall we go to the canteen?"

"For all that's sacred, Angelica," he snapped, frustration thick in his voice. "I've compromised. The least you could do is answer my question."

I tilted my head, a slow smirk tugging at my lips. "So needy, King Blackbone," I drawled, fully aware I was poking the beast. "Good to know that when you're busy being an insufferable arse, Cadet Grim could always step in as your more agreeable replacement–"

His stern stare dug so deep into me I fell quiet, and I felt the weight of his undivided attention. His fist balled against the wall as he backed me up against it, and I was worried he would punch through it as his black essence rose from his feet, covering us waist deep in it.

"Ben," I said calmly, but inside me, fear was a step ahead of that calm. How deep in the essence could I stand before it killed me?

He looked at me with such a devastated gaze and waited, clearly keen on every word I would speak. "You don't need my words. You know where you have me."

He closed his eyes and grunted as if still trying to get the image of Cadet Grim kissing me out of his head. His shoulders dropped, resigned. Close to me, he curved his body possessively around mine.

"Ben?"

"Um," he moaned, his face clenched in agony, as if I was interrupting him claiming me.

I cocked my head up to get my lips near his ear. "I am your woman. And only yours." I paused until I held all of his attention. Then I whispered. "I love you."

Those were the words that really made him come undone. I could feel the shift of power from his body turning into something deeply lethal and protective. His breathing steadied from his rage but became deep with arousal instead.

"Good," he managed to growl out between his teeth. "Then I shall make that clear to everyone else in this world as well."

"Perhaps tell me how you intend to do that before you do it." I kissed him gently, and it was as if something inside him grew even more possessive of me.

"I intend to do it with any method necessary so that every single person understands it."

He gave me a gentle kiss in return that held so many more promises than pure passion, and that was all it took for me not to argue with him.

23

After dinner, we took the shortcut through the courtyard to the sparring hall. The enormous room with high vaulted ceilings and walls made with block stones was again full of ambitious cadets. Most of them would die before they graduated. I was probably in that quota, too.

"No. You'll not be in that quota. I won't let that happen," Ben growled.

"That surely was a passive thought."

"Keep your shield up. We don't know how many in this outpost can read minds."

That was a creepy feeling, and I understood why Ben had taken so much time learning who everyone was and what their magic could do.

From one end of the room to the other, I let my glance sweep over everyone here. Zayd was in the eastern corner training a few first-year cadets I didn't know by name. He met my gaze for a second before looking away; ashamed. He should be. An apology would come soon enough, but he wouldn't make a scene in here.

Ben must have seen our exchange in eye-contact because he placed his palm at the small of my back and pushed me towards an area in the last row of mats, which had four available spaces next to one another.

Considering the death magic cloud I had stood in before dinner, I was still edgy when he touched me.

"May I ask how your magic works? I was in the midst of it, and still I was safe."

Ben kept an eye on Zayd as we walked further into the hall. *"The black smoke is a residue, and sometimes it transmits death magic, but it's not death itself. It's like a scale. I can balance the magic without hurting anyone when I touch them, but when my emotions are disturbed, it's akin to too much weight on one side of a scale and the magic becomes unbalanced. That's when it oozes out of me uncontrolled, and it fills with charge that travels through the smoke and kills whoever it touches. I can let out the black smoke deliberately with no charge in it to conceal us without it being lethal-unless I lose control."*

"Risky game."

"Not a game. Not around you."

"Thank you for telling me about it."

"I aim to please my woman." He smirked at me, clearly enjoying I had accepted the word.

Nesso, Davis, Commander Daffron and Murben followed us with their eyes vigilant, assessing anyone and everyone around us as a potential threat.

"I want you to train with Davis today," Ben said, stepping up on the mat, beckoning for Davis. "I want to show him one technique before you start. Just don't break my soldier."

"I'll be his greatest misery. But out of respect, I'll not cross the line of breaking him." I smiled at Davis, who returned it with a playful chuckle.

A few seconds into their training, and Ben having lost focus on me, Murben came to stand by my side.

"I haven't seen King Blackbone smile like this since his mother was alive. Not a sneer, not a smirk, not a leer, not a grin, not a mocking smile or a playful smile. A pure and simple smile from being happy. In love."

I observed Ben's face, and it seemed lighter somehow from when I had spoken to him in the Black Wing Territory. "Who's the lucky woman?" I flashed Murben a cheeky grin.

He snorted, but his face dropped to become serious. "It would be strange if you hadn't worried about him being truthful. The situation you're in is complicated, I realise. But I'm willing to bind my words in a curse and accept a painful death if I'm wrong. I can promise you that his love for you is genuine."

The hair on my arms pricked at the grandiosity in his utter belief of what made his king happy. Me. Little insignificant me.

He leaned closer and softened his voice. "King Blackbone wouldn't have severed one of his soldier's thumbs if he hadn't lost his head seeing you hurt with the mark of shackles. Shackles make everything worse, even if they were only superficial marks. He has issues about failing his mothe–"

"Cadet Coraly, your turn!" Ben called out, and it made me jump. "Use daggers today, but Davis, draw no blood," Ben warned him, and Davis's eyes widened. Ben turned towards me. "See what you think about how Davis moves and his way of fighting."

I took my boots off and stepped up onto the mat at the same time as I unsheathed one dagger, knowing it was my fault he was weaker with his thumbless hand.

We moved around each other, and every time he struck at me, he stuck out his tongue and gave away which direction he would launch. Great! He fought the same way as Zoe, and I knew that style by heart already. That made it so much easier to avoid his attacks, as I'd know exactly where he'd leave himself vulnerable.

We fought for a good while and with more than a five points advantage, sweat dripped down my cleavage, so I held up a hand to pause the match to drink some water. A figure appeared at my back, and still drinking, I turned, almost spitting out water as I coughed. Navy-blue uniform. Tall and muscular body. Gelled up hair. Very sad blue eyes.

Zayd rubbed his shoulder nervously and his eyes were those of 'I have really fucked up' that I had only seen once before when he had gone out with other cadets clubbing in the city, forgetting my sixteenth birthday. It was the time when our friendship had bloomed into romantic feelings, and I had been so upset that he had forgotten about me. Especially since it had been the year after my mother's reveal, and my father was put into the Royal Castle dungeon.

"I'm very sorry, Angie. I didn't mean what I said. It's hard for me. I…" He sighed and looked down at the floor. "I miss you."

My heart melted. This was the Zayd, who I had always known. How could I stay angry with him?

"Because he's a prick!" Ben's voice roared in my head.

I snatched my head to see Ben glare our way, and I glowered angrily at him. *"You're walking a really thin line of being a prick yourself. Stay out of my passive thoughts."*

"Keep your shield up!"

I locked the mental shield in place and twisted my head back to look at Zayd, who had clearly seen me looking at Ben.

"Are you looking towards him now to help make your decisions for you?" he asked, his voice full of hurt.

"I want to cut you up into pieces," I barked. "He's the merciful one." I was lying, obviously, but I had answered a harsh reply to a harsh question.

"Damn it, Angie! I'm sorry." A few heads around the room turned our way – he was making a scene.

Ben was trembling, fighting to remain in control of himself, and Murben got punches in on him because of his lack of focus. I desperately wanted to know what was going through Ben's mind. Perhaps if he could do it to me, I could have a little peek into his mind, too.

I extended my bond and dug deeper than I had before. Suddenly, I saw his mind like two forking lines of light. One was white, and the other had a silvery tone. I followed the darker one, which I assumed must lead to his inner thoughts.

"I love her so fucking much! If he as much as touches her, I'll lose my shit."

I jumped right out of his thoughts and panted.

"Are you all right?" Zayd asked, and struck his hand out to steady me. I freaked out by the touch and swatted it away as I looked over at Ben. He hadn't seen it as he had spun around in time to miss it, but now he was back to facing me.

It had been so dark inside his mind. There was so much anger and hurt that it had knocked the wind out of my lungs. How could he breathe or even stand upright with that much weight on his shoulders?

"Angie, can we go somewhere and talk in private? The tree, perhaps?"

Tree? That gave me an idea. Zayd needed forgiveness and Ben needed to show me he was the strongest male. If I was right, I knew just the thing to accomplish both without bloodshed. If I was wrong, this situation could get horribly worse.

"You want me to accept your apology?"

Zayd nodded, and it looked as if he wanted to touch me; get closer to me, but he refrained, for which I thanked all the nine Spirits.

"Then you'll show me great sportsmanship and you'll shake Ben's hand when he beats your top score on the obstacle course."

Zayd looked stunned. The top score had been his pride the entire year and it would hurt him to lose it, especially to Ben. If he could handle that, it would be proof enough of his respect for me, and I'd forgive him.

Ben had heard me and had abandoned Murben to stand close to my back. I hadn't turned around to see him, but I could sense he was there. If I hadn't sensed it, I could see the way Zayd lifted his stares above my head. "What if he can't beat my record?" Zayd asked.

"I will!" Ben's voice was razor-sharp.

I tied my boots and went out to the obstacle course with Zayd and the black-wings following me. Rumours that Ben was going to do the course spread through the building like a virus and over three hundred people lined the side of the field. There were also people leaning out from their windows in the military building to watch.

Ben stood by the starting line, rolling up his sleeves with an expressionless face, as if this was an ordinary challenge. As if he couldn't see the enemy soldiers staring at him, hoping he would fail.

I looked around, reflexively searching for Emroyce to take the time, but he wasn't there. Hurt echoed through me for his family's hardships. I would find him and Fern later to see how they fared.

I had to push past a few cadets and then walk between Murben and Commander Daffron, who parted to let me through to join at Ben's side.

"I'm sorry I put you through this. This wasn't what I had intended."

"I'm glad you did. Now I can show them all at once rather than having to prove myself repeatedly. This way is more efficient."

"What if you…" I didn't want to think it nor show him I feared it. I did have faith in him. "Fail?"

"I won't."

I rubbed my arms, feeling a chilly breeze, and wished I had brought a jacket. I looked around at everyone once more and wished I could tell them all to go back to minding their own business.

Ben touched my elbow. "Don't worry. Camp Leader Watson's record is four minutes and thirty-seven seconds. I can do it in four minutes and fifteen seconds."

I crossed my arms over my chest. "How do you know that?"

"I had excellent maths tutors and the motivation of my father. Angle. Speed. Wind. Strength. Length of track. Gravity. Give or take two seconds, but I'll still be faster than him." He growled out the last word as Zayd came to stand next to us.

Zayd flicked his wrist to look at his watch. "Are you ready to start?"

"You'll not be keeping time. Cadet Coraly will. You can double-check if you like to ensure she isn't cheating."

"Cadet Coraly doesn't cheat."

"I guess he doesn't know you as well as I do." Ben winked at me before he put his foot on the starting line and lowered his back.

"I don't cheat!"

"Cheat. Steal Black Blades. All sorts of mischiefs. You take what you deserve. I love that about you. Now time me."

I stared at my watch. "Five…four…"

"Oh, for fuck's sake, just start it!"

I snorted. Fine. Have it your way. "Ready. Go!"

Ben sprinted, his muscles flexing into mountainous bulges, his fists tight as they swung at his sides and his boots beat the soft soil which had grass patches in scattered areas and puddles on others that hadn't drained away from the last deluge. He practically flew over and skidded under the six bars and was up the net wall so fast, taking the roped squares two steps at a time. I had never seen anyone this fast. The monkey rings didn't need to swing much for him to grab the next one and the last one he didn't bother with as he jumped to the landing platform.

I was so proud of him and wanted to tell all the spectators that he was my man, but no one around me cared as they chatted so loudly it was hard to hear my own thoughts. There was mostly booing but Zoe, Kate and the black-wings were cheering him on. Mazdon looked at him quietly but nodded every so often as if Ben had impressed him, too. I smiled but kept my eyes on Ben and the time.

Like a wriggly worm, he crawled under the long strip of net and sprinted up the wall without using the rope at first. Once gravity pulled his momentum to a halt, he quickly grabbed the rope and climbed the last bit of the wall before hauling himself up by his arms, his hands gripped over the top plank, and he swung his legs over to the other side. He was abseiling down at a speed that would develop blisters on his palms for sure. As I had, he dropped the last bit and landed expertly on his feet. Without hesitating, he jumped up on the balance bar, arms outstretched for balance as he crossed it in long strides. He threw himself into the last challenge without having made a single mistake, jumping the steppingstones one at the time without hitting down too hard to lose time. When he was over the finish line, I checked the time.

"Four minutes and sixteen seconds." *Wow!* That was impressive.

Ben panted, supporting his hands on his knees. But he stretched up tall when Zayd approached him. The entire field went silent as if the wind had died, scared to blow at them as they squared up. Every cadet turned to stare at them, following their every move with a tension that could have made more than a few magical abilities collide.

Zayd gritted his teeth as he stretched his hand out. "Well done."

I couldn't believe it. Zayd actually yielded to me and would shake the black-wing king's hand merely for my forgiveness. I saw a glimpse of Ben extending his hand to shake Zayd's before Zoe hung around my neck.

"Wow! That was something!" she chirped. "No one will ever beat that. Ever."

"Yeah, he's pretty great," I muttered, sour for having missed the handshake of the century.

"Imagine how he'll be in bed, honey," she said, raising her brows at me.

"Zoe!"

"Come on! Give me some gossip," she whispered. But she fell a few steps away from me as the crowd parted like a bow splitting the sea when Ben walked my way.

"You were one second over," I mocked.

"With the wind, I did say give or take two seconds."

"I didn't say it was acceptable."

He chuckled softly and watched me, as if we were the only two in this world. He wrapped an arm around my shoulder and pulled me tightly to him and kissed my forehead; a gesture of affection in public I wasn't prepared for. As if he wanted to show everyone in the entire Bensguard Outpost that I was his woman. Maybe it was even a silent threat for the other cadets not to dare harm me. He wouldn't have made such a statement without a cause.

When he removed his hand from my shoulder, I noticed there was a handprint of blood on my shirt. He was bleeding. Most likely from the rope having cut through his palm. My chest tightened. He hadn't winced or grimaced at the pain. Had he even realised the injury was there? What upbringing had he received not to even notice a wound like that?

"What did you think of Davis's technique?" he asked, as we were walking back to our room.

"That is what you ask after all that?" I threw a glance over my shoulder to see people pat Zayd on the shoulder whilst he sulked, looking at the ground.

He shrugged his shoulders. "What else would we talk about?" He smiled down at me, as if the difficult trial he had just undergone had been nothing.

Instinctively, I wanted to punch his shoulder but stopped myself, fearing he had more injuries from the obstacle course that he didn't moan out loud about. "Davis was all right. Not a bad soldier."

"Anything else you took note of?"

"You can't assign me to fight your men and then become jealous."

He grunted the way he did when contemplating something. "I'm not jealous. Should I be jealous?"

"Always," I teased and walked into our room as Ben held the door open for me.

I retrieved the cream from the bathroom cupboard where I had stored it after the last time I used it, treating Ben's lash wounds.

"Sit!" I demanded.

"Yes, my queen," he said, lowering himself onto the mattress of his bed.

I took out bandages from the wardrobe and treated his hand, cleaning it with a damp cloth, applying a thin layer of cream and then wrapping it in the bandage. Every touch of his skin sent tingles down my spine as he sat motionless, simply observing me whilst I took care of him.

I nestled the last strip of bandage beneath the edge of the rest. "There. Done."

"Thank you. That was nice." His eyes moved to the top of their sockets as he glanced at me. "You do know that I can't keep this on tomorrow during lessons? I can't show any sign of weakness."

"I am aware. That's why I didn't drag you by the ear to Mewer to get him to heal it. Sleep with it and see how it looks tomorrow."

"May I stay at your place tonight?" he asked timidly, as if we owned a castle each at either side of a continent.

I looked over my shoulder at my small bed that I barely fitted in myself, but when he joined me, it seemed bigger; greater, somehow. Nonetheless, squeezing into one single bed wouldn't provide him with the rest he needed, as we would be like sardines in a tin, unable to move.

"Why don't you move in with me?" I asked.

"What?" He looked confused, searching my face for clarification.

"Move the beds together," I demanded, flicking my finger between the beds.

He chuckled and stood up, pulled his bed out from the wall by hooking his toes under the front frame before he walked around it and kicked it to stand flush against mine.

I took a step back to admire the result. "Much better. Oh, and one other thing."

"Yes," he drawled.

"Keep your boxer shorts on, or you'll be too tempting."

He came closer and caressed a strand of my blue hair behind my ear. "I'm sure you can handle a pinch of temptation."

I swatted his hand away. "Keep them on, or you won't sleep in my bed, which now means you'll have to sleep on the floor." To prove my point, I grabbed his pillow and tossed it into the corner where his bed had been a moment before.

He stalked after it and immediately flung it into my face. Before I could remove it, he had tackled me down into the bed and rolled me over him to lie by the wall.

"And what will little you do to get me out of your bed if I decide to stay? Ants are strong, but they can't move mountains."

"You grossly underestimate the female methods that I'll use to get what I want." I tugged up his shirts from his trousers and unbuttoned them.

Then, going lower and lower, I kissed a trail down towards his cock, and whilst I did, I watched it grow.

"Angelica," he growled my name in warning. When my fingers hit the lining of the boxer shorts, he pushed down on my hand to stop them. "No. This is too dangerous. I get your point, and I yield. I'll keep my clothes on."

Those words stung inside me as if my elevated hot desire had scolded me from the inside as it sizzled out. Would I never be able to touch him? Wasn't there a way for him to learn how to control his magic enough not to kill me during sex? Would my fantasies of it throughout an entire lifetime be enough? It had to be enough for tonight, and I tugged my hand up and rested it gently on his heaving chest.

24

Neville had that normal 'if you mess with me, I'll kill you' look on her face when she strode into the Zoology classroom with fast, long strides. Her short, blonde hair was windswept, and her iron-grey eyes glistened with fury, adding to her 'I really want to kill someone, right fucking now' look.

"Third-year Cadet Sarah Victory died two days ago from drinking a venom that should have been harmless had the labels been placed correctly. Don't mistake your vials! If it becomes a norm that cadets do it on purpose…well, good luck for your third year."

The second challenge was tomorrow, and Neville was, to say the least, testy.

We had practised several times with handling the snakes, but Ben had never let me stick my hand down a terrarium myself. He said he would do it. I did it anyway, of course. I needed to prove to the other cadets, and to myself, that I was as equally skilled as them. When I graduated, I wanted to deserve going on the Spirits' Trek. Ben grunted a lot during classes.

I watched Ben intently as we worked because Neville had grabbed my arm and stopped me after class the other day to tell me about her suspicion that Ben could have a second magical ability. She had told me that Terence would never have accepted someone in his territory and the fact that he was so calm around Ben was unnatural. There was no way anyone could convince her otherwise.

I planned to confront Ben about it when the time was right, but for the time being, I simply observed him.

I was glad to see Emroyce back at class, even though he wasn't his cheery-old-self, and his mind often seemed to be somewhere else. After I visited Fern and Robin, I could understand why. What Counsellor Desry had done to that poor boy had made it almost impossibly hard not to cry when I saw Robin. The tiny three-year-old's eyes were completely cross-eyed, one eye pointing to the floor and the other at the ceiling. He had been sitting by the kitchen table in Fern's quarters with a plate of food in front of him, which I doubted he knew was there, his drool hanging down the corner of his lip.

What had got Emroyce fighting again was when Ben had told him that perhaps if he reached the Spirit's Heart the Spirits might gift him magic to reset Robin's mind. 'The Spirits gift the magic you need most', Ben had said to him. I loved him for it. It had awoken my friend again and given back some fighting spirit in his amber eyes, and every day he seemed to get better. The dark patches under his eyes were gone, but he still had some weight to get back onto his body.

After completing my task, I returned the bright green snake with the yellow underside into its terrarium and labelled the vial of its venom. Then I carefully slid the vial into the stand in the case at our workshop's table.

Emroyce was also finished with his snake, and I nodded for it, proud of him for not having let the last snakebite deter him. "You have a rather large snake on your arm."

Emroyce looked at it for a second and grinned at me. "You should see the one I have in my trousers."

I chuckled, relieved to hear his usual banter, even though the joke hadn't entirely touched his eyes. Even Ben seemed pleased with Emroyce's effort and didn't make any threats to what he would do if another male showed me his dick.

Class ended, and the day carried on with English class and mathematics. Both of which seemed to bore the black-wing king who was used to the best private tutors that silver coins could buy.

The following day came all too quickly, and I nervously tucked in my black uniform shirt that was already smooth against my hips.

"You look perfect," Ben repeated for a third time, as we got ready to go to the challenge. "You've extracted venom more than twenty times. You know how to do it."

"Even if you successfully do it a million times, it takes only one bite for you to have reduced magical ability like Emroyce."

He grunted. "You don't use your magic, anyway."

I threw an angry glance at him over my shoulder where he stood by the wardrobe, buttoning up his trousers. "You don't know that. Me seducing you to sleep in my bed could be my power."

"That's a power all right, but not your magic. I hope one day you'll trust me enough to tell me."

"Why? Why does it matter? I don't use it, anyway." My voice had come out a bit more aggressive than I had intended, so I inhaled a large breath.

Ben came to stand at my back and circle his enormous arms around my front, resting his chin atop my head. "I want the best chance to protect you, is all. But at this moment, there aren't many threats around, so I'll wait. Perhaps instead of assuring your affection through trust, you could offer me those three little words again."

I snatched my daggers from the bed and shoved them down my leg holsters. "You're an arse."

"That's four words."

"Not if you use a contraction. Have you not paid attention in English class?"

He chuckled warmly into my ear, and the heat from his breath made my sex tighten but all my other nerves relax.

We left the room and walked into the Zoology classroom, seeing every cadet standing at their workstation with straight backs, ironed black uniforms and polished black boots. Four navy-blue uniform-dressed Camp Leaders stood at the front with their arms crossed over their chests and feet wide apart as they watched cadets fill the room.

Zayd nodded at me when we made eye-contact, but Neville's, Ward's and Tomason's faces kept expressions hard as stone.

Tomason is here.

Wrath boiled inside my blood, as I noticed she exchanged a brief look with Ben.

Neville started pacing the front when everyone stood still and ready. "As you can see, your workstation has a number from one to twenty-five taped to the space in front of you. You'll find the same number on a note taped to the glass of the terrarium. Idiot proof, right? When I call out for the challenge to start, you go to your terrarium. Gently pick up the snake! Make it bite the edge of the glass cup! Extract venom! Put the snake back whilst the other teammate labels the vial. It's easy! You've done it many times over by now. If your time is quicker than all the other groups, and you're the first one to give me the vial, you win a ten seconds' head-start on the Classifying Herb challenge next month. Simple task. Simple rules. Hurt the snakes and you'll forfeit your win. Kill a classmate and…well…a shame, but step over them and carry on with the challenge."

Spirits! Neville was pricklier than a cactus today. More emotionally deprived than my brother.

"And you wanted me to date her?" Ben almost looked as terrified as I felt.

"Why not? All cuddly and soft."

"I'd rather sleep with my sharp and cold sword collection."

"You mean, my sword collection?"

"The Black Blade was never yours."

I wasn't going to have that conversation at this moment when my nerves warmed my stomach, and it felt like I had a snake there coiling around restlessly.

"Go!" Neville shouted. No counting down from five, not even Ben's mercy of providing two words 'Ready' and 'Go'?

Ben and I rushed to the terrarium labelled twelve and Ben gently lifted out a bright red snake with yellow spotted dots. My head snapped to my right when I heard a scream and saw a female body on the floor and a snake slithering under their workstation.

My chest started heaving. There was a snake on the loose!

"Cadet Coraly," Ben said sternly. "Focus."

I would, if I knew where the venomous snake had gone. At this moment, I wanted to climb up on the worktop.

I didn't even know the name of the woman who had died, nor had Emroyce given her team a name representing her character. There were more screams as Gravelhorn had made it his mission to snatch the snakes out of other cadets' hands and let them loose on the floor. Was this their tactic, as I noticed his teammate, Cadet Malloopa, kept working nimbly at completing their task. There were snakes hissing and slithering everywhere; on the workstations, on the floor and in cadet's arms. I backed up against the wall lined with terrariums as a thick brown snake came towards me.

"Stay calm, Angelica, and it won't bite you. Let's carry on. Come to my side," Ben said calmly.

I panicked and hyperventilated.

"Look at me, Angelica. Come. Take deep breaths. In through your nose and out through your mouth."

Another small male cadet sat down, leaning his back towards the low cupboards under the line of terrariums. He looked groggy, but was still conscious, obviously bitten by a snake with weaker venom than the dead woman lying beside him on the floor.

I'm going to die. My skin was crawling. Ben put the snake back in its home and squatted down in front of me, severing the line of sight to everything else in the room.

"Breathe."

I calmed a bit but still couldn't get my mind to clear and stay focused on the task.

"Do you want me to lift you up and take you out of here?"

Weakness. No. The other cadets couldn't see me weak. I shook my head.

Ben helped me to my feet, and I saw the intense concentration on Cadet Dixon's face from the Underdog Team, and his teammate, Cadet Toran, was already putting the snake back in the terrarium. They seemed to be ahead of Gravelhorn, but the bastard was also on his way with his vial to the front. Worse than my panic of the snakes, I couldn't let the Angry Team win. I wouldn't give fear space to grow and acid my gut. Before I could think clearly, I scanned the floor for a path clear from snakes and rushed to cross Gravelhorn's path, stalling him for a few seconds, which was the only time Cadet Dixon needed to get to Neville first.

Gravelhorn jabbed a hard fist on my shoulder blade for having lost him the challenge. My vision was overshadowed by the desire to faint, but I held myself together. Although, the punch would leave a substantial bruise.

Well worth it.

Neville looked at her watch. "You beat the other teams. Your team wins!"

Team Underdog had won the ten seconds head start prize at the Classifying Herb challenge next month. Good for them. They deserved it.

"When you have put all the loose snakes back into their homes, you are dismissed."

When I turned towards Ben, I froze in place, as I watched him pick the snakes up as if they were nothing but mere sticks before he returned them to their terrariums. Some of the snakes seemed to stroke at his arm when he petted them, as if they worshipped him. Neville must have been right. She knew these snakes like they were her own babies. Magic was at play, and it was a magic Ben hadn't told me about, which begged the question. Why not?

I looked around to find Zayd helping the cadet who had been bitten to get to his feet and lead him towards the infirmary.

"Camp Leader Neville!" Ben shouted across the room to where she was still standing, frowning at the dead woman on the floor. Ben was holding up a long brown snake to show her. "I believe this is Terence, and not that snake in his terrarium at the moment. Get the other snake out and I'll put Terence back."

The fear that I had held at bay erupted to full strength. If Terence had bitten the woman, no wonder she had died instantly, and now Ben was holding the viper in his hands like it was the cuddliest thing ever. Even if he was using his magic, how could he be so certain that Terence wouldn't bite him? One tiny bite and Ben would be dead in a heartbeat.

I wobbled a few steps, everyone's words from around me slurring into an unfathomable language, echoing against my skull. My vision swayed like I was watching the cadets from under the water surface.

I heard Ben from somewhere near me. "Cadet Coraly?"

Then it all turned black, but not peaceful. In my subconscious, snakes slithered around me, hissing and snapping at my throat. There was blood smeared on my body, on the classroom floor, and over my friends.

I awoke screaming, drenched in sweat that felt like blood. Ben flew up to sit on our bed and when he saw the state of me, he cupped my face with his massive palms.

We were in our room. It was dark. Night. Ben was in his boxers. I was in only my underwear.

I was panting hard. "You could have died!" Tears seeped down my cheeks.

"I'm unharmed. We're safe in our room."

But the panic held a tight grip on my heart that didn't let me breathe. "There was blood, and the cadet died and the other got bitten and…"

"Look at me, Angelica!" Ben said softly, trying to angle his face to get eye-contact.

My eyes still darted to my body to check for blood. "You were dead. Lifeless on the floor," I cried, frantic panic gripping my throat anew.

"Angelica! Look only at me," Ben instructed sharply. "I'm alive. I'm here."

My hands were all over him, touching him to verify I wasn't still in a nightmare. His bulging pectorals were indeed wrapped in warm skin and his shoulders were tight with bones and muscles. My hand carried up both sides of his neck and curved his cheeks, where I finally nestled my hand into his hair before I let out my ragged breaths.

The black-wing king was truly here with me. He had stayed with me and taken me to our room to shield me from others' eyes; eyes who couldn't see me this weak.

"Was I carried here?" The thought made my stomach twist.

He didn't want to answer it as I had told him not to but nodded.

My nails dug into my palm. "Did everyone see it?"

He shook his head.

Good. So why was he so grief stricken about it? I flashed him a quizzical look.

"Tomason carried you. She cloaked you. No one saw more than her touching your arm before you were gone from sight."

Ah! I just discovered that jealousy was a worse feeling than fear or shame. Camp Leader Tomason would never have carried me to my room under an invisibility cloak unless she did it for Ben. What hold did he have on her to cooperate? Were they lovers and was he cheating on me? Maybe it wasn't clear to him that I only had exclusive relationships. Maybe in the Black Wing Territory, they weren't monogamous. The darkness grew inside me. I had an issue with trust, I realised. It wasn't easy to allow people to get close when your own mother had been the biggest traitor in your life. I had never suspected anything, and that was how easily Ben could be fooling me, too.

Ben was simply observing me and waited for my reaction. When I gazed at him again, he pulled an impish grin. "Good. Jealousy is better than fear. Jealousy, I can settle easier."

What? The bastard had known! He had waited for my emotions to switch on purpose.

"Yes," he said, pushing back my wild hair. "There is nothing going on between me and Camp Leader Tomason. I want *you*. The woman who could love her enemy. The woman who'd die for her friends. The woman who has been surviving and fighting when others would have crumbled, going through the hardships you've had to face. A woman who does not desire a king but has true devotion to the man beneath the crown." He inhaled a deep breath and let it out slowly, shifting his eyes to mine. "A woman who I hope will forgive an ignorant young man's mistakes."

Jealousy turned to fear once more. What mistakes? What awful things had he done that he couldn't tell me about? Were they so terrible that he believed I couldn't forgive them? That reminded me of what Camp Leader Nar had told Theo Grim when he had pretended to be Ben.

"In war updates, Camp Leader Nar told us that the black-wings were about to attack Pansery. That's where Camp Leader Nar and General Denor's families live. Why are you attacking them? You must pull back the soldiers. I'm sure my brother will allow us to go there if you must tell them to retreat in person."

His jaw clenched at the same time that he averted his gaze from my eyes. "Let's get some sleep."

"So, you won't pull them back? White-wings will die! Children! Innocents!"

"It's not up to me…I can't…" he whispered, cocking his head low, gazing at the floor.

"You're their king! If you can't find it in you to make the right choice, then we can all go to the Underworld!"

He scoffed, looking up at me as if every word I had said cut right through him like a knife. "Don't make the mistake of believing you know where my moral compass points."

The look on his face told me he wouldn't do anything about it. He thought he could hide in my bed whilst his soldiers killed my people.

A wrath, comparable to learning about my mother's betrayal, struck hard and hit like an iron ball bouncing against my ribs. I got off the bed, took out a tracksuit from the wardrobe and pulled open the door after I had dressed.

"Angelica, where are you going? It's the middle of the night."

"I'm going to sleep on the second floor!" I bit back before slamming the door.

The torches in the sconces on the wall running along the stairs weren't lit so the steps were hard to see, but after my mapping of the building when I was young, I knew them by heart and let my memory muscle bring me up to my family apartment. With hard and determined knocks, I was ready to wake the dead to get inside. I was not sleeping next to Ben tonight, and I'd let him believe I had stayed with Zayd.

My brother opened the door, rubbing one eye with a knuckle. He'd had the decency to pull on a pair of yellow uniform bottoms. "Angie, what in the world?"

I pushed him aside and walked inside. "I'm sleeping in my room tonight."

But I gasped as I looked into it from the doorway. "I was gone for only two years, and you turned my room into a gym?" I headed for the room that used to be his before he had moved into our parent's room. "A gentleman's room?" There was a poker table in the middle of the room and a bar at the end, topped with flasks containing colourful liquids. Two sofas were pushed up against the corner by the window and the air had a hint of a cigar smell.

Harvey gestured for our parent's bedroom. "We can both fit in my bed. But no pushing your cold toes up against my thighs like when we were kids. And you must stay on your side, no star-fishing across my side. I remember that you could sprawl across the entire bed even when you were so tiny." He walked into the bedroom and pulled the pillows apart and got under the covers. "I need to leave for Pansery in the morning, so I need the rest. When I come back, I expect my flat to be empty."

He could *say* whatever he wanted, but I'd *do* whatever I wanted. I knew he wouldn't kick me out using force.

Fully dressed, I crept down beside him without saying a word, grateful that he had taken me in without greater reprimand. He could have told me to go away, and I would have had to fight my way inside, gaining more bruises. Because 'no' was not an option tonight.

For a while there was silence between us until he said, "So, you can even piss off a king."

"I haven't pissed anyone off," I snapped. "He pissed me off."

"Do you want me to remove the soul bond?" he asked even softer, his voice loaded with remorse.

My heart hurt at the question and that it prompted me to voice my decision. "No, I want to keep track of his movements." I paused and sighed. "I asked him to remove his troops from Pansery, and I stupidly thought he cared enough about me to do it, but he said he couldn't."

Harvey was quiet for a while. "Did he tell you why not?" His voice made him seem so eager to know, yet reluctant to spy on my private conversation.

"No. He didn't even have the decency to explain why. He plainly said he couldn't."

Harvey let out a large breath. "Good."

"Good?" I flew up to lean on my elbows.

Harvey didn't turn around and he closed his eyes, ready to sleep. "Not good, obviously. I just meant; that's it then. Nothing more to consider."

Oh okay. I guess he was right. Ben's refusal made his relationship to me clear. He and I could never find mutual ground. He would always be my enemy.

25

Harvey had already left the apartment when the alarm on my watch went off. Mewer's herbology class started in an hour and my first problem was that I didn't have a uniform. I really should have thought about that yesterday, as I'd absolutely not go back to my room and confront Ben.

I sighed, thinking of solutions.

Zoe might have a spare one in her room. I wouldn't even care if I had to dig it out of her laundry basket.

When I had made my way down the stairs and arrived at her door, I knocked gently, hoping to avoid any other cadets' attention. Zoe opened the door, and as soon as she saw me, she waved me inside and closed the door behind me. She had already dressed in her combat leathers, and she had armed herself fully with weapons. "Angie, have you come to see me off? You know I kick-arse, honey."

I frowned, and then it clicked. "You're leaving for Pansery?"

"You didn't know?"

I shook my head, looking around the tiny single room the lucky agent didn't have to share with anyone.

"Your brother needs an intel agent on site." She pointed both thumbs at herself. "That's me."

I leaned my back against the door, crossing my arms. "You don't seem worried. You know you'll be in the midst of war?"

"Of course, that's what I trained for. I have been stuck here for over two months with nothing to do. It's boring." She turned on her heels, rummaging through her drawers and her wardrobe for stuff to pack, like keeping herself busy would protect her from my steel gazes.

"When will you be back?" I needed her here in order to keep my sanity.

"Hopefully by the end of the week. But if you aren't here to hug me farewell, and that is obviously a crazy thought since you don't do goodbyes, then why are you here?" She paused her step, her hands gripping her daggers, staring at me.

I cleared my throat, feeling awkward. "Did the launderers supply you with a spare uniform by chance?"

She looked me up and down, noticing my tracksuit, and threw a quick glance at her watch. "Do I even want to know why? You and Ben fighting?"

I unfurled my arms from my chest and crossed them at the small of my back. "No. Not anymore. I walked out on him yesterday. Stayed the night at my brother's."

She tossed her daggers onto the bed next to her backpack that was packed to the brim. "How did Ben take that?"

I flashed her a broken smile. "I don't know. I slammed the door and left."

"He won't be happy."

"*He* won't be happy? Whose side are you on?" I threw my glances up at the ceiling to steel my patience.

"His, I guess. He's providing me with a lot of fun in the north this week. Give my thanks. Tell him I'm sorry for all the soldiers of his I'll have to kill."

"Knock yourself out! He refused to pull back his troops when I asked!"

"Oh, honey. You can't expect him to just change overnight. Give him time. Here," she said, handing me her room key. "Sleep here until I'm back, so you can cool off. The uniforms are in the wardrobe but obviously use one of my daggers to peel the magic rank emblem off, or you can get punished. And in return for my hospitality, please get some breakfast and eat so you don't get any thinner. Other cadets could break your body in half just by looking at you."

I hugged her tightly and for longer than normal. "Thank you. You're a true friend, Zoe. I won't say goodbye, so…see you later."

"See you later!" She left, and I hurried to get ready, as I had promised her I'd eat breakfast, and I kept my promises.

In the canteen, I found Emroyce, Kenyard, Mazdon, Kate and Zayd already halfway through their breakfasts, so I fetched mine quickly and sat down next to Zayd. He smiled at me briefly and resumed to focus on his cereal. The pear and small bowl of strawberry yoghurt I had on my tray looked like a tiny snack compared to his assortment of bread, a boiled egg, and a tall glass of orange juice. Zayd stood out in his navy-blue uniform to the others around the table wearing black, and when I swept my glance around the canteen, I spotted the other camp leaders; Ward, Mewer and Tomason at another table. It was admirable in a way that Zayd had stayed seated with his friends rather than with leadership.

Zayd noticed I was still looking at him and hadn't touched my breakfast, so he flashed me another smile, which I returned with much affection, and it was at exactly the right timing as the black-wings pushed through the doors. Ben saw the looks Zayd, and I had exchanged, and I felt his rage inside my chest. I had to use all my concentration not to rub over the sore spot and to keep my damned shield strong.

Zayd pointed at the broken stitches on my left shoulder. "This isn't your uniform."

"Central depot stocked my wardrobe with the incorrect garb. I peeled the emblem off," I lied.

A stupid lie, since central depot never got it wrong.

"Ah," Zayd scoffed. "I thought it had to do with not staying in your own room last night."

I glowered at him. "How do you know?"

"I ran into your brother this morning when I came back from my jog."

I stirred the spoon mindlessly in my yoghurt bowl. "He has no business telling you about my private life."

Zayd chuckled so low no one else would pay attention to us as Emroyce and Mazdon discussed the next challenge. "Harvey is my best friend, Angie. Obviously, he'd tell me to take advantage of the situation."

I glowered at him with an overload of annoyance. "And will you?"

"Shamelessly," he said without hesitating. "If you need a place to stay, my warm bed is always an option."

"Thank you. I would have taken you up on that, but someone else offered up their bed before you." I held up the key to Zoe's room before tucking it down in my pocket again.

He gawked. "Who?"

"The person in this world I care about the most."

"Ah," he scoffed and prepared a spoonful of cereal, lifting it to his mouth. "Zoe."

I nodded. "Please don't tell anyone. Not yet. I want some solitude." I bit into the pear and tore off a chunk.

"I won't tell a soul. Cross my heart and hope to die." He made the sign over his chest.

"You still say that? Like when we were kids."

"When it's important. Although, it begs the question. If you and Ben aren't stuck to the hip, can I take you out again?"

"You *are* shameless!"

"Guilty as charged. So, is that a yes?"

I hated to see that his blue eyes held so much hope. "It's too soon. I'm too broken to know what I want."

It felt like a blanket of sadness swept across me as I realised that I wasn't as confident as I used to be. Where had my fighting spirit, my goals and my ambition gone?

"Fair enough," Zayd said. "I'll start by picking up the pieces and gluing your heart back together and after the glue has set, I'll ask you again."

"Sure." I nodded.

"I have about an hour free after your herbs and poison class before I have to teach battle tactics to third-year cadets. If you want, I can show you useful books in the library for your test, or we can go into the woods, and I can help you identify some herbs you'll be using."

"I'd like that. By the water pools where we used to play when we were kids?"

"Perfect. It's a date." He winked before looking down on his tray.

"It's not a date. It's two friends studying herbs."

"First piece of the puzzle," he said, and stood from the bench.

How had he finished his breakfast so fast? I had barely touched mine. I hurried to scoop the yoghurt into my mouth and swallowed as I kept listening to Kate lecturing the men on how she would be better than both of them combined in the herbs and poison challenge.

"Have you finished?" Emroyce asked, looking at me, as they had been waiting for me.

I grabbed the tray and nodded, my voice seeming not to work today. We walked together to the herbology classroom. Its layout had fifty double desks spaced out over ten rows to host a hundred cadets. I sighed, knowing a confrontation was on the horizon as I'd have to leave a space free for Ben to sit next to me or everyone would realise that we were fighting. It didn't mean I needed to look at him, though.

Walking through the rows, I knew I had to be careful as I had no weapons with which to defend myself if anyone planned to attack. The rules of the outpost didn't allow for that, of course, but some did it anyway, and took the lashes as punishment, knowing they had eliminated some of the competition. I picked a table at the end of row seven and slouched onto a seat with feet stretched out and arms crossed over my chest. A soft frown manifested on my face as I inspected the plants that Mewer had placed on all the desks.

Ben appeared in the doorway without the other black-wings at his side, as they had been divided into the other group. His gaze swept over the room, and he sauntered my way as he saw me and sat down on the empty chair next to me.

I ensured to keep my mental shields up, seeing in my peripheral view that he was staring at me.

"Did you have a…good night's sleep?" he asked. His muttering was low, and the tone clearly suggested he was jealous.

I had insinuated that I would stay the night with Zayd on purpose, so I had expected his dark mood. Without moving my eyes his way, I ensured they stayed on Mewer, who walked into the classroom. "No. Can't say I got much sleep."

He grunted angrily. Did he really think so little of me that he thought I had rushed to Zayd's bed to have sex with him? Maybe because he couldn't give me such sensual satisfaction himself, he worried I would source it elsewhere. The thought was heart-breaking. But so was thinking of all those who would die because he didn't order the retreat of his soldiers from Pansery.

Mewer had his long golden hair curling over his back, and it was uncommon to see him this clean, with no splotches of blood on his navy-blue camp leader uniform. His green eyes glimmered, showing how much he liked his profession and everything that had to do with healing. He was such a caring and compassionate man even when his tall frame and wide shoulders equalled the other warriors, making him look beastly.

"Cadets!" Mewer voiced over everyone to get the class to settle. "You're embarking on the third challenge of your first year. Well done for being alive. And thank you to those who haven't increased my workload in the infirmary." He looked around the room approvingly. "This challenge is about ensuring you stay strong during battle. If you're wounded, you must know how to identify herbs around you in the forest that you can use to heal. It also includes knowing what berries not to pick, which are poisonous and how to identify poisons, which your enemy may have smeared onto their weapons. Identifying that will help you prepare the correct blend of antidotes for the quickest recovery."

He held up two tubs of creams. "The white cream is the one many of you have seen and used already. It's a healing cream with an antibacterial effect. It's slow-working, though. I still prepare it because it helps minor injuries and because it's easy and quick to make with herbs, which are quite common in our woods. This other green one," he said, holding it up, "is a very rare cream, whose qualities will seal up a nasty cut in mere moments. However, to make it is a lengthy process and you can only find its ingredients in the Black Wing Territory and high up on their mountains. The final test of this challenge, for me to declare a winner, is in two parts. The first part is to gain knowledge and to use it to create a cream with the best healing effect. The second part is to show you can grow herbs and give them the correct care. This basically means that you must keep the plant on your desk alive for the month and not kill it. It's a Zincrics herb from the east Katagoon province and it's your job to find out how to nurture it. There are lots of books about it in the library."

"Aw. Our first baby. But I'm sure you'll kill it, as you do to my people," I muttered to Ben below my breath.

He didn't respond. Not a single word in argument to defend himself.

Mewer splayed out his arms, gesturing for a table filled with mature herb plants. "Today's class is about making a blend you can eat to settle your stomach from nausea. I'll keep the classroom open so you can get whatever book you need from the library and return here to use the herbs to create your mix. You may begin."

Ben stood from the chair. "I'll get the book. You don't have any weapons, so stay here near Emroyce."

I waited for Ben to leave the classroom before I strode to the front, ripping off peppermint leaves and stuffing them into a tea bag net together with ginger and a slice of lemon. I tied the net together with a string and then held it out to show Mewer. It wasn't really fair, as this class hadn't changed tasks for years and I had known it by heart already. It was Mewer's trick to emphasise talking about creams beforehand to confuse the cadets that he was looking for a cream when he had used the word blend, but I had known this task was a brew; a tea in which herbs should be dipped into hot water to work.

He smiled at me proudly. "But you could have at least waited a while to give the secret away to the other cadets." He winked and ushered me a step towards the door with a friendly hand on my back. "You're dismissed."

Ben returned, and I crossed him in the doorway, snatching the book out of his grip. "Thank you. I'll need that for later."

He gripped my arm and stopped me from the quick escape I had planned to make. "Where are you going?"

"Zayd has offered to take me out to the forest to teach me about herbs."

Wrath burned in his red eyes, and his arms trembled. He quickly dropped my arm so as not to hurt me.

"Another non-date with Camp Leader Watson?"

I kept staring at the wall to avoid eye-contact. "I don't know if it's a non-date. I guess it's open season now." I stole a glance at him out of the corner of my eye, but my pride was still too stubborn to lower my shields.

The silence was thick with unspoken words. "We had one little fight."

I pinned him with my stares. "You, attacking my people, isn't something insignificant to me. It's the breaking point between us. You must see this?"

Ben didn't avert his gaze, but was far from caving first, not budging on his decisions.

Fine. Nor will I.

"Put that issue aside for now. This challenge is too important to lose because of our temporary squabble."

"I guess we'll have joint custody over our plant. You can have it this week and I'll care for it the next."

I rushed off before he could put in another word, my resolve weakening every second I was near him. My body craved to be close to him and my mind wanted his company all the time. It was a bloody curse.

In Zoe's room, I flicked through the herbology book until the time when the class should have finished and borrowed a pair of hiking boots and a small shoulder bag from Zoe's wardrobe.

The corridor was quiet as I left Zoe's room, but when I was about to turn the corner, I heard a vicious dispute between two voices I could identify. I pressed myself against the corner to eavesdrop.

"She will hate me if you don't let me tell her the truth," Ben growled.

"You're preaching to the wrong crowd, King Blackbone. When she hates you, she runs to me," Zayd replied.

Ben snorted. "Just because you slept with her last night, it doesn't mean that she'll come running back to you. She already left you once and that was before she even knew me."

Zayd seemed to choke on his breath. "Is that what you think happened last night? Oh, if you insinuated the same to Angie, she must be so pissed off with you for thinking so little of her."

That's actually what I had thought.

"If you did," Zayd carried on. "She might be tonight, though."

Don't be too confident of that, Zayd! I peered around the corner.

Ben stepped closer to Zayd, closing the space between them. His fists were tightened at the side of his legs and his chest rose and fell in sharp breaths as he squared up with Zayd. His jaw clenched and every muscle in his body coiled like a predator ready to strike. He stared hotly into the eyes of the man who wanted to steal away his woman. Ben's eyes were dark with fury, daring Zayd to make the next move. Tension crackled in the air, and it seemed each second made his pulse thunder more and more in his veins, yet he held his ground, but I'd guess one wrong word from Zayd at this point was all it'd take to wreak havoc and start a fight to the death.

My heart raced as I watched them, taking notice of every little twitch that could set them off. I held my breath for so long it burned in my chest.

After a brief moment, Ben veered to one side and carried on down the corridor the other way towards our room.

I sighed out a mighty, lungful breath, and having waited for a while after Zayd had cleared the corridor, I headed for the tree and climbed up to my branch to ponder what Ben had said. Zayd…leadership was prohibiting Ben from talking to me. Why? Why would Ben care to listen to them? Zayd and Harvey would never put a threat on my life, would they? Would I really put it past my brother not to do it in the name of defending his territory? Who really cared about me? *Ben did.* He was here with me when he should be up north, leading his war.

"Angie? Ready?" Zayd shouted from the ground.

I climbed down from the tree to where Zayd waited for me. "I feel so angry. Perhaps, it's a better use of my time if we spar."

Zayd stretched his hand out for me to take it, but I walked past him.

He didn't seem to be offended by it and simply chirped, "We can't go there right this moment, as the hall has restricted access for the hunger challenge for second-year cadets. But I'm happy to practice some lunges at you by the water pool."

Zayd needed to be back within an hour, so that left us little time, but we rushed around the area and had found some frog leaves and salvia to make a soothing paste for insect bites before we returned. Zayd had been helpful, but the words between him and Ben had echoed in my mind the entire hour. When we returned to the military building, I immersed myself into books in the library. But they were not only about herbology, I also read up on historic disputes between the territory.

Oddly, there was no information older than twenty-six years when it seemed the wars had started. That was roughly about the time when my father had hiked the Spirits' Trek. The narrative about the war was always vague, with no detail about battle strategy, with focus only on how many had died in the attack and how much destruction the war had left in its wake. I spent four more days in the library from morning to night, trying to ignore Ben, and he never approached to talk to me.

Tomorrow was another of Mewer's classes and I would have to sit next to him. Lying in Zoe's bed without energy to do much, I contemplated reporting myself as sick and staying in Zoe's room for the rest of the week. I had enough pity chocolates and toffees to last me for a month.

Almost not finishing that thought, there were three gentle knocks on the door. Who would visit Zoe and not know she was on a mission? I pulled open the door and saw Ben hunched over with his forearm supporting himself on the door frame. He had cut his hair shorter, so his wavy black quiff finished by his ears, and he had shaved. He looked younger in appearance, but his tired eyes made him look ancient. Could it mean that he was as exhausted of fighting as I was?

I leaned against the spine of the door. "How did you find me?"

"I followed the humming in my ears and the tug of the bond." He focused on his hand, curling his fingers in the air. "Please, come home."

I crossed my arms over my chest, ready for a fight. "And where exactly is my home?"

He didn't take the bait, keeping his voice calm. "Our room. In my arms. Anywhere where we're not apart." He leaned into the room as if he wanted to get closer, but he kept himself anchored with his forearm on the door frame.

"And what about our disagreements? Should they simply be ignored?"

"Whatever list you have made of things you're angry with me about. I accept responsibility and I apologise for them all."

I took the step forward to show him I wasn't backing down and leaned my hip against the door frame. "Did you really believe it would be that easy?"

He huffed, raked his fingers through his hair, and pinned his hands to his sides. "I'm sorry for believing for one second that you would have intimate relations with Watson."

"So, for calling me a whore. What else?"

He stared at me hard. "I did not call you a whore, and I wouldn't have blamed you if you had stayed with Watson. Believe me, I understand the severity of our conflict."

Spirits! Severity of conflict? Did he think he was talking to one of his war commanders?

"So, I'm permitted to make love to Zayd?"

His teeth gritted for a moment. "If that's what you want."

"No, Ben! That's not what I want! I want you to trust me with your secrets. Let me in." I tapped a firm finger against his chest, right by his heart.

He clamped my hand against his chest to keep it there. "I asked for some time to fix things, and you accepted that only a week ago."

"That was before I knew you planned to invade Pansery."

"You know there are wars in the north."

I snatched my hand free. "Wars you can end. So, where else have you planned to attack? Bensguard?"

"Angelica, please." He closed his eyes. He looked so broken. "Let's just…let's take a walk under the stars."

"No! I want to know. Tell me, King Blackbone. Where do you plan to attack next? I doubt I can warn anyone in time, so just tell me. Which city are you sacking next?"

"I don't know!" he roared.

I took a step backwards. My heart was in my throat. Ben had never shouted like that at me before.

"I'm sorry," he whispered, composing himself. "I don't know. Is there no way you can see beyond the crown and simply love Ben?"

That's why he had roared. Calling him King Blackbone had struck a nerve.

"Give me something, or I'll ask my brother to give me another teammate. He already offered to do it when I spent the night in my family apartment, so I know he'll do it."

"So, that's where you were." He stared at my feet, his mind absent in thought. "I'll tell you one statement, but there can be no questions about it.

That's all I can give you at this moment."

I nodded. A silent agreement I was dying to make so I could be in his arms again. I timidly walked closer to support my hip against the door frame, but kept my arms folded over my chest. He held out his hands as if to accept me into his arms, but when he saw I wasn't going that far, he rested them at his sides.

"I'll have to…" he tapped at his head.

Right. Mazdon could be listening.

"It's not the black-wings who are attacking the White Wing Territory. And, if King Emille found out you knew who, he'd kill us both."

My eyes widened and I blinked a few times. *"What? Why?"*

"I guess because of your magic, which is why I want to know what it is, so that I can assess what the threat is and how much I can tell you."

I reflexively shook my head. *"I have no magic."*

"Angelica…"

I pushed my fingers through my blue strands. *"But who else could be–"*

"No questions, I said."

"If I had magic, and I told you what it was, would you tell me what you know?"

He shook his head. *"I can't promise that. It depends on your magic."*

My hand paused at the top of my head, halfway raking through my hair, and I looked at him, still baffled. *"I have no magic."*

"Okay. Let's discuss it later. I gave you something. Can you come back to our room now?"

"I said I would keep you as my teammate if you gave me something, not that I'd share your bed again. For that, you'll have to give up another piece of information that has nothing to do with war and everything to do with you."

The impatience was evident in his eyes. I wasn't sure how much farther I could push him. He had been taught to negotiate like a king, and he had given up too much for nothing already.

"And what is that?"

"Tell me what your second magic is, and you'll have me naked, begging for your body on top of mine within minutes."

He froze, staring at me in silence.

I narrowed my eyes at him. *"Are you about to deny that you have a second magical ability, King Blackbone?"*

"No," he growled. *"That's information I wouldn't mind sharing if it wasn't because of the nature of it. I fear you'll cannot love me after I tell you what it is. The offer of you naked beside me will definitely be off the table."*

I swallowed. Was he an intrinsic like General Denor? Had he manipulated my mind? What magic did he have that could be unforgivable? What magic could be worse than his death-magic?

"We can never be us without me knowing. You can wait to tell me later or rip the

plaster, but sooner or later, I'll want to know. It's up to you if you think time will lessen my anger about it."

"No, it won't. It'll only get worse." He inhaled deeply. "I can…I instil… My magic makes living things trust me."

I gasped. *Trust magic.* There it was. The crack in my heart I had always expected him to make. I backed up one step and saw him frown before I slammed the door in his face, hiding the bite of hurt behind a thick plank of wood.

I sank to the floor, not sure it was still there as it appeared to have been ripped out from underneath me. A hollow ache blossomed throughout my chest with a relentless agony, making it hard to breathe. The crushing weight of my heartache seemed to sink deep into my bones.

I had trusted him. Believed him when he said he loved me. Now I could never know if his words were true. Tears burned at the edges of my vision, so I hasted to dry them with the heel of my palm. An enemy king wasn't worthy of my tears.

I saw the nausea remedy teabag that I had made in class on the desk, but I had no way of boiling water. Maybe hot water from the tap would suffice. On the top shelf of the cupboard in the kitchenette I found a mug, so I took it and turned the tap to the hottest setting, cussing when I was trying to fill the mug because my hands were trembling so much that water squirted everywhere. I put the mug down on the counter and tossed in the tea bag.

Tears streamed down my cheeks, and this time I let them fall, as I slowly sipped the tea.

Did this mean we were finished? I could never know whether Ben had made me trust him or made me love him. If he told me he had never used the magic on me, he could be using his magic to make me trust his words. How could I ever know that my feelings were my own when he was near me? Was he using me to get to my magic? What if he told me to trust him to gift my magic to him? He was dangerous. More than I had realised.

My brain worked out that he must have used his trust magic on the snakes. That's why they had worshipped him like a Spirit. The same way I worshipped him. Spirits! I was such a fool!

Although I felt like retching my insides out completely, nothing came up. Perhaps the tea had helped.

There were soft knocks on the door. "Please, Angelica, talk to me." Ben talked through the wood.

He was still here? I pressed my hands over my ears. "Not another word from you."

"We can't spend our entire relationship not speaking." His muffled voice through the door made it feel like I was in a bad dream, and I wanted to wake up right fucking now!

"Or touching, or being next to each other," I added.

There was a brief silence until I heard his remorseful, soft voice. *"I'll do anything."*

Shit. I could never escape him. He was in my head. I'd have to tell my brother to unbind our souls.

"Please don't do that. We can fix this ourselves. I swear it to you on my…on my mother's grave that I've never used my trust magic on you. Not once."

He had listened to my private thoughts again, crossing that line I had set for him, but what he had sworn dug deep into my soul.

I walked towards the door, tracing my fingers down the wood as if it was his cheek. "You loved your mother."

"I love you more!" he roared, as if I was stupid for not understanding that.

"Shush! Keep your voice down. You're in the corridor." I shouted through the door.

"I don't care! When will you get it? All I do is for you. To keep you safe and happy."

I wanted so badly to trust him. *Wait!* Was that my true feeling, or was he using his magic on me at this very moment?

"Stop using your magic on me!"

"I'm not using it on you! Please trust…please *believe* me. I'd never use it on you. I'll do anything for you."

"Like giving me the Black Blade?"

There was a brief silence. "Except that," I heard him mutter through the door.

"Your list of exceptions goes on and on. What about gifting me your trust magic?"

26

It was quiet.

I snorted to myself. *Thought so.*

I looked towards the bed. I needed to lie down.

"Okay," Ben grunted.

My heart stopped! I halted and turned around, walking back to the door. "Okay?" I dropped my jaw.

He would gift me his trust magic? I mean. I didn't want it. Didn't need it. I couldn't even handle another magical ability because I'd go mad before the day ended from so much power. But that he had agreed blew my mind.

I opened the door slowly and looked at him; his black hair, red eyes, handsome face and muscular build. "You'd gift me your magic?"

He sighed, his forehead wrinkling. "I mean, it's good to have when convincing my soldiers not to attack the White Wing Territory, but if it's what you need to repair any distrust between us, it's yours."

I stared at him, assessing what I thought about it all. "Not once?"

The wrinkles in his face softened. "Not once have I used it on you."

I drummed my fingers one after the other against the door. "Not even when I poked the tip of the Black Blade at your heart?"

He shook his head. "I knew you wouldn't stab me. Well. I didn't know. But I was confident enough. With you, one never knows." He flashed me a smile that didn't meet his eyes.

"You're a gambler, King Blackbone."

"Never once have I lost a bet. And some have involved substantial wagers."

I raised my brows, so he continued to explain.

"Staying a captive of the white-wings after you had offered to free me. Bonding to another soul, who isn't very liked at this outpost and risking death with her. Letting you leave on a non-date with Camp Leader Watson. Placing my heart in your hands, even when I know that with every secret

I'll reveal, I'm jeopardising you stamping on it. And a few other things I'll tell you about another time."

I looked at him for a while, deliberating over my next move.

"So," he muttered. "So have I earned what you said about your body on top of mine, yet?"

I pinched my lips between my fingers. "Not quite, but I have a counteroffer." I stepped out into the corridor, closed and locked Zoe's door behind me, and rushed for our room, hearing Ben keeping up behind me.

"I know that look in your eye, Miss Stone. What mischief are you up to this time?"

"Telling you would ruin my fun." I unlocked our door and hurried to the wardrobe to bring out an iron fighting rod.

The way he cleared his throat was loaded with suspicion. "You want to beat me up?"

"You tell me how beaten you feel when I'm finished."

Once I levelled the rod horizontally, I pushed it at Ben's abdomen to herd him backwards towards the edge of the bed.

"Sit, leaning against the wall and hold the rod. Don't let go until I give you permission."

"Yes, Mam!" He shuffled himself up and made himself comfortable. "You want me to do sit-ups or something? When I was in the war camp in Uppland, the soldiers used to challenge me by–"

"Shush. Not talking. This isn't a training programme. It's your punishment for keeping secrets."

I stripped in front of him until I was only wearing a pair of blue lace knickers.

He swallowed hard as I crawled up onto the bed by his feet. "I wish I could tell you more secrets if this is my punishment."

"Shush! No talking! No moving! No protesting!"

"Protesting?"

My fingers nimbly unbuttoned his trousers and when he realised what I had planned for him, his eyes widened in horror. "No! Angelica."

I kissed his abdomen. "I said no protesting."

"I can't. The magic. I must keep a leash on my emotions."

"Don't let go of the iron rod."

"So, that is what it was for! But my magic transfers through the air, too, not just by the touch of my hands. What if–"

"Shush. Apparently, kings aren't good listeners. Not another word!"

I grabbed the lining of his trousers and tugged them down until I could remove them entirely together with his socks and discarded them onto the floor. After that, I started tugging down his boxer shorts but stopped teasingly before I had a glimpse of anything beneath and instead went for the buttons on his shirt. Ben was panting harder and harder and as my head came closer to him, he brought his hand to my cheek. His eyes looked deeply mesmerised as he breathed, "You're so beautiful."

I pulled my cheek away. "No talking. Hands on the iron!"

He snapped his mouth shut and clamped down on the rod. I pushed the opened shirt to either side of his torso and kissed his hard muscles.

He cocked his head up as if in agony. "Angelica, I don't think I can take this," he groaned.

"Speaking again invokes a penalty. Now, it's going to be worse for you."

He chuckled and said a quick prayer to the Spirit of the Living that we both would survive this. It didn't frighten me. He wouldn't hurt me. He wouldn't let me do this to him if he didn't desperately want it.

Kissing lower and lower, I reached his boxer shorts and tugged them downwards to reveal his impressive length.

I grunted playfully. "Hm, not bad."

His smile was crooked but kept quiet. *Wise.*

I gently kissed the round tip, hearing him release a strained breath. More kisses around his shaft made him squeal out, "Fuck!"

Something inside my stomach coiled in excitement when I took his length inside my mouth, and he leaned his head back against the wall. *He likes it!*

I moved my mouth up and down, sliding my tongue against him, making him wet and warm and hard. He panted as if he had just returned from a flat-out run, his hands keeping a white-knuckled grip over the rod.

Going faster on him, he whispered to no one in particular, begging for mercy. Black smoke whipped around us, making him unsettled.

But I wasn't in a mood to be merciful, not caring whether he might kill me in the process, as I was quite confident that he would keep his magic controlled.

Faster and faster, I pumped his cock with my mouth and with a gentle suck. He began uttering soft groans, clearly getting closer to erupting.

Dark magic covered every area of our room's floor, and it swirled ominously towards the ceiling. This was so savage and sexual at the same time. Death magic had built up inside him to dangerous levels. Abruptly, I stopped, knelt back and got off the bed, walking over to stare out of the window, seeing thick grey clouds hanging over the outpost, hiding the stars.

His eyes followed me as he panted. He made a low grunt after a while.

"Now, I get your mischief…and my punishment."

There was a mix of emotions on his face. Relief. Frustration. Hurt. He got off the bed to lock himself in the bathroom with the shower at full power.

I had been cruel, and in a way I regretted it, but he had to understand that I won't kneel to him as my king, nor any man; not him, not Zayd, not Harvey and certainly not General Denor. They couldn't treat me however they liked without suffering the consequences. I couldn't accept Ben into my life if he didn't let me into his. Fully. He kept secrets and that meant our relationship wasn't complete – just like his blow-job. Hopefully, he would get the message and understand how frustrating it was for me, and the reason I couldn't forgive it.

With my hands hooked around the bed frame, I pulled his single bed apart from mine and walked around to shove it against the other wall with my foot where it had been originally. No more sharing beds until he committed fully. I was not his plaything.

I left the room and went to the sparring hall, but its locked doors stopped me from entering, and there was a sign explaining the hall was in use for the hunger challenge. Angry, I stomped to the herbs and potions room where Mewer was tidying up his tools and the Smoking Team; Ivan Crow and Gregg Hefany sat on their desks, exhaling something which gave off green tendrils of smoke that smelt minty and sweet.

Cadet Hefany's eyes were so intense periwinkle it was unnerving the way they stared at me. He kept bending smoke into pictures of snakes with his magic as I stopped next to Mewer. Their team was the most divided in loyalty as Cadet Crow was a gold bender and wanted to team up with Axel Hillip in the Jealous Team who could create gold. No doubt he wanted them to take over his father's jewellery shop in the capital and become filthy rich.

Mewer smiled at me whilst stacking a few of the study books on top of each other. "You look…" He appeared to weigh his words carefully. "Ready to murder someone? May I suggest a jog in the rain to cool yourself off before you hurt those you love most?"

Through the window, I could see that it was raining again.

"Appreciative of your advice as I always am, however, I think this time your wisdom comes too late." A cool breeze from the humid rain air came in through one of the open windows and made a chill run down my arms. "Maybe not. Maybe I'll go for that jog, after all."

"I knew you wouldn't pass up the opportunity to find Katagoon Water Hemlock by the riverbank, whose flowers only turn outwards when it rains," he said softly, so the Smoking Team wouldn't hear him, and finished with a wink.

'Thank you,' I mouthed. "Do you need help tidying anything?"

"No. But thank you for asking. Although, you could take this book to make my pile lighter." He handed me a thick book titled, 'Herbs & Healing Potions'. "Keep it until you graduate, as it's particularly useful for cadets during their third year."

I would think that Mewer had a soft spot for me, but by now I had learned to keep my guard up against all men. He pushed the book towards me and paused, looking over my shoulder before he pushed it the last bit and then carried on picking up a pile of mint leaves from the desk and stuffing them into a tea bag. Whatever he was preparing, it always made me curious, but the feeling turned to annoyance as a hand appeared on my shoulder.

"Camp Leader Mewer," Ben greeted.

"King Blackbone," Mewer returned.

His hand pinched at my shoulder. "*You left me.*"

"I thought you needed time to cool off."

"You're playing a cruel game."

"I learned from the best." I cocked my head up to watch his reaction.

"Mewer, may I ask?" I quizzed. "What would you do if one of your close friends possessed trust magic?"

Ben stiffened behind me, his grip on my shoulder tightened. *"Careful, Angelica. That is secret information."*

"Mewer won't tell anyone. I trust him…or have you made *me trust him?"*

Ben must have lost control of his mental shield, because I could feel his irritation through our bond like a furious beast trying to claw himself out of his cage, slamming again and again against the bars but being restrained – for now.

Mewer's golden eyebrows rose, his green eyes calculatingly assessing my question. "I guess I would trust the people I love, or there would be no reason to love them. If loyalty needed time to grow in an environment without that magic at play, I would ask Cadet Charney in second year to bound the magic temporarily to block it until trust settled."

Ben's hand squeezed even more possessively over my shoulder. *"Cadet Charney is from Emendroth Outpost, his father serves in the Infantry. I certainly do not trust him. Even if I did, I don't want anyone else to get involved in our relationship problems."*

He didn't need to trust Cadet Charney, but I could use that information to my advantage, anyway.

"What relationship? What problems?" I snapped at him.

"We're no longer together, then? Is that what you're telling me? Is that why you've pulled our beds apart?"

"Well," Mewer said, clearing his throat, clearly having seen the stares between us and noted our internal feud. "Once you're done with that particular volume," he said, tapping his hand gently on the cover of the book, "please hand it back to me personally. I hope you'll have a successful run."

"Run? It's raining," Ben barked. "You could catch a cold."

"What I catch or not, would be none of your concern unless we were soulmates…oh wait, we are! But that can't be right as soulmates tell each other everything."

He smiled. Why was he smiling?

"You called us soulmates, and not what we are; soul bound."

"Soulmates. Soul bonded. Whatever."

"There is a big difference," he corrected, still grinning.

Lumping the comprehensive book into my arms, I turned on my heel, ready to leave. "Thank you, Camp Leader Mewer. You're always so enlightening."

Mewer returned to sorting his herbs, minding his own business. "Always happy to help."

When I got into our room, Ben was still on my heel, and I was still ignoring him as he had mentioned he would come with me and I had firmly said no.

After I had flicked through the herb book, I had realised that it was full of notes in Mewer's own handwriting. One in bold on the water hemlock page advised using gloves when picking them. The book was practically a key to all the medicines he created. My heart filled with such admiration for him, it was hard to focus my emotions on being pissed-off with Ben.

"I'll get my gloves," Ben muttered, having been reading over my shoulder.

I snapped the book shut and put it down on the desk, every one of my movements sharp and final. "You're not coming."

He held my gaze as if he wanted to scan me for a loophole or a weakening link, but I showed him none. That I had put up a wall between us last week had clearly made him think twice about the battles he picked to fight with me, and he was being careful. He likely waned to use his demanding kingly tone with me to get his way but knew that if he went down that route now, he would only dig himself into a deeper hole. I kept one eye on him as I searched through the wardrobe drawer for my leather gloves.

He pinned his hands on his hips, his fingers digging in tightly to his flesh. "You cannot go out there by yourself, in the rain, hunting for poisonous plants and on the outpost premises where fellow cadets call you mutt."

I donned the waist-long, black leather jacket with the Bensguard Outpost key emblem on the collar and pulled on the black gloves.

"Watch me."

I left the room and the building; walking at first, but as my frustration hammered in my chest, I began jogging. Icy rain fell on my head, sleeking my hair to my face and seeping along my skin to the inside of my jacket. It was needed to pacify the agony roaring in my mind. All I wanted to do was to stay with Ben, banter and smile at each other like we used to do when we were in the Black Wing Territory, where my mission had felt easier than the reality I faced here. To imagine my naked body against his was as easy as breathing but refraining to be with him because I couldn't have the full extent of his mind, was a struggle I didn't know how to beat. He was a king, and I was a nobody; I got that.

I halted by the treeline, hidden by the dense forest branches, as the words sank in.

He is a king, and I'm a nobody.

My heart ached to the point I wondered in a fleeting second if I was having a small heart-attack. There was no possible future for us. What was I doing with him as my teammate? I was no warrior. I was a spy and had enjoyed my special missions to retrieve various items for my brother. Maybe I should beg him to transfer me back to that post. Slowly, I walked towards the pond by the foot of the mountain, considering my choices and where I could find somewhere to call home. I thought of Zoe, Kate, Mazdon, Emroyce, Fern and Zayd and even Harvey, Brian and Valentina but then my thoughts circled back to settle on the fact that Home was at Ben's side. The humming in my ears from the bond to him heightened the further away from the building I jogged. The constant reminder that he was always with me. I had to find a way to ensure I was by his side and not hidden by his shadow.

The water hemlock by the pond was indeed blooming and enjoying the rain by the bank. I squatted down and took out the paper bag from my shoulder bag and opened it with a wide mouth before setting it down underneath me to keep it as dry as possible from the rain. The hemlock stems refused a quick snap, so I turned and twisted to pick them, careful not to let their clustered white flowers shed and land on any part of my skin.

The humming in my ears was distracting me and kept amplifying until it was a scream. I jerked my head up. *Ben!* Was he attempting suicide? He was flying too far away from me. The bond angered and it felt like my soul was a thinning string nearing snapping point. Where was he going? I supported my hands on the wet stone, the agony unbearable, as I tried to keep myself steady. I didn't want to fall into the pool when the sound made my vision tunnel, and I feared I might faint. After a few moments, the screaming in my head ebbed and I could breathe normally, adequately enough to carry on. But I made a mental note to scold him later.

It took me a while to fill the bag and as I looked up to put it into my shoulder bag, I noticed something glinting in the water before seeing a distorted reflection of someone on the water surface. By reflex, I twisted and looked up to see a blonde man who I didn't recognise, raising the largest sword I had ever seen. Just letting it fall from its own weight would cut my head clean off from my shoulders.

His eyes were filled with intense rage as he looked at me for a moment before he began bringing his sword down, calling out the word, "Mutt!"

My daggers were difficult to draw the way I was squatting, so I knew I wouldn't have time to get them out. Panic numbed me and I held my hand up, turned my head away and screamed.

I waited for the pain that would be momentary before death. The darkness. The peace. But I only heard a thud among the drops of rain falling onto the water surface of the pond. My head twitched to my right towards where the blonde man lay on the grass beside me, black veins running thinly beneath the skin of his face. His eyes were vacant, and he wasn't moving, his chest didn't rise with his breaths.

"You cannot defend yourself if you look away from your opponent. You really aren't going to use your very powerful magic even to save your own life?" Ben rebuked.

Ben was here! Saving me. I wanted to throw myself into his arms, but my pride held a nasty grip around my emotions.

"I was just about to use my magic when you killed him," I lied and stood up. "And I have my daggers." Hopefully, he couldn't see how my knees wobbled.

He grunted and I knew it meant he saw straight through my lie. "You couldn't draw your daggers the way you were squatting."

"I had him," I snapped. "And I told you not to follow me."

"I wanted to live." There was no excuse in his voice. "And I wasn't following you. I was on my way back, flying overhead when I saw this guy," he said, and gestured at the corpse with his hand, "sneaking up on you."

"Where were you?" I asked to keep to that subject, but I didn't expect an answer, only more secrets, so it surprised me when he answered.

"I was collecting comfrey root for Camp Leader Mewer's class, which can only be found in the Black Wing Territory and high up on the mountains." He patted the shoulder bag laying on his hip. "I also got marjoram, lemons, chamomile, lavender and basil, so I can make you a soothing tea when we get back."

"That sounds an awful lot like the blend to remedy a foul breath. Do you think I taste bad?"

He closed the gap between us, and I could hear his boots squelch on the water-soaked grass. "I can't recall. Let me see." There was a smile curling at the end of his lips, but it wasn't confident. He brought his lips slowly towards mine, as if checking whether I would allow it. "There may be more places I must taste on you to be certain of you being delicious." His breath hit my mouth.

I groaned, my sex tingling with need for him to be closer. Inside. His lips brushed mine and my core tightened with anticipation. Heat pulsating through me with the thought of his warm touch travelling down my naked body. I bit my lip to ensure I wouldn't completely unravel at this very moment, but it was nearly impossible as every brush of his hand made my body burn with longing to claim him as mine.

"Your breath first, though. Breathe on me." He pulled away to make eye-contact and had the biggest grin on his face.

He was fucking teasing me. Was he retaliating because I was pushing him away and now he'd hold me at an arm's length? He was cunning and intelligent, but he was also on my playing field.

I lowered from having risen to my toes. "Not to worry. I don't want to bother your Majesty. I'll ask someone who cares…hm, maybe I can ask Zayd when I get back."

He roared, grabbed the back of my neck, and pulled me close to his face. "I love you. My chest almost collapsed from fear because I thought I wouldn't get to you in time to protect you from the blonde guy. I'm doing everything in my power to be near you, to respect your wishes, and at the same time keep us alive. And that is a dangerous balance in this place, I can assure you." His grip was hard and uncomfortable, but I didn't dare complain.

Instead, I drove the conversation deeper. "People don't keep secrets from those they love."

"And yet, you do the same," he defended, staring straight into my soul, it seemed. "The secrets I keep are those which aren't mine to share. Ask your brother. Pester him about learning the truth. I'll defy him and tell you the secrets if he won't, but not until it's safe for you to know. When I'm on my turf and can protect you. Here, I can't ensure I'm around you all the time when you need it."

"Let go of my neck. You're hurting me," I finally voiced, as his anger put more pressure on his grip.

Immediately, he let go and let his hand slack at his side. "If you want to know all the truths, we can flee to my territory together and you can join me in fighting my battles."

"We would still be bonded."

"I'm glad for that and I don't see the bond as a problem. I don't have any intentions of ever removing it. If you were bonded to me for the rest of our lives, it would make me a happy man. You have many choices in life, but they're yours to take. I'm here, by your side, whatever you choose to do. The rain, I could do without though, if we could carry on this conversation inside our room."

The rain was riveting down his black hair and falling off the tip of his nose. He was here, soaked, for me. Together, we were standing in the pouring rain, arguing over something that should be so simple. I loved him, too. I wanted to let him into my heart, but my mother's betrayal had cut me so deep.

"I want to pick some chive leaves, nightshade, stickleback, burdock and sorghum before I'm done. It'll only take an hour and then I'll come to the room."

He crossed his arms over his chest and nodded. "I'll wait."

I rolled my eyes at him, but in earnest, I was happy for his company. He even helped me pick the ingredients I needed and when he was bending low, I pushed him over to roll on the wet grass. He dragged me with him and wrestled me to my back. We laughed and bantered, and for a moment, I forgot about the world around us, and even the rain went unnoticed.

When we were back in our room and donned dry uniforms, we made our way to the canteen for dinner. None of my white-wing friends had arrived yet, which was a relief, as I didn't want to be split in deciding whether to sit with the white-wing friends or the black-wing group. Gravelhorn, Malloopa, Crow, Hefany, Grim and Randall sat at a table near the back wall and a chill bristled the hair on my arms when their creepy stares followed me as I went to the service station. It smelt lovely, of rosemary and honey. My mouth watered as I was starving after the hike through the woods and the rain.

I lifted the lid and saw thick slices of ham and in the next pot there were roast potatoes. This was the warm comfort food I agreed with. Even though I was starving, I served myself a small portion, knowing not to eat with my eyes. Ben copied my movements, and side by side, we walked to the table and sat down next to Commander Daffron; Ben taking the seat opposite me.

"Where are Murben and Davis?" I asked, and Commander Daffron only shrugged his shoulders and looked at Nesso, who did the same, looking like a young pup compared to Commander Daffron.

Nesso's silver hair was damp, as if it had recently been towel-dried and so was Commander Daffron's. Although, Commander Daffron's black hair was combed neatly in a side parting at the top and tight to his neck at the back, whilst Nesso's was wild at the top as if he had shaken himself dry like a dog. Both the commander's amber eyes and Nesso's storm-grey with black flecks surveyed our surroundings between every bite.

Commander Daffron was no chatterbox, but Nesso was, so I aimed my question at him.

"So," I started. "What have you been up to today?" I pointed to the window to indicate the rain.

Murben walked through the doors before any of them had answered me, and looked around the canteen, barging deeper into the room like a storm when he laid his eyes on Ben. I had never seen him this focused and there was anger on his face. He normally didn't show any emotions, and his face was always a mask of calm, so whatever had happened had greatly upset him.

He hadn't yet made any eye-contact with me as he stopped behind Ben's back and whispered something into his ear.

In the instant that followed, Ben's eyes went wide, and he launched himself across the table and shoved his fingers into my mouth, prying out my chewed food and chucked it back onto my plate. He swung his legs over the table and wrapped his arm around my shoulder, bending me into his torso and nestling his hand under my arm, as if he was ready to keep me upright if my knees buckled. He pressed me close to him and led me towards the canteen exit, away from the evil laughter and the men's ensemble to our right.

"What's happening?"

"Nothing."

I stiffened. "More secrets?"

He pushed harder at my back, so I had to carry on walking.

"I'll tell you in our room."

"Did you like the ham!" Cadet Gravelhorn bawled out in laughter before the canteen doors closed behind all the black-wings.

My veins heated to a near scolding, and I snapped my head up to look at Ben. "They didn't?"

His face was grim, and he wasn't looking back at me. I saw the angry forking veins underneath his skin from the strain of controlling his rage. "Murben just reported that someone has broken into their room. Flora is missing."

The taste of the ham fillets and gravy on my tongue made me feel nauseous, and reflexively, as bile rose to the back of my throat, I gagged. They had killed Flora and made me eat her! My stomach twisted violently, and a sickening wave of horror left me breathless. No! This couldn't be real! Memories with Flora flashed before my eyes. Her small nuzzle and round form. Always happy to see me.

Now she was inside me.

I clutched around my stomach, and I shuddered. Panic clawed at me as my throat closed so tight I couldn't even scream.

Ben's focus lay on the corridor ahead and on getting me to our room as fast as possible. He didn't ask how I was. He could probably sense how distraught I felt through the bond. I tried to hold my tears in, but like opening a valve, they came rolling down my cheeks and I sobbed out a cry.

My legs buckled, but Ben held me up. He got us into the room and lowered me to kneel on the floor, where he knelt on both knees, his knees touching mine, and he wrapped his wings around us.

I wasn't sure I deserved it, but I had made the black-wing king kneel, comforting me over a pet pig. I had heard he had never knelt for anyone, although I didn't believe this counted, either.

"I loved that stupid pig."

"I know," he simply whispered and held me in silence as I sobbed into my hands with his arms curved around my back and his cheek resting on my head.

One arm eased from my back and cool air swept in before I heard Ben click his fingers. The door closed, so I assumed the black-wings had still lingered in the doorway.

"Murben will get us some dinner," he whispered, and his arm returned to nestle around my back.

It didn't feel like I would ever have an appetite again. I couldn't think about eating now.

"After that, can I go back and kill Gravelhorn?"

"He's provoking you. He isn't allowed to murder you unless it's during the challenges, but if you attack him, he's allowed to defend himself. And if you were to die in that defence, it'll be easier for him to get away with it. Don't fall for it."

I tore and twisted inside his frame to get free, but he held me tightly. My desire to plunge a dagger into Gravelhorn's chest burned hotly inside me like an unbearable itch beneath my skin. That was the problem with him, wasn't it? That he knew how to get on my nerves. The way it made me loathe him made me worry that I was falling for his tricks. If the moment came when I let my guard slip around him, he would ruin me first.

27

A new day had dawned, but it brought no relief, only deeper aches and fresh wounds to layer over yesterday's pain. I woke feeling like Leadership had taken a cheese grater to the inside of my chest, each breath scraping against raw nerves. A gnawing sorrow curled tightly around my ribs; a quiet torment that wouldn't let go.

I drifted through the morning's academic classes in a haze, my mind too burdened to focus. Words blurred on the page. Voices sounded distant, like echoes in water. I didn't speak unless spoken to, and even then, it was through clenched teeth.

After lunch, I prepared for another herbology lesson with Mewer, slipping my weapons into place by muscle memory more than thought. The recent threats on my life had agitated Ben. He wasn't just watchful anymore; he was a blade ready to be drawn. His eyes swept every corner of the corridor relentlessly. He barely spoke, his muscles flexed and his expression intense. His hands never strayed far from the weapons strapped to my hips and thighs, as if he expected danger to leap from the shadows at any moment. Honestly, he could probably unsheathe my blades faster than I could myself.

In the herbology classroom, I slid into my usual seat on our shared desk. The familiar scent of dried leaves and bitter roots hung in the air, grounding me for a moment.

But Ben didn't sit right away. He hesitated, posture taut.

Five desks to our right, Cadet Hefany let out an obnoxious snort, like a pig, unmistakably intended to mock. My stomach clenched.

I looked bitterly at Gregg Hefany, his black hair and the thin rim of periwinkle around his dilated pupils.

Murben had found out last night that he was the one who had slaughtered Flora, and it made me grateful Ben had held me back from attacking Gravelhorn yesterday.

I had something entirely different in mind for his punishment. If I couldn't kill Cadet Hefany openly when he could defend himself, I would poison him. Scare him a little. He was a heavy smoker, which was logical considering his magic to bend smoke, and I had just the thing which could kill you if you smoked it. An overdose of hemp should make him regret killing Flora. The anticipation of the revenge coiled like a snake in my gut. I had prepared, plotted and waited for the moment to strike, vicious and agonising to make up for the hurt he had caused me. My fingers twitched as if I could hurry the action, but I forced myself to remain composed. *Not yet.* The revenge couldn't be rushed. It must bite him when he didn't see it coming.

Cadet Hefany laughed softly and turned his head to look forwards as Mewer entered the classroom. Lucky for him, as Ben seemed ready to stalk over to him and snap his neck. The black veins forked over his hands from holding in his death magic. I touched his hand, and he immediately pulled it away and turned to me in shock.

"Are you unharmed?" he asked.

"I'm unhurtable. Sit down."

"You can't touch me when I'm that angry," he muttered, as he lowered himself to the seat.

Mewer held up a glass with a light-green liquid inside. "Today, we'll learn to make a cold relief brew, which can help bring down fever. This could be very useful for when you have an infection, which you'll likely catch after a few days on the battlefield."

"Few days!" One of the girls in the Horse Girls Team shouted.

"Yes, a battle can take several days before one side has won, and it's important to have the knowledge to care for yourself if there is no one else around to help you." He swirled the liquid inside the glass. "As you can see, this is a tea blend with a green colour. Green colour is good when it comes to things you consume. Red is normally deadly. That's good to bear in mind. Today, I want you all to get a glass from my desk," he gestured for the ten jugs full of the same coloured liquid and the towers of glasses stacked beside them on his desk, "and replicate the tea blend by using your smell and taste to identify the ingredients. You can test your theories by making different blends using the leaves over there." He pointed for the table along the wall that had about four dozen glass bowls filled with leaves, with a label in front of each to name the herb. "Write your final blend down on a paper with your names on it and I'll announce the teams who got it correct during our next lesson."

The cadets started moving around the room to fill up their glasses and returned to their desks.

"I'll go up there and retrieve the glass. You stay here," Ben commanded with finality, and I decided not to pick a fight this time.

Ben returned with a full glass, sniffing it as he walked back to me.

"I can smell elderflowers…primrose…and honey." He put the glass down on the desk and pointed at the pen and paper Mewer had supplied in the top left corner on the desk. "Write it down and let's get out of here."

I raised my brows. "Well, that lesson was fun. Couldn't have left some investigating for me?"

He smirked. "You could have mentioned the one hundred and fifty millilitres of boiled water needed to brew the leaves, if you wanted to take credit for something."

I threw the pencil at him, but he deflected it, turning a shoulder.

"You're going to have to write it down," he said, clearly not finished in taunting me.

Ben lifted the glass to sip the liquid. "Make it two teaspoons of each herb, but only one of honey. Especially if it's served to you, who is sweet enough."

There were no more pens to throw at him within reach, so I glowered at him, and stole the pen he had picked up from the floor and tucked behind his ear.

I jotted the tea blend ingredients down on the paper and put our names at the bottom. As I stood up, there were noises coming from the Smoking Team's table. I craned my head around Ben to watch what was going on.

Cadet Hefany was having fits on the floor and his teammate, Cadet Crow, was hunched over him, calling for him to try get a response. But Hefany was unresponsive even after the fits ceased. The large man simply stared at nothing, his skin turning a bluish tone.

"Out of the way!" Mewer bellowed, squatting down next to Hefany. Mewer put two fingers on Hefany's pulse and counted but pulled away as he saw blood and saliva foam from his mouth. "Water hemlock poison. Quickly retrieve the vial of the thick, sand-coloured liquid in the second drawer of my desk."

Mewer started performing mouth to mouth, ignoring the foaming blood around Hefany's mouth. He'd do just about anything to save anyone's life, even if they didn't deserve it. I admired Mewer for that. Heck, I wanted Hefany to survive if it made him happy.

Hefany suddenly took some shallow breaths that sounded raspy, and Mewer pushed two fingers into his mouth to push down his tongue. "Quickly!"

Crow was at the desk drawer, searching through it, making glass vials clonk against each other.

Mewer inspected Hefany's eyes. "Hurry Crow!"

Crow launched himself from the podium, landing on top of the nearest desks before jumping between them to get to Mewer faster as cadets filled the aisles in his path.

He handed Mewer the vial and Mewer quickly poured it down Hefany's throat before tipping him up slightly and then waiting, observing him for any sign of life, keeping two fingers on his pulse.

A moment passed, and the classroom was dead silent. Every single cadet held their breaths. Waiting. Hefany looked truly dead already, though.

"Everyone!" Mewer shouted. "Take your glass of tea blend to your room and finish the assignment there before breaking for dinner. You can hand your notes to me during the week." Mewer looked at me. "Everyone, except you."

Mewer hadn't invited Ben to stay, but it didn't look like Ben was going anywhere.

Whilst the cadets were filing out of the room, Crow leaned down towards Mewer; his normally neat blonde hair dishevelled, and his amber eyes glazed over. "Is he…. Is he dead?"

Mewer nodded. "I'm afraid so."

Crow snapped his head towards me. "I'll make you pay for this."

When the room had emptied of cadets, Mewer looked at me. "Tell me you didn't take my kind advice and made a murder weapon to use against your own people."

"Me? Camp Leader Mewer, I swear it on my life. I didn't do this. I had planned to make him sick from hemp, considering what he did to Flora, but not to kill him. Someone else got to him first. I'm innocent."

"If you say so, I'll give you the benefit of the doubt." He sighed and looked at the dead man by his knees. "Any theory as to the motive of why this happened?"

I glanced over the corpse. "Because he was a dickhead?"

Ben chuckled behind my back but stopped as Mewer looked at him.

Harvey walked into the classroom then. "I hear of another cadet's death outside of challenges. You're going to have to be less generous with your herbs if this continues."

"Yes, Captain Coraly. Although, the death was due to water hemlock poisoning, which I don't provide the cadets."

"Of course. Fill out the paperwork so I can contact his parents. This isn't the first son his family has lost, as they run a Fire Prevention organisation in Gaithbry. Prepare his casket to be sent back to them."

Mewer scooped up the corpse and carried him out of the classroom whilst my brother held my gaze with his intense sky-blue eyes. He had come back from the war, his face seemed to have more shadowed hollows than last time I saw him, his chiselled jaw sharper. His dark-blonde hair had grown almost reaching his shoulders. I almost considered whether I should be worried for him.

I took a few steps to close the gap between us. "How convenient that you knew so much information about a random first-year cadet so soon after his death."

He stared down at me so hard Ben stepped closer to my back.

Harvey didn't look up at Ben as he said, "Next time, you clean up your own mess. Don't allow our family name to be weakened by those easily removed. People should fear attacking us. Understood?"

I gasped. *My brother had done this?*

"On that note, Captain, there is a dead body in the woods by the pond." That was all Ben stated with no remorse or offered excuse, completely in character for a king who was merciless, and not the Ben I knew.

Harvey nodded once with what looked like gratitude, turned around and left. I stood baffled, staring at the void he left behind. Harvey had avenged Flora. Something inside me wanted to dare to smile. My brother had stood up for me. He could mask it with his pride if he had to maintain a captain's authority, but the quarrel that had led to Hefany's death had been over a pig and not a death threat on my life. I guessed Ben could handle those, and Harvey had stood up for Flora. Secretly, maybe he had liked her, too. She had been a part of the family for ten years.

Ben snorted as we left the classroom and headed down the corridor, so I turned to look at him. "What?"

"I'm pleased. When I can't be near you, your brother is clearly looking out for you in his own odd way."

On the way to our room, we met Zoe and Davis in the corridor, dressed in their combat leathers; a sheathed short-sword hung from their belts.

I hugged her tightly. "Zoe! You're back. How did it go?" The hug was brief before I took a step back, giving her some room.

Zoe's face turned grave, and she sought Ben's eyes.

"Oh, no, you don't!" I shouted at her. "You don't get to keep secrets with King Blackbone from me. What in the Underworld is going on?"

"It was a quick mission, honey. I didn't do much." She gestured for Davis. "Leadership has just announced the sparring hall is clear for use, so we were on our way there. Care to join us?"

Ben grunted at my side, looking stiff again.

I narrowed my eyes, throwing him a questioning look. He didn't react to it and waited for me to answer Zoe.

I had never seen Zoe look with such familiarity at anyone as when she gazed at Davis. I wondered whether she had wanted to spar alone with him and not have us dragged along. It almost made me envious that Zoe had chosen not to come and find me when she had returned, and instead had, intentionally or not, run into Davis.

I glanced between them before looking at Zoe. "You sure you want us to join you?"

"Absolutely, honey. I think I can take you this time. Davis has helped me practise."

"When?" I blurted out. I wasn't sure why I did. It wasn't like it was strange. We had spent a lot of time with the black-wings.

"Whenever both of us have a spare moment."

Ben grunted again, and I purposely stepped on his foot to quieten his discontent.

"Well, I guess we have nothing better to do," I muttered. "Herbology class was cut short due to 'death of arsehole'."

Zoe raised her brows but didn't look too bothered. "Someone died? Who?"

I bit my nail, feeling the unease run down my spine from all the crazy shit that was going on this morning. "Gregg Hefany."

Zoe dismissively waved her hand in front of her face. "Oh, yeah, total arsehole."

"He murdered Flora and made me eat her."

"What?" Zoe shouted, her hand reflexively moving to the hilt of her sword. "I'll kill…wake him from the dead and kill him again."

"Thanks," I giggled.

"Are you okay, honey?" A compassion that no one got to see often entered her eyes.

I threw glances around, seeing the men waiting. "It's what it is. I'll tell you the details later."

"Unhurtable as ever!"

"You bet your arse! And you said something about thinking you could kick *my arse*?"

"Oh, I don't think so. I know so, honey!"

We made our way to the sparring hall and found two vacant mats next to each other that was next to the windowed wall. Through the window, the view was towards the woods at the back of the building where Kate and Captain La Roy practised fire wielding by the tree line. Kate was getting better from all their training, seeming to put in the hours every time the sun came out to chase the rain clouds away. No wonder Harvey was in such a foul mood lately. Kate could have toned it down after I had revealed his feelings for her. I worried she was playing the jealousy game too hard.

"Don't interfere in your brother's love life," Ben warned from my side. "I know what you're thinking, but some matters are best left alone."

"They belong together. You should have seen my brother during the summers at the cottage when they–"

Ben plucked a dagger from my leg holster before I could defend it. "Miss

Stone, focus on your own survival."

"Is that so? You're challenging me? I thought you knew your limitations."

He chuckled and moved around me, pressing his front against my back, and he lowered to nip gently at my ear with his teeth. "Pushing boundaries amuses me."

I thought of the boundaries he was pushing, the border between the Black Wing Territory and the White Wing Territory beyond the mountain pass.

I sighed, shaking the subject from my mind and worked hard to find a new one.

"Why did you grunt before when we saw Zoe and Davis in the corridor? Please, don't say it was nothing, or I'll nail your bed to the wall so we can never move it back next to mine again."

"I'll trade that secret in exchange for moving my bed back to where it should be. Next to yours!"

"Deal."

I had been chattering my teeth all night after returning from the hike in the rain, so I'd gladly steal his body heat in the nights to come.

He leaned over, supporting his hands on his legs and I felt his breath warm on my ear. "Look at them."

I watched Zoe and Davis spar on their mat, laughing and teasing each other.

"They seem happy enough. Flirting a bit, perhaps. Are you worried Davis will fall in love with a white-wing? Does his family hate white-wings, or something?"

Ben pinched my chin and turned it back. "Look closer."

I watched them spar for a while and saw no foul play between them. Both were following the rules, drawing no blood. They tumbled over the mat and Davis tickled Zoe before he let her up. Zoe had spent a long time in the Black Wing Territory, so I knew she saw no problem with black-wings and considered them as equals.

I shrugged my shoulders. "Looks like we should give them some privacy."

Ben grunted. "Let me spell it out to you and give you a lesson in battle techniques at the same time. Look at the concentration on their faces. Look at how they bend their bodies and take about the same amount of time to react to each blow. See how their arms bend and jerk upwards when they parry. They both push out their tongue in concentration. Now, note something else. Their height. The shape of their noses. The bend of their legs."

"So, they have the same body build. Are you saying they should practise with someone who's more unlike them for better training?"

"No. You're a clever woman, Angelica. Think. What about their magical powers?"

"Zoe can make hearing portals…and Davis can do the same…can't he?"

"Yes. You're getting closer." Ben's hands swept along my curves until they rested at my hips where he could draw another of my daggers in a split second. The touch was highly distracting from his lesson.

I inhaled a deep breath, steadying my focus. "You think they're soulmates? A perfect match."

"No. I believe they were born at the same time, and of the same blood."

I gasped. "You think they are siblings?"

"Twins."

"Spirits!" I tore myself out of Ben's arms, which were circled around my stomach and sprinted up onto their mat, separating them from a wrestling hold. "My turn!" I called into Zoe's face.

Ben was chuckling darkly from somewhere behind me.

I drew my sword and blocked her swing, as her sword came down at me. She wasn't one to be taken off guard and not seize the opportunity to attack me when I was unprepared.

"I almost got you there," she leered, and we circled around each other.

"Careful, I'm only wearing the cotton uniform."

"Should have brought your combat leathers. Your mistake, honey."

She came at me with quick steps, and she was light on her feet, so she had planned offence rather than defence. We hammered swords together for a good while until Zoe eventually said, "I was thinking about these rough days you've had and thought that we could finish this week by forgetting about them. How does the Diva Den tonight sound? I'll order you a cocktail that makes you forget your name."

"I already have trouble remembering my name from all the spy missions. Let alone without also adding *Mutt, Miss stone*, and *Traitor* to the list."

"Good. Then it'll be an easy best friend task. Shall I pick you up at nine o'clock and we head down to the city?"

I jumped a step to my right as Ben hovered over my shoulder, closer than my own shadow. "Spirits!"

"What about the city?" he growled.

"Zoe and I are going on a girls' night out."

"Good grief, what fresh poison is this?" he muttered. "I wasn't really in the mood. What is the dress code?"

"Uh…being a girl…"

"But keeping male bodyguards. You, going on your own, is out of the question. What time and where?"

"King Blackbone," I said firmly, balling my fists. "I'm going dancing with my best friend. You're not invited. Maybe the men are having a poker night or something that you can attend."

Would he dare to oppose me when we were finally making some progress, getting closer to one another again?

I had to pick my fights with him and this time it was his turn to surrender.

His eyes lowered. Was he yielding? At least he was contemplating it. When his eyes lifted, I ensured to lock my stares on him as hard as I could, unwavering, silently demanding his submission.

His mouth twitched, not from amusement, but from a warning, willing me to break.

My stance was solid as stone, confident like someone who knew they would win.

Back down, king!

28

"Miss Stone," his dark voice resonated through my bones.

He was going to protest, so I held up my hand in front of his face. "Should I get the hammer and nails for your bed?" I warned.

He rolled his neck on his shoulder, his calm slipping. "Who else is going?"

I looked at Zoe, who blinked a few times. "I hadn't really given it much thought. We could ask Valentina, Fern and Kate."

Zoe circled Davis, and I assumed she was planning a surprise attack after having sneaked around him.

"Sounds great. Kate won't go. It's not her thing, but you ask Valentina, and I can visit Fern. I wanted to stop by the infirmary anyway to see how Robin is doing."

I launched another attack on Zoe's right side as soon as she was clear from Davis, but she blocked it, flashing me a smug grin.

Ben ran a hand down his face. "This really isn't wise."

"And why not?" I asked, keeping my eyes on Zoe.

"Drinking alcohol will reduce your ability to think clearly." He quickly drew the other dagger from my other leg strap. "*What the heck! Leave my weapons alone!*"

"Just proving a point, love."

Zoe laughed as if this was a game and walked around in another circle. "Being involved with you already shows poor judgment on her part, honey. So how much worse could it get?"

Ben cocked his head to the side to stare at her before he looked at me again. "And will there be other men?"

"It's not a 'women only' club. Who knows who I might meet?" I teased him. "It isn't like our relationship is set in stone."

"Oh, I'll get a chisel, if that is all it takes."

Zoe swatted her hand in front of Ben's face. "Stop this pointless jealousy. You're not chains she wears."

Ben towered over Zoe. "And she doesn't wear my chains, either. So, she should be a bit more understanding of my position."

"Stop squabbling like children and set the plan in motion," I instructed Zoe. "I can already feel my hips sway to the music like the time we went to Deadly Dolly's in the Black Wing Territory. Do you remember that?"

Zoe nodded, her eyes hungry for more mischief.

Ben pinched the bridge of his nose. "If the Diva's Den is anything like Deadly Dolly's, you're definitely not going."

"Relax. I'll be back before you wake up in the morning and you can always..." I tapped my head. *"Talk to me in my mind."*

I stepped off the mat, but Zoe wasn't following me, so I frowned at her and nodded towards the exit.

"You go ahead, honey. I might take another round with Davis."

"Davis? No. I think he has that...that patrol to do." I dug my stares into Ben. "Didn't Davis have that patrol he has to make now?"

"Yes," Ben drawled in a confused tone. "The one by the stairs to the leadership floor in the west wing. I want to know everyone that goes up and down during the next three hours."

Davis didn't question Ben and only nodded curtly before he left, as one would to a king who had already severed one of his thumbs.

With that sorted, I left the sparring hall and walked the winding corridors to the infirmary, finding Emroyce sitting cross-legged on the floor with Robin. He was trying to show Robin a wooden figurine of a bird he had carved, but there was no response in the boy's sweet little eyes. Emroyce looked relaxed with his long, black hair out and he was wearing brown trousers and a cream-coloured tunic. He also appeared devoid of daggers.

He stood up as I walked towards him with Ben on my heel. The infirmary stank of mint and a man was coughing repeatedly from somewhere deeper in the room.

"No change yet?" I asked, as I was by Emroyce's side.

He shook his head. "No. He's...just gone." Emroyce looked at the three-year-old replica of himself when it came to facial features, his amber eyes and ebony hair, but Robin was thin like a skeleton, pale as a ghost, cross legged and cross eyed. Then he turned his head to look back at me. "Do you think that with your..." He looked at Ben, hesitating. "You know. Could you set him straight?"

I pondered it. It would be tricky. "If I could charge the light crystal and...you know...I got access to what I needed." I cleared my throat. "Maybe."

Emroyce glanced at Ben and then back to me, whispering. "He doesn't know?"

I shook my head. "I have no magic."

His arms slackened by his sides. "About Flora. . .I'm so sorry."

"Cadet Hefany got what he deserved."

"Yes…You didn't?"

"No. Not me."

He smiled. "Good. One candidate less for us to defeat."

I nodded. "I actually came here to speak with Fern. Where is she?"

Emroyce swung his hand up, pointing for the bed in the corner. "Last patient on this week's rounds before she is off."

"Some girls are going out to the Diva's Den tonight."

"No!" he moaned. "Don't drag her into that shit."

"That's what I said," Ben muttered behind my back.

I twisted. "Weren't you going to get a chisel?"

He grunted.

Fern seemed to work hard on the coughing man, and I recoiled, not wanting to catch whatever he had. It sounded exhausting. "Emroyce, I don't want to interrupt Fern when she works, so can you tell her to meet us in front of the building at nine o'clock?"

He sighed. "Sure. No problem."

We walked out from the infirmary hall via the inner passage and headed for our room through the winding corridors, and I was eager to check on the Zincrics herb plant. It had to be alive if we were going to have a shot at winning the third challenge, and I had paid too little attention to it lately.

Ben fell into step next to me, focused on a thought that had clearly riled him. "Angelica, about what you said to Emroyce…" He wasn't looking at me and kept an even pace to mine. "I know you want to help him, but dealing with the magic that goes into those light crystals is dangerous. They can overpower your soul."

I opened our door and entered, looking towards the windowsill for the plant. "I know."

Ben watched me as I inspected the plant. It had grown, and it was rich with leaves, thanks to Ben's care. *Impressive.*

"You're sure you can handle it?"

"I don't know." I poked the soil to find it perfectly moist.

"I don't like when you gamble with your life."

"You mean your life. If the magic in the light crystal claims my soul, will it claim yours too if we're bonded?"

He was looking at me as if he wasn't sure why I didn't get it. "I'm using all of my trained ability to shield you out. If I didn't, you would understand how much we're connected through the bond. Every emotion, every touch, every word spoken around us you'd experience the same. What I see you would see. I could even learn your magic and use it and you could probably tap in to use mine if you prioritised the time to allow me to train you. We. Are. One. So, yes, love, if magic claimed your soul, the crystal would trap mine the same as yours. But this isn't my concern. Captain Coraly won't keep us bonded forever, only for as long as it's beneficial for the white-wings. Once we're separated, I cannot help by protecting you from threats like the mind bending of General Denor or the powerful magic in the light crystal."

I trembled at the thought of seeing General Denor again.

"Okay. I'll be careful with the light crystal magic until leadership separates our souls again, and then you don't have a say in my actions."

"So, my love counts for nothing?"

"Correct. Only if we were a couple would it count, but at the moment, there are secrets standing in our way."

"You can still love me and trust me, even if I keep secrets about politics and war unrest in my territory."

"With your trust magic, and only the Spirit of the Living knowing what else you're hiding, no."

"You're being unreasonable."

"No. I'm perfectly in my right."

I took out my duffle bag from the wardrobe and stuffed it with a towel, a black outpost tracksuit, my underwear, a hairbrush and my makeup.

"What mischief are you up to now?" Ben asked, as he watched me dart around the room to pack my things.

"I'm going to the bathing chamber. It's underground in the east wing."

"I know where the bathing chamber is," he growled. "The problem is that you're avoiding me and going somewhere I can't protect you. I have no female guards here."

Discretely, he had placed himself between me and the door. I snorted. Did he really believe I didn't notice that he was trying to stop me from going? Or even worse, did he believe he had a say in where I went and that I wouldn't absolutely crush him if he didn't move?

"You're becoming a tad overbearing, King Blackbone. Back off."

The insult didn't make him waiver. "You can use our shower."

I lifted the strap of the bag over my head and rested it onto my shoulder before taking a few steps to push up against him, glaring at him. "If you don't move out of my way, we'll have an argument. Do you really want to start a fight when I'm going out in a sexy little dress, getting drunk and dancing with handsome men when I'm extremely pissed off with you?"

He tensed, the black essence oozing off him to curl around our legs. His red eyes shone brightly with hot rage, but I kept my stance firmly before him, chin held high and waited for his reply.

After a few moments, he very slowly edged away to one side, but kept his eyes on me the entire time, not speaking a word. The way his muscles had flexed, the way his hands had coiled into fists and the way his essence flowed, I didn't dare push him further, so simply swept past him and walked towards Zoe's room to pick her up along the way. My heart was pounding with my steps the entire way, as I had the gut feeling I had pushed Ben to his limit this time. Not that I could imagine what he would do if he overheated. Not in a million years did I believe he would do anything that caused me harm. Maybe he would kill a few others, though, to get it out of his system. I prayed the beast would remain inside our room until he calmed down.

Zoe's smile, as she opened the door, made my tension simmer out. "Ready?"

She was, her duffle bag already slung across her shoulder. "I've not been to the bathing chamber since I returned. I'm really looking forward to it."

In the changing room to the bathing chamber, the Horse Girls Team was on their way out, having just finished as we entered. We put on our black Bensguard Outpost bikinis with the key symbol embroidered in golden stitching on the tops and bottoms. I noticed a few dents in Zoe's black bikini that she had tied tightly to her body to perk up her breasts. One of the dents was at the side of her left breast and the other at the small of her back.

"What's that?" I asked, fingering at the three-centimetre bulge on her bikini bottoms but quickly realised when I touched the hard iron. "Folding knives? Really? In the bathing chamber?"

"A woman can't be too careful."

"Well, I didn't bring any, so you'll have to protect me."

She winked at me, and we walked into the main hall. I gasped at the sight even though I had seen it many times before. I had forgotten the impact of being in here. It was stunning with sand-coloured, high vaulted ceilings made of squarely chiselled stone with a flower rim around the arched doorways. Round pillars supported the vaults, connecting to the walls and large plants with colourful flowers hid their base. Along the edge of the pool, workers had lit candles, providing the room with a dim yellow glow, amplified by the copper lanterns with glass sides hanging low from long chains attached to the ceiling. On the far end, a three-tiered waterfall cascaded into the pool, sending a soothing sound into the space.

The water was hot, and my muscles instantly agreed as I sat down on the submerged seat below the surface, waiting for Zoe to take the seat next to me. I played with my toes on a floating lily, watching the white statues of the nine winged Spirits kneeling in alcoves along the walls around the pool as if they were praying to the water.

"So!" Zoe called out and sat down beside me. I recognised the tone. I was about to get the third-degree questioning. "What's the issue with you?"

"With me?" I spat, knowing exactly what she was referring to.

"You have a handsome king pining over you and yet…nothing. Is he cruel to you in private?"

"No!" I bellowed.

She kept an elbow on the edge of the pool and looked closer at me. "Are you…you know…not into men, honey?"

I averted her intensely quizzical gaze, looking at the floating lily by my toes. "Zoe, you know me. Don't be ridiculous. He's great."

"So, why then are you pushing him away?" She gasped. "Is he awful in bed?"

I hesitated, not having much experience to speak of.

"Oh, no. What a bummer, honey." Zoe cringed and looked at me with her pitiful, grey eyes.

"Agent Hammerton," I cursed her. "You're not to pry in the royal sex life."

"Fine." She slouched down into the water to wet her purple hair and wore a smirk on her face. "I understand."

"Understand? What do you understand?"

"You're worried he won't be as good as Watson."

"What? No, that's not it. It's just that his magic…its dangerous when he loses control. He doesn't want to harm me."

She darted to sit up straight. "So, you never…He must be a virgin then? Spirits! The fucking black-wing king is just scared as shit about his first time. That's kind of sweet."

Fuck! I hadn't expected her to make that connection.

"You're an enigma," I told her and lowered myself to be just above the surface with my chin.

"Thank you, honey."

"It wasn't a compliment."

"I took it as one, anyway. Well, whatever you say, I like the black-wing king."

I hesitated to answer for a while as I breathed in the hot steam. "He keeps secrets from me."

Zoe's eyes widened at that, and she knew I had seen it. Whatever she had learnt on her last mission north was something awful she hadn't even been able to tell me about. I narrowed my eyes at her, leaning in a little closer and tilted my head in a silent encouragement to share her secret. *Come on, just tell me!*

There was an idle moment of hesitation and uncertainty flashing across her face. "I promised your brother I wouldn't tell you. It's not safe for you to know."

"The same repeated answer as Ben. From my best friend, who normally doesn't shy away from telling me things straight. Great."

"For the hate of all demons, I cannot," she hissed, seeming more frustrated than I had ever seen her before.

"You can tell me. I won't tell my brother."

Even that comment didn't make her talk, and she kept her lips sealed in a straight line. We both toyed with the same water lily, trying to pull the petals off with our toes.

Eventually she looked at me, and not as confidently as I was used to. "I hope that isn't the only thing that stands between the king and you. Because the secrets that I know, are not only proving that he's a super good guy. They also mean he's prioritising protecting you over the risk of losing you." There was silence between us once more until she huffed and sat up, the water rippling around her. "And what is your issue with me flirting with Davis, anyway?"

I was quick to shake my head. "It's nothing."

"Then you don't object to me slipping into his bed when we get back drunk tonight?"

I closed my eyes and cringed. "Spirits, no. Don't."

"Tell me, Angie!"

"If you can keep secrets, so can I," I muttered.

"Very mature."

"If I can't trust the information from my intel officer, you won't get feedback from your field agent. Simple. Trust works both ways." I hated the word and thought of Ben. *Trust works both ways.*

"But I do it because I'm protecting you."

"And I'm doing it to protect you."

Her brows knitted. "Why? Is he a psycho or something? He'll kill me in my sleep?"

"No one could kill you in your sleep. You wake up if someone so much as breathes in the same room."

She crossed her arms over her chest, accusing my comment of being unfair. "You breathe so loudly I could hear you from your room, honey."

"I breathe! Or I would die," I emphasised, making an irritated face at her.

"That's why I compromised when we lived in our apartment and put earplugs in when sleeping." She grinned back at me.

"Thanks! I love you, too."

She stood up. "I'll be right back. I forgot my water bottle in my bag, and I get really thirsty in here."

Zoe took her sweet time, and I frowned, as she hadn't returned yet. Suddenly, a wrestling ball of two bodies in black bikinis plummeted into the pool, and a struggle continued under the surface. I rose to my feet and watched, trying to see what was going on. I could only spot purple hair swirling around with long white hair belonging to someone with a tall and lean body. Cadet Aurora Darling of the Party Girls Team.

I plunged deeper into the pool to get closer, swept my hand through the water to catch a fist full of long white strands and yanked hard. Both women surfaced, spitting out threats. Darling turned her hateful, yet mesmerising, big blue eyes my way, and her beauty immediately intimated me. She was the most stunning woman I had ever seen, wrapped in tight skin in the colour of silver under a sunset. She was tall, slender, with lovely framing collarbones under a sharp chin running up to high cheekbones. Her skin was flawless and so were her full lips and winged eyebrows.

She brought up her hands as if she was ready to strangle me. And she went for it. Her hands clasped around my neck, and she pushed me under the surface. Water streamed in through my nose and into my air pipe and by reflex I tried to cough but only swallowed more water. The distraction had made me lose precious seconds and then she had her body weight behind her assault, pushing me down in such a hard grip that I doubted I could free myself.

My eyes stung from the chlorine as I searched the shimmering surface just above my head, the pale glow, so close, yet so teasingly untouchable. The cool tiles were slick beneath my bare feet, providing little grip to throw her off me. There was no hint of mercy in her leg lock around me. My screams died in a rush of bubbles and every movement I made to try fight her off was dulled in the water. The panic was as suffocating as the water, and my lungs burned, needing air.

29

I clawed at her hands to get them off my neck, but she had clamped down and anchored them with nails deep in my flesh. Her grip was so hard, it hurt like needles pushed onto my flesh, and I couldn't focus on anything but pain. I kicked out my foot against her abdomen, but she was solid as a rock and folded her leg over mine so I couldn't move my legs again. It was then that a sense of arousal entered me, as though I enjoyed being murdered, finding it sexy. The touch of her sensual magic was heavenly, like I belonged with her fingers wrapped around my neck and there was nowhere in the world I'd rather be. I no longer wanted to fight her, and my arms slackened at my sides. If she wanted to murder me, I'd gladly accept it.

"Angelica?" Ben's voice was loaded with concern. *"Your pulse is slowing. What's going on?"*

My mind was blurting out things of its own as my active and passive thoughts merged. My shield dropped to the ground, leaving the connection between us wide open.

"I'm dying…" My subconscious sang through a calm abyss.

"Where the fuck are you?"

"I'm dying…" My voice was small, echoing softly in the dark void.

"Are you in the bathing chamber?" He must not have kept his shield up because I could feel his panic through the bond. It was humbling. I had meant so much to him.

"I'm sorry…sorry…sorry…" My words were eaten up by something dulling my brain.

Suddenly, my head jerked upright and out of the water. Zoe's expression was vicious, and she held one of the foldable knives in her hand. As I spewed up water, Darling stood at a distance, hissing over a stab wound to her shoulder.

"You bitch! You brought a knife to the bathing chamber?"

"Not in vain, honey, I may add!" Zoe snapped.

Zoe put a hand on my shoulder and looked at me but still kept an eye on Darling.

"Are you okay?"

"Thanks to you." I noticed movement by the large plant behind Zoe's back and saw Darling's teammate, Beatrice Courtney. Her curly silver hair around her perfectly feminine face was dry and the golden glow of her eyes was hungry for death. She hunched low, palming the surface.

"Shit!" I pushed Zoe in front of me to get out of the water.

"What's her magic?" Zoe barked.

"Ice wielder. Move!"

We didn't make it to the steps to get out of the pool before the ice caught us by the hips. My teeth chattered from the cold, and I instinctively wanted to cross my arms over my chest to keep warm, but my hands were stuck, frozen inside ice.

Darling walked over the ice with a predator's prowl, clicking her tongue.

Zoe cut the knife in the air in front of her to warn Darling to keep her distance.

Darling avoided Zoe's strokes and snapped up Zoe's wrist in the same snatching grip as she had used with the snakes, prying the knife out of her grip. Then she laid down on the ice next to me, playing with the blade over my skin, cutting thin lines on my stomach that coloured red.

"I honestly thought you'd have some powerful skill to kill us with, Mutt," she gloated, making a deeper cut right above the swell of my breast that sent blood seeping down to stain my bikini top.

I groaned at the sting but kept frowning at her. "I have no magic." My words came out in sharp furious gasps before I clenched them tight to stop them from clattering.

I knew that if I exposed my magic, I'd have to kill them both so they wouldn't talk. I hoped for another solution, but as the ice bit into my captive skin, my options were few.

"And," she crooned. "I assumed you'd have admirable intelligence because you could wrap the black-wing king around your finger. But nothing? Little old me can just kill you this easily?"

I roared, thrashing against the ice magic, but the cold only tightened its grip, spreading a numbness up my arms like creeping vines. Helplessness clawed at my chest and my mind raced, searching for an escape, but it left me the same as the warmth drained from my body.

"What a shame. I'm so disappointed," she taunted. "But I won't regret killing you and taking your place in bed next to King Blackbone. I'll seduce him and give him the most pleasurable experience he's ever had right before I slit his throat."

Anger tore through me like lightning, possessing me. My magic surged around inside my veins, building up. The ice underneath Darling vanished, and she plunged into the water, but it didn't hold her back, and as she surfaced, she wrapped her arm around my neck and put the blade to my throat.

Ben, Murben, Davis and Nesso rushed inside the chamber and skidded to a stop by the pool edge as they saw Darling holding the knife against my skin.

Ben's pupils had dilated in the dim light, appearing almost entirely black, and together with his set jaw and tenseness, he looked completely merciless. "If you don't remove the blade from Cadet Coraly's throat immediately, you'll not be walking out of here alive," he said grimly. As Darling hesitated, he added. "Your mother will be dead by the morning and your sister won't arrive at this school next year. My bodyguard will make sure of it. I hope I have made myself clear that this is a threat on everyone in your family."

Darling let her hand drop to her side, crossing the pool floor to ascend the few steps to get out of the water and closer to Ben.

"Be careful. Don't let her touch you. She has seduction magic," I told him.

"I'm aware," Ben growled. "And a touch of my hands kills. Her choice." Ben didn't move away from Darling as she moved closer; only watching her.

Darling thought better of touching him and passed him to walk through the door leading into the women's changing rooms. Courtney walked around the pool, using another path before she followed her teammate through the same door.

Davis was at the edge of the pool, beckoning Zoe to get out. He clasped arms with Zoe and lifted her out of the water whilst Ben was waiting for me by the steps. I hung my head, staring at the bottom of the pool as I walked out.

"Second murder attempt in two days. Aiming for a record, Cadet Coraly?" Ben muttered, his eyes scanning over the cuts carved into my skin.

"What?" Zoe bellowed. "There has been another one? Why didn't you tell me?"

I cocked my chin high and stared into Ben's eyes. "I guess we all have secrets."

Still soaking wet, I exited the bathing chamber via the doors leading out to the reception, as I couldn't very well go into the changing room and risk being murdered again. "Davis! Please can you collect my things and bring them to my room?" I called out and pushed open the steamed-up glass doors, hearing a, '*Thank you for saving my life,* would be nice,' from Ben before they shut.

The entire way along the corridors, men wolf whistled as I passed by in only my bikini. My wet blue hair was branching out to cover most of the thin strips of blood across my body. When I reached my door, I realised that I didn't have a key on me, and I swore my most colourful verse of foul words.

It didn't take long, though, before Ben caught up with me and opened the door. I hesitated, not entering the room. I couldn't swallow my pride, even though the hair on my skin bristled from the freezing water drops coating my body.

He sighed. "What now?"

I glanced down the corridor. "I thought Davis was coming with my things, I'll get my dress, and then I'll head to Harvey's apartment to change."

He had saved my life, again, so I should just drop my guard, but keeping him at a distance was the only way I knew how to protect my heart. Because I really…really didn't want to be fooled twice and earn my own title as a traitor rather than just riding on my mother's reputation. She had ruined Father's legacy, and I wasn't going to add to it. I swiped away a tear from my eye.

Ben put a hand on my shoulder, about to say something, but gasped. "You're so cold." All courtesy was out the window, and he hurried to scoop me up into his arms and carried me inside, kicking the door closed with his foot before he continued into the shower.

"What are you doing?"

"Getting you warm."

He turned on the hot water and simply stood there with me in his arms, the hot water wetting us both.

"This won't change anything," I sniffed, even if in my twisted heart I knew it did. The ache for him was relentless. Even when I had pushed him away so many times, he was still my anchor. Why couldn't love be enough? It took all I had not to break and forgive him. But I was betraying my own heart because I desperately wanted to wrap my arms around his neck and kiss him ferociously to satisfy my need for him. *Why did he have to be so fucking perfect? Why couldn't he be the bastard I thought he was when Harvey forced me on the mission to kill him?* I reminded myself once more: *I'm a mutt, and he's a king.*

"You're perfect," he muttered, his eyes begging for mercy.

I gasped and wriggled myself out of his arms, darting for a towel. "You're not allowed to listen to my passive thoughts." I stomped towards my wardrobe.

"I know. But I like those more than the words you speak."

I screamed out in frustration, and clasped my hairbrush, tearing it through my hair. "You violate me when you listen to my passive thoughts.

We agreed we wouldn't, or have you forgotten that?"

I looked over my shoulder to see him lean with his shoulder against the door frame to the bathroom, looking so…heartbroken.

"You agreed to bind your soul to me. You can't have expected everything to be clear cut."

"My brother forced me! I had no choice!" I screamed but calmed and looked at my watch. It was eight o'clock, so I only had an hour to get ready and be at the front of the building for our girls' night out. "I don't have time for this."

"What?" he barked, his patience dissolved. "You're still planning on going?" Irritation marred his voice.

"Why wouldn't I?"

"Oh, I don't know. Because you were almost murdered less than half an hour ago." He scowled, his gaze travelling down my body.

"All the more reason to drink and forget my sorrows." The shouting had made me feel light-headed, reminding me I had eaten little today.

He poked at his chest in a gesture resembling an arrow to his heart. "Am I one of those sorrows?"

"Definitely. There are nothing but daggers between us and any steps closer will only draw blood."

His eyes tracked my reaction. "You've a demon's determination to be the bane of my existence."

He stared at me from the doorpost the entire time as I styled my hair, applied my makeup and added more eyeliner than usual. Finally, I dressed in a skimpy silver dress covered in shiny sequins that barely reached my knees. When I bent over to tie the laces of my knee-high boots, I realised all too late that Ben could see right down my cleavage and noticed his black essence slip again, inking out of him in thrusts like an angry octopus.

"Knock it out," I hissed.

He circled into the room. "Don't drink too much. Keep your thumb on the bottle opening when you're not drinking, so no one can slip a drug or poison into your drink. Make sure you locate all escape routes leading to the street. Count the guards to visitor ratio and identify those who look likely to cause trouble. Don't go to the women's bathroom alone or walk through any dark corridors or alleyways. Keep a knife in your purse, and if attacked, go straight for the jugular. If you're cornered–"

"Yes, yes. I get it. I was a general's daughter, so I can handle myself, and this isn't my first time going dancing." I donned my waist-long black leather jacket. "And we have a lot of magic between us; bone breaking, hearing portal, and speed."

"And yours."

"I have no magic."

He grunted whilst he strode up to me. "You're gorgeous." He cupped my cheek and cussed. "You're still freezing cold."

I snatched my cheek away, but Zoe's magic, formed a blue hearing portal at my side, interrupting my response.

"Are you ready to go?" she asked.

I craned my head closer to the portal as if she could hear me better if I was shouting into it, although I wasn't sure how it actually worked. "I'll be there in a second." The portal was gone the moment after, and I grabbed my matching silver sequinned purse from the desk, stealing Ben's key and putting it in before heading out. "Don't wait up! I might not be back until Sunday afternoon!"

I deserved the pang of hurt I felt through the bond, then.

I was early to the front, but so were the three other women, clearly eager to leave this place, even if only for a while.

"You guys look stunning," I chirped as I joined them.

Zoe was wearing a top and skirt set in purple leather that showed off way more skin than my skimpy dress did. Valentina wore a grey outfit that matched her eye colour and whose patterns and dress cuts made it look similar to armour and not dancing clothes, but that was just the way Valentina was comfortable. She even had one dagger in a thin belt around her waist, which I wasn't convinced the guards of the Diva's Den would let her enter with.

Ever since Fern had been raped, she wore clothes that covered most of her body, so she was wearing a lovely black dress with a boat cut neckline and the skirt reaching to just below her knees. She had her long black hair flat against her back and a rich red lipstick accenting her amber eyes.

"Are you safe?" Ben muttered through the bond.

"Spirits! I haven't even left the premises." I tuned him out and turned to Fern. "I'm glad you could come. How's Robin?"

She twisted as if she still felt uncomfortable talking about Robin, keeping her gaze on the darkness enveloping the outpost. "He's sleeping now. Emroyce is with him."

"Emroyce is such a sweetheart."

"The best brother one could wish for," Fern said giving a sweet smile.

"Sure you don't want to swap then? Captain Coraly has his moments," I asked, and she laughed as if I had asked her to swap sweets for poison.

"Why are we leaving early?" I asked Zoe.

"I wanted to walk through the city to see all the Turning of the Year decorations."

Valentina was the one taking the lead towards the city. "Oh, my Spirits, I should have told my parents we were purely doing that! I thought I might not make it out tonight, and when I had finally convinced my parents to allow me to go, they kept nagging me on safety protocol."

I snorted. "Ben was the same."

"Ben?" she asked, brow low.

I felt like I was standing in the spotlight under the moonlight. The thousands of stars staring at me in scrutiny. "Sorry. King Blackbone."

Fern's fleeting glances roamed over me. "You use first names?"

Zoe pulled down her skirt as she walked. "They'd be married if the king had a say in it."

Both Fern and Valentina gasped. There was unmistakable intrigue shining in their eyes. "Tell us all about it," Fern urged.

"No. It's girls' night out. Let's not speak about the men at the outpost and only drool over those inside the club."

"Uh oh! That doesn't sound good. He's not up to scratch?" Valentina asked.

"I'll not speak about my relationship with the black-wing king."

"So, you are in a relationship?" Zoe smirked, as if she knew she had tripped me up.

"No!"

Valentina scratched her head. "Would any other woman be able to start a relationship with King Blackbone?"

"No!" I barked.

"Okay. I think I get it," Valentina said, lifting the strap over her handbag over her head to have it lay across her chest because it irritated her when it kept sliding down her shoulder.

"What?" I snapped.

"You need a lot of alcohol tonight," she said flatly.

I nodded. "Yep, you got the gist of it, all right."

We all laughed, and Zoe filled Valentina and Fern in on the murder attempt in the bathing chamber on the way.

We gossiped and chatted, passing by houses that were decorated in winter blossom and lavender for the festival of the Turning of the Year. Many people went through great lengths to invoke the generous and happy atmosphere, and some clearly competed with their neighbours about who decorated the best. There were colourful lights hanging along the edges of the roofs and pine wreaths hung on doors, their size seeming to depend on how rich the family was who lived there.

We reached the area where bars and taverns filled the street corners.

"Are you safe?" Ben asked, and I almost tripped, as I was stepping up onto the payment where the line to get into the club ended.

"I'm not even inside the club yet."

Fair play to him; as long as I answered, he stayed quiet thereafter, although the humming in my ears for being further away from him was still distracting.

Fern, Valentina, Zoe and I queued up for a while before we were let inside the Diva's Den. We claimed a round table surrounded by black leather upholstered sofas, the music blasting into my ears. Zoe immediately beckoned me to the dance floor whilst Valentina went to the bar to get the drinks, having the most vicious elbows to get ahead in the line out of us all. Before we had joined the academy, she had even broken a bone or two if someone pushed her back and not allowed her through to make her order. Fern stayed to guard our purses as she enjoyed sitting and watching rather than being an active dancer. This was how she was happy with her leg bouncing on one knee under the table and an orange juice in her hand.

I danced with Zoe and Valentina all night, always with a drink in hand and after a handful of them, I noticed the room spinning even when I was standing still. This didn't deter me from rubbing up against the girls as we released three months of built-up tension from classes and challenges. For a moment, all my troubles seemed to disappear with the beat of the music. The music was totally my style. It was so loud it almost overpowered the soul bond humming in my mind. Not to mention it was so loud one could barely hear one's own thoughts. Although, evidently, I could hear Ben's.

"Are you still safe?"

"Yes! Stop asking. My friends think I'm crazy, seeing the weird look on my face when I talk to you in my mind. Aren't you going to bed soon? It's..." I looked at my watch. *"It's after midnight."*

"I am in bed. This will be the last time I'm checking in on you."

"You really haven't sent any secret spies to spy on me?"

"Nope."

"A momentary lapse of judgment on your part?"

"No. I thought crossing that boundary with you could be more dangerous than the one I crossed when entering the White Wing Territory."

"Those wise decisions are what make you a great king."

"Or a very dead one. The night will tell."

"Oh! Got to go. There is a very cute man by the bar. Last chance to confess your secrets and claim me as yours." I realised that not once during the night had I cared to look at another man, but I wouldn't give him the satisfaction of telling him that.

He only grunted into my mind.

"Fine. Suit yourself. Sleep tight! I'm sure I won't!"

I made my best attempt at putting my shield up and carried on dancing with Zoe who didn't seem to be interested in other men, either, and that worried me. I would have to have the talk about Davis with her tomorrow, and I wasn't looking forward to it. A group of men surrounded Valentina on the dance floor, salivating over her like she was takeaway food, so she was happy. I glanced over at Fern who seemed uncomfortable at the interaction between them, and I believed that no matter how much I told her that Valentina could take care of herself, it wouldn't help.

I looked at the time again and it was closer to three o'clock in the morning, so I hooked onto Valentina's arm and dragged her away from the beasts eyeing her.

"I'm all danced out and near to vomiting up all alcohol I have managed to swallow. Can we go home now?" I begged.

She nodded with a smile. "I thought you'd never ask."

Zoe and Fern agreed as well, and we wobbled home, which probably took us double the time it had taken us to walk into town.

I fumbled with the key in the lock, seeing more than one keyhole, and I was clearly imagining dark essence swirling out by the bottom of the door frame. Finally getting the door open, a wall of black essence hit me, and I couldn't see a thing inside my room. I swatted my hand in front of my face, which also vanished from sight inside the darkness beyond the doorpost.

"Ben? Are you in here? What has happened?"

"Are you unharmed?" he muttered, his voice coming from the direction of his bed.

"Yes," I barked, coughing as the black essence dried my throat with a smoky taste.

"Are you…alone?" His voice was so dark and solemn it hurt inside my chest.

"Yes. Where are you?" I took a few steps in and closed the door behind me.

"Don't come close or touch me. I'm a tad upset. Just get into your bed. The essence will have cleared by morning."

"What a shame. I so felt like finishing what I started the other day…involving your mid area." I added in case I hadn't been clear.

"Miss Stone, stop toying with kings."

"Why? It's so much fun."

"It's not polite."

"You want polite? Okay, I'm coming to you and crawling under your covers."

"No! Don't get near me!"

"Oh, yes! I'm coming."

"This is the momentary lapse of judgment I talked about."

I stumbled and supported myself on his bedside table, hurting my hand on something sharp and metallic. "What in the world is this?" I felt with my finger along metal that wasn't a blade.

"A chisel," he muttered, his careful tone betraying the fear of leaving his vulnerability unguarded.

The symbolism of wanting to carve our name into stone was oddly the things that made my brain click. I knew at that moment that he was mine, and that he truly wanted me.

As if the chisel cracked the hard shield around my heart, my defiance relented. I had fought our love, denied myself from feeling it, buried it beneath hurt and anger. The weight of the shield I should have held up in front of my exposed heart was too heavy to bear and the truth slammed into me.

I love him.

Like flying and snapping away my wings, trusting him to catch me, I let myself fall – fall for him.

The heat of that love melted away all my hesitation. I crawled under the cover, and he flinched like a skittish animal as I put my head on his chest and relaxed.

"You're still freezing cold," he muttered.

A few moments passed until he had calmed and could wrap his arms around me and that's how we fell asleep – as one.

30

The door closed with a thud, and I felt along the sheets with my hand, finding the space next to me empty, so I pulled the blanket over my head. Although, I was pretty sure it wouldn't do anything to help my headache.

The sharp scratching sound of a whetstone against steel started.

I sighed under the blanket. "Must you do that in here?"

"I'm not allowed to carry weapons outside this room, and you aren't keeping your blades sharp enough."

His message was crystal clear. This was my punishment for last night. I tried to go back to sleep even when the light from the window was streaming in because he had fucking pulled open the curtains, evidencing it was way past noon.

"You were reckless last night," he said, his voice coming from different directions inside the room. I guessed he had stopped sharpening iron and taken up pacing. "You touched me when I told you not to. I could have killed you!"

Oh! We were talking about that. That was unexpected. I thought he meant the clubbing.

Considering I had been up too late and become overly drunk, my headache was made worse with every word coming out of his mouth. "That was yesterday. Right now, your loud voice is killing me. May I schedule this fight for later this afternoon? Or, I don't know.. never?"

"You cornered me in the bed. Unable to move away from you, I could have hurt you. I was terrified."

"Oh, my Spirits! You make it sound as if I assaulted you against your will."

"It *is* against my will when I'm not in control of my emotions! I was angry. Jealous. Worried, and–"

"And you would never have hurt me. I knew that with certainty, or I'd never have risked our lives. Considering last night, perhaps it isn't even plausible that you can harm me with your magic, as we're one and the same whilst soul bound."

There was a thud and the mattress sunk beside me as Ben sat down. He flipped over the cover and put his hand on my forearm, and we both saw my veins turning black and forking up my arm. He immediately let go. "I can definitely kill you with my magic."

I crawled to my knees and stretched a leg out, swinging around to sit straddled over his lap and nestled my fingers through his hair. "But you wouldn't. Because we love each other."

His eyes opened wide. Slowly, a satisfied grin followed. His happiness, and his gorgeous face, made my heart ignite and my stomach tickle. I kissed him, and he responded with brutal fierceness, as if he had believed we'd never kiss again.

But then, he pulled back and narrowed his eyes at me. "You're still freezing cold. What did the ice wielder do to you?"

I grinned and kissed him again, pushing my tongue into his mouth and caressing along his. "Nothing that you can't thaw."

I ground myself over his crotch. He instantly went hard beneath my weight and wrapped his hands around my arse. I wished I could stay in this moment forever, but the wish was short-lived as he lifted me off him.

"Let's stay away from that thought."

"So what? You forbid me from kissing you now? I thought that was what you wanted. I certainly want romance."

"You want romance?" He fetched one of my uniforms from the wardrobe and held it out to me. "You never struck me as a romance-kind-of-woman."

My brows rose. "What?"

"Well, I haven't yet had to wear a rowan cross around my neck, burn sage, or had to ask leadership to allocate me another room because I tediously must wrestle you out of my bed. Although yesterday came damn close to that."

I rolled my eyes at him.

"Well," he scoffed. "If romance is what you want, I shall see what I can do. But first, we have work to do."

"Work?" I flopped back into bed. "It's Saturday and I have a hangover."

"Yes, but Zoe has been perkier than you and has been sparring with Davis all morning, so it's time we talked to them."

I flew out of bed. "What?" I didn't really want to face that confrontation. "Maybe we should wait until we have more evidence than a few similar mannerisms before we say anything."

"My spies already confirmed my theory. Have a hot shower before you catch a cold. Although, I have learnt a tea blend to cure that, compliments of Camp Leader Mewer."

I walked up to him and wondered whether there was any way I could seduce him to make him forget the whole thing and stay in bed with me all day.

As if he had read my thoughts, he griped my hands and put them together between us so I couldn't get closer to him. "I know it's difficult to be the bearer of bad news to those you love, but it's the right thing to do to tell them."

The secrets he held must be truly bad then if his integrity pushed him towards telling the truth, no matter how much it hurt. I looked into his eyes, lit the colour of fire, yet as tranquil as smouldering embers. "I was stupid to ever think that you could harm me, or that you would hurt me with your secrets."

He shrugged back and the embers that had been peaceful ignited a flame of agony. "I never said that the secrets wouldn't hurt you. I only said that they had nothing to do with my love for you."

I snatched my hands out of his grip. "That's how you want to play it? Walking on the line of technicalities? You know what? I don't really care anymore. You can keep pushing me away to a distance where you think I'm safe, but I'll find a way to get so close to you that our passion will burn away all the barriers and all the technicalities until they're nothing more than cinders of a memory."

He smirked, and I could feel through the bond how the other half of my soul, his soul, fed on my words.

I stomped into the bathroom, and as I slammed the door shut, I had a second view of his smirking face. Ah! Kings!

As I showered in scolding hot water, the residue of Cadet Courtney's power trickled off me like small pearls of ice until it was out of my system. Thereafter, the water burned, so I turned it off.

Without a word or look towards Ben, I got dressed in my combat leathers and collected the daggers he had so kindly whetted this morning together with my sharpened headache. Ready to leave, I found Murben leaning against the wall with one ankle crossed over his foot in the corridor. No longer having a pig to protect, I guessed he was back on bodyguard duty. There were shadowy bags under his eyes, though, so I worried Ben had been pushing him too hard. Murben was about thirty-five years old but today he looked ten years older than that. Although, his mature demeanour could have something to do with that. No matter how rough he looked, he still maintained his air of danger, with his dark skin, tight muscles and the shadows that set over his eyes. He had kept his charcoal black hair short that curled in small locks.

A small greeting was all I managed before passing him, so I'd gain a head start on Ben, but soon enough, they were flanking me all the way to the sparring hall.

"How come Cadet Coraly is in such a splendid mood this morning?" Murben asked Ben over my head.

"Because apparently she prefers blunt blades," he replied, continuing the private conversation over my head.

"Can I assume that my benevolent king was kind enough to help her sharpen them this morning?"

"I did. Although, I don't believe Cadet Coraly considered it a kindness, and she showed no gratitude."

I glowered at them both in turn and received impish smiles in return.

"Murben, don't you think Cadet Coraly has beautiful eyes?" Ben continued tantalising me as we walked.

"Indeed. Like the clearest sapphires under the glistening sun. It certainly compliments that gorgeous smile she has."

I grunted irritably at them.

Murben cleared his throat. "My king, are you sure you've said nothing this morning which Cadet Coraly needs further clarification on, or perhaps…I don't know…an apology?"

"No. I don't believe there's anything unsaid."

I stared at Ben, and he flashed me the face of someone who could do nothing wrong.

"Maybe," I growled. "You want to think harder? Maybe *there are* words to be said."

I picked up my pace to enter the sparring hall first. For the first time, since leadership had recently opened it up after the temporary use for the hunger challenge of the second-year cadets, I found the hall empty. "I guess most cadets have better things to do at noon on Saturdays than to train. Like sleep," I hissed at Ben, who made his best attempt to hide a smile into his hand. "Zoe and Davis aren't here."

I walked around the hall and heard a noise from behind one of the supporting pillars of the vaulted ceiling.

"Jason," Zoe laughed.

Jason? First name? No! "His name is Sergeant Davis," I muttered softly, and perhaps only Ben had heard me, as we rounded the pillar.

What we saw made me gasp. Davis was sitting with his back against the stone pillar and Zoe straddled over his lap. They both paratactically flew off the floor and stood up, smoothening their combat uniform to their bodies.

Zoe cleared her throat. "I didn't hear you coming, honey."

I just stared at her, lost for what to say next. *"It's too late. Perhaps we shouldn't tell them now?"*

"Miss Stone! We must inform them or we're not very good friends."

"You do it then."

"I really think it would be more gentle on them if you told them."

I sighed. "The black-wing king says you aren't allowed to see each other."

"Miss Stone!" Ben warned, his hands resting irritably on his hips.

Zoe looked pissed off. "Angie, what's going on?"

"Well, the thing is that when we checked backgrounds…Well, we believe–"

"We know," Ben corrected sternly.

"Yes, well. We know that maybe–"

"With certainty," Ben bit in once more, and there was no mercy in his tone.

"Are you telling her, or me?" I snapped.

"I pray to my two Spirits that you become more direct when crowned queen."

Queen? The thought soured my stomach. I was an undercover spy who didn't want to be seen whatsoever. Attention was the last thing I wanted. A queen was the complete opposite. *"If I become queen."*

"Oh. That's happening."

"With or without secrets, right?"

"Yes, Angelica. I'll spend the rest of our lives sucking up to you if that's required after you learn the secrets. I'll not spend the rest of my life dealing with my subjects by myself. You'll have to carry some of the burden."

"Oh, there is the romance you promised."

We attacked each other with our eyes, and it rapidly grew into a competition as to who could hold it the longest without peeling away.

"Guys?" Zoe asked, interrupting our staring contest.

Murben answered in my stead. "I think this is an aftermath from yesterday."

Ben turned to Davis. "Zoe is off limits."

"Yeah, that's real smooth. Much better than how I was going to put it."

"As I recall, you didn't put out any words."

I screamed with my mouth closed and took Murben's hand. "You'll train me today. Zoe, I'll tell you in private later." I dragged Murben two mats away and rolled my shoulders as I got ready to fight.

"Never put me through that again," Murben muttered when we stood face to face.

"What mischief have I done now?"

"I didn't get any sleep last night. Ben stayed in my room until midnight, whimpering and in a state of flat-out panic. 'What if she gets hurt?'. 'How does going out help her situation?'. 'Am I not enough for her?'. 'What if she meets another man?'." Murben jabbed a fist at my shoulder.

"Ouch!" I huffed.

"Then he came back just after midnight. 'She has spotted another man, and I worry she won't return until tomorrow. Should I go after her?'. 'What if he kills her in her sleep?'. 'What if they don't do any sleeping and she doesn't put her shields up and I have to feel it all?'." Murben jabbed a fist at my other shoulder, but this time I was ready to block it with my forearm. "Good," he snorted before he carried on with his rant. "At one point, I thought I'd have to lock him in the dungeon so that he wouldn't hunt you down. I barely had any sleep and when he left, I had to sleep with the window open so his magic residue could clear."

Vulnerability brought my eyes to the mat, but I had to be ready for his attack, so found my courage quickly. "Ben and my relationship is complicated. There are secrets in the way," I muttered. "If you want to sleep better, you could tell me what the secrets are."

"There is a simple solution to find out what those are." He kicked at my side, and I swatted his leg away irritably.

"What?" I lowered my guard and because of it, his second kick hit my thigh with a mighty whack that made me sway before catching my balance.

"Just marry him, and those secrets become your entitlement."

"Stop being facetious. He hasn't proposed. Nor do I want to accept *before* I know the secrets. And I think I know a better solution for your sleepless nights."

"What is that?"

"I'll make you a beauty cream to get rid of those black bags under your eyes."

He circled around me. "Oh, in a mocking mood today, are we? I wasn't going to push you, but we'll train with our wings out then. I want to see how well you can swing a sword and still keep your balance with your wings out."

"Uh, that's not how we fight. Soldiers always fight with their wings in so that they don't get damaged or cut off."

"*It is* how we train if you take nine seconds to bring them out when you need to flee."

"Ben told you," I growled, and twisted my head to see Davis watching Ben and Zoe spar. "I'm not wearing the uniform with the slit at the back."

Murben quickly moved around me, pulling my dagger from my leg-holster in a swift move and cutting a long rift into the leather at my back. "You do now."

I threw a quick look over my shoulder and gasped. "You destroyed Bensguard Outpost property. And you could have cut my back!"

"And risk King Blackbone giving me an early death? Not likely." He gestured towards my back. "Cadet Coraly, shall we get started?"

Hesitating at first, I put in some more effort as I struggled to get the wings out. The choice to unfurl my white wings wasn't to insult Ben, but to avoid trouble if any other cadets would walk into the hall. As the plumes snapped out, I stumbled to my knees but was quickly on my feet again. "I'm okay."

Murben rubbed his fingers over his forehead as if I was an utter disaster. He held up the dagger he had stolen from my leg straps. "Let's stick to the daggers instead of a sword. I think that is difficult enough for you if you can't even stand on your feet."

I glowered at him.

"Good. Use that anger to focus, and for goodness' sake, keep your wings tucked along your sides and off the floor. Imagine you're on a battlefield where weapons could be strewn on the ground. If you drag your wings across the blood and dirt, they might get caught on something sharp. Then you won't be able to fly at all. And if you flex them around you, anyone can simply cut them off."

That picture of war was horrific. Again, I missed my undercover agent work. My muscles strained from just below my neck and all the way down to my tail bone, as I squirmed around, trying to flex the wings tightly to my body.

"Are you having some sort of after-party from last night?" Murben asked, looking at me as if he was wondering what the heck I was doing. "Is this really how bad it is?"

"I've never liked flying. The wings are heavy."

He shoved my dagger back into my leg strap. "I didn't want to believe King Blackbone when he told me how bad it was. Okay, no problem. Tomorrow morning, at six o'clock, I'll enrol you to my training camp and we go out for a run and then some press-ups and so on."

"Between you, Ben and Zayd training me, I won't have a life."

"Nor will you keep your life during a battle if you don't improve your proficiency at using those wings."

The snap echoed softly in the hall, as I return my wings. "I'm done. At the edge of the mat, I donned my boots before holding an arm high into the air. "Zoe! I'm having lunch. Coming?"

"I'm starving!" she called, and scurried after me as I had already crossed the hall, taking the shortcut to the canteen through the courtyard.

Once we had filled our plates with a steak pies and chips and sat down, she leaned over the table and said, "Now, tell me what's up with Davis?"

"It's bad news. Are you sure you want me to tell you here?"

She nodded, and I believed her, as I had never seen her in tears.

"Ben's spies found out that your mother was a white-wing, who once loved a black-wing."

"That's awesome. I don't blame her, honey."

I leaned forward, my stomach twisting into tight knots as I prepared to speak the words I knew would shatter Zoe's world. The truth pressed down on me like dark rain clouds, each syllable a burden and all I wanted was to avoid the storm. Her eyes, bright and trusting, the same as Davis's, met mine, unaware of the deluge of bad news I was about to unleash.

"Zoe," I began, my voice barely above a whisper, "you know your mother died during childbirth, but that's not the whole story. You weren't born alone. You had a twin, a brother with black wings. Your father had to take him to the Black Wing Territory, but he couldn't take you. So, he left you at the orphanage."

Zoe's fork paused mid-air, her gaze stayed on her plate as she processed my words. The canteen seemed to stop, the clink of cutlery and murmur of conversations fading into a distant hum.

"Jason Davis," she muttered, her voice flat, as she absently stirred her chips in the brown pepper sauce. Her expression remained unreadable, but I could see the subtle tremor in her hands, the slight tightening of her jaw.

I had rehearsed this moment countless times, trying to find the right words to soften the blow. But nothing could have prepared me for the way Zoe's face fell. Her smile, once warm and genuine – mocking even, now appeared strained, as if the very act of curving her lips upward took immense effort. The sparkle in her eyes dimmed, replaced by a hollow emptiness. Her shoulders slumped, and her breath slowed.

I reached out instinctively, wanting to comfort her, to fix her sadness somehow and take away her pain. But before I could move, Zoe stood abruptly, the chair scraping harshly against the floor. The clatter of her fork hitting the porcelain plate echoed in the sudden silence.

"Excuse me," she said, her voice tight, "Excuse me, I'm going to go…" She pointed for the door. "I need to be alone." Without another word, she turned and walked away, her footsteps quick and purposeful, each one silent yet thunderous with the turmoil she was feeling.

I sat there, rooted to the spot, my heart aching as I watched her retreating figure. The hurt in her eyes, the betrayal she must have felt, haunted me. I wanted to chase after her, to apologise, to explain. But I knew she needed space, time to process the truth I had just laid bare.

With a heavy sigh, I stood, leaving my untouched food behind. It felt like weights had been strapped to my ankles, each step an effort as I moved towards my tree. I climbed to my branch, seeking solace in the familiar embrace of the branches.

As always, it didn't take long before Zayd joined me. His presence was a comfort, a silent understanding passing between us.

I fiddled with an acorn in my hands, avoiding his gaze. "I've started to believe you only use your magic of far-sight to see when I'm here."

Zayd chuckled softly, the sound a welcome distraction. "It's certainly a useful tool for that. Why are you here this time? Did something happen when you were out last night?"

I shook my head, unable to find the words, but then I muttered, "I gave Zoe some bad news."

Zayd's expression shifted, concern etching his features. "And she didn't take it well?"

I hesitated, trying to form a guess but failed. "I don't know. She left. I don't know where she went."

Zayd placed a reassuring hand on my shoulder around the trunk. "She'll come around. Give her time."

I nodded, though doubt gnawed at me. The uncertainty of Zoe's reaction, the fear that I had lost her trust, lingered in my mind. But for now, all I could do was wait and hope.

I frowned suddenly. "You knew about last night? Ben told you I went clubbing?"

"No! Many people at this outpost keep an eye on you. Your brother told me."

"My brother…is keeping an eye on me?"

"Crazy, right?"

I snorted and my stomach churned as I watched Zayd polish a bright green pear on his navy-blue shirt. He stopped his momentum and looked at me. "Have you eaten anything today?"

I shook my head, and as I did, he immediately offered me the pear. He hadn't even hesitated. It was so easy with him; the kindness, the conversations, the confessions. I wished I could be in love with him now as I had been in the past and ignore all this drama with the black-wings. But the things in life you really want were those you fought hard to gain and keep.

"Wow," he scoffed, as he watched me. "That frown." He looked pointedly at my forehead. "You need some serious cheering up. Let see if I remember what used to make you happy. Ah! Do you remember when we used to play that game with the leather ball? You held onto it and tried to get past me to touch it down beyond the painted line before I tackled you backwards. Tackle ball, I believe you called it. How many points in total do you have now?"

I laughed at the memories as they grew vivid in my mind. "Sixteen. I scored like two a year since I was eight."

His ocean-blue eyes shone with playfulness. "What? You thought I'd simply give the points away? You have to earn them," he chuckled, his smile full of hope that I'd take the bait and bite back.

He had already succeeded in making me giggle and lose that frown. I nodded. "Okay. Let's see if I can score another today."

He had already dropped to the ground when he said, "I'll get the ball and be right back."

He was back within five minutes with the ball under his arm, beckoning me to join him on the field. We played the game for a long while, and in earnest, the distraction was welcomed. Although, the bruises I could have lived without. Once we were done, my body ached as if I had constantly been crashing into a wall. He was clearly far more muscular now compared to when we were younger. I hadn't scored a single point either.

We had shared nostalgic looks, though, which was a far more dangerous game than tackle ball.

31

The alarm pierced into my ears at five-thirty in the morning, and I immediately regretted agreeing to practise wing exercises with Murben this early on a Sunday. I rolled over and was about to shove the blanket over my head when I noticed Ben staring at the ceiling as if he had been awake all night. We hadn't talked yesterday after I had got back from the game with Zayd. I had been busy with other things until late evening, and I had thought he had been asleep when I returned to our room, considering his back had been towards me the entire time. Clearly, he hadn't slept well, if at all, his hair was dishevelled, and he looked pale.

"You look too handsome to look like shit," I muttered.

He didn't turn his head and kept staring at the ceiling. "The Spirits have struck me with quite a few punches over the years and I've learned to take them with grace," he muttered in the same sarcastic tone back at me.

"What have I done now?" I propped my elbow on the mattress and leaned on my hand.

"Mischief as always, Miss Stone. Mischief as always."

"Is this about me playing with Zayd yesterday?"

"Funny how you guessed correctly on your first attempt."

I exhaled sharply, pressing my fingers to my temples, frustration tensing my nerves. *Not this again!* "Had you preferred to be the one playing?"

"Much preferred it, yes."

"Okay. I'll tell Zayd that you want to play with him next time."

Ben grunted, his eyes burning with equal frustration. "You're evil. You know that's not what I meant."

He had no time to react before I crossed the space between our beds and threw my knees around his waist, bouncing on his abdomen. "Don't be so grumpy."

He folded his arms under his head to emphasise that he wouldn't touch me and that he hadn't forgiven me.

I tore my nightgown over my head to sit in only my blue lace underwear and nothing covering my breasts.

"Evil," he repeated, trying to pin his eyes on the ceiling, but I saw them twitch as if it was too tempting not to look at me.

I got off him and stood at the side of his bed, my arms crossed over my breasts and leaning on my leg with my hip out. "When I say I want to fight for you, you push me at a distance. When I give you space and socialise with others, you get angry that I'm not prioritising you. How do you want it? Do I mean anything to you, or am I purely a tool for your political ends?"

"You can have friends, but some may think it's polite if you keep a distance from your ex-boyfriend!" He frowned. "And please stop pushing your hip out like that. It's too tempting when I know how perfectly it fits inside my palm. Play hard but play fair."

"You're not the one to speak about being fair. You have about three minutes to declare your intentions, King Blackbone, or I'm out. And I don't only mean to train with Murben, I'll go to my brother and beg for my old job back. I'm done playing your pawn."

"*My* pawn," he scoffed between clenched teeth.

"That's it! I'm gone!" I turned towards the wardrobe.

He swooped his legs over the edge of the bed and sat up in a swift move, grabbing onto my hips with his colossal hands. "Please. Stay."

"You better have something damn good to say to convince me to continue being your teammate and risking my life for you."

He nodded, and he had that pondering gaze on his face. He swallowed and looked into my eyes and pulled me close to lean his head against my stomach. "After my parents died, I became a teenager without an adult who would pay attention to me; watch me earn my achievements and to praise me for all I accomplished. My life has felt as if without purpose, and no matter who else supports me, it doesn't feel as if I care whether or not they're impressed by the goals I achieve. But when you look at me, you see me. I have that purpose back where everything I do feels important. That is how I know I love you. That's how I know I have loved no one else."

Okay. I hadn't expected that. Talk about playing hard and not fair!

"I don't have any parents, either. But you don't see me pushing you away whenever the going gets tough. You don't hear of me keeping secrets from you."

He grunted darkly.

"What's that supposed to mean?" I asked.

"You just did…push me away and give me an ultimatum. I'm the one who has been trying to keep us together. You've been pushing me away since the moment you saw me."

"Because of the secrets you deliberately separate us with. I've ignored that our love is against the rules, that my brother doesn't agree with it, that I'll lose my life if anyone murders you and that you're the king of my enemy! Those are obstacles not in our control, but the secrets are in your control!"

"Of course." he sighed. "You're right. I'm still terrified of how deeply the secrets will hurt you, and I don't want you to regret anything between us when you find out." He leaned back and looked at my naked form, slowly pushing his hand up my side to cup my breast. When black veins started seeping up underneath my skin, he immediately stopped and pulled his hand away. "I can't even touch you without hurting you."

"It doesn't hurt!" I tore my fingers through my hair. "I'm fucking unhurtable!"

He grunted and subtly shook his head, not agreeing with something that was on his mind. "You better get ready for your session with Murben."

I swept my hands through the air. "See! Pushing me away."

"Do you want me to come with you?" He searched my face for an invitation, bracing himself for a rejection, as if holding back hope that he hadn't overstepped.

My fury dissolved as it was obvious how his nerves were knotting his entire body. "Probably for the best, or there might only be a puddle left of me after he has run me to the ground."

He let out a low chuckle, the sound a little too forced, as if laughter could remove the tension in his muscles. I tried to look away from those muscles as he got out of bed to get ready, but I think I gawked most of the time – *I'm only human.*

I spent the rest of the day with the black-wings, but constantly tried to watch my surroundings, hoping to spot Zoe. She was nowhere to be seen. As we trained near the field, we could see Zayd's relentless attempts to claim back his top time on the obstacle course, but I suspected he was also doing it to keep an eye on us.

It quickly turned night and a new morning, and not surprisingly, my entire body hurt from the training the previous day, especially my back muscles. Ben had praised my hard work and purred into my ear that my butt had become firmer.

The weeks passed with me in hard training, both physically and mentally. Ben guided me on how to keep the mental shield strong and attempted to break through it so many times it gave me a constant headache. Murben and Davis timed the speed it took me to bring out my wings, and I strengthened my back muscles with sessions in the weights room.

Unavoidably though, the day of the third challenge arrived. My nerves throbbed under my skin as we walked through the corridor and I was holding the pot of the Zincrics herb plant in both my hands, and thanks to

Ben, the plant looked healthier than when we received it. Although, admittedly, the leaves looked a tone of ash from all the death essence.

We had to halt in the hallway between corridors when cadets stampeded across towards the Battle and Tactic classroom on their way to their challenge-test. As usual, we passed the Admission Office, the Infirmary, the Assembly Hall and the zoology classroom before we arrived at the herbology classroom adjacent to the canteen.

Mewer and half the class were already inside, and he looked up from his desk and pointed for the shelf along the wall with three dozen Zincrics herb plants on it already.

"Ensure your plant has a sticker with your name and leave it on the shelf before you take your seats."

I followed Mewer's instructions and sat down at the place Ben, and I had claimed for this classroom. Kate smiled and waved at me from the other side of the classroom and Mazdon gave a curt nod, as did Emroyce, sitting one desk behind him and next to Kenyard.

When everyone in this morning group had sat, Mewer stood up.

"Let's begin. Today is challenge day and whoever wins will earn the rare healing cream." He held up the transparent tub again with the green cream inside. "The task is to be the quickest to make a healing cream that will close a minor wound on my hand. You can find all the ingredients you need on the table over there," he explained and pointed. "Cadet Dixon and Cadet Toran who won the last challenge have a ten second head start and the rest of you will have three minutes. If no one has provided me with a cream when the time is up, no one wins. Is that clear? Or does anyone have any questions?"

The bond crackled in my head, and I waited for Ben to speak to me.

"When we start. Get me vitamin E oil, nut oil, zincrics leaves and beeswax, and I'll get the coconut butter and pestle and mortar. Plus, I'll add the comfrey root I collected from the mountain in the black-wing district."

I nodded towards him, as Mewer started the countdown for the challenge.

"Five. Four. Three. Two. One. Start!"

Cadet Dixon and Cadet Toran both went for the herbs, looking through them as if they had trouble identifying the items presented and knowing what was needed. After five seconds, Mewer started a five second countdown for the rest of the class.

"Five. Four. Three. Two. One. Start!"

I darted toward the front of the classroom to get the ingredients, having to wrestle Emroyce to share some of the nut oil into a transparent tub. *"Vitamin E oil, nut oil, zincrics leaves…what was the last thing?"*

"Beeswax."

"Okay. Got it!"

I sprinted back to Ben, pouring what I had in my arms out onto the desk.

"Great. Thanks." He pounded all the ingredients together in the iron mortar with his bulging muscly biceps, looking so deliciously focused.

When the ingredients had become a creamy substance, he stirred the pestle around in the mortar rather than pounding. His intelligence, having such knowledge of most things, was impressive. I looked around the classroom to identify if there were any emotional manipulators here, but found that no one was paying us any attention, so I guessed the infatuation for him was all on me.

I closed in on the back of his chair as he sat by the table and couldn't help but push my arms down his chest and lower my face to nip at his ear, kissing his neck.

"We don't have time for that. I really need to win the challenge for you, especially considering your wing-weakness-situation. Not that the cream can patch you up if you fall from a great height."

"Way to go killing the buzz."

"There is no buzz. Unscrew the lid and hold the empty tub up for me, so I can pour in the cream. It's almost done."

I held the tub up in front of him and was ready with the lid in my other hand. With the pestle, he scraped the light-green cream into the tub.

"Be ready to sprint."

I put my footing into a sprinting position and as he removed the pestle, I launched myself forwards, screwing on the lid as I ran to the front, and punched the tub down on Mewer's desk right in front of Emroyce's face.

"Done!"

Mewer nodded for me, and I turned to grin at Emroyce, who responded with a playful pout. My heart was in my throat and the anticipation was unbearable. Ben came to stand behind my back like a solid anchor against the waves of untamed nerves. We watched Mewer as he unsheathed his dagger and made a thin cut in his palm and then unscrewed the lid to our cream and applied it generously. After a minute, he dried the cream off with a tissue and looked at the wound.

"It has healed enough." He inspected a register fastened to a clipboard that laid on his desk before he looked up at us. "Congratulations. You were faster than anyone in the earlier groups. You're the winners." He tossed the tub with the green healing cream towards Ben, who caught it mid-air before making a curt bow.

Ben slid the cream into my side pocket over my trouser leg and ushered me out of the classroom as all the cadets streamed out. "Come with me," he said, a dark mystery hiding at the depths of his voice.

Did he think I, the queen of mischief, wasn't able to recognise trouble when it dangled in front of my face? "Where are we going?" I asked, the accusation not subtle.

"Since it's a sunny day, I'm taking a shot at the romance stuff you said you wanted."

"Really?" My brows raised at him. Okay, I was way off. That wasn't the mischief I had expected.

He took my hand and guided me out of the building and towards the mountain ridge and the river pool. When we arrived at the pool, Murben stood by the bank and it was beyond me how he had got here before us since I had seen him at the challenge moments ago. He stood with his arms crossed over his chest and legs spread wide as if he was guarding something. Getting closer to him, I saw a red blanket hidden between the long grass and on it a feast of delicacies was laid out. There were sandwiches, chicken breasts, a potato salad, and for pudding there was chocolate mousse topped with strawberries and whipped cream.

I twisted to look at Ben. "I approve."

"I'm glad to hear it. Murben worked hard on it," he said and leered.

I burst out a laugh. "Thank you, Murben."

"You're so welcome, future queen."

I glowered at him, feeling my eyes ablaze with a warning, and my jaw tightened, letting him know that the word 'queen' rang in my ears like mockery. It wasn't his right to rewrite the story of who I was, and to make me wear a crown that wasn't mine.

Murben's lips curled at the edges, even when he tried to be serious.

Ben waved at him. "Now, make yourself scarce."

Murben left, and it was only the two of us. I lay down on the blanket and popped a strawberry into my mouth.

Ben lay down next to me. "Sweet before savoury, Miss stone?"

I groaned. "Yet, not sweet enough." I rolled on top of him, claiming his mouth, and he responded by sweeping his tongue over my lips before dipping it into my mouth. My sex tingled so potently it surged right through my core, and by reflex I ground against his crotch, surprised to find he didn't push me off. With a speeding pulse my breaths grew more shallow and a flush crept up my neck. All I could think about was him as he touched my sensitive areas, making my toes curl inside my boots. Everything about him unfolded me like a treasure map waiting to be explored; the world seemed to bow at his presence alone, his voice dangerously seductive like a lure from dark shadows and his scent made me want to close my eyes and surrender my being to do with what he willed.

We spent the afternoon talking about innocent things like nature, flowers, animals and places we had visited that were wonders of the world.

That was when we weren't making out and relaxing in the grass under the sun. I had forgotten where I was until the sky had turned dark and Ben announced he thought it was safest if we returned to our room. Disagreeing, I suggested we could sleep under the stars, but apparently, I didn't have a say in the matter.

"You passed the test," I told him as he put the key into our door and opened it for me to enter first. "You were very romantic today."

"Thank you. It pleases me to hear you're happy with my efforts."

"And Murben's efforts."

"Let's not forget." He closed the door and removed his boots next to the wall beside it. "And where do we stand on the beds now?"

Spirits, he looked so gorgeous when he had that begging look in his eyes. "You can move them together again, if it pleases the king."

"It pleases the king very much that he can sleep next to his queen."

He didn't hesitate to pull out his bed and push it towards my side. When he looked up, he must have seen my distant look.

"What's wrong?"

"You keep mentioning that so breezily. You know that to wed someone means a permanent mark on the neck sealed by the Spirits after you've said those vows? The mark is irrevocable. It means you would have made your choice for life. Forever belonging."

"*You* say it, as if you think you must teach me how it works. I know what commitment the ritual pledges to the Spirits, and my vows are yours when you want them."

He undid two buttons of his shirt before he swept it over his head, releasing a set of tight abs and a shelf of pectorals.

Unintentionally, I let out a moan.

"Bedtime," he said teasingly, and I wondered when he'd ever make love to me to pacify that ignited flame that burned so fiercely the moment I looked at him.

In only our underwear, he tucked his arms around me to hold me close to him, skin against skin, and that's how we slept peacefully all night. It was the best night's sleep I'd had in weeks. But as I woke up in the morning, I was hit with the realisation of a new timetable to practice for the fourth challenge; a balance test that was impossible unless you had incredibly steady hands.

After breakfast, I dragged my feet alongside Ben towards the navigation classroom, intimidated that Camp Leader Seon Nar was going to lecture us about steady hands and balance. Simply seeing the air wielder's face, or hearing her sharp voice, reminded me of General Denor and made my bones shatter like a wind chime.

"You shouldn't judge her," Ben said, walking next to me. There was a serene calm about him this morning, which was unnerving since my nerves drummed me into attack mode.

"What? You're on her side now? Did General Denor alter your brain before or after my brother lashed you? She hates you."

"She is also struggling with a war against her village where her elderly parents live with her older, and very greedy, sister."

"Haven't you been busy getting to know everybody else's business? Perhaps you should make a running commentary about my life, and I may learn something I didn't already know."

He looked away from me and grunted darkly. Were there things about me he knew that I didn't? That made my stomach even more unsettled.

We entered the classroom, and I noticed it hadn't changed since I last saw it. On the wall were maps of all the three provinces in Skyberg and topographic drawings of the land. There were binoculars, magnifying glasses, compasses and other tools that helped in navigation tasks in baskets on shelves along the walls. The tables were arranged much like in the zoology classroom, but instead of tall workstations for people to stand around, these desks were low for sitting at.

We sat down at one workstation together with Kate, Mazdon, Emroyce, Kenyard, Penya and Maruto. Cadet Ashton Hall, and his father Sergeant Enzo Hall, who were the expert archers, also joined us today. Ashton and Emroyce looked quite alike with long black hair slithering over their shoulders and bony faces that finished in sharp chins. Ashton, perhaps, looked a little more serious than Emroyce, who enjoyed showing off. But that wasn't the way of those from the Pharanir province. Their way was very much like Camp Leader Nar now strode in with confident steps and had zero play in her expression, and just like Camp Leader Neville, she spat instructions at people, too. None of them were much for coddling cadets. It made me wonder why they had applied for leadership at all.

"Because they're good at what they do. They care. They know what's out there, and they know the cost if they were soft towards us." Ben clarified.

"Listening in on my thoughts again, are we?"

"You were loud. Perhaps a tad hateful?"

"For as long as she has General Denor's back, she'll get no sympathy from me."

"So unforgiving. And I'm the one who got lashed."

"Aren't you the one who always reminds me that we're one and the same?"

"Touché."

"And what the heck is this thing in front of us?"

I looked at a square platform that had another raised circular part centred over it. On top of the wooden circle was a fist-size granite. At the side of the contraption was another similarly sized stone.

"It's a balance board."

"Shut up and listen!" That was Camp Leader Nar's greeting, but in fairness, it got everyone's attention. "The task is to swap one stone on the balance board for the other without triggering the magical red warning light. The one who can do it the fastest without triggering the alarm during the challenge wins a muscle massage by an elite specialist in the city, as well as being one win closer to going on the suicide mission through the Spirits' Trek. If you didn't understand those instructions, ask a friend…if you have any here." She waited for a moment as she stared at us, not caring that her long ebony hair flapped with irate wind across her face and partially obstructed her view. "Well! Start practising! Once you're fed up with it, you can bring it to your room and practise some more. I won't hold any classes about this as I need to dash off to the war in a few days, but anyone who needs guidance can seek me or any of the other Camp Leaders out. I'll be back on challenge day on the thirtieth of December. May the Spirit of Luck be with you!"

"And also with you!" the class answered the standard response in unison.

After her rousing speech, she left the classroom.

Emroyce leaned towards me. "Not sure who I'd like to cuddle with most, her or the viper that bit me."

I choked on a laugh. "If you ever give her a try ensure you bring an antidote."

He laughed out loud, and many cadets turned to stare at us, so I cocked my head low and looked at the simple contraption in front of me. I attempted to swap the stones out, but each time I removed the first stone, I triggered the red alarm that flashed around the circle.

I growled lowly, and looked at Ben, who was watching me intensely by my side. "How is this relevant to the mission task in real life?"

He sighed. "Patience isn't your virtue. Do it slower and more gently."

No matter how slowly I did it, it triggered as soon as I started pushing the second stone onto the circular platform. "It's so sensitive." I looked around and saw that Ashton was doing well even though he too triggered the alarm, but he had got further than I had.

"What is Ashton and his father's magic?"

"Not anything that helps them in this task. They can possess other people."

"Great. That sounds fantastic."

"I wouldn't suggest you attempted it for fun. I've heard it isn't a pleasant experience as their life-force drains yours for as long as they are in your body."

Ben dragged the tool closer to his space and separated his knees, patting at the seat between his legs. "Sit here."

I scooted across and he wrapped his arms around me, guiding my hands in his. The way he touched me, with his breath falling onto my neck, I barely noticed the gentleness with which he moved the stones across, and I gasped when I realised he had placed the second stone on the circle without triggering the alarm.

"How did you do that?"

"With patience and gentleness. You try it again."

I tried it a few more times. "This is impossible!" Both stones fell off the circle and clonked onto the desk. "I'm taking a break. I need air, and we can practise again after lunch."

Ben smiled. "I'll take the balance board to our room and meet you in the canteen."

I nodded. "I should also see if I can find Zoe. No one has seen her since I told her about her twin brother."

He followed me to the corridor, where we parted ways. When I walked towards the river pool, I noticed that some of the second-year cadets and third-year cadets were following Ward and a few of the other sergeants in the Air Force Unit out on patrol again.

It reminded me that we were the unit who was sent on suicide missions, but the General Operations Unit cadets were the ones who went out to war, so leadership expected them to attend patrols even before they had graduated.

As I walked the forest path between the pine trees I heard a twig snap behind me, but before I could turn around to see who was there, someone wrestled me to the ground and pulled a fabric bag soaked in chloroform over my head.

32

"*Ouch! My head.*" Not that my sore wrists were any better. My tail bone throbbed, and my foot could possibly be broken.

"*Angelica? Angelica!*" Ben called, his voice loaded with panic. "*Can you hear me? Where are you?*"

"*It would be a surprise if my head was still attached to my body with this headache. Was I out dancing last night?*"

"*Last night?*" The tone of his voice made it clear he wasn't in a mood for jokes. "*Angelica, you've been gone for a month.*"

"*A month! What?*" Cold dread washed over me, and my mind raced with a thousand thoughts. "*What happened? Where am I?*"

I turned but couldn't twist as my wrists and ankles were bound to a chair. Darkness surrounded me, as I tossed my head around. "*I'm blindfolded.*"

"*Fuck!*" Ben cussed, and I could feel his stomach twist into unforgiving knots of unbearable terror. "*Don't panic. We'll find you.*"

"*I'm not panicking. You're panicking.*"

"*Can you blame me? I have been driven to madness for a little under a month, and so have your friends. We have done everything in our power to find you.*"

"*You've been working with my friends?*"

"*Yes. Even Watson.*"

"*Awe, for me?*" I regretted mocking him. "*Ouch, my head really hurts.*"

"*My love. Focus. Tell me what you can hear around you. What can you smell? Are you outdoors or indoors?*"

"*Can't you just find a cadet who can track me?*"

"*We have tried that. And wind whispering, animal whispering and sending out hearing portals. I've tried everything. Even the humming in my ears has been kept on a constant low frequency, so I can't tell if I'm getting closer to you or not. Mazdon is here, so give us a minute and we'll go outside, and you can scream your loudest to see if he can hear you.*"

That was a horrifying thought. *"If I scream, I think my brain will split in half."*

"Just do your best. Can you tell me anything else?"

I sensed that Ben had gone into warrior leader mode, desperately seeking a clue to resolve his mission. He was really suffering from not knowing where I was. His anxiety levels would soon blow the roof off his sanity.

I held my breath to listen to my surroundings. *"There are droplets riveting over stone. I can hear a soft echo." I inhaled. "And it smells damp, like…"*

"In a cave?"

"Yes."

"Okay, we're outside the military building. Can you scream for me?"

I drew as much air as I could into my lungs and screamed. *"I did it. Could you hear me?"*

"Mazdon says he can't hear you." Ben sounded even angrier than before. A dark seething rage lay hot just below the surface of his merciless temper, burning through every rational thought. *"I'm going to fucking kill the one who is doing this to you."*

"That's nice…" My mind was blurring like I had smoked too much hemp. *"I'm so hungry and thirsty. And I feel so weak."* Whatever magical effect I had been exposed to was a whole new level of agony.

"You've probably been starved for a month. Like a magical coma. If that's the case, you might not have long until your body shuts down after the magic was removed from your system. Stay with me." There was a promise marring his voice, indicating he would destroy the world to get to me.

He was fighting his destructive thoughts, but they were nearly shattering his control.

"You must save yourself. Tell Mewer to break the soul bond."

"Never! If anything happens to you, I'll meet the Spirit of Death by your side." The harshness in his tone left no room for arguing. It was clearly an alternative he couldn't even begin to imagine how to survive.

"Please, Ben. I'm not worthy of you, anyway. You're a king, and I'm a traitor's daughter."

"Don't you ever tell me that. You can't give up. I will find you."

His shields were weak, making me exposed to his torment and every second felt like a blade twisting deeper into his gut. The abductor had made a fatal mistake in making an eternal enemy of Ben. When he found the perpetrator, there would be no mercy.

"I'm really cold." I swallowed hard, trying to steady myself to make the uneven gasp deepen into something I controlled but the relentless worry gripped tightly around my throat.

I clenched my fists to make my hands at least stop trembling.

"Fuck!" Ben swore again. Powerless. *"Can't you save yourself with your*

magic?"

"I have no magic."

"Really. Even in the face of death, you won't use it?"

"I can't. Not now, anyway."

"Okay, so what do we know? You're in a cave, perhaps low down underground, as it's cold. Anything else?"

"I don't know. My body hurts." Sounds faded into a distant hum and a dull pressure throbbed in my skull. Dark spots danced in my vision and grew larger.

"My love. Be brave. I'm working as fast as I can."

"Where are you?"

"I'm flying over the mountain ridge. But the potency of the humming in my ears isn't changing. I think there must still be some sort of spell on you to fool me."

I felt so tired that I didn't even have the energy to speak to him in my mind. It was a struggle to hold my head up and every time I let it hang, the back of my neck stretched uncomfortably. The blindfold was pressing hard at my eyes and the pounding in my head didn't ease.

A month. I had been out for a month.

Who had done this to me? Gravelhorn? Crow, as revenge for Hefany? But I hadn't been the one poisoning Hefany.

"I'm just going to sleep for a bit."

My body felt strangely weightless and unresponsive, and my pulse seemed to be slowing with my every heartbeat.

"No! No, no. Stay with me. You must remain awake. Can you scream again?"

"I can't. I'm too tired."

The silence seemed to make his anxiety worsen. *"Please, Angelica. Don't give into it. Fight!"*

"I can't. I'm sorry. Please, hurry to Mewer."

The air became too thick to breathe, and I struggled to fill my lungs.

Ben's roar echoed inside my head. *"Do you know who is most worried about you?"*

"Is it not you?"

"Of course. I mean after me."

"I hate guessing games."

"Your brother. He has gone ballistic on everyone at the outpost, ordering them to pitch in with the search."

There was a span of silence before he called out my name once more, but I was too tired to answer. It felt as if my mouth was glued shut. My mind could have been in a sandstorm where my ears heard the swooshing sound of sand blowing through my mind, numbing everything between my ears.

"Angelica!" He shouted above the breezing sound of sand in my head.

"Please, answer me."

I attempted answering him, but I couldn't tell whether my voice had been pushed down the soul bond to reach him or not.

"Angelica, can you coo into the space around you to identify how large the cave is?"

Coo?

I didn't have the energy to answer him.

"Please, Angelica. Fight! Think of your mother's treachery. Think of General Denor putting you in the infirmary. Think of Counsellor Desry who destroyed Robin's mind. Get angry. Scream!"

I inhaled a large breath that seemed to almost drown me with the damp air before I screamed; the sound echoed around the stone walls. *"Maybe a room as big as the sparring hall."*

"Good girl. I can't be far away." Helplessness clearly still clawed inside him even if he tried to mask it with a calm voice.

"You're a terrible liar. You've no clue where I am. What does Harvey think?"

"They are all asleep at the moment."

"Asleep?"

"It's three o'clock in the morning. Only Mazdon is here with me."

"Tell him he has been like a big brother to me. Better than Harvey."

"You can tell him that yourself when you see him."

There was silence for what felt like an hour, and my head dipped as I occasionally nodded off. *"Are you there?"* I asked him.

"I'm here, my love," he answered gently, but I sensed the edgy desperation beneath it.

"What's happening?"

"I'm circling the mountains and I'm landing every twenty minutes to rest, but the search is difficult in the darkness."

"I must sleep. I love you."

"No! You're not someone who says goodbye. Especially not like this. Not to me! Spirits be damned, you'll fight for me, Angelica!"

He wasn't accepting my defeat, but there was little I could do as the fog rolled through my mind and darkness threatened to take me over. *"I can't do this."*

"Give me just two more hours. I have searched almost the entire west side."

He had left his mental shield wide open in his search for me. I could clearly perceive the fear he suffered, coiling around his ribs and tightening his chest until he couldn't breathe. He was so worried of being unable to stop the inevitable, of losing me. There was no thought on the fact that he'd die too, like it didn't matter to him. The only thought running through his mind was that of saving my life.

There was silence again, and I listened to the dripping sound of water striking the cave floor. I tried to bounce on the chair to tear at the restraints and break free, but instead I fell over, hitting my head on the stony ground. *"Fucking ouch!"*

"What happened?" Ben asked with such worry that I thought my heart would break.

"I fell over and hit my head. I don't think it'll help, but I'm on a wooden chair."

"Can you smash it to pieces and free your hands?" The small hope in his voice could have killed me right then.

"I'm sorry. I can't even get off the floor." I tossed with my head, trying to get the blindfold to come off, but it had been tightened too securely. I rested my forehead against the cold stone, and it soothed my headache.

Ben growled, his patience so thin I imagined it was transparent by now. *"I wish I could identify what I hear around you."*

My brows scratched along the stone as I raised them. *"You hear through my ears?"*

"Yes. But not very much. The sounds are very faint."

I lifted my head, feeling a severe head-rush as my consciousness was slipping, but I had to stay awake a little longer. *"Ben, find Mewer and have him bond Mazdon to your soul. Mazdon will be indirectly connected to me, and he can listen to what is around me."*

"That should work! I love your extraordinary mind!"

There was silence once more, and I rested my head against the rocky ground again, trying not to feel the pain as the weight of me and the chair clamped down on my left hand.

"Angelica! Angelica! Angelica!" My name echoed inside my mind until I registered it was Ben shouting for me.

"Yes?"

"We have been trying to contact you for two hours. You must have slept. Please, stay awake. Mazdon can't use your senses otherwise."

"Hello, Angie!" I heard Mazdon in my head.

"Hello, Maz!"

"I'm so happy to hear your voice. But, Angie, now I need you to be very quiet. Try to hold your breath for as long as you can and be completely still."

I inhaled a large breath, then ensured I didn't move a muscle whilst I waited.

"Okay," Mazdon called. *"I think I know. I can hear running water, leaves blowing in the wind and there is an owl hooting nearby. Best guess is that she's in that cave near the river pool that has a small waterfall."*

"I have already checked there a few times," Ben barked.

"Yes, but with the mind games at play, let's check again. She could be concealed in an illusion."

"Okay. Hold on, Angelica, we're coming."

I relaxed and let go of my breath, feeling my mind drift off.

When my consciousness brought me back to the world of the living, my blindfold was off, and I saw tree branches swishing by. My back rested against someone, and I was sitting…on a horse…swaying to its quick walk. I was wedged between two muscly arms which held onto the reins. I cocked my head up and Ben looked down at me. "Hello, love." He smiled, and the intention in his eyes wasn't as playful as he meant it to be. "It's not far to the infirmary now."

The blindfold was off. My eyelids blinked, my vision blurry at first from the very shadows I had drifted through in my subconsciousness. I saw Ben and I really looked at him now as if he was the only thing in the world that mattered. He was here. He had saved me. I had been sure I'd never wake again to see those lovely ruby eyes staring back at me.

His face was lined with exhaustion, but it still managed to light up the moment our eyes met. Raw emotion was buried deep in his gaze, but there was also a lingering agony of his worry that I wasn't in safety yet. His shoulders were tense, and he held me with an iron grip as his glances snapped sharply around to scan our surrounding for threats. He didn't force me to talk, and every so often he leaned down to plant a kiss on my head.

I couldn't keep awake, my body was breaking at the seams, shutting down, and the world became a dark place once more.

Deep green eyes and golden hair greeted me when I opened my eyes once more.

"Mewer?" I croaked, my head lolling between my shoulders on a soft pillow.

He palmed my forehead and put two fingers on my neck to check my pulse. "You're lucky to be alive. You were closer to death this time than the last."

I tried to keep my eyes open to see where I was. In the infirmary. A corner bed at the far end. The blue drapes pulled to shield me from view. I was wearing a white infirmary gown and was covered with a sheet that was tucked under my armpits. How long had I been out for?

A hand squeezed around mine at my other side, so I turned my head.

Ben smiled at me, but there was still that tint of worry in his eyes. "How are you feeling?" His deep voice was gentle, as if I'd break if he put some weight behind it.

I blinked my eyes shut momentarily to rest them. "Not entirely alive," I admitted. "It hurts all over."

My arm tightened inside a calloused palm. "A small prick," Mewer said, as he inserted a needle into the crock of my arm and emptied a cylinder with a transparent liquid into me. "Whatever magic was used, it did some extensive work on your mind." He looked up at Ben, his gaze relaying a hidden meaning, and then he put the cylinder down on a tray on the side-table. "I'm surprised you couldn't feel the magic through the bond. Must be dealing with someone with advanced skills." Mewer put a plaster over the leaking prick hole and put his hands into the pockets of his brown healer coat.

Ben squeezed my hand tighter. "But Cadet Coraly should concern herself purely with recovering and I'll take care of finding who's responsible." He flashed me a smirk. "Teamwork."

I smiled at him, feeling too hoarse and weak to say much.

"I'll inform Fern you're ready for lunch. Perhaps start with your favourite; strawberry jelly," Mewer said.

The fond childhood memories made me smile. I had consumed more than a hundred jelly pots during my countless visits to the infirmary.

My happy memory was short lived as both men looked up towards the door, their faces turning grim simultaneously. Ben shot out of his chair to stand tall, pushing his chest out, and Mewer's hand drew back his brown healer coat to rest his hand on his hilt. The curtain was drawn in a way that meant I couldn't see who had entered the infirmary hall, but by their reactions, it made my heart pound harder. From the way they slowly turned their heads, their eyes pinned on the same source, I could tell that whoever it was had walked closer.

"I heard one of our star cadets momentarily visited the demons."

General Denor.

I couldn't stop my entire body from trembling. The voice turned my nerves against me, and I was immobilised with fear; almost unable to breathe.

His thin, long face, sharp nose and jaw disgusted me. His cheeks had a richer colour than before, and his face and neck marked with more scars, most likely earned during the war in Pansery during the last month. The short, black hair wore a few more grey streaks in it despite his young age of thirty. He had donned his armour over his red general's uniform with the star between two horizontal chevrons on his shoulder and three circles of magical potency on the other, as if walking into the Bensguard Outpost was as much a war as the one in the north.

"Get out!" Ben growled.

"No fists required today, King Blackbone. I come in peace to witness the remarkable recovery first hand."

"You don't know the meaning of the word peace," Ben said darkly.

He ignored Ben and looked at me. "So, the men collected you from the cave in time. Well done. How did they–"

"I never told anyone where I found her," Ben growled, and his fists tightened at his sides.

"Nor did I," Mazdon added, approaching through the hall with Emroyce, Kenyard, Brian and Valentina and her teammate Treylieh at his back.

Emroyce was finishing chewing on something, and Valentina had a water bottle in her hand, so they had probably rushed here from the canteen as soon as Mazdon had picked up on our conversation with the general.

General Denor scanned the arriving cadets, his eyes flickering among them as if he was searching for someone in particular.

Ben observed his behaviour, following the general's glances with a suspicious gleam in his eyes, as if he had just figured something out.

General Denor relaxed into his usual self-confidence and sniggered. "Training can take place in the most inventive of places."

"Training!" Ben roared, pushing up his chest even higher, filling it with air.

"Yes. I needed to test how long it took for two people who are soul bound to find each other, once applying appropriate motivation."

Ben stalked towards him, murder in his eyes.

"No!" I shouted, and was about to get out of bed to stop Ben, but Brian held me down against the mattress. "You've not healed enough yet to interfere," he whispered.

"Ben, don't!" I begged him.

If he attacked General Denor, the general had the right to lash us both at best, or murder Ben in self-defence at the worst.

Ben didn't get to General Denor before the general's magic latched onto Ben's mind and brought him crumbling to his knees with agonising grunts. Even with the potent power the general possessed, which could destroy Ben's mind, Ben kept fighting it and crawling closer.

"Release King Blackbone," Mewer demanded. "I don't want a fight in my infirmary. Sick and injured soldiers are trying to rest in here."

"I'm sure the general can see reason," Treylieh said calmly, clearly using his persuasive magic, and everyone behind Mazdon's back turned to look at him as if a ghost had spoken.

He never spoke, and now he had dared to use it on the general.

General Denor released his grip on Ben's mind, looking wearily at his audience.

Ben was on his hands and knees, panting in pain, rubbing his palm at his forehead.

"I believe disciplining cadets is in order." General Denor looked to be counting how many of us there were. "Forty-five lashes in total."

"You shall die for what you did to Cadet Coraly," Ben swore.

"Another threat to a general's life? Are you certain you want to do that? It adds more lashes."

"Don't bother counting," Emroyce said. "There will be no lashes. If we don't agree to draw a line under this incident, you're not walking out of here alive. You've no witnesses, and I doubt any of us will say other than that you attacked first, and we defended ourselves. I doubt you can render all of us dumb or dead before one of us is fast enough to kill you."

General Denor snorted and shook his head as if the threat had been petty. "I've brought down legions, boy, so your threat doesn't scare me."

"He's meaning to kill someone before he leaves," Kenyard warned from behind Emroyce's back, obviously having used his magic to listen to the intention in the general's voice.

Despite Kenyard's warning, Valentina took a step closer to General Denor, staring up at him. "I'd reconsider that if I were you. How long does it take for you to render me unable to use my magic compared to me snapping your spine in two?" Valentina asked. "I can break your bones in a blink of an eye."

Valentina looked so tiny as she faced off with the general, almost small like a child, but she was fierce.

Then Valentina's body collapsed; her head hitting the floor with a vicious thump, her purple hair spilling over the stone. Her grey eyes were wide open but vacant. She wasn't breathing. Wasn't moving.

"I guess it took me half a blink," the general sneered, lacking empathy when observing the corpse where it lay lifeless at his feet.

We all gasped in unison.

Treylieh threw himself over his dead teammate, checking her for a pulse and nudging her shoulders. Shock fed on all of us for a moment as time seemed to freeze, the world narrowing into a single, horrifying sight before my eyes. The scene burning into my mind. My breath hitched and caught between a gasp and a strangled cry. A claw gripped around my heart to hold me captive in a paralysing disbelief. *This can't be real!*

Mewer also seemed stunned before he reacted and crouched to examine her.

Valentina was one of my best friends. I had known her forever. It was like someone had just punched a fist through my ribcage and ripped out my heart. I wailed in pain and hurt, ready to get off the bed, fetch my daggers and attack the general.

Ben helped Brian wrestle me back down into bed and pin me to the mattress. *"Don't move or make a sound to draw attention to yourself!"*

I gripped Ben's arm hard to hold onto my sanity. *"The general has killed her!"*

33

Treylieh stood up quickly and stared the general straight in the eyes. "You feel merciful and will bring Cadet Karson back to her original state, having only wanted to demonstrate your power, but not to kill her."

The general laughed. "I do feel that tug and compulsion to obey you, but I'm too advanced in magic for you to be able to push me that far." He pointed at his three circles where Treylieh only had two.

My brother in his yellow uniform appeared between my friends in black, separating them to get through. He cleared his throat at General Denor, but said nothing, and only stared at him.

"Fine," General Denor muttered.

I focused on not dropping my jaw. Was General Denor that afraid of my brother's magic…of our inherited magic that he yielded?

The next second, Valentina squirmed on the floor, moaning in agony, but alive.

Harvey glanced at her quickly before turning his look back on General Denor. "My work to train these cadets into soldiers is redundant if you keep killing them. Lash them if you must but leave them able to fight our war."

I guessed that was more protective than I had expected my brother to be. Harvey turned on his heel and walked out of the infirmary. General Denor looked at us all as if we were vermin, but his gaze stopped on Ben.

"You took your teammate's lashes the last time. How many will you be sacrificing yourself for this time?"

"All of them. You can hand me ten of them during every coming month for five months."

"No! I'll take my own!" I yelped.

Ben couldn't do this. General Denor could scar his back permanently. The ten lashes he had already taken were still showing between his shoulder blades. What if they scarred the tissue around the wing flaps, hindering him from bringing his wings out?

Everyone else also objected, calling out that they would take their own punishment, but General Denor held up his hand to silence them. "I accept King Blackbone's proposal." He twisted at the thought as if it gave him pleasure, and I bet it meant that he'd visit our outpost once every month over the next five months to lash him personally.

"Please, don't do it." I begged.

"It's what he wants. He'll find ways to torture everyone else until he's satisfied. This might settle his sadistic need somewhat."

"The cost is too great. My friends say they want to help us. Let them help."

"I'm born to bear this responsibility as king. I accept my fate." There was a finality in his tone that I knew was futile to argue against.

"Good," the general mused. "Be in the torture room in an hour. That is long enough for me to sharpen the iron studs on the whip," he said, as he walked away from the infirmary.

I gasped and cried out, tears falling down my cheek.

Ben wiped them away. "I'll be all right."

My friends gathered around the bed looking at one another. No one dared to protest against the black-wing king, but I knew what they were all thinking. They would gladly have shared the burden.

"Who can stay with Cadet Coraly whilst I meet with the general?" Ben asked.

"Kenyard, Mazdon, Kate and I have our challenge after lunch," Emroyce said, looking at his watch. "In thirty minutes."

"What?" I rose onto my elbows. "We have the challenge in thirty minutes? Where is my uniform?"

Ben pushed me down like a restraint jacket. "We're skipping this challenge. You're not well enough. Camp Leader Mewer has cleared it."

"I decide whether or not I'm well enough!" I hissed.

"Sure," Ben said, holding his hands straight out. "Hold your hands out like this without them shaking and I won't say another word. You'll complete the challenge for us whilst I play with General Denor in the torture chamber."

He was right, but I really wanted him to be wrong. I hadn't even been able to keep my hands steady enough not to trigger the alarm on the contraption before General Denor had kidnapped me. How in the world would I be able to win the challenge today without practising, and being malnourished? I attempted Ben's test anyway, realising my hands were shaking uncontrollably as if my nerves were revolting, trying to crawl out of my body.

I dropped my hands to rest on the mattress at my sides, looking away from Ben as he flashed me a I-told-you-so look.

"Treylieh and I have the heat challenge," Valentina whispered from the chair that she had managed to pull herself up onto.

"Spirits Valentina, you were dead a minute ago. I'm sure you're not allowed to compete, either," I scoffed.

"If you give Camp Leader Mewer that idea, I'll break your bones, Angie!"

Nope. Certainly didn't want to do that. Breaking bones hurt like suffering all the pain in the underworld. I frowned. "You sure you're all right?"

She stared a warning at Mewer. "I feel normal. Don't fuss over nothing. I'm doing my challenge."

I expected nothing else from Valentina. She could have gone to the Underworld, slaughtered the Demon King and come back up again, ready for the next challenge. No problem.

I saw Ben move his gaze to Brian.

"Winter and I have the magic challenge," Brian muttered.

"What about your brother?" Ben asked.

I snorted, but Ben didn't seem amused. "Oh, you were serious?"

Ben looked at Mewer, who held up his hands. "I can stop by once in a while, but I can't ignore the other wounded because I need to guard her all the time."

Ben shook his head, almost bit his tongue, but said it, anyway. "What about Camp Leader Watson?"

There was so much hurt in Ben's eyes from suggesting it.

"I'll be okay on my own. You'll only be away for a short while."

Ben dug his stare into Mazdon.

Mazdon nodded. "He's in his apartment. I don't believe he has anything today." He turned to his side. "Emroyce, you're the fastest. Will you get him?"

Emroyce disappeared out of sight so fast, it made me glad that his speed seemed fast like always. The snake bite couldn't have reduced it that much.

After two minutes, Mazdon nodded. "Camp Leader Watson is coming. He didn't hesitate." Mazdon tapped his palm comfortingly over my shoulder and walked away with the others, who followed him out of the infirmary.

Ben leaned over to kiss me when we were alone. When he pulled away, he said, "Never do that to me again. Never try to go up against the general without a better plan than an up-front attack."

"I'm sorry I make you worry so much."

"It's a strange situation, really."

"What do you mean?"

"Well. If we weren't soul bound, this month would have broken me.

But as we are, the outcome seemed irrelevant, as wherever you go, I will follow. Don't get me wrong. I want you to live. I want to live. But if you would have died, I would have died with you and not had to feel the grief of loss. A beautiful algorithm."

"I'm not that fond of maths," I sneered. "Let's stick to surviving. Together."

"Yes. I'm going to have to fight to survive what comes next." He grunted. "When Watson arrives, the rules are; no kissing, no sharing lovey childhood memories, no touching, no exchange of caring gazes, no planning of non-dates, no–"

"So, basically, he can stand with his back against my bed and guard me without saying a word?"

He nodded as he took in the suggestion. "Yes. Pretty much. That would be preferable. And if he could avoid breathing the same air as you, that would suit me even better."

"Ben! He's a large part of my life. You're going to have to trust me. Ironic isn't it."

"I do trust you. It's him, I don't trust."

"Considering, he comes to guard me without hesitation, cut him some slack." I nodded deeper into the hall where he came walking towards us between the row of beds. He was wearing a navy-blue t-shirt and black hiking trousers, appearing casual on his day off.

"Camp Leader Watson. Thank you for coming. I won't be but a minute," Ben explained.

"Take your time. I got this," Zayd said, but then drawled out an, 'I think', when he saw my angry stare at him. After that, he returned his gazes to Ben. "And if you accidentally kill General Denor, I'll help you bury the body."

"Good to know," Ben answered in his kingly tone as if he had made himself a new ally.

"Emroyce told you what the general did to me?" I asked.

Zayd nodded. "And to Valentina. Everything."

Ben rounded the bed to square up with Zayd. "And will you stand up for Angelica if he comes here before I get back?"

Zayd looked unsure, his glances shifting between Ben and me. "I'll try."

"That's not good enough, Watson. Die for her if necessary! I would!"

"Ben!" I warned. "That's enough. General Denor is powerful. We all do what we can to defy him but keep ourselves alive."

Ben took a step towards me and bent down to kiss me, probably to show Zayd his claim, and whispered. "Remember the rules." There was no apology in his eyes before he threw a glance at Zayd.

I rolled my eyes at him, although I couldn't be entirely sure Ben had been joking. Murben joined Ben's side as he had poked his head in the moment Ben was about to leave. Ben leaned towards Murben, his eyes lethally icy. "The general fears someone at this outpost. Someone not in leadership. Tell Nesso to find out who," he said as they walked away together.

How could Ben know this? The general feared someone? Didn't seem plausible. If he did, that person must be short of a spirit or a ghost.

Zayd's shoulders relaxed when we were alone. "How do you deal with that powerhouse?" He nodded for the space where Ben had stood a second ago. "Are you using your magic to control him?"

I chuckled. "No. I use my female powers and wrap him around my finger."

"Like you once did to me. I guess you were always good at that. And you almost left me again without saying goodbye."

"Not funny."

"I guess not. Lucky, your brother heard about the commotion and came to push him back this time."

"Yeah, my brother came, but didn't even stay for a minute to ask how I was."

"He's in a foul mood this week, having lost five hundred soldiers in Pansery, twenty on an undercover mission in Banaly at Duke Gastling's Manor and three spies he kept in the Ivory Castle." Zayd sat down in the chair Ben had used.

"My brother spies on our king?"

Zayd leaned back and the wooden chair creaked. He folded his arms along the armrests in an attempt to look relaxed, but the intensity in his eyes gave him away. One boot crossed casually over his knee. "He has his reasons," he muttered, the true meaning behind the words held back.

I narrowed my eyes. "Why are you telling me this now?"

He hesitated, watching me, already knowing his standpoint. "He's my best friend," he said finally, tone held with unmistakable loyalty. "And he doesn't deserve the cruel role he's forced to play in this war. He's not the villain you've made him out to be. He needs your understanding. Maybe even your forgiveness."

My traitorous heart ache at the thought. "Well, if he wants forgiveness, he knows where to find me. He can use his own damn mouth to ask for it himself. He can talk to me. He can invite me to dinner; invite me into what used to be my home."

Zayd sighed through his nose, leaning forward slightly, his shadow cast onto my lap. "He has his reasons," he said again, as though repetition might shape the truth.

I scoffed, arms crossed tightly over my chest. "Yeah, he has his reasons," I muttered, mocking Zayd's loyalty.

A pause hung between us. Then Zayd lifted his chin and offered a crooked smile. "I'll invite you to dinner at my apartment."

I blinked. "You've learned to cook?"

"Not in a million years," he admitted with a smirk. "But I can have the chefs prepare something. I'm not above bribery."

A laugh slipped from me, unexpected and unguarded. "I'll pass," I said, grinning. "Just in case you get any heroic ideas and try to cook anyway."

Besides, I could guarantee that a dinner with Zayd would have been on Ben's list of objections if I had allowed him to carry on listing them.

"I was thinking of fire-roasted poison," he teased.

"Well, that does sound like something you'd serve your guests," I coughed a laugh, grateful the tension between us had lifted.

There was a span of awkward silence, so I thought of something to say to break it. "Your hair looks cool. You've shaved at the sides."

"I know you prefer it long, but it–"

"Makes your neck sweaty and you can't focus as it tickles your ears. I remember."

Zayd's cheeks flushed red, and I think mine might have, too. So, I moved on. "How did your third-year cadets do in the last challenge, the Battle Tactics test that you taught?"

"Brian and Winter scored admirably, but John Somers and Richard Crawly won."

I stared at the ceiling as I pondered the name. "Somers? Isn't there a Captain Somers in the Abarath Outpost?"

"Yes, that is Captain Giovanni Somers. John's father."

My neck hurt, even with my gentle movements as I tipped it down again. "No wonder he knows about Battle Tactics then." I quickly realised my insult. "Not that your tutoring wasn't what made him so awesome, of course."

He looked relaxed, slouched into the seat where he chuckled at me. "Remember that I'm the one tutoring the combat training, too, and I can take it easy on you or make it very, very hard."

I closed my eyes to rest them from the light as I groaned. "That starts after today's challenge. Combat is the fifth challenge, isn't it?"

"Yes, as of Monday, you're in my care, my little warrior."

I hadn't noticed that Ben had returned and was almost by my bed with his long strides.

Zayd stood up as the threat approached. Ben held his black uniform shirt in a tight grip in his left hand, as blood flooded in forking rivers down his back, and with his other hand, he pointed his finger at Zayd's face. But he didn't touch him as he growled with lethal calm, "She isn't your warrior.

If we would have been in the Black Wing Territory, you'd be dead for even thinking about claiming my queen."

Zayd hovered his hand above where the hilt of his sword would have been if he had been wearing his uniform. "We're not in the Black Wing Territory, and as far as I know, she hasn't accepted to be your queen yet."

"I'm well fucking aware!" Ben spat.

I hissed at the pain as I moved my neck. "Calm down, Ben," I whispered lowly. It was obvious he was in no mood to take feedback on his orthodox ruling. "We were only bantering. I don't believe that was on your rule list."

"I hadn't finished it," he snapped at me, his eyes glowing red with anger…or jealousy.

"What rule list?" Zayd asked, looking disgusted at hearing that Ben had put restrictions on me.

"No looking at her. No speaking to her. No smelling her. No listening to her. Definitely no tasting or touching her!"

Zayd frowned. "How am I supposed to teach her combat next month if I can't touch her…or any of that other stuff?"

Ben lost it; the look in his eyes foreign to the man I knew. He shoved Zayd backwards, so his shoulders slammed into the wall behind him. Zayd's stare intensified, and he moved low, striking a punch at Ben's side, who folded, losing his breath.

"No fighting in the infirmary!" Mewer bellowed from the other end of the hall, hurrying our way between the beds.

Ben drew a breath to stand ramrod straight, crossing his arms over his chest to show he wouldn't strike a punch, but his entire face told me he would have liked to retaliate.

Before the healer had reached us, Ben muttered to Zayd, "Good of you to come and guard Cadet Coraly whilst General Denor forced my attendance in the torture room."

Zayd leaned in closer to Ben's face, as if telling the black-wing king he hadn't been frightened by him. "As always, it wasn't for you." Zayd turned to me but didn't get any closer to avoid angering the beast. "See you in class, little warrior." After a quick and impish leer to taunt Ben, he rushed out of the infirmary before the black-wing king's merciful streak would falter.

Ben forced his breaths in and out with harsh and rapid stints to pacify his wrath. I didn't speak to let him focus and gain some sort of manageable control.

He immediately turned to Mewer as he arrived. "Can I move Cadet Coraly to our room?"

Mewer bit his lips and cocked his head sideways. "If it were a physical injury, I'd say okay, but it's her mind. General Denor searched through it thoroughly. I'd like to keep her under observation for another day or two at least. I want to give her a few more treatments to provide her the best chance at your next challenge."

"Combat," Ben uttered, as if it was a curse.

Mewer nodded. "But she's stable and comfortable here. Let's see what we have to work with when it comes to your own wounds." Mewer gestured for Ben to hop up to sit on the bed next to mine.

He inspected Ben's back where the iron ends of the whip had torn open his flesh. I was happy Ben was blocking my bond to him so I didn't have to feel what must be excruciatingly painful. Although, Ben wore that pain without a tick of his jaw.

Mewer poked gently at his back and squinted his eyes to see where to start. "This was entirely unnecessary. You know you can't attack a general without consequences," he muttered.

Ben leaned around Mewer's shoulder to see across the three metres between his bed and mine. *"What do I answer to that? That the general can't attack my soulmate and break her mind to the brink of death?"*

"Soul bound. Not soulmate," I corrected and licked my lips as I gawked at his naked torso, his muscles curving so tightly to his body that every time he moved, they flexed deliciously.

He grunted down the bond. "*Take that mischievous look off my body, Miss Stone. This is an infirmary, a place of pain, not of pleasure."*

"One doesn't necessarily exclude the other. I'm in a lot of pain, but I want you to pleasure me. Once you're all healed and bandaged up, we can draw the curtain."

"Here I was, thinking you were going to help me with my argument against the healer?"

"What argument?"

He grunted once more. "*Never mind."*

"These don't look good," Mewer muttered as he pushed at a flab of skin which hang down.

My arousal immediately vanished, seeing Ben frown from the agony as Mewer applied a cream.

"Where is my uniform? Ben, you put the green cream we won in the challenge in my pocket. Put the cream on your wounds."

"I helped remove your clothes…since we had to do it with urgency, considering the state of you. There was nothing in your pockets."

"Then the general must have stolen it."

Ben grunted and his fingers curled around the mattress at the side of his thighs. "I won't stand for that. He can't steal from me and get away with it. Where can I find him?"

"You'll not confront him again, Ben. I forbid it."

Ben jumped off the bed even when it looked like Mewer was in the middle of applying healing cream, and he pushed his arms into his shirt and started to do the buttons. "The general has an apartment here, doesn't he? On the leadership floor next to your brother's?"

"Ben! Don't even think about it!" I panicked, stretching for him, and almost fell out of the bed.

"Okay. I won't confront him. I'll not pay him that courtesy. I'll break into his apartment and take it back."

"You can't do that! He'll have a reason to kill you!"

"Haven't you learned anything?" Mewer gasped.

My heart thundered. Was Ben serious?

34

Four days had passed and Mewer promised to dismiss me tomorrow morning. That left me the entire Sunday to settle back into my room before the academic classes started on Monday. For my benefit, Zayd had postponed the combat training until after the Turning of the Year holidays, but the war updates and the core subjects were still on as normal.

I was in dire need of a shower even though Fern had tried her best to wash me lying down, and a few times standing as I had tested how my legs held up with the weight of my body. All seemed okay. They were just coddling me like a child for no good reason. At least I knew it wasn't Ben's doing as he had begged Mewer many times to be allowed to take me back to *our* bed. Although, I don't think the use of the terminology *'our'* bed had helped his case.

Only one more night to go, sleeping in the infirmary bed with the creepy ordeal of one of the black-wing guards taking turns to watch me at night.

"Do you have to go?" I begged Ben as we waited for the commander of his entire army forces to arrive to babysit me "Commander Daffron is so serious. He doesn't talk much."

Ben stroked his thumb over my hand that he was holding. "He does. He just doesn't like you." There was a gleam in his eyes as if he wanted to be playful, but this situation had tested his patience too much to shake the irritation.

"Oh, great." I rolled my eyes at him.

"And it doesn't matter, because it's nighttime and you're supposed to sleep," Ben hurried to add to the matter to keep my attention, as if he couldn't stand that we weren't also connected via eye-contact when I didn't look at him.

"With someone who doesn't like me from enemy territory watching over me," I muttered. "I'll sleep like a baby."

"Commander Daffron is loyal to me. He won't harm you. If it ever seems as if he forgets, remind him he has a wife and two daughters."

A chill ran down my arm. "You wouldn't!"

"He knows I would." He looked up and deeper into the infirmary hall, breaking the eye-contact he had desired so much. "May I remind you that in the Black Wing Territory, I'm not the same man as here. Here, I'm a first-year cadet. There, I'm the king." He hadn't looked at me even for a split second as he spoke. The thought must have really upset him.

I recalled the day he punished Davis and cut his thumb off just for marking my skin red with cuffs. I swallowed. There was an element of fear drumming through my blood at the comment. I knew of his statue; though I wasn't sure I could live with it. That was a man better forgotten.

He grimaced, clearly having picked up on my fear through our bond.

"Does Commander Daffron have any magic?" I asked.

"No." Ben shook his head, his eyes serenely resting on mine. "His achievements have been earned by hard work alone, and rigorous training at his older brother's manor."

Commander Daffron sounded terrifying, but he would be if he was so high in rank. It wasn't a job for those with weak stomachs.

I twisted my hand to lace my fingers into Ben's. "Commander Daffron has a brother?"

Ben's sigh was heavy as he kissed my fingers. "Yes. Duke Hartmore. A man I hope you never meet again."

"Duke Hartmore! Did not see that coming. Really? There is no resemblance between them."

"Commander Daffron doesn't like talking about it. They don't see eye to eye. And I have been contemplating cutting the duke's eyes out ever since he got his eyes on you."

I twitched, squeezing his callous hand. "Don't be morbid. There is no harm in looking."

"It could be for him."

"Stop it. He has a manor in Banaly, right? In the south of the Black Wing Territory."

"Which you'll never visit," he growled, and I could feel the vibration of his expelled words on my skin where his lips touched my fingers.

"Why? Is he not a nice man?"

"Women say he's handsome. Wealthy. Charming. Well liked throughout the province of Banaly. A charade for the masses, to be sure." Ben held my gaze in a challenge, waiting for me to shoot the duke down in favour of him, but underneath his words lay real jealousy.

"And is this man not arrogant, not stating he's the king every two seconds, not bossy and overprotective?" I asked.

"That sums him up."

"Hm," I put a finger to my lip. "Maybe I have chosen the wrong–"

Ben swiftly pulled the pillow from underneath my head and whacked me with it.

I bawled out in laughter. "Put that back like I had it, King Blackbone."

Ben unhooked his fingers from mine and stepped sideways to get nearer to my head.

"And fluff the pillow first," I demanded.

He snorted and smiled. "Now who's the bossy one." He lifted my head carefully to put the pillow back, tucking it in by the neck.

"Comfy?"

"Very. And by the way." I looked up at him. "You owe me a massage."

"How is that?" He didn't drop that gorgeous smile that told me he would do just about anything for me in this moment.

"Because you couldn't find me sooner. It cost us the win of the fourth challenge."

"That wasn't my fault. And you don't need a massage. You need daggers and to get stronger. And our healing cream."

"So, you only win when the prize is something I need?"

"Yes."

"Well, I need a massage, and you owe me one."

He wiggled his brows. "I'll prepare some lotions." But then he frowned. "So," Ben muttered, and I felt a serious conversation coming on as he sat back down on the chair again. "There are only three more days until the Turning of the Year eve. How do you normally celebrate it around here?"

"Well, for the last two years, Zoe and I have shared a bottle of wine…or three…on the rooftop of our apartment in the Black Winged Territory, exchanging gifts as we watched the stars. The three years before then, I had dinner with Harvey the day after the eve, as he had taken on patrol shifts, saying he didn't have family to celebrate the eve with." I sighed, thinking further back in time. "Before the year my father was imprisoned and my mother was exposed as a traitor, the entire family used to share a big meal during the eve that I helped Mother to prepare. Zayd, Emroyce, Fern and the La Roy brothers were invited, too, as they didn't have any parents or other family." I snorted at the memory. "I used to worry when the men sized up Flora the moment the food took too long to arrive at the table, fearing they would chop her up and grill her in the fireplace."

Ben's expression went solemn. "I'm sorry about Flora."

"I know. Thank you."

"What about the gift? I assume I'm entitled to give you one."

"You don't need to do that. It's difficult for you to venture into the city and it could even be dangerous."

"As I said, entitled. I want to give you something. You know I have my resources. What would Watson have bought you when you were…dating?"

"Nothing special. Chocolates. Flowers. Something I would have needed at the time. Something that showed he cared and that he knew my likes and hobbies. I mainly gave him weapons or cologne."

"Quite impersonal," he mused, as if it was a triumph.

"It's not supposed to be something grand. It's not like our job pays us well, although my undercover pay was twice what I get as a cadet. Mazdon and Kate also give each other a bit more, as they have money in the fund the Royal Family set up for those families whose parents walked the Spirits' Trek and died during service. Obviously, the Coraly's and the Bengrey's didn't get that as our parents were traitors to the crown. Zayd told me Harvey and I were lucky to keep our jobs from the sound of a king's counsel meeting he attended. Zayd also has access to his fund, but he doesn't like to use it. He says it's filthy money, considering what his father did to him. He does claim the spot on the royal counsel table when summoned, though."

Ben's lips stoke over my fingers pensively. "What happened to his father?"

"His father was in the team that went on the Spirits' Trek with my father. But he was tormented by something that happened during the trek. I don't know much about it as Father didn't like to talk about it, but Zayd's father became hooked on alcohol and women in brothels. That's why Zayd never drinks alcohol or would consider a one-night stand. One day a patrol found his father with a dagger through his chest in a backstreet. A few months later, a worker came to Father's office with a basket that a woman had left on the doorsteps to the military building. Inside the basket was baby Zayd, and a letter from his mother to explain who his father was. Abandoned by both his mother and his father. He grew up with us at the outpost and lived with a maid who worked in the kitchens who died when he was fifteen. That's when he started staying at our house and shared a room with Harvey."

"I didn't know you were *that* close."

"He moved into a dorm room when he turned twenty to undertake the academy education. I didn't see him much for that year, but during the Battle of Bensguard, he protected me and consoled me afterwards. Harvey was too occupied with his own grief after Father was sent to the Ivory Castle dungeon. Harvey also had to shoulder the responsibility of becoming the captain, as Denor was promoted to general. Spending more time together, my romance with Zayd bloomed and–"

"And that's where I'll stop this story. No need to tell me more. I garner the rest. He had issues with people not committing to him because his parents abandoned him, and you have issues with committing to people because your mother betrayed you. Sounds like a match that was doomed to fail from the outset."

"I don't have issues committing!"

"No? Then come with me to the Black Wing Territory and marry me?"

"I'll not take that as a genuine proposal, and no, because I'm *committed* to complete the Spirits' Trek to reinstate the honour to the Coraly name that my father worked so hard to earn and which my mother squandered in a day."

"Committing to a task and to a person isn't the same."

"I have committed to you as much as I can. You know that." Irritation marred my voice. Ben was walking on the damn tightrope of my patience again. "You know you sit on secrets that'll hurt me when I learn them. So be fair. And when is your commander coming? He seems pretty preferable to have around right now."

Ben chuckled warmly. "Does his presence really bother you that much?"

"Yes! He looks at me as if he's ready to slit my throat as soon as you give him the order."

"I won't."

"I bloody hope not."

He sighed. "If you want me to stay, I'll stay." Ben stood up and clasped both my hands inside his enormous ones and kissed them.

He offered more of himself than he should. I could tell from the tired look on his face that his heart was stronger than his mind. He had stayed with me all night yesterday, too, when I had asked him, and it wasn't fair that I asked him to sit through another sleepless night. He had barely had the time to recover from all the hours of sleep he lost when looking for me as I was hidden away in the cave.

"I'll be fine. I can pretend to be asleep before he arrives."

"I'm sure he would have preferred that, too, but it's too late, I'm afraid."

I looked the other way to see Commander Daffron approach dressed in complete combat leathers. It wasn't obligatory by the Bensguard Outpost rules to wear them when off duty, but he never wore a cotton uniform. The same as all the black-wings, he wore no weapons, but his stares could certainly kill.

Ben approached him and exchanged a few words before he returned to the bed and kissed me as if to remind me not to forget him overnight. "Good night. I'll be back in the early morning."

I lost eye-contact with those beautiful red eyes and then he was gone, and Commander Daffron took his place on the chair with his stares on the floor, avoiding me. I observed him for a while; his wavy, black hair that reached to his neck from a side parting, his horizontal eyebrows above wide horizontal eyes, a small nose and pale lips. He had a square jaw with a chubby chin, and when his mouth moved, it created small dimples on either side of his cheeks. The rumours about him seemed to be accurate. Merciless. Muscly. Arrogant. And too young to be a commander at an age of thirty-five.

He tucked his hair behind one ear and straightened up in the chair, looking uncomfortable as if he had seen me stare at him in his peripheral view.

That he was uncomfortable made me nervous, and I grasped for anything to say.

"When is Ben's birthday?" I asked, not coming up with anything better to say and I realised I didn't know the date.

His stern look made me press the back of my head harder into my pillow.

"*King Blackbone's* birthday," he empathised, "is on the thirteenth of July officially, but he was born on the fourth of April."

"He has two birthdays?"

"He doesn't want to celebrate on his actual birthday as it would take away the focus of the Spring Festival, which is an event for the people."

Awe, that was so sweet of Ben to move his birthday to keep his people happy. I doubted King Emille would do that for the white-wings. There were still four months until Ben's birthday, but I drew a blank of what else to talk to Commander Daffron about.

"What do you think he wants for his birthday? Has he mentioned to you that he needs anything?"

"Soldiers for the war and to go back to the Black Wing Territory to command them. A black-wing heir to secure his position as the head of the royal family. Use of magic that can mend a large rift in the land."

Wow. He sounded bitter. I guessed he missed his job. "Tall orders," I snorted. "I was thinking more like a new watch or a dagger."

"He seems to like chocolate kisses." There was no humour in his voice as he said it, as if it was simply a matter-of-fact.

I blushed at the memory, and the fact that Ben had obviously told the commander about it. I looked up at the vaulted ceiling, smelling the peppermint ointment used on a sergeant five beds to my right. At least it was better than two days ago when a guy unfortunately died and stank up the place with the tangy smell of blood.

"What's your wife like?"

Commander Daffron snapped his stares up from the floor and stabbed them into me. "Don't feel as if you need to engage in small-talk. I'm more than happy to guard you in silence."

Considering his tone, I contemplated staying silent for a while but decided not to. "I really care about...*King Blackbone*, and he respects you. It'd make me happy if we could reach some level of common ground. We don't need to be friends, but...I don't know...maybe tolerate each other."

There was a long silence. I supposed he had said all he felt obliged by duty to say. I let go of the tension in my muscles and rested on the pillow, feeling my eyelids become heavier.

"She's beautiful," he muttered suddenly. "Long, black hair that reaches the small of her back. Her eyes are a jade green like the moss in our garden." He cleared his throat and adjusted himself on the seat. "She smiles at me as if it's by reflex when I come home from work." He closed his eyes and inhaled a large breath. "She smells of sweet honeysuckle and summer. She's kind and courageous and when she gets angry, I flee her sight."

I chuckled softly, finding it hard to imagine him hiding from anyone.

"Thank you for sharing. She seems lovely. You must miss her. I'm sorry if that's my fault...that you're apart."

"I only wish our house wasn't so close to the north when I can't be there to protect my girls."

I didn't want to push him and ask about his daughters. He had shared more facts with me than I had expected already.

"What is there in the north that you fear?"

He didn't answer and remained silent. Probably as instructed by Ben.

"I can understand now why you hate me."

"No. Not even close. I have many more points. Not noble. Not educated enough. Too weak. Not a pure black-wing. Not committed to the king because he has secrets. Too involved with your ex-boyfriend–"

"Thank you! I didn't ask you to read me the entire list in one evening."

He bowed his head low, looking at the floor again.

I sighed. "Perhaps there is one thing on the list of things I can work on to start earning a piece of your respect?"

"Will you take us back to the Black Wing Territory? Can you become a black-wing of noble birth? Can you–"

"No, I was thinking more in the lines of getting you a cup of coffee or maybe training harder during the combat challenge. Spirits! When you guys go all out, you go all out."

"You could learn how to fly better."

I moaned. "Ben told you?"

"About your weaknesses? Yes. Murben and I are the king's closest associates. We must ensure His Majesty is protected. He tells us everything."

My weaknesses? *Bastard!* Ben told them everything? I wondered. Really?

"So, he told you we have not yet made love?"

I thought it would make him blush or squirm uncomfortably, but he simply answered.

"Yes. And I know of the reason."

He called my fucking bluff without hesitating a breath. If he knew that many details about me, there really was no reason to be polite and make the effort to small-talk.

I turned to lie on my side, so I didn't face him, tugging my white nightgown so that it didn't cling tightly to my body. "Good night," I muttered, but received no reply.

Ben returned to my bedside early in the morning, as he had promised, and there was no sight of Commander Daffron when I woke up. Mewer dismissed me from the ward with the promise that I'd stay in bed today, and Ben and I walked to our room together.

I raised an eyebrow at Ben as he fell into step beside me. "Commander Daffron told me about his wife."

"Yes, she's a stunning woman with a lovely brown skin tone. It's not as dark as Murben's but a milky coffee sort of shade. And his daughters; Anja is eight and Breanne is six, look like small copies of their mother."

"It didn't surprise me they were beautiful," I told Ben, as we arrived at our door. "I was stunned that he spoke to me about them. Maybe there is hope to start some type of friendship."

Ben shook his head. "I instructed him he had to answer all your questions, which didn't relate to war. His girls are his world, and he doesn't befriend anyone, hence you'll have his loyalty at best. It has always been his choice, considering his position as a commander and being targeted on the battlefield, with a high risk of dying young. He doesn't want to add grief to anyone's life. But I'm pleased to hear you spoke at all. Your time wasn't completely insufferable then?"

"Oh, it was. He had a long list of things he didn't like about me, too. I guess you didn't order him to keep quiet about those."

"My apologies, milady. I'll make sure to mention it next time."

"Don't bother and there won't be a next time." As Ben opened the door, I gasped, seeing what looked like sticks of firewood in a pile by the wall. "What happened to the desk chair?"

"Apparently, it doesn't hold if you throw it into the wall." His eyes darted for the part of the wall where some paint had peeled off and there were indentations and scarring on its surface.

"They are normally built to sit on," I clarified, looking around the room but saw no other signs of his angry outburst. He had made the beds. The stationary was neatly placed in the organiser on the desk. No dishes. No dirty laundry strewn about.

He cleared his throat as he rocked back on his heels. "I tidied everything else."

"I can see."

I entered the room with my first mission to get a shower and a change of clothes, and the time I took in the bathroom seemed to frustrate Ben as he kept asking if I was okay through the door.

I came out from the shower, annoyed. "Don't you have anywhere else to be, or any royal duties to perform? Go see what your minions are doing. Actually…that reminds me…" I hurried to don a tracksuit and dug around in the desk drawer for a pen and paper, huffing extra hard as I had to stand to write the message since there was no chair. Once finished, I rolled the message into a scroll and wrapped a red string around it.

I held it up in front of Ben. "Please, could you do me a favour?"

His brows narrowed. "Theoretically, always. But what is it?"

"Can you give this to your spy, who sources things for you in the Black Wing Territory?"

"It has no wax seal," he muttered. "Anyone could open to read this without you knowing."

"I trust you won't read it."

"Who shall my spy give it to?"

"Your spy can open it and execute the order inside it, but I don't want anyone else to know or find out about it."

"Cryptic. As king, I should know what the order is before I give it."

"No. You're not allowed. See it as a trust exercise. Trust is more fickle than love, so don't let me down."

He grunted at me before putting it into his pocket.

I leaned back against the desk. "Tell me what your plan is to get our healing cream back from General Denor, so I can treat the lash wounds on your back?" At first, the thought terrified me, but then I recalled all my undercover spy missions where I had been in much tricker and dangerous situations. Pointing a Black Blade at the black-wing king being one of them where I had gambled with my life. The prospect of the mischief, and the anticipated adrenaline, made me feel excited and alive.

"When you're well. We'll discuss it."

"I'm well now, and I'm going up to the second floor to get the cream back, whether or not you come with me."

His eyes widened, clearly understanding I meant it. "Camp Leader Mewer ordered you to stay in bed for the rest of the day."

"Mewer is a healer and doesn't understand the ways of spies." I walked towards the door.

"Where are you going?" Ben asked.

"To get the cream back."

"And you have a plan?"

"Yes. To go up the steps to his apartment on the second floor, pick the lock, go inside, find the cream, and then leave."

He raised his brows at me. "That's not a plan."

"It is."

"Not a good one."

"Since you have none, it's better than yours." I smiled my mischievous grin that he recognised and got his legs going to catch up with me.

"Let me knock on the others' doors, at least."

"Sure. Lead the way."

We picked up Commander Daffron, Nesso, Davis and Murben on our way and hurried along the corridor to get to the apartment General Denor held at the outpost. That it was so early in the morning and that General Denor's schedule had been to leave Bensguard yesterday was already in our favour.

Davis circled our backs as Murben inspected the lock to the apartment door. "I don't like this. Five black-wings on a restricted access leadership floor of a white-wing outpost. I can see many things going wrong," Davis muttered.

Nesso slapped a playful hand over his back. "If we get into trouble, we could always use our soul bond to call Captain Coraly for help."

Davis cringed. "Very funny. The captain doesn't bother to speak with me through the bond."

"I bet if you shouted into your mind that you were about to force an entry into the general's apartment, he would listen."

"Guys!" I hissed lowly. "If you're not quiet, my brother will likely hear you from inside his apartment by simply using his ears." I glanced at my family apartment's door only five metres away.

Before I could offer to pick the lock, Murben swiped his hand across the coil. There was a click as it unlocked, and he opened the door and simply walked inside. Murben had magic! Unlocking magic! I felt my jaw drop, and as the others sneaked into the apartment, I beckoned Ben with my finger to stay with me in the corridor.

Ben poked his head into the apartment and hissed at the others. "You guys start looking. We'll join you in a minute."

He already looked guilty for the Underworld as he strode up to me.

"Explain," I snapped.

"Murben can unlock doors." Ben put his hands into his uniform pockets and rocked on his heel with a look of complete innocence on his face.

"That wasn't the puzzling part. When I saw you in the dungeon and wanted to set you free, I risked my job, my reputation…my life! Why didn't you just walk out of the White Wing Territory if Murben could unlock the gates?"

"That's a part of one of those secrets," he muttered, lashing his gazes down onto the floor.

So, he had stayed at the outpost for a reason, and he wouldn't tell me why. My rage spiralled out of control, and I clenched my fists at my sides.

"But…" he said, holding up a finger as he noted my fists. "But one truth is because I couldn't leave you here not knowing if you were safe."

"No wonder that none of the black-wings have tried to come to save you. You don't consider yourself captive." I couldn't think straight when I was this angry and had the time pressure of finding the cream, which I contemplated whether Ben deserved now. "We'll talk about this later," I spat and barged past him and into the apartment, seeing Commander Daffron stretch to look at what was on a tall shelf in the bookcase. "I think I see it," he muttered as he turned around and saw me.

I went over to him and lifted a foot up. "Clasp your hands and hoist me up, and I'll get it."

Commander Daffron did as I had ordered him, but with a gentle moan. "Spirits, you're heavier than you look."

"It's the weight of both wings." I supported my hands over the bookcase, trying not to lose balance and fall out of his hands.

"Isn't that a problem when you fly?" he asked hoarsely, as he lifted me higher.

"It is. I don't fly much. I don't like it. Ask Murben."

Murben came our way. "She's getting better."

"Really?" I hissed, turning around. "Because I don't believe I have made any progress. Or so you point out every time."

Murben shrugged his shoulders.

"Guys," Commander Daffron prompted. "Can we focus on the cream?"

I stretched across the shelf and fingered at the cream tub that was just beyond my reach but was coming closer as I fiddled over the lid. "Got it!" I called at the same time as I heard Nesso curse out loud.

"Well, well. What have we here?" I heard General Denor's voice from the doorpost.

My blood ran cold hearing his dark and amused voice, promising severe punishments.

He wasn't supposed to be at Bensguard…and we weren't supposed to be in his apartment.

Five black-wings and no witnesses.

The fear of meeting his merciless gaze made my limbs lock down when my instincts wanted me to take a step back. Working against us was that he was a young general of thirty years who hadn't grown tired of challenges to show authority. He had grown rapidly in rank because he was ruthless and had powerful magic.

His posture was rigid, ready for a battle. He'd show no leniency. My body screamed at me to move. But where? We were trapped inside his home as he blocked the way out. Even if we could push our way out, the general's mind games could kill us all in an instant. We had made a terrible mistake coming here and now we'd pay the price.

35

I stepped down from Commander Daffron's hands, my heart burning and expanding with fear inside my chest to the point I thought it might burst. Ben came to stand in front of me like a shield against iron, not thinking of the fact that General Denor's weapons weren't those of physical pain, but something that could go through Ben and hurt my mind.

"Let see how many rules you're breaking this time."

He walked into his apartment, not seeming the slightest bit scared of any of us…or all of us put together. Casually, he dropped his keys into a bowl on a side-table by the door, as if he would have come home like any other day. He was wearing a red tracksuit with his emblems on them and there was sweat coating his temples as if he had been out running.

"Your presence on the leadership floor. One. Breaking into the general's apartment. Two. Stealing a general's property. Three. Attempting to assault the general. Four."

"We're not assaulting you," Nesso snorted.

"True. But who would believe you, black-wing?" He then ignored Nesso and targeted Ben. "Deducting the ten lashes I've already given you, I'm still owed thirty-five. And how many of you are in here?" He counted Commander Daffron, Nesso, Murben, Davis, Ben and finally settled for me. "Five lashes for four assaults each for the six of you. One hundred and twenty more."

"No!" I shouted, watching Ben to see if he'd accept just to get us all out of here. If he did, I'd crumble.

General Denor held up a finger before anyone could comment and stared at Ben. "But, I'm willing to forget all about this heist if you let me have ten minutes alone with Cadet Coraly. You can even keep the cream."

"I'd rather take the one hundred and fifty-five lashes," Ben said calmly, as if he was in charge, and with such boredom that it even irked me how good he was at playing this game.

"I didn't offer you to take your friends' lashes. This time, I'd like everyone to bare their own twenty lashes, even Cadet Coraly, unless I can have ten tiny minutes with her. You can time me if you like."

"No," Ben said with such finality I almost forgot I had a say in the matter.

"Yes," I said, moving around Ben. "I accept."

Ben glowered at me. "You don't know this man. The lashes will be far more lenient than what damage he can cause in ten minutes."

"Leave. Now," I growled at Ben, my tone uncompromising.

His teeth clenched, and he stood quiet for a few seconds, purely staring at me. Then finally he said, "Ten minutes. Not a second more." As the black-wings left the apartment, Ben added. "I'll be right outside the door."

"Great," Denor said and closed it, trapping me inside. His gaze wandered from my head to my toes and up again with a look of intrigue and hunger in his eyes.

"Powerful weapon indeed. You're an extraordinary woman."

"Get to the point, fast. You only have ten minutes," I growled.

"So impatient," he sniggered, amused. "I thought to make a deal with you."

I wrapped my arms around myself as protection from his stares. "A deal? I have nothing to offer."

"Oh, but you do. Don't you know how special you are? No one has told you, but I know because I've been inside your mind. If you want to know just how special you are, how much any man should worship you, then all I ask is for one simple deal. As you are aware, I'm due to visit the Bensguard Outpost each month during the next four months to lash King Blackbone with ten lashes per visit. If instead, those times I visit, you date me, I'll forfeit the lashes on King Blackbone. I might even force you to give them to him if you don't want to take me up on my generous offer."

I wanted to stop breathing, but I needed to keep my wits about me if I was going to walk out of this apartment at an advantage, or as myself…or at least not dead. What had my father taught me about negotiating? Don't walk away from the bargain without a counter proposal.

"I might consider your deal if you also agree to fix Robin Bengrey."

"Interesting," he purred, moving like a viper deeper into his flat and sitting down on a crimson-coloured sofa. "Yes, I heard about the tragedy of what Counsellor Desry did to the poor boy when he couldn't interrogate an adult who knew you. Captain Coraly had, with such convenient timing, sent you all out on a mission. Apparently, Counsellor Desry has also expressed an interest in learning more about you." He tapped his fingers on the armchair in the same rhythm as my racing pulse, as if he could detect it, maybe even control it. "Now, I'm wondering how much you'll sacrifice to help little Robin?" he muttered to himself. "I believe the price of our deal just went up." He crossed one leg over the other and seemed to ponder the terms in silence.

"You better think fast. The time…and my patience, is running out," I told him with more calm than I had expected.

"So, to summarise," he said, clearly enjoying every single second of this. "I won't lash King Blackbone, and additionally, I'll right little Robin's mind, in exchange for; four social meetings alone with you, and that during the First Year Ball in Gaithorpe Palace you will act as my date and give me one public kiss."

"Not as a date. As friends."

"Sure, you can tell people we're friends, although we'll be more like lovers by that time."

I snorted. "Never! And you cannot manipulate my mind at any stage."

"Are you sure? You might like it."

A warm sensation swept through me, as if someone was caressing my skin and every nerve with a lover's touch. Involuntarily, a moan escaped me from the pleasure, but I quickly straightened up.

"Stop that! That is my deal. You're not to touch me with your mind."

He stood up and crossed over the rug, only stopping when he was right in front of me. "Then I'll add another date. Our first date being you celebrating the Turning of the Year eve with me. And you must wear something nice, no uniform." The thirty-year-old general held out his hand with five bony fingers. "Deal?"

I wanted to confirm the terms with Ben, but the bond was quiet. "You're manipulating my mind now by cutting off the soul bond, so how do I know you'll stay true to the deal?"

"First of all, we haven't made a deal yet, so I'm breaking no rules, and secondly, I'm not touching your mind, I'm touching Ben's and Mazdon's, keeping them both out of our conversation. I promise you they're not harmed, only muted. And they'll stay unharmed for as long as you tell no one of your magic. You're mine. Understood?"

Well, what I understood was that I was trying to stay alive treading mud, and that he wouldn't stop coming after me until he got what he wanted.

"Why the kiss?" I asked, looking at the hand he still had held out between us. "Do you simply want that part of the deal to create a fight between Ben and me when I tell him?"

He shrugged his shoulders, showing he wouldn't make any excuses for it. "Guilty as charged."

He was driving a hard bargain. I really didn't want to agree to his terms, and Ben would go ballistic when I eventually told him. But if I didn't, I'd lose the opportunity to save Robin.

"No kiss. But the rest is agreeable. And you must right Robin's mind immediately."

"Then, no deal." He kept his hand out as if he knew I would yield.

Fucking bastard.

If Emroyce found out I had declined the deal to help Robin because of one little kiss, he'd never forgive me.

I guessed the general knew that and would, without a doubt, use it against me. What I also guessed was that Ben would kill General Denor before this was all over. That thought made me smile. I held out my hand to grab his to shake on the deal at the same time as Ben poked his head inside the apartment to call out that the time was up. He saw us shaking hands and frowned.

I tore my hand out of the general's and stormed for the door.

"I'll pick you up for our date at eight o'clock the day after tomorrow," Denor said loudly enough for Ben to hear before I slammed the door shut.

"Date?" Ben scoffed.

"It's not a date," I growled.

"Perhaps I should ask you out for non-dates, too, then at least I'd get somewhere with you?"

I halted in the step to stare at him. "Don't fuck with me right now. I'm in no mood."

I noticed Murben was behind his back, so I continued towards the stairs to descend to the ground floor. Ben didn't seem to take the hint that I wanted to be alone and chased after me. "What happened? Tell me why you were shaking hands."

"Not so much fun being on the other side of the secrets, is it?"

"I'm keeping mine in order to protect you."

"So am I!" I bellowed and took the steps quicker. I stopped at the bottom of the stairs, shoving my face up close to Ben's. "I need a few moments of solitude. Don't follow me." I retrieved the healing cream from my pocket and tossed it to Murben, who caught it expertly. "Here. You put it on your king's back."

Then I left them by the stairs with quizzical looks on their faces, as I darted outside and climbed the tree to sit on my branch.

I got no more than two hours of solitude before people came looking for me, but this time it wasn't Ben or Zayd, but Emroyce and my brother.

"Come down here immediately," my brother said sternly, making my stomach twist.

What now?

I hadn't even put both feet on the ground when Emroyce embraced me so hard I found it hard to breathe. "I'm not sure what you did but thank you!"

I had never seen Emroyce in tears, but that was what was on his cheeks; actual tears. He wiped them away quickly, of course, and stared at me.

"General Denor came to the infirmary and just…he just healed Robin's mind. Robin is back to normal. Completely fine. Then the oddest thing happened – General Denor said I had you to thank for it, and then he left."

I couldn't say he was welcome as Counsellor Desry had destroyed Robin's mind in the first place because he had wanted to get to me, so I just smiled. That obviously didn't sit well with my brother, who looked grimly at me, knowing there was more to the story. It always was when I was involved. *I don't seek out mischief – it finds me!*

"What did you offer in return?" my brother asked.

"You don't believe General Denor did it from the goodness of his heart because he and I are such good friends?"

"No," he said, unyieldingly.

No? I wouldn't have thought so, either. "It's none of your business," I muttered.

Oh dear, my brother could actually get more irritated.

He looked red in his face as he blurted out at me. "None of my business? Tell me how that could be when I'm the person responsible for this outpost, and I'm the head of our family."

"Family?" I snorted. "Since when were we a family? You never speak to me anymore. You never invite me to my own home! You don't take time out of your schedule to train me. Oh, and, you forgot my birthday. Zayd took me out."

"I knew he was taking you out. I was the one who suggested it and approved his leave and swapped around his patrol schedule. We don't socialise because cadets will target you as a threat if they believe you get favourable treatment. I don't train you personally, but I've instructed Zayd to do it, and you don't seem to have any issues coming to my apartment to sleep, so I assumed you'd come around when you wanted to dine with me. You're always welcome. Furthermore, I have organised the best protection you could possibly get, having King Blackbone's soul bound to you."

I almost dropped my jaw, feeling gobsmacked. Harvey hadn't said these many words to me in five years. "Well," I grunted and put a hand on my hip. "If you're the head of the family, you could invite me more often. And you could have given me a birthday gift," I muttered.

"Fine," he huffed, pushing his dark-blonde hair to one side as the breeze had flipped it the wrong way and he smoothed down his yellow uniform as if he was patting himself to calm down. "I'll host a dinner, as we normally do for the Turning of the Year, and invite our friends who have had no family to return home to. But you'll have to help me cook."

I cringed. "Can we have the dinner the day after the Turning of the Year eve?"

His strained smile dropped. He signed deeply. "Of course we can, but it begs the question as to why."

I glanced at Emroyce, who had stood silently and listened beside Harvey. I bit my lip, contemplating how much I could tell my brother without starting a war among the leadership ranks. "Apparently, I have to spend the eve with General Denor."

Harvey tipped his face up into the sky and sighed hard once more, reeling in his anger. "So, he got his claws into you, anyway."

"I'm a big girl, Harvey. I can handle myself."

"I really doubt you understand the extent of this problem. He makes King Blackbone look tame."

Emroyce leaned in, a frown lay deep on his forehead. "Was this the cost you paid for Robin?"

"That and a few other things. But it was worth it."

Emroyce shook his head. "I appreciate whatever you've agreed to, and if there is anything I can do for you, you only need to ask. I'm in debt to you."

I flashed him one of my famous, mischievous grins. "Oh, don't worry. I'll call it in at a later date. You might get a front-row seat to the trouble I'll cause during the First Year Ball, as I assume…" I looked at my brother, "that you won't allow the black-wings to attend."

"No. They aren't invited to attend. Do I even dare to ask about it?"

"No, never mind."

"Have you told King Blackbone about your involvement with the general?" Harvey asked, as if he expected I had, and that Ben would automatically be there to protect me day and night.

"Not yet. I still have that pleasure to look forward to."

Harvey patted my shoulder. "Let me know if I can help in any way. If I don't hear from you, I'll see you at three o'clock on the day after the Turning of the Year eve and we'll prepare a meal together for our friends."

I nodded and held my breath through another lung-crunching hug from Emroyce before I watched them walk back into the military building.

I climbed my tree again and felt like a coward when deciding to tell Ben about the deal from here where I was at a safe distance.

"Ben?" I called.

"Here," he answered sternly.

I swallowed. *"Where are you?"*

"In our room, waiting for you to come back and tell me what is going on."

"I made a deal with the general."

"I saw that. Can you come and tell me about it?"

"I'm telling you now."

"Was it that bad that you can't even tell it to my face?"

My heart was pounding wildly, and the shame scolded it to a point I thought I might faint and fall out of the tree.

"He agreed to mend Robin's mind and remove the lashes on us all on a few conditions."

"This is ridiculous. Where are you? I'll come to you."

"I'd rather stay here…alone…please let me finish." Ben remained silent, so I continued. *"I need to go on four non-dates with him and spend the Turning of the Year eve with him."* I waited for his outburst, but there was no sound connecting through our bond, so I guessed whatever he said or did, he didn't convey it to me.

"Is that it?" he asked after a long moment had passed.

I hesitated, almost scared of telling him the final point. I inhaled and exhaled deep and slow. *"I also have to go as his date to the First Year Ball."*

"Out of the question. Royal officials and noble folks go to that ball and will see you with him. I can't go, so I don't want you to go at all."

"And I have to give him a public kiss during the ball," I blurted, as if ripping off a plaster.

My heart was thundering in my chest, and the silence made it even worse. I waited for any word from him for a while.

"Ben?"

"Give me a minute." That was all he said before the connection between us went silent. His voice had been dark; murderous. *"Fuck!"* I heard him roar, but it was faint, as if it was a very potent passive thought and he hadn't meant for me to hear it.

"Please, don't destroy more of our furniture."

"You should have told me that sooner." He sounded out of breath and in pain.

"Are you okay? I'm coming."

"No. Don't come here now. You won't be able to see anything, anyway. My death magic spiralled out of control and filled the room again. The magic is balanced but I'm using everything I have to ensure it stays that way."

My heart couldn't handle letting him suffer by himself as it throbbed with this inexplicable need to share the burden. I climbed down from the tree and went to our room, opening the door up to an attack of black essence that billowed out, hitting me straight in my face, and filling the corridor.

"You're going to kill the entire outpost," I muttered, real concern growing that it could probably kill me, too.

"I'm trying not to," he retaliated, and there was no humour in his voice. He sighed, his patience dancing on its last nerve, it seemed. "I told you not to come here."

"Yeah, well, you need me," I said and opened the window to air out the black essence.

When the essence had cleared enough for me to see him and the room through a thick layer of grey cloud, I noticed that Ben had wrecked the three doors to the wardrobe to splinters. Some shards on the floor had traces of blood, so I walked towards him and grabbed his hand to inspect it. There were small cuts over his knuckles, but nothing major.

"This was unnecessary," I cussed at him. "You can't tell me you're threatened by me spending a few hours with the general to settle a deal."

"I had made plans for the Turning of the Year eve for us. Romantic stuff you wanted. I guess I'll have to cancel them."

The hurt in my chest was like someone hacked away with an axe at my heart. Of course, it made sense he was disappointed. I hated the situation, too.

I brought images of Robin to my mind to keep strong so as not to break apart in front of him, making the torture even worse for both of us.

"A bit of competition is healthy, I guess," Ben finally muttered. "Although, I'm not sure how I can compete with a man who can alter your mind to like him."

"The deal specified that he isn't allowed to use his magic on me."

"And you believed him?"

"I did, but even if I didn't, I had no choice. He mended Robin."

"Yes, but he took your soul. Hefty price to pay."

"And I'd do the same deal again if it saved Robin."

"I didn't mean for you. I meant it was a hefty price for me."

"Ow." I swallowed and walked into his embrace. "No one can ever have my soul but you. I'm yours."

He grunted, and his shoulders relaxed. "Did he mention if he knew anything about your magic?"

"Nothing specific. He mentioned he thought I was extraordinary. A better compliment than you've ever given me," I mocked, thinking the worst of our argument was over, but his voice told me it was far from over.

"I thought so," he said grimly.

I got the feeling he knew something about me that interested the general and it was information Ben was withholding from telling me.

Another secret. *Wonderful.*

36

Ben wasn't in bed when I woke up this morning, nor had he spoken to me much before we had fallen asleep last night, and I hadn't seen him all day. At one point, the humming in my ears had been ear-deafening, and I had known he had strayed close to the black-wing border, but since then, I had no clue where he was. I had asked the black-wings, but none of them had seen him, either. I guessed he wanted to stay away, not wanting to see me get dressed for my non-date with General Denor this evening.

I was in my underwear, brushing through my hair, when he finally returned to our room, pausing in the door for a second to look me up and down before he entered.

He was wearing his flight leathers, and the wind had clearly torn at his hair when flying. "Here." He held out a red box that was about ten centimetres deep and long but only about a centimetre tall. "The spy returned with your order."

Commander Daffron's gift. "Perfect." I took it and stored it inside one of the paper gift bags by the door where I had put the others' gifts.

"What's inside it?" Ben asked. "The spy told me it cost triple the normal fee, especially considering the short notice."

I opened my underwear drawer in the wardrobe and brought out one of my money pouches. "How much do I owe you?"

"Only an explanation."

"I'd rather pay. How much?"

"I won't accept your money."

"Then I'll have to find another way to pay you back."

He looked at the bags by the door. "Who is the package for?"

"Not you."

He gripped at his chest as if he was having a heart-attack from the lack of control he had over me. "You'll be the death of me."

"Not likely. I'm quite fond of you, whereas there are many others who actively want you dead." When I saw the pain in his eyes, and knowing today would be difficult for him as it was, I waved for the paper bags. "They are Turning of the Year gifts for the black-wings."

"That's nice of you. You didn't have to give the servants gifts. They surely will have nothing for you."

"That's not the point of gifts. It's my pleasure to give *my friends* gifts."

He grunted. "I'm heading there after you leave. Do you want me to take the bags to them?"

"No need. I'll do it on my way out." I stretched up onto my toes to kiss him on the lips before I took the dress I'd picked out off its hanger. "Don't want you snooping through what I got them."

Ben got comfortable on the bed and propped up onto pillows against the headboard. Playing with a dagger, tossing and catching it tip to tip, he watched me dress. The ice-cold anger in his eyes wouldn't thaw by any number of kisses, or me telling him the non-date was a chore, not a choice. He muttered something about mixed messages by the look of my red dress that had a high slit up to the middle of my left thigh and my dainty designer high-heels. Ben threw the knife into the same chipped piece of wall as he had been aiming for all week and sighed through his nose for the millionth time in the last hour alone.

It was nearing eight o'clock, so I draped on the white fur coat Zayd had given me for my fifteenth birthday after his first salary as cadet, realising I had grown no taller since then.

Ben jumped off the bed and came to my side, as if being close enough to touch me somehow marked me as his. "I'd remind you of the safety protocols, but I know that is futile, since if General Denor can't protect you, no one can."

I finished applying my lipstick. "I think you've given him better compliments than you've given me this evening," I said pointedly and swiped my hands in the air to indicate my looks.

He appeared to swallow a cocktail of irritation and jealousy as he watched me. "No woman in the world can compare to you," he growled, and grunted even louder as he heard someone knocking on our door.

I had told General Denor to wait for me at the front of the building so not to anger Ben further, but he clearly hadn't listened.

"I'll get it," I called out, but didn't get to the door before Ben had yanked it open.

"General Denor," he greeted, clearly counting on him responding in the same way and emphasising his own status.

Not sure if he thought he'd win my admiration with some sort of verbal bucking of horns.

"King Blackbone," the general greeted as Ben had planned, but appearing completely unbothered about it, which jarred Ben even further.

"Have her home before eleven o'clock. Safe. No scratches. Happy preferably, but at the least sane," Ben growled, his knuckles going white from the grip he held over the door handle.

General Denor chuckled. "You'd be a better comedian than king." Then he ignored him, looking at me, holding up a hand for me to take it. "You look absolutely otherworldly. Marvellous."

"No uniform," I muttered. "As agreed."

"And you've matched to my general's colours." His black eyes looked at me hungrily, as if he could eat me, despite knowing I was poisonous, like the reddest berry of the Lily of the Valley plant.

I hadn't thought about the colour of my dress when I donned it, and now I desperately felt like changing, not to match his red surcoat with gold hems and buckles over a black shirt and breeches, which were tucked into black knee-high boots. Oddly, his attire bore no sign of rank or outpost emblems on them. He had brushed his short black coif in a side parting, and he was closely shaven. Over one shoulder, he carried a bulging duffle bag which caught my curiosity.

He held up one red rose in front of me and I took it, not knowing what else to do. "Are you ready to leave?" he asked.

"Yes." I grabbed onto the handles of two paper bags. "I only want to drop these gifts off before we leave."

Ben looked at the bags. "I told you I could drop them off for you."

I kissed him on the cheek. "You're not my messenger."

General Denor guided my hand to rest on his biceps around his crooked arm but turned towards Ben in the door. "Any last words for the evening? I'll mute your bond as soon as you shut the door."

I noticed the black essence that seeped out of Ben's palms the second before he slammed the door in the general's face. The connection between Ben and me died with the shut door, it seemed, but the humming in my ears remained as a reminder that he was still a part of me.

After I had dropped off the gift with Murben, the general and I started walking towards the city under a sky peppered with stars. I inhaled a big breath to ready myself for the night's performance, as he had demanded it to be as close as possible to a real date.

"How would a person who tears people's lives apart spend a festival based on giving and generosity?" I asked him, failing to be polite at my first attempt at being civil.

"I won't tell you," he said mysteriously, ignoring my misstep. "I'm planning on showing you."

Entering the heart of the city, I smiled at seeing the beautiful lanterns hung from each porch this time of year, casting their warm light on the cobblestone streets. This festival especially always brought out the best in the people of Bensguard. People put on their best wear and were in their most delightful mood as they clustered together in front of market stalls. House flags and decorative banners added to the colours as well as the pine reefs, winter blossoms and ivy wreaths that hung on doors. Small pine trees dusted with snow stood like sentinel by porches. From open doorways scents wafted out that were sweet from baked goods.

The normally stale city square pulsed with holiday spirit. Extra stalls had been set up for the celebration, selling everything from sugared buns and pies to meat skewers which roasted over open flames.

In front of the centre fountain, a group of singers bawled their merry tunes, drawing small crowds.

Although, I tried to shake it, the joy was infectious, making it almost impossible to remain bitter about the company I was keeping.

"Why do you think I'm the general of the Special Missions Unit of the king's forces?" Denor asked, his voice casual as we stepped into the bustle of the square.

I didn't answer immediately, distracted by the savoury breads rolled in sugar. My mouth watered instinctively, and I licked my lips before replying. "So you can torture cadets and because you've used your mind-bending magic to claw your way into power."

He chuckled, low and amused. "That's the how. I was asking if you knew the why?"

"Beats me, General Denor. Really beats me."

He cleared his throat. "Please, for tonight, call me Wallan."

I gave him a sidelong glance to show he didn't have the right to ask me that.

"Because I'm a patriot," he said simply, ignoring my defiance. "I'd do anything for these lands in order to protect our people so they can live in peace. Nights like this? They're my reward."

His answer caught me off guard. I raised a brow, searching his face for some trace of irony, but found none.

"Then I like Wallan better than General Denor."

He laughed a heartfelt tone, and before I could stop him, he was leaning over the bread stall I had been eyeing. He exchanged a few coins with the vendor and pointed to one of the golden-baked flaps. The woman slid it onto a paper plate and handed to him with a knowing smile.

We continued walking, the smell of the warm bread drifting toward me, but he neither ate it nor offered it. Cruel, indeed. The man had torturing down to a fine art.

A little farther on, we stopped at another stall glowing with lanterns. A row of jacket potatoes steamed beneath a glass cover, each piled high with fillings. He ordered two with spiced chicken and handed me one without comment. "Food before pudding," he said, digging in with a wooden fork.

I tried to eat with dignity by taking small bites, but hunger gnawed at me. I hadn't eaten much earlier today, too anxious about what Ben thought of all this. I looked for him now, half-expecting to spot his silhouette among the crowd, but saw only strangers and sweeping shadows.

We stepped into the threshold of the house of worship, where hymns echoed off stone walls. A priestess stood near the altar, preaching about love and peace. I sat beside Wallan on a pew, my plate warming my hands as I finished my potato.

Once we had finished, the warmth of the spiced chicken still lingering on my tongue, we walked outside again to sit on a park bench overlooking the square. General Denor handed me the flaky pastry he'd bought earlier, and its scent hit me instantly; apples, sweet vanilla, and a pinch of cinnamon.

"Have you ever had this before?" he asked, his voice gentler than I was used to hearing.

I shook my head, watching the steam curling upwards. "No. I don't think I have. What is it?"

He smiled faintly, and eyes momentarily went distant. "My mother used to make them when I was a boy. It was my favourite then. Still is."

I took a bite. The crust flaked apart in my mouth, giving way to the warm, spiced apple filling. The sauce was silky and rich, melting into the crumble with each chew. The taste was truly sweet and comforting.

"It's gorgeous," I murmured, surprised by how moved I was by a pastry.

"I told you," he said, grinning as he leaned in to take a bite from the opposite end, his fingers brushing mine. The movement felt too intimate, so I moved further away from him.

Then he glanced at me, the humour in his eyes dimming. "I know you believe I'm cruel, because of how I treat the black-wings–"

"And me," I snapped, my voice razor-edged. "You kept me in a cave for nearly a month, or have you forgotten that detail?"

He didn't flinch. "That was a controlled trial, so I could assess how long King Blackbone would take to find you. To understand how far he'd go. And he did. He scoured the realm like you were the sun he needed to survive. His pure source of life."

"Because I was," I hissed, the warmth from the dessert turning to ash in my mouth. "We're soul bound."

Denor's tone remained maddeningly calm. "You were never in any real danger. I had full oversight the entire time."

"And *Valentina?*" My voice cracked slightly. "You killed her. You murdered my friend."

The festival noise faded into a dull hum as I stared at him. He didn't even blink.

"I didn't kill her. I rendered her unconscious. That's all. My magic's not strong enough to cheat death, even if I wanted to. I can't resurrect someone truly dead." He casually took another bite of the flap, like we were simply two lovers sharing a treat.

I clenched my fists and glared at him. "That makes it all okay, then?" I spat, the sarcasm sharp enough to draw blood. "Is that why you think I'll forgive you now? Because you brought me out to mingle with cheerful strangers and gave me something sweet to eat?"

He swept a hand through the air to gesture to the crowd surrounding us. Families holding hands, children chasing one another with wooden swords, lovers huddled close to keep warm against the evening chill. "I need you to see this," he said quietly. "Our people, living, laughing, safe. There's so much good we can do here, within our borders. Why stretch ourselves thin chasing demons across them?"

I looked away from him, my throat tight from holding back the curses I wanted to spit at him. I didn't have the perfect answer, not one I could bear to say aloud.

"We're all people with feelings and needs. I think we should help everyone we can who needs it. No matter where they live or what colour wings they have."

"Yes, I couldn't agree more. Theoretically. But if manpower and funding don't allow for such wishes, how would you choose whom to save and whom not? Isn't it a fair delegation of duties to say that the black-wings should fight and care for the black-wings and the white-wings manage their own responsibilities? And if the black-wings attack us because they think we have a better living or more riches, don't we have the right to defend ourselves?"

"I don't believe King Blackbone is attacking us because of riches. He has that already. There is something in the north that he can't control, and I think he needs our help."

"Is that so? And what has he told you about the situation in the north?"

He was gleaning information. I could feel it in my bones. He pretended to be a caring man, like a rose with a thorny stem, sharp at every turn.

"That the northern people are a troublesome lot. Like you," I said, flashing him a mock smile.

"Perhaps he has bigger plans in order to satisfy his needs. Maybe he wants to rule both lands."

"He isn't like that. He doesn't even want to be king and would give it all up if there was someone else who could rule justly in his stead."

"Is that so?" he said, voice low but pointed. "Perhaps you have too high expectations of a man you barely know, or perhaps you've been fooled by a master of deception. I wouldn't blame you. No one can fault King Blackbone's intelligence." He paused beneath a lantern. "If I may, with your consent, I can show you my latest memory from two months ago, during the battle to protect Pansery."

At the mention of entering my mind, a shiver crawled its way down my spine. I wrapped my arms around myself, a reflex that had become as natural as breathing. Too many people had been inside my thoughts recently – some with permission, too many without. Each intrusion left a mark, subtle but lasting, and I was running out of unscarred ground in my own mind.

But…the north. The question of what had happened up there haunted me like a ghost. I'd imagined it so many times and filled in blanks with guesses and half-truths. The general was offering me a piece of that truth. Of course, it would be to Ben's disadvantage. Denor didn't do anything without an angle, but if this glimpse removed just one more barrier between Ben and me, if it gave me even a shard of clarity, it might be worth the risk.

I hesitated because it was hard to imagine what I might see. How I might feel afterwards.

But I nodded.

Denor's hand tugged at my elbow to pull me off the bench and away from the crowds. "Let's find some privacy," he said. "Just in case you feel the urge to vomit."

He guided me across the cobbled square toward the edge of the festivities, where the lights faded into shadows. We stepped beneath a quiet alcove overgrown with ivy vines. The sounds of the festival became muffled behind us.

I stopped, suddenly feeling uncertain. Cold fear twisted in my stomach, and a light sweat broke across my neck. Was I truly ready to see through his eyes, even for a moment? To feel what he'd felt, to witness war through the senses of a soldier who'd fought in it? My body tensed, torn between dread and determination.

"You look pale," he observed, his voice softening. "Are you sure you want to see my memory?"

The shadows pressed in around us, the only light was a single flickering lamp hanging above a nearby doorway. I looked up at him, jaw clenched. For Ben – for the truth – I nodded again.

Darkness clasped me in an iron grip, and the world around me vanished as my mind focused in on a war. I had never been to Pansery, so I didn't recognise the battlefield, but I saw black-wings attacking white-wings with weapons raised and anger flashing on their faces. Soldiers dressed in iron armour chased innocent women, slaughtered children and burned houses. The white-wings tried to defend the city, but they were outnumbered and couldn't protect everyone. White-wing soldiers were losing limbs and lives one after the other, and blood seeped through the soil to form red puddles.

I gagged, bile with the taste of cinnamon raising at the back of my throat, and Denor brought me back to the Bensguard alleyway. I almost vomited, but I held it in and held myself together. The stone walls of the surrounding buildings swayed, and a tunnel formed at the black edges of my sight. I was about to faint.

Denor wrapped an arm around my waist to keep my wobbling knees from making me buckle under. "No!" I panted.

"It's only natural that the black-wing king would lie about it to cover it up."

I wanted to cuss at the general and tell him it wasn't true, but I had seen it in my own mind as if I had been there personally. Ben had ordered the attack on Pansery and the black-wings were attacking the city, killing innocent people. How could I ever love him after this? There was no action that could redeem him and earn my forgiveness.

Once the strength was back in my knees, Denor let go of me and took a step away. "There are a few things I still need to do tonight before I take you home."

We walked a few streets down, the images of the battlefield looping continuously in my mind. People greeted the general politely and with fondness as we passed, as if he were a celebrity everyone knew personally. He seemed…liked. I hardly registered my surroundings, as Denor knocked on a red door to a three-floor town house.

A young woman a few years older than me with long blonde hair and dressed in a long apricot-coloured dress opened the door and instantly got a hopeful look in her bright-blue eyes.

"Yes," the general told her, and the woman started sobbing into her hands. Denor brought up a large envelope from his duffle bag and handed it to her. "All the information is inside, the address and collection point and date. I have covered the costs, so now you only need to enjoy your new little bundle. Congratulations."

The woman called out for a 'Malkner' who arrived beside her. The man gasped as he saw the envelope and was quick to shake the general's hand.

The couple hugged each other, and the man looked at the general. "How can we ever thank you?"

"No need. I'm happy to help. Happy Turning of the Year."

"Happy Turning of the Year," both of them said in unison and slowly shut their door as the general turned his back towards them.

He turned the corner, and I fell into step beside him. "What was that all about?"

"Mistress and Mister Dunsdabad are unable to conceive children, so I searched out a mother who didn't want her child and have arranged for the Dunsdabads to adopt it."

"That's so…so…sweet of you."

"Don't say you're starting to like me."

"No, I definitely wouldn't go so far as to say that."

He smiled and gestured for me to enter a printing shop.

"Why are we going in here?"

"You'll see."

Denor walked up to the counter and greeted the man behind it whilst I waited by the door. The owner was a middle-aged man with sparse brown hair and ink staining his apron and hands. After the greeting and the exchange of a few pleasantries, Denor also handed this man a folder with documents inside.

When we returned to the street, I only lifted my eyebrows as a question.

"The shop was going bankrupt, so I found an investor who wanted to print his political propaganda, and they can now both benefit from the profit and keep the shop going so the shop owner can provide for his family."

"So what? You're assisting the Spirit of Family now?"

"Something like that. I find myself drawn to the Spirits like a calling in life. I want to keep them close to my heart."

"So, what is your next act of impersonating a Spirit?"

"Master Corso. An artist who is incredibly inspiring and creates outstanding paintings, but no one pays a nobody any attention. It so happens I know a wealthy lady in Gaithbry who loves art and has a gallery. She has agreed to showcase Master Corso's paintings in next month's exhibition, and I only need to put a letter into his letterbox with the details. He isn't home at the moment, as this night gives him far too much inspiration, so he sits on the hills on the outskirts of the city to paint the bustling streets and the fireworks."

"And after you've posted this letter, will I be allowed to return home?"

"I only have a young widow who needs a handyman around her estate, and a homeless man, to pair together, and then we can watch the fireworks."

"Fine. Then you'll take me back?"

He nodded. "And at any time, if you want to swallow your pride and decide to stay in my apartment tonight, my bed is big enough for the both of us."

I frowned. "Dream on, old man."

"Oh, I might be ten years older than you, but I can still show you how sex is supposed to feel. I find it interesting to know that you haven't made love to Ben yet. It must mean that you're still not committed and are open for when something better comes along. And believe me. I'm definitely better. Pleasure guaranteed, as I can twist your mind to believe it was the best thing you'd ever experienced. I can make you feel as though your orgasm lasted for days."

"Ew! No! And you promised to stay out of my head and not garner information about Ben and me. That was the deal." We had arrived at the artist's door, so he pushed a brown envelope through the post box slat in the door.

"That piece of information I garnered before we made the deal. So I have broken no rules. You don't need to decide now. You should think about my proposal. With you by my side, we could become the king and queen of the entire Skyberg."

"What you're saying is treason." I almost lost my breath. "Is that what you think? That because my mother was a traitor, I'm a traitor, too? Or is this some sort of test that you'll inform King Emille about?"

I turned on my heel, ready to walk away from him, but he took a hard grip on my arm and placed a gift box in my hand. "Think about how many people we can protect and help like I have tonight."

I snatched my arm away, unable to argue that he had acted admirably tonight, but his intentions weren't entirely pure. "You can watch the fireworks by yourself. This date is complete. Don't speak to me until next month."

He only grinned, straightening up tall and watched as I left without another argument.

This evening had been awful. My heart hurt so badly, I pressed my hand over it as if that could stop it from cracking. Ben had been lying to me. The general wanted me to betray my king and sit as queen next to him. All I wanted was to restore honour to my family name. Maybe I'd had avoided all this heartache if I had only pressed that Black Blade into Ben's heart when I had the chance.

Tears started falling down my cheeks and I had no way of stopping them. I tried, but failed, wiping the back of my hand over and over to clear them from my face. A park bench empty of people stood under a tree in a secluded area just before the road forked in the direction of the outpost, so I sat down, contemplating what to do next. Would I just ignore Ben for the next three years, or could I crawl on my hands and knees in front of my brother, begging him to release me from the soul bond. Then my brother could do what he wanted with the traitorous black-wing king.

Mindlessly, I fiddled the lid open on the gift Denor had given me, and saw a black bladed knife. Small but effective. The hilt was adorned with jewels, and it looked expensive – beyond his pay grade. Not even Ben could source something like this for me. It wasn't the Black Blade with Spirit magic, but it was a black blade!

Spirits! I should go back to the general to say it was too much and that I couldn't accept it, fearing I'd be in debt to him if I kept it, but I couldn't. I really wanted this blade. With this blade, I could send Ben straight to the Underworld even if his death magic would survive.

I shook my head, rubbing my hand over my forehead. This didn't feel right. General Denor had planned tonight, shoving his memories into my mind and a black knife into my hand. He had wanted me to be the tool to kill the black-wing king all along. Question was whether it was the right thing to do even if the method he used to trick me was dubious.

With determination, I stored the blade in my handbag and discarded the packaging into the bin next to the bench and headed up the street to the outpost.

"Where are you?" I asked.

"By the campfire in the forest clearing," Ben answered. *"He has already let you leave?"*

"Yes. I'm coming." I'm coming for you all right. To kill you.

"You don't sound happy. What lies has the good general fed you tonight?"

"A jacket potato and a cinnamon flap." I answered sharply.

"Typical northern taste for food," Ben snorted.

Funny how you can know that, as I doubt your men ask about Pansery recipes before they murder them!

Ben was already on his feet as he saw me approach the clearing. Zoe wave from amongst the group around the fire and I could hear Nesso playing the harmonica I had gifted him.

Shit! I didn't want this big a crowd. If I killed Ben and died myself, I didn't want the others to take their revenge out on Zoe. I stiffened as Ben put his arm around my shoulder, his thumb stroking gently over my cheek.

"You're cold." He flexed out his wings and wrapped one around me. "How did it go?"

I looked up into those big red eyes of a complete stone-cold liar.

"It was fine. I'm fine."

"Are you sure? I could ask Camp Leader Mewer to have a look at you. 'Fine' in two sentences in a row must be bad."

"I'm fine!" I hissed, and when he stared at me in frozen shock, I rolled my eyes. "Let's join the others and sit down."

I'd have to lure Zoe away somehow before I struck. She was sitting next to Davis, and they seemed to be having a civilised conversation, so maybe she had accepted the fact that they were twins.

Ben sat down on the grass with his legs apart and patted on the ground between them for me to sit down. I did as asked, and he wrapped both his wings around us.

Nesso played extra loudly on the harmonica and stared at me as if to say a thank you and Commander Daffron shockingly nodded his head in a curt bow, seeming to have thanked me for his gift, too. I looked at Murben who shoved his breast out, showing that he was wearing the bodyguard pin I had given him featuring the two small Bs which were Ben's official emblem, but also had a larger B for 'Bodyguard' around them, protecting them.

"My men were moved by your gifts…and so was I. They were very thoughtful. I never knew Murben wanted a public sign of gratitude, and I don't think he'll ever take that pin off. Nesso had missed his harmonica, and I don't think he has ever had such a fancy one with jewels and his name engraved on it. Davis loved the sword handle you fashioned for him to drape onto the normal hilt so he could hold it better without his thumb. Very clever. Did you come up with that design yourself?"

I nodded, but my heart was too heavy with grief to say more words than were absolutely necessary. I hated how beautiful Ben looked, and how vulnerable he had let himself become the way he sat among those he trusted. Not the monster they said he'd become. Not the villain I was supposed to see. Just the man I loved.

How did we get here?

A thousand memories surged at once; his laughter under the stars, the way he said my name like a vow, the feel of his heartbeat pressed to my ear on nights we pretended the world would never turn cruel.

I don't want to do this.

But I have to.

He grunted a low purr. "Now. The one you gave Commander Daffron, that made me want to marry you that instant, as I saw the look in his eyes. A pocket-sized painting of his girls to keep with him when he can't be with them. I thought I saw him tearing up."

"I'm glad they liked them," I muttered.

I stared into the enormous flame that Davis kept feeding to become larger and larger. Somewhere in my mind, a voice kept whispering his name like a prayer begging for another way – another world where we weren't natural enemies.

"Now, I wonder. Where is my gift?" he asked.

I sought for my purse to ensure I had it by my side and discreetly snapped the clip open, fingering over the black blade knife. The weight of the blade was nothing compared to the weight in my soul.

I'll gift you death in a minute!

"It's in our room. It's a gift best given in private."

"Well, I have one for you," he said, handing me a small deep-blue box.

He opened it for me and held up a chain with a circular pendant, featuring his emblem with the double B. After a brief inspection, he clasped it around my neck. "It's a seal that you can use in an official capacity. Any instruction you write, whose wax you seal with the stamp of the sigil will be law, as equal as if I'd have given the order. Anywhere you're in the Black Wing Territory, they'll follow your order if you show it to them."

"Thank you," I muttered, but the gratitude towards what he had given me was underwhelming.

He had literally placed his entire territory into my hand; at my mercy, and all I could muster was a mere 'thank you'.

He sighed, obviously noticing something was wrong, and began to gently massage my tense shoulders instead. His touch felt so good. I wanted him to be who he had said he was. I wanted us to be together. His closeness felt so right. I straightened my shoulder again and twisted my head around to stare at him. "If you use your trust magic on me, I'll kill you," I hissed quietly, so no one else could hear me.

His eyes widened instantly, blinking as if he hadn't heard me right. For a heartbeat, he just stared, frozen, like his brain needed extra time to process the words. His brows pulled together, not in anger, but in wounded disbelief, like he'd just been slapped and didn't know why.

"I'd never use my magic on you. I told you that. What's wrong? Did the general upset you?"

I snapped my head back round to look into the flames. "I'm fine."

But I wasn't fine. I had to kill him. It was the right thing to do. Something I should have done a year ago, but I had hesitated then. I had been given another chance. It was now or never.

Pushing my hand into my purse, I clasped around the black blade knife, and in a swift movement, I turned around and launched my arm into the air, aiming to stab at his heart.

37

He didn't stop my hand from coming down at him, his love for me flashing in his eyes. How could my heart so strongly believe he was innocent when I had seen all the lives he had taken?

I halted with the tip poking against the fabric of his shirt, just like I had the last time I had pointed a black blade to his heart.

"I can't do it," I cried, and tears burned my eyes before they flooded like a deluge down my cheeks.

I grabbed my purse and stepped over his knees to get away. The harmonica went silent, and I heard gasps around the fire.

"And you said it would be fun to piss the general off," Commander Daffron grunted.

Nesso chuckled but stopped when Ben grunted.

I hadn't heard that Ben had come after me as I walked across the field. But he passed me and held up his hands in front of me, not touching me, but so intrusive I had to stop, or I'd slam into him.

"This is way beyond a little problem, which I suspected your many 'fines' meant. Tell me right now what is wrong. You almost killed us both and damned our souls to the Underworld."

I hadn't contemplated that if I'd have stabbed him with the black iron blade, I'd have also eternally condemned my own soul to the Underworld. An icy chill ran down my arm at what I could have just done.

"You're a lying piece of shit! That's what's wrong!"

"Okay, sure, but why? What has the general told you?"

"He didn't only tell me, he showed me his memory in my mind. I saw your army attacking innocent white-wings in Pansery. You ordered all their deaths. The blood. The horror…the children! I saw what you've done!"

"I see," Ben said curtly, looking hurt. "And you believe this, do you? You truly believe that what you saw was real and that I would have done that?"

"I saw it!"

Murben came to stand at Ben's side. "They are fake memories, Cadet Coraly. No black-wings have attacked any white-wings. I assure you. The general has the magic ability to show you whatever he wants with his mind."

"I…I saw…I…felt it. It felt so real."

"Sure it was," Ben said, gritting his teeth. "And so conveniently, he gifted you a black blade straight afterwards. I wonder what he imagined you'd do with it. A clever game. If he kills me, there will be war, but if you kill me…one problem less for him. And you fell straight into his trap, so quick to believe him. That I would…" Black essence ripped from his palms and oozed out from the fabric of his trousers. "The deal might have been worth it to save Robin, but as I said, a hefty price for me." He turned around and walked towards the outpost building.

He had walked away from me, each step that widened our distance made the separation feel more permanent. I had broken our trust, and my chest hurt as if something vital had been ripped from my insides, leaving only aching emptiness behind. I had deserved it. I had hurt him.

My eyes watered, my vision of him blurred like looking up at the sky from the bottom of a murky lake. My knees buckled to the ground, devastated, I cried into my hands. Murben stayed with me, crouching down and wrapped his wings around me, holding me for a long while, as my body was shaking with silent sobs. I clung to Murben's shirt, fearing that if I'd let go, I'd shatter completely. His hand made soothing circles over my back, the gesture reminding me that the black-wings were not my enemy. The other hand enveloped my entire front in a hard grip as if he was concerned I'd slip away from sanity and turn into stone if he didn't hold me together. It could be the truth of it since it was the first time in what felt like forever, that I was this heartbroken.

My sobs eventually hitched, and I calmed enough to speak. "What shall I do? What have I done?"

"Don't despair, Cadet Coraly. King Blackbone loves you. He'll forgive you," Murben consoled. "Question is whether you can forgive yourself?"

"No!" I cried out so hard he had to hold me tighter. "I love him so much. It hurt so much to think he was evil. My heart broke. I don't deserve him! I'm a mutt. A traitor!"

"No. Your heart is pure, Coraly. I've never regretted meeting you, no matter what pain it'll cause me. King Blackbone knows the tactics of warfare and what the general will do to weaken him. He won't blame you for this. Go to him. Tell him how you feel. Please. Before he loses control over his magic."

My chest hurt, my breath rasping out of my lungs with each cry, making it sore. I calmed my breathing once more and nodded.

Murben let me out of his embrace and gave me a wide berth to stand up. "Please, go to him," he urged again.

I caressed the soul bond between us. "*Where are you?*"

"At war, but not against innocents, it seems."

"Please, Ben, you say I must live with your secrets and that isn't making it easy for me. You knew that would be the case from the moment you stayed here when you could have freed yourself. This cannot be what destroys us."

There was silence. The bond calmed, and he wasn't arguing.

"I'm in our room."

I made my way to him, and as I entered the room, I went straight for the drawer and brought out my gift to him. Ben was sitting at the foot of the bed, throwing five of my daggers into the cracked wall, the damage growing larger. He hadn't spared me a single glance as he fetched the blades from the wall and started anew.

"I'm sorry. It shouldn't have taken me so long to realise that I could never love someone this much who would be that cruel."

"There was one tiny lie made up about me and you were so quick to believe it. Wanting a reason to hate me for being a black-wing like your mother. And if you have forgotten, let me remind you that you too have black wings."

He continued throwing the blades at the wall without looking at me, but in my mind I heard him speak to me, as if that was making it easier for me, or perhaps it was his passive thoughts and he hadn't realised I'd heard them.

I could feel his anger through our bond…no, not anger…hurt. He wasn't ready to forgive me at this moment, so I put the gift down on the bed, grabbed a tracksuit and left the room. I changed in one of the common toilets and went to the obstacle course to blow off steam.

I watched the obstacle course in front of me in almost pitch darkness. It would hurt to miss a step and fall off any of the obstacles, but who cared? I deserved pain. It was ironic that I had never imagined myself doing this on the eve of the Turning of the Year. Alone and miserable. My mother had really screwed me over big time. Six years ago, I had been eating a hot meal in our family apartment, laughing and being loved. Today, I had no parents, no hot meal and nor was I laughing. "Spirit of Family! Can you stop fucking with me?" I shouted to the black void above. "Spirit of Love…Life…or Death, or whoever is in charge…" What? What would I tell the Spirits? Whatever! Fuck them all. Perhaps it was easier to only have two Spirits as the black-wings did, and there was only one to pray to for the living. Simple.

I focused my eyes on the first obstacle and sprinted for the first hurdle, wanting to push aside all thought of everything wrong in my life and only focus on the adrenaline.

When I cleared the six hurdles, I tore at the net wall to climb it before launching myself at the monkey rings, then I was down on my knees and elbows crawling under the net roof before finding the rope in the dark to climb the rope wall and abseil down the other side. I was going fast, probably using the energy of my rage, thinking of General Denor, and how he had purposely destroyed my relationship with Ben. I jumped up on the balance bar, and although I could barely see it, I didn't slow my speed.

"Where are you?" Ben roared.

The distraction caused me to lose concentration, to fall off the balance bar and plummet to the ground, hitting down hard with my shoulder.

"Ouch!"

"Are you okay?"

"I think I dislocated my shoulder."

"Who are you fighting?"

"The ground."

"The ground?"

"I was on the balance bar when you shouted. Now, I'm on the ground."

The bond went silent, and I stared up at the stars, smiling as I saw the Golden Stallion constellation said to be the Spirit of War's horse and which all warrior's prayed to for strength on the battlefield. I stayed on the ground, waiting for the pain to settle, counting the constellations I could see in the dark sky.

After a while, Ben's face popped into view. "Let me help you up." He shoved his arms under my thighs and back to lift me up.

"Ouch! Ouch! You don't need to lift me. It's my shoulder that hurts, not my legs. I can stand."

"Okay," he muttered and stopped, putting me back on the ground and laying down next to me. He held the box out that I had gifted him, but he had removed the lid, so I could see the ring inside. "What is this?" he asked, both with hope and fear marring his voice.

"I thought it was self-explanatory," I muttered.

"No. I want you to explain to me exactly what you mean by it."

"Well. It's a promise ring."

"A promise of what?"

I pinched the ring between my fingers and yanked it out from its hold and held it up. "It's my promise to you that I'll be yours. Forever. My heart and…" I angled the ring so he could see the inside where the jeweller had melted glass over a drop of my blood, and next to it were the words, 'I'm yours', "…and that I'll give you my blood and all I am. You don't have to like me in return. I just…I'm yours, anyway," I stammered, my confidence reduced to a puny size.

I slid the ring onto his ring finger, and considering the black blade situation, I was extremely relieved that he accepted it. When it was on, Ben swiftly pushed his fingers through my hair and cupped the back of my head, pushing our lips together. A stone lifted from my chest from the relief that he hadn't forsaken me. My desires ripped through me, as did the need to have him. All of him.

He wrapped his arm around me, pulling me closer, his mouth claiming mine like it was vital for his survival, and his tongue slithered inside my mouth to touch mine with a gentle caress. My body heated, filling with a powerful arousal I knew would go unsatisfied, yet every little piece of him I was given was the air I needed to breathe.

"Your heart," he panted, and sucked on his own finger before he slid it down my tracksuit trousers and beneath my knickers. "Even if it's in pieces…each piece is larger than the heart of anyone I've ever met. I love you so fucking much."

He might have been a virgin, but the way he massaged my clit with his wet finger didn't seem to be with inexperience. He hit the perfect spot, and my arousal grew tenser and stronger. I moaned his name onto his mouth between his kisses and I moaned out all my pleasure so he could hear what he did to me. His fingers quickened and my breath deepened. "I'm going to…this is…Ben…" I moaned.

I looked up at him and saw his satisfied gaze on me and his victorious smile. "I want to pleasure you. Take it."

"Out here?"

"Everywhere!" He kissed my neck, moaning hot breaths at my skin. His fingers worked even quicker on my clit. "You're amazing," he whispered against my mouth. "So beautiful like this. Submissively pleasured at my complete mercy."

I reached for his cock, but he pulled his hand out of my knickers and clamped his hand on his trousers to stop my entry and broke our kiss. "I can only handle one thing at a time. You today. I want you to thaw for me." His hand returned inside my knickers, and he added a second finger to press at my clit and made wide circles, undoing my control.

My orgasm ripped through me, sending my back into arching fits towards the stars and the pain throbbed in my shoulder at the same time. I ripped the grass out of the field with my cramping fingers and moaned loudly as the pleasure burst through my seams. Ben pressed his lips like a lid over my mouth to eat the sounds erupting until my back collapsed feeling spineless.

With closed eyes, I lay silent for a few minutes to catch my breath, musing with the throbbing of the aftermath.

When I opened my eyes, I saw him smiling at me. "At least Mazdon knows where we are now."

"I hope he enjoyed the show." It made me pray, though, that Zayd hadn't seen us from his window with his far-sight and had watched me cum around Ben's fingers in the middle of the obstacle course.

Ben pulled his hand out from my trousers and tucked it under my tracksuit jacket, palming my stomach.

"Maybe we should get inside. It's not safe out here after dark without any weapons."

Ben's face was nuzzled into the crook of my neck, kissing me gently. "Murben is on guard duty and around somewhere."

"Oh great! So, he saw me unravel at his king's touch!"

Ben chuckled. *"If he didn't. I'll be gloating, telling him about it in detail tomorrow."*

I slapped at his shoulder and his chuckle echoed through my mind. He sounded so happy, it made my soul purr.

As we watched the stars together, my eyelids became heavier and heavier.

When I opened my eyes and felt I was waking up, the sun was shining high in the sky. Murben was standing with his back towards us, guarding us…still on the grass under the balance bar on the obstacle course. I moaned and Murben turned around to see me flashing him a quizzical look. He tapped at his bodyguard pin with the proudest grin on his face as if to say, 'I've got your back' and turned his back towards us again to carry on with his duty.

I nudged at Ben's side. "Wake up. We fell asleep." I turned my wrist around, my watch informing me it was lunchtime.

"Hey!" I nudged Ben once more. "It's lunchtime."

He tucked me closer to him. "What a perfect day. Orgasm, then sleep straight to lunch."

"Yeah, and if I'm not ready and in my brother's apartment in two hours to help him cook for ten people and a toddler, he'll kill me."

"You can cook?"

I slammed an elbow into his chest. He coughed up a laugh.

"That's your question? If I can cook? Not what *you* should do all day missing me?"

"No, I'm intrigued by this new side of you that I've never heard of before. I would really like you to cook for me one day so I can decide if you'll make a good wife."

"Oh, you'd have to hire a food taster to ensure I won't poison you."

"Your cooking is that bad, hey?"

He earned another elbow to his chest, and he gladly took it with another mock laugh. "Poison you on purpose!" I scoffed.

He continued his endeavour of staring at me lovingly, still not getting off the grass and still having Murben guard us. He nestled his hand into my hair and stroked his thumb over the hairline at my forehead. Then he grunted, frowning low. "I know you haven't coloured your hair this month, and you were unconscious during the one before that. How have you had time to do your hair? It's still blue at the roots."

"My parents had someone put a permanent glamour on it when I was five."

"So, what is your natural colour?"

"I can't remember, but I have always assumed it's like Harvey's."

He grunted again, pulling at some strands.

I attempted to sit up, but he pushed me back down and placed gentle kisses over my lips. "Is it your turn today?" I asked, wiggling my brows. "In the sunlight."

"No. Why? Had you wanted to go again?"

"Behave King Blackbone, or I might invite you to the big family dinner."

He stroked his hand along my head. "I don't mind going with you."

I froze. Stunned. "What? You want to sit through that ordeal? Dinner with my family?"

"Yes. Why not? I hope to be a part of it one day."

I opened my mouth to say something but closed it and tried again but drew a blank on what to say. "Are you sure you don't mean that you want to flee from it like the plague?"

"No. Who will attend?"

"Well, Zayd will be there for starters." Ben just looked at me as if that didn't bother him and for me to go on. "Mazdon, Kate, Zoe, Brian, Captain La Roy, Emroyce, Fern and Robin. And Harvey and me, of course."

"Sounds delightful."

"Sounds deligh…? What? You might have too much blood flowing in your head. We should get up and go back to our room to give you a release."

Ben stood up and held out his hand to help me up and I had forgotten the pain in my shoulder until then and cussed under my breath.

"Are you okay?"

"I'm fine."

"Oh uh," he raised his brows at me. "Last time you said you were fine…"

I glowered at him, and he kept quiet, pinning his lips into a thin line.

We started walking towards the military building, and that's when he added. "Just don't stab me, okay?"

"Really? You couldn't refuse?"

"Come on! It was funny."

"Well, let's see how funny you think it is during the family dinner. There might actually be real stabbing."

"Your family sounds lovely."

When I glowered at him this time, he flashed me a wolfish grin. And to add insult to injury, the bastard winked at me.

Ben told me he would run to the liqueur store to buy some wine whilst I got showered and dressed and I told him to get something much stronger, as I could anticipate that I'd be needing it. When I had dressed in a deep purple dress, tightly fitted around my body, he returned with a bottle of whiskey. I opened the bottle and poured some into an empty water bottle before taking a swig at it.

"That was a gift for your brother for having us around for dinner," Ben muttered.

"Well, he'd have opened it and shared it with us during the dinner, so I'm just helping him along." I felt the warm buzz seeping down my throat and into my stomach. Much better.

Ben showered quickly and got dressed in black trousers and a purple shirt that matched my dress.

I kept my eye on the time. Harvey didn't like it when I wasn't punctual, and he had said three o'clock. When it was five minutes to three, I tapped my watch to indicate that we had to leave. "Let's go!"

Ben slapped on some cologne, grabbed the three bags containing the gifts I had bought and the bottle of whiskey before he opened the door into a quiet corridor as most of the cadets had returned home for the holidays. We climbed the stairs to the leadership floor, and I took a moment to ready myself outside Harvey's door.

"Okay, so a few rules before I knock and before the others arrive. Don't speak to Zayd about his parents, or that you beat him on the obstacle course, or taunt him because…actually, don't speak to him at all."

"If he asks me a question, may I answer it?"

"If you're polite. Don't push Harvey or Kate about their relationship as their situation is complicated, or in other ways tease Kate about her frankness, because you'll risk her setting fire to the apartment. And don't ask about how her fire wielding is going because Harvey doesn't like that Captain La Roy has taken an interest in teaching her privately in his spare time. Don't compare my brother's and Captain La Roy's skills at being captains. Don't ask Brian what he will do after he graduates this year. He's stressing about it. He doesn't really want to go on the Spirits' Trek, but he's in the lead of wins so far in their year. Don't whisper anything to me you don't want Mazdon to hear. Don't mention the snake bite to Emroyce. Obviously, don't mention the war between black-wings and white-wings. And I don't even know what the deal is between Zoe and Davis now, so perhaps don't bring that up, nor that–"

"Spirits, I should have brought a notepad to write all of this down. Can you propose a conversation topic I *can* talk about?"

"Uh…um…maybe just smile."

"A teethy smile, or with my lips closed?"

I glowered at him, and he smiled at me before knocking. "Don't worry. I'm tutored in conversing in public events as well as diplomatic affairs."

Why did it feel like that didn't apply when entering my family home?

"It's not like Watson will open, and I'd ask him if he saw me giving you an orgasm out on the field last night," he added.

My eyes opened wide, and my heart burned. "You wouldn't?"

38

Harvey opened the door before Ben could answer.

Timed to perfection, I'm sure.

"Oh, you came as well?" Harvey muttered, glancing at Ben.

Ben opened his mouth, and I stared at him. He closed his mouth for a second and just smiled, but then said, "I can leave if you like."

"No," Harvey drawled pensively, shaking his head, and gesturing for us to come inside.

Ben handed Harvey the opened bottle of whiskey, and my brother looked at it with raised eyebrows.

"Don't look at me," Ben said in defence. "Your sister started the party downstairs all by herself."

"Aren't you in a gossipy mood?" I growled.

Harvey put the bottle down on the dining room table without a word about it. "King Blackbone can set the table, and you can prepare the creamy potatoes and the salads and I'll do the meat," Harvey instructed, like the leader he was used to being.

I looked at Ben to confirm if he was okay with doing a servant's job and he only shrugged his shoulders, nodding. I pointed towards the glass cabinet with all the fancy plates and silverware. "If you steal any of the silver, you'll be in trouble," I whispered to him.

Ben wrapped his arms around me from behind and bent down to whisper into my ear. "Maybe I just need to steal something little then to see what might happen. I might like this promised trouble you mention."

I shoved him away and glared at him, pointing a finger in his face. "Behave."

He raised his palms up. "I'll be good. Promise."

I joined Harvey in the kitchen and felt strangely at home when I opened the cupboards to bring out the ingredients I needed. Harvey hadn't moved any of them, so I found the items in the places they used to be stored by our mother. We cooked next to each other in silence for a while until Harvey sighed and glanced at me.

"How did it go with General Denor?"

Somehow, it was kind of nice that my brother had asked me. That he had cared to ask. "Yeah, it was fine."

Ben appeared in the doorway to the kitchen. "If she says she was fine, hide the knives." He pointed with a thumb towards the living room. "Which glasses do you want me to set out, the tumblers or the ones on foot?"

"Do both. The one on foot for the wine and the tumblers for water if they don't want to drown their miseries with whiskey," I hissed, glowering at him.

"If there's any left when the guests arrive," he mocked before he returned to the living room.

"What was that about knives?" Harvey asked.

"Nothing. Denor said something that made me want to stab Ben, but I didn't, and we worked it out."

Harvey whistled lowly. "Complicated relationship."

"Nah, I'm sure wives want to stab their husbands all the time. Pass me the salt."

I had expected him to say something about me not getting too attached to the enemy king, but surprisingly, he didn't and just passed me the salt.

"Problem is," Harvey began. *Here it comes.* "I don't have to help hide other wives' husband's bodies."

I stood stunned. He had made no attempt to forbid our relationship, only meaning that he didn't want the trouble of having to clean it up.

"Awe, you would do that for me?"

"Of course. You're my baby sister."

Ben arrived again, leaning on the doorpost, and smiled. "What are you two bonding over?"

"Who of us should bury your body," I replied, and his playful smirk widened.

He flashed one right back at us. "It doesn't surprise me that you two can even bicker about that. It'd be polite to give me a heads-up as to who won."

Being distracted when I shoved the potato tray into the oven, I accidentally burned my wrist. Ben immediately darted to my side to look at it.

I snatched my hand away, remembering the lessons my brother taught me about not showing weakness. "I'm fine."

Ben looked up at Harvey with a playful cocked brow. "Hide the knives," he whispered before he stalked out into the living room again.

Harvey snorted. "He seems genuinely fond of you, despite your blue hair."

It was almost a compliment if I ignored the disbelief in his tone and I was near to confessing that Ben had given me the sigil that gave me the same power as a queen in the Black Wing Territory but thought better of it. If anyone found out, they could use it against me, forcing me to take actions I didn't agree with or write letters I didn't stand for. No, better that it stayed secret.

"Maybe I made a mistake joining your souls," he continued saying, as I had remained silent. "My offer still stands to remove the bond if the connection becomes a burden."

He was treading into dangerous ground, on a topic I didn't want to discuss today. "I'm fine!"

Harvey pushed all his knives to his other side and further away from me and actually gave me an impish smile. I hadn't seen one of those on his face in a long, long time.

I grabbed a bottle of red wine. "I see you're taking King Blackbone's advice."

"One can not fault a king's knowledge of battle tactics."

I rolled my eyes at him and continued preparing the peppered sauce, adding a dash of red wine and drinking a dash straight from the bottle.

"Sure. That's okay. I've got more bottles," Harvey muttered, focusing on cutting the sinew off the meat. "Does King Blackbone want a glass of wine whilst we wait for the others?"

"He can share my bottle." I kept stirring the sauce to ensure it wouldn't burn to the bottom of the pan and checked into the firewood compartment of the oven to check the flame was still going. I put another log in for good measure. "Do you think our parents are looking down at us now and wishing they were here?"

"Angie…" Harvey signed. "Well, I bloody hope that they ended up in different places because I don't want to watch them killing each other and ruining my peace when I join the Spirits' sides."

I laughed. "You should have told me about our father's execution. I could have come with you to Gaithbry to support you."

"I didn't want you to see that. It was gruesome enough for me to have to swing the sword at his neck."

"I know father appreciated your courage."

He turned around from the kitchen counter and leaned against it, knocking back the last sip of whiskey from his tumbler. "Father gave me his last magic gift before I…you know. Carried out his sentence."

What? Father had another gift? I just stared at him, waiting.

He cleared his throat. "As you know, our magic should stay a secret as it gives us the advantage of the element of surprise, and because the one we both have might earn us a dungeon cell in the Ivory Castle. The magic Father gifted me was the ability to shut off emotions. It's very liberating. It was also very generous of him to do so when he had to face death. He was a great man." He looked down to the bottom of his empty glass, his face agonised by forced composure. The secret he had revealed lingered in his eyes like a quiet, aching sorrow, as if he was waiting for my judgment, or worse, pity.

"He was," I muttered.

That was all he got. No pity, or forgiveness. In my opinion, he should have launched a rescue party and broken him out of the dungeon. *Coward!*

I thought about the magic. It explained some of his behaviour lately. Particularly the time Ben had been angry enough to kill Zayd and Harvey had stopped it. Today though, Harvey had all his emotions on display, and I recognised the brother I knew growing up. For the days he was on duty, he could use the magic, he'd need it as a captain.

"Just don't use it when it comes to Kate," I teased. "She likes you, you know."

"And I love her," he said plainly, setting the tumbler down on the counter.

"Oh, so that numbing magic is completely off right now, then?"

"You know I've always loved her."

"Yes, but I thought you were too afraid to admit it to yourself."

"I have been, and I'm not saying I'll act on it. She deserves better than me. I'm in the crossfire of some very powerful people and I'd only cause her pain."

"Sure. Perhaps so. But isn't that her decision to risk taking? I know I'd rather live a short life with Ben than a long one with someone else."

His brows lowered again. "Is it really that serious between you?"

I stopped stirring and dragged the saucepan away from the heat on the stove. "I'd marry him tomorrow if I didn't think it futile, considering we could die in the challenges the day after."

He sighed. "So, you'll not listen to your big brother when he tells you…he asks you not to get involved with him? That it'll leave you hurt at the end."

"We're not going there today." I smiled softly at him.

"You're right. Not today. But another day I'll oppose to it."

We both chuckled, and he filled up his tumbler with more whiskey.

We finished preparing the food and Ben tasted my cooking from behind my back, providing remarks on my skill until our guests arrived and the seats filled up with those I considered my family. There was laughter and banter, and Ben kept smiling and being polite, as he had promised.

Before pudding, we exchanged gifts, and I gave Harvey a new sheath, as his was worn by wars and age. Harvey gave me a box with our mother's old things. "Technically, these are mine. My inheritance," I said, rolling my eyes at him.

"I was going to burn them but thought of giving them to you just before I lit the match, so be grateful."

I was, and I looked into the box of various items like it was a boxful of old treasures. I'd have to wait to go through them another day, but I was already intrigued as I spotted the necklace Mother always wore, letters and a glass figurine of a cat that she had liked.

On the sofa behind me, I saw Mazdon give Kate a pair of fireproof gloves, so as not to burn up anything else in their dorm room, and hiking clothes. Kate gave him a new axe and tools for the cottage.

I reached into my bag to bring up a pair of leather training gloves for Zayd, so he could get faster at the rope wall on the obstacle course.

"And you said I couldn't tease him about the obstacle course time," Ben muttered from my side at the table.

Zayd gave me a box of my favourite chocolates, and I sighed in relief that he hadn't given me anything inappropriate. But then he went to my brother's bedroom to retrieve another large white box with a big red bow attached to the lid. Crap! I didn't want a fight to break out. He set it down gently onto the table. My heart skipped a beat as I saw the box move in small nudges. Zayd opened the lid slowly and a small pink snout popped out, sniffing the air.

I gasped, folding my hands over my mouth in awe. It was the cutest little piglet, its folded ears flopping just above its eyes.

"Meet Fiona," Zayd said, lifting her out of the box and hugging her to his chest.

He slowly walked towards me, stroking her gently as she looked around, making soft oinks. Zayd had fitted a red collar on her with a golden plaque hanging off it with the engraving 'Fiona Coraly'.

"Awe, Zayd, thank you. She's lovely."

"I know how much you loved Flora. I have prepared a spot for Fiona in the stables and told the stable master to restrict the area, so no other cadets have access to her. That should keep her safe. I know you can't be committed to keeping her in your room and having to walk her, considering you'll spend most of your time on training for challenges…or in the infirmary."

Everyone but Ben gave a low chuckle at the joke. I stared at him in warning, and he pulled up a smile that didn't extend to his eyes.

Zayd handed me my new soft, pink friend to hold in my arms.

"I'm going to teach you how to sit, lie down and roll around just like Flora," I told her.

"And like most men, it seems," Emroyce blurted, putting a teasing hand on Zayd's shoulder, and glancing over to Ben too.

Everyone laughed.

When Zayd showed me Fiona's travel cage in Harvey's bedroom, and secured her inside, we exchanged a sentimental gaze that contained so many memories of our past. For a moment, I forgot to keep my distance, and I took his hand and squeezed it gently. "Thank you."

He took a step closer. "You know I was put on the doorstep of the outpost, never having known my parents. People come and go in this outpost and the only thing I have in my life that is worth…everything to me, is you. I know no one else. You're my world and I'll never stop fighting for you. For us."

"Zayd," I moaned, and dropped his hand.

"I know. I don't care if you have a fling with the black-wing king. We got involved so young and you need to experience something else, too. I understand it must feel powerful to get the attention of a king. But when it settles, I'm going to be right here for you. No matter what. I just wanted you to know that. To never be afraid to come back to me or tell me when you're in trouble."

"You've also got Harvey," I muttered.

He smiled at that. "Yeah, it'll be him and me together forever. Although, I think I saw him making advances towards Kate tonight."

"Yes, it seems this evening has brought out generosity, kindness and a sprinkle of bravery in all of us."

"As long as he's subtle about it. I don't want a vendetta between the captains. Captain La Roy won't give up so easily."

"Nor would I expect him to play dirty. He's very righteous."

"Let's hope that righteousness isn't only an act that'll crumble when Harvey removes what is important to him."

Returning to the living room, all the commotion had settled. I was about to join Harvey and Kate by the window, but I hesitated as I saw Kate open a velvet box with a pair of diamond earrings inside. With no warning, Kate kissed Harvey, clearly ecstatic, and surprised at receiving a gift from him tonight. I turned around after seeing my brother blush, thinking it best if I left them alone for the moment. Perhaps my brother would finally pull his shit together and ask her out.

As I turned around, I saw Zayd by the fireplace, leaning into Ben to tell him something privately. I could only guess that it wouldn't be something polite. I feared a brawl breaking out and my heart sped up. Zayd continued making his way to join Emroyce, Robin and Captain La Roy who were singing by the piano and I homed in on Ben, circling the edges of the room before joining him at the other end.

"What did Zayd say to you?" I demand to know.

Ben smiled at me like he had been challenged with something that wasn't a match for him. "He said, 'beat that'."

His light spirit was suspicious. "And what did you reply? You didn't tell him about the ring, did you?"

I felt his desire to touch me through our bond, but he refrained. "No, nor did I thank him for the chocolates he gave you that I'll be tasting straight from your mouth. See, I can smile and be polite."

I passed looks of incredulity over him and watched Emroyce play the piano and sing with Robin in his lap.

When my glance swept over Mazdon, I saw him frown at Zayd and I wondered if Mazdon ever regretted trading away his inherited fire wielding magic for the super hearing. Hearing everything must get annoying at times.

Fern was sitting on the sofa chatting to Brian, seeming to take the opportunity to relax as Emroyce was entertaining Robin. She congratulated him for his and Winter's win in the Magic Wielding challenge. Fern also admired Emroyce's gift in her hand. He had given Fern another teacup to a set she collected. Emroyce had also given Robin a real iron sword, and as Robin waved it around sitting on his lap, the worry lines on Emroyce's face deepened. Fern had knitted extra thick socks for Emroyce's hikes and next year's navigation challenge. Robin had made him a drawing, as cute as the ones he used to make, proof that his mind was back to normal. Brian had given Fern a lovely necklace with a diamond drop pendant like the sigil on her uniform for serving the infirmary guild.

Fern had hugged me many times over and thanked me for the deal I had made with General Denor to save her son, and I felt guilty as she had saved up to give me a gold bracelet with a heart-shaped charm hanging off it. I had provided the rest of my friends with a mere bottle of wine, as I normally gifted them. Fern got a scarf, as she had sworn off alcohol. In return my friends gave me more of my favourite chocolates, having gone through a lot of effort to source them from Gaithbry.

Ben kept an appropriate distance for a teammate, not to rile anyone up unnecessarily tonight, but leaned in to whisper. "There will be a lot of kissing for the next few weeks." He earned another elbow to his abs, this time softer and more playful.

I slipped into the kitchen to get the three dishes of peanut butter cake, which was a recipe my mother always used. It was Zayd's and my favourite, but I never ever got it to turn out quite the same as when Mother made it. I put the dishes on the table and called out that pudding was served.

As everyone was taking their seats at the table, Harvey leaned in towards Ben, attempting to be discreet, but the entire table silenced as he spoke.

"I'm sorry I didn't have a gift for you. I would have got you something if I knew you were joining us." My brother's words had been without an ulterior motive, probably having observed everyone else opening presents but him.

"Oh, that's okay, Captain," Ben replied simply. "I already got the one thing I wanted." He casually supported his arm and hand on the table, not to show off, but to let people around the table notice the promise ring on his finger.

Zayd's eyes widened, disbelief flashing across his face as his gaze was dead caught on the ring. The ring symbolised that Ben had got everything he had ever dreamed of having. Any match he intended to challenge Ben with, he had lost. A muscle in his jaw ticked and his lips parted as if gasping for an explanation. It was gut-wrenching to see his reaction.

Ben kept his eye on Zayd the entire time, seeing the unquestionable shock shaping his face.

And Ben smiled.

39

Training for the fifth challenge was brutal. To excel at combat was a matter of pride for most cadets, and a necessity for your survival. The cadets parted as Zayd walked into the sparring hall, stepping up onto the mat. I had forgotten how much other cadets admired him. It reminded me of how much I hated women's gazes hungrily glancing over his muscular form when we were going out. Looking around, it was clear which men tried to show off their muscles as they had rolled up their sleeves so tightly on their biceps to make them bulge that they'd soon have no blood left in their arms.

Zayd was barefoot and he wore his navy-blue camp leader combat leathers. Most of his weapon collection donned one or other part of him to show the full and appropriate combat attire during war. I wasn't sure though if it was for demonstration purposes or to use in the war Ben had started with him during the Turning of the Year holiday. I inspected him and saw a baldric on his back holding two crossing swords, daggers in arm and leg holsters and a few throwing stars tucked in a case secured on his belt. If he had meant it as a threat, it was flawed, as I'm sure Ben took it as a compliment if Zayd thought he needed all those weapons to succeed in killing him.

There was a movement as someone crept closer to my back. "A punch to the face that floors him, and he won't need any of those weapons," Ben muttered.

I twisted my face to shush him over my shoulder.

Zayd spun around on the mat, looking at all the cadets' faces with a sense of regal stance, puckering his chest out like a cockerel among hens. "Challenge five!" he called out over the soft whispers. "Many say it's the last safe training before the serious work of this academy begins. The last chance to build yourself up for the hard trials when exercises push you to your limits…and beyond."

"What do you mean, 'beyond'?" Cadet Courtney, the fucking ice wielder, who had almost turned me into an ice lolly, asked from the front row on the opposite side of the mat.

Zayd tuned so I could only see the back of his head. "Death!" his dark voice echoed between the stone walls, taking a step closer to her. "I mean death cadet. During my time as a cadet, we were still one hundred and eighty cadets alive at this point, but by the end of my last year, there were only thirty of us left."

"What a waste of soldiers," Ben again muttered, clearly not wanting to be tutored by my ex-boyfriend.

I shot an elbow backwards that I think hit low on his abdomen.

Zayd must have heard him because he amplified his voice as he continued. "The challenge will be settled by a few stand-offs in combat and the losing team in each fight will be out. This is the only challenge that isn't completed in one day, but over the entire month, so you must stay focused at all times, as killing will be permitted all month if you're inside this sparring hall." He looked around the cadets' faces once more to gauge their reactions.

Ben's broad frame brushed up against me, guarding my back closer than was possible without our skins being attached. This month would be exhausting for the both of us to ensure I stayed alive.

Zayd glared hatefully above my shoulder where I knew Ben stood before he continued his speech. "There are eighty teams left, and every team will have one fight the first week, knocking out half the cohort. The second week, those remaining will have another match, eliminating half once more, leaving twenty teams remaining. The third week, we bring it down to ten teams and on the last week you'll have two fights if you win the first before you fight the final." He moved effortlessly around the mat like a predator prowling his domain. His hand moved in fluid strokes as he spoke, emphasising his words with short gestures. There were no wasted motions, no unnecessary dilly-dally, only discipline and deadly efficiency. "The prize of the challenge will be a day off, but you must take it before the summer break. The schedule of when your matches are, and what weapons will be allowed, will be posted on lists outside the Administrations Office, so make sure you're vigilant." Zayd put his hands on his hips and sized up everyone, his sharp gaze never wavering, tracing everyone's shift in posture and sign of hesitation. Even standing still, his presence commanded attention, his posture straight and his muscles coiled with controlled power. "Today, there will be free training, so I can see what I have to work with and then I'll make a plan for your training and pair you up from what I see could be a beneficial exchange. I might even mix some of you up with the other group. Bear in mind that depending on when your matches are, you'll get more or less training than others." He clapped his hands dismissively. "Get going!"

There were only forty mats, so he had divided the groups into two sessions of forty teams each, one for the morning training session and one for after lunch. Normally, the camp leaders didn't group the black-wings together with their king, but Zayd had put Davis and Murben in our group. That was why Zoe had come and now sat leaning against the wall to watch her brother train. A few of the second and third-year cadets had also come to watch, some of the third-year cadets clearly trying to calm down from having been pissed off in their dispute management class.

Everyone scattered around the mats and Kate came my way with a smile. "Can I train with you? Maz wanted to have a round with King Blackbone, saying he needed some training where he's actually challenged."

"Men!" I scoffed and saw Ben and Mazdon step onto another mat next to Kenyard and Emroyce.

"Yes. One of the Spirits' mysteries and sloppier work," Kate muttered.

I guessed things weren't going as well as she'd hoped with Harvey after the kiss at the Turning of the Year dinner. I pinned her with a tiresome look. "Why don't you just ask him out?"

"He's the man. I was waiting for him to make the move."

I'm just going to fucking say it. "He won't. He doesn't believe he's worthy of you, but if you ask him, I doubt he's strong enough to resist."

"That sounds romantic, and a great start to a happily ever after," she sneered. "Up with your palms and I'll practise hitting them. Don't keep them still, making it too easy."

I lifted my arms and held my palms up, ready for her as she punched at them, and I was surprised to discover that she had a vicious force behind her fist. "You know it's not like that. My brother has always loved you. He's just…a man."

Kate giggled, punching a two-one pattern, and I worried I'd get a nose-crunching fist in my face if she missed.

Christopher Charney, a mahogany-haired second-year cadet, who had been leaning against the wall now crouched down next to the mat as he watched us. "Women are too weak. Do you know how hard it's to breathe when you have the sharp edge of a broken rib clawing at your lung? I got that during one of my matches last year."

"Thank you for that useful advice," I snapped at him and focused on Kate's incoming punches, as she hadn't paused, ignoring him completely.

"Five cadets died in this challenge last year from heart failure, brain damage and blood loss. Some who survived lost limbs and earned deep scars. A shame to get a scar on those pretty faces."

He was a muscular man, but leaner than the other cadets with winged brows and a crooked nose on a colossal head, and dressed in the cotton uniform, showing three circles for his magical adeptness.

"Thank you for that compliment, Cadet Charney," Kate chirped, not looking his way, nor at his teammate Daro Jenson, who was still leaning against the wall with his arms crossed over his chest, laughing menacingly.

Now I understood why Emroyce had named them the Scare Tactics Team. The picture he painted of last year's combat challenge sounded horrific.

"What are you two doing here, anyway? Aren't you supposed to be on survival training in the woods?" I asked. "Hiding from Camp Leader Tomason?"

"This is the perfect place to gauge what magic people have, and I heard you don't have any," he leered.

That spurred an idea into my mind that made my heart race. An idea that could definitely work and would be worth a few injuries. I focused on Cadet Charney and almost got punched by Kate, who tumbled forwards a few steps as I moved.

"Oh, sorry." I told her before focusing on Cadet Charney again, holding out my hand for him to shake it, and as a challenge. No one in this outpost truly believed I had no magic, so it'd be interesting to see if he'd be brave enough to touch me. "Thank you for the solid advice."

He stretched up to stand tall and looked at my hand, and I looked at it too, hinting it could be poisonous, just to make it extra fun. He glanced over my face and then stared at my hand again. I kept it out and waited, flashing him a sinister smile.

"You know my magic is to block other people's magic, right?"

"Right. But this is just a hand." I turned it over in the air, as if to show a child I hid no monsters in my palm and kept it out as a challenge to him.

The apprehension in his face was amusing to watch as he slowly took my hand and shook it at the same time as he stared at me like he thought I'd grow a second head. The longer I could hold his hand, the better.

"Are you blocking my non-magical hand? You look scared of touching a pretty, little woman," I taunted, hoping he would give me a few more seconds.

"Do you think this will make us friends?"

"Oh, why would I want to become your friend? In four months, you have challenge eight. Your teammate will tie you up in ropes and fly you over a deep gorge. Statistics show that more than half of the cadets die in that challenge. I don't find the dead good company."

He snatched his hand out of mine and stared over my shoulder. Obviously, Ben was standing at my back. I sighed.

Cadet Charney left the sparring hall, and I turned around to stare at Ben.

"You take all the fun out of antagonising my fellow cadets when they run shit scared at the looks of you."

He didn't seem amused. "What mischief are you up to now?"

"Oh, you'll see. Meet me in our room after this session."

He crossed his colossal arms over his chest, clearly disapproving. "You're scheduled to get flight training with Murben."

I mirrored his stance, not giving in to his harsh stares. "You'll want to postpone that practice for about an hour."

Frustration tensed his muscles. "No. Not really. It's important that you improve."

I squared my shoulders so close to him our black leathers touched, and I planted my bare feet firmly on the cold stone floor as if turning one with the stone. Unmovable. "I dare you to tell me that again."

His red eyes swiped across my blue, searching my face as if hoping for a reason to push back. A retort balanced on his tongue, but he pressed his lips together, swallowing his words. He didn't agree but he'd accept it.

I gestured for him to step aside, so I could continue my training with Kate. We carried on punching each other, and she wasn't holding back her frustration, either.

When Zayd called out to dismiss everyone from class, I was about to grab Ben and pull him to our room, but Zayd stopped me.

"Great work today, Angie. Your right hook is sharp as ever. It reminded me of the time I stood you up at the Spring Festival Dance."

"I remember. Harvey had been more important than me. Fishing trip, was it?"

"Anyway," he cleared his throat. "You still have that problem with your left leg dragging. Stand flat when you swing but try to be light on your feet to move around between punches."

As if that was my problem. No. If I failed, it'd be because of my stupid wings. The bread and butter of any soldier. "Thank you. I'll work on it." I was eager to get around him to join Ben, who was waiting for me by the door.

"Will you join me for lunch in the canteen today?" Zayd asked, and he sounded so hopeful.

"I have flight training with Murben." *And before then, I have other plans.*

"Good," he muttered. "You need the training. Perhaps another time."

I smiled and nodded. "Great session," I said, patting him on the shoulder as I passed, running for Ben.

Ben's overload of scepticism of my new mischief forced me literally to drag him by the hand through the corridors to our room. As soon as I shut the door, I went for the window to pull the curtain closed and then I ripped off my leather jacket and the thick combat shirt beneath. The skin over the swell of my breasts chilled, covering me with goosebumps.

"Get naked and into bed!" I ordered. "We have an hour tops."

I hurried to unbutton my trousers and pushed them down to the floor and stepped out of them. By which time, Ben had only unbuttoned his shirt with slow movements, staring at me with suspicion. I darted to him and began helping him off with his trousers and couldn't get them off fast enough.

"What is going on?" he asked, bending his knees one at a time and tugging off his trousers.

"My good king, I've seen your hands draw a dagger much faster than this. Come on! I want you now!"

A strained exhale. A guilty look in his eyes. "You know we can't…I can't…"

"During the next hour, you can. Here, touch me." I held out my hand. "Use your death magic."

"Angelica," he moaned.

"Do it! Go for it! Give it your best shot! Then you fuck me like there is no tomorrow. I need you inside me now and I have waited long enough."

I couldn't stand even the smallest slither of space between us for much longer or I would go mad. Using up all my patience, I fought to keep in control of my wit.

Ben laced his fingers into mine and sighed. He was about to stroke the other hand into my hair, and he leaned down for a kiss, but instead, he pulled back, looking at my hand. "My magic doesn't work on you. Why isn't it working?"

"Like no tomorrow," I reminded him.

"How?"

"We've got one hour. You really want to waste it on questions?"

"You're using your magic, aren't you?"

I grinned at him. "I have no magic. Nor do you. Do you want to fuck me or not?" I hesitated. "I mean…we don't have to do this now if you're not ready."

The glow in his eyes changed in one blink, turning into those of a beast with ravenous hunger. His hands were behind my back in an instant and the clip to my bra came undone before it was flung across the room. I followed the path of the fabric, but slammed my eyes shut when warm kisses swept over my breasts, and I moaned his name loudly. His tongue rubbed around my nipple, sending a tendril of arousal downwards to tighten the ache of my clit. It throbbed painfully, and even more so when Ben finally granted me access to dip my hand into his boxer shorts and grab his hardened shaft.

Ben lifted his head and hovered his mouth near mine, and moaned my name, tightening a grip at the root of my hair on either side of my head. He went for a kiss that was so deep the passion burned my stomach. I pushed him away, kneeling in front of him and tugged down his boxer shorts, taking the impressive length of him in my mouth. Ben roared loudly, his chest heaving, and as I looked up, I could see the throb of his pounding heart beneath his skin.

He steadied, shoving his hand against the wall so the grit between the stone crumbled.

When our eyes met, I saw his feral need; wild and uncontrollable. I had awoken the beast beneath the calm exterior, and I couldn't wait for him to obliterate me into shattered pieces.

He crouched suddenly, picking me up and dumping me, oh-so-not-gently, onto the bed.

"You're mine," he growled. "Forever." His touch was passionate, brutal and a sweet pleasure all at once. And I wanted more of it. Faster. Sooner.

He covered my body like a lunar eclipse, yet my soul had never shone so brightly. His hands swept all over me, down and around my hips and up again, tracing the curves of my hips, my breast and around my neck. His naked body shaped alongside mine and he was trembling with excitement. Excitement of being with me. Touching me. Like a worshipped queen. Someone he had waited a lifetime to find. Someone to save him from himself; the abomination he thought he was. And in his arms was the only place I felt loved and safe. It was the only place I didn't feel like a traitor.

He ripped my lace knickers apart. "Sorry, I'll buy you new ones," he barely breathed as he ravished my mouth, twirling his tongue around mine. Supporting himself onto his forearms, he pushed my knees apart with his and settled between my legs. "Are you sure about this?" he groaned. "I'm from enemy territory."

"You are my world." I moaned as his kisses trailed down my neck, nipping gently at my skin. "Am I the one who you want to lose your virginity to?"

"I lose nothing and gain everything. I haven't been more sure about anything in my life. I want to be inside you." His hand pushed further down my skin and over my apex. "You're so wet," he moaned as he pushed two of his fingers into me. "You are so ready to take the whole of me."

"Then shut your damn mouth and pleasure me, King Blackbone."

It finally happened. He grabbed one hand around his cock and pushed it inside me.

He was inside me!

An extension of me. Truly one and the same. One soul. Joined by feral love and passion.

Blood abandoned my head.

"So wet. So warm. Such perfect fit," he moaned at each thrust, identifying new sensations. "My perfect match. You're mine," he crooned with the possessiveness of a mate.

I had no brain capacity to answer and only relished the smooth skin and hard thrusts that filled me with *him*. My blood overheated and sweat beaded on my chest.

"Mine!" he roared once more, as if he was threatening Zayd or any man who dared challenge that fact.

I ran my hands along his pectorals, pushing my palms down his ripped abs like a rolling wave over an unforgiving ocean and finally brought them behind his back to cup his buttocks. I let my hand bob with the movements of his thrust, which had become harder, hungrier. We had an hour, and I feared he wouldn't last that long doing this. I circled my legs around him, pressing my locked feet to help him settle deeper inside me. He roared again as if a tad bit more of his self-restraint was slipping.

"Don't undo me yet, love," he growled, panting at the top of my head as he slammed into me.

Wrestling him to his back, I folded my legs on either side of him, lacing my fingers in his, and used his crooked arms against the bed as support to lift myself up and ease down on him, again and again. I rode him as hard and fast as I could, the tension of my own lust building up, tightening painfully. I wanted him with all I had. Wanted his pleasure and wanted him to feel my pleasure. He was staring at my bouncing breasts, but his gaze snapped up and focused into my eyes when I lowered my shield to let him into my emotional pockets; letting him feel how aroused I was from his doing. I was locked into a madness; a state I wanted to be my entrapment forever. The burn of release grew closer.

"Fuck!" he cursed, not prepared for the emotions that slammed into him through our soul bond.

He frowned as if it was painful holding himself together and not shattering into pieces. His chest heaved from drawing breaths like the first one after breaking surface from almost drowning, like I was that air he needed. "This won't work. I get too close, too fast." He pushed me off him, pinning his arms against my back to press my front against the mattress. He twirled around on his knees to kneel over the back of my kneecaps, clamped his large palm over my hips and pulled me up towards him, stabbing into me from behind. With each thrust, he grunted as if it hadn't been a well thought out plan. *"This damned gorgeous body…it'll be my undoing."*

"I heard that."

"You were meant to. It's your fault I'm weakened to my knees. Literally."

"How dare you cuss me when you're in this position?" I shoved my arse backwards, making him take me deeper.

He roared.

I did it repeatedly, and he urged me to stop; to slow down.

"You know how you say I'm always mischievous."

"Yes?"

"When you say I can't do something, I'll prove you wrong?"

"Yes?"

I turned around and flashed him a smile, to which he looked truly terrified, before I gave him my all. I pushed back so hard, and repeatedly, he stood no chance of keeping himself together.

"No, no, no. Stop! I can't focus. I'm going to cum. Slow."

I didn't. I wanted him. More of him. I wanted to hear him roar that deep, dark tone of pure satisfaction. He slammed at me harder, faster, and faster, as if the motion couldn't be stopped now. The die was cast, and the lust spun out of control. And then it broke free; the roar of the untamed beast that filled the room.

I came apart. A violent shudder tore through my body. I erupted with him, whimpering out my climax, arching my back and pushing down my shoulders as the pleasure hit in throbbing waves that crashed against my sanity. He collapsed onto my back and my arms couldn't hold us up. Still inside me, he lay still, panting into the curve of my neck with small echoes of his mighty roar. A ripple through time that could never be revoked. The wheel of time had turned, the future had been altered, our love had been chiselled into the very stone of this world's foundation.

Once my breath had settled, I turned so that our fronts were close to one another, and our lips met for a sensual caress of the powerful eruption. Then Ben stroked my hair and only watched me in silence, as if everything in life had been set back onto the course the world should always have been on.

"I don't have sympathy, but I have gained some understanding now," he whispered hoarsely.

I looked at him quizzically, stroking over his pectorals that I loved touching. "Of what?"

"Of Zayd. I would rip apart this world if that made it possible for me to keep you. The poor bastard must have been heartbroken when you left him. I know it would destroy me."

I averted my gaze from his and stared at his pectoral where I had my hand. "I'm not good at goodbyes."

"I hope you'll never need to say it to me. After having had a taste of that, you can be sure I'll never let you go. Because making love to you was the best experience I've ever had."

I smirked. "Great. Thanks." I tapped at his pectoral with an air of urgency. "Now I must dash. I mustn't be late for Murben's training." I teased, starting to get out of bed, but didn't get far as a muscular arm wrapped around me.

"Oh no, you won't. I've heard that it's customary to spend some time cuddling afterwards before you leave."

"I'm sure the king doesn't have time for such triviality."

"Oh, yes, he has." He flicked his wrist to look at his watch. "I might even have time for another attempt at this."

"Attempt? You were perfect."

"Yes, no arguing there, but with practice, I could get more perfect, for longer."

"Awe, you'd do anything for me, wouldn't you? I got you wrapped around my little finger so tightly I think I could almost make you sit, lie and roll around like my other pets."

He chuckled. "Although, if you think about it. I've *already* got you to sit, lie and roll around. The sitting, being particularly enjoyable." He winked.

"You're terribly…king-like."

I sat up and honed my gazes in on where my clothes had ended up before collecting them off the floor, getting new knickers that weren't torn to ribbons. Ben tipped onto his back and folded his arms under his head, watching me dress from the bed.

"I like the striptease better than the dress tease."

"Ripping my clothes off and apart doesn't count as a tease, but an instant gratification."

"Kings aren't known for being patient. Which brings me to my next point. When will you be back from the flight practice so we can do that again?"

"I should have specified that it was a one-off occurrence." I relaxed my magic nerve and gestured towards him. "You should have your magic back now."

Black essence oozed out of his hand, and I'd have thought he was only testing it if it weren't for the angry frown on his face.

"Something bothering you, my king?" I asked, tying the laces of my boots to my knees.

"One-off! What fresh poison is this? That's torture."

Having finished dressing in my flight leathers, whose leather was tougher than the combat leathers, I kissed him quickly on the cheek. "See it as practice for the torture classes in year three." I tore away from seeing his tempting naked body, feeling equally affected by the same torture, and left the room to find Murben.

I found him leaning against a tree at the end of the field with his ankles locked and his hands inside his pockets. He looked bored to have been waiting, but he'd never tell me that out loud.

When I was close enough, he pointed a thumb over his shoulder and into the woods. "I saw a boulder in a clearing twenty minutes west. Let's go."

I fell into step beside him, observing his serene chocolate-brown face. "And what plans do you have for this boulder?"

He didn't look my way much as he was scanning our surroundings. "I want to see your landings."

That sounded nerve-wracking…and painful. "You want me to take flight from on top of a boulder?"

He held a branch away from the path and gestured for me to pass. "No. I want you to glide and land."

I twisted back and waited for him to catch up with me. "Only glide and land?"

"Yep. Glide and land on your feet. And I want you to test both wings to see if there is any difference."

I stared up at the boulder as we arrived beneath it. It seemed a feature piece of the clearing with a view of the blue sky. Most of its top was covered in light-green moss and it smelt dank, so it was probably slippery. Thankfully, there also seemed to be a thick layer of grass around it – crash padding. *Lucky me.* "And how do I get up onto it?"

"Climb, fly, be dragged up there, your choice."

"You couldn't have brought a ladder?"

Murben crossed his arms over his chest, and I turned to look for grips or outcrops I could use to climb the damned rock. "Or a rope with a grapple hook," I muttered.

Once I finally got up onto the boulder, I looked around at the silver birch and pine trees surrounding us. "The trees are too close."

"Any other observations that feed your reluctance, Cadet Coraly?"

"Yes. The clearing is too small."

"I believe those two parameters are the same issue."

"Yes. Because *it is* the problem."

"You have padded flight leathers on. Come on! Get going!"

I twitched my back from side to side to flick open my white wings before backing up on the boulder to the opposite edge from which I was going to launch myself off.

"What are you doing now, Cadet Coraly?"

"I'm making space for a running jump. Is that allowed, Bodyguard Murben?"

"That's fine. Just start."

I cocked my head. "I don't know if I've ever actually heard what your first name is."

"It's Jonathan. Now, go!"

"Jonathan. That's a lovely name. It suits you, Johnny. Johnny the brown teddy bear."

"Cadet Coraly?"

"Yes?"

"You're stalling."

"Tell me you're my teddy bear and I'll be good."

He looked up at me for a moment, squinting at the brightness of the sky, "I'm your teddy bear."

I smiled and was about to sprint when I stopped. "Ben told you to obey my every command, didn't he?"

"He did."

"Overprotective prick."

"I heard that. Put your shield back up." Ben told me through the bond.

"Well, sorry, but you are overbearing sometimes."

"Like when I'm on top of you…thrusting."

"I'm at training. You're distracting me."

"Okay, but tell Murben I want you home in one piece."

"Dead or alive piece?"

He only grunted at that.

I poked my head around the edge of the boulder where Murben was waiting for me to perform my suicidal acrobatics. "Ben says he wants me back in one alive piece."

"I had planned that, too. Now glide and land."

Right, better get this painful experience over and done with. Wings angled upwards, feet firmly on the stone, bent knees and arms at the ready, I darted for the edge and jumped, holding my wings steady so they wouldn't fold along my body with the gravitational force that pulled me towards the ground.

I passed the clearing and slammed straight into a tree and tumbled down the branches. What made the embarrassment worse was that Murben was below, catching me before I hit ground.

I fought to get out of his arms and onto my own feet. "I swear that tree wasn't there when I jumped!"

"I saw it move, my queen," Murben said with a smirk on his lips.

I glowered at him. "Although it moves less than Ben. Why is he staying here in the White Wing Territory and risking his life every day? Why does he even bother with someone like me? And why can't he tell me about what is going on in the north and about all his secrets? Can you explain to me why he's so bloody stubborn?"

"Because he's the king."

"As if that explains it."

"It does." Murben pointed to the top of the boulder to indicate he wanted me to go again.

"I thought you were on my side." I stomped back towards the boulder.

"Nope. I'll never be able to side with you against my king. But I like you, though."

I brushed leaves off my flight leathers before I began climbing up the boulder. "I guess that's something, and more than the commander."

"Yep. Although you warmed him up pretty good after your gift. It was very thoughtful."

"He told you about it?"

"Yes. He showed me the portrait of his girls. His spirit has lifted significantly since then and every time he takes it out of his pocket to look at it. A realistic painting like that can only have been done by a great artist and must have set your purse back by a lot."

I wouldn't know. Ben had paid for it.

"Has he told all the others about it, too?"

"I don't know. Are we learning the art of gossiping today or are you actually going to attempt to glide and land once more?"

"Do I really have a choice?"

"Nope. Turn your wings even more upwards like this." He angled his enormous black wings above his head. "Beat them at the same time as you sprint and then take off."

I did as instructed a few more times and an additional few more times with my black wings. Each time enduring that sandpaper rasping feeling against my flesh, as I switched them inside my back and brought the other pair out. Whatever I tried, I seemed to either fall flat on my face or hit into a tree trunk. The bark had frayed my black flight leathers, and the branches had scratched my face and hands, and my ribs had been beaten badly once or twice, but other than that, there were no broken bones or deep flesh wounds. Still hurt like fuck, though.

"Let's try another tactic. No use of a boulder this time."

"What? No! I can't do it from a flat surface, the wings are too heavy."

"I think you only believe so because you've never thought that you could do it. We're changing that perception starting right now. Do it."

"Fine."

"Fine?" Murben lifted an eyebrow.

"I don't have any weapons on me to stab you with, Murben! What do I do?"

"Let's see if you can just lift off the ground a few centimetres by flapping your wings."

I beat them in the air, feeling victorious when I could get them synchronised to flap at the same time. But Murben didn't seem as pleased as I felt, considering his dark frown.

"What in the world…are you doing…with your arms?"

"I'm preparing for take-off."

"The balance is in your wings, not gained from flapping your arms about like an idiot."

I relaxed my wings to my sides and put my hands on my hips. "Are you supposed to call your queen an idiot?"

"Absolutely not. But you're not yet my queen."

"So only when it suits you, you call me that?"

"Yep. That's the way the world works. Marry him if you want it to change."

"If this whole bodyguard thing doesn't work out for you, you can always become a wedding planner," I snorted.

"And if you fail and don't go on the Spirits' Trek, I'd propose that you don't transfer to the Air Force unit."

"They'd be lucky to have me."

"Oh, I'm sure Camp Leader Seon Nar will be more than pleased to carry on torturing you in my stead, having stolen the attention of General Denor; her planned future husband."

"What? She likes General Denor?"

"Wasn't that obvious?"

"Look at us, Johnny, gossiping and giving each other advice for the future. People could think we're friends."

He only grinned and pointed toward the top of the boulder. "If you can learn how to angle your wings, we can move on to the next lesson on how to ascend and bank sharply."

I practised a few more jumps before he called it quits to grab a bite to eat and escorted me back to the military building. I practically dragged myself into my dorm room, limping from a hit to my thigh.

Ben had sourced new wardrobe doors and a new desk chair, and was sitting by the desk writing letters as I walked in.

"My muscles are aching all over."

Ben turned his head to scan for my injuries; his gaze darting all around my body. "Understand why Murben is my bodyguard yet?"

I was in too much agony to banter or even glower at him and only held up a rude finger towards the king.

40

Neville was the camp leader on duty and delivered her characteristically frank and unedited gruesomeness-report during war updates. Because of her short blonde hair, I could tell she had fresh cuts running above her ear on her left side, which were ugly enough to leave scars. She spoke about a few raids occurring by the iron mines, and their frequency and hostility were getting worse. The black-wings hadn't accepted responsibility, saying it must have been rogue rebels in the area.

"I think it's more than a few raids. Harvey seems unsettled this week," Kate whispered.

"I don't think it's the black-wings' doing. Not officially, anyway. Ben wouldn't have ordered the raids," I said, and looked at Zoe, who seemed pale. "What do you think, Zoe?"

"I don't know, honey," she answered quickly, and turned forwards to listen to Neville.

"Whatever it is, it's far away from the Bensguard Outpost. The Emendroth Outpost would have to deal with it before we do," I told Kate, and Maz nodded in agreement from her side.

Camp Leader Neville dismissed us with fifteen minutes to spare. Her information always went faster than the other camp leaders'. She was efficient, I'll give her that.

When we stepped out of the assembly hall, I saw a yellow uniform standing out among all the blacks.

"What is my brother doing here on the floor with the commoners?" I joked, exchanging a look with Emroyce who was talking to Kenyard to my right.

Harvey nodded at me for attention, so I excused myself and told Zoe I'd join her in the sparring hall in a moment.

When I arrived at his side, Harvey didn't acknowledge my vibrantly enchanting personality and was back to his stone-cold focus on being a Camp Master and Captain. I guessed he only gave the luxury of his warmth and caring behaviour during the holidays.

"I have noticed that Kate is falling behind in her magic practice and…" he said, hesitating, pulling me by my arm to a quieter spot. "Captain La Roy is giving her more attention than normal. Could you…help Kate. Take some time off La Roy's hands?"

"It depends." His stare bore into me, but I didn't back down. "When are you going to ask her out?" I asked bluntly. "I'll not ruin her chances with Captain La Roy if you never plan to ask the poor girl out. She has been waiting for almost a decade."

He was twisting in his skin, clearly uncomfortable with asking me this personal favour when his demeanour always pushed him to be professional. "I don't know." He didn't seem frustrated with me, only unsure of how to proceed.

"Then you can offer to train her yourself. Or ask Zayd."

He paused his reply as cadets passed us before leaning closer. "He's a camp leader and very busy."

He wasn't focusing on me, so I demanded his eye-contact, shifting my weight to be face-to-face. "And you don't think I'm busy trying to control a king?"

"Controlling?" he snorted.

A layer of my patience peeled off. "Fucking ask her out, or I'll ask Cadet Ashton Hall to possess you and help you along."

Fear crept into his eyes then. "You of everyone should know what people like General Denor could do to destroy you by harming those you love. King Blackbone, Zayd and I lived through torment the month Denor held you captive, not knowing if you'd return to us alive. Denor has no interest in breaking King Blackbone, he's out for us, so you can imagine what the general could do if he found out how I feel about Kate."

"You're such a cowering donkey!" Spirits I loved my brother, but most of the time, he was so stubborn it made me want to scream. "What difference does it make if you lose her to him or the challenges, or even in the war afterwards? At least gamble on a happily ever after rather than giving it up to Captain La Roy."

He pinned his lips tight and there was a second's flicker in his eyes as if he was thinking about it. "I'd rather her live happily with Captain La Roy than being tortured to death because she chose me."

I pressed my fingers against my temples as if I could physically hold back my irritation. "Then I have led the cowering donkey full circle. There is really no point in me interfering in Kate's schedule. Let her train with Captain La Roy. I don't have time for this. *I'm* still fighting for the one I love despite that he's the king from enemy territory that is soul bound to me and whom I could imagine each and every one of the cadets here would love to have a shot at killing."

"Can you at least tell her to be careful?"

"I'm sure Maz can relay the warning…or write her a letter or something. You know Kate, if you send her messages through someone else, she'll retaliate causing you tenfold of misery."

A smile curved his mouth, and he nodded before he turned away from me, disappearing between cadets.

Among the cadet-packed corridor that smelt of leather and sweat, I noticed Ben sneaking out the front of the building, even though the dark clouds in the sky had rolled in bringing thunder, and the lightning sporadically ripped through the sky towards the ground. He was up to something, delivering his letters. Maybe I was the fool, and not my brother, trusting a man with more layers of secrets than an onion. I shook my head to clear it. It was important that I trusted him, or I'd go mad.

Zayd exited the Admissions Office to my right and saw me. Instantly, he pulled an easy, uncomplicated smile. "Come on, Angie, let's get to combat practice."

I asked him about the iron mine raids on the way, but he didn't have much more information than Neville had told us, and he didn't seem worried about them as they were so far away from our outpost. He told me that Camp Leader Ward had seen nothing suspicious on his patrols, either.

We arrived at the sparring hall, and he didn't dismiss me from his side as we ventured deeper inside. Dim light shone through the window and onto the mat Zayd normally used for lecturing and demonstrations like a glorifying spotlight. On our way there, I looked over my shoulder and grunted seeing Ben walking into the sparring hall with Tomason tailing him. He walked across the hall with such authority in his step it seemed that the air itself parted to bow for him.

Desire flared in my chest. Clearly, I couldn't shut down the attraction when I wanted to.

They didn't speak before they broke up and Tomason went to watch Brian and Winter train at the far end.

"Don't worry," Zayd whispered to me. "I'll give him a hard time for it."

"No!" I breathed, but Zayd only winked in response before he took up his spot in the middle of the demonstration mat.

What the heck had he planned to do? It wasn't safe to irritate a king who possessed death magic.

Ben pushed through the crowd of cadets, as if they were nothing but muddy water rippling to his sides and stood behind my back, so close our arms brushed. I threw a glance over my shoulder but didn't lift it to his face as my cheeks already burned at seeing his firm arse in the black leather trousers and at eye-level I saw the golden crown emblem of his rank on the shoulder of his t-shirt. Other female cadets seemed to have noticed the same and were staring at him as if hoping for a marital proposal to secure a royal title. "Eyes forwards, cadets," I hissed to the people closest to us, making Ben smirk in silence as he too focused his eyes forwards.

"Listen up, cadets!" Zayd shouted. "Yesterday, I saw a few good moves but even more of them which we need to build on to improve your technique. I've decided we need to start with the basics, which means we'll have to go through the curriculum quicker. That also means you're going to get a lot of homework, so that everyone has time to get up to the same level and stand a better chance at the challenges, especially towards the end of the month. We'll start with parry, as I saw many yesterday who were just punching into raised hands, which won't happen on the real battlefield. To show how a block should look, please..." he looked out over the crowd of cadets. "King Blackbone, can you volunteer to help in the demonstration?"

Shit! No! What is he doing?

Ben pushed past me and strode up onto the mat to face Zayd.

"What we're going to do," Zayd said, glancing around at the cadets. "Is that first I'll launch a strike at King Blackbone and you can observe his technique at blocking as I expect he has been trained by the best, and then he'll come at me and I can show you the moves slowly whilst I describe how you need to keep your arms up to protect as much of yourself as possible." He waved his hands in the air to help illustrate his instructions before he returned his gaze to Ben and began rolling up his sleeves. "Are you ready?"

Ben grunted, watching Zayd's charades with utter boredom. "I don't normally block in a fight. I attack, but sure. I'll gladly do defence today since I'm sore from having *played* with Cadet Coraly last night." Ben flashed Zayd a cheeky grin, leaving no doubt about what he was referring to.

Tense on the sideline, I was trembling, the heat from my adrenaline rushing up and down my insides. *Please don't do anything stupid, Zayd!*

Zayd's eyes turned incensed, and he came at Ben in a full-blown attack, jabbing out his fist towards Ben's face. As Ben held one hand in his pocket, he purely used his right forearm to swipe Zayd's strike away just at the right moment, causing him to stumble past him to his right.

Zayd straightened and walked back to his starting position. "As you guys saw, he swiped his forearm to deflect a direct threat," he had a growl to his voice. "Now, King Blackbone can launch a strike, and I'll show you another method." Zayd beckoned with his hand for Ben to come at him.

Ben took two long strides, brought his arm back and like a battering ram slammed through any defence Zayd had tried to put up, punching him straight over his nose. I heard the crack of bone. Zayd stumbled backwards, landing on his arse. The downpour of blood from his nose quickly covered his hands and the chest of his navy-blue uniform.

Ben walked up to him and folded double, leaning over Zayd to inspect the injury. "Your brain seems to be leaking through your nose. Do you want me to take over your training, *too?"* he asked, smirking.

"No. Go practise in your pairs, so I can get the bleeding to stop." He waved at the cadets to go to their mats.

"Okay," Ben chirped and turned to grin at me. "Let's see what you've got."

My rage boiled inside me at this point. *"Why did you do that to Zayd?"* I stalked over the mat to get to him.

"He was fighting worse than a demon who swings hard without thinking or aiming."

"Spirits!" I inspected Zayd, who so willingly let me tip his head up and care for him. "I should take you to the infirmary so that Camp Leader Mewer can look at this. Your nose might be…probably is…broken…badly." It was angled sideways like a crescent moon and the skin was cut just below the bridge.

"Yeah. It does sting a bit." His eyes were watery, but he complained less than he probably should considering the severity of the damage.

I pulled an arm around him to help him up and threw another angry stare at Ben.

"What?" Ben scoffed. *"Are you surprised? Did you really think I was going to let him get away with striking me in front of all the cadets?"*

"Arsehole!"

Dizzily, Zayd swayed a few steps, so I put my hand on his chest to steady him. He put his hand over mine that rested on his heart, staring into my eyes lovingly; the promise of undying love speaking louder than any words he could say. There was a shine to his eyes, as if he was memorising a precious moment. A soft smile of affection hid beneath the fresh blood that still poured from his nose.

"If I knew you were going to coddle like that, I'd have let him strike me." Ben grunted.

Yeah, maybe this hadn't been such a great idea, as Zayd seemed to read more from it than what it was.

"Shut up, Ben! I can't believe you punched him like this."

"He wasn't focused. Would you have preferred if I'd riled him up by telling him how he must be kicking himself for having lost you? Especially considering the awesome sex that undoes a man. How else could I make it clear to him that I'd do anything to hold on to it? Punching his face included."

"Don't be so cocky, or I'll make sure it was a one-off event."

"You wouldn't dare punish me by abstaining sex."

"Try me."

"Maybe I call you out on your bluff. See how long you can keep away."

The infuriating resolve in his voice sent heat rushing up my neck. I forced myself to cool the frustration that coiled deep in my gut. If I didn't deliver my punch with a levelled voice, he'd marvel in his victory.

"Nah, it wasn't that good," I lied. It had been otherworldly.

He didn't have a comeback for that and Zayd was making the most of me holding him and helping him to the infirmary.

Even Mewer cussed as he saw the injury and gestured for Zayd to take a seat on one of the available beds. "What did you do? Fly straight into a tree?"

Nope. I knew how that felt, and this looked worse.

"Combat training," Zayd muttered.

"Yes. The cadets are supposed to come to me looking like this, but in all my years here, I've never seen this on a camp leader."

"I like breaking records," Zayd hissed, as Mewer cleaned his nose with an alcohol-drenched cloth.

"Well, I think that it's King Blackbone who has broken all the records, literally," Mewer added, glaring at me.

I glowered back at him, nervously playing with my fingers over the hilt of my dagger. "What are you looking at me for? I'm here taking care of Zayd."

Mewer focused on carefully dabbing at Zayd's nose. "Coraly, couldn't you control King Blackbone better, so this doesn't happen to good people?"

"What? Zayd was the one challenging him. I say he has himself to blame for this one."

"He didn't have to strike so hard," Zayd objected and hissed from the sting of alcohol to his wound. "It was only a demonstration."

His blatant lie made me want to punch his nose and add to his pain. "It was a show-off of strength, and you know it."

When Mewer had cleaned Zayd's nose of the blood, he poked at it gently. "I can probably heal most of it and tape it up, so you don't need stitches. The scarring will be minimal that way."

I crossed my arms over my chest but immediately regretted it, seeing the blood covering my sleeves, and the waft of its tangy smell made me want to shower. "I say, leave a scar as a reminder of his stupidity right on his nose. Perhaps he'll think twice before he picks a fight with the king again."

"I'm the one in pain and bleeding here. Maybe you can pick my side this time? You know I'd happily bleed for you, so you could cut me some slack."

I roared out in frustration and turned on my heels to walk away. "Happy bleeding!"

With Zayd's blood covering my hands and having ran down my forearms, I rushed to my room to shower and get into a clean uniform. As I finished brushing my hair, there were frantic knocks on the door. I had barely opened it before a parade of women carrying paper bags pushed into my room with their mouths all in thin serious lines.

"We brought lunch," Kate muttered still wearing her combat uniform, and hesitating in her step, looking at the beds which were pushed together. "Whatever," she just muttered and crawled up onto them, unpacking her lunch.

"I brought yours," Zoe said, sitting down on the desk chair wearing her casual clothes; a purple tunic and black trousers.

In flight leathers, indicating she had just returned from survival in the woods practice, Valentina jumped up to sit on top of the desk, dangling her feet freely. Lastly, Fern moved daintily across the room in her burgundy infirmary uniform and sat down at the edge of the bed. "I can't stay long. I'm only taking a break from work for lunch," she said, as she placed her salad box on the bedside table.

"Okay," I drawled. "Is this some sort of intervention because Ben punched Zayd?"

"No," Kate spat. "This is a rant meeting." She leaned against the wall and opened the lid to her salad, the smell of tuna wafting out.

I guess Harvey has made no advances then.

Zoe handed me a salad box and a bottle of water, and I sat down next to Fern on the bed.

"If you won't ask. I'll tell you! Your brother sucks!" Kate said, pointing her fork at me before stabbing into a cube of cheese in her salad.

I turned and looked at her. "I don't disagree with you there. But, to add to that, he's doing it to protect you from those who want to hurt him, and he says there are many of those in the capital."

Kate looked horrified by that. "People want to hurt Harvey?"

"I think it has to do with our…his magic, being a traitor's son and a high-ranking officer. This outpost has the Special Mission Academy Programme for magically gifted, so naturally everyone wants to climb the ranks at all costs. If he earns the loyalty of most cadets, King Emille will see him as a huge threat."

"But Harvey isn't a traitor. He'd never harm anyone or be disloyal."

"Not sure you know the Harvey they know in the capital. He treats you differently than anyone else, even me."

Her cheeks blushed, and she waved with her fork towards Zoe. "Moving on."

Zoe glared at me for an instance. "Well, I made out with my twin brother because someone didn't warn me in time."

"That *someone* would be Ben, because I only found out before we went dancing. So don't you point your fork at me. How is it between you two now, then?"

"Well, in general, men are stupid, honey."

"Agreed!" everyone called out in unison.

Zoe spoke, clearly not caring that her mouth was full of tomato. "All of a sudden, he has become this noble protector, as if I'm delicate. I'll keep kicking his arse and see how long it takes for him to back off. But it's kind of nice to have a brother. Family by blood, and all that. He gave me some beautiful jewellery that covers the entire ear for the Turning of the Year. You know…because of our hearing magic."

"That's nice."

"Yes, it's nice, but I want a real man's man. Someone brutal and strong. Perhaps you can ask King Blackbone if he has any friends who he can hook me up with?"

"You want a black-wing?"

"Why not?"

"Okay, I'll see if he has any friends he wants to never hear from again, or maybe an enemy."

Zoe flung a tomato at me, and we all laughed.

"What about you Fern?" I asked after I had picked the tomato off the floor.

"No. I have Robin and Emroyce. That is more than enough."

Fern looked uncomfortable talking about her romantic relationships, seeming to quickly want to move the attention onto someone else. If I had known who had raped her, I'd fucking cut his balls off. She was such a gentle and lovely person and was the last one who deserved her life in ruins.

"I guess we have boyfriend problems all around. What about you, Valentina? Any boyfriend on the horizon? Or can you join in to curse men anyway?"

She hooked her legs together and swiped some purple strands away with the back of the hand she was holding her fork in. "Is it weird that I think General Denor is hot?"

"The guy who momentarily killed you?" Zoe asked, baffled.

"Yeah. So powerful. He brought me back," she defended.

"Camp Leader Seon Nar likes him, too. Would it not scare you to compete with her?" I asked.

"I wasn't going to marry the guy, just…loosen him up a bit. He kept you in a cave for a month, for Spirits' sake! He's a lunatic!"

I thought about how General Denor had helped those people during the Turning of the Year eve. There was more to him than met the eyes. Although his methods were ruthless. He didn't take no for an answer.

"And from what I hear, he's dating Angie now," she told everyone with a leer.

"Hilarious. I thought I had enough problems with men in my life. But the Spirits love tearing me a new one."

"You guys should have seen it," Kate laughed, her messy red bun ruffling against the wall. "King Blackbone punched Zayd so hard I thought we'd have to look for his nose inside his skull."

Zoe, Valentina and Fern gasped.

"Poor Zayd," Fern moaned.

I stopped drinking from my water bottle and held out my index finger, signalling with it. "No, not poor Zayd. He was stupid enough to ask Ben to volunteer and then struck first."

"Come on!" They shouted again in unison.

"I hear voices inside our room. Are you unharmed?" Ben asked.

"Kate, Zoe, Fern and Valentina are here. We're ranting about men as none of us are thrilled with the men in our lives right now. Come inside and tell us how come men are so stupid."

"I just remembered that I have something else to do. Very important king stuff. I'll come back later."

"The king of the Black Winged Territory, who has fought wars, and has killing magic, is fleeing from five small women?"

"With the wars, I planned the attacks, worked around the locations, deployed a strategy and had thousands of men backing me up. I didn't haphazardly walk into the heart of the battle to be picked apart."

"Coward!"

"Absolutely. If being king has taught me anything, it's knowing how to pick my battles. I'll leave the flowers by the door. Give me a shout down the bond when it's safe for me to return."

"Sure."

"I can imagine the mischievous smile on your face."

"And I can imagine you grunting with your arms crossed."

I waited until he had been quiet for a while before I fetched whatever he had left outside the door.

"What is it, honey?" Zoe asked.

"Ben left flowers. Or more accurately, a rose plant. That's unorthodox. I had expected a bouquet." It was beautiful, over twenty flowering roses in a clay pot. I put it down on the wide windowsill.

"A plant pot?"

"I didn't want my apology to ever die."

"Smooth. But I'm still angry with you."

"I must confess, I'm not accustomed to apologising, so it's good to know that I need to put in more effort then. What do you suggest could be sufficient? Jewellery? A new

gown? Picnic? A horse? Me devouring your vagina?"

I choked on my salad and had to swallow down half my water bottle to clear my pipes.

"It sounded like you reacted to my last proposal."

"Definitely not. Stay away from me and mind your own damn business."

"Are you okay, honey?" Zoe asked.

I pointed at my head. "Ben is grovelling."

"I swear, that man is so in love with you, he'd do just about anything for you. You should test him. Ask him to get you a light crystal, or something."

"He already gave me one for my birthday. Not charged or anything, so it can't repel evil spirits or amplify magic."

Not yet! But I'll soon make Cadet Bostee charge it for me.

Everyone gasped.

"So, what's the problem, honey?" Zoe asked.

"He won't give me the one thing I want; the answer to his secrets…and the Black Blade," I muttered. "He says he isn't responsible for the war in the north. He says there is something else up there, but he refuses to tell me what. How can I love a man who doesn't trust me with his secrets?"

Considering he had trust magic, it was a real punch in the gut of irony.

Strangely, I noticed Zoe tense up and she shovelled the last bit of her salad into her mouth as she stood up.

"Well, I'm going to get going. I've got patrol duty with Ward in a bit."

I was sure she knew what was going on in the north. Although, it was beyond me why she hadn't told me about it. What hold did Ben…or my brother, have on her to keep her from gossiping to her best friend?

41

Ben didn't return to our room last night, which fuelled my anger as I woke up alone in the huge bed. I dressed for combat training and headed for the sparring hall. I took the shortcut through the inner courtyard and heard Zoe shout at someone and changed my direction to join her.

"Oh, look who has come to your rescue. The mutt," Cadet Darling sneered and both her and Cadet Courtney looked me up and down as if it was a rehearsed move.

An ice-cold shiver ran through me when I saw them and recalled our last fight in the bathing chamber.

"Leave us alone, Cadet Darling," I muttered, I'm in no mood for a cat fight this morning.

"What? Haven't you read the administration lists? We meet you and King Blackbone in the first challenge, and we're allowed to use our magic. I'm looking forward stealing King Blackbone's desires from you."

"If you fucking touch him, I'll plunge a black blade into your heart." I still had the one General Denor had given me tucked into my boot – and I was one snap of sanity away from using it.

She looked a bit taken aback by the threat, but she soon found her footing. Zoe had, however, had enough and took a step towards her with a raised fist. Courtney intercepted, grabbing Zoe by the throat, clenching hard, her nails pushing into Zoe's skin.

"You attacked, and I'm allowed to defend myself," she sneered, and the icy-blue tone under Zoe's skin climbed up the veins towards her chin.

I froze with fear. She was going to kill my best friend.

A dark shadow fell over us and before I had time to react, Ben hooked Courtney's throat between his thumb and fingers, and he lifted her off the ground so that she lost her grip on Zoe.

"Why are we grabbing each other by the throats today, Cadet

Courtney?" Ben hissed at her, who gasped, clawing at his hand.

Black death magic grew from his hand into her veins and climbed up her face, reaching for her eyes.

"No, Ben! Let her go!" I screamed.

If Ben killed someone, who was defending herself, he would earn more lashes as a minimum.

Ben put her down on the ground. The black essence receded, but he didn't let go of her throat. "Be thankful that Cadet Coraly has a big heart. Next time you threaten her or Agent Hammerton, I won't listen to her words of mercy. Have I made myself clear?"

Cadet Courtney didn't acknowledge his warning, and his jaw tightened.

"She can't say anything or move because of your hand," I hissed at Ben.

Ben removed his hand and Courtney squeezed out a 'yes' before she scurried away with Cadet Darling's hand around her shoulders.

"That was awesome," Zoe stammered, as her teeth chattered from Cadet Courtney's ice touch.

"Are you okay?" I asked her.

"Yeah, honey, just my pride that's hurt. I need to go to work. I'll see you later."

She left, and I crossed my arms to shield myself from Ben. "So, you protect all damsels in distress now, not solely me?"

"Zoe is one of us."

My anger grew, but I had to remember that we were in the open in the courtyard where everyone could see us. *"Us? Us, is a word hanging in the balance. Where did you sleep last night? With Camp Leader Tomason?"*

The prick smirked. *"You're jealous!"*

"I'm not. Just curious, as you didn't come home last night."

"You never invited me back. I waited."

"That didn't answer my question."

"I stayed with Murben and Davis."

"You slept on the floor?"

"Spirits no. Davis did."

I rolled my eyes at him and walked to the sparring hall without checking whether he was following me. Zayd had rolled out the weapon racks and placed them right by the doors. Great. Blades. I could count on some cuts today, then.

Seeing the huge tape over Zayd's nose made me cringe. The others would surely think it made him look weak. I gathered around the mat with the other cadets and smiled at him as his glance swept over me.

"As some of you know," he said, his voice nasal, "I've put up lists for your first matches on the Administrations Office announcement board."

"So, am I forgiven yet?" Ben asked from behind me.

"I want a horse."

"What colour?"

"Shut up and listen to the lesson."

"I had this lesson when I was eight years old."

"You can go around the mat to watch from the other side, so that I can focus on Zayd. We're not joined by the hip."

"No, we're joined by the soul." He shoved his fingers into my side to tickle me and I yelped.

Everyone turned our way.

Ben grunted and cleared his throat, not having known how ticklish I was.

"Good," Zayd said, looking at Ben. "I thought you'd worry about volunteering again, King Blackbone. You should have more than enough experience with a sword."

Ben straightened and looked at Zayd, who was the same height as he when Zayd stood on the mat. "Why would I be worried? You're the one with a broken nose."

Zayd gestured for the mat to invite Ben up. Ben shrugged his shoulders, but his eyes gleamed as he walked around me and up onto the mat. "Glad if I can be of help. Do I get to have a sword for this?"

"Cadet Hillip! Fetch King Blackbone a sword."

Cadet Hillip and his teammate Rebecca Donally – the Jealous Team according to Emroyce because Cadet Donally was infatuated with Zayd. Her hateful stares from across the mat clearly told me I was in her way. But they were aimed at me in vain, as it wasn't really up to me who Zayd loved. Zayd had never been into red-heads, and I knew Zayd found her arrogant and spoilt, letting Cadet Hillip do all the hard lifting in their challenges. I surely hated her after she had declared that she respected my pet pig more than she respected me.

Cadet Hillip hurried across the hall to retrieve a sword from the weapons rack and returned with one of the biggest swords there was in the rack that had the bulkiest handle. On top of it, he added weight to it by turning the crafted iron hilt into solid gold with his magic. The sword was meant to be wielded using a two-handed grip. He probably thought that Ben would find it hard to use, but Ben simply gripped it and launched some test strikes in the air with a one-handed grip, as if the sword weighed nothing. I saw a few of the cadets' mouths drop as they stood next to me.

"Nice work, Cadet Hillip," Ben praised, inspecting the gold. "If you ever need another job after you graduate, let me know." Then Ben turned to Zayd. "So, what's the lesson?"

"Let's demonstrate a beat and block sequence."

"What will that teach them?" Ben gestured for the throng of cadets with his free hand.

"To strengthen their muscles and feel the hack of the blade. Some of them have never held a sword before. Not everyone was born with a sword in their hand."

"Fine," Ben grunted, and circled around Zayd, waiting for him to strike first.

They swung a few times at each other. At every turn, the attacks became more heated. I became nervous because Zayd was wearing iron arm guards reaching up to the crook of his elbow, but Ben wasn't.

"I've taught girls with a stronger swing than you," Zayd mocked.

"Oh, I'm not giving you my all, or you'd be dead. How's your nose, by the way?"

They sped up, and it wasn't just an exercise of beating and blocking anymore. I bet Zayd had forgotten he was giving a lesson. He was whispering something to Ben that I couldn't hear. I twisted to look at Mazdon quizzically.

"You don't want to know," he answered and returned to watching them.

"What's going on?"

"Watson says you'll soon tire of me and that he knows what you like the most. Please, can I punch him again?"

I felt like slapping my hand over my face. *"No."*

"Can I tell him I think you like when you sat on me the most?"

"No."

"Not even hack off an arm and–"

"Smile and be polite!"

Ben pulled up a smile as instructed, but it made the whole matter worse, as now it just looked as though he was mocking Zayd.

I wished I could use Rebecca Donally's magic and shrink myself to a tiny size and fly away from here undetected.

Sweat coated Zayd's hairline and his eyes were tearing at the edges as if his nose was giving him grief. Ben simply focused on defence, not breaking a sweat, and smiling. Zayd changed tactics and made a few stabbing attacks that Ben blocked, although the tip of the sword had been close to his chest.

"If you think he's attacking you for real, then stop and get off the mat." I urged.

"You're worried about me?" he purred. *"No need to be. I'd beat him blindfolded."*

Okay, so maybe Cadet Donally wasn't the most arrogant one in here.

Zayd finally held up a hand to stop Ben, even though Ben wasn't attacking him, and checked his nose. He cursed below his breath as he realised blood had seeped through the tape.

"Everyone, get to a mat and practise beating and blocking until lunch. You've got a history lesson in the afternoon, and tomorrow morning, we start with the first matches." Then he left the hall with his hand over his nose.

The cadets cleared from around the mat and joined their teammates on a free mat whilst Ben strode like a cunning predator towards me.

"So, this is the first time I'll be able to size you up with the sword. Except for the ones you pushed up against my heart."

"And you don't let me play with that sword anymore."

"You might get to play with it again when you can handle it responsibly."

"You mean, when I'm not intending to kill kings with it?"

"Oh, feel free to hack away at King Emille if you like."

I shook my head at his words. "I'll just get a sword. Do you want me to get you a lighter one from the rack?"

"No, this is a fine weapon. The balance is off since Cadet Hillip added the gold, but the blade is sharp."

"Good, no reason for sharpening it in the early mornings, then."

He laughed, nodding for me to get going.

"Prick."

"I heard that."

"You were meant to."

"Miss Stone, you should be more careful about who you insult. Insulting kings could be considered treason."

"Not if you're the queen."

"Touché."

I returned with a short-sword in hand that I normally used when sparring with my father and held the blade up, ready for battle.

I beat and blocked as per the lesson specifications, but with a few sneaky moves in-between, adding both low and high blows to attempt catching him off guard.

"Not bad. Not bad at all. I might even dare to say impressive, unless it inflates your ego," he mused.

"Inflate away. It isn't as if it could get bigger than yours."

"Feisty today, are we? Anything to do with you imaging me with Rella?" he whispered into my ear after he had locked my sword in a position above my head.

"Camp Leader Tomason," I corrected. It was infuriating that he had said her first name as he otherwise always used proper titles.

He smiled as I attacked him harder, and he swapped his sword hand to fight with his left, teasing me with how easy it was for him. That riled me up even further. I gripped the sword tighter around the hilt. His smirk deepened and he deflected my strikes effortlessly, mockingly.

"Are you even taking this seriously?"

He cocked his head, the bastard making no effort to hide his amusement. "Are you?"

I bit back a growl rising in my throat. My pulse pounded in my ears, but I lunged again, faster this time, yet in the blink of an eye, he had twisted away from my attack, tapping the flat side of his blade on my shoulder.

After an hour and a half of him telling me all the things I did wrong and with my stomach churning for lunch, I angrily stomped off the mat, returning the sword to the rack and headed for the canteen. I picked up a steak pie and found Zoe sitting with the black-wings, shouting over the table at Murben.

"You're lecturing me about manners? That guy bumped into me on purpose!" She pointed at an empty spot, whoever had been there had already left.

"And if you were polite and had any sense of self-control, we wouldn't be having this conversation," Murben retaliated, looking at Davis for support.

Davis held up his hands in surrender. "Hey, she's my sister. I have to be on her side."

"Thank you, Jason," Zoe added.

Murben shook his head as if it was all madness. "Punching every cadet in the face who bumps into you isn't an appropriate response."

"It is, honey."

Murben seemed pleased with her calling him honey, but Davis just shook his head at Murben. "The use of the world 'honey' is an endearing name for those she believes are stupid."

"I don't adhere to sarcasm, hence I'll take it literally," Murben said and picked at his food.

Zoe growled out loudly, grabbed her tray and stormed off, shouting, "Good luck with taming him."

I sat down on the bench next to Murben. "What's up with her?"

"She has no self-control." Murben watched Ben sit down opposite us with admiration to his king in his eyes, like his loyalty to Ben was intertwined with his fate and as unbending as iron.

I looked at my steak pie oozing out hot steam as I dug into it with my knife. "She has never had that. What's new today?"

"Don't know. She seemed tense."

"Really?" I lifted my brows. "What gave it away?"

"Her screaming, mainly." Murben looked at me with a flat expression.

I shoved meat into my mouth and panted as the gravy burned my tongue. "I was being sarcastic."

"I know. I was being polite."

Ben chuckled as he gathered food onto his fork.

"What's so funny?" I snapped.

"Do you want some Aloe Vera because you just got burned!" Ben mocked.

He wasn't talking about my tongue but the annoying fact that Murben never got offended or budged from being professional, so there was no chance of winning a competition of sarcastic banter with him.

"Stay out of this," I barked at him.

He chuckled even harder.

"What?" I asked.

He let go of his fork and held up his hands in surrender. "Just feels like you've been a part of this family since forever, is all."

"Well, I think Zoe is a fresh breath of air to our boring dynamic," Nesso chirped, the harmonica I had given him in hand ready to play, but I prayed to the nine Spirits he wouldn't do it in here or he'd be beaten up.

I made eye-contact with Commander Daffron sitting next to Nesso, who only gave a curt nod before focusing on his food.

When I had finished my lunch, I walked back to the dorm room with Ben following me as if everything was back to normal.

"Just so you know," I told him as I unlocked the door. "I haven't said I've invited you back in yet. I'm still mad at you."

He followed me inside anyway. "Is that so?" he sniggered, grabbing my hand and spinning me around, so I ended up with my front flat to his chest. "I say it's about time you start to trust me." He held up a black blindfold with the Bensguard Outpost golden key emblem on it.

I swallowed, and the memory of the last time I was blindfolded in the cave, surfaced.

"Which I know might be hard for you, as you don't even trust your own hearing when fighting," he added. "You must use all your senses on the battlefield, not just your eyes. When I'm done with you, you'll be able to fight battles even if blinded."

I stared at the blindfold as if it was murderous to the touch. "Why don't I just close my eyes and punch you in the face?"

"Oh, you thought the blindfold was for the battle? No, it's for you to wear in bed when I lick and kiss every little bit of you. I know you fear the tiny piece of cloth and that'll be detrimental to our future challenges if you seize up in panic when the camp leaders put it on you, so I'm going to make you love it. Make you associate it with pleasure until you beg me to put it on you again and again. Now, get naked and hop onto the bed."

My toes curled against the floor at the thought of his promise. "It will not become a rule that we'll have sexual activities every night."

"Not a rule, but it's highly recommended." He watched me undress, flashing a wolfish grin.

42

The playful, teasing Ben, from yesterday; the one who had blindfolded me and whose tongue had sent hot desire through me, was gone. This morning, he was cold, distant, his mood sharp as a blade. Black essence was rolling off him as he paced the room, muttering about how we should have fled to the Black Wing Territory, how the combat challenge was too dangerous, and how I could get seriously hurt.

I had only snorted in response, crossing my arms over the black combat leathers. "Your ego is too big," I reminded him, arching a brow. "The law doesn't care if you're a king. Your death is just as fair game as mine. Now, let's go before we're late."

Mazdon and Kate, and Murben and Davis also had a combat challenge today, and it was probably the reason my brother had come to the sparring hall to 'inspect the educational progress' of our outpost, which really meant he was shit scared that Kate would suffer.

Zayd had pulled together the smaller blue mats to create a larger squared one in the centre of the hall for the challenges, and cadets were flocking around it.

I stopped next to Emroyce and peered between the shoulders of the Archery Team, Ashton and his father, Sergeant Hall, who were up after Kate and Mazdon. Currently on the mat Cadet Oscarson from the Prank Team was in an arm lock with his face pushed onto the mat. Surprisingly, his face was under the knee belonging to Cadet Wells from the Earth Kissing Team. Cadet Wells and his teammate, Cadet Quill, were among those with less muscular builds but instead used more of their brains in the academic classes. It seemed Cadet Wells was using a taught technique rather than brute force when twisting at Cadet Oscarson's wrist. The one dagger we were allowed to use was still sheathed on his belt.

Emroyce had his long, black hair tied in a tight ponytail that draped over my shoulder as he leaned in. "This match will be a tie and must be settled on scores as Cadet Lerren used his faint breath magic to knock the 'nature whisperer' out in seconds of the previous round."

Zayd called the match. Cadet Wells won, who pushed his spectacles higher on his nose and got off Cadet Oscarson.

"When do you have your match?" I asked.

"After lunch. Which is fortunate because Kenyard likes to sleep in the mornings."

"Who are you up against?"

"The Serious Team. Cadet Seabass and Cadet Conrad."

"Uff, and who will take on Cadet 'heat you up with my eyes' Conrad?"

"That would be me, as I can move faster around him. Besides, Cadet Seabass likes to torment his opponents verbally, as his increased taste buds help little in combat, so that works out well for Kenyard who can use his magic to read his intentions from his voice, unless Cadet Seabass has enough control over his split tongue to keep it inside his mouth."

"So, if he likes to taunt people, why have you named them the Serious Team?"

"The taunts he makes aren't distasteful jokes, but more informative facts about our enemies and miseries of the world," he explained, flashing Ben an accusing look, who stood like a protective wall behind me.

I looked over my shoulder to see how Ben took the comment thrown at him, but his face was like a stone statue. I had expected his indifference, as he'd never admit his wrong doings to other men, the way he did to me.

My heart leaped as Zayd called Kate and Mazdon to the mat, but my stomach settled when their opponents were Elinor Maruto and Klint Penya. My guesses were that my brother had something to do with that match, as Cadet Penya and Cadet Maruto were referred to as the Healing Team and none of them were interested in combat. They were the kindest people I knew in this outpost, and both had only one circle of magical ability. Penya was no match for Mazdon, who was four years older, and had served a year in the Air Force before going back to the academy. Apart from that fact, and being the second sweetest man in the outpost, Maz rivalled Zayd in muscle build and could hear every step on the mat that Penya would take.

Kate was up first, and Maz prepared her by tying her wild red hair into a ponytail with a leather strap and checking that she had secured her belt tightly around her waist and that the dagger wasn't stuck in the sheath. Kate rolled her jade eyes at him. I glanced over at where my brother stood by the windows and saw him tense, reflexively putting his hand on the pommel of his sword as if he could do something to help, even though he knew very well that he could do nothing to interfere with a challenge. In the challenge, it was permitted for cadets to kill one another. King Emille would take

Harvey's head if he interfered with that rule, not accepting any further missteps from the Coraly family.

The women walked up to the middle of the mat. Cadet Maruto looked extremely uncomfortable in her black combat leathers, tugging down the jerkin and trying to twist it as if it wasn't a good fit around her slim body. She liked looking beautiful in fashionable long dresses, and like Penya, they both had velvety, black hair cascading down their backs. Her black eyes scanned the mat to avoid eye-contact with Kate, her hands trembled at her sides.

Zayd ordered the start, and Kate frowned as she focused on shaping fire into her palms. Small flames flickered to life in front of her and she was ready to throw them at Maruto. But Maruto retaliated by turning her fingers in her palm, summoning a whirlpool of water, blocking the incoming heat balls with a sizzling sound.

A fire wielder against a water bender? That was interesting.

The air between them where their magic had clashed steamed in a fight between heat and condensation.

Kate moved sideways and fired another fist of flames, but Maruto dodged her fist with a move as fluid as a river, sending a whip of water that caught Kate's hands. Maruto gathered a torrent like a tidal wave, pushing Kate across the mat, knocking her off balance. For a breath, it seemed Maruto had the upper hand but then Kate created a blazing spiral of fire around them, trapping them in raging flames.

The smoke of the fire was suffocating, and the heat forced the crowd backwards, Ben strapping his arm across my front from behind for my protection.

Maruto conjured up larger amounts of water to eat the fire that flickered and then died. Both of them were drenched and panting, as small igniting sparks sporadically sputtered in the wet air around them.

They'd get nowhere with the use of their magic. Kate pulled her dagger, and my heart pounded harder. I knew Kate was merciless, but would she really be able to kill sweet Maruto?

Kate launched for Maruto with her dagger, but Maruto flinched, holding her hands up like a dainty noble lady in complete dismay, Kate eased off on the stroke and missed skin, cutting over leather.

Penya bent over the mat to whisper with a kind voice, "Maruto, the dagger. Use your dagger."

Kate even waited for Maruto to get the hilt into her hand, and I couldn't help shaking my head as she gripped it like a cooking knife and managed to cut her own finger.

Kate dashed around Maruto and gripped one arm around her waist and brought her dagger to Maruto's throat but didn't cut. Maruto yelped, dropped her dagger to the mat, and froze in terror. The poor thing.

"Say you yield," Penya whispered to her, not caring about winning and securing a seat at the king's counsel or getting chosen for the Spirits' Trek. Unlike most greedy and egotistical cadets in this place, they only wanted to survive and eventually get stationed close to home. Unlike cadets like Floyd Gravelhorn, who'd not yield purely to keep his pride; I guessed Ben was also in that category.

"I…I…I yield," Maruto stammered in ragged breaths.

Penya rushed up onto the mat and wrapped his arm around Maruto to lead her off and kept his healing hand over her cut finger before returning to the mat for his own match with Mazdon.

None of their magic could be used as weapons, so they instantly drew their daggers, and I noticed Penya was left-handed. At the first swipe Penya made against Mazdon, he twisted to his side to avoid it. Then Maz moved closer to get behind Penya's elbow and gripped over his wrist with his free hand, putting his own blade close to Penya's neck.

"I yield," Penya said quickly and dropped his dagger to the mat.

Gravelhorn muttered under his breath at what a coward Penya was and as my attention tore his way, I saw Cadet Darling wink at Ben.

Emroyce must have seen it too, because he whispered to me, "Don't let that get you riled up."

I bloody hoped that Ben would kill her after I had taken care of Cadet Courtney in my match, but I doubted he would because she was a woman.

"Now, this is the match I came here for," Emroyce said excitedly.

"Thanks," I spat.

"Oh, I really don't want to watch your match. You can't use your magic and you're up against the Ice Queen? No thanks. I'll go to the common rooms and get a fire going. And King Blackbone against Cadet-sensual-wielding-Darling, that's just cruel on you. I hope you'll make Zayd suffer for it. But this match," he said, nodding at Murben and Davis as Zayd handed them one dagger each for the duration of the challenge. "Hated black-wings; a bodyguard to the king and a sergeant, killing allowed, against the Archery Team? Now, we're talking action."

I watched as Sergeant Hall's steps made dents into the mat from his ox-sized body. The veteran soldier's face was set grimly, clearly not finding repeating the academy's challenges entertaining. He had tied the front of his shoulder-length brown hair to the back of his head, showing more of the many battle scars that littered his face.

A tremor ran through me, wondering how many battles he must have been in during his lifetime. All I knew was that he looked angry and tired of it, probably thinking that he didn't want the same life for his son every time he was training Ashton. He scratched at the thick, brown beard that covered most of the lower part of his face. The dagger was already in his other hand, as he waited for his opponent to face him.

Ben moved behind me, and I twisted to see him crossing his arms over his chest, his eyes set on Murben, who stepped up onto the mat.

I reached out to Ben. *"Are you okay? Are you worried?"*

"I'm always worried that my servants will get hurt."

I turned back to watch Murben toss the dagger in his palm and spin it around to check its weight and balance. He flicked his thumb over the edge and tip to test the sharpness, and the more he seemed to prepare himself, the more my heart raced.

"Murben's combat skill is second only to Commander Daffron's, so unless Cadet Hall gets a lucky strike in, he should win."

"Will Murben kill Ashton's father?"

"I can't answer that. He's allowed."

I swallowed, feeling my legs shake.

Zayd started the match, and the men circled each other, both warriors by trade, each step and each move of their arms calculated.

Murben's black brows were set low, and his dark-brown eyes were completely focused on Sergeant Hall.

I held my breath for so long, so as not to distract Murben, that I became light-headed. My grip around the hilt of the dagger my father had given me clasped so hard the pattern of the runes was indented into the skin of my palm.

They attacked, tumbling into a brawl in the centre with hands raised to block stabs and fists struck out to punch at exposed areas. Murben's dark complexion made it easier to distinguish between the two when they quickly spun around each other. Each attack made my heart pound harder inside my chest.

Sergeant Hall had ten years and probably ten kilos on Murben, but Murben was fast and knew how to anticipate moves, his technique mirroring Ben's in many ways.

The match had me enthralled with fear, and my eyes hurt like they'd been scratching against sandpaper each time I blinked.

"Calm down or put up your shield," Ben growled.

"You have no right to tell me to calm down when I'm watching a match where my friend could die!" I barked.

"He's not your friend. He's a bodyguard. And if he dies, that's the Spirits' will."

"You sound like my mother. That was what she used to say. Or my brother, who apparently now has emotional blocking powers. Just like you, it seems."

"So, that was his second power that he used on me so I wouldn't kill Watson. Interesting."

"Yes, so whilst you two can easily watch people die around you, I find it hard to

watch my friends when they are in danger."

"Do not assume that I find this easy to watch. Murben has been my bodyguard since the day he turned eighteen and I was nine years old."

Murben danced around Sergeant Hall, and as Hall swung his blade at his face, Murben ducked and waited an extra second for Hall to pull his arm back before he planted his dagger in the crook of Hall's shoulder. Then he quickly pulled it out and backed off.

Sergeant Hall roared and pressed his other hand over the wound, but the ligament to the arm seemed damaged as he struggled to raise his dagger.

Murben danced around him on light feet.

Don't get cocky. Don't get cocky. Don't get cocky.

But Murben wasn't the cocky type, nor did he leer at Hall from having inflicted him pain. There was only that sense of duty in his dark-brown eyes.

I prayed to the Spirit of War that Sergeant Hall would yield, but I knew there was little hope of a war veteran surrendering before his last breath. His only weakness seemed to be the love he held for his son. What could I do to make Sergeant Hall choose to keep his life to help Ashton through the three years before graduation?

"You have that mischievous look in your eyes. Stop it," Ben warned. *"You'll suffer grave consequences if you interfere in a challenge."*

"I'm sure the general can make exceptions for his new favourite pet if I let him add to our deal."

I could feel Ben's gazes burning at the back of my head as he grunted. I didn't know what could make him more riled up than mentioning the general.

"Murben wouldn't like that you put yourself in danger for him. He's the bodyguard not you," he said with a levelled tone.

Sergeant Hall jerked out his leg, striking at the back of Murben's kneecaps, felling him to his back.

I closed my eyes and exhaled. *Please, Spirit of Life. Don't take Murben.*

Sergeant Hall placed all his weight on top of Murben and swapped his dagger over from his damaged right side to his left hand, raising the dagger high. He stabbed down. Murben anticipated the veteran would go for the jugular, so he dodged sideways, pushing at him with his elbow at the same time to tip Sergeant Hall off. Swiftly, Murben swung his leg in a high arch to lift his knees off the mat and straddled Hall's back, twisting the knife out of his left hand and holding it tightly against the side of his neck. It was such an impressive move my jaw hung wide open. The soft murmur of the onlooking cadets fell away to a complete silence.

"Yield," Murben demanded.

Sergeant Hall attempted to flip Murben off him before he realised it was pointless. Murben pressed the dagger harder into the veteran's skin, drawing blood.

"I yield," Hall muttered.

Murben got off him and walked past Zayd to hand him back the dagger before taking a stance beside Davis.

As Davis took a step towards the mat, a hearing portal formed in the air halting him, and Zoe's angry snarls threatened him not to lose before it vanished.

"Nice sisterly advice," Ben mocked.

"It's not like you have offered me any at all."

"Don't get cold feet."

I turned around to flash him my most annoyed look to see him grin at me. Shaking my head at his pun, I turned back to see Ashton and Davis standing face to face, waiting for Zayd to give them permission to start.

As soon as Zayd did, fists flew wildly in the air until both of them walked off to either end of the mat, panting for a brief break. Ashton's body suddenly became relaxed, still standing, but his head was hanging with his chin almost touching his chest. The moment after, Davis squirmed, the dagger in his hand flinging right and left uncontrollably in the air in front of him until it dropped to the floor, and so did Davis.

"Coward," Ben muttered. *"Ashton is using his possession magic."*

"No! I won't yield!" Davis shouted in vicious spasms, lying on the mat.

Davis rolled around three turns, and it was awkward to see the unnatural jerks of his body. Fist after fist, he punched himself in the face, cracking open his brow and nose until blood poured out of his nostrils.

Davis rolled around again, thrashing around on the mat. He struck out with his right hand to grab onto his dagger beside him on the mat before plunging it into his own thigh. "Get out of me!"

"Davis!" I roared and launched myself forward.

Emroyce was quick to wrap his arms around me, holding me back. "You can't interfere."

He shuffled me backwards and into Ben's arms to hold me back.

Ashton roared out in pain from his own body, as if he would have felt the same pain as Davis.

Davis pulled the dagger out of his leg and stood up, looking incredibly pissed off with Ashton who clearly was back in his own body now. Davis threw the dagger towards Ashton, who dodged it, and if Zayd hadn't leaned to the side, it would have hit him instead of the wall behind him.

"Careful, Cadet Davis," Zayd warned.

But Davis was in no mood to play anymore, and went full on warrior on Ashton, beating him to the mat, bending him into a leg lock that would soon break Ashton's leg.

"I yield!" Ashton hollered, his shameful eyes immediately seeking his father's with the look of a beaten dog.

I breathed out when their match had ended. No one died. Thank you, Spirit of Life.

Now, I only needed the Spirit of Life to carry on his good work when it came to my own match against the ice wielder, Cadet Courtney.

"Do you want to take on the Ice Queen first, or do you prefer I start?" Ben asked when we walked up to Zayd so that Ben could get a dagger.

"I'll take the first match," I told Zayd. "So, I get it over and done with. She needs a…" I looked at Cadet Courtney, as she swaggered up onto the mat with her curly silver hair and golden eyes looking smug. "Size ten body bag," I muttered to Zayd.

I pulled my dagger from my leg holster and clenched it for comfort. *"Any last piece of advice?"*

"Don't give up until the Underworld freezes over? Demons don't like the cold."

"Thank you. I meant actual useful advice. Never mind. I'll just kick her arse."

"That's also a good plan."

Zayd looked at me, but was trying to keep his face straight, as he said in a low voice. "Don't underestimate your opponent, you might misstep when gloating. Keep your dagger in a tight grip and go for the stabs at her abdomen, she finds it hard to block at the height of her elbow. Her uniform has reinforced leather above her heart, so don't even think about jabbing there. She's also good on her feet and jumping, so don't waste time swiping out with your leg. She knows her combat technique is weak, so she'll try to use her magic, so don't let her touch you or the dagger as her ice magic can travel through objects as well as flesh."

I nodded in thanks and glowered at Ben. "Now, that was solid advice I can use."

Ben grunted out loud, as I passed to square up in front of Cadet Courtney.

Zayd counted down for this match to ease me in, and I refrained from rolling my eyes, keeping them on the smirking diva in front of me, who I was sure wouldn't hesitate to kill me now when she had the chance.

I smirked right back at her because I had tricks of my own. Using incredible speed, I moved around her, and with a mighty jab, I impaled my blade into the back of her side. An ear-piercing scream rang out. A sense of satisfaction coursed through my veins.

"That was for freezing my legs into ice lollies in the bathing chambers."

She moaned and pressed her hand to her back. But she didn't curse insults at me, knowing bloody well that this was a part of the game.

Her silver locks flung forward once more when I moved around her, but she stood still as if the strike had crippled her. But I wasn't about to underestimate her. It could be an act. If she wasn't going to do something,

I planned to stay put over at my side, waiting for her to bleed out.

She squirmed awkwardly as she put her hands together, summoning ice, but then she was clearly unable to lift her hand to shoot it my way. She kneeled, palming the mat and a circle of ice built outwards from where she sat, but the layer was so thin it melted away before it reached me. Her face was the perfect portrait of frustration and fury.

After a while of staring at her knees, she sighed heavily, waving for Zayd to stop the match. "The bitch must have hit something. I can't go on."

"So, you yield?" Zayd asked.

She lifted her head, and her stare shot daggers at him. "Yes. I yield."

"Cadet Penya, could you escort Cadet Courtney to the infirmary?"

Penya nodded and fetched Courtney from the mat, leading her out with a supporting shoulder tucked under her arm.

"Luckily, the demons don't have to live with the Ice Queen, then," I said to Ben and shrugged my shoulders.

"I'll tell them to thank you for it after you've sent me there."

"Behave. And maybe I don't. Your turn to play with Cadet Darling 'Big Bosom'."

He snorted. *"It'll not be easy. I don't even know where to strike without hitting or touching any of her private areas. They seem to be all over her."*

No one could argue she was a truly stunning woman. Any man would want her even without her using her seductive magic on them. She was wearing a tight leather corset that made her breast almost pop out, and which I couldn't believe central depot had supplied. It looked more suitable for sex games in the privacy of the bedroom, with buckles and silver hoops hanging off it.

"Why don't you have a uniform garb like that?" Ben asked.

"Because it's slutty."

"Maybe for night duty in our room?"

"Focus on the match!"

With one long leg overlapping the other, Darling swayed her way towards Ben, who had placed two firm feet on the middle of the mat.

Zayd waited for her to take her stance opposite Ben but instead Cadet Darling sneaked up behind Ben and began swiping her hands along his body. She touched him, palming the skin around his neck seductively before the match had even begun. Ben didn't stand a chance by the time Zayd called the start. He was already under the thrall of seductive magic and only stared at her mindlessly.

"Are you okay?"

I didn't receive any answer, and I couldn't pound through his shield to find out what was going on at the other side. Cadet Darling cupped her hands around his face and dragged the back of her hand down his cheek, her blue eyes glistening as she toyed with him.

"Ben!" I shouted and waited. Nothing. *"King Blackbone!"*

I moved to the side to get closer to them and Darling noticed the commotion I caused, taking her eyes off Ben for a second. His hand jutted out to clamp over her throat and her veins blackened in forking rivers towards her cheekbones. She focused back on Ben, locking her eyes into his with more intensity, and followed him as his knees buckled to the mat. She leered, pressing gentle kisses to his lips as she unbuttoned his shirt and exposed his ripped chest. *My chest.*

What the fuck!

A guttural growl muttered in my throat.

Take your hands off what's mine.

Her hands were in his hair, and I saw her foul little tongue enter his mouth.

Okay. That's it. The bitch had to die.

She folded him down on his back and straddled around his abs.

I rubbed my forehead. This was so highly embarrassing. Zayd stood watching them, seeming to have no intention of stopping the public display of the black-wing king being seduced in front of the entire first-year class of this outpost. Was this Cadet Darling's goal? She seemed to have no intentions of drawing her dagger and using it.

Ben still had his hand cramped around Darling's throat, which was my only consolation, as he only needed one moment of sanity to kill her.

"Come on, Ben! Shake it off!"

Cadet Darling's hands slid down his chest, her breasts almost in his face. It made my blood boil with rage. Emroyce came to my side and circled his arm around me and folded me into his chest. "Don't do anything stupid. Don't watch if you can't handle it."

I looked around the room and found Kate and Maz on the other side with their brows deeply set with empathy.

When Darling unbuttoned Ben's trousers, Emroyce had to hold me back.

I searched Ben's red eyes, but they were void of anything I recognised.

"Ben! Snap out of it!" I screamed. *"Please!"* The voice in my head was a sob.

The shield weakened, and I received words back. *"Why? I fucking love it!"*

"You fucking love it?"

I knew Darling's magic was influencing him, but how could he say that to me? He should be stronger than this. Maybe if he truly loved me, he could have fought off these dark desires.

My heart fell, as I saw the death magic grow under Darling's skin, but it wasn't because he wanted to kill her, it was because he was aroused, and his emotions were out of control.

I rushed over to Zayd. "Camp Leader Watson, stop this!"

"I guess," he said, looking at them, "unless he yields, it's allowed…" he said, not sounding too confident.

Cadet Darling had heard my plea, and now she was rubbing her palm over the bulge of his unbuttoned trousers. "Do you want to yield, King Blackbone?"

"No," he answered firmly, but in a voice I didn't recognise.

My world shattered. I wanted to die. Ben was the good and unspoilt element of my miserable life, and now Darling had taken that away from me, too. The air in the hall suddenly felt so thick it suffocated me, drawing out the stunned gasps I barely registered as my own. I watched Ben enjoy another woman. Agony pressed against my lungs. I was frozen in my sorrow and utterly unable to breathe. Their bodies tangled together in an intimacy I couldn't tolerate no matter how fake it was. It was as if I felt the floor crumble beneath me as I watched the man I love become a stranger in an instant. My stomach twisted and burning nausea churned, threatening to erupt, and when I swallowed it had the taste of raw betrayal, heartbreak and utter devastation. I wanted to scream, cry, but it'd only make me look weak. The space in my chest filled with panic and my whole body trembled, but there was nothing I could do.

The damage is done.

I could never look upon Ben the same way as before after this. The memories of this would forever scar my mind.

43

I tore out of Emroyce's embrace, fighting tears of rage. Every fibre of my being screamed for me to act, to stop the abuse. I marched over to my brother by the windows, holding the heat of fire in my eyes. "Call the match off, or King Blackbone might kill everyone in here if he loses control of his magic."

That part could be sort of true.

I wasn't sure if Ben's magic could technically do that, but nor did I want to find out, and I'd say anything not to keep watching their display humiliate me.

"I cannot interfere," my brother said coldly. "Camp Leader Watson is judging the matches. I trust he'll stop it if he fears for the other cadets' lives."

"Thanks, brother!" I hissed and stormed for the doors that lead to the shortcut through the inner courtyard.

My legs felt wobbly, but they had to carry me until I could reach the field. I forced one foot in front of the other, my eyes stinging with tears at all Cadet Darling had destroyed. After rounding the corner of the building, I ran across the corner of the field, slamming into the rough bark of the old oak. I cried out. Heartbroken. Why hadn't Ben been strong enough to fight it? Strong enough for me? I pushed my footholds, climbing to my branch in the tree to sulk in solitude.

I knew it was lunchtime when Zayd joined me on his branch opposite mine, holding out a brown lunch bag towards me. His blue eyes were downcast, his gaze holding a hesitation over whether our friendship had ended.

I didn't accept his peace offering and crossed my arms over my chest. His shoulders slumped and each of his breaths sounded heavier than the last as if his guilt stabbed at his heart. Regret etched itself into every line of his face. Clearly, he was restless from all the shame he carried. Shame he had to bear because it was his duty, no matter that I was his ex-girlfriend that he wanted back into his life.

That didn't make it easier to forgive.

Ignoring him, I looked the other way, abruptly sitting up straight as I saw Kristine Bostee walking across the field and there were no royal guards tailing her.

Sweet. Just what I needed.

"Don't approach her. That is an order from your camp leader. If you want to blow off some steam, we can play tackle ball once the matches finish."

"Can I use my magic when I tackle your arse to the ground?"

"I don't know. There are a lot of cadets out and about today, and I'd worry about what you intend to do and who might see us."

"Never mind. I'm not on talking terms with you."

"We don't need to talk. You can just beat me up if you like. Just come and get me after you've finished fighting with King Blackbone."

"Who said there will be a fight? Who said there is anything to fight about?"

"I know you. There will be a fight."

"Which begs the question. Did you pair Ben with Cadet Darling in a match just to piss me off?"

He nervously rubbed his palm back and forth across his spiky gelled hair. "Oh uh, here comes my fight."

"Did you really think that letting Cadet Darling seduce Ben would drive me into your arms? That must make you the most stupid man at this outpost, of all outposts, in the entire world!"

"No. It wasn't my intention for Darling to get a chance to use her magic on Ben. I thought she'd be an easy match for him and that you could get your revenge on Courtney. Which I think you did pretty well. She was so embarrassed having to limp off with what looked like a minor injury to the other cadets."

"She was embarrassed? I was embarrassed! My boyfriend was making out with another woman in front of me, in front of the entire class, my brother, you!"

What Zayd also didn't know was that Ben had 'fucking liked it'.

"Boyfriend?" Zayd choked a scoff in sudden surprise.

"He was, but not anymore!" I bit off bitterly. My misery suddenly overwhelmed me, and my tears kept falling faster than I could wiped them off my face. "These are your doings."

The bastard had the nerve to look remorseful. "Angie, I'd never hurt you like that."

"Well, you did! And when my legs don't wobble so much, and my heart isn't threatening to burn a hole through my ribcage, I'll march up to my brother and tell him to revert me back to my old contract and send me on a mission far, far away. Maybe I'd be useful in the north with whatever they're battling there."

"No! No, Angie, calm down."

"Don't tell me to calm down!" I screamed at him, and he held up the lunch bag between us as a shield against my fury.

"We'll figure it out. Ben will probably be as mortified about this as you are."

"I highly doubt that."

"Please, Angie, be reasonable."

"Reasonable?" I barked.

"Okay." He held up his hands. "I recognise that was the wrong thing to say. Forgiving. Merciful. Understanding. Pitying even."

"To forgive something like this, I'd have to be a fucking Spirit."

"All I'm saying is that you should busy yourself for two or three hours and then I'll be off duty, and I can take you wherever you want to go and we can do anything you want to do to distract your mind from what happened. You've always wanted to go see that weapons museum in the city which displays your father's sword. I could take you there."

"I'll occupy myself during the next two to three hours by packing!" I shouted at him.

His face dropped. "I guess I should be happy if I get a better goodbye this time than the last."

Ouch!

"Bastard," I moaned at him and snatched the lunch bag out of his hands, biting down on the fold before climbing down to the ground and stomping towards the infirmary. I met Fern at the door. "Where's Davis?"

She pointed at a bed somewhere in the middle of the hall. "Over there." Then she rushed away, clearly having a busy time during the challenges.

"Thank you," I called after her, but she was so far away already, I doubted she heard me.

I found Davis's bedside and Murben, Nesso and Commander Daffron were crowding around it. Davis's leg was bandaged up, so he looked to be okay.

"Clever thought to stab yourself when he possessed you," I muttered.

"Thank you," he said curtly, and looked around at the others, who tensely stood not moving a muscle as if I was about to either combust or fall apart.

"I was impressed by your moves too, Murben."

"Thank you, my quee–"

I glowered at him.

"Cadet Coraly," he finished.

He looked so unnerved that I thought he'd jump to the ceiling if I dropped a pin to the floor.

"When is your match, Commander Daffron?"

"Tomorrow after lunch." He looked on edge, too, twisting faster in his movements than normal, his eyes scanning the room for threats every other second.

There was silence lingering in the air each time I stopped speaking, making me feel unwelcome. I made a muttering sound. "Murben, is there somewhere I can go where you know Ben is not?"

He cleared his throat. "None of us have seen King Blackbone since he won his match, Cadet Coraly. He told me he wanted to be alone, so I don't know where he is."

"He has been gone for three hours, and his bodyguard doesn't know where he is?" I asked.

"I'm afraid so. I'm sure his Majesty will turn up at some point."

"Turn up? He's not a lost dog…Actually. Retract that. Dog. Pig. Bastard. Whatever. If you see him, tell him I'm going to be in the field this afternoon, so he should avoid it, and you can also inform him that he will sleep in your room tonight."

"Oh, man!" Davis moaned.

"Tell Ben it'd please me if he slept on the floor as Davis is injured."

Davis smiled at that.

"I'll do so. Good day, Cadet Coraly."

Good day? Spirits how formal. They must be extremely worried, either of my magic or Ben's wrath.

I angrily turned on my heel and took the door leading to the inner corridors, climbing the stairs to the second floor. When I walked into the Captain's Office, my brother wasn't there. I sighed and sat down in his chair to wait and ate the sandwich from the bag.

When I had finished my lunch, he had still not arrived, so I decided to take matters in my own hands and find myself a suitable mission. All his secrets must be hidden away in the drawers. I slid one open and saw documents with the red classified stamp on them. I took one out and read about a Lord Dann in Gaithbry who they suspected stole money from the cotton field factory and Harvey had deployed a spy called Agent Kamrel to ascertain who the lord was collaborating with.

On deeper thought, I realised that somewhere in here there could be information about the war in the north, so I rummaged through the drawers, trying to find the word north on any of the papers, when I suddenly heard someone clear his throat. I looked up and saw my brother's stern face.

"What are you doing?" he asked, even though he could clearly see I was snooping.

"What can you tell me about what is happening in the north?"

"That is classified." Harvey came closer, his hands folded around the back of his yellow uniform.

"You keep telling me that."

"You keep asking the same question."

I closed the drawers and pushed the chair to roll away from the desk. "Were you using your emotional block magic today when I pleaded for your mercy?"

"Angie, what are you doing here? I'm sure it isn't to tell me what a lousy brother I am."

I cocked my head from side to side. "No, that's just an added bonus. I want my old contract back. Send me to the north."

"Declined."

"Fine. If not the north. Send me to help…" I looked for the paper in the drawer again and held it up, "this guy. Agent Kamrel has a mission to spy on Lord Dann."

"That is also classified information."

I put the paper back down and slammed the drawer shut. "You should have a lock on your drawers…and your door."

"Unsolicited entry is punishable on this floor, so I don't need to have locks."

"Fine. Punish me. Send me to the Ivory Castle's dungeon. I don't care. That sounds peachy right now."

He rubbed his palms over his entire face. "Angie…" he sighed. "He never…got naked. He stopped it, and he looked drowned in despair when he snapped out of it."

"Don't tell me you have sympathy for the black-wing king? And don't tell me it was nothing. What if Captain La Roy would have seduced Kate, wrapping his tongue around hers, touching her breasts and undressing her in front of everyone? Sliding his hand down her trousers to–"

"Stop!" His chest was heaving with rage, his blue eyes intense as if all sanity had left them.

"Remove the soul bond on me and send me on any mission you like, just away from here," I barked.

"All right. There is a mission I can send you on."

"With a high probability of dying?"

"Not a high probability, but there are always risks. I'll write up a report to General Denor and put a folder together with the details. It's about monitoring the iron trade raids outside Emendroth Outpost."

"Good. I'll go pack." I darted for the door to get the heck out of here before he changed his mind.

"I have one condition," he called out to make me halt.

I dropped my shoulders and turned to look at him. "What?"

"You finish the fifth challenge and then you go. It gives me the option to say you're on a special mission and if you feel like carrying on with the academy training once you return, you'll have that option, too."

"So, you're just sending me on a quick one-month mission?"

"Three weeks. At first. Then we'll see."

I shook my head. "Fine. Whatever. Even a bit of Emendroth air will do me good."

"Let's hope so. I've heard the air is thick with deception down there."

"No different from here, then, brother."

I left his office and descended the stairs two steps at a time and turned the corner sharply to get to my room. There wouldn't be too much to pack for a three-week mission. It could wait until after the challenges. Right now, I could do with that offer of playing tackle ball with Zayd.

I gawked when I opened the door and stepped inside, seeing ten more plant pots with vines, featuring big red roses, climbing along the walls, and in the middle of the room, Ben sat on both his knees, facing me.

On his fucking knees!

"I'm so sorry," he said instantly, and tipped his head down to stare at the floor to show submission.

In his short glance up at me, I could see his eyes were bloodshot. My heart hurt for so many reasons, like a damaged dam that was ready to burst through its cracks and flood my insides until I choked.

I walked over to the bedside table and found the sigil to the Black Wing Territory that he had given me inside the drawer, and chucked it at his chest, where it bounced to lie in his lap.

"Here, you should have that back," I said, as I walked to the wardrobe and brought out my duffle bag and started packing my casual clothes into it even though it was way too soon, but I didn't know what else to do with myself.

"What's happening?" he asked, his voice marred with panic.

"We're going to fight our next matches until we lose…" I turned to him. "Unless you want to tell leadership that we forfeit because we're unfit to compete."

"But we aren't unfit to compete."

"Not me, at least," I muttered into the wardrobe. "After that, the rest is none of your concern. I think my brother phrased it as 'classified'."

"You're going on a mission?"

"I'm going back to being an agent, and Harvey will arrange to bond you to someone else."

"Angelica, please."

"I'm quite convinced I'm 'Miss Stone', at the moment."

"Please. I'll do anything. I'm a king and I'm here, in front of you, begging you on my knees."

"The roses were a nice touch, too," I said coldly.

"You must realise that I don't like Cadet Darling."

"No, I think you said that you 'fucking loved it'."

"It was her magic talking."

"Funny, because her magic sounded exactly like your voice. There was also no hesitation in it, or strained vocal cords, showing you were trying to fight it. You freely took all the pleasure she gave you. Like a leech."

"I did fight it. I stopped it. But you didn't see when I did because you left."

"Because I was too heartbroken…too embarrassed. I took a chance on you even when my heart was screaming no and all my friends said I was naïve. I thought I could prove to everyone else that the black-wings weren't the enemy, and that…I don't know. That my mother hadn't been a traitor. But I was wrong. She plainly stabbed my father in the back, and you stabbed me, so lesson learned. And now everyone is going to keep calling me a traitor and a mutt until the day I die. The only difference is that now I deserve it for being such an idiot."

"Please, tell me what you want me to do. Abdicate as king? Marry you and brand us in front of the Spirits? Scream off the top of the Bensguard Outpost roof that I love you?"

"I want you to pack your bag and stay in Murben and Davis's room. On the floor. Davis is injured."

"You can't mean this. This can't be it."

"I'm sorry. But…it is. I'm going to get out of the room before you go all death-smoky in here, and I want you gone by the time I come back."

"Where are you going?"

"I'm going to play tackle ball with Zayd."

"So, him, you forgive? But not me? He was the one setting me up."

"I don't care about him, what he did. I cared what you did, and Zayd wasn't the one with his tongue down Cadet Darling's throat."

"No, but he has been down your throat and will do anything to do it again. Ironically, he doesn't know you plan to ditch him again."

"Maybe this time, I'll give him goodbye sex before I leave, and maybe I'll even *fucking love it!"*

There it was. The black essence of his death magic seeped out from the skin on his hands as he lost control of his emotions. He clenched his hands shut, trying to contain it to the point his fists were white-knuckled. "You told me you were mine forever." He glanced at the promise ring on his finger.

"And I meant it. I will love you forever. But that doesn't mean I'll stay by your side when you mistreat me and do unforgivable things. Sitting on your knees and buying me flowers isn't enough."

"So, what is?"

"Maybe nothing is enough."

Tears were threatening to burst out, so I left the bag on the floor and got out of the room as quickly as I could, not wanting to experience his sorrow for one more second. I didn't want to feel the Spirit of Death's hand as it clamped around my heart and tried his best to rip it out of my body.

I sprinted as fast I could up the stairs and knocked on Zayd's door. When he opened, the deluge fell from my eyes, flooding my cheeks as I crashed into his chest. With no hesitation, he wrapped his arms around me. That's when I realised, although Zayd was not blame-free, that this was where I had come. I'd had nowhere else to go where I felt safe.

Zayd stroked the top of my head without saying a word. The breath of a sigh landed there, too. Zayd held me tightly until I had managed to collect myself. He tilted his head down to watch me, pressed at his chest. "I guess I should take at least a quarter of the blame for these tears."

"I'll give you some colourful bruises to pay for it. Get the ball."

"You sure you don't want to hang in my apartment and read in front of the fireplace? I still have some of your old romance books in the wardrobe."

I snorted at him. "You scared?"

"Absolutely." He picked up the leather ball from the hallway armchair and cupped his arm around it before he pushed me out into the corridor to lock his door. We walked side by side out to the starting line on the grass field where he passed the ball to me. Immediately, I sprinted across the line, trying to take him by surprise, but he was onto me and tackled me back and I flew to my arse, cussing. I got up on my feet again and tried to dart around him, shoving my shoulder hard into his chest when he blocked my path. He was like a stone wall, and my shoulder throbbed with pain. It had clearly not healed fully after last week when I crashed into a tree training with Murben, or even before then when I had fallen off the balance bar.

My next attempt to dive between his legs and stretch the ball across the line, failed too, as he pinned my chest to the grass with his knees.

"Almost got me there," he chuckled, and waited for me to retreat before he let me go, so that I wouldn't go for the line again as soon as he relaxed. Which I totally would have done.

I tightened the grip on the ball, and exhaled a sharp hiss of frustration that my willpower alone couldn't win me a point. Getting an outlet for my rage today would be a win on its own, but I wasn't someone to settle when there was more to be gained. I wanted a freaking point. I had to think up a new tactic.

I looked him up and down, looking so confident and stable. Then a new plan popped into my head. Taking a few steps back, I drew back my arm and flung the ball as far beyond him as I could. When he looked up, I circled him and ran to catch it on the other side. He turned quickly, catching up fast. I yelped, laughing, hammering my feet faster onto the grass, stretching up my hands to catch the ball as it plummeted. At the last moment, Zayd jumped high into the air and caught the ball before I could reach it, and as he landed, he crashed into me. We tumbled on the grass with the impact and finally came to a stop on our backs.

"This is ridiculous!" I beat a palm on the grass. "You could have let me have that one."

"Oh no. Never," he laughed, twisting his head to look at me at his side. "I'll never let you win on purpose. You have to work for it."

He stood up and held out a hand to help me up before we walked back to the starting line, and he looked at me with concern as I muttered a few complaints about my sore body.

"Maybe we should stop while you're still in one piece, considering you have a match next week. You do still have a match next week?"

"Yeah, Harvey said I have to complete the fifth challenge before he could send me away."

"So, you're still planning on leaving," he muttered.

"Regretting that you matched Ben up with Cadet Darling now, aren't you?"

"I feel awful. Will you kill me if I say that King Blackbone shouldn't be judged on the account of what your mother did? I know you find it hard to trust anyone again, but he seems to really care for you. I mean, if he comes to a family dinner with the Coralys when he doesn't have to, he must either be a sucker for punishment, or he's really trying hard to make it work with you."

I glowered at him, half playfully, and half in warning. "He's a blackwing."

"And what are you?"

I sighed. "I don't know anymore."

"Maybe you want to figure that out before you say something to him that you can't take back and damage your relationship beyond repair."

"You know you're talking up your rival, right?"

He shook his head, a sad smile curving only at the edges of his mouth. "Only your misery is my rival. I want you to be happy, Angie. You deserve it."

"I don't know. Maybe my soul is as damned as a demon's."

"Don't say that. Your soul could never be damned. It's just burdened with a black-wing king."

I snorted a laugh. "So, who am I fighting next week then, except for Ben?"

"Not too happy about it, but I had to match you up with the Backstabber Team. If I give you another easy one, cadets and leadership will start to talk about me giving you preferential treatment."

"Another easy one? The last one broke me!"

"Yes, I know. But you know what I mean. Physically. But at least neither Cadet Grim or Cadet Randall have magic that they can use as a physical weapon. That's the best I can do for you."

"Thank you."

We walked back to the building, parting at the forking junction by the stairs, and I slid into my room and found Ben lying on the bed, reading Mewer's herb and potion's book.

"You're still here?" I muttered.

He didn't look up from the book. "You're naïve if you believe I'll give up on you after one argument…or…well…ever." Then he closed the book and put it down on the bedside table. "I thought I'd have to wait up longer before you'd return. Have you eaten? Can I get you something?"

I refused to meet his eyes, knowing they'd cool the fire inside me that had started to become a comfortable normal. It was for the best that I ignored him as my every muscle was tense like a coiled spring ready to snap at the slightest push. He could apologise all he wanted, but I wasn't about to snuff out the anger burning inside me. "I need something that can wash off your betrayal," I snapped, marching over to my bed and grabbed my nightgown from underneath my pillow before I locked myself in the shower room.

The silence was still thick with resentment when I finished and had towel dried my hair. I crawled over the bed, right up against the wall, and pulled the blanket up to my shoulders. It didn't take long until I felt a weight push down the mattress beside me.

"Where are you going on your mission?" His voice cracked, sounding like it came from a broken man.

Maybe Zayd was right, and he cared for me more than I comprehended anyone could. More than I could ever love myself, and maybe that's why I couldn't understand him. But my pride was something I had camped with for far too long to lower my shields and let him back into my heart.

"I'm going to…none of your business land," I told him, but regretted it, hating to treat him like this. I loved him so much, and I just wanted to turn around and be swallowed up by his muscly arms.

There was a deep sigh and a moment of silence. "How long will you be gone?"

"How can you be so sure I'm planning on returning?"

"Are you planning on telling me anything?"

"Nope."

"I can't lose you," he murmured, so softly I wasn't sure he had spoken. It was the sound of someone who was hoping for the slightest sign of forgiveness, or even that I'd turn around and look at him.

"I'm sorry." I replied coldly, keeping my emotions bottled up. "You've already lost me to the demons from my mother's betrayal." I wrapped my arms around myself like an anchor to ground myself enough so I wouldn't turn around and face him.

"It can't have permanently scarred you to never love again. Think, Angelica! What do you need to chase all your demons away?"

The weight of his words was almost too much to bear and I let the silence stretch to calm my breathing so my words would come out measured. "You tell me. What do I need to do for you to stay away from me?"

I prayed to the Spirit of War that he wouldn't put his hand on my arm. I could feel him close to my back and if he touched me now, I'd crumble. I wasn't ready for that. Zoe had been right that I should never have left the undercover mission in the Black Wing Territory and come here having to deal with people who always ended up hurting me – betraying me. There was a good reason why I didn't put my trust in people. As soon as I let them into my heart, they ripped it wide open.

"I'm not a demon." He grunted, frustration clawing at his throat. "I need a herbal tea for my headache. But I'll be back."

"I won't hold my breath." I whispered the harsh words as I knew they'd cut deeper than if I had screamed them at him.

My lip was trembling now, and I blinked hard to keep the tears that were threatening to fall, but he'd have heard that my voice was filled with a quiet pain.

"Good, because if you don't breathe, you'll die, and I'm planning on living the rest of my life by your side."

"That's not what it means," I muttered into the wall.

He swallowed hard, the rejection finally seemed to be settling in. "I know what it means, Angelica, but sometimes things can be looked at from many angles. Life is complicated and filled with trials. It's your decision on how to look at them."

44

Still angry with Ben after a week had passed, I couldn't bear the sight of him this morning, either. I climbed over him as he slept, and I went to the sparring hall alone for target practice, throwing knives at the target board on the wall. It took me an hour to completely disintegrate the cardboard into ribbons, only having missed a handful of times.

Ben entered with Murben, and they started training on a sparring mat not far enough away from the breathing space I needed from Ben. I assumed they were warming up for the matches this morning, but in truth, it most likely camouflaged keeping an eye on me. Ben didn't look my way. Smart man. I threw another knife at the target. Harder. It was six o'clock in the morning and no one else was stupid enough to be up before first light, so I felt guilty that Ben had dragged Murben out of bed because Ben was too much of a coward to confront me alone. Although, I supposed he had tried every day for a week, and I hadn't taken it well.

"I can feel you staring at my arse. Please, keep to yourself over there," I hissed.

"Minding my own business, and staying away from you, all the way over here," he retorted. Then he fucking took off his shirt and added. *"But I can feel your eyes on me, so you're not really playing this fairly."*

I threw another dagger on the target board and walked to the wall to retrieve the three I was practising with.

"All your rights went out the window the moment–"

"I had my tongue down Cadet Darling's throat. I know. Could you sleep any last night to rest up for today's match?"

I dared a peek over my shoulder and saw fists flying between the two black-wings. *"I didn't lie sleepless pining over you, if that's what you're asking."*

"I thought you'd stab me in my sleep, but you just left without a word this morning, which was an interesting choice." His tone dripped with sarcasm.

Ben was panting down the bond and grunting from flexing his muscles as he manoeuvred around Murben.

"You were lucky. I was contemplating killing you," I hissed.

"Ambitious," he crooned.

It was hard to pull my eyes away from their sparring, as every one of Ben's muscles tightened and bulged with each move, his perfect skin glistening in the dim morning light through the windows. I swallowed at the sight of another forceful punch on Murben where Ben's biceps balled, both when he struck his arm out and retracted it back to his chest.

"I think you have some drool at the side of your mouth," Ben chuckled.

I pushed the back of my hand across my mouth. *"I do not."*

Watching him like this, the temptation to touch him was too great, so I headed to the canteen to get breakfast with Zoe and Fern before returning for our challenge with the Backstabber Team.

The weapons rack held only iron fighting rods today. Great. I'll go to bed bruised tonight. At least I didn't expect to make love to anyone anytime soon and have to miss out because of my sore flesh. *Silver lining, I guess.*

Avoiding Ben, who stood among the black-wings, I ripped a rod out of its bracket and made my way to Zayd, who was holding the score papers in his hands and looked perky as ever in his navy-blue combat uniform. Not that I expected our tackling exercises this week would have worn him down.

Zayd glanced up at me when I got to his side. "So, still not speaking to King Blackbone, uh?"

"I can't wait to cut the bond between our minds." I nodded at his lists. "Who am I fighting, so I can get this over with?"

He pointed the back of his pen towards Cadet Theo Grim, who leered at me and stepped up on the mat.

"Iron rods and magic allowed," Zayd called out. "Ready. Go!"

Cadet Grim circled me with light steps, almost skipping like a girl. Clearly, this match amused him. He immediately resorted to magic, his corporal form flickering, and it was hard to look at him for a moment as he shifted, appearing in front of me like he had once before; as an image of Ben.

I leered to myself. Hadn't he heard about Ben and my last match? If he thought that this would make it harder for me, he was very, very wrong. This was exactly what I needed. To punch the shit out of someone who looked like Ben, but who wasn't him.

I swung my rod as hard as I could, hitting over his arm, and even when he had blocked half the impact, it still struck him over his upper arm. He hissed. Gone was the smirk and the playful glint in his eyes. Instead, it had turned sharp, focused…deadly. I assumed there would be no more holding back from his part. This fight had just become serious.

"I take that as you're still furious with me," Ben said. *"I'm glad I didn't ask you*

to spar with me this morning."

"Shut up so I can concentrate. I only get this one chance at beating the shit out of you, as I stand no chance of scoring a hit on the real you."

"You flatter me."

"If you thought that was flattery, you might want to look away now."

I attacked fervently, but focused on using the techniques Harvey and my father had taught me, proud of how I managed to mind my steps and keep perfect footwork at the same time as I blocked the incoming blows. A lucky hit to his head knocked him unconscious, to which I finished with a display of twirling the rod around my body until I punched the short side down in a final thud onto the mat.

"Damn!" Ben barked in my mind. *"That was hot!"*

I glared at Ben. *"Maybe you should contemplate sleeping in Murben's room tonight."*

"Yes, maybe I should."

I walked off after Zayd had ordered the Twin Team to carry Cadet Grim to the infirmary, slammed the rod back in place into the rack, and left, not caring to watch Ben's match.

Zayd found me in the canteen at lunch.

"I rescheduled some matches and put you in a fight with the Jealous Team in two hours' time, if you're up for it. You seemed on fire today, so I thought you wanted to make the most of your anger. The faster you complete your matches, the sooner you can leave…if that's what you still want to do."

"Thank you, Zayd."

"You're welcome."

When he left, I saw Zoe in his stead, who had been standing behind him. She looked cross, clenching her hands on her hips.

"You're leaving?" she spat.

"Did you not hear about Ben and Darling?" I retorted with the same tone.

Zoe sat down opposite me. "I don't really care what is going on between you, or any of your lovers, but you had planned to leave me without saying goodbye. That just sucks. If you're going on a mission, I'm coming with you, honey."

I smiled. "Thank you, Zoe. That would be nice. Like the good old days."

"So, when do we leave?"

"I still haven't got the specifics from Harvey, but he said I had to finish the fifth challenge before I left. It's only a boring patrol mission to the iron mines."

"Since when did you and I go on a mission which was boring? Last time you moaned that you got too much action, remember?"

"Because you didn't send me backup!"

"Let's see what other fun we can have this time."

"I'm regretting this already."

"No!" she drawled. "It'll be fun. You and me on the road. Like two orphan outlaws with no one to condemn our mischiefs. If you and Ben aren't together anymore, maybe we can even find ourselves some handsome black-wing bad boys."

"I'm fed up with bad boys. Maybe next time, I'll go for someone steady, who won't betray me."

"Nah, if that's what you wanted, you'd have stayed with Zayd. You want someone powerful who can beat the shit out of anyone who calls you a mutt. You must set your bar a little higher than someone who doesn't betray you. Like someone muscly, tall, handsome, powerful, with magic that no one wants to mess with. Someone who makes people push up against the wall when they pass by. Someone who'd do anything for you. I don't know…someone who'd lock himself up and risk his best friends' lives in enemy territory just be near you."

I frowned. "You're just describing Ben."

"Am I?" she scoffed sarcastically.

"We're not talking about this."

"Okay, honey, but you're being stupid."

"Thanks for the pep-talk. You should find Harvey and let him know that you want to come with me on the mission before he assigns another team. I need to collect my thoughts and focus on my next match, which I assume will be against Cadet Donally."

"Break a leg…well, not literally, but you know…may the Spirit of Luck be with you. Although, she'll be easy to beat. Just go at her like a ballistic lunatic and strike a few blows, and she'll yield like a coward."

"I can do that. That's right up my street today. Thanks for the advice."

"Always got your back, honey."

She walked me out to the inner courtyard before she left for the leadership floor, probably on her way to see Harvey, and I turned to enter the sparring hall. There were a lot of murmurs in the hall, as the challenges hadn't started up after lunch yet. Many were practising in their teams on the mats around the perimeter of the centre mat. I looked at the weapons rack.

Chain flails and a spiked ball. Not my favourite, but it'd certainly make it easy to look like a lunatic, swinging that about.

I grabbed one off the rack to get the feel for its sharp spikes and weight and how the handle felt in my hand and sat down on the wooden bench running along the wall. My stomach knotted. If Cadet Donally struck my head with one of these, I could forget my mission. I'd have to spend days or even weeks in the infirmary.

Zayd walked in and stopped in his step, finishing the mouthful of his lunch and swallowing. "It's only Cadet Bengrey and Cadet Kenyard versus Cadet Nesso and Commander Daffron, then it's your turn against Cadet Donally."

"I know. Thank you," I said, letting my fingers follow along the spikes of the iron ball in my lap. "Did you inform Ben of the match, considering I'm not on speaking terms with him?"

He gave me a pitiful smile. "Yes, I told him." Then he continued walking to the mat.

There were so few cadets in the sparring hall at the moment. Most were having lunch or couldn't be bothered watching a black-wing match, so I got a good view even sitting down on the bench.

This match was still in its first round, so they were allowed to use one dagger. Magic was also allowed but the black-wings had none. Nesso and Kenyard's match was a quick affair because Nesso danced around Kenyard, making Kenyard increasingly annoyed more than anything. Kenyard grew fed up eventually and made his first and only strike.

Emroyce and Commander Daffron's match, however, made me lean forward in my seat to watch intently. Emroyce used his super speed, yet the commander seemed to time the strikes as if he wasn't even watching Emroyce and blocked at just the right moments, the blades ringing as they made impact. Had the black-wing commander undergone the same training as Ben showed me with the blindfold, listening to the movement and anticipating the angle and speed to fight as if blind?

Commander Daffron was fifteen years older than Emroyce, so he'd had time for more practice in his days. But Emroyce was fierce, strong and fast; one of the Bensguard Outpost's best warrior cadets. I glanced around the room, but Ben was nowhere to be found, or so I thought, until I spotted him in the courtyard, peering in through a paned window. Why was he out there?

I reached out through our bond. *"Why are you standing out there?"*

"I'm staying away from everyone."

"Have you pissed off the commander, too?"

"No," he chuckled. *"And look, we're on speaking terms."*

"No, we're not. Bond communication isn't speaking."

"Good to know."

"So why aren't you watching the match and giving your support beside the mat?"

"Because there are a few people who I can't stand to watch die. Daffron is one of them. I wouldn't know how to break the news to his girls."

"Emroyce won't kill him unless he has to in self-defence."

"Excuse me if I'm not as confident as you."

Emroyce sped around Daffron, and his dagger snagged the combat leather on the commander's arm but didn't draw blood. Emroyce was so fast.

Suddenly, I felt the worry turning in Ben's stomach. He must have lost his focus on keeping his emotions to himself. I wanted to comfort him, but I was still so mad at him. I had to get away from here, or it'd tear me apart.

Daffron knelt and spun on his knees in one swift move, punching out and striking true into Emroyce's stomach as the faded edges of his speed passed by, making Emroyce fly backwards and land with a thud onto his back. The commander threw himself onto Emroyce, wrestling him to his front and pinning his arms over his back until Emroyce screamed in pain. When he didn't yield, Daffron pressed the blade of his dagger beneath Emroyce's ear, pressing the tip in harder and harder.

"I yield!" Emroyce finally called out and Daffron let go of his grip and walked off the mat.

My eyes widened. Emroyce had used his speed, and still, Daffron had won. Daffron had beaten Emroyce. Unbelievable. My jaw still hung open as Emroyce dragged his feet off the mat and sat down on the bench beside me.

"How's your ego?" I asked him.

"Smaller than my cock."

"So, still very huge," I said with an impish smile.

He snorted in reply. "Damn right!"

Ben walked up to us and made eye-contact with Emroyce. "You fought well. Commander Daffron is my best warrior."

If he was trying to show kindness to my friends to butter me up, it wouldn't work to earn my forgiveness. I pushed off the bench and passed by him, deliberately letting my shoulder shove gently at his, and without looking at him or saying a word.

He grabbed a flail from the rack and sauntered after me towards Zayd.

"King Blackbone, you'll fight first," Zayd explained, and pointed at Cadet Hillip, who was jumping on the pads of his feet, warming up in the corner of the mat as he talked to Cadet Donally.

The chatter around the mat was of a degrading nature. Mainly, cadets commented on whether we had made up, or if the three of us had got together. Others took bets on whether Ben would screw Cadet Hillip the same as Cadet Darling, who was known to swing both ways. This was exactly what I had feared, and my face burned with embarrassment as if it had caught fire, the heat creeping all the way to the tips of my ears. I could feel every pair of eyes drilling into me like stabbing knives. The humiliation made me want to sink through the floor as easily as the ocean surface could swallow me up and end my misery. But I could do nothing other than stand there and take it, coating myself with another layer of tough skin.

Cadet Hillip joined Zayd and Ben and leaned in to say something to Ben. Ben's fists balled at his sides, and it looked like he was about to jump him when Zayd pushed Ben backwards towards the mat, telling him something in private. I was counting the seconds until this nightmare was over, and feeling the tug to flee, I backed into someone. I turned around. Murben.

"You're not abandoning your teammate during his match, are you?" he asked.

"Does Ben have to tell you bloody everything about our private disputes?"

"I guess he doesn't have to, but he provides me with a better chance of protecting you both when I know the details."

"Did he tell you how I whimpered when he pushed me into a climax, too?"

"Yes." He said stone-faced, devoid of any tone of apology or mockery. He really didn't lower to sarcasm.

I frowned. "And how is that detail remotely helpful in protecting him?"

Murben opened his mouth to answer, but he was caught in his thought process, so he closed it and tried anew without success. "Maybe that detail was purely him gloating."

I grunted at him and tried to move around his enormous frame.

"That didn't come out well. Give me another chance to explain. When Ben was nine; the year I met him, his entire family cheerfully celebrated the Turning of the Year together in the court before they dispersed on various duties during the year. When he was ten, he got this handsome black stallion for his birthday. At the age of eleven, he was praised by his father for a great achievement. At only twelve years old, he won the flight cup. When he reached the age of thirteen, he got his first crown, and the lords had to swear fealty to him as the rightful heir to the throne. When he was fifteen, he found the Black Blade. And then there were a few dark years after that, with his parents dying, the war, the betrothal and the new duties of his role. But then he met you."

"You've lost me, Murben. What has this got to do with him telling you about our intimate activities?" I asked, but my mind was stuck on one particular word. Betrothal?

"King Blackbone has had many triumphs, but I've never seen him so ecstatically happy as when he came to my room telling me about your intimacy. And I've never seen him as heartbroken as last week."

I tried to push past him again, but he blocked my way. "Good then, that I'll not be the source of his torment any longer."

"I heard you're leaving. But know that whenever you want him to come to you, tell any black-wing you need him, and the king will find you. Because King Blackbone would rather let everyone around him die than lose you. He's purely trying to keep as many as possible alive to remind himself of his humanity."

"And…" I contemplated not asking. It would give the impression I cared. But my curiosity-vein demanded answers. I twisted, trying my damned hardest to ignore it, but the question crawled along my spine. "You mentioned betrothal?"

"Did I?" Murben said so plainly that I wasn't sure I had heard him right.

Cadet Donally screamed, so Murben cocked his head to look up and I twisted to glance behind my back.

I hadn't even realised the match had started, but Ben was holding a tight grip over Cadet Hillip's throat, his face blackening. Cadet Hillip's eyes dropped to the bottom of their sockets, and his muscles went slack. Ben let go of his throat and the cadet's body collapsed onto the mat under its own weight. Dead.

Cadet Donally screamed.

Everyone began murmuring indistinctly until a cacophony filled the hall. Murben and I walked closer, as Zayd rushed to Cadet Hillip and took his pulse. Everyone silenced until Zayd looked up at Ben. "You killed him."

"Isn't that allowed?" Ben questioned.

"Yes…but…it's frowned upon."

"Frown upon the rules as much as you want, but you made them."

Cadets debated amongst themselves and many shouted threatening remarks at Ben. Others protested to Zayd that it wasn't right, and that he should have Ben executed. Zayd was reiterating the rules of challenges to everyone who approached him, but he was getting cornered.

"King Blackbone, take Murben and Cadet Coraly back to your dorm room!" he shouted over the crowd.

Murben circled his arm around my shoulder to shield me from any weapons being thrown our way. But I had no desire to be locked in a room with the two of them, so I tore out of his grip and hissed that I'd make my own plans. Before Ben had reached Murben, I was out the front door and heading for my tree for the second time today. Next time, I might as well bring a blanket and sleep perched on my branch if Ben was going to behave like this.

I waited for Zayd, who I was sure would come to argue with me when everyone had calmed down, but my stomach begged for dinner, so the level of my crankiness wouldn't be in Zayd's favour when he arrived.

The sky was dim when Zayd stepped out of the building and jogged towards the tree. With ease, he wrapped his hands around the trunk and branches to swing himself up to his branch opposite mine.

"How are you feeling?"

"Hungry. When is it safe to go to the canteen?"

Zayd looked at his watch. "In fifteen minutes, I'd say." I could feel him staring at me as I watched the stars in the sky. "You know…Cadet Hillip had it coming. I heard him tell King Blackbone that he was going to kill you. That is why King Blackbone killed him."

"Why are you telling me this? It's not in your favour."

"You have spent too much time with King Blackbone. I don't pick and choose the information I tell you so that it suits my end game the best. I tell you things I think you want to know. Not because I expect something in return, but because I love you."

"Well, Ben can't just go around killing everyone who says they want me dead. There won't be many soldiers left."

Zayd sighed. "I'm glad you have him."

My eyebrows lifted as if almost by themselves. "What?"

"Yeah, I mean it. I guess I understand now why your brother paired you up with him. He's not restrained by compassion for others when it comes to you. It's like it's black and white. No one else matters. His world revolves around you. It's kind of cool to watch. Like the stars," he added and tilted his chin up to look at them.

I was gawking at him, though. "He has made you his wing man now?"

"No. Just saying, he'll protect you in a way I can't. I would hesitate to consider the stakes, but for him, you're the biggest stake. If someone threatens your life, it's clear cut to him to eliminate them. I can't do as much for you; I couldn't even sway the camp leaders' choices in the leadership meeting for your next match tomorrow morning."

I cringed. "Who am I fighting?"

"Cadet Floyd Gravelhorn."

"Really? You couldn't pair me with anyone else?"

"I'm afraid not. I did what I could, but leadership overruled all my reasoning. I can, however, influence what weapon you'll use. Any preference?"

I scratched at the back of my neck, which I was severely worried would come off tomorrow. "I need blades, considering he's stronger than I am. No fighting sticks, or he'll bruise me black and blue and break my bones. A clean, quick death is better."

"Angie," he drawled, rebuking me.

"What? Can you say you'd be surprised if he killed me? Especially after Ben killing Cadet Hillip today."

"I guess not. I'll talk to Harvey to see if he can send you on the mission sooner to get you out of the challenge tomorrow."

"Don't bother. It was his decision for me to finish the challenge, and he used his captain's stare when making the deal. Let's use the butterfly blades for the match. That could be fun, right? Three stab wounds at once will make my death more efficient."

Kristine Bostee walked out to the field then without her teammate Cadet Wix or any of the royal guards on her flank, yet she was dressed in the iron armour King Emille had ordered her to wear at all times. Her eyes emitted light, making her easy to spot through the evening hue. This was my chance. I quickly climbed down from the tree, with Zayd hissing at me to stay put.

I ignored his warning, traversing the grass field and holding out my hand to her with a kind smile on my face. "Hi, I'm Angie. Captain Coraly's sister."

Sceptically, she shook my hand, using her other to push blonde hair behind her ear. "I know who you are. Everyone is talking about you."

"Nice. So, my fame has reached you."

"Well, the other cadets are mainly debating how you'll die, so not sure it's a good kind of fame."

"Like yours?" I challenged.

She pulled her hand back an awkwardly long moment after, looking at me as if it had been a threat.

But I was fine with that. I had done all the greeting I needed. "Well, may the Spirit of Luck be with you in the survival in the woods challenge."

She snorted. "As if I'd be allowed to participate. I'm only allowed to do the challenges King Emille deems safe."

"That must get boring."

She shrugged her shoulders. "Probably nicer here than when I eventually must serve at his side. Queen Miriam doesn't want other females around her husband and quickly sees their death in her soul reading magic. At least here, I get the entertainment your boyfriend causes."

Zayd gripped over my shoulders as he had caught up with me, and flashed Bostee a smile over my head.

"Let's leave Cadet Bostee in peace before we all get into trouble. You head to the canteen, and I'll find out where Cadet Bostee's guards are."

"Sorry," I muttered towards her and turned on my heel. "Goodbye."

Zayd followed in my steps. "So, to her you say goodbye? A stranger you just met."

"How many times do I have to apologise for that?"

"Once would be nice."

"Okay, well. I'm sorry! If it makes you feel any better, it was the hardest thing I ever had to do."

We walked up the steps to the building.

"It does make me feel a little bit better," Zayd muttered, his eyes retreating to a painful memory in the past.

"Spirits! Men!"

I veered right towards the canteen whilst Zayd went to the Administration Office to see what was going on with Cadet Bostee's guard change.

When I had picked up my lasagna, I looked around the room, tray in hand. The black-wings, Zoe and Valentina were sitting at one long table, but I saw none of my other white-wing friends. *Shit!* I contemplated taking a seat at a smaller table by myself. But that'd probably raise more questions than I wished to talk about, and I could probably get away with silently sitting down next to Zoe, even if it was opposite Ben.

Everyone shouted a greeting at me as I approached, but Ben didn't look at me as I sat down and continued eating his food as if nothing. As if he hadn't killed a man minutes ago.

In the awkward silence, Nesso suddenly spoke, "Zoe, what would you do if someone betrayed you?"

Ben levelled him with a hard stare, but Zoe, who sat next to Ben, couldn't see it.

"Cut out their tongue." she answered.

Nesso cleared his throat, looking nervously at Ben. "What would you do if someone hurt your friend?" he asked Zoe, clearly worried Ben thought he overstepped a line.

She shrugged her shoulders. "Break their neck."

"What would you do if someone cheated on you?"

She frowned this time. "Cut off his fucking balls, honey."

Nesso then turned to Valentina sitting next to him. "Valentina, what would you do if someone betrayed you?"

Valentina continued eating as if it was a straightforward question. "Kill him."

"And what would you do if someone hurt your friend?"

Valentina again said casually. "Kill him."

"And what would you do if someone cheated on you?"

"Kill him."

"Him? Why do you assume it's a man?" Nesso asked.

"Of course it'd be a man. Who else would do those despicable things?" she spat.

Ben pointed his fork at Valentina. "I'm with her on this one. Her rules seem simple."

"Thank you, King Blackbone. Why complicate matters?" Valentina blurted.

"You cut so deep, Valentina," Nesso said, stabbing his lasagne.

Valentina stared at him. "What does that have to do with cutting people?"

"Nothing. I just desperately wanted to change the topic. Do you know how to skin a rabbit?" There was silence around the table, so Nesso continued. "Well, I'll tell you that–"

Valentina jerked her gaze up from her food, looking annoyed. "I love the part where you skip over the fact no one asked."

Spirits! Valentina was in a bitter mood today. More so than usual.

I tuned out as Nesso carried on asking random questions.

"Zayd told me why you killed Cadet Hillip, but it isn't right. Why did you do it? You'd have won, anyway."

He lifted his brows to look across the table, lines forming on his forehead.

"You're talking to me?"

I cut my lasagne into smaller pieces. *"I thought we established that communicating through the bond isn't 'on speaking terms'."*

He stirred in his seat. *"Showing strength is better than winning at this outpost. He should have known better than to threaten your life, and now the rest of the cadets know what happens when they do."*

"Zayd said he admired your commitment to protect me. Did you threaten him to tell me that, too?" I felt tense, crossing my shins under the table, but being careful not to stretch them too far so they'd touch Ben.

"No. But the camp leader is right. That it's my primary priority." Ben pushed the tray away so he could cross his arms over the table and purely focus on staring into my eyes.

"That's the first time you've agreed with Zayd." I pushed a bite of pasta and meat into my mouth.

"It's the first time he has been sensible."

Spirits, his stares were unnerving, and sexy and… Stop that!

"So, that is what you call murdering Cadet Hillip? Sensible?"

He nodded in silence. *"Yes. And don't worry. Cadet Hillip will resurrect in the Underworld. It wasn't like I killed him with a black blade. I had to hide that from you, remember?"*

I stabbed my fork into another bite. *"It was a shame I didn't get to use it first."*

He smiled playfully. "It wasn't for lack of trying. *You'd have made me into a roast spit if I hadn't been so charming. Thankfully, you aren't as merciless as a demon."*

Resigned, I rested my arms to either side of my tray. *"Sounds like your ego is bigger than a demon's."*

He cleared his throat. *"The reason I didn't hesitate to kill him, except for the obvious fact that he had threatened you, is because your brother is making the challenges harder this year. Why do you think that is? Actually, no matter the reason. If he needs to cull the numbers, I'll be helping him, and making damn sure it won't be you."*

"And who prays to the Spirit of Life for Cadet Hillip?"

He scratched at his neck. *"Another Spirit of yours?"*

"Yes."

"Well, I can say a prayer tonight if it makes you feel better. As a king, perhaps the Spirits will do me the favour of resurrecting Cadet Hillip with some common sense this time."

"Because I'm the almighty ruler of the black-wings. I decide everything because I'm king," I mocked.

"You should have my job. You're very good at it, I hear."

I gave him a rude gesture with my finger, gripped the tray, and walked away.

"Prick!"

"I heard that!"

"You were meant to!"

45

"Must you come to bed after I'm asleep and get out of bed before I wake up? We could lie for a while and talk about our issues," Ben moaned, as he arrived at the sparring hall.

"Be glad I haven't separated our beds." I observed Cadet Gravelhorn and Cadet Malloopa spar on a side mat before the matches were about to start. *"Besides, it's redundant, since I'm about twenty minutes away from dying, anyway."*

Ben was rolling his black sleeves up to the crook of his arm with irritated flicks. *"If you do, you're going to have to help me identify all your nine Spirits when we see them. Spirit of War. Spirit of Luck. Spirit of Life. Spirit of Death. Spirit of Love. Spirit of the World. Spirit of the Sea…and…"*

"Spirit of Family and Spirit of Magic."

"Right."

"So, you've realised you can't always protect me? That you can't interfere in my match?"

"Oh, I would, but I doubt killing everyone in here will work out well for me."

I rolled my eyes at him, but he ignored it. He pointed at Malloopa. *"The guy looks as close to a demon as one can whilst still being alive."*

My chest tightened with worry. I couldn't bear it if I had to watch Ben die. *"Be careful,"* I muttered reluctantly.

Ben winked at me. "As it happens, I'm used to fighting demons," he whispered into my ear and planted a quick kiss on my head before he gathered my hair up into a ponytail and tied a leather band around it.

"What are you doing?"

"You will not fight Gravelhorn with your hair in your face."

He turned to Commander Daffron, who was guarding me from behind my back. "Protect her," Ben commanded, as he pointed a stern finger at him before walking up to Zayd, who had arrived with Ben's butterfly blade in one hand.

I agreed that Ben normally had lots of demons in his head, but today I feared they'd distract him, a distraction he couldn't afford since Malloopa wasn't an easy contender. My stomach cramped seeing the three circles on his uniform to show his advanced magical skill. With just a slight touch on Ben, Malloopa would learn everything about him and his fighting technique. Ben would have to stay the heck away from his hands.

My insides hurt from the anxiety as my stomach rose to my throat. What if Malloopa got one swing to Ben's neck and killed him? I didn't want to imagine a world without Ben. Not that the bond would allow me to suffer that option. However comforting that sounded, and however pathetic my life was without a reason for staying alive, I still felt that there was something important I had to accomplish before I died. I wasn't done walking the soil of this realm.

Malloopa wasn't someone who showed off, so when he walked onto the mat, he held his blade tightly without swinging it around in an artistic display like Ben did to intimidate his opponent. Malloopa glided his steps forward like a ghost with a pale expressionless face. His eyes shone in orange as they watched Ben, and his long, black hair spread over his shoulders. He had wrapped leather bandages from his wrists to his elbows for support and wore tight combat leathers that were shaped to his body, so he could move freely. He also wore fitted iron shoulder guards and shin guards, which I considered to be cheating, especially since leadership hadn't provided Ben with any of those, either.

"I pray for a clean fight today," Zayd called to them both.

Ben walked around the edges of the mat and passed by where I was watching. *"And to who of your many Spirits would you pray to for that?"*

"The Spirit of War…Love…or Luck in your case. It depends. Now, focus on your match!"

Zayd beckoned them into the middle before he backed off. "Ready! Go!"

Fearlessly, Ben struck at Malloopa, hooking his butterfly dagger into Cadet Malloopa's, and tearing it out of his hand, flinging it beyond the edge of the mat.

The anger on Malloopa's face was palpable, making me want to take a step back, but I couldn't because Commander Daffron was flush to my spin and behind him was a wall of cadets who were watching the match in suspense. I cocked my head up to make eye-contact with Commander Daffron. "He'll be okay, right?"

Commander Daffron only nodded and resumed watching the match.

The gesture wasn't too comforting. My skin was crawling and every nerve-ending told me to sprint up onto the mat and help Ben eliminate the threat. The memory of him and Cadet Darling making out on that mat was the one thing that kept me grounded.

Malloopa bent his knees to get low and spun around, flailing out an arm, attempting to catch Ben so he could use his magic, but Ben jumped out of his reach.

I exhaled, took a new breath and held it so tensely I forgot to breathe.

Ben slashed the three-pointed blade towards Malloopa's throat, but Malloopa snapped backwards, avoiding the impact. They circled each other with mirroring steps, as if they were counting down to attack simultaneously. Abruptly, they sprinted for each other. Ben hacked down with the butterfly dagger towards Malloopa, who blocked it with his iron arm guards.

Malloopa retaliated, swinging iron at Ben, who blocked with his forearm and immediately attacked after. Ben spun around Malloopa and jabbed at his lower back, but Malloopa got his knee up and kicked away Ben's blade. It went flying towards Kate, and Mazdon folded his body in front of hers for protection. The second before the blade could jam into his back, Emroyce caught the handle mid-air and swirled it around his wrist in a cool move. I exhaled and shook my head at him. He cocked an eyebrow and smirked.

Now, neither of them had any blades to fight with.

I turned back towards the match and held my breath again, feeling dizzy as my lungs demanded access to more air than I had been providing them in the last few minutes.

The two men had begun a dance to a deadly rhythm of kicking and hitting at each other. Their eyes locked on their opponent and muscles taut, their bare feet shifted with careful precision, searching for an opening to strike. The jabs were bursts of brute strength, Malloopa punching a sharp fist at Ben's ribs. Nothing seemed to crack. Ben tried to grip Malloopa, intending to use his death magic, but Malloopa knew about his magic and wouldn't allow himself to be caught. Malloopa struck up a lightning-fast heel towards Ben to keep him at a distance. Ben pushed it higher with his wrist in a block, grabbing the back of Malloopa's leg, kicking out the leg Malloopa wasn't using for balance and felling him to land face first onto the mat.

I crossed my arms over my chest. If I hadn't been so upset with Ben, I'd have been in awe of his strength.

Ben straightened his back and rolled his head around his shoulders, trembling with a purr, as if he had felt my hunger for him through the bond.

Bloody great!

Ben turned around to smile at me, and annoyingly, I was too stuck between Commander Daffron and the mat that I couldn't turn around or look away to ignore him.

Malloopa sprung back up and launched himself at Ben. I panicked, waving my hand at him to turn around. My breathing was so erratic, I thought I might collapse.

Ben didn't react until the last moment, then the *nonchalant* bastard turned around and struck out a foot straight across Malloopa's abdomen, sending him sprawling backwards.

Malloopa tried to stop the flight by steadying his foot against the floor, but the floor was too far beneath him. He plummeted downwards and fell on his arse. The impact to the back of his head against the stone floor echoed in the room, and he didn't get up.

Zayd rushed to him to check his pulse and released a big sigh of relief. "He's breathing. Take him to the infirmary," he called towards two second-year cadets in the corner who I had never noticed at the outpost before.

Ben collected Malloopa's butterfly blade off the floor, and Emroyce handed him the one he had caught before Ben slowly sauntered to Zayd and held them out to him. There was no rush, no fright, no sign of weakness over Ben. How did he make it look so easy?

"Next match, you need to be more focused. You're arrogant and one slice across your jugular will end us both."

"Nah. I'm only playing." He smirked at me in passing.

"Prick!"

I barged up to Zayd to wait for my match with Gravelhorn to start.

"I also heard that!"

"You were also meant to!" I didn't turn around to look at him.

"Do you know what I call those who call me a prick in the Black Wing Territory?"

I rolled my eyes but carried on as if I didn't have an arrogant quiz master in my head. *"No."*

"Dead."

I snorted down the bond. *"Are you saying you want to kill me?"*

"No, I'm saying you're getting away with murder."

"How poetically ironic."

"I know."

To stand next to the navy-blue uniform gave me a familiar comfort like an anchor in a raging storm. I didn't know why. Maybe it was because, as a camp leader, Zayd had authority over these people, and no one would touch me as long as he forbade it. Not that he could forbid it for long. I had to compete, and he'd had no say in who I had to be fighting.

I looked up at Zayd, who was clearly concerned about how the next match would turn out.

"Would you feel better if I told you my goodbye now?"

He dug his stare into me. "Angie!"

I sighed, trying to still my racing heart in vain. The adrenaline had already conquered my body and was the sole ruler over my actions. "Any last advice in this match?"

"Avoid the blades."

I stared right back at him. "You sound like Ben. Any *useful* advice?"

"What do you want me to say, Angie?" He sounded stressed. "Gravelhorn's magic is strength, and he's pretty solid in combat. I know of no weakness. And you chose the butterfly daggers. Not one, but two! Weapons he seems confident with, too."

I rolled my eyes at him, and took hesitant steps up onto the mat, inspecting Gravelhorn's physique; his blonde blowback hair, his wide chin and muscles that rippled at each of his steps. He was tall, almost two heads my height. I swallowed. The scar under his right eye that he had earned in a brawl at the iron mines made him look even more grim, as he watched me like an eagle honing down on his prey. His hazel eyes followed my movements and swept down to watch how I held the hilts of the butterfly daggers, now regretting having asked to use two blades instead of one.

My stupid heart pounded so frantically, it was distracting me from observing him back. My senses were registering his intentions a second too late every time he moved.

This was probably the most important fight I'd have in my lifetime, so I should better get a grip over myself. He wanted to kill me, and on the mat at this very moment, he was allowed. The two butterfly daggers he held casually in his hands certainly had the weight and sharpness of making the job easy for him. One wrong step, one swipe over my jugular and it was nighty night.

Gravelhorn got to the centre of the mat first. "Come on, Mutt. Come play with me."

An intense rage tightened around my heart. Wrath burned like wildfire, scorching every rational thought in its path. My body started to tremble from the sheer force of the turmoil. Emotions flooded the bond between us that wasn't mine, and Ben growled gutturally from where he watched us next to Commander Daffron.

An icy chill ran through me and down my arms. Shit. This was it. I was about to die.

"You're not afraid, are you?" Gravelhorn teased, and backed up a bit to provide me with a larger berth to dare walk farther onto the mat.

Arsehole.

I'd be stupid not to be afraid but telling him that wouldn't give me any advantage. The words 'mutt' and 'traitor' echoed inside my head.

"You can win," Ben said confidently. *"Your father trained you for this. Don't let his size detract from your skills."*

"Shut up. Busy dying over here." I snapped, as I positioned myself at the

centre of the mat.

Ben was right, though. All I wanted was to reinstate the glory of my father's legacy, and the training he had given me was part of it…of me. I could do this. I stared at Gravelhorn; straight into his hazel eyes. "Let's play."

I knew blades. I was good at throwing them and hitting my target and had practised endlessly this week, courtesy of being pissed off with Ben. Not letting Gravelhorn have a moment to assess my strategy, I threw one of the butterfly daggers at his chest. Even if it wouldn't be a killing blow, I could injure him and make him slower. That would be my tactic. Picking him apart, piece by piece. It would be tedious, and I'd have to be patient, but it was the only way I could survive.

The blade forced the wind to split as it soared towards Gravelhorn. He sidestepped in time and Emroyce caught my blade at the edge of the mat.

My arsehole opponent leered and clicked his tongue. "Now, you only have one weapon left."

"You're more arrogant than I thought if you think I need more than one to kill you."

I launched myself at him, stabbing straight for the soft tissue below the ribcage. He blocked with an easy swipe, and I took a step backwards, surprised he didn't counterattack immediately. Without hesitation, I went for close combat, striking out and blocking until I had worked up a sweat, but he simply kept blocking.

Sure, you keep blocking, arsehole. One time or another, you'll fail, and I will get you!

I faked a left move and went right, dragging the three tipped weapon in the air to cut his side. It snagged his leather shirt, but didn't even tear it. *Shit!*

"Nice one," he praised mockingly.

Next plan. I tossed the blade behind him, so he followed it with his gaze. Then I balled my fist and aimed for his balls. Rolling past him, he succeeded in blocking my strike before I ended up on his other side and picked my blade up again.

"That was below the belt, Cadet Coraly," he sniggered.

Why wasn't he going for the kill? He'd had plenty of chances to end me. What was he waiting for? Did he want to put on a show for the other cadets about how he toyed with me…a show for Ben?

I went low, bending my elbows, supporting both hands on the mat, and struck out my leg to swipe behind his kneecaps. He didn't jump…or fall. In fact, it had no effect on him. It was like I was trying to cut down a tree with a wooden spatula. He folded over me, trapping my body under his, so I couldn't bend my knees to kick at him. The wrist of my blade-hand was clamped inside his hand and pressed onto the mat. He stole my blade and stabbed it towards my wrist. I waited for the excruciating pain when the tips would impale my flesh, but it never came. I opened my eyes to inspect my hand, and I realised he had pinned my wrist between two of the three forks and into the mat. The stuffing of the mat emerged through the tear.

This close to him, I could really see his hazel eyes glowing vengefully above the large scar on his cheek. I punched his face with my other hand, but he caught my wrist after only one swat, and held it down, bringing his face close to mine.

No! I can't move. I'm trapped.

I can't believe he trapped me. Caught under his weight, I had no chance. I was nothing more than a flapping fish out of water.

Gravelhorn nipped at my earlobe with his teeth and whispered. "I think we should put on a show, the same as King Blackbone and Cadet Darling did, to make the king suffer. Want to play along, or should I just break your bones into submission?"

He twisted my wrist backwards and sideways to seek my pain point. I didn't want to scream, but the sharp sting shot up my wrist, my forearm, and stabbed at the connection to my shoulder.

"Cadet Gravelhorn!" I heard Ben shout in warning.

Gravelhorn turned his head towards Ben. "Oh, no." He leered. "She's my toy now, and there is nothing you can do about it. Not when I do this…" He turned me around to my stomach and my pinned arm tore into an unnatural angle. When he put his knee onto my back and pushed down with his weight, something in my forearm snapped.

I cried out loudly, tears pouring from my eyes.

"He fucking broke my arm!"

Gravelhorn laughed, a tone that was dark and malicious. "Nor when I do this…" He wrapped the crook of his arm around my head and was about to snap my neck when Ben roared.

"That's enough, Cadet Gravelhorn. You've made your point." Ben had one foot on the mat as if he was ready to interfere.

Gravelhorn twisted my head further.

Pressure twisted and tore at my throat. I had been calm until I noticed the creeping darkness at the edges of my sight. I had mere seconds to decide if to scream. Still, I didn't. My pride screamed louder.

A terrifying reality hit me.

I might not get out of this alive.

My inner spirit screamed at the pain lacing down my neck. My body wanted relief, but I refused to yield. If I wasn't going to be a cadet still standing when graduation came, it'd be because I was dead.

He grinned at Ben. "I have the right to break her neck unless she taps out."

"She can't tap out! You have trapped her hands, and you're clenching her jaw shut."

"Oh, too bad. I'll do the world a service by ending her traitorous little life…unless you think her soul…and yours, are worth begging for. On your knees."

"Let her go," Ben growled between his teeth, black essence floating around him in a thin, tight layer, like a second uniform.

"Beg. On. Your. Knees. King," Gravelhorn demanded.

This was so degrading for Ben. I believed Gravelhorn would spare my life if Ben knelt, but I knew Ben wasn't the type of king who knelt to anyone. In this instance though, if he wanted both of us to live, he was out of options. The agony in his eyes showed a resignment stretched too far, like the inability to control the situation had destroyed the core part of himself, and the sight of that scarred me. I had to do something. For his sake. I reached deep inside me to grab the magic I had been tucking away for so long, and had been told repeatedly by my father, and then my brother, never to use. I kept still as it filled me up, zapping through my veins like a static charge. It scorched me worse as I rushed it, but I worried that it took too long otherwise, as Ben's resolve was weakening.

What's it going to be, King Blackbone? Kneel, or I'll snap her pretty, little neck right now."

Ben tugged at his trousers, and he began lowering his knees towards the mat.

No!

Ben's knees were almost down. I couldn't allow it to happen. With equal strength to Gravelhorn, I pushed myself upwards, tossing him off me.

Gasps erupted, filling the hall as they witnessed Gravelhorn flung across the mat, slamming hard into the wall. But I could only feel the pain of my broken arm and make out Ben's silhouette as he threw himself over the mat to get to me. My vision tunnelled, then closed my world in darkness.

46

I blinked open my eyes and recognised the infirmary. That was nothing odd. I had woken up in the infirmary millions of times before. But the shadow that cast from a pillow was new. The pillow lowered down onto my face with such force that it cut off the air to my lungs immediately.

"I can't breathe!"

Panicked, I clawed around the pillow at forceful arms, but the muscles I found there were rock hard.

"Help!"

"Angelica?"

"Someone's suffocating me with a pillow!"

"What!"

"Where are you?"

"I'm more than seven minutes away. And a heavy storm is rolling in fast, so I might have to land and walk. I won't make it to you on time. You need to scream!"

I wriggled on the bed and pounded on enormous biceps, trying to get the pillow away from me enough to get a sip of air. But all it did was amplify the pain in my newly healed forearm.

"They are too strong. Help! I can't breathe!"

"For Spirits' sake, use your magic this one time to save your own life! We'll deal with the consequences."

Hadn't he known that I had used my magic when levelling off Gravelhorn from my body? What had he thought that was? My own muscle strength? It didn't matter. My magic couldn't help in this particular situation.

"I've tried, but it's of no use against him."

"Can you grab something around you? Kick the bed frame to make noises?"

"I'm fucking trying!" I was panicking, which was the first rule of what a soldier should not do. *"Where is your black-wing guard detail?"* I bellowed,

accusatory.

"The white-wings were on guard duty. Angelica, focus. Claw at their face. Go for the eyes. Bend their fingers back."

"I have no chance! I can't breathe! Save me!"

"Shit! I'm on my way." I heard his dark growl down the bond. *"I'm going to have to put up my shield against the bond, or I'll drop from the skies. You're losing consciousness, and so will I if I keep the shield open."*

He yelped suddenly.

"Ben!"

"Just some lightning striking a bit too close."

"Land!" I ordered, but my voice was weak, and I felt faint.

The bond went quiet. He had put his shield up. There was blackness filling my mind into a narrowing tunnel, again. My lungs burned, wanting air that they were denied. My arms fell to my sides, no longer obeying my command to fight.

There was a soft touch on my lips. Air. Sweet air filled my lungs. Once. Twice. Five times. There was pressure onto my chest. Once. Twice. Five times. The moist lips covered my mouth once more.

Air!

I recognised the taste of caramel.

"Angie! Come on!" Zayd roared.

Pressure.

"Don't leave me! Damn it, come back!"

Air.

Pressure.

Lips.

My chest heaved. I drew in masses of air into my lungs.

My lips tighter against lips.

I opened my eyes, and Zayd had his lips clasped around mine. I wrapped my arms around him, broke the life-saving act that had faded out into a kiss and panted into the fold of his neck. His arms were quickly wrapped around my back; one hand stroking in comforting circles. I looked up and realised I was still at the infirmary.

Cadet Tony Wix, the storm wielder, lay bleeding out beside the bed; one dagger nailed to his shoulder and another impaling his heart.

Spirits! This is the son of the captain at the Dashqaz Outpost and Kristine Bostee's teammate. This can't be good!

I tried to smile at Zayd. "It took you two blades?"

He rolled his eyes at me and exhaled in relief. "Good to see your sense of humour is as sharp as ever." Zayd looked at the cadet with a mix of grievance for a life lost and relief that he had done what had needed to be done. "I threw the first dagger from across the hall when I couldn't clearly confirm what was going on. When I saw the pillow, and him killing you, the next one went straight for his heart."

"I can't believe Cadet Wix wanted to kill me. Why?"

"Don't know, but I'll sure find out. Maybe he considered our greeting with his teammate, Cadet Bostee, a threat? Whatever his intentions, it'll get messy, considering his mother is the captain at the Dashqaz Outpost."

The thought pounded at my head. Then I punched a fist into the hollow of his shoulder. He moaned, pulling away from me with a quizzical look on his face.

"You were on guard duty."

"I was only away for a minute to fetch Treylieh to guard you because I have another match to judge in ten minutes." Zayd gestured for Treylieh, who stood as motionless and emotionless as always by the head of the bed. He held up a hand in greeting but kept quiet in his normal way.

"It was evidently more than a minute," I muttered.

"I'm sorry. If killing a cadet to save your life isn't enough, I'll make it up to you later."

I grabbed the sleeve of his navy-blue uniform so he couldn't leave. "Who is still left in the matches?"

"The Black-Wing Team won against the Twin Team and Emroyce and Kenyard won against the Fistfight Boys Team. So, the final will be Emroyce and Kenyard versus Murben and Davis."

"But Davis is injured."

"He's a tough bastard."

Zayd nodded towards the door only a few beds over where Ben stood leaning against the frame, wet like a drenched cat. That's when I noticed the deluge and thunderstorm outside the windows facing the front courtyard. It seemed to be calming down, though. "I assume King Blackbone will want to take over the guard," Zayd told me softly.

Perhaps. He didn't seem pleased, though. How much had Ben seen of Zayd having had his lips around mine? Well, Zayd had saved my life, and I hadn't *'fucking loved it'*.

Ben walked to the foot of the bed, and his hands curved around the footboard. "I'm glad to see you awake."

That was all he could muster to say when I had almost died twice today? Just because he was jealous.

My blood heated instantly. "Zayd, can you get Mewer before you go, so he can separate the king's soul from mine?" I said, looking past Ben as if he was a ghost I couldn't see.

Ben frowned. "Are you angry with me for this, too?" I didn't answer him. "Watson, tell her that you were the one on duty."

Zayd stood from the bed. "I have."

I crossed my arms over my chest, but instantly regretted it, as the pain from my forearm shot white-hot pain before my eyes. "Get Camp Leader Mewer," I growled through gritted teeth.

Ben rubbed his hand over his forehead tiresomely and looked at Zayd. "Have you ever won an argument with Angelica?"

"Nope. We never argue. She looks up at me and I know to shut up. You should have done that before she started giving you the silence treatment. It takes weeks to come back from that."

"Those are the best word of advice you can give?"

"Yep." Zayd patted a hand on his shoulder. "That, and try to enjoy the silence whilst it lasts. May the Spirit of Luck be with you," he said, as if Ben was about to fight the demon queen herself. "Come Treylieh," Zayd called. "I believe your training tomorrow for the survival challenge will be far preferable than staying here."

Ben frowned and looked up and deeper into the hall, sauntering away to get Mewer and bring him back to my bed.

"Cadet Coraly," Mewer said with that kind voice that he used when he was glad his patients were still alive. "The outpost needs a budget for you alone, with as many visits as you make here." He signalled for two larger infirmary workers who had arrived with a stretcher to remove Cadet Wix's body. "Although, I guess this mess wasn't your fault." He pointed at Wix's corpse. "Camp Leader Watson told me what happened. It's a shame. He was a strong contender for the Spirits' Trek."

I was in no mood for light-hearted jokes, nor apologies. "Please, can you organise matters so we can remove the soul bond as soon as possible?"

"Harvey decides that, and he needs to prepare shackles for King Blackbone, and guards."

I hesitated, seeing Ben shifting his weight to his other leg and his eyes lost their focus, as if it caused him discomfort at hearing the word 'shackles'. "Fine," I drawled as I turned my focus back to Mewer. "Tell my brother to do that, and quickly. And could you do something for me? Could you find out if the black-wings are okay?"

"They are fine," Ben spoke directly to me, knowing the question was better directed at him had we been on speaking terms.

Mewer scratched the back of his head. "I'll see what I can do."

When Mewer left, Ben's glances scanned me up and down a few times, as if he scrutinised every single part of me to ensure there weren't any new scrapes, bruises or cuts. Thankfully, he didn't lift my infirmary gown to check underneath, as I was sure he had contemplated it. The blanket was crumpled up at the foot of the bed, so he gently arranged it and draped it over my legs with a double fold over my waist.

He beckoned for someone at the door. "I'm going to change out of these wet clothes."

Commander Daffron came into view and eased down into the chair next to the bed with a watchful eye on everything around us. When I looked back towards Ben, he was gone from my bedside. I sighed, not really having wanted him to leave, but not wanting him near me either. I was so confused.

I rested in silence for a long while, but the commander's eyes turned up to watch me as soon as I moved to rearrange my blanket.

"You know," I told Commander Daffron. "When I was injured as a young girl, my mother used to make me this amazing peanut butter cake." I sighed. "I tried to make it for the family gathering the day after the Turning of the Year, but every time I attempt making it, it never comes out right. It doesn't taste the way she used to make it, even though I follow the recipe to the letter. I think she used a secret ingredient that died with her."

"Don't feel you have to talk to me. I'm more than happy to guard you in silence."

"Of course. Sorry." At least he was consistently rude.

I relaxed my head onto the pillow and rested. I must have dozed off because when I woke up, Murben had swapped guard with Commander Daffron.

I smiled at him. "I'm surprised you're already here. How did the final go?"

"We lost."

"Honourably, I'm sure. Fighting against Emroyce and Kenyard can't be an easy match."

"I had Kenyard to the mat in the first five minutes, but Davis is more brute than speed, so Emroyce got a good few punches in before he knocked him out. Neither a fair nor honourable fight from Cadet Bengrey, I'd say."

"Emroyce has always been more of a show-off than a fair fighter. He likes the glory of winning."

"Davis has been in our room, licking his wounds for an hour, so let's see if he'll change guard with me later, or if you'll have to endure me for a double session."

"I don't mind. You're a delight to be around, Murben. At least when you're not telling me to fly into trees."

"I didn't tell you to fly into them."

I giggled as he flashed a crooked smile.

A small infirmary worker appeared by my bed and she handed me a letter. "For you," she said, clearly in a rush before she was off to another bed.

I turned the cream-coloured envelope over to see the red wax seal. It was from the royal castle, but the sun symbol wasn't the emblem of the Royal Family.

"I wonder what this is?" I muttered, seeing Murben's curiosity as he leaned forward in the chair.

I slid my finger beneath the fold of the envelope lid and opened it, fishing out the letter and folded it open to read.

Dear Cadet Coraly,

I have received the unfortunate news about the hardship you faced in your challenge against Cadet Gravelhorn and, furthermore, about the death of Cadet Wix.

Although anger and vengeance have been soaring the winds across Gaithbry, I want to assure you that our meetings and your attendance at the First Year Ball will be unaffected by such rumours and your safety is guaranteed.

Having approved Captain Coraly's request for your suggested undercover mission, I agree to postpone our next date until your return.

I send my most sincere regrets for your hardships in these matters and pray for your speedy recovery.

Until we meet again,
Yours faithfully,
General Wallan Denor

When I had finished reading it out loud, I looked at Murben. "Not sure if this is polite, well-wishing, or a threat. He has obviously looked through a few minds if he already knows about Cadet Wix, who died mere hours ago." I flipped the letter and envelope over as if I could see a magic signature on it. Because how the heck did it get to me so quickly?

"What's your plan for the matter? You can't go to the ball."

"Why not?" I narrowed my eyes at him. "I'm going."

"It'll destroy King Blackbone."

I put the letter back inside the envelope and placed it on the side-table. "You don't have to worry. We won't be soul bound."

"Not what I was referring to. I was referring to the public kiss and the despairing state he'll be in not knowing whether you're safe."

"Murben," I called sternly. "What I do and don't do whilst Ben and I aren't bonded, is none of his business since…well, you know since when."

He crossed his arms over his chest. "And what about the twenty minutes' flight to cross the sky between Skyberg and the Gaithorpe Island? If you fail, you'll plummet down, far, far down, to the ground below to the realm where the wingless people live, who will rip your corpse apart to examine your species, which they don't know exists."

"Nice picture. But if I'm dead, I'm dead, and it doesn't matter if they pick me apart."

"That wasn't my point. I'd prefer it if you lived."

I scoffed and turned my head to see Zoe and Kate come into the infirmary, each holding a tray loaded with buckets and plates full of snacks, and two bottles of white wine.

"Ditto," I said, looking at Murben. "You might want to leave if you want to survive. Zoe's got that menacing look in her stare."

Before Zoe had fully arrived at my bed, she shouted across the gap between us. "Was it really necessary to rip Kenyard's arm open with your sword?"

I gasped. "The final was fought with a sword?"

"It was only a graze," Murben replied.

"Whatever. I'm not talking to you, honey," Zoe spat, and put her tray onto the mattress at the foot of the bed as Kate put the one she was carrying onto the side-table.

"You look like shit," Zoe told me.

"Will you be ready for the mathematics test tomorrow?" Kate asked. "I can bring the books here and help you study for it."

"Leadership hasn't changed the tests in fifty years. I know the answers by heart."

"Okay, whatever, cheater," Zoe spat.

"Be careful how you address the black-wing queen," Murben warned.

Here we go. Now, it was convenient to call me 'queen'.

"She has been my best friend for four years, honey. I call her whatever I like," Zoe retaliated.

"I insist you don't, or I might have to ensure you can't call her anything ever again."

"Oh, yeah?" Zoe pushed her chest out. "What are you going to do about it?"

Murben rose to his feet. "Destroy anything that threatens my queen."

Zoe reached out her hand and snatched up an empty syringe Mewer had left on the side-table and hurled it at him, nailing it to Murben's neck.

Murben yanked it out quickly and rubbed his neck. "What the fuck is in this?" Before he got an answer, he had to duck, as Zoe had gripped the chair meant for the next bed over and hurled it at him, too.

"Agent Hammerton," Murben drawled a warning. "Stop, now."

Kate and I exchanged a look. Spirits, what was going on between them?

"Why? Because you think I'll hurt Angie like men seem to hurt all women in this place?"

My eyes were wide open with confusion.

I saw the yellow captain's uniform before I registered my brother's face, as he joined my bedside, too. It certainly was getting crowded. Harvey held a mission folder in his hand and Murben gawked at it as if it held the cure to save his life.

"You're causing a commotion in the infirmary," he scolded us.

"I was rebuking Agent Hammerton about her–" Murben started saying when Harvey cut in.

"Rebuking Agent Hamm…" Harvey sighed. "You have a lifetime of moments to make poor judgements ahead of you, so can I interrupt this one?"

Murben nodded, although I didn't believe my brother had asked for his permission.

"Agent Coraly, here is your mission file. You leave tomorrow after lunch. You'll sit your mathematics test in the morning. Make sure you get enough rest to recover."

Agent. The word felt heavenly to hear. Not cadet – that alias had been a disaster so far.

"Thank you."

Murben was clearly not pleased. "And who will protect Agent Coraly on this mission?"

Harvey looked down to speak to me instead of indulging him with an answer. "Cadet La Roy will come with you."

"Cadet La Roy?" I gasped.

"Don't ask. It's a personal favour. Gives him a breather from the dispute challenge with…well…a break from drama. I'm also sending Cadet Crawly and Cadet Dessen."

So, a fire wielder, a memory wiper and a torture specialist on a patrol mission. One of them was a second-year cadet, and the other two were third-year cadets.

"And…Air Force Sergeant Karson will be in charge."

"Valentina's father?"

"He has mission training and knows…" he looked at Murben, "…the area. Agent Coraly will also have Agent Hammerton's assistance."

Murben glanced over us both. "That smells like trouble. And for how long will Agent Coraly and Agent Hammerton be away?"

"Until the mission is successful. It's more imperative now than ever, since a crate of black iron was stolen from the forge vault and with no sign of forced entry. If the iron reappears, Agent Coraly's mission will be shortened." Harvey answered before turning to me once again. "I've arranged for the soul bond you have with King Blackbone to be transferred to me once you have finished your lunch tomorrow. That will enable him to move around rather than having to be cooped up in the dungeon, unless he'd prefer that," he said, after I had nodded. Harvey then left the infirmary.

Stolen black iron? No sign of forced entry? Unlocking magic. I stared at Murben, who avoided eye-contact and raised the chair that Zoe had hurled at him upright and sat down.

I looked behind his back and glanced around the hall. "Where is Fern, by the way? If she isn't on duty, she should come and have snacks with us."

Kate pointed at a bed in the far left row by the front facade windows where Fern sat hunched on a bed with no patient in it. Brian held his arm around her. "She was delivering the child of another infirmary worker this morning, but the baby didn't make it. She has been crying all day."

"Spirits, how sad."

"Emroyce wasn't focused on his match today because he had been taking care of Robin most of the day. I thought I'd go there when you chuck me out of here to help him," Kate added.

"Do you think Fern has started to look chubby?" Zoe asked abruptly.

"Zoe! At least consider your words before you blurt them out," I hissed at her.

She shrugged. "I think she is expecting. That's why the whole thing has upset her so much."

"Expecting what?"

She paused her popcorn in front of her mouth. "A baby, honey." She made a gesture with the popcorn towards them. "I think Brian is the father."

I thought about it. Zoe might be right. Fern hadn't been consuming alcohol when we had been out to the Diva's Den dancing nor during the Turning of the Year dinner. Brian had also given Fern a diamond droplet pendant during the dinner of Turning of the Year and for her birthday he had given her an adorable bracelet with a house, an apple and an F charm hung from it.

No wonder Brian wanted to get away for a while if he was getting overwhelmed with the thought of becoming a father. But why go on a what could become a dangerous mission and risk Fern becoming a single mother to two children?

Kate and Zoe sunk down to sit on the bed with me, and we chatted for a while about anything and everything whilst we consumed most of the snacks and drank the wine, almost forgetting that Murben was sitting at our side listening.

Eventually, Zoe threw open a hearing portal. "We need air. Come out for a run with me."

"Leave me alone," Davis answered from the other side of the portal.

"Stop licking yourself like a beaten dog and take me out, honey, as no one else is offering," she spat, throwing a glare at Murben.

When Davis didn't respond, Zoe closed the portal and jumped off the bed. "I'm going to go and kick my brother out of bed. You want to join me, Kate?"

"Sounds fun. Maybe I'll set his bedsheets on fire. That will get him going."

They laughed as they walked away, but their presence was immediately exchanged for Mewer's, who checked my eyes, my pulse and my temperature. "You're good to go. I'll discharge you but refrain from any activities for the rest of the day and drink plenty of fluids. And by that, I mean water," he said, tapping his pen on the empty wine bottle. "Do you want me to send for Zayd to help you to your room?"

Murben stood up. "No, I'll escort Agent Coraly."

Mewer nodded, and as always, he didn't linger before helping his next patient.

I donned a black tracksuit and a black t-shirt with the rank of first year that I pulled out from the side-table drawer, sticking Denor's letter down my trouser pocket. Then I tipped the left-over snacks on the tray into one bucket, tucked it under my arm and let Murben support me back to my room.

"You know that you'll be missing flight practice for the flight slalom challenge next month by going on this mission?" he muttered. "You know you need the practice."

"I promise I'll practise harder when I return. If I return."

He threw me a glance as to say that wasn't funny.

Inside my room, I felt quite exhausted and perhaps a tad drunk, so I laid down on the bed. That warm, fuzzy feeling gave me a pleasant buzz, making it easy to fall asleep, if it wasn't for Murben tapping on my shoulder.

"King Blackbone is waiting outside the door and asks for permission to come in and see you."

"I thought kings didn't ask for permission, but for forgiveness," I snarled.

"The rules are different for you."

Really? He's not going to bite on that sarcasm? "I don't want to see him."

"Okay, may I speak freely then, and not as a messenger from the king?"

"If you have to."

He crouched by the bedside to get his face levelled with mine. "You shouldn't be too quick to judge the king. He deserves to be cleared from the charges of what happened with Cadet Darling."

"Yeah? How so?"

"Because by the Spirits, I believe what he feels for you isn't love, but something deeper. Your souls matched each other's on all levels before you were even soul bonded. And I fear for the world and what King Blackbone would do to it to keep you safe. Please, talk to him. If you can't forgive him, at least end on good terms before you leave tomorrow. You don't know how many times he has kept you alive, and a kind word from you could be all it takes to keep him fighting the evil in this world. You don't know him, but I do, and he'd have his head severed from his shoulders before he knelt for anyone, but he was going to kneel to save you."

I rolled my eyes at his drama, but something in my chest had tightened at his words.

"If I sent a message through you, would that count?"

"It's better than nothing, if that's truly all the strength you can spare him."

"Tell him the roses better still be alive when I come back."

Murben looked at me as if he had seen the first sign of the world falling apart.

"He has already asked plenty of times for your forgiveness and if you don't give it to him, he'll lose himself. If he'll have to choose between you and himself, he will choose you."

"Or Cadet Darling."

Murben scoffed.

"What's funny?"

"Your ignorance of how much you meant to him."

"Stop Murben. You really need to open that match-making business. You're really good at talking the man up. What do you tell him about me, I wonder?"

"I remind him that your soul suffered a rift five years ago, and that he has touched on the part of your soul that's hurting the most from being betrayed. I tell him to be patient and give you time to heal. It takes time to get to know someone to the point the love is worth more than all the light crystals in the world."

"Wow. That's decent advice. What…what might Ben have answered to that?"

"Why don't you ask him yourself?"

"Never mind," I said, flinging myself out of bed and walking to the wardrobe. "I need to finish packing."

Murben straightened out his legs and followed me. "Should I let him inside?"

"It's his room, too." I pulled out the larger backpack that I had already started to pack and rested it towards the desk leg to finish packing.

Ben sauntered closer, the hair on my skin bristling because of his otherworldly energy that pushed against me. He looked at me for a while, probably hoping I would make eye-contact, but I kept on ignoring him. He reached for the bucket of left over snacks that I had put down on the desk.

When Murben had left the room, he asked, "What are you eating?" He looked inside the bucket. "Popcorn, onion rings and…" He smelt my breath. "Wine. The old classic." He raised his brows at me.

I didn't reply. He sighed. "How long will you hold this grudge?"

"It might take longer than it's worth it to receive my forgiveness. Until the thorns of the lovely rosebushes that you bought me have grown so thick, that it'll be impossible to enter this room."

"I said I'll give you forever, if that's the time you need to heal. And I'll kiss your soul every time you doubt my love for you."

"Oh! Kiss my arse."

"I'd love to." His hands closed around my waist.

"Stop it. Please, can you let me pack in peace?"

He held up his hands in surrender and threw himself onto the bed.

Angrily, I shoved down a few uniforms into the backpack, trying not to get them wrinkly. The bag had specific side straps where I could fasten my daggers, and one longer strap underneath to secure a blanket. I carried on packing, and each time I looked over my shoulder, I saw him watching me from the bed. It irked me how his tender eyes sent warmth streaming up and down my body. Involuntarily, I sighed more heavily each time I took a peek.

"Looks like you have that problem with drooling again," he said, and although I didn't look, I knew he had a cocky grin on his face.

"Bite me."

"You keep sweetening my deal. Kissing… Biting…"

I closed the lid to the backpack and clicked the buckles together. Then I turned around to look him deep into his eyes. "Harvey told me a crate of black iron had been stolen from the forge storage facility. Without a trace. As if someone had simply used unlocking magic to open the vault and closet it once the theft had been done. No sign of damage or forced entry. Then I remembered that you were more than seven minutes away from saving my life. Where were you, I wonder? So, I'll ask you, and if you lie to me, you'll have no chance for redemption in this lifetime. Think carefully about your answer before you give it. Did you steal the crate of black iron and give it to black-wings in your territory?"

His frown lowered and his eyes darkened. His chest rose and fell slowly with shallow breaths; not looking so confident lying in bed anymore.

He sat up with his feet firmly planted on the floor and raked both hands through his hair. "Yes. I took it."

"Why?"

"I can't tell you that."

I snorted to myself and slung the heavy bag over one shoulder. "I'm staying with Harvey tonight, and I'll see you in the infirmary after lunch tomorrow to remove the soul bond."

"You're still going to go through with the mission, even after what you've been through the last twenty-four hours?"

"Yes."

He raced to the door before I got there and kept his hand on it. "Please, don't go. I can't protect you off the Bensguard Outpost premises."

I griped the door handle. "You haven't protected me in the last twenty years. I think I'll manage on my own."

"I wanted to. I just hadn't found you yet."

"Remove your hand," I seethed, staring hard at him, and when I twitched to stand straight, he flinched, removing his hand.

A jolt of shock rippled through me, momentarily freezing the rage burning in my chest. *He flinched.* Satisfaction from a win against him was hard earned and instantly drowned beneath a layer of disbelief still scolding my gut. Power hummed in my vein, and it was intoxicating. *Maybe I have more power over him than I thought.* The king who had ruled over all black-wings since he was nineteen years old, and had a reputation of being ruthless to his bones, had flinched at my anger.

The question was whether he'd reclaim that power at a later date when I least expected it. Make my hurt insufferable. Heartbreaking. It worried me that he could break my heart – *and that I'd let him.*

47

The questions in the mathematics test hadn't changed this year either, and my only challenge had been to complete it in time since Emroyce had kept hissing at me to tell him the answers. Ironically, I had whispered them ever so softly, I had put a smile on Mazdon's face. Surprisingly, the bond to Ben had been extra quiet this morning, and I had only been hearing the soft hum of it pulsating in my ear like calm waves washing up on the shore. Ben had handed in his answer paper before anyone else and left the room.

"Where are you?" I asked once I handed in my paper and exited the exam room.

"Socialising with peers to garner who are our allies and who are our fiends."

One way of sugar-coating spying. *"Get your arse to the Infirmary."*

When I entered the infirmary hall, he was there waiting for me next to Harvey and Mewer.

"How did the test go?" Harvey asked.

"As well as if I'd had the answer sheet at hand."

"Right," Mewer voiced. "Let's do this quickly because I've a cavalry soldier with internal injuries, and an infantry man poisoned with night shade to attend to. Join hands."

Harvey clasped over Ben's hand as if it was a normal procedure by a captain, but I hesitated to hold my hand up in the air between Ben and me. Ben gazed at my small fingers before he sensually laced his fingers between mine. My heart pounded with the need to touch more than his hand, and to say what was left unsaid between us before I left. But I held myself together like an agent born and bred at the Bensguard Outpost, just like my brother.

I focused on Harvey's hardened resolve to find the strength to keep me going.

Mewer cupped one hand over mine and Ben's, and his other he folded over Ben and Harvey's grip. With a soft light, the bond shifted between us, and the humming in my ears died. The tenderness Ben's soul had provided me, like a subtle caress in the background, was gone and it made me feel like an empty bottle where someone had just turned it upside down and poured out all its contents.

"There," Mewer finally said bowing curtly. "Captain."

"Thank you, Camp Leader Mewer." Harvey put his hand on my shoulder. "The squad is meeting you in the stables. May the Spirit of Luck be with you."

"And also with you," I whispered, thinking this mission had nothing to do with luck and all to do with the skill of the monsters he had shaped here.

He nodded with a smile before he left me alone with Ben. Ben looked heartbroken and as empty as I felt. Despite that I repeatedly told him I preferred he stayed away, Ben followed me to the stables. I think I was up to about a hundred times that I had told him I wasn't good with goodbyes since I had met him almost two years ago.

Today, each time I lectured him about it, he had answered that this wasn't a goodbye because he would see me soon. He hadn't talked much this morning, dragging his feet around, sombre and sulky. He had stopped begging me to stay after General Denor had signed the mission orders – stopped talking; only answering when spoken to.

I prepared my horse and waited for the others to ready theirs in the stable and come outside to join me. At the corner by the side of the hitching pole, I sat slouched on a hay bale, watching as Ben was checking my work, tightening the cinch, clearing caught mane from the bridle and going through the packing to see that I had everything I needed for the journey.

"All in order, Inspector Blackbone?" I asked when his arms fell to his sides.

"It depends. Where are you going?" he asked for the thousandth time.

"It's classified. Don't worry. It's a low-risk mission."

His glance wandered up and down my body. "Then why are you armed to your teeth with weapons?"

I looked down at my flight leathers; the thickest garb the outpost provided and wearing them meant I was prepared for any assault - *from my own clumsiness or by others' vengeance.* It was true I had filled every strap, sheath and pocket with sharp iron. "It's the latest fashion," I mocked.

"Can you at least tell me when you'll be back, so I know when to come looking for you if that time lapses?"

"Nope. Classified. You're stuck being *soulmate* with my brother and won't be able to go anywhere until you've been on the mission through the Spirits' Trek."

"That's not an inspiring picture. If your brother's messed up mind doesn't kill me, the trek will finish me off."

"And if you survive both, I'll pick you off when you get back from the trek."

He smiled. "I don't doubt it." Then his shoulders sagged again. "Please, tell me you're joking, and I'll see you before I graduate in three years' time." Insecurely and probably worried about my answer, he slowly stroked his hand across the brown mare's rear.

Did he mean he would stay at the Bensguard Outpost when I wasn't here, and wait for me for three years until I came back?

"I haven't decided yet. Aren't you glad we're on talking terms again?" I smirked at him.

Yet inside of me, I was missing the mind communication the bond provided. It was comforting and fulfilling somehow.

His eyes darkened below his lowered, black brows. Slowly, he sauntered across the scattered hay on the ground between us and knelt on the stone, pushing in between my knees and putting his hands on top of my thighs.

"I count my small blessings. In earnest, I thought you'd never speak to me again. You can be quite stubborn." Longing surged in his eyes, wanting something he couldn't have.

It was incredibly difficult not to shove my fingers through his thick, black hair and lean forward to press my lips to his. My heart was certainly betraying me, pounding with its desire for him, filling my chest with a warmth I tried so hard to reject.

"You were going to kneel for me," I whispered, recalling him at the edge of the mat as Gravelhorn had me nailed to it.

"I was. For you, I will. I knelt for you in our room earlier, and I'm kneeling now. But you won't let me into your heart, won't trust me."

"Kneeling before me in private is one thing, but you were going to kneel in public. In front of all the cadets, only for Gravelhorn to spare my life," I clarified.

"For you, I'd turn Skyberg into dust."

I rested my hands on his strong shoulders. "Perhaps don't do that. And you know trusting is difficult for me."

"Maybe start small. Give me a location?"

I put my hand on his chest to push him backwards, so I could move my leg around him and get up. "Nice try. You almost had me there, and had you used a tad of your trust magic, I might have caved."

He stood up and followed me to the mare. "I'll never use trust magic on you for my own benefit. I told you that."

"You say that, but how would I know?" I moved the wooden stepladder to the side of the horse and untied her rope from the hitching pole, readying to leave.

I had to get away from Ben or I feared I'd break. The goodbyes really weren't my thing.

"For starters," he voiced, as he watched me mount. "If I had used it on you, I'd have taken you back to the Black Wing Territory. I'd have convinced you to forfeit the fight with Gravelhorn and for certain, I'd have had more intimacy the last week rather than fighting. But instead, I have given you space and respect. You're going on a mission without me, on which I neither know the location, nor the duration of your absence; for fuck's sake."

"Hmm," I pondered out loud. "And is it the space or the respect you imply by keeping the secret about why you have stolen a crate of black iron? What you have done with it, and who you're planning on stabbing? Are you planning on stabbing me with one when I least expect it as revenge for the time I almost impaled you?"

"Twice."

"What?"

"You've held a black blade to my heart twice."

"And how many times did I actually stab you?" I asked rhetorically, kicking the horse's flank, steering her in a circle.

"That you intended to do it still hurts," he muttered.

Ben leaned against the wall, crossing an ankle over his foot and shoved his hand into his pockets, nodding in greeting as Zoe, Brian, Cadet Crawly, Cadet Dessen and Sergeant Karson passed by, riding their horses out from the stable.

Zoe was the first one out, riding her favourite cream-coloured stallion whilst the other men had mounted dark-brown horses, except for Sergeant Karson, who rode a black charger. This made him look like our leader, although he was from the General Operations Unit and had no say over the cadets in the Special Missions Unit in normal circumstances.

Then we set off south towards Emendroth and it took all my strength not to look over my shoulder to see Ben one last time. Not seeing him, not hearing him, and not feeling him inside me made me feel so incredibly soulless. Had he felt the same when the bond broke? To me, there was no way of telling whether these feelings were caused by the broken bond, or if his soul had shattered my heart on the way out of me.

The convoy would be on the road for three days and there was a forecast of grey skies with a roof of heavy rain clouds, and light drizzle. There was a day's ride to get to Candir Outpost, reaching Dashqaz Outpost on our second day before we arrived at Emendroth Outpost on the third day.

Although, considering Zayd and I had pissed off Captain Wix, murdering her son, I'd rather sleep in the coal mines outside Dashqaz border than stay in the outpost. Thankfully, the Spirits had ruled in my favour for once, as King Emille had summoned Captain Wix to a counsel meeting by the time we arrived there.

We re-stocked our supplies and set course for Emendroth early in the morning to give the horses more leeway to rest during the day and not need to push them so hard. Brian was particularly keen on pointing it out, as he had always been fond of horses. That he and Winter had won the Horse Race Challenge last year hadn't come as a surprise.

Cadet Crawly rode up next to me. He flicked his wavy white hair to one side and looked at me with his big brown eyes. "You know…my best tradable good is sorrow," he said, and smiled pitifully at me.

I raised my brows at him. "How can one trade in sorrows?"

He was a second-year cadet and teammate with John Somers, a team Emroyce had named the Boss Team. Cadet Crawly had been kind to me during the entire trip, and I had learned that his mother worked in the kitchen in the royal palace when she got pregnant with him by someone with powers, but no one knew who, or could recall how he looked like. Many of the workers had speculated that it had been a black-wing, since his mother wouldn't say, claiming she couldn't remember. So Crawly wasn't too keen on having Ben and the rest of his entourage around the Bensguard Outpost.

"Many pay good money for me to wipe their memory of whatever causes them grief."

Zoe rode up to us and aligned her horse to his other side. "If you touch Angie, I'll wipe you off the face of this damn floating island, honey."

"I was just offering a relief, is all," he muttered, and no one questioned whether Zoe meant what she'd said.

"Thank you. That's very kind, Cadet Crawly. I'll think about it."

"You'll do no such thing," Zoe hissed. "If you fuck up the type of love King Blackbone offers you, I'll kick your arse until you can't sit again."

I moved around in the saddle. "I already feel sore enough to avoid sitting for at least two days."

"And that's without enduring something so painful as childbirth," Brian added.

Both Zoe and I turned in our saddles to look over our shoulders at Brian. "Or so I heard," he muttered, and looked to his left where Cadet Dessen walked his horse. "But Cadet Dessen is the torture master, so he should know."

Cadet Dessen was a beefy man, although I couldn't know whether it was simply his golden armour that made him look massive or if there were muscles underneath. His silver hair curled down to his back over a black cloak and his hands occasionally buzzed with the deep magenta charge of his torture magic. Its touch was said to be so crippling that even the generals and captains would not stand too close to him. They shrugged away from Cadet Dessen's father, who was the Torture Master at the King's Dungeon, even more.

"I've never endured childbirth, so I wouldn't know," he said curtly with that mix of humour and seriousness I didn't know how to interpret.

I could tell on Brian's face that he wasn't sure whether to laugh at the joke or be quiet. He could very quickly end up being Cadet Dessen's next victim.

"Kids! The Emendroth Outpost is just around the next bend," Sergeant Karson shouted from the front, leading the way along a narrow bridleway with trees blocking the sight of the path's destination on either side of us.

I couldn't wait to get to the Emendroth Outpost, or more accurately, I couldn't wait to get off the horse's back. In all my life, my butt had never been this sore. The times I had accompanied my father to the capital when young, we had always taken more time on the road and made more stops, gazing at the stars, or roaming through city markets and attending dances before carrying on. Mother had always stayed behind 'cooking' and 'cleaning', which I now knew were just other terms for 'spying' and 'covering up her tracks after relaying information to Ben's father'.

I let that thought linger. Harvey had caught and killed Mother five years ago, but Ben had become king two years before then. Had Ben known about my mother's mission? What if he had known and not called it off? He had told me he had known who I was the moment I had put my foot into his territory. Perhaps that wasn't because his spies found out about me, but because he already knew my family's circumstances.

"I don't like that look on your face. What is it, honey?" Zoe asked me, and both she and Cadet Crawly turned my way.

"Nothing. I'm tired."

Cadet Crawly stretched, probably sore as a sinner, too. "I hope they'll greet us with good food, a comfy bed and pretty whores when we arrive."

"Whores? Really?" I asked.

"Yeah," he turned to Zoe. "Will you share the cut and join me this time?"

"This time?" My jaw dropped, completely unhinged.

"Nope," Zoe answered.

My eyes grew wide open as I stared at Zoe.

But Crawly moaned. "You were more fun three years ago. Since when did you start denying yourself some pleasure?"

"Since I…since you started to look worn out and full of parasites, honey."

"Sure. Whatever," Crawly twisted in the saddle. "La Roy? Up for it?"

The thought clearly appalled Brian, and I doubted his righteous upbringing by Captain La Roy would ever allow him to accept that type of activity.

"I'll pass," he replied firmly but politely.

Zoe turned around to face Brian, her purple hair moving across her shoulders. "Are you sure, honey? You might have a few sleepless nights ahead of you."

"Yeah," Crawly added. "I heard that you don't want to fall asleep on a watch close to the iron mines."

That wasn't what Zoe had referred to, and I glared at her to ensure she wouldn't elaborate on her point. To which the bitch rolled her eyes at me.

Rounding the bend, the full force of the Emendroth Outpost came into view. An enormous sand-coloured fortress with two large keeps enveloped in masonry walls topped off with crenels. It rose majestically from atop a rolling hill, with the mountains that bordered the Black Wing Territory like a wall to the west.

Even though the Bensguard Outpost had the Special Missions Unit Academy, Emendroth Outpost was three times its size. A shiver ran down my spine as I took in its dark silhouette and the mist that clawed at the base of the wall. Seeing the banners of the lightning bolt instead of the key symbol felt sinister, like the air around it whispered to me that I was entering rival turf, and it reminded me I was far from home. I could feel it too, as our magic abilities weakened the further away from the Spirit's Heart we travelled. This was the outpost closest to the capital and a marker of a grand seat of power; a warning for all those who dared to cross past the portcullis.

The only relations I knew of, who were stationed at the Emendroth Outpost, were Cadet Charney's father in the Infantry Unit who possessed blocking magic, and Cadet Lerren's father in the Air Force who had breath that made you faint. So, my biggest threat was that Gravelhorn's family lived near the iron mines, and I'd definitely try to avoid running into any of them. If Gravelhorn had notified his four older brothers of how much he hated me, I could well be their next game, and they'd be suiting up for hunting as soon as I set foot in the camp outside the mines.

"What would you call a demon crossed with a Spirit?" Zoe asked, as we slowly neared the outpost.

"I'm too tired. That's more of a Nesso-game."

"Oh, come on. Don't be boring. Humour me. What would you call a demon crossed with a Spirit?"

"A fictional character," Crawly answered, not familiar with the games the black-wings played at lunchtime.

"A Demi-Spirit," I answered.

"No, that's when a mortal without wings on the ground below mates with a Spirit. Maybe you get a 'Spirit-damned' pain in the arse," Crawly retorted.

"Fine. Whatever. Sounds like your father might have been a demon, honey."

I snapped my head Zoe's way, sending her a warning with my narrowed eyes, and then at Crawly, who seemed cool-headed and well versed with Zoe's manners.

"You get a Demon King," Zoe answered. "What would you call a black-wing king crossed with Stone?"

I rolled my eyes at her. "I don't know, but I'd certainly beat Ben with a stone if I thought it'd make my words bear more weight."

"Correct," she laughed. "Dead weight!"

I actually laughed. It was kind of funny.

We eventually arrived at the outer courtyard of the Emendroth Outpost, receiving no welcome party, and soldiers with old-looking uniforms scurried around the place, carrying out their tasks without as much as looking our way.

"Since when did leadership start looking through the city gutters to find soldiers?" Crawly gasped.

"That's not helpful, Crawly," I rebuked before sliding down my horse, not able to wait a second longer to get off.

"I didn't come to help. I came along to mock," he replied, also swinging his leg over the saddle and sliding to the cobblestones.

A pressure in my temples began building. A headache coming on, and I gathered that this trip wouldn't be the respite from my problems as I had thought.

48

The tension in the air was thicker this morning than the southern humidity, and I realised that Zoe and my decision to keep daggers under our pillows wasn't a failed judgement call. We met up with the squad, each member with bags under their eyes from lack of sleep and walked the corridors aimlessly trying to find Captain Blingster. The conversations in the halls slowed as we passed, heads turned, and eyes lingered on us just long enough to assure us we were unwelcome.

The raids had become so frequent that leadership had ordered a squad from the Special Missions Unit of the Bensguard Outpost to come here. That had clearly made us an intrusion and an insult to those who considered they were capable of handling themselves. No one moved to make space, elbows remained stubbornly spread and if I'd break the fingers of those pointing at us with a disgusted look on their face, there'd be few soldiers left who'd be fit for battle.

Although, it surprised me how few soldiers there were at the outpost, and I guessed that leadership had sent most of its forces to the north to fight the war around Abarath. Procedures had been tightened because of the recent advancement from Commander Daffron's older brother, Duke Hartmore. I could only assume that the other part of the army had been sent to guard the iron trade in the mines.

We found Captain Blingster in the stable surrounded by the three camp leaders for the Infantry, the Cavalry and the Air Force. They were discussing hotly about various strategies, which we seemed to be interrupting. He turned around to give us a few instructions, the hostility in his voice sharp and the answers to our questions clipped and dismissive.

Once we had been briefed on our mission and saddled our horses, I could have sworn I heard my butt complain as I swung my leg up on the brown mare Captain Blingster allocated to me. The sharp pain and bruises were etched onto my butt bones and my muscle aches were running down my thighs. With this in mind, I cussed, remembering how I'd missed out on the prize of a massage from challenge four that the Agility Team had snagged when General Denor had trapped me in the cave. He should pay for that, although I was convinced that he wouldn't mind massaging my butt to repent for his sins. I shrugged. Horrible thought.

"Kids! Let's be vigilant about anything out of the ordinary today," Sergeant Karson said, as we cantered for the iron mines.

It only took thirty minutes to reach the mountains and the mines. The camps around the mines were as I had expected from the descriptions. Except, they were dirtier. Workers scurried back and forth, loading iron rocks into carts secured behind sturdy working horses. They fashioned grey overalls that looked filthier than a decade of working deep in the mines, especially around the knees where the fabric was significantly frayed.

There were five main cave openings into the mountain and their entrances had been framed with thick wooden beams, and iron rails the width of the carts' wheels run along the middle of the pathway so the workers could push the cart deeper into the mines. The horses then delivered the carts loaded with iron to the Ivory Forge on the southwestern coasts, where they melted it down and made weapons.

From atop my horse, I peered into the cart specifically meant for black iron, finding it was almost empty, and there was no horse strapped before it. Maybe it was because it could take days to fill it.

I looked up and deeper into the camp area and the vast field at the foot of the mountain, identifying hundreds of small barracks divided into drifts on either side of a dirt road. On one side, the wooden barracks were painted white and on the other side, they were painted black. On the black side, there were more horses and carts readied to pull iron loads towards the Black Wing Territory. This was the part of the deal and trade agreement.

A middle-aged man with brown hair reaching his neck, dressed in a new grey overall with a sword and a lasso whip at his sides, spotted us arriving and approached with determined strides. He was cleanly shaven and not as dirty as the other men and was even adorned with a few gold rings on his fingers.

"I heard Bensguard leadership was going to send the special unit down. Did not expect they could spare six of you."

I couldn't tell by his voice whether he was impressed, or if he thought it had been an insult. But he carried on. "I'm Foreman Daral." He was looking Valentina's father in the eye when he spoke, most likely being a veteran raised in the olden days when there wasn't so much magic around and age meant strength and wisdom.

"I'm Sergeant Karson and this is Cadet La Roy, Cadet Dessen, Cadet Crawly, Agent Coraly and Agent Hammerton." He pointed at us in turn.

"We're here to help stop the trade raids, so let us know what we can do."

"I guess you guys could accompany the next cart rolling for the Ivory Forge. See if you can scout any spies. Apprehend them if you can. As long as we have one hostage to question, we might make some progress."

Seemed easy enough a task. Scout a spy, catch it, and protect the cart in the event of an ambush. Although, I had wished for my task to be off the horse's back.

A group of workers had gathered near one of the entrances and were speaking in hushed tones, staring at me.

"Don't mind them. They are black-wings," Forman Daral said. "Get back to work!" he shouted before turning back to us and pointing at a horse that had begun walking with a driver on a small seat fashioned at the cart's front. The driver was accompanied by two guards. "You can join that delivery if you catch up."

Sergeant Karson nodded and kicked his heels into the black charger's flank. The charger reacted instantly and trotted forward, and our horses followed his lead. Having greeted the three men in the delivery party, we settled into a walk beside them. The guards' tension seemed to ease off, their shoulders not as tightly set below their ears and their sword hands moved from where they had rested on their laps near the hilts to now lazily hold their reins. Their eyes kept scanning the road ahead, though, but not as vigilantly as before. It was understandable. Every trip was a gamble, every delivery a test of luck.

A chilled breeze swept over my neck, so I folded the collar of my uniform up to protect against the winter winds rolling over the hills on either side of us. Gone were the leaves on the trees that fell in autumn and gone were even the smallest gaps in the clouds to let through sunlight. We rode side by side for an hour, talking about trivial soldier topics like our favourite weapon to wield, how uncomfortable the thick winter socks were and comparing the food in our canteens. It sounded like our squad ate gourmet food compared to them. But there was only so much soldier talk one could take when every movement sent a jolt of soreness through my body. I had been on a horseback for too long and my bones complained about it. It felt like my thighs had been rubbed with sandpaper, my knees locked in a constant position of agony and my lower back throbbed relentlessly. My fingers cramped, which I might, or might not, be able to straighten out ever again.

A thud sounded against the cart, and we all looked towards the sound. An attacker had lodged an arrow into the side of the wooden cart. Two more arrows thudded into the other side of the cart, and Sergeant Karson's charger reared, but he got it to settle and was off, galloping beyond the hill the arrow had come from with Cadet Crawly and Cadet Dessen not hesitating to follow.

Not the first time under attack, the horse strapped to the cart clearly recognised the threat and galloped off in full pelt. The two mine guards hurried after it, but I veered my mare towards the hill from where the first arrow had come, in the opposite direction of where Sergeant Karson's team had headed.

"La Roy, cover me!"

"No! Coraly!" he yelped but soon gave up trying to persuade me to stop as he knew I wouldn't, so instead he blazed fire at both my sides, hiding me in flames.

Brian and Zoe weren't far behind me when I reached the top and saw three men flee on foot down the hillside and into the forest beyond. They were splitting up and running in different directions, so I shouted for Brian and Zoe that I'd follow the one to the far right.

Harder, I kicked the mare's flanks and raced towards the treeline, but I quickly realised that the forest was too dense to cover a vast distance with my mare.

I flung myself down to the grass and drew one dagger in hand before sprinting into the darkness below the canopy of naked branches.

It was a damn shame I needed to catch the man alive, or I could have tortured him with my magic, but if he lived and talked, he could snitch that I had used it. He wasn't a big man. I'd say he was about my height, my weight and thinner than me, so a collision between us would be evenly matched. But damn, could he run fast.

I ran my damned fasted to catch him, still, the gap between us remained. Strange was that when we got deeper into the undergrowth, he kept stopping and turning around briefly as if to check that I was still following. He had a quiver full of arrows, so he had plenty of time to stop, anchor, aim and let loose an arrow towards me before I reached him. So why didn't he? He was luring me towards something. The warning grew in my gut, and I ceased the chase, letting him go. But he, too, stopped and turned with a curious expression on his face. The bastard even took a few steps closer to me.

But as someone pushed aside bushes on my right and stepped closer, the small man lowered himself into the high grass and seemed to vanish. Three enormous men clad in warrior leathers; filled to the brim with daggers and two long-swords crossing in the baldric at their backs leered at me.

All three warriors had short, blonde hair that was shaved at the sides, long faces with sharply chiselled jaws and multiple scars over their faces. They all held an expression of being pleased to see me, as if they had expected me, yet simultaneously seemed disgusted by the sight of me. I had been prepared to engage in combat against one man, against three and wherever the fourth one had gone, that fight wouldn't end well for me.

I backed up as the three men moved towards me.

"What a nice coincidence to run into you out here, all alone, Cadet Coraly," the oldest of them, who walked in the forefront, purred.

I swallowed at the loaded threat in his voice. Their handsomely rugged looks were not too far off from…from…Floyd Gravelhorn. These could be Gravelhorn's older brothers. The Gravelhorn family lived in these parts, so it wasn't a far stretch to assume. If they were, their magic was strength – and I was dead. Gravelhorn's older brothers were experienced soldiers, having already survived the challenges of the academy.

Flames of fear engulfed me, and my gut twisted with nausea. Hopefully, they knew me from being the captain's sister rather than by my disputes with Gravelhorn. If so, I could reason with them. But I knew that hope was slim to none. They all stared at me like I was a small insect they'd enjoy crushing with their boots – if I was so lucky to get a quick and painless death.

The man I assume was the eldest, because he had a weathered look from experience and carried himself with more authority than the others, spoke again. "Our little brother has told us all about you, black-wing-lover."

Crap! There died the last bit of hope I had of making it out of this alive.

He laughed menacingly. "We'll kill you now," he informed, as if he was giving me a heads up. "The question is just how and what we'll do with your corpse." He turned around to his blonde brothers, littered with more scars than Gravelhorn. "What do you guys think? Should we split her in six parts and send King Blackbone a map, so he can go on a treasure hunt?"

"I say we send her head in a gift box to Black Castle," the second oldest suggested.

"Let's push an iron rod through her body whilst she's still alive and then hang her from the Ivory Castle, somewhere high up where it's hard to get her down, so that everyone has plenty of time to look at her treacherous corpse whilst it rots," the third one said.

My legs wobbled under my weight. What if Ben had to see those images of me? Parts of me.

"King Blackbone will kill you," I croaked out, my voice breaking from fear.

"Undoubtedly. If he knew who was responsible, but who will tell him?" The oldest brother flailed his arms out to gesture at the calm nature surrounding us, which was nothing more than naked trees, boulders and a brown forest floor with the odd clusters of mushrooms. No one but ants and birds were here to witness my murder.

"Zoe! Brian!" I screamed.

"I don't know the other guys who attacked your cart, because that wasn't us. But thanks to them, your friends aren't even close to here. They won't hear your screams."

My heart pounded so hard it hurt. I really couldn't see how I could get out of this with my life intact. Oddly, the thought that I had failed Ben was the thing that came to my mind. I wanted to at least try to fight for my survival, but it wasn't for my sake, it was for his. I couldn't die like this, like a slaughtered boar in the woods. It was undignified for a former general's daughter. But my mind didn't let me see past the logical outcome of three brute men against a small-sized woman. I trembled so hard I felt numb, and worse still when the oldest brother drew a sword free from his back.

"I feel like hunting. The adrenaline rush makes the kill more satisfying. I'll give you a three second head start, then we're coming for you. One…"

I turned on my heel, sprinting for the treeline.

"Two!" I heard him shout from behind me. The amusement was evident in his tone, like he was thoroughly enjoying this.

I looked up. The treeline leading to the road was too far away to make it there before the Gravelhorn brothers would catch me, and I was within reach of an arrow the entire time.

"Three!"

They were coming!

I jumped over tree roots growing close to the ground, careful not to trip, and hammered my boots harder on the dirt pathway, but Gravelhorn's brothers were close to my heel and breathing down my neck already. I knew they'd catch me. Like a rabbit running from wolves, my heart belaboured my ribcage as I fled.

What would they do to me once they'd caught me? Immediately run me through with that enormous long-sword? Capture me and bring me back to their home to drive an iron rod through me? Beat me to death first?

A heavy weight folded over my back and wrestled me to the ground, crushing my lungs and beating the air out of them. My nose hit the soil, and my cheek scraped over gravel. I had to close my mouth, to not eat dirt. The older brother grabbed me by the collar and lifted me up towards him, where I saw the rage glistening in his hazel eyes. Hunger for revenge and anger coiled deep inside them, and the terror I felt was suffocating, as I knew Gravelhorn eyes would be the last thing I saw before death.

There was a tree right behind me, giving me little wiggle room to move as each attempt to swing at him made my flight leather scrape against bark, and I had lost my drawn dagger in the fall.

An arrow thudded, and the brother jerked forward, pressing me up against the trunk before he looked down at his chest. There was a tip of an arrow emerging straight through his ribcage having torn open the leather of his jerkin.

Another arrow lodged to the side of the first.

I screamed as his grip on me became slack, my back grating along the bark, and my feet touching the ground as he collapsed at my side.

More arrows ripped through the forest, aiming for the other two brothers standing a short distance away from me, gawking at the sight of their dead brother. None of the brothers reacted in time, and several arrows lodged into their backs also. The man, who had hidden in the long grass, now reappeared and stood before running away.

Something pricked my neck. Had I been hit? I searched the area with my hand and found a small dart. Poison?

My legs numbed, lowering me to the forest floor. I had to get back up again to get to the treeline and call for help from the others. I needed an antidote. Fast. I got to my knees, but my feet tickled, going numb.

Shit!

Stand up, Angelica!

You need to get up! I screamed at myself.

The ground before me fanned out and merged back together, repeatedly, making pebbles and twigs appear in duplicate. I hadn't done the hallucination training yet, but I'd have to pull through, anyway. I folded up my knee and put my foot on the ground, but because my foot was numb, I couldn't really feel if it was firmly planted. With my double vision, I could only hope I had put my foot at a balanced distance away from my body. At least, I think I saw my knee wobble in the air.

Lift!

Lift yourself up!

One. Two. Three.

The force I used pushed my balance off centre and I stumbled to land on my hipbone.

Ouch!

Again, I attempted getting up and found my footing.

Two steps. Three steps.

I was going forward, at least.

The ground came up at me, or I fell, I wasn't sure, but my chest scraped against the forest floor for a second time.

Damn!

The fall scraped skin off my chest and my collarbone could have broken, but now my whole body was numb, so I couldn't tell whether it was bad or only superficial.

A shadow fell over me. The weight of someone's foot pressed my back down and my panic spiralled as I had no control over my body to do a damned thing to fight the incoming threat.

"Just stay down," a deep male voice instructed, not belong to any of my friends.

An unfamiliar foe.

Shit!

49

Am I dead?

I pulled air into my lungs.

Do I still have all my body parts?

I tested them, and yes, they all moved and were intact. Head, shoulders, arms, legs and toes, all seemed okay. I blinked my eyes open. This wasn't a dorm room. It was a castle bedchamber.

The bed that enveloped me was huge, with a canopy of brown fabric with gold embroidery; an emblem with a circle around the letters PH. The room had a high ceiling, and the wallpaper was in a soft brown with beige patterns. Beige curtains gleamed like molten gold as the sunlight outside the windows streamed through. There were large golden framed paintings of battles and nature hung in a level line across the walls. A wardrobe, a vanity and a desk were pushed against the opposite wall, their wood had been carved into detailed flowery patterns.

I had seen nothing like it before.

The room was gorgeous.

And I'm alive.

Odd.

I stood up and a long white nightgown flowed to the floor around my feet. It was in a romantic design with lace and cut tightly around the waist like a corset. Spirits! This wasn't my style. Where were my flight leathers and my weapons? I glanced around the room but couldn't find them.

The giant iron door was the only escape route I could see, and judging by its thick frame, it would be heavy to open. I inhaled, gathering my strength before tugging at the handle. A gleaming iron spear shot out to stop me from exiting as soon as I peered out into the hallway, which was also decorated in brown and gold, with a dark-brown carpet running along the centre of the corridor.

"I'll alert the duke you're awake," a sinister voice said, and it wasn't the same man who had kidnapped me in the forest.

I quickly inspected the guard, completely covered in shiny new iron armour.

Duke? PH…Patrick Hartmore? Could I be in the Hartmore Manor in the Black Wing Territory?

The guard shut the door with force, pushing me backwards. If he thought that could keep a special mission agent in captivity, he was stupid!

Darting to one of the windows, I pulled the drape aside and climbed up onto the wide windowsill, fiddled open the locks and pushed the window open. A vicious gust of wind tore my hair back, and I gripped hold of the bars across the window so as not to fall off the sill. A zap of magic hurt my hands, so I immediately let go of the iron. They had been warded with magic! Fuck! I leaned forward, careful not to let my forehead touch the bars when looking out. I swallowed. Okay, perhaps that way hadn't been a viable option of escape anyway. Beneath the window was a one hundred metre drop along a cliff face that ended in a lake. I supposed it could be possible to survive the plummet into the water if my wings failed me and if I could stay clear of the outcrops of the rock face, and if there were no rocks beneath the surface. But that was a lot of ifs I wasn't willing to gamble on even if I could break the wards and force the iron bars apart.

A maid with a large basket walked into the room and stopped to stare at me with a terror-filled look on her face. She lowered her gaze and put the basket down on the floor by the vanity, bringing out a brown gown with gold thread running through it. With its delicate details, the dress was more refined than everyday wear, yet it didn't carry the lavishness of a true ballroom gown.

She folded it over the chair before she brought up a makeup box, hair items and finally a pair of brown shin-high boots. Then she stood still behind the vanity chair, waiting in silence. The woman was so calm I dared to approach her. She was in her forties, I guessed, with a frail body squeezed into a cream dress with a burgundy jacket laced tightly around her waist, and she had dainty, black wings tucked close to her frame. She was pale, as if she was malnourished, which contrasted with the black hair she had tied up in a bun at the top of her head.

I crept down from the windowsill, and she gestured for the dress. "Please, let me help you."

Her quiet sophistication was inviting, so I took a few steps closer and as I reached the chair, I pinned the fabric of the dress between my fingers. "Where are my flight leathers?"

"Duke Hartmore thought this was more appropriate for lunch."

"Then Duke Hartmore can wear it. Where…"

The woman giggled into her hand. I hadn't expected that.

"I'm sorry," she apologised. "You'll understand why that is funny when you see what a proud gentleman he is. Please, let me help you dress."

"Is it fair that I know the name of the person who wants to dress me?"

Her smiles came easily. "My name is Miss Verona Gretel."

"I'm–"

"Miss Angelica Coraly." A soft, knowing smile tugged at her lips and there was a familiar recognition in her gaze even though I was certain I had never met her before. "Everyone knows who you are."

My brows rose, stretching out my entire face. "Do they?"

"Well, everyone at this manor has been warned. There is a representation of you painted in blood on the Black Castle proclamation board, so it's safe to say the entire Black Wing Territory knows. Although, I'd say it doesn't do your beauty justice."

I recalled the ordeal with Davis's severed thumb and a beat of agony pounded at my chest.

Miss Gretel laced the dress at my back so tightly I could hardly breathe, and my lungs already throbbed in pain from Gravelhorn's brother having wrestled me to the ground. How would dressing like this leave enough airway open to my lungs to think straight?

When she finished, she gestured for me to sit down.

I watched her through the oval mirror of the vanity; her thin ebony eyebrows folding over black eyes darkly rimmed with eyeliner and subtle wrinkles etched at the side of her eyes. Her lips had the same burgundy colour as her jacket and as she smiled at me, I noticed two lines of straight and white teeth. She was clearly treated well as a servant, although she wore no jewellery, not even earrings.

"What's the Duke like?" I asked, as Miss Gretel applied my makeup.

"He's not his brother."

I don't think anyone was alike Commander Daffron. He could possibly be his own species.

"What does he want with me?"

"He wouldn't tell that to his servants, but he has always been jealous of what King Blackbone possesses."

Great! I was in the middle of a power struggle between two men fighting over the same toy. I had seen Duke Hartmore a few times, and we had danced once or twice during one of Ben's balls that I had attended before I had fully caught the king's attention. I recalled one of the times when the duke was about to ask me for a dance and Ben had interfered and sent him away on business matters.

Later that night was the first time Ben had danced with me. Never had people stared at me so much as during those three minutes. But I hadn't cared. The crowd had faded into nothing when the two of us swayed on the dance floor of our own world. I relished the moment to the core of my soul, the attraction too strong to ignore already then. I recalled the melody, desperately wanting the memory to take me back to that day. The ghost of his warm touch tingled over my skin and making my heartbeat race. That I was an undercover spy intensified the moment and though I had expected nothing more than a formal dance of duty, it had meant something deeper as he seemed able to look straight into my soul. For solely those three minutes, I had let down my guard and felt like myself, like the person I wanted to be.

Those three carefree minutes were gone now, tarnished by the hardship of lovers of warring sides, a war my mother started.

Not wanting to think down the path leading to pain from the day Mother had labelled me a traitor, I shook my head to focus back on Gretel.

I picked up some of Gretel's pins. "Can I have these?"

"Of course. Do you want me to put them into your hair?" She had almost finished putting up the front of my hair into a bun at the back of my head, from which the rest of my long, blue hair hung to the small of my back.

"No. I'm going to fashion a weapon with them."

She smiled. "I understand perfectly why King Blackbone chose you, my queen."

My heart almost stopped. "What?" Had she just referred to me as her queen?

The guard opened the door before I could ask her to explain.

"Time to go!" the guard shouted.

Miss Gretel rushed to pack up her things and then whispered into my ear. "The king knows you're here." Then she curtsied towards me before she scurried outside with the basket strapped over her arm.

Quickly, I uncoiled the pins and spun a few around a thicker one, making it look like a tiny knife before shoving it down the side of the fashionable boots I had been provided.

The guard looked at me as if he wondered whether or not I was coming. If I'd had a choice, then not!

I sighed, following the guard as he escorted me through endless corridors, and all the guards I came across during the walk wore shiny armour, covering every bit of their body except their eyes, nose and mouth.

So, this is where all the iron had gone.

The luxury of this castle couldn't compare to any other place I had ever seen. Black Castle was known to be...well, black. It had dark stones, and not all of this fancy decor, with floor to ceiling mirrors wrapped in gold frames, the brown and golden drapes around each alcove where sconces were holding torches lit by a magic flames, and enormous portraits and paintings on the walls. Duke Hartmore obviously liked the more extravagant lifestyle.

Brought along a labyrinth of brown carpets, we finally arrived at a golden double winged door. The guard opened it ajar and pushed me through the gap. The door closed behind me in an echoing thud.

Wonderful.

I took a few steps deeper into the majestic dining hall, gawking at the view of a vast lake through the massive windows. The hall had a table in its centre, large enough to easily host over fifty people. A throne-like chair at its head had been pushed half a metre away from the table, and in it sat a well-dressed man, his back straight like a rod made from the iron he'd been looting.

Duke Patrick Hartmore.

He licked his lips as if the guard had brought him a treat. I approached him slowly, inspecting him from top to toe to locate any weapons. Peculiarly, he wasn't wearing any.

He wore black trousers and a tailcoat, with a brown handkerchief tucked into the left breast pocket. Beneath the surcoat, he had a brown suit vest over a crisp white shirt, where a brown bow tie tightened around his collar. White gloves covered his hand and at the end of the shirt sleeves he had fastened golden cufflinks. Golden hair curled around a tall, black top-hat, and his face was groomed to perfection. He might even have had some makeup on his face to make it look impeccably smooth. As a display of grandness, he had his black wings spread wide behind him, the tips coloured in the same teal colour as his eyes.

"Stunning," he exclaimed when I was right in front of him.

I crossed my arms over my chest, causing the iron wires that supported the corset to press up against my lungs, making me feel even more caged inside this prison. "Why am I here, Duke Hartmore?" I panted, getting little air.

"I wanted to meet you in a more private setting. I've heard so much about you…and King Blackbone."

"Well, we aren't on good speaking terms at the moment, so what you've heard means jack shit now."

He pinched his pointy chin between his thumb and fingers. "Interesting. Let's discuss it over food and wine." He rang a golden bell before putting it back down onto the table next to a paper.

A row of servants entered the room and placed platters of meats, potatoes, vegetables and gravy onto the table before leaving.

"Please, sit," Duke Hartmore said, and I slowly edged myself between the chair and table at the spot beside him. Before I sat down, he vanished and appeared again behind the backrest of my chair, his white-gloved hands tucking me in.

"What in the world?"

He smiled down at me and winked. "I can winnow between shadows."

I threw an accusing gaze over my shoulder. "Commander Daffron doesn't possess that magic."

"No, my brother has this silly notion of living by hard work without magic. My magic was a gift." He leaned back in his chair.

The rapid movement was going to give my neck grief. "Really? Gifted or taken?"

Either or, a man who possessed magic, but hadn't touched the Spirit's Heart, or had their magic inherited, would soon go mad. Their body wasn't built to contain magic.

"I hear my brother has rubbed off his healthy amount of scepticism on you," he snarled. "How is my dear brother faring these days? Trapped in the white-wing academy at the Bensguard Outpost, is he? Still a loyal commander who follows our beloved king's every command?"

My teeth grit at hearing the tone he used when speaking about Ben and Commander Daffron. "I wouldn't know. He doesn't talk much."

"Classic Valence," he snorted, crossing his leg over his knee like a gentleman and resting both arms on the armrests.

Valence? Was that the commander's first name? It was beautiful.

He gestured for the food on the table. "Shall we start?"

"I'd rather leave." I kept my voice level. I couldn't afford to work myself up as he antagonised me. My primary objective was to breathe and not faint in this dress. "Where are my flight leathers?"

"You can't leave already. The party hasn't even started." He leered shamelessly, clearly aware and amused by my lack of air.

I clenched my jaw and glared at my captor. "What party?"

He laced his fingers and rested them on his lap. "I have much in store for our future."

Every word that dripped from his mouth was obviously deliberate to test my patience with his vague riddles and unnecessary theatrics.

"Our future? Duke Hartmore, I'm not one for games and I'm growing bored." My fingers curled into fists at my sides, nails biting into my palms. "Is there a point to all this, or are you stalling purely for the fun of it?" I forced a breath out and back in, feeling dizzy. "What do you want from me?"

"An alliance." The words came out in a purr as if he thoroughly enjoyed hearing himself talk.

"Surely, you must discuss that with King Blackbone. I have nothing to offer you. No lands. No title. No army."

"No, but you have the king wrapped around your little finger. So, if you obey me, I control him and thereby the kingdom."

He dragged out another meaningless sentence, my irritation burning hotter. If he didn't start to make sense soon, I'd launch myself across the room and into his lap to strangle it out of him.

"I think you got your facts confused."

"Really?" He leered at me as if he pitied my ignorance. "Because it took all but an hour after your arrival here before I received the king's threatening letter. You must clearly be a very interesting person if King Blackbone hasn't tired of you yet."

My nails were now cutting into the flesh of my palm so hard it wouldn't surprise me if it had drawn blood.

He stood up as he picked up the letter from the table and paced in front of the fireplace to read it to me.

"Duke Hartmore," he read and paused. "Duke Hartmore? No, 'Dear Duke'. 'Hello Duke'. 'Good greetings, Duke'," he mocked, but carried on. *"Cadet Coraly is in your care, and you will care for her like you would a queen."* Duke Hartmore ensured he had my eye-contact before he gestured at the table. "Do you feel like I have treated you like a queen?"

I averted from his gaze, proudly looking out at the lake view.

"If I see a bruise on her skin, a cut to her flesh, swellings, or learn that you have removed a hair from her body, I'll scatter the remains of you in so many places you will neither see any Spirits or any Demons before I pulverise this world into dust. You have four days to return her to the Bensguard Outpost. Failing to do so will be an act of war. I will spare no effort or expense in a retaliation. King Blackbone." Another short pause. "Fascinating, isn't it? Never have I seen his composure falter, but this…this reek of desperation." He looked closer at the letter, twisting it slightly in the light. "And I think he has even signed his name with his blood, as if the threat of his words weren't enough." He tossed the letter into the fire, where a corner ignited first before the rest was set aflame. "And it intrigues me how you can even stand looking at him after what he did to your family."

"That wasn't King Blackbone's doing. It was his father's," I muttered lowly, watching the letter burn with his words that still echoed in my mind.

Words he had written to protect me even though I had pushed him away.

"Yes, of course." He gazed into the fire before holding out his index finger to me. "But then again. When your mother begged him to be alleviated from the mission after his father died, King Blackbone denied her request and ordered her to continue with the deceptive game."

My mother had begged Ben to stop it?

The knowledge stung and tightened my already compressed lungs.

"Hurts, doesn't it?" he mocked. "To be betrayed. Over and over again.

Love is redundant." He gestured for the fire where the letter had burned to cinders. "Although I admire King Blackbone's quite poetic letter about your safety, it said nothing about me marrying you. When you marry me, you won't get love, but you'll get all the luxury you'll ever need."

"Marry you?" I almost choked on a snort. "You're delusional if you think I'll ever marry you."

"Oh sorry, honey. Did I forget to bring in my bargaining tool before mentioning that?" He rang his gold bell again, and a guard popped his head in through the golden doors. "Bring the hostages in here," Duke Hartmore commanded.

Hostages?

Six guards escorted three men inside the room wearing dirty and blood-caked Special Missions Unit's flight leathers and brown fabric bags over their heads. No woman, though. Zoe wasn't here. My heart cramped. The guards kicked at the back of their kneecaps to make them kneel on the brown carpet that stretched from the doors to the fireplace. The men grunted in pain and gurgled words, obviously gagged. A chill of dread ran down my arms. Then the guards yanked the bags off their heads.

Cadet Crawly, Sergeant Karson…and Brian!

Their faces were swollen and the skin across their eyes and cheeks was bruised a tone of blue with dark black edges.

My hands flew up by reflex to cover my mouth, and tears stung in my eyes.

"My problem was your stubbornness, Miss Coraly. You see, I knew I could beat you black and blue and break all the bones in your body, and you'd still rather die than have the Spirits mark your skin with our union. But then I found a solution. Your weakness is your compassion for those you love. So, now your problem is, Miss Coraly, that I have a priest ready to wed us in an hour, so you have very little time to decide. If you refuse, your friends will suffer the consequences of your choice."

I gawked at him, shaking my head. *No! This can't be happening.* "Please, don't," I pleaded.

Ben had told me that this man was someone he hoped I'd never meet again in my lifetime. Now I understood why.

"Let's start with the oldest then, shall we?" The guard next to Valentina's father lowered his dagger to place it against his throat.

Sergeant Karson looked at me, not weakening his resolve. He knew what it was to be a victim of war. He wasn't blaming me for being in this situation.

"No! Stop!" I screamed.

Duke Hartmore held up a hand to halt the guard. "Stop? So, are you coming with me to the chapel?"

Marriage. The mark of the Spirits would be permanent, and the Spirits would strike me down if found guilty of adultery with Ben. How could I agree to a lifetime by Duke Hartmore's side? To give up Ben? The ultimatum had made me realise how much I still loved Ben and although I was hurt, I'd never forsaken him, forsaken us.

Surely, he was bluffing. If he wanted me to cooperate, he couldn't kill my friends.

"I…I…I can't," I stuttered.

Duke Hartmore flicked his hand at the guard, a merciless command that fell like a blade itself. I turned my head to the guard who moved behind Sergeant Karson. A sharp blade glinted as it caught the reflection of the sunlight streaming in from the windows. The moment stretched, frozen in time yet unbearably swift. There was no hesitation. The guard wrenched the sergeant's head back and in one single, practised motion, he slid the dagger across Valentina's father's throat. The sound was sickeningly soft, a whisper through the room's silence. I gasped at hearing the sharp yelp and the wet gurgling. The jugular expelled masses of blood, spilling in dark lines down his chest.

"No!" I screamed, pulling at my hair. "What have you done?" My mind struggled to accept what had just happened.

Sergeant Karson's eyes flickered then turned vacant and his body went limp. His body swayed for a fraction of a second before the guard pushed it forward to fold onto the carpet with a thud. The space between us quickly filled with the tangy scent of blood, my body heaved, and I almost vomited. Watching the tears that streamed down Brian's face made my vision water.

The guard simply wiped his blade clean on a cloth from his pocket, his face unreadable, as if he had done nothing more than complete an ordinary task. He didn't comprehend that he had murdered my friend's father.

The duke watched, satisfied.

How would I find the strength to tell Valentina her father was dead? She'd be devastated when she found out. How could I comfort her, hug her tightly enough, when I had caused his death?

My breath caught in my throat. *I can't breathe.* I fought to stay conscious. The warmth rose in my body and the faded edges of nearly fainting threatened to take control of me.

When the guard, who was towering over Brian, put his blade to Brian's throat, my knees buckled and hit down on the carpet. My heart beat with severe palpitations. Tears welled down my cheeks as I clawed at my face. "Please! Stop! Please!" I cried as loudly as I could, pouring all my panic and pain behind the sobs. *No! Not Brian! Not Brian!*

I searched his kind eyes for forgiveness but found no blame in them. We shared this trauma. The terror was as evident in Crawly's eyes, who kept his head down and gaze low not to bring attention to himself.

"Okay, I can see you're suffering, so I'll make you a deal. I know you want to complete the academy and hike the Spirits' Trek to restore your father's good name. I'll allow you to do that, if you return to me straight after and marry me. You'll have to make your oath with the use of an oath caster's magic, of course, but I'd let you and your…two remaining friends go."

What choice did I have? I couldn't let him murder Brian and leave Fern's child fatherless. I had already made Valentina fatherless. At least this way, I had a chance to find magic that could reverse the oath or at least have a few last moments with Ben before it was time for me to say goodbye.

If I could muster to say the hated word.

I nodded, wiping the tears and snot off my face. It was to little avail, my tears kept coming each time I looked at Sergeant Karson's corpse.

"Bring in the oath caster!" Duke Hartmore ordered the guard in charge, and he turned to walk out, but returned only a few moments later with an elderly man by his side who had a crooked back as he slowly walked forwards.

Seeing the oath caster enter the room, made my chest become heavy, as if the Spirit of Death had filled it to the brim with rocks. This brown-robed man with sparse grey hair and light-grey eyes would destroy my life. Duke Hartmore had been right. I'd have rather died than live and suffer with this curse hanging over my head. But if it saved Brian and Cadet Crawly's lives, I had no other choice.

The old man held up a thin, wrinkly hand, beckoning me with a gnarly finger to put my hand in his. The tension of the moment pressed on my chest, battling to steal a breath from my lungs that my dress had already robbed me of. This man was asking me to make one single vow, an irrevocable oath that would sever any hope of a future with Ben. My heart screamed with pain. To find another way. To refuse. But the image of my friends, bound, beaten, and waiting for a salvation only I could secure, burned behind my eyes.

I swallowed hard and held out my hand, hesitating at first. I sighed. I knew the stakes. Finally, I rested my hand on his cold bones. He then turned to look at Duke Hartmore. "Tell me the conditions of the oath."

"Miss Angelica Coraly shall return to wed me no longer than six months after her graduation, or immediately, if she decides to drop out of the academy before she graduates. With the oath said, she won't be able to engage with anyone else."

The old man turned to me. "Do you, Miss Angelica Coraly, understand the conditions of the oath and the consequences should you fail to honour them?"

My pulse pounded in my ears from the fear I felt sensing the oath caster's magic thrumming in the air, waiting. *Once I speak the words, it's done. There's no going back.*

"Yes," I whimpered, finding it even harder to breathe in the dress.

I was certain the duke had made me wear it on purpose for his own protection. I couldn't reach the make-shift knife in my boot to kill him or even make a quick escape wearing this.

"And do you willingly take part in this oath?"

"I kind of have to," I snorted, my mind caught between love and duty.

"You must state you're doing it willingly, dear, or the oath will not latch on." He patted my hand gently as he waited for my response.

Could he tell that I was being forced to do this? Did he know even? Did it matter to me if he did? He was doing it anyway.

My lips parted, but the words stuck for a moment. "I'm doing it willingly," the pained breath spilled out against my will, sealing my fate.

A distinct glow coiled around my wrist and a golden tattoo curled around it like a fancy bracelet, or in my case, shackles. It bound something deep inside me, and I felt my heart and hopes shatter.

"Once you have honoured your oath, the oath will break and the symbols around your wrist will disappear." He looked at me with sad eyes. "Okay, dear?" He gently patted over my hand again, seeming to ease his own burdened heart.

I nodded in understanding, still feeling like the duke had poisoned my heart.

"Good," the duke said. "And I haven't bruised your skin, cut into your flesh, caused swellings or removed a hair from your body, as warned by the king. The guards will escort you to the outer courtyard and a carriage has been prepared to take you to the Bensguard Outpost with haste, as I believe we're running out of time before King Blackbone declares war and orders my brother to pay me a visit."

I gazed down at the oath tattoo etched into my wrist, the golden ink burning like shackles of a future I hadn't chosen – and the one I had lost. My eyes snapped back up to meet his, blazing. "I like your brother much better than you," I said, each word sharp as a blade, wielding something sharp when I couldn't reach my hair-pin knife.

He smirked, as though my fury was nothing more than a breeze against his armour. "But you won't be marrying him. So, you better get used to liking the look on my face. Thankfully, my brother and me look nothing alike."

That part was true. The duke's features were noble, his golden hair and light features painted him like some storybook prince. But the commander was carved from something darker. His eyes were like storm clouds ready to break, his onyx hair wild and severe. Still, at least their differences would make it easier not to hate Daffron for his brother's curse. No. The duke had earned that hate all on his own.

My hands clenched at my sides, my breath coming faster. Rage boiled in my chest like molten iron, burning up the last thread of my restraint. My vision blurred at the edges with it, as if homing in on a target I had to kill. "Maybe you'll allow me to make a few adjustments of you first," I snarled, my voice trembling with the force of my fury. I swung my fist toward his infuriating face, aching for the satisfying crunch of bone under my knuckles, but he vanished in a blink, reappearing by the door before I could even fully extend my elbow.

Coward.

He calmly folded up his sleeve, smug as ever, revealing the matching oath tattoo inked onto his wrist. A mockery of unity. A chain in the shape of a symbol. "Looking forward to seeing you again soon, Miss Coraly…or shall I say, Duchess Hartmore."

My jaw tightened until it ached. My nails bit into my palms as I fought the scream building in my throat. He had no right to say my name like that. No right to claim me for eternity.

50

The forest passed in a blur of shadowed trees and the creaks of the carriage wheels. Each day on our journey home bled into the next with the dull rhythm of hooves stomping on packed earth. Mist clung to the moss in the early mornings, and the scent of pine filled the air, but I noticed none of it, not really. My thoughts circled endlessly around the duke and the sick satisfaction in his eyes as Sergeant Karson fell. Karson, who had saved my life more than once, who'd laughed like thunder and treated me like an equal in a world of commands and politics. He hadn't deserved to die. And the Duke would never be forgiven. Nor would Valentina forgive me, either.

Brian and Crawly had convinced me not to tell Valentina that my initial refusal had caused her father's death, but to say that he died in combat in the wood before the guards took them.

Other than that, none of us had spoken much during the journey. I had mainly cried quietly, shoved up against a corner, and on occasions, Brian had patted my back to console me. He had made a few awkward attempts at conversation before giving up, and Crawly seemed to sense the tension and kept to himself, only occasionally glancing at me. The silence in the carriage was unbearable with all the unspoken thoughts. The men had promised me they'd not tell Ben about the oath, and to let me break the news to him myself. Not that I knew how or when. Each time I was pulled back to the thought, it felt as if someone was pounding a stone at the window to my soul and it was cracking more and more at each pound.

What would I tell Ben? That I had been a coward? That I'd stood there, helpless, as the duke's guard delivered the killing blow? That he tricked me into marrying him? I didn't know if the truth would break him, or if it'd drive him to vengeance, just like it was doing to me. Either way, it'd destroy something…maybe everything.

The days were long, the nights restless. Even when we camped and the fire crackled low, my eyes remained open, staring into the flames as if they could burn away the memory. But they never did. I didn't want them to. The hate kept me from falling apart.

By the time the forest thinned and the first signs of the mountain ridge, dividing this land from the Bensguard Outpost, came into view, I felt no relief, only a deeper sorrow. The carriage halted. This was as close as it could be to the outpost without leaving the Black Wing Territory.

We got out, and the black-wing escort turned the carriage around with haste. We faced a terrain that would still take us at least two hours to hike before we reached the military building. Thankfully, I was no longer wearing the tight dress. Our backpacks had been in the carriage when we climbed in and mine had contained my flight leathers that I was wearing, even if it was dirty and stained with Gravelhorn's brother's blood.

By the time we walked across the training field outside the military building, my legs were burning with exhaustion, and I couldn't keep my shoulders from curving inwards.

Ben sprinted across the field towards us, likely notified by one of his spies of our arrival. He caught me with one hand hooking around my waist just as I felt like buckling onto the grass and the other hand pushed into my hair as he crashed into me with a relief-filled kiss. My lips stung with an electric charge in warning and the tattoo bracelet on my wrist burned. Ben broke the kiss, frowning at me, clearly having felt the discomfort too.

Damned oath caster! He hadn't mentioned that the oath demanded I stay faithful until I wed the duke.

I had thought I'd get a few precious moments with Ben before the wedding, but that fire was snuffed out with all rest of the hopes of living happily ever after.

When Ben noticed how tired I was, his face softened.

Zayd and Harvey were also on their way out onto the field, and when they got to us, I was sandwiched between them. Harvey pulled me into his arms and pushed Ben away. "No romantic relationships are allowed within the unit."

I feared he would punish Ben with more lashes, but Ben quickly said, "That wasn't a sign of affection. It's a tradition in the Black Wing Territory that we kiss the warriors to welcome them home after their missions."

Zayd cupped the back of my head as he glowered at Ben. "Let's test that theory, shall we, because I'm also very happy she's back safely." He pushed up close to kiss me. The oath once again warned about affection towards another than my husband to be.

Dark essence I hadn't seen in a while leaked from Ben like ink in water, and I pushed my lips up harder on Zayd to distract him whilst I flapped with my hand behind my back to order Ben to stop that. Kudos to Ben, he refrained from letting his stone-set face show his rage, knowing that if he did, leadership could punish me with lashes, too.

The painful zaps over my lips intensified, and Zayd pulled away from me. "What the fuck, Angie?" Zayd hissed lowly at me and touched his lips as if I had bitten him.

Harvey pushed Zayd away and wrapped his arm around me, leading me towards the military building. "Angie, you must follow the rules even if it means we must repeatedly prove that we aren't associating with black-wings. We're loyal to the white-wings."

I glowered at Harvey, but he didn't see it. He was in full captain mode with his head held high and his eyes focused forwards. "Then you shouldn't have teamed me up with one!"

"I wanted to team you up with a white-wing at first, but my request to team you up with Emroyce was declined. It's a test from King Emille!"

"What?"

"There are a lot of things at stake. Go to your room. Rest. And attend the flight practice with Camp Leader Nar tomorrow. I'll see what I can do to help you to stay away from the black-wings."

Yeah, that has just become harder, considering I'm due to marry one!

We stepped inside and walked through the corridor side by side. "Harvey, have you heard anything about Zoe and Cadet Dessen?"

"I received a report yesterday evening that they were safe at the Emendroth Outpost, having captured one of the black-wings, who was behind the trade raids. Cadet Dessen is torturing him to see what information we can get out of him."

I was about to tell him not to bother. I knew it was Duke Hartmore who was responsible for the trade raids. But since the duke was going to become my husband, my life would be less complicated if my brother didn't know of his obsession of shiny items. The Spirits only knew what would happen to me if they captured and executed the duke whilst the oath was still intact. The oath caster seemed to have left out a fair bit of information regarding the terms of the vow. Would I be freed from it, or would I die with the duke? Like the soul bond package deal.

I nodded and was more than happy to go to my room to sleep and shut out all my hardship to welcome the nightmares, which couldn't be worse.

Harvey and I parted by the stairs to the leadership floor, and I carried on to my room, passing third-year cadets who were doing their sleep deprivation challenge, looking worse for wear than I did. At my door, I realised that the key was in the backpack that Ben had removed from my shoulders to lessen my weight when I arrived. I sunk down onto the floor outside my room, waiting for him.

Ben appeared in the distance, his large body taking up most of the space between the walls. I instantly stood up but averted my gaze from his pitiful smile, my shame so overwhelming I couldn't even look at him. With one hand protectively at the small of my back, he unlocked the door to let me in. Inside the room, the beautiful roses were still alive and had grown bigger since last week.

I stripped off my uniform, had a quick shower and dressed in a floor-length black Bensguard nightgown with long enough sleeves to cover my tattoo.

After I had tucked myself into bed, Ben lay down, curved along my back, stroking his hand over my arm. "Tomorrow, we'll get the bond reinstated. I don't feel whole without it."

"I don't know," I muttered. "Harvey might team me up with someone else."

His fingers paused on my skin. "Why?"

I didn't answer. My eyelids were too heavy for any type of conversation.

"Angelica, talk to me." The need for acceptance was so thick in his voice, I feared he would choke on it if I said nothing.

But there wasn't much I could say to explain my new predicament without having thought it through. Words to a king on the verge of unleashing war had to be chosen carefully.

"There is nothing to say. I'm tired."

"What did the duke do to you? If that bastard broke you, I'll rip him apart."

"At least we can agree on something." I sighed. "That was a man I had never want to meet again."

His grunt was guttural. "Tell me what happened?"

"Is that a royal order? If not, I'd like to sleep." I guessed if I was to become a Duchess in the Black Wing Territory, I'd become Ben's subject and have to live by his rule.

Ben gripped my arm gently. "Why are you talking to me like that? Are you still angry with me?"

I shrugged his hand off my arm, and he let it fall off. "Please, can you sleep in Murben's room tonight? I'd like to be alone."

I felt his sigh on my neck. "You really want me to leave?" The hurt in his voice cut like a knife into my already bleeding heart.

"Yes." I held my breath in, fearing I'd break with his next words.

I felt the mattress lift as Ben stood up, and the warmth behind my back was eaten up by cold air. He didn't argue. The door clicked shut and then there was silence.

I had held it together this long, but the moment he was gone, the weight of it all crashed down on me. I let out a shaky first breath, the aching blossoming through my chest. I curled my knees up, the grief rolling over me in waves.

Spirits, I had wanted him to stay and hold me. But I couldn't face him, not now, not having made a vow to another man. The pain was too raw and unbearable to control.

I pressed my face into the pillow to muffle the sobs that tore free. Tears dampened the pillow as I cried myself to sleep.

In the morning, I got dressed in clean flight leathers, tied up my hair in a tight bun, and was ready to practise flying…well…falling a lot. The challenge was to fly slalom between twenty poles, turn around the last one, and still manage to stay airborne before taking the same trip back to the start line.

When I arrived at the practice field on top of the lowest and narrowest mountain ridge at the far north of Bensguard City, it was also clear to me that Camp Leader Nar was still raging over the war in Pharanir and wouldn't cut me any slack. A few times during the practice, I think she even made it harder for me than the other cadets, throwing gusts at me using her air bending magic.

Murben leaned into me as I assessed the gaps between the poles, the angle and the wind resistance. "Do it just the way we have practised."

"Flying into trees?"

"There are no trees here, Cadet Coraly."

"No, only twenty poles and an incensed camp leader."

"That, there are, but try not to fly into either of them."

Hesitating, I glanced around the practice area, seeing Ben being friendly with Mazdon at another station with its own set of twenty poles. I had intentionally ignored him all morning, fearing the consequences as my love for him grew stronger with each breath, and would become impossibly hard to reject when the time came to step into my Duchess shoes.

"Ready?" Murben prompted, deliberately honing my attention back to my task and away from Ben.

I nodded, took a few steps backwards and flexed my white wings before sprinting into a launch. At the eighth pole, my wing caught and spun me around, making me lose balance and tumble down the side of the ridge, scraping my right hand and left cheek against rocky outcrops. When I had come to a halt, I moaned and got to my feet to climb back to the top where Murben stared at me tiresomely. "Again!"

"I'd say you're training me too hard, but I guess you don't want me to drop your king during the roped flight of the eighth challenge next year?"

"I'm working on preventing that, yes." He gestured for the starting line. "Again."

"You might possibly be a demon, Murben."

"They are far uglier than me. With regards to the king, I believe your rejection will kill him before him falling to the ground will. Again!" he gritted between his teeth.

Fine. He could have a dig at me. It seemed all black-wings were grumpy this morning, and I could imagine Davis would be even more pissed off with me for having to sleep on the floor…unless it had been Murben's turn.

"Sounds like you weren't happy sharing your bed with him last night," I teased Murben.

"The king slept on the floor. Simpler than a peasant." I could hear in Murben's voice that he was scolding me. The king being disrespected was a matter he held with no humour.

I raised my brow. "He didn't order Davis to leave his bed?"

"No. He said he wouldn't get much sleep, anyway. Nor did I, with all his questions about what could be wrong with you until the early morning." He pinned his eyes at me quizzically.

I ruffled my feathers to ready them. "You're confusing me, Murben. Are you fishing for information, or are you rebuking my behaviour?"

He sighed. "What's going on between you two is none of my business, so I guess I'm just cranky from lack of sleep." Then he grinned.

"What?"

"I heard you wore a pretty gown at the Hartmore Manor. Hard to imagine you without black leather and the daggers."

I swallowed. What did they know of what happened?

I pointed at the flight path and took another step over the uneven mountain cap to get closer. "I'm going to do this again now."

His grin hadn't fallen from his face. "Wise choice."

I made it all the way to the end of the twenty poles, turned, although clumsily, and made it half the way back before a pole whacked over my thigh. That would colour the inside of my thigh blue come morning. With my back still against the ground, I gently massaged my leg before getting up and limping back to Murben. He simply inspected me swiftly and said, "Again!"

This time, I flew through all twenty poles, but I was unable to turn around with the small berth needed to make it back. Again, I tumbled down the side of the mountain and added to my scrapes and bruises.

My back bent too far backwards with a jerk, so I put a hand on my small, feeling my entire body ache. "Why don't you show me how it's done?"

Murben snapped out his plumes to an impressive span and sprinted toward the course, folding his wings close enough to his body so they made him into an arrowhead, fitting snugly between the gaps but remaining wide enough to carry his weight. Like a water snake, he slithered between them, turned around the last pole with his back right up against it, and made his way back with the same efficiency. Finally, he stopped in front of me, with steady feet on the ground and crossed his arms; his left side framing the bodyguard pin I had gifted him.

"I don't want to play with you anymore," I muttered.

When I looked around, I realised that the other cadets had been practising this manoeuvre for two weeks already when I had been on my mission – *getting engaged*. The challenge was the day after tomorrow and I wasn't up to scratch.

I sat down to tie the laces on my boots tighter and Murben squatted beside me.

"If you don't want to tell the king, why don't you tell me what's bothering you?"

"Wouldn't you tell the king?"

"Yes."

"Then, telling you is the same as telling Ben."

"So, there *is* something to tell."

I narrowed my eyes at him. "Well played." The anger fuelled my speed this time, and all I knew was that I got to my feet, sprinting towards the flight course.

But the next thing I noticed was crashing against the last pole, my nails scraping the rock as I spun over the edge of the cliff. Then I was hanging from my hands off an outcrop with a fifty metre drop to the ground beneath my feet.

Shit!

I tried to heave myself up, but my feet found no traction on the wall, slipping off at each attempt to get a good foothold, as the wall crumbled under my soles. I couldn't possibly let my grip go. There was no chance I would find the balance when falling so that I could fan out my wings and glide down. So, if I failed to pull myself up, I'd die a painful death.

Shit! I cussed again. I'd have to call out for help. This was so embarrassing.

I inhaled a deep breath. "Help!"

Murben's head leaned over the top of the cliff. "How are you doing there?"

"Almost good."

"Almost. Maybe this is the motivation you need to progress. You've plenty of space to push off the wall and make your landing below."

"Want to bet your life on it? Ben won't be pleased if I die. Although lately maybe I've given him reason to give up on me."

Murben laid down on his stomach, propped an elbow on the ground and his hand on his cheek as if he was listening intently.

Having very little grip on the stone surface, my fingers slid off more and more with each passing second. "Help me up, will you?" Another few seconds and I'd be free-falling through the sky.

"Is there anything you'd like to tell me?"

"Yes! You're a sucky friend!"

"I'm not your friend. I'm your servant."

"Well, since you're not serving me, you suck at that, too."

My right hand dropped from the outcrop, and then I lost the grip with the other. Panic soaked me through.

Murben caught my wrist the second after I was airborne, but I was already a complete wreck by the time he lifted me up to him. Hysterically, I pounded at his chest.

He pulled me into his embrace. "I've got you."

My heart was still racing, and my emotions were all over the place. I was completely unravelled, clawing into Murben's back. "Murben, I can't do this. I've lost him," I complained, as he offered me a shoulder to cry on.

He pulled me to a distance, cupped my face and wiped his brown-coloured thumbs across my cheeks. "You can never lose him unless *you* choose to. Talk to him. His intelligence and his skill in negotiating diplomatic solutions might surprise you."

Not against unbreakable oaths, he isn't. There was nothing he could do.

Ben was watching us from across the ridge, so I straightened and pulled down my flight jacket. "I'm fine. All is fine."

Murben looked deeper into my eyes. "The last time you said you were fine, you almost stabbed the king with a black blade."

"I think I know how a stab to my heart would feel. We have both done a fair share of backstabbing."

"I'm sure you didn't believe loving an enemy king would be easy. He comes with a backpack heavy with conflict. You know this."

I scoffed. This time it wasn't his backpack of problems that was heavy, it was mine. "Sometimes the thing you leave behind can be the heaviest thing to carry." Mine was losing Ben to marry the duke.

Camp Leader Nar called out that the lesson was over, and I shot off towards the military building before Murben could ask about what I had meant by that.

"Lunch," I muttered, and began walking down the ridge when most other cadets flew down. Murben and Ben had the good judgement to leave me to walk back alone, guarding me from a few metres behind.

When I arrived at the canteen, I got my food; steak medallions with potato wedges, and sat down on the table with Nesso, Murben, Commander Daffron, Brian, Winter, Valentina, Mazdon and Kate. Ben wasn't there, though.

There wasn't much conversation going on today, and I too put my head down to eat in silence. Nesso was the only one chatting away and Murben was grunting only to acknowledge his comments. After a while Nesso, who was looking over his shoulder, stiffened.

"Guys, there is a cockroach on the floor."

I grimaced. Ew!

Murben turned in his seat to look at it. "That's a fine example of the specimen," he only remarked and turned back to his food.

"But...but..." Nesso stammered. "Commander Daffron, can you see it? Kill it?"

Commander Daffron cocked his head to look at it, but focused back on his lunch without a word.

Nesso seemed to be freaking out about it, which was odd. He was a mighty warrior, but he couldn't handle a cockroach?

"Now, where did it go?" he muttered, keeping both his boots on the bench.

Valentina, whose face had been a mask of composed anger during the entire meal, got off her feet and stomped on it. "There. Dead," she blurted before taking her tray and leaving the canteen.

There was the pain in my heart again. She must have obviously heard the news about her father. Brian only lifted his eyes up slightly to look at me before he too left quietly.

After lunch, I hiked back to the mountain ridge to keep practising the slalom flight alone. I chose a course in the centre of the area and not at the edge of the cliff face, since I wouldn't have Murben to depend on to lift me up.

By evening, when I returned to my room, Ben didn't show, nor did I see him the day after. Whilst speaking to my brother on updates about Zoe I had asked if he could sense where Ben was. Harvey had simply said that the king had shielded his mind behind something stronger than black iron, which was interesting since I'd have described his shield as a caressing curtain I could peer behind if I wanted to. Harvey did tell me, though, that the humming in his ears was pleasantly mild, so the king was around here somewhere.

I went to bed at night unable to sleep, staring at the shadows stretching across the ceiling. I had pulled up the blanket to my chin, but it still didn't offer the same warmth and comfort as Ben. When would he return? Probably not tonight. The unresolved tension was a barrier keeping us from getting close again. My stomach twisted, but whether it was from the lingering ache of our argument or the looming sixth challenge tomorrow, I couldn't tell. I needed rest, yet my mind refused to quiet. Every time I closed my eyes, doubts clawed at me, unsure if whether or not Ben would show up. Not that it truly mattered. Not in a million years could I win the flight challenge, nor was the prize of some mead and wine useful to me. Although, the party that leadership threw after this challenge every year had always been grand, and I had slipped into it many times, even though my father had forbidden it. This year, I should seriously consider not going. Alcohol and keeping secrets were not a great cocktail.

Because I did carry an unforgivable secret around like a loaded crossbow, and eventually, I'd press the trigger to the truth waiting to be spoken; accidentally or with a good aim.

I exhaled shakily and turned onto my other side, as if shifting would somehow free me from the weight pressing down on my chest. It didn't. Instead, the emptiness inside me deepened, stretching into something unbearable. *I have to tell him*. But when? How?

51

The remaining one hundred and forty first-year cadets had gathered atop the mountain ridge after lunch the following day. Camp Leader Nar called out the start of the races one by one and recorded the times on a register secured to a black clipboard.

Not seeing Ben around, I contemplated leaving, so I didn't have to suffer the humiliation, even knowing that deserting the challenge would earn me lashes. Then a shadow fell over me. Glancing over my shoulder, I saw the enormous man behind me. Ben wasn't smiling and his eyes focused on watching the races instead of looking at me. It was so stupid the way my stomach still fluttered when I observed him. But he was so gorgeous, especially in his black flight leathers, with the golden crown rank on his shoulder and the Bensguard Outpost key symbol by his collar. His hair had grown longer again, reaching down to his shoulders, and he had a stubbly beard; a look which I hadn't seen on him many times. Only when something distressed him.

I turned forward, and endured the acid raising in my stomach, as I watch the other cadets performing the slalom admirably.

"I wish we could get the reward before the competition. Downing a bottle of wine before flight is preferable," I muttered.

Ben didn't respond with a comment, and he never looked my way. He was the first one to line up for the challenge when it was our turn. He bent low with a leg stretched out behind him, clearly ready to give it his all, even when he knew I would fail.

At the word 'Go!', Ben set off with an astonishing speed, hurling himself around the first pole and bending his body to snag the other poles, curving around the last obstacle and was back before I got my jaw back into place from the awe of this man. No one could have done that faster than him and the discontented look on Camp Leaser Nar's face confirmed it. Ben sauntered towards me and stopped at my side, his arms crossed over his chest. But he didn't speak a word to me.

Right. I dragged my feet to the starting line, cringing at the poles as if they were demons risen from the Underworld, ready to make it hard for me at every turn.

"Go!" Camp Leader Nar shouted. My boots pounded the ground, and I had a good start, my wings at least lifting me off the ground. I swirled through the poles and made a successful turn, thanks to the training I put in over the last two days, and only whacked into the last pole on the way back, which bloody hurt. Still, I remained on my feet, running past the finish line.

Ben still didn't speak to me as I went to sit down on a rock to wait for the others to finish, but he moved to stand behind me. I wished that he at least could have acknowledged my efforts and told me I had done well.

Last up was the Healing Team, and both Penya and Maruto were incredibly fast. Probably even faster than the black-wing teams. Emroyce had probably been faster than any of them, but Kenyard had missed the turn, so that had probably cost them their win. Gravelhorn and Malloopa had been too bulky and clumsy through the poles, so I didn't think they had done well at all.

Camp Leader Nar dismissed everyone and headed off without lingering or making small-talk.

Cadet Darling pulled out two wine bottles from her backpack and held them up in front of Courtney. "Let's get the party started!" She hoisted the backpack up on her shoulders and swayed her sassy hips passed Ben. "Join me later, darling," she said seductively, and set off towards the military building.

Well, that made what I was about to inform Ben about a bit easier. I waited until everyone had left the mountain until I stood up to face Ben. The tension between us was short of killing me. He knew something was wrong but was oblivious to the storm raging inside me.

There was a level of trust in his expression, as if I'd never do anything to hurt him, making this so much worse. My throat dry, the words I needed to tell him were impossible to get out. My fingers twisted together, a silent battle against the overwhelming guilt. I hated to be in this situation, knowing my words would hurt him deeply. He wouldn't understand the sacrifice I had made. He wasn't there. The image of Sergeant Karson having his throat slit flashed in my mind.

I wished there was another way; a way to break the oath. But there wasn't.

"I have made a few arrangements for you tonight." My chest tightened as if I was bracing for a blow.

"Oh? How so?" he said with mock surprise.

I crouched to search in the side pocket of my backpack that I had by my feet and brought up a small herb ball I had stuffed into a tea bag made from camomile leaves, elderflower, a tad of hemp and a few other things. Not taking a step closer to him, I held it out. "Chew on this, but don't swallow it. It should have a calming effect."

Slowly, sceptically, he eyed the ball, shaking his head. "I prefer to be in control of my emotions."

"Okay," I sighed. He had rejected my peace offering. "Maybe I'll need it in a bit, anyway."

The sun was halfway below the mountain line in the distance, casting a warm orange glow on us, which seemed fitting. It felt like the agony from the rift I was about to make between us would soon bath me in flames and set my world ablaze. The sadness clamped over my heart felt like a fire licking my insides.

He crossed his arms over his chest in a signal that he was waiting for me to talk to him.

I cleared my throat. "I've convinced Harvey to place you in the dungeon cells tonight so that he can enjoy the party without all of the black-wings in his head. In the early morning, when the party has died down, Murben can unlock the cells, so you can escape to the Black Wing Territory. I've packed a bag with some supplies; water and weapons, in the cave by the lake for you."

He stood still like a spotted doe. "What?" His eyes darted inside their sockets as he stared at me. "You want me not only to leave your bed but also the territory?"

Even with my best efforts, I couldn't stop the single tear that ran down my cheek. "Yes," I whispered. My insides screamed no!

"You're a coward," he told me plainly.

"I'm a coward?" Rage boiled inside me.

I was a coward? All I did was try to keep him safe and happy, no matter what pain it caused me. This was how I saved him!

"I'd call you much worse if I didn't love you. If you could only sacrifice a fraction of what I've endured for you, perhaps we'd have stood a chance. I have waited. Patiently. But now you're pushing me away. Why? What did Duke Hartmore do to you?"

I had to be strong. If I told him what the duke had done, Ben would start a war and innocent people would die. I didn't want that on my conscience. There was nothing either of us could do about it, so the best thing was to distance myself and soon enough he'd forget about me.

"Nothing! I just…nothing. It's over between us." I flung my backpack up on one shoulder and barged past him. If I stayed another second, I'd shatter into a million pieces in his presence.

Ben gripped my wrist and spun me around, clearly not ready to let me go. As he held my wrist high, my sleeve sagged down and that's when he saw the tattoo bracelet.

Dammit!

His face crumpled. "What is this?" His growl was feral.

I snatched my arm back and pushed the sleeve down to hide it. "It's nothing."

"I get the feeling it's what would make me want to turn the world into dust. So don't tell me it's nothing."

"It's the reason you have to leave." I took another step in the direction of the military building.

"That looks like an oath tattoo, and Duke Hartmore loves making oath deals. What have you agreed with him? To spy? To kill me?"

"No!" I shouted, turning around. "I'd never agree to that! I love you!" The words were out before I realised what I was saying.

The chest he had held up so proudly suddenly relaxed, his breathing slowed, and the anger evaporated from his face. "That was all I needed to hear. Tell me about the deal and we can resolve it together."

"It can't be resolved. It's too late. Just leave me alone!" I screamed, turning around and hurrying away.

"Angelica!" he roared so loudly, the sound echoed between the mountains and the air inside my lungs rumbled. "You'll tell me what is wrong this very instant, or I'll send word to Black Castle and march all my armies down to the Hartmore Manor and extract the information from him. One way or another, I'll find out. But many soldiers will fare better if you tell me now."

My next step halted on the ground, and I turned around, looking at him. He wasn't bluffing. His eyes had darkened and locked on mine. He was determined, his fists curled and loosened at his sides.

"No matter what it is, I'm not going anywhere," he promised.

He would drag the truth out of me piece by piece and puzzle it together. Not protecting me and not loving me, weren't options he'd consider.

As much as I wanted to keep the secret buried, I knew deep down that Ben would never let me face the prison of my oath to the duke alone.

"The duke put Cadet Crawly, Cadet La Roy and Sergeant Karson in front of me; made them kneel." My voice was barely more than a whisper, trembling. "The guard held a dagger towards Sergeant Karson's throat." I vividly recalled the memory of the terror in Sergeant Karson's eyes and felt the churn of nausea clawing its way up my throat, thinking of all the blood. "When I refused the duke's deal the first time…" My throat closed, but I forced the words out. "The guard slit Karson's throat." Tears burned hot trails down my cheeks. "The guard put the blade against Brian's throat."

My voice broke and I came out of the memory and looked at Ben. "I believe Fern is pregnant with his child."

Ben's expression shattered, his usual composure cracking at the edges, his wrath barely contained. "So my spies tell me," Ben admitted softly.

Distraught, it looked like he wanted to step forward, to cross the space between us, to pull me into his arms. But neither of us moved. He stood motionless, every muscle in his body coiled, his breath too controlled. His jaw clenched so hard it could crack stone, the tendon in his neck twitching with restraint. His fingers itching for a weapon, for an outlet, for something to break. His eyes were focused on me, not blinking, but burning with a seething fury, like a tangible force in the air, and a promise of destruction.

A single muscle ticked in his jaw as it seemed the words sank in. Every word about my suffering, about how I had been deceived, clearly twisted like a knife deep into his soul, but he didn't lash out. Not yet. But I was certain that the duke would pay for what he had done.

I nodded in understanding of how much effort he applied to keep himself calm. "I couldn't refuse the deal a second time. Couldn't let him slit Brian's throat. So, I agreed. Once I stop my education at the academy, graduate or come back from Spirits' Trek; whatever happens earliest, I'll marry him in front of the Spirits."

His rage was a beast barely caged, pacing behind the trained calm. But his silence was more terrifying than a roar, more deadly than an unsheathed blade. And when he finally spoke, his voice was lethally icy. "Marry? He'll force you to marry him?" His chest began heaving heavily, his fist balled, and the black essence started storming around him.

There went his control.

"Go back to the military building. It's not safe for you here," he growled.

Before I could understand why, he sprinted towards the cliff edge and jumped out, flexing his wings wide, sailing into the sky and beating his black plumes to fly higher and higher. The sky filled with his black essence, forming an enormous cloud that blocked out the sun, and concealed him from view. The cloud of death magic grew thicker and wider, and if I wasn't to die from the touch of Ben's magic, I'd have to move before it was upon me.

I hurriedly hiked back, and when I got to the front of the building, I saw Murben and Commander Daffron staring up at the black cloud expanding across the mountains and reaching towards the Bensguard Outpost.

"I assume you talked to King Blackbone," Murben sneered.

"Yeah. That was your brilliant advice," I sneered back, walking past him. "A courtesy from your brother, Commander Daffron," I spat, passing the commander.

"You should inform Captain Coraly to keep everyone inside the building and close all the windows. Just in case," Murben muttered.

Shit! Did Murben believe it could get that bad?

I hurried to my brother's office and found him gazing out of the window. "Ben's a tad upset," I said, strolling up beside him, looking out.

"You don't say," Harvey muttered, shoving his hands down into the pockets of his yellow uniform.

"Murben told me to advise you to keep everyone inside and to close all windows."

He went to his desk and brought out pen and paper. "I'm taking advice from black-wings now? The Spirits help me." He scribbled something down on the paper. "Zoe returned today. Can you tell her to send out hearing portals into all halls and the surrounding practice fields to inform people to get inside?" He handed me the note. "On my orders."

To hear that Zoe was back was music to my ears. I hurried down the stairs to the ground floor and I rushed to knock on her door.

My purple-haired friend yanked open the door, and I threw myself into her arms for a hug. "You're safe! Thank the Spirits!"

"Yeah! No, thanks to our leadership, honey! No one around here seems to want to talk about where you went?"

"Duke Hartmore captured me."

"Spirits! Are you okay? How did you escape? Being bad-arse, no doubt." She stared at me with that girl-power-look and took a step away to inspect me from top to toe.

"No. I bargained my way out, but it was costly. I must marry the duke."

She gawked and her grip was hard over my arm as she pulled me towards the window. "Well, that explains that," she said, pointing at the black cloud. "You told him."

I cringed. "He has this tendency to overreact."

"You call that an overreaction?" She lowered her voice and muttered. "I don't want to see him when his anger is justified."

I handed her Harvey's note. "I'm afraid it has caused you extra work. You're on clean-up-my-mess duty."

She read the note and waved me away. "I need some space for this, but I'll see you…you're not wearing flight leathers to the party tonight, are you, honey?"

"I'm not in the mood for partying."

"What? Of course we are, honey."

"Did you see the death cloud above our heads?"

"Even more reason to have fun in our last few hours. If you don't support me in this, I'll not be your bridesmaid."

"Not funny! There won't be a wedding ceremony like that. It's a threat, not a joyous occasion." Or at least I hadn't thought it'd go down like that, but it wasn't as if we'd had time to discuss the details of the arrangement before I left.

"What? I'll not be your bridesmaid? Wow! Now, you really owe me a party."

"Let's play it by ear and see what happens to Ben. Maybe I can stop by the courtyard later and at least help your drunken arse into bed."

"I've missed the party two years in a row, being out on our mission, so I'm planning on making up for it!" she shouted after me, as I left down the corridor to go to my room.

Despite what I had said to Zoe, I knew I had to attend the party for my plan to work tonight.

I showered and laid out a sapphire blue dress on the bed that had a silver thread sewn into it that was so fine you couldn't see it if you didn't look closely, but it glimmered like shining stars when hit by light. As I was putting on my dangling diamond earrings, Ben entered the room. My heart did a double take, not prepared to see him so soon and deal with the unspoken issues between us.

I felt my puppy-dog eyes settle on him. "Feel better?"

I noted he observed my not-yet-complete attire; my knickers and bra set in sapphire blue lace.

"Not really. But I gained my control back." He walked closer, his frown deepening with each step. "You're going to the party?"

"Yes. We have a plan. Remember? I have to distract them from going close to the dungeon and catch you escaping."

He shook his head. "I'm not leaving."

I had to support myself on the desk and hung my head. "Why not? Don't make this harder on me than it already is. I beg this of you."

"If I leave, Captain Coraly will know you orchestrated my escape, and that you knew about Murben's magic. Leadership would call you out as a traitor."

"I know. What does it matter now?"

"You know nothing of the extent I'll go to for you. Listen carefully as I say this. I will not give you up." He nestled his hand behind my neck and brought it upwards to cup my head, gripping at the root of my hair, pulling me closer to him. "You are mine. I will find a way to break the oath. I have assigned Nesso to order his spies to search through the entire Skyberg and find out where the best Oath Breaker is and bring that person to me."

"You think there is something that could break the oath?" A spark of hope ignited in my chest.

"If there is, I'll find it. And if there isn't, I have a few other options in mind."

"Wait a minute. Nesso spies? Like what? He has an entire army of spies?"

"Of course. He's my spymaster."

"What? Nesso is a spymaster?" I cocked my head, looking at nothing in particular, picturing the eighteen-year-old with his playful way, his kind blue eyes, smooth facial features and a bouncy mop of silver hair. "That's hard to imagine. He's so chatty."

"Exactly. He creates social networks faster than anyone I know. He has a prowess for it. And no one suspects him of anything sinister because he's…well, he's Nesso."

"Definitely didn't see that coming."

"He can make mean physical webs with his magic, too."

"Nesso has magic! Spirits, it's like I don't know him at all."

"Good quality for a spymaster, isn't it?" Ben said and winked at me.

"I guess, but I still have more questions for later, but now I must hurry to get dressed."

"Since you haven't dressed yet, can we make the most of it?" He slid the back of a finger down my naked spine.

"Feeling murderous today, aren't you?"

"I can control myself."

"If you could, I'd already be dressed. You're distracting me."

"Would it help sway your choice if I removed my shirt?"

I glowered at him. "You know how the oath works and how it will protect a betrothal. I won't be able to commit adultery."

"I think I could be more powerful than the oath magic, and if not, it'll be well worth the pain."

I slapped his shoulder. "You're awful. Well, if you'll not escape tonight, please can you dress in something nice and accompany me to the party? And can you remove the black cloud in the sky? It kind of puts a damper on the evening."

"I'll come and be nearby to watch you, and maybe have one dance, but I don't want to anger your brother any further by showing everyone my affection for you."

I accepted his compromise and left for Zoe's room as soon as I had made myself ready. She opened her door in a short, black dress that barely covered her arse.

"Nice!"

"Ready, honey?" She grabbed her key, shoved it into her bra and brought the door with her on the way out. "Do you know if Murben will be there?"

My brows narrowed. "Murben? He's so…vanilla and you're so…rainbow."

"I thought with some alcohol we could rainbow him up tonight."

"Jeez! I hope the Spirits hide tonight."

"Yeah! So us demons can come out to play, honey."

The courtyard was full of cadets of every year and everyone in leadership, except Neville and Nar who always volunteered to be on patrol during this evening.

Zayd had dressed in black trousers and a blue shirt that matched mine. He was oddly joyous. The friends around him obviously having drank a few tankards of mead too many already, and he was dealing admirably well with them, considering Zayd never drank alcohol. He sat at one of the picnic benches with Mazdon, Brian and Penya, watching as Kenyard and Emroyce arm-wrestled. Brian was judging them and barking as soon as one of them cheated or lifted an elbow off the table. To their side, Mazdon and Penya were tossing a copper coin into a small mug, and if someone scored, the other had to drink.

Zayd caught my arm and pulled me onto his lap when we got closer, whilst Brian moved closer to Emroyce to make space for Zoe.

"You look beautiful," Zayd said, eyeing me up. "I think you wore this dress at my graduation party, if I remember correctly."

"I'm impressed you recall."

"One doesn't forget a sight like this," he murmured, his gaze lingering on me with an intensity that sent a shiver down my spine. There was hunger in his eyes that he likely felt every day but kept buried beneath layers of control. But here, in this moment, in the comfort of this relaxed atmosphere, he let it slip through, and I could feel nostalgia from our past settling between us.

"Who's your bet on?" he asked, nodding at Emroyce and Kenyard.

"If you don't say me. I'll take offence," Emroyce barked.

"If you don't say me," Kenyard pitched in, twitching his head to flick his dark-blonde fringe aside. "You'd lose!"

I laughed. "Can't it be a tie?"

"No!" both called out in unison.

As I watched the games, I let my shoulders relax, and I swayed to the music emitting from four magical speakers in each corner of the courtyard, compliments of a third-year cadet's magic to cast sound. Not a shabby beat, to be honest. He had good taste.

Zayd handed me a bottle of white wine and I sipped on it for a good while, feeling it warm my insides and my worries in life drifted further and further away. We all cheered for Emroyce when he finally pressed Kenyard's knuckles onto the table. Next, Mazdon put his arm up against Zayd, and even though I was a distraction sitting on Zayd's lap, it was an even match for more than fifteen minutes before Zayd won.

Zayd shouted with glee, shoving both his hands into the air, and then tossed a victory copper at one of the mugs, which also scored. In his excitement, Zayd clamped both his palms around my cheeks and kissed me.

The oath zapped warning energy between our lips that stung like a bolt of lightning, and I pushed away, rubbing over the numbness. Zayd also jerked, toppling me off his lap and onto my knees on the cobblestones. I got up quickly, without making much of a scene. That's when I noticed Ben, who stood leaning against the door frame to the open balcony doors of the library with his hands casually in his pockets. Ben was gorgeous as always, except for the angry looks he gave me now. His black hair lay around his royal face, and he had dressed in a black shirt that had silver embroidery swirling at the front, matching trousers and a pair of low black suede shoes.

Ben crossed the courtyard and grabbed my arm, pulling me closer to him, clearly not liking me sitting on Zayd's lap in the first place and the kiss certainly overstepped the limitation of his patience.

"Angie doesn't like it when you touch her that way," Zayd spat at him. His gaze fell to where Ben held my arm.

"Now, she does," Ben replied harshly, with no playfulness in his eyes. He let go of my arm and instead circled his hand around my back to clasp his hand at my waist.

Zayd snorted. "You think your black cloud trick scared me? Your words won't bring me to my knees," he said, standing up from the bench, closing the space between them.

Ben tilted his head to crack a tense muscle in his neck, probably trying to maintain his ever-fading patience. "I don't want you on your knees in front of me. But Spirits when Angelica is," he said with a taunting purr in his tone.

"Guys," I barked between them, trying to get them to stop squaring up against each other, but Zayd ignored me, swiping away the hand I had raised between them so that he could get closer to Ben.

"Be careful how you speak to me," Zayd hissed. "I'm a white-wing camp leader."

Ben chuckled darkly, not backing off one bit. "I'm a king."

"That doesn't make you special in this territory. I've known Angie all my life."

"Ironic," Ben leered, pushing his face even closer to Zayd's. "Because it only took two months for her to fall in love with me." Ben took another step closer to Zayd, which I hadn't thought possible, as they were too close to one another already. "And next time you've your lips on Angelica, I'll kill you." Ben glared deep into Zayd's eyes, meaning every word he said.

"Ben!" I warned and pushed him back a step.

I glanced at the men sitting at the table for help, but all of them put their heads down, avoiding eye-contact.

Zayd leered at him. "Next time she has her lips on my mouth, it's because she has begged me to put them there."

"Zayd!" I rebuked and pulled at Ben's arm to leave.

"Yeah," Ben scoffed, bending to my will and following me, but speaking over his shoulder. "You're right. You're no threat."

I dragged Ben away and towards a table at the other end of the courtyard where Murben, Nesso and Davis sat. Although, I'd preferred to have taken a seat two tables over, where Valentina, Kate, Winter, Maruto and Fern were enjoying some cake and water.

Zoe hurried after me and sat down next to Murben. I noticed that all the black-wings were wearing similar clothing to Ben, not a far stretch from their uniform. I rolled my eyes. *They could have made more of an effort.* Although, Nesso seemed to have attempted gelling his silver hair backwards into some sort of style, even though it had torn loose and streaked in every direction, which didn't look too bad, either. Davis had combed his towel-dried hair sleek against his head with a neat side parting.

I punched Ben over his shoulder. "You said you were going to keep a low profile."

He flailed out his hands as he sat down. "How was that not a low profile? Did you see me throw him across the table? Was I engaging in a fistfight? Did I kill him? No! I kept a low profile."

"Spirits!" I massaged my brows with my fingers and thumb as I sat down next to him.

"And what I wonder in all of this is," Nesso chirped, looking at Ben. "What would you choose? Would you rather watch as Angie kisses Watson, or kiss Watson yourself?"

I glared at Nesso in warning, and so did Ben before he folded his arms on the table in front of himself and hunched over them, huffing a low grunt.

"Oh, come on! It's a party."

"Kiss Watson myself," Ben answered, and I dropped my jaw.

"Really?" Nesso asked, looking as much in shock as I.

"Yes, but I'm the king, so I'll order you to do it for me," he said, smiling cheekily at Nesso, who erupted in bawls of laughter.

"And Angelica kissing Watson looked awkward. I bet his saliva was as poisonous as a demon's," Ben muttered, throwing an angry glance at Zayd, who had sat back down and engaged in the games at their table.

"Please," I moaned. "Can we talk about something else? Anyone heard who won the sixth challenge?"

"The Agility Team and the Healing Team tied," Zoe answered.

I looked at Penya and then over at Maruto. Good for them.

"I'm not looking forward to challenge seven. Archery," Nesso muttered.

"Only the Spirits know in what direction all those arrows will fly. I wouldn't be surprised if I had an arrow in my shoulder before the first week is up."

"I'll happily shoot you," Zoe said, and then turned to Ben. "Can Murben take me out for dinner?"

I blinked at the question that had been so out of the blue and my glance switched between Murben, Zoe and Ben.

Ben cringed and rubbed his neck with his large palm. "He isn't trained for such an extreme assignment. Not sure he'd know what to do with you." Ben looked at Murben as if to ask if he knew about her request before she made it. Murben shook his head but seemed amused by the prospect.

"He can buy me dinner, honey," Zoe snapped.

Had Zoe just called the black-wing king 'honey'? I had no idea in which direction this conversation was heading. I kept quiet, observing them. At least we had moved away from the topic of Zayd kissing me.

"So, you can shove it down his throat?" Ben asked.

"No! To eat," Zoe snapped.

"I fear you'll eat him."

"I wouldn't…yeah, I would. So, that's a yes, then?"

Ben gestured a hand at Murben as if to say 'sure, go ahead and take her out if you dare', but immediately afterwards, he stood up and pulled me towards one corner of the courtyard, serving as the dance floor.

Nor him, nor I, wanted to witness the awkwardness between them, considering their flirting so far had been Zoe throwing medical syringes and chairs at him, and him trying to lecture her about her uncontrolled behaviour.

Ben started moving in subtle motions to the rhythm of the music, folding me into his torso and rubbing up against me, almost as if we were standing still and making out. His hands were all over me, caressing sensually up and down my body. His lips nipped over my lips, my chin and my neck, angering the oath but it was also causing heat to circle down to my stomach and coil at my sex, making me wet for him. The otherworldly energy he exuded flowed from him and his muscular chest, peeking out from the three open buttons of his shirt.

The heat, the lust, the love, they were all I wanted and nothing I could have. A cruel temptation. His knee slid between mine, his thigh rubbing gently against my groin as he moved to the music like the beat to an orgasm. His callus hand palmed over my naked back. His hand travelled upwards to my neck, his fingers curving around my throat. Our lips met; a light touch. Teasing. A dangerous game that could earn us both lashes. His warm breath brushed my face. I wanted him closer. I wanted to let him in; tell him about my magic. Accept him as mine.

Fear still stopped me, though. The way he slid his body along mine, he'd soon erase all my shields, breaking all the barriers I'd put up between us. His muscular body towered over me, enveloping me in raw power. He was looking at no one else but me, the same way I wanted there to only be us two in the courtyard, so I could rip off his clothes and make love to him right there and then.

"You have that mischievous expression on your face again, Miss Stone."

Oh, fuck all my oaths!

I took his hand and pulled him to our room, the alcohol not helping when trying to avoid the corners along the corridors. Our tongues were already in each other's mouths when we barged through the dorm room door, zapping us with pleasure and pain from the oath. Ben kicked the door shut with his foot, not keeping his hands off me, tugging my dress and underwear off.

I began undoing the buttons of his shirt, but he had no patience and ripped it off with no regards to his seamstress. He balled the fabric in his hands and tossed it to one side, his pectorals flexing with the movement before he pranced at me, wrestling me into the bed, like a snake eating a mouse in one bite. He kissed my breasts, and I arched into him, moaning.

His breaths came out in ragged gasps, his hands trembling as they traced the curves of my body. The death-magic clawed its way to the surface, curling with black mist around his fingers, drawn by the storm of emotions raging inside him. Ben gritted his teeth, forcing it back to keep it buried, but it was like trying to hold back the tide with bare hands. It pulsed out and across my body, demanding freedom to roam over every part of my skin. His eyes darkened, clearly trying to fight it with everything he had. I didn't know how close the darkness was to becoming charged with death, but understood it was a power that drained him as he held it at bay. He wanted this, *me,* more than anything. I could tell, but if he lost control the magic would kill me.

Somehow though, I felt safer than ever. I knew he would never harm me. The problem was the oath. Each sensual touch and kiss stung more potently in warning than the one before, the oath magic getting more and more agitated. Ben removed his trousers and boxer shorts, still holding a hand cupped behind my head and kissing me. The naked man in front of me was all I ever wanted. He was perfection. Mine. Every part of him fit around me like a glove that finally found its matching hand.

He rolled over me, supporting his elbows on the mattress and grunted from the pleasure of our naked fronts meeting. Balancing on one elbow, he guided his cock to my entrance and pushed inside.

It felt like my veins froze with ice and shattered around me, the pain of the sharp shards rasping against the inside of my flesh.

He pulled out of me roaring, tears forming at the edges of his eyes. He must have felt the pain, too, and probably even worse, being the intruder to the oath magic.

He tipped himself over to lie on his back and put his forearm on his forehead, seeming to ponder whether we could defy the magic and attempt that again. I curled up to rest my head on his chest in silent mourning of our trepidation.

He sighed and stretched for the bedside table, opened the drawer and brought out a tub of white cream. "I believe I owe you a massage, at least."

"You can't heal me…this…" I said, rubbing my thumb at the tattoo as if I could erode it from my skin, "with a massage."

"I know, but if we want to maintain some level of intimacy, we must start somewhere. Flip over to your stomach."

When his warm hand slipped over my back, applying cream on my tense muscles and ironing out the knots, I admitted to myself that he had been right. With my mind, I followed his every touch over my body and enjoyed the sensual atmosphere it created between us.

"I have something for you," he said after a while, when he had done my entire back and legs. "I was going to give it to you after the challenge, because I thought you might have been upset…because…because let's face it, you weren't going to be the fastest."

"This is ruining the mood."

"Sorry." He went to the wardrobe and got something off the shelf and came back to sit on the bedside with a white paper box and unravelled it.

"A peanut butter cake?"

"Commander Daffron told me it was your favourite pudding."

I sat up against the headboard and brought it to my lap. "Yes, but not just any peanut butter cake. My mother…" I shook my head. "Thank you. The gesture is very sweet."

I picked up the chocolate covered peanut butter cake, and took a bite, savouring it and…What? How? This tasted exactly like my mother's. The taste triggered happy memories from my childhood in an almost paralysing hold. It was like my mother was still here, standing beside me whilst she let me try the first bite. Just the way we used to do in the kitchen after waiting for the chocolate to set. I pictured her baking, having her black hair tied into a bun and I could hear her laughter in my mind as her gleaming eyes watched me try to keep it on my tongue for as long as possible before it melted away and I'd ask for another bite. The vivid memory was overwhelming, twisting my heart with both longing and loss. How could something so small bring back so much of her?

My hand trembled slightly as I nodded at the cake. "Where did you get this?"

"Why? Is it good?"

"It's perfect. Like I haven't tasted it in five years."

"Well, then I won't tell you from where I got it, so I'll ensure to have a hold on you, or to give you a reward when you have been good."

"Bastard!" I called out playfully and rushed another bite into my mouth, closed my eyes and pressed the chocolate against the roof of my mouth in the same way as when I was a child, and moaned.

"Shall I leave you two alone? Sounds like you've all the pleasure you need."

I smiled, but didn't open my eyes, as the next reality hit. Information the duke had told me. My heart fell even further into a pit of misery.

"My mother begged you to stop her mission two years before the Battle of Bensguard," I whispered.

Ben stiffened, and there was a span of silence when he just looked at me. "Yes, she did," he whispered.

I lowered the box with the cake to my lap. "How could you do that to me?"

Instantly, I could see it on his face that he knew this conversation could only turn out badly. His face was normally unreadable, but it betrayed him now. The lines of his expression drawn tight with resignation as the consequence of past decisions caught up with him. His eyes weren't as commanding but dimmed with regret. Insecurely, they searched my face for forgiveness…or maybe the fact that I wouldn't be wounded beyond repair. He raked his fingers through his hair, his knee bouncing as his foot tapped the floor. His lips parted and I waited for his confession.

"I didn't know you then, Angelica. My father had just died, and I had become king at an age of nineteen. I was trying to keep the kingdom afloat. I didn't know what your mother's mission was or what damage it did to you." He leaned closer and took my hand to hold it steady, as if he was afraid I'd vanish if he let go.

His explanation still didn't excuse what he had done to me. It was a mission he shouldn't have given to anyone. He had been young, reckless with power, blind to the consequences of his command. But that didn't absolve him. Question was, if it didn't absolve him, did it absolve me? I had gone to his territory on a similar mission to kill him, and he seemed to have forgiven me for that.

"And I'm trying to keep myself afloat now. How did you expect me to react after hearing that it was on your order she came back here and that the Battle of Bensguard happened? That I was labelled a traitor to my people."

Perhaps all our issues weren't resolved – *maybe none were.*

He swept his gaze towards our hands as he stroked his thumb over my skin. "I guess I'll sleep in Murben and Davis's room tonight."

He exhaled a slow, shaky breath, then dropped his gaze for a fleeting second, perhaps the only sign of weakness he'd allow himself. When he looked back at me, his stance remained strong, but the hollowness in his eyes spoke volumes.

It appeared as if he thought that this was the moment he'd lose me. That he'd deserve it. He had done an unforgivable act.

"No!" I said sharply. "We're not doing that, anymore. Nothing will keep us apart. We'll fight whatever comes our way. And you must definitely taste this peanut butter cake. It's the best."

I held it in the air and when he went for it, I smeared chocolate across the side of his mouth. "Oops." I seductively brought my mouth over his and licked gently.

The playful gleam in his eyes returned, and he tried his best to remain motionless, but it didn't take long until he couldn't control himself anymore and ravished me, wrestling me backwards and spinning me around in the bed, pleasuring me all the ways the oath magic allowed.

52

Ben kept me in bed and shamelessly offered a replay of last night's activities if I stayed. He had nothing to lose, considering Harvey didn't allow him to attend the assembly, and the archery training didn't start until after the weekend.

Harvey was holding the war updates this morning, as Zayd had been called to the capital to attend a royal counsel meeting, so I definitely couldn't skive.

I crawled under his muscular arm and slithered myself out of bed. "Ben, you know I have to go."

Bra, knickers, socks, shirt, trousers, I grabbed one after the other as I found them scattered across the floor, dressing quickly. I put my hair up in a ponytail, laced my boots and gave him a quick peck on the cheek before I was off.

I was almost late and sat down next to Zoe in one of the top row seats. Harvey began the session by praising Zoe's achievements from earlier this week, both for the mission and for the work on warning everyone about Ben's death cloud. To that, I rolled my eyes and gave a 'Really? You get praise for that?' look at Zoe.

Harvey dismissed the second-year and third-year cadets after the war updates, and when the hall had quietened down again, Harvey continued to inform the first-year cadets about the First Year Ball. He spewed out the details as if it was a mission drill, conveying the appropriate dress code, behaviour expected, activities that'd be held and what dignities were going to attend. Not to mention the importance of upholding the professional ethos of the Bensguard Outpost for continued financial contributions and support.

When he finished lecturing us about it, we were dismissed, and I found Ben waiting for me in the corridor. His knee was bent, his foot on the wall, one hand in his pocket and the other held a bottle of water. The waves of his black hair fell forward as he looked at me. "So, what do you want to do today?"

Some of my friends and the black-wings, except for Nesso, were also circling around us, seeming not to have decided on their agenda for the day.

"We might as well practice some archery. Leadership has set up more target boards at the end of the field for this month's challenge."

"Okay." Ben pushed off the wall.

Kate waved a hand at us. "You guys go ahead. I've got a session to practise my fire wielding with Captain La Roy."

I cringed. Why did she have to carry on flirting with him? Why didn't my dumbass brother pluck up his courage to ask her out? "Captain Coraly should train you. Have you asked him?"

Kate looked at me tiresomely. "He said he was busy. And I prefer to train with Captain La Roy."

"Why?"

"Because Captain Coraly has this 'you must succeed, or you might die in the future' approach whilst Captain La Roy is more of a 'do your best and you'll improve as you go along' type of teacher."

"And what approach do you think will keep you alive in a real battle?" Ben asked casually, still with one hand in his pocket, but holding the water bottle out for me.

Kate flashed him a rude finger and walked off.

"Well, that finger will chase away the demons for sure," he told me, and winked.

I laughed and took Zoe's back as we walked out to the archery field. "Cool that you can spend the day with us? You don't have any mission lined up?"

"Your brother is preparing a mission for me up…well, it's classified, but it isn't until next month, so I've got some time kicking your arse at archery."

I grunted, not happy that my best friend and brother were keeping secrets from me. The same secrets my boyfriend and his entire inner circle clearly knew, too.

The sun was out, and I smelled the scent of spring coming in the air, like grass and wildflowers blooming. We all gripped a bow and a quiver with ten arrows each from the weapons rack and gathered around the last target track before the treeline to our right. The birds were chirping, and the branches were swaying gently in the wind as I watched Zoe take her stand at the mark and anchor her arrow.

Two arms snaked around my waist and Ben's head lowered to rest on my shoulder. "After this, can we go to see Camp Leader Mewer? I'd really like to get half of my missing soul back."

"I thought that by giving it some time, you'd come to enjoy my brother's soul equally as much."

He chuckled warmly into my ear and bit at it. "It's like cuddling a porcupine."

"And I'm a fluffy lamb?"

"Spirits no." He yanked me closer. "More like a hedgehog."

I cocked my head up to see his impish smile. "I get the impression you don't like needles."

His nose snagged against mine. "Not unless they're used to sew our souls together. Then I'll endure them."

Zoe turned around and took a theatrical bow, so I fought Ben's hold to crane around her and saw the arrow lodged into the bullseye. I clapped, and the others joined in.

Emroyce pushed his longbow down like a walking stick next to us. "I'm intrigued to find out how well a black-wing king can shoot. Your turn, King Blackbone."

He lazily let go of me and gripped the bow he had leaned on the weapons rack behind us, pulling up one arrow from the quiver sitting on the ground before stepping onto the mark. Where do you want it?"

"Where do I want it?" Emroyce looked confused. "In the bullseye."

"Yes," Ben snorted. "But do you want me to put it on the edge so that we don't get into trouble with the ladies and uphold the appearance of being gentlemen? Do you want it just to the right or left of Zoe's arrow? In the same groove? Splitting it down the middle?"

Emroyce glanced at me, to which I shrugged my shoulders. I had never seen Ben shoot before, so I couldn't tell if he was bluffing. My preference was that he shot it straight into Cadet Darling's chest, who was practising ten targets down from us and kept throwing stares our way, but I doubted Ben would agree to do that.

"Uh… A centimetre to the right of Zoe's. That should prove your aim and not do better than the lad…" Emroyce paused. "Although, can you call Zoe a lady?"

"Emroyce!" Zoe barked and punched him in the hollow of his shoulder.

"See," Emroyce huffed towards Kenyard, holding in the pain. "Not a lady."

The black-wing crew laughed, and so did Mazdon, having heard the conversation with his super hearing even though he was standing further back, talking to Penya and Maruto.

Ben turned towards the target. "I have to say, it's been a while since I've done this." He pulled the string tight.

"Don't start making excuses now, your Majesty. You were portraying your confidence so well," I chirped, standing close at his side.

He smiled at my remark, rested his thumb on his cheek and closed one eye to aim, starting high and lowering his aim until he let go of the feathers. The arrow hit exactly where Emroyce had instructed him to place it.

I applauded, and Emroyce joined in after he had picked up his jaw from the ground.

Ben made a mock bow, too, albeit not as deep as Zoe's.

Bending my arm around my shoulder, I pulled out an arrow from the quiver I had slung over my back and walked towards him. "So, where do you want me to put mine, King Blackbone? Cleaving Zoe's?"

Emroyce, Kenyard, Davis and Zoe cheered at the dare.

Ben raked his fingers through his hair and licked his lips. If I wasn't mistaken, there was an ignited shine to his red eyes. "I'd get extremely aroused if my girlfriend was that skilled at archery."

Girlfriend? In public? Aroused? Wrapping him tighter around my finger? Game on!

About to pull the string, I hesitated and lowered it instead as Nesso sneaked up to Ben and whispered something into his ear. Ben nodded to him before Nesso scurried off again. What in the world had that been about?

Ben looked up and saw me frown at him, but he simply smiled back and crossed his arms, nodding for the target.

"You'll be my servant and carry my lunch tray for the next week if I hit true?" I challenged, keeping the string stretched.

"Sure," Ben scoffed, and his arrogance fuelled my will to fucking split that arrow down the middle.

"You're in trouble," I heard Zoe whisper to Ben. "Angie can take that shot."

For a moment, I closed out all the surrounding sounds; the birds, the cadet's chatter, the swooshing sound of the wind. My vision narrowed like a tunnel between me and the target. All I could see was the bullseye and the rings rippling from it. I pulled the string tighter, my biceps clenching, my thumb resting on my cheek. One eye shut, one deep breath, aim…and I took the shot. My heart pounded as I waited to hear the thud. I blinked and focused on the target. There it was. Bang in the centre, cleaving Zoe's arrow down the shaft with curving strands on either side of mine.

I released my breath.

My skill had clearly shocked them to a stunned silence, as I could hear only one set of applause. I shook off my gloating smile before I turned around. To my horror, I saw that the only one who was applauding was General Denor. My friends were clenching their fists at their sides. The general wore his red uniform, and he walked in perfectly polished boots. I scanned over his pointy facial features, the blowback, black hair and the almost black dark-green eyes set in dark hollows.

Ben had placed his colossal frame in front of mine, blocking most of my view of him.

"That was mighty impressive, Cadet Coraly," General Denor said, the unfriendly tone not amiss as he stared at Ben. "Servant for a week. You might find your calling yet, King Blackbone."

"What do you want?" Ben growled at him.

Mazdon, Penya and Maruto had come closer to stand next to Zoe, Murben, Commander Daffron and Davis. Emroyce and Kenyard closed in on my sides.

"I have come to inspect how the seventh month's challenges are going, and I especially like the second-year cadets' horse race. Karson and Treylieh look strong, thanks to some help from Cadet La Roy, who I believe won the challenge last year. But I've also come to Bensguard to arrange for my next date with Cadet Coraly."

"Non-date!" Ben and I called out in unison, and Ben turned around to flash me a triumphant grin.

"How sweet," General Denor crooned. "The more delicious it'll be to tear you apart. Oh, wait! Duke Hartmore has done that already."

As Ben launched himself forward to attack the general, Emroyce quickly placed himself in front of Ben, holding him back. Murben rushed to Emroyce's side to help him. "It's not worth it," Emroyce warned Ben. "He's just riling you up to trap Angie into more deals."

Ben calmed by sheer force of will, his muscles taut with the urge to strike. There was still an unspoken threat lingering in the air between them as his fury simmered beneath his calm exterior. His eyes were locked on the general with a stare filled with such hatred I shrugged back. "Leave Cadet Coraly alone. It's me you want to torture, playing your mind tricks like a coward."

General Denor's smugness wavered slightly, as if sensing the shift of power but hid it well with his smirk. "Coward? You think I need to hide behind my magic to earn my merits?"

"You're nothing without your magic. Thirty years old and already a general, but whom no one has seen even throw a punch."

General Denor snorted, amused, and laughed to himself before he craned around Ben to seek eye-contact with me. "Unfortunately, Cadet Coraly, it sounds like there will be no restaurant visit for our next date. I'll be taking you to the sparring hall where King Blackbone and I will have a fair, non-magical, no weapons, old-fashioned fistfight to which you'll have a front-row seat. I'll return to the outpost on the thirty-first of March for the fight, so you'll have some time to train for it." He leered at me. "I'll pick you up for our…non-date at eight o'clock, and you can witness how a real man fights."

Anger burned in my chest, but it was a waste of time arguing over our deal. "May I wear my uniform this time?"

"Wear something casual that you're comfortable in and you won't mind getting dirty with a few bloodstains. The front-row seat can be a splash zone. That'll be, unless King Blackbone rejects my challenge and prefers that I take you out on a romantic evening in the town." The leer he gave Ben was so aggravating, there was no chance Ben could pass up the challenge.

Ben pushed Murben to one side and took a step closer to the general. "There will be no punishment if I beat the shit out of you?"

"No," General Denor crossed his arms over his chest. "Off the records."

Ben was still tense, his tall body guarding me like a brick wall, but after a brief pause, he nodded in agreement. "I'll be there."

General Denor's lips curved. "Looking forward to it." He gave a bow towards me before he sauntered the length of the field, stopping to speak to other cadets and inspect their skills.

We continued practising and spent most of our efforts on Maruto, who had never held a bow before. Maruto explained that in her small mountain village in northeast Pharanir, it was customary that the men protected the women and were the ones hunting for food, hence she had never needed to know how to wield weapons. No one had told her she would receive magical powers, and it wasn't until she turned sixteen, and had got caught in a vine and almost drowned in the river that she had found out. If it hadn't been for her magic clicking into place, allowing her to bend water and drop her down onto the bank, she would have died.

We practised some more before we decided to break for lunch. Kenyard and Penya stayed behind to give Maruto some more training, but the rest of us walked back to the military building. We passed by the Angry Team and Gravelhorn drew back an arrow in the string and followed my movement. He couldn't let go, of course, as General Denor would execute him on the spot if he killed me outside a challenge. He hated me in general, but if he had heard what had happened between his brothers and me in the woods, I was sure his eagerness to kill me had grown tenfold.

The only thing he achieved by aiming his arrow at me, though, was to put Ben in an even fouler mood.

In the canteen, Ben snatched the empty food tray off me as we got in line to the serving units behind Emroyce, who created a bottleneck asking for extra cheese on his chicken wrap.

"I believe I lost a bet," Ben said.

I tugged at the tray, trying to take it back. "I wasn't being serious. I can get my own food."

Ben held the tray high in the air so I couldn't reach it. "I'm a king who honours my bets."

"I was always going to make that shot. You forget I grew up here. The year Zayd did his archery challenge, I spent every day of two months on that field." Shit! Could have avoided talking about Zayd. That wouldn't alleviate his annoyances of the day. "Just saying, it wasn't a fair bet." I tugged at the tray when he lowered it, but he didn't letting go.

"Miss Stone, you're being unreasonable."

I didn't let go of the tray either, and looked him in the eye. "Says the king, who makes rules up as he goes along."

His face came closer to mine. "No, I don't. And you've always been unreasonable."

I exhaled a large breath. "Fine. Have the tray." I let go and crossed my arms over my chest.

He froze and glanced behind him where the black-wings loitered. "Uh oh! Murben! Hide the cutlery!"

I rolled my eyes at Ben and followed in his footsteps as he received the food plate from the chef and balanced both trays towards one of the longer tables.

Everyone seated along the benches and tucked in to eat chicken wraps with mixed vegetables. Even Nesso had joined us again, sitting down opposite Mazdon. It was interesting to see who of the men would resort to cutlery and who'd just eat the wrap with their hands. Surprisingly, Commander Daffron was more of a fine diner than I had expected.

An awkward silence settled between us until Nesso barked out, "Could you hear that?" He looked at Mazdon for an answer.

Mazdon's eyes darted around the canteen. "Hear what?"

Nesso leaned over the table towards Maz. "My thoughts."

Mazdon snorted and picked at his wrap with his fork. "My hearing magic doesn't work like that. I cannot hear thoughts."

Nesso tried to make eye-contact with Maz again, appearing eager to learn. "But I thought the words very loudly."

Zoe flashed him a 'you're-such-a-lost-cause' face. "Oh! You're so stupid, honey."

Murben, who sat next to Zoe, frowned and looked at her. "Weren't you using the word 'stupid' and 'honey' interchangeably?"

"Yes," she huffed, as if it was obvious. "Best to use both words to make sure Nesso understood." She scoffed down a large part of her wrap and leered at Murben.

"Hey, Zoe!" Nesso called to her. "Is there snow in the Underworld?"

Zoe dropped her shoulders. "How would I know, *honey*?"

Nesso stroked his silver fringe from his eyes before resting his forearm on the table again. "I thought you might have checked before you crawled out of there!"

Everyone giggled under their breath, and it lightened the mood. Even Ben seemed to relax somewhat.

I turned to Zoe giving her a look to stop their banter before it turned ugly and brought out two small gift boxes from my pocket, which were wrapped the same, and handed one to Zoe and the other to Davis. "Happy birthday!"

Everyone at the table moaned out about how I always remembered everyone's birthdays and looked guilty for having forgotten.

Zoe and Davis opened the gifts and held up the matching golden bracelets with the word 'Twin' engraved on a wolf-shaped plaque. On the inside, the other twin's name and the birthday of the twenty-sixth of March were engraved.

"Thank you. This is really cool," Zoe said, and both of them smiled at me before they put them on.

"You're welcome. Are you excited about your mission next month then? I'd like to hear about it."

"You're going away again?" Murben asked, surprised. "I mean…you're assigned to go on a mission?"

I had momentarily forgotten that they were having a thing…a very odd and confusing thing.

"Well. It's sort of classified. Up north…" she said, nodding upwards as if north was in the sky. "You know."

Murben's expression shifted in a instant, the light in his gaze was replaced by a guarded sharpness as if the mask of his easy-going facade had been ripped from his face. He clearly didn't like hearing about her being sent to the war front.

"Ah," he muttered. "We should start your training for that. What's your sharpest weapon?"

"Her tongue," Nesso spat, tapping his tongue with his four-pronged fork.

"Agreed," Mazdon and Emroyce said at the same time.

Zoe smiled at Nesso as if they were best friends. "And I'm sure Murben has no experience handling that one." She held her hand up high for Nesso to slap it in a high-five.

"If her blade-skill was as precise as her tongue, she wouldn't need help training," Murben said plainly.

"Oh, I don't need training. Put your hand on the table if you dare, and I'll show you how well I handle a knife, too." Zoe wiggled her eyebrows in challenge, which made it humiliating for Murben not to accept, so he placed his palm flat onto the table, leaning in with his body to emphasise that she didn't scare him.

"Are you sure you want to do this?" Emroyce asked with lowered brows.

"It can be his birthday present to me." Zoe stared angrily at Emroyce before she barked at Murben. "Spread your fingers!"

Murben complied and Zoe speedily hacked down with her food knife between his fingers, stopping when she had done all the gaps twice without touching any of his fingers.

"Kiss that, honey!" she spat when done, dropping the knife onto her plate and taking her tray to leave.

I wondered whether her eagerness to leave was to get away from more of my questioning of her mission.

I returned my focus to my food but glanced at Murben with raised brows. "I'm impressed. I didn't know you'd be so confident she wouldn't miss."

Murben followed Zoe with his gaze as she left. "Oh, no, I thought she'd stab me, if not by missing, then on purpose, but I decided it was worth the pain to prove my point."

"Well, that fell flat, didn't it?" I laughed, but Murben still looked serious.

"Yes. To my delight. I prefer her being proficient with blades rather than in need of training. Leadership sends her on dangerous missions, and I don't want her to get hurt."

I nodded. "That's so sweet of you to say."

Davis wriggled the fingers of his thumbless hand in front of Murben. "Speaking from experience, it's quite neat to have all fingers intact, too."

Nesso pushed Davis's hand away, as if it was nothing to complain about if you were a true soldier. "So, did you ask Zoe out yet, Murben?"

"Mind your own business," Murben growled at him.

"That's kind of not in my job description now, is it?"

I laughed, knowing now that he was Ben's spymaster. "So, did you?" I prompted.

Murben looked at Ben.

"What?" Ben scoffed. "Don't look at me. You might have to answer your queen."

I noticed that the white-wings around the table tensed at that comment and stared between Ben and me. The word 'traitor' rang loudly in my mind.

Murben cleared his throat. "I was hoping to get access to a full suit of armour for the occasion, but if she's going on a mission…maybe there isn't much point."

Ben chuckled under his breath, clearly amused by Murben's inexperience with wooing the ladies.

"Better you do it before she goes. Maybe there are handsome soldiers up north and you could–"

"My love," Ben purred at my side. "Perhaps don't torture my servants. Leave him be."

I rolled my eyes. "Fine!"

Ben, Murben, Nesso and Davis pushed their food knives to hide them under their plates. Commander Daffron, who sat at the far end, hadn't reacted or spoken any, as he only listened and focused on his food.

"Guys!" I barked at them, crossing my arms over my chest. "That's getting old."

"Yes, but highly relevant whilst you two aren't bonded," Nesso defended.

"Well, you don't have to be worried for much longer. Ben and I are heading to Camp Leader Mewer now to remedy that."

Ben frowned and avoided looking at me. "Actually, I thought we better wait until after my match with General Denor."

"You're kidding, right?" I almost spat in his food, and he turned his face to look at me, so I stared at him with as much disdain as I could muster.

"My fistfight is against the general of the Special Missions Unit of the White Wing Territory. I'm not expecting to get away without a few bruises. If we're bonded, you might feel them, too. Better we do it after."

"That's four days away!"

Nesso leaned closer to Murben. "Uh oh, the king is in trouble."

I flashed Nesso an irritated glare and took a deep breath. Why was I so angry about this? "You're the one who has nagged about getting the connection restored. I thought you were worried about having my brother in your head."

"I'm getting used to your brother. He's quiet. I had assumed someone would murder him before you, but now that you've got the general's attention, I'm not so sure," he teased.

I picked up and threw the food knife at him, ensuring that the flat side would hit his chest and not the sharp edge.

He held out his arms to show me the tomato stain I had made on his shirt and couldn't stop laughing.

"We will bond straight after the fight has ended. We'll arrange with Camp Leader Mewer for ten o'clock or something."

"Sure," he said, leaning back in his seat, having finished his food. "May I escort you to our room so I can get out of this dirty shirt and have you to myself for the rest of the day?"

"Sounds like a reasonable request."

Nesso snorted. "It's so funny that Angelica still believes our king requests actions when they're demands back home."

"I do miss home," Ben told Nesso in warning. "But I'm glad to hear that Miss Stone can be reasonable in some matters."

I stood and lifted my legs around the bench to get out. "When it involves you naked, always."

"Ugh, please. Hurry to your room. That's too cheesy for me," Emroyce complained, shaking his head as if the words would fall out of his ears.

I shoved my hip against his side. "I thought you liked extra cheese."

Emroyce looked up at me, cringing. "There's a limit!"

I rolled my eyes and stepped closer to Ben. "Will you clear my tray as well?"

He looked down at the items on the tray as if that would sway his answer. "That wasn't a part of the deal. I can do it if you want. But it'll cost you extra."

"Don't worry." I flicked my head sideways to flip my hair back so it wouldn't fall onto the dirty smears on my plate. "I'll do it myself. Although, out of curiosity, what would the cost have been?"

Ben smirked and pushed me forwards with one hand, carrying the tray with his other. "Definitely something with you naked."

"I can still hear the cheese, guys!" Emroyce called as we made our way out.

We took the shortcut across the inner courtyard on the way to our room. I couldn't wait for the naked wrestling to start. Just looking at him, knowing he had called me his girlfriend in public, made me want to rip those clothes off and feel his skin along mine as soon as possible.

Although, it wasn't only about desires anymore. That was the scary part. It felt so natural walking next to him. Like I knew him, and we had always belonged to each other.

I thought about his life and his friends, wanting to know more about him, to take up a bigger part of his life. "Commander Daffron?" I drawled, not sure if it was the right moment to be nosy.

"Yes," Ben replied, not seeming to be the topic on his mind.

"How did he and his wife meet when Daffron doesn't talk?"

"Remember, I told you he does talk to people he likes."

"Sure. Yes. But how did he get to like her?"

"His wife, Juliette, is a veterinarian and used to tend to the animals around my castle before she had their daughters. She followed my father's troops to the northern camp ten years ago to care for the warhorses, and that's where they met. Commander Daffron had a black stallion that he really liked, Gallion, he called him. During a battle, a spear impaled Gallion's hind leg and Juliette spent days trying to save him. The damage was too severe though and when the horse died, she comforted Commander Daffron, which was interesting since no one else in the camp dared to go near him; being brutal and a son to a duke and all."

"You said he spoke a lot to people he likes."

"Yes, but he doesn't like a lot of people. For some reason, he didn't push her away. I provided a house for them closer to the north, so that he could visit her and their one-year-old baby, Anja, when I promoted him to become the commander of my army three years later, after my father died."

"And what about Nesso? What's his story to have become a spymaster being so young?"

"He's eighteen now, but he has been my spymaster for three years."

Baffled, I turned my head to look at Ben as we walked. "He started working for you when he was fifteen?"

Ben nodded. "He was born for the role. His family worked at the spice field in the very south of the province of Banaly. The manager of the operation beat him to work harder, until one day when he was twelve years old, he actually hid in a waggon heading towards Black City to flee for his life. He lived on the streets for three years, rummaging through the bins for scraps of food when I met him. I took him in like a stray dog and he has been loyal ever since. He knows the back streets like the back of his hand and is skilled at blending in with the shadows, so he has proven to be a superb spy."

The taunting thoughts about Nesso's unfair childhood settled after a few moments. "But, if Nesso is used to living in the back alleys, then what was that in the canteen the other day? How come a cockroach fazed him?"

We had reached our door and Ben focused on getting it open but patiently answered my questions at the same time. "A cockroach once crawled out of his mouth when he woke up after having slept against a bin outside a side alley of a restaurant."

"Oh, that sounds awful. Poor thing."

"Don't let that make you soft. I want you rough and feral in there." He flung the door open. "Get into bed!"

"I guess that wasn't a request?"

"You're damn right, that was a demand!"

I squealed as he chased me inside and ripped my clothes off.

53

Today, Ben was stepping onto the mats against General Denor, and if the rumours were true, it wouldn't be a fight, it would be a bloodbath with equal losses on either side.

It was amazing what gossip one could hear between the blur of arrow shafts and taut bowstrings during archery lessons. It was strange, however, that the last day of March had arrived, and Camp Leader Nar had yet not set the date for the challenge.

Lying face to face in bed, I gently flicked my finger over Ben's lip. "The general won't kill you, will he?"

Perhaps the fear of dying was why Ben had spent the day tangling himself around me, as if he could imprint his touch onto my very soul before stepping onto the battlefield. Knowing Ben, he was too confident to fear losing. He probably wasn't scared of dying, just worried about aching too much to cuddle me afterwards.

Ben exhaled a quiet chuckle, but there was no amusement in it. "I doubt he'd face consequences if he did. I, on the other hand, will be carved into tiny, unrecognisable pieces if I stop his heart from beating." His breath landed on my lips, and when he had finished speaking, I got to taste it as he pushed his tongue against mine. He tasted of the painful zapping oath energy and the sweet strawberry jelly we'd had after dinner.

"I can't get enough of this," he purred, trailing his fingers lazily down my bare side, his eyes dark with hunger. "Of you."

We rolled together in bed, exploring each other with eager hands and needy lips, losing ourselves in intimacy, not knowing what state Ben would be in after his fight. Triumphant. Beaten to one breath away from the grave… Dead.

Ben had kept his promise, and I no longer trembled when he tied the blindfold around my eyes. He had made me love the blindfold, made me crave the surrender of sight, made me beg for his touch in the dark.

"It's not fair," I scowled between flares of desire. "Do you want me to kick his arse for you? At the very least I should slip some poison into his drink, or–"

"Hush now." He pressed his lips over mine to silence my anguish. "Don't waste time worrying about me. I'll be fine. Focus on pleasing me until the last minute before I've to prove my worth as king." He threaded his fingers into my hair, deepening his kiss with his tongue playing inside my mouth.

The oath still bound my body's loyalty to the duke, forbidding Ben from claiming me fully, but we had found other ways to satisfy the ache. Again and again, until the darkness outside brought the evening….until desire could no longer distract me from the dreadful thought of what was coming.

As the sun dipped lower, we remained locked away, cocooned in each other's warmth, too entwined to acknowledge the world outside. Nesso had been tasked with bringing us dinner, his smirk a silent acknowledgment of what kept us confined within these walls. But beneath the heat of Ben's touch, an icy fear pooled in my gut. He had never been one to waste a moment, yet this, this felt different. This felt like the final touches before a goodbye. As if he believed this could be his last day in the world of the living.

As his tongue tangled with mine, I wished more than anything, that I could freeze this moment in time. Because after tonight, everything could change. I panicked thinking about a life at the outpost without Ben at my side. Why hadn't it been me who was challenged to fight the general? He wouldn't kill me…or I didn't think so, anyway.

"Are you sure you don't want me to kick his arse for you?" I offer again, entirely serious as Ben removed the blindfold.

At the very least, I could try to get Ben out of the fight that was for no good reason other than their bucking of horns.

He nestled his arms around me and pulled me to lie on top of him. "Sending out a woman on the battlefield to fight for me? I'll never do that again."

I froze, mid-stroking his pectoral. "Again?"

He looked at the ceiling with a gaze shadowed with memory. His eyes wistful. "That's how my mother died."

As I rested my head on his chest, I could hear his steady heartbeat. "I remember you told me she died on the battlefield. Was she a great warrior like you?"

I cocked my head upwards and saw pain seeping into his eyes, dulling the fire that had burned there a moment ago. The next moment, his thoughts weren't here in the room with me. I was certain he was putting himself through the torture of what happened the day his mother died. His jaw clenched. A muscle ticked beneath his skin, and he tensed as if bracing for a blow that had already landed years ago.

He swallowed hard, but it was like a lump was stuck in his throat, clearly suffering a guilt that never left him. "I don't like talking about that." He gently rolled me off him and got out of bed, crossing the room to get to the wardrobe to don his combat trousers.

I tilted to lie on my side and pulled the blanket up to my waist before propping an elbow onto the mattress, supporting my head on my hand. "I wished we were soul bound. I wouldn't fear you dying if I knew I'd go with you to meet the Spirit of Death." My chest tightened and I flung myself to sit up straight as realisation hit "Did you suggest we bond after the fight because you worry that you'll actually die?"

He pulled a shirt off the hanger and slid his arm through it. "It's a possibility."

"Damn you, Ben!" I was quick to fume, hot and angry, my heart burned in my chest for a completely different reason than it did a few minutes ago. "That's my decision to make, and did you ever consider that if you die, my brother dies, too. I'd lose you both."

"Considering I wasn't planning on losing, that's a small risk I'm willing to take. But I'd never gamble with your life."

"You've not thought this through. If you die, my heart will turn to ashes anyway. Bonded or not."

"No, it won't. You can get back with Watson and live a long and happy life."

How dare he make that statement in this situation? "I'm so angry with you right now!"

"No, you're not," he mocked, and leaned down to kiss the top of my head before buttoning up his shirt with the crown emblem on his shoulder and tucked it into his black leather trousers.

Lastly, he fastened the wide buckle of his leather belt and rolled his sleeves up to his forearms.

A knock on the door made me jump. Ben glanced at his watch, then at me, sitting naked on the bed. "Although General Denor said you could dress casually, and something you were comfortable in, I don't think he meant naked. Get dressed."

I sashayed past him to get to the wardrobe. "And what if the general prefers a naked dress code? Maybe I can live a long, happy, naked life with him instead of Zayd."

"Get. Dressed," Ben growled through clenched teeth.

Another knock. Spirits, the general was so bloody punctual.

"Yes! Give me a minute!" I yelled through the door.

I quickly yanked on tight white trousers and an ocean-blue tunic before concealing from Ben that I pocketed my light crystal from the bedside table. If Ben's life was at risk tonight, I might need to use it. Then I went to open the door, still pulling up my socks. "Are you in a rush to get beaten up?"

General Denor smirked, leaning against the door frame, as he waited with arms crossed. He was wearing red combat trousers and a matching shirt with the sleeves rolled up all the way to his biceps, pinching them tightly to make them protrude. "I was actually very excited about our date."

He was wrong on so many levels, but I didn't bother correcting him. This was definitely not what I considered a 'good' date.

I pushed my feet into my boots and laced them up in the corridor as Ben stepped out and locked the door, keeping one eye on the general.

"As this is a date, it'd be proper that I held your hand on the way to the sparring hall, Cadet Coraly," the general teased.

"Lift a hand towards her, and I'll promise you, I'll cut it off the next time I hold a blade," Ben warned, and then looked at me pleadingly as if to ask permission to start the fight here in the hallway.

I put my head down and followed General Denor to the sparring hall. To my surprise, he greeted many outpost residents as we walked through the corridor, receiving the respect expected by a general. Cadets pushed up against the wall and stared at the floor whilst those who knew him better patted a friendly hand on his shoulder, asking if he had time for a drink before leaving the outpost again.

"General, do you know why leadership has delayed the archery challenge?" I asked.

The general threw a stare over his shoulder at Ben before lowering it to meet my eyes. "We've decided to hold it next week on Monday the fifth of April."

"Why? The challenges have always been held within each month?"

"It's a leadership decision," he said politely, but didn't offer further explanation.

We arrived at the sparring hall where all our friends had gathered. It was strange to see familiar faces dressed in casual clothing. General Denor veered off to the left to greet a few third-year cadets who seemed to worship him. They were looking at him like he was one of the Spirits. They'd probably wag their tails and run off fetching a stick or to do any other bidding he asked of them.

I joined Mazdon, who stood around a section of newer looking dark-blue mats that had been joined into one big square for the match.

Ben stripped out of his boots and stuffed his socks down into them before stepping onto the mat. He bounced on his pads of his feet, testing the surface and making a few test swings into the air, warming up his strikes.

Maz sighed as he looked down at me. Worry strained every piece of skin on his face. "I gave Camp Leader Mewer a heads up about the match and he said he would stay in the infirmary until it was over. He cursed you for making so much work for him."

"Mewer would never cuss me." I wanted to smile at Maz, but I couldn't. Nothing about this match was funny. I was worried sick over what General Denor might do to Ben. Would he cheat and use his mind to destroy him?

"Maybe not in so many words, but he did make a big sigh."

Yeah, that sounded more like something Mewer would do.

Emroyce and Kenyard carried one of the long benches along the wall and placed it parallel to the mat, and I sat down next to Kate with Captain La Roy on her other side, who was wearing his formal yellow uniform.

I leaned forward to intercept his glances at the general and the king. "Captain, can't you do something about this?"

"You want me to tell the general he can't fight whomever he wants? No, thank you. I'd like to see tomorrow's sunrise. I heard it's going to be beautiful, like a dance of fire," he said with his gentle voice, and then he gazed at Kate with those besotted amber eyes as if she was his sunrise.

Gravelhorn entered the hall with eight other guys at his back, and together with Malloopa, they moved out a bench and put it opposite ours, the mats between us. The Backstabbers Team and The Fistfight Boys Team were among them, clearly making a point of siding with the general.

Cadet Kwi in the Fistfight Boys Team concerned me the most, as he had the magic that could weaken other's magic. I didn't think that Ben would cheat, but if his life was threatened, I wanted him to be able to resort to his death magic. Half of Kwi's face and the beginning of his hairline had been clawed off by accident, fighting his teammate. His good burgundy eye on his left side traced the movement of the combatants. His teammate, Cadet Lewis, was sitting beside him with his palms curved around the bench's edge, his claws clicking on the wood. He wore a leather vest that showed off all the odd blue tattoos covering his arms and both his cheeks below a mop of yellow hair. He had his wings out, and I had noticed that about him before. It was like he had a hard time having his wings and claws out independently of each other.

General Denor crouched to remove his boots and socks but also his red general's shirt. He folded it neatly on top of his boots, grinning at me. "I haven't packed many shirts and don't want to get it stained with blood."

I rolled my eyes at him and his theatrics, but I didn't complain when Ben removed his black shirt, displaying his rippled abdomen all the way to where his black trousers were fastened low on his hip.

Ben passed by me and handed me his shirt. "Cadet Coraly, you're drooling again," he whispered, and winked before turning to walk to the centre of the mats.

I didn't care. Ben was fucking hot! And he was mine.

General Denor beckoned with his whole hand for Ben to approach. Oh, okay then…I guessed the match had started.

Ben didn't hesitate. He barged straight for the general, made a swift left-right move to avoid the general's fists, then planted his own into the general's abdomen. "That was for tricking my girlfriend," Ben said, pulling back sharply to assess the general's counterattack.

I felt a blush heating my cheeks, noticing many were staring at me, stunned at having heard the black-wing king call me his girlfriend. Kate smiled at me and bumped my shoulder lightly with hers.

"I told you, King Blackbone," the general panted, folding upright again. "Your biggest enemy is one of your own subjects. A king who can't even control his peasants must be as weak in bed as he is on the throne."

Dammit! That was Ben's weakness. He'd lose focus in his anger if the general kept tormenting him about Duke Hartmore's deceit. That was another type of mind-game not against the rules!

Ben attacked with pure rage, the lack of focus passing the advantage over to the general, who got in three punches to Ben's side before the general caught him in a neck lock. Ben fought to twirl out of it quickly, and once freed, he struck an uppercut at the general's jaw that snapped his head sideways. The general staggered backwards, shaking it off.

Denor's fighting skills actually impressed me, and I realised he didn't simply talk the talk, but could walk the walk. He clearly merited his stature as a great leader and fighter.

They clashed into a flurry of punches and kicks in close combat. Blood sprayed from their noses and when they broke apart, both of them had cuts over their brows.

I didn't want to watch, but I couldn't look away, fearing if I did, Ben could die.

"Go for his left thigh!" Valentina bellowed from behind me.

She and Treylieh had appeared just then, stinking of horse. Crawly stood behind her, and I pressed my lips into a thin line as we exchanged glances. Brian and Winter weren't here, so I assumed they were busy with their trust exercise challenge with Mewer.

The spectators on the other side roared, so I turned my head back around to see Ben's forearms bulging as his fists repeatedly pummelled the general's face.

Denor swung himself low and struck a leg behind Ben's knees, felling him onto his back. Swiftly, he straddled Ben's stomach and launched punches to his face, throat and chest. The punches to Ben's throat seemed to break his focus from blocking the rest. Anxiety rippled through me. A voice in my mind wanted to scream for them to stop. Tears welled up in my eyes as I watched the general strike blow after blow. *Please, don't kill him! Please, don't kill him!*

Maruto, who sat to my right, took my hand and held it softly. With my other hand, I pressed Ben's shirt to my face to inhale his scent, but it was like trying to draw a warm breath in a snowy landscape and felt nothing but ice. It only made the panic worse. The blood in my veins ran cold like frozen solid. I couldn't move, couldn't think. The water wielder's hands were warm around my cool skin, a reminder I was alive. A reminder that for as long as there was life in me, I'd use everything I had to help Ben.

Denor showed no mercy. Blood smeared across Ben's face. Oh Spirits! No, no, no! Ben couldn't lose. He couldn't leave me. I needed him by my side to survive this academy, to…simply survive!

I couldn't take it anymore, couldn't allow the general to steal him away from me forever. I flew onto my feet. "Ben! Get up!"

Ben twitched my way, as if my voice had guided him like a beacon of light through the stormy dark sea back to the match. He slammed his heels into the mat, arching his body with raw force as he twisted, flinging Denor off him in one powerful motion. The general hit the mat with a grunt. No respite, Ben barely made it to his knees before the mind bender lunged at him again. Ben retracted instantly. He yanked back, using the momentum to drive the general's head down between his knees. Releasing a fierce growl, Ben locked his arms around the general's torso, heaving him up and over his head. The crowd gasped as Denor's body crashed onto the mat with a sickening thud. Ben released him, rolling smoothly to his feet.

Cadets roared around the mat, their voices colliding in a frenzy of excitement as they cheered for their favoured opponent. Their roars went wild with suggestions of punches and kicks that could be the winning strike. Cadet Lewis from the Fistfight Boys Team stood on the bench, thrusting his fist skyward, calling for a flying kick. Amidst the chaos, Gravelhorn sat motionless on a bench, his eyes locked on me, burning with vengeance and venom so palpable it made me nauseous. It wouldn't be enough for him that Ben died. Gravelhorn wanted me sent to the Underworld.

Ben circled the mat, his chest heaving, muscles taut with fury from his injuries. He wiped blood off his mouth with the back of his hand, his gaze lethal.

His voice was sharp as a blade as he said, "Have you landed enough punches on me, so not to feel ashamed of your efforts?"

"Me? Ashamed?" the general scoffed, rocking his torso back and forth as he held his fist up in front of his face. "I've done more damage on you."

Ben tilted his head, smirking. "Just tell me when you're ready to give up, and I'll finish this. I don't have all day. I need to get back into bed with my woman."

Denor's lips curled into a sneer. "Is that the prize to the winner? Maybe I'll have her in my bed tonight instead."

That was a mistake.

He should *not* have said that.

All of Ben's muscles tightened into bulging mountains, rage rippling through every single one of them. He shot forward like a predator locked onto its kill, arm cocked, bicep flexing with terrifying force. One brutal jab to the temple sent the general crashing to the mat.

The general wasn't trying to get back up. Out cold, he didn't move. Was he dead?

Ben limped over to me with a hand on his swollen throat, clearly hurting. He carefully craned it to test its pain threshold. He took his shirt from my hands to put it back on. Then he grunted, circling his foot in the air.

I stood up to get closer to him. "Did you…did you kill him?" I asked gently.

"No," Ben panted. "He's just unconscious. The bastard will get up eventually, but I don't think he'll wake for a while. We should go to the infirmary. I'd like to get my soul…" He softly poked a finger at my heart, "returned to me, and get you back to being naked in our bed."

My heart warmed as if his love had streamed from his finger and pierced through my ribcage. I blushed, looking at him. He had fought for me. Shown his strength as a threat to others, hoping it would protect me. He had fought himself bloody to show everyone I was his. I stroked my thumb over his brow. "And Fern can tape this."

He hissed at my touch, and circled an arm around me, hopping slightly on his other foot after picking up his boots.

"General Denor was better at combat than I had expected. He's truly dangerous if he can fight as well as he can uses magic. I hope you realise what you've got yourself into meddling with him."

I was well aware that Ben didn't like me near him, but I wouldn't go back on my deal and have Robin's mind obliterated once more. That was simply not an option.

"The difference is, he isn't fond of you, but he likes me," I teased.

We exited the sparring hall to an empty corridor and Ben moved his hand from my shoulder, grabbed at the root of my hair, and cocked my head up before planting a seductive kiss on my lips. "That's what I'm afraid of. Powerful men never like sharing their toys."

Tingles raced down my stomach and settled at my groin. "Like you?" I moaned over his lips.

Ben kissed me so teasingly softly I barely felt it. "Exactly like me." He let go of my hair and pushed us forwards to make our way to the infirmary. Soon after, Harvey joined us, as Zoe had informed him of the situation through a hearing portal.

As Mewer transferred the soul bond over to me from Harvey, the light crystal in my pocket, containing pure energy that powered magic, throbbed with pulsating waves against my thigh. The power transfer left me slightly dizzy, but nothing that Mewer, Harvey or Ben noticed.

This time when the bond connected, the humming sound that had first irritated my ears, then turned to a song of love, now roared like a thunderstorm inside my mind. The bond was clearly not willing to give into Duke Hartmore's oath, fighting hard to sever it. The erratic slicing pain through my head, and the flickering aches behind my eyes were incredibly distracting.

Ben grunted repeatedly, as I supported him all the way to our room once we were finished at the infirmary. "Since we're all patched up now, I wanted to ask you for a favour. And not a pleasant one." He closed our room door behind us, and my hands were busy steadying his balance.

"A favour? The great King Blackbone needs a favour from little Miss Stone? I can't imagine what you could possibly want…or what it'll cost you. I believe you already owe me a favour from when I wanted to set you free from the dungeons."

I left him to balance next to me, as I untied my laces and tugged off my boots.

"It depends on how you count favours. I haven't killed you after threatening me with black blades."

I felt his palm cup my arse before I straightened up again.

"That doesn't count, unless you truly intended to make good on your intentions." I helped him closer to the bed, even if I thought he genuinely didn't need it, just because it was nice caring for him, anyway.

"No. I never contemplated ending your life. Who'd be a thorn in my side if I didn't have you?" He smirked at me.

"Nesso seems to do a pretty good job."

He laughed and stroked his thumb over my cheek lovingly. I swatted his hand away and tipped him off my shoulder so that he could get comfortable in bed. I knew his loving gaze meant he had something to ask me which I wouldn't like. "Ask me your favour then. What is it?"

He pulled his shirt over his head and laid down.

Yeah, getting naked, that'd help his case. I was weakening already; probably drooling. He was playing dirty, and he knew it.

His hand stroked up my thigh and clasped at the fabric of my tight white trousers, pulling me closer. *"Would you consider coming with me to the Black Wing Territory? I only need a few hours to show my face at the Spring Festival."*

My heart almost stopped. He had asked in our minds to hide the request from Maz. The favour sounded extremely risky. Could I trust him fully?

What if he took me there and decided not to return to the White Wing Territory?

"It'll be quick, I swear," he emphasised, his big eyes trying to garner my reaction. *"You'll just have to stay out of sight while I make a speech and have a few dances with noble ladies and then we'll come back here."*

Why was he so adamant about informing me that the visit would be quick? Was he hiding something? Or Someone? One of the noble ladies he had to dance with, perhaps.

Then a thought hit me.

Had General Denor postponed the challenges on purpose to test whether I'd go with Ben? He obviously knew of the festival and Ben's expected appearance during it. Was he waiting for me to take the bait, so he could call me out as a traitor the moment I thieved the cheese, releasing the trap that'd decapitate me?

It seemed everyone was playing a game around here; a game that could have a deadly outcome for me. When had I gone from being the predator as an undercover agent, to becoming the pawn in my own damned game? I was no longer holding the rule book, it seemed. But who was?

Ben wouldn't have asked me if it wasn't important to him, unless it was a part of his game. I was a white-wing warrior, and I owed him nothing. I could say no. But he had stayed here to keep me safe and if I didn't go with him, maybe he'd find he had a usurper on his throne when he returned. The thought of him having to fight his way to reclaim his rightful place, and possibly dying in the process, thawed my heart. Although, I didn't like the fact that he wanted to hide me away like a sleazy mistress when we should walk side by side, considering that was what he claimed he wanted of me.

Ben was still watching me, waiting for my answer, his fingers stroking up and down my leg.

I took a step backwards to get out of reach. *"If I go with you, I can't even join the party?"* I remembered Commander Daffron had told me about the festival being on Ben's actual birthday. It'd break my heart not to spend it with him. If he was serious about me, he should want to make a public commitment. *"Is it so you can hide me away from your betrothed and enjoy the festival with her without having me be a thorn in your side?"*

His teeth gritted, and a vertebra in his neck cracked, as he pressed his head to the side. *"Who told you about that?"* He sat up on the bedside with his feet swung over the edge to be flat on the floor. I took a step backwards, suddenly feeling uncomfortable with the narrowing space between us.

Shit! If I told him the truth, Murben might lose a thumb, or worse. "Duke Hartmore," I lied.

He supported his hands on his knees, his shoulders tense, pushing upwards, making him look far more threatening. "You're a good liar. Your problem in this case is that Duke Hartmore doesn't know about the betrothal."

"We're not talking about how I found out," I cut in, my voice sharp. "We're talking about how you never told me you're promised to someone else. Another secret. One that has nothing to do with the war in the north, or secrets that could destroy your territory."

A tremor of anxiety surged through me, my heart slamming against my ribs. I pressed my hand to my chest to steady the violent palpitations bruising my insides. *He didn't deny it.* He has someone else. To stay calm was an ambitious goal, so I aimed for control. I needed to breathe.

I'm jealous. Yes, it was true. Pure, ugly jealousy coursed through my veins like venom. I had thought he was mine, but that was far from the truth. He belonged to someone else, and I was only a toy until he had to face his commitments. We were on borrowed time. Borrowed toys must be returned. It was the end of this. The end of us.

My stomach churned rebelliously, breaking into my poise. My head spun. Desperation split me in two. I had dreaded to ask him, burying the truth beneath layers upon layers of denial.

I hadn't given his love life much thought since it had slipped out of Murben's mouth. But now it was burning through me like a disease, turning my insides rotten.

Ben's eyes darkened, filling with the resignation of a man who knew there was nothing he could say that could fix this. "I'll break the betrothal off when we get back from the Spirits' Trek."

"In two and a half years?" I spat.

The words tore from my throat like sandpaper, like I had swallowed and then hurled back up a fucking desert. "And an even better question…" I palmed my forehead to ground myself, feeling dizzy. "You're still committed to another woman while you sleep in my bed?"

He stood up and moved towards me. "It's nothing–"

"Don't!" I shot a hand up, pointing a finger at him like a blade between us. "I'm so furious with you right now." I paced the room like a caged lioness, but it was impossible to process the information with the anger in my chest building like a storm about to break.

He had told me he hadn't made love to anyone else. But there were other ways. Kisses. Naked skin pressed against one another. Public affection. Who had he been intimate with and promised his heart to before he met me? That thought stung like a thousand burning nettles.

Ben grabbed his shirt from the foot of the bed, his jaw clenched. "Should I sleep in Murben and Davis's room again tonight?"

I froze by the window, looking out, my fingers gripping the sill so hard the wood caved under my rage. "I'm contemplating it!"

54

It was the first of April; a day of tradition when people played pranks making fools of one another. I woke up feeling like the biggest fool of them all. Ben lay asleep beside me, which I had barely accepted after our fight yesterday. His breathing was steady despite the struggles he faced in my territory. *He shouldn't be here.*

Even in deep sleep, he looked beaten worse than an interrogated enemy who refused to break. Bruises coloured his cheeks, dry blood caked his cheekbones and jaw, and a cut near his temple ran across his tanned complexion. His lips, usually curved in teasing arrogance, were parted to breath out his exhaustion as he rested. His swollen nose was probably blocked.

Yet, despite everything; the fight, the pain, the secrets between us, he was still here. He had stayed at my side.

Even though it was against my better judgement, I had decided to go with Ben to Black Castle, so he could pacify his subjects. But I'd let him stew in insecurity for a while longer before I'd tell him. The shadows of his betrayals and secrets cast over the love I felt for him, clearly hadn't darkened the light and hope of what could develop.

I inspected his face thoroughly. Ben couldn't walk into Black Castle looking like a man who'd been beaten to the Underworld and back. If he did, regaining his authority after seven months away would be a battle he'd already lost. But we didn't have time to let him heal naturally, not if we were planning on reaching the festival by the fourth of April. Nor did I want him to have blatant confirmation that I possessed magic, so I settled on removing the swelling, cuts and bruises on his skin whilst he was still sleeping.

I clenched my jaw and got to work. My fingers ghosted over his swollen skin, willing the bruises and cuts to fade, feeling his tissue mend beneath my fingertips. The sight of him battered and vulnerable poked a hard finger of accusation at my heart through its cage of ribs.

I didn't care what it cost me, he'd wake up with his face restored, and I'd deny with my every breath that I had anything to do with it.

But as I worked, my anger grew red hot every time I looked at him, imagining him kissing this other woman to whom he was betrothed. My hands shook with the effort to keep healing when all I wanted was to shake him awake and demand answers. When I had finished healing him, I counted my blessings that he was still sleeping, so I could sneak out and calm my nerves. Although, it was perhaps a futile exercise, as I was certain I'd blow up with raging anger once again when I laid my eyes on him.

I sauntered around the outpost after having spent an hour in my tree, and found Valentina and her teammate, Treylieh, in the stables. They were still getting a few last days of practice done before their horse race challenge as their challenge had also been postponed to the fifth of April.

Tired to the point of fearing I'd fall off the saddle with all the magical energy I had expelled this morning to mend Ben, I still rode out with them. It'd do me good to feel the chill morning air on my face.

We took the route west where the horse track was located, and the horses seemed to pull in that direction on their own, as if they knew what fun awaited there. The sunrise was bright orange this morning with a thin line of yellow, like a lid suffocating flames. I had brought out the brown mare I often borrowed from the stables and Valentina had chosen a white charger for her challenge while Treylieh had picked a taller black stallion. I took great care in noting how all the horses in the stable performed, establishing I wouldn't pick this short mare for my horse race challenge next year.

We started with a slow walk to warm them up but then pushed hard and rode faster, racing each other. Valentina pushed her white charger over a fallen trunk, and from my angle, I watched as her lightweight body flew off the horseback and into the forest, landing between the trees on the other side of the trunk.

Treylieh and I veered our horses around the trunk to see how she was doing. She was pissed off, that was for certain. Bones cracked as she used her magic to correct something that had obviously ended up where it shouldn't be. She ejected a sound that wasn't a painful cry but more like a furious complaint that her bones had failed her. Even if she could mend her fractures, she'd be extremely sore for a while after. There was also a wound on her thigh that was bleeding, having cut herself on the sharp stone beside her.

"It was the stupid horse's fault," she spat. "He hesitated and stepped wrong. Or Brian's fault, who said this horse was the best fit for me. Now, look what the thing has done to me. If I don't heal in time for my challenge in five days," she shouted and looked at the horse. "I'll make a hamburger out of you!"

Treylieh and I exchange an amused look. "I'll take you back to the infirmary to get you examined," Treylieh said, as he dismounted to help her up, probably having used some of his persuasion magic as Valentina didn't argue.

I snorted to myself, realising that Harvey had made a great judgement call, matching them together.

"Do you guys mind if I don't come along? Mewer will kill me if I show up with more work for him, and I wanted to head down to the city to get something."

"I don't need help," she growled, standing up before Treylieh got to her, and hopping on her good leg towards the horse.

The horse moved a step away from her where it was grazing, probably sensing her hateful energy. To be fair, I would move further away from her too when she was in this mood.

She gave it the evil eye and hopped closer. "Stay!"

The horse moved again, and Valentina roared. "Move again and I'll break your bones, too!"

This time the horse was wise enough to be still, and Valentina put her boot in the stirrup and mounted. Treylieh followed behind Valentina as they headed back to the outpost after Valentina had waved her hand over her head and thrown a 'see you later' over her shoulder to me.

I carried on forwards. Not used to praying to the Spirit of Luck, I paid him thanks as not a single person crossed my path into town. I didn't have much time as I had to get back to class at ten o'clock. That gave me an hour to find a craftsman who could create the object I wanted to give Ben on his twenty-sixth birthday this Sunday. A gift fit for a king. I only had one idea as to what to give him, so there was no room for failure. The 'Magical Shed' was my best guess to source the item. The owner was an old man stemming from a family who had supplied various types of magic to customers for generations; to non-magical people and regular white-wings alike.

The name of the shop was fitting, as it was a small rickety house at the east outskirts of the city. The walls were simply erected wooden planks devoid of paint, and as I walked inside, I noted that it hadn't been redecorated since seven years ago when Father had brought me here last.

Closing the door behind me, I could still feel a faint draft sneaking through the wooden beams. Shelf upon shelf lined all sides of the walls, each overflowing with wondrous artefacts, aged tomes, vials of shimmering liquids and relics that hummed with power. Feathers, dream catchers and animal teeth hung from leather cords from the low ceiling, their presence both eerie and enchanting. Some swayed gently, moved by an unseen force, whilst others remained perfectly still. The more colourful potions; ruby red, deep violets and shimmering golds were carefully arranged in glass jars on the shelf behind the worn wooden till from where the shop keeper, Mister Frayor, smiled at me.

"Miss Coraly," he croaked, and there was a twinkle in his eyes as if he had been expecting me. "A sight for sore eyes. It's been almost a decade since I last saw you."

He looked kind through and through, like his age had washed away all his calls for vengeance. He still had his thick grey hair and warm brown eyes set in a thin face that I thought looked more frail than last I saw him. The clothes he wore were the same as I remembered; a brown overall with a white apron that was dirty from potions, ink and oils.

I neared the till and caught the scent of herbs and old parchment but also a sweeter smell, like melon, which could be from anything; a midday snack, or the traces of a dissipated spell.

"You recognise me?"

"Oh, yes. Yes. Very much. What happened to your family was a travesty, indeed. My thoughts have been on you once or twice every year."

Probably on my birthday, while people were reminiscing about the Battle of Bensguard. "Thank you for your thoughts."

He placed his hands on the till and leaned over, eagerly wanting to please his customer. "What can I do for you, child?"

A ray of colourful light fractured across the room from a prism hung in the window. Only the Spirits knew if the prism was just a trinket or a relic with dormant magic waiting for greedy hands to claim it. Or had it wanted to warn me? I hesitated. "I wanted to gift someone my oath." I rubbed my arm, looking around at the bric-a-brac in the shop. "Not really sure what I'm looking for."

"You want an oath to be made just like the one you have?"

I gawked at him before looking at my arm to verify that my sleeve was still covering my oath tattoo. "How did you know?"

"I'm an oath caster. I can sense these things like an ant crawling down my neck."

Swiftly, I put my arm on the till and pulled the sleeve up to show him. "Can you remove it?"

He shook his head, clicking his tongue. "No. There is a big difference between an oath caster and an oath breaker."

Saddened, I stared at the tattoo bracelet on my wrist. "Do you know any oath breakers? I'd really like to get it off."

He took my hand in his cold grip and inspected the tattoo. Then he sighed, shaking his head again. "This is a very potent oath, made by someone highly adept at magic. You'll find it hard to source someone who can break it."

Shit!

Did Duke Hartmore know this? If I found something that he desired more and wanted to negotiate my freedom, would he know anyone skilled enough to remove it? My stomach knotted. *It couldn't be permanent!*

"Okay. Thank you for taking the time to look at it."

His face wrinkled even more. "I'm sorry I couldn't help you there, but maybe I can help by making you the other oath you needed. Tell me about it."

"I have come into possession of a black blade."

Mister Frayor gasped and patted the arms I was resting atop the counter. "Dark item. Dark item, indeed."

"Yes." I scratched the back of my head with a finger. "I'd like to promise someone I'll never use it on him. To cast a spell that makes it impossible for me to stab him with it."

"Oh dear. Sounds serious. But a good idea. I can help you with that." He pulled out a few drawers in the counter and searched through them until he settled on something and closed the last drawer shut.

A leather band floated up to hover in the air in front of me on account of a movement from his fingertips. "This band can hold such an oath. You'll put it on the person's left wrist."

I took out my coin pouch from my pocket. "How much will the oath cost me?"

"It's fifteen coppers, my child."

Fifteen coppers! I barely kept my words from spitting across his face. That was three quarters of a month's salary. I sifted through my pouch, counting the coins.

"I'll have to come back. I only have fourteen with me today."

"Nonsense. I'll give you a discount."

I looked up from the pouch. "Are you sure?"

He nodded once curtly. "Positive."

"Thank you, Mister Frayor."

He closed his eyes and muttered a few foreign words and with them, black swirls printed onto the band.

"The oath only works once. Once you have put it on someone, the band will evaporate," he explained, handing it over to me.

"I understand. Thank you. Perhaps the next time I see you will be sooner than a decade."

"Let's hope so, Miss Coraly. Bye."

I took the forest road back, hoping to avoid any unwanted encounters. But luck, ever a fickle thing, turned its back on me – twice lucky in one day was clearly too much to ask for.

I cursed the Spirit of Luck, as General Denor blocked my way. His crimson uniform marked him as on duty. I inspected his face and the way he moved, not giving away any agony from yesterday's brutal fight. He must have used his magic to mend himself and maybe Mewer had helped heal the physical injuries.

I reined my horse to a stop, scanning him with narrowed eyes. "Why is it that no matter where I go these days, you always seem to be there?"

He smirked in a way unlike the general he was rumoured to be. "Because you make any excuse to see me?"

I tapped my finger against my lip, feigning thought. "No, that's definitely not it."

"Maybe it's because when Camp Leader Mewer dismissed me from the infirmary, Valentina was admitted, raving like a madwoman about your little adventure in the woods by the horse track. I figured I'd check if you were still in once piece."

Dammit! I had told Valentina to keep her mouth shut in front of Mewer. My jaw tightened as I shook my head at him. "I think you make every effort to piss off a certain black-wing king."

"Guilty."

"As you can see, I'm okay, so off you go!"

He aligned his beautiful black stallion next to mine; the horse was a fine example not normally seen around the Bensguard Outpost. He brought up a wine bottle and two glasses from his backpack.

"If you're going to follow me. This will count as your third encounter with me," I told him, trying to make my horse go faster to lose him, but his horse seemed to follow my mare by instinct.

"Sure. A glass of wine?"

That was odd, as it was early morning on a Thursday. Perhaps he was trying to drink his shame away from having lost his fight against Ben. "I can't. I have a class in thirty minutes."

"If the general in your line of command, who can manipulate people's minds, tells you to drink wine with him, you drink wine with him."

I stared into the distance, counting to three, gathering what sliver of patience I could muster with each number. "Fine! Fuck the glass and hand me the bloody bottle!"

He handed me the bottle and I took a large swig. We talked for a long while about the outpost in the olden days, the challenges and he even touched on conversations about his family, as our horses walked towards the outpost, the general supplying me with two more bottles before we circled the edge of the treeline surrounding the outpost. My horse had started to sway more and more beneath me, although I guessed it was just me getting more drunk.

General Denor told me about his family and growing up in the wilderness at a small cottage in Pansery in the east mountains in the Pharanir province. His father was a hunter who killed and skinned animals for clothes and ate their flesh for nourishment. The general even told me the story of how his father walked the Spirits' Trek by himself and another black-wing ten years ago without having army training and received his magic. His father had then passed his mind bending magic to Denor, and that's how the general had ended up in the Bensguard Outpost in the first place.

The stories were so personal that I wondered whether he'd let me keep the memories or wipe them clean as soon as we arrived back at the outpost.

"Have you been drinking?" Ben's voice echoed inside my head like a terrible hangover.

"Can you feel that through our bond?"

"Yes. Your shield is down."

"I'm busted!" I giggled nervously, my stomach tickled, unsure about what he'd think of me.

There was a tug of annoyance through the bond before I shielded my mind. Not surprisingly, and not what I wanted in my current state, Ben was at the stables when we returned. *Damn his excellent spies!*

I leaned over to chide him for spying on me and being so overprotective but lost my balance and propelled my arms in the air without gaining grip as I fell off the horse. Ben caught me before I was even close to the ground, his lips sliced into a thin line, and he shook his head. "You've an archery academics lesson in minutes. How will you sit up straight for that?"

"It's okay. Camp Leader Nar and I are this tight," I said, crossing my fingers.

He clicked his tongue. "That's how tightly she despises you."

Ben was staring daggers at the general; a silent threat for him to leave.

"This was a fun date," Denor mocked, veering his black stallion around.

"Non-date," I slurred my defence to his back.

When the general had left our sight, Ben looked at me. "Can you walk?"

I giggled. "I'm better at fucking."

"I don't disagree, but right now, walking is more appropriate."

"Are you sure?" I whispered. "No one ever goes to the back of the stable where Fiona lives."

He headed for the military building without putting me down. "First of all, the notion of your pig watching us as we're intimate isn't something that arouses me, and second, you know we can't because of the oath."

"Oh, right. I'll give you a blowjob, then."

Ben halted for a brief moment before carrying on. "You're drunk."

"Only a little."

"Or perhaps a lot. You'd not know the difference whether I stuck my cock or a carrot into your mouth."

"Well, life is full of surprises."

He sighed, clearly not amused. As Ben lowered me into our bed, I gripped a hold of his belt, trying to get it off. Ben swatted away my hands. "That's not appropriate now. I'm going to have to tuck you into bed, tell Camp Leader Nar that you're unwell and hope she doesn't care to know the truth. I'll probably go with a migraine."

"Yes. *You* are my migraine. Now, take your trousers off." I fiddled my fingers around the buttons.

He swatted my hands away once more as if I was a persistent fly. "Spirits, what did the general give you?"

I flipped onto my back and saw the ceiling spin. "Love potion," I said, laughing.

"I'll put Cadet La Roy on guard duty at our door if he isn't on his trust exercise training. I'd hate for Camp Leader Watson to walk in on you when you're in this state."

"You're jealous. So jealous!" I slurred, rolling my eyes.

He bent low and kissed me. "That, I am. Now, sleep off whatever this is, and I'll be back soon. I'll take notes for you during the lesson."

"But I'm still fucking horny. What will I do with that?"

"If you're still aroused when I return, maybe I can help you out with that then."

55

A firm shake rescued me from my nightmares of violence and blood and death. I turned over groggily and blinked against the morning light. My head throbbed with a pulsating rhythm behind my temples.

Ben sat on the edge of the bed with a brown paper bag in his hand, his fingers crumpling its edges absent-mindedly. "Breakfast."

I rubbed a knuckle in my eye and yawned. "Breakfast? What happened to lunch and dinner?"

He smirked, setting the bag beside me. "You slept straight through them. It's been so calm here at the outpost with you sleeping all of yesterday, I contemplated not even waking you up for breakfast."

"Very funny." I rubbed my entire face. My skin tingled and the headache lodged in my skull refused to fade.

"But unfortunately for you," Ben continued, pushing off the bed and striding to the window, "it's Friday. We've got classes today, and if we're not on the field in an hour, Camp Leader Nar will have our heads." He swept the curtain aside with one tug, letting in even more sunlight.

I groaned and yanked the blanket over my head. "I know how to shoot, *and who!* Close the curtains!"

"That may be true, but we still have to attend." His voice was holding back amusement, but I also detected assertiveness in his tone, telling me he wasn't going to let me wriggle out of this just because of a mere hangover. "Come on! Rise and shine!"

"No." My voice was muffled under the blanket. "There is no rise. There is no shine. Go away. Preferably as far as Black Wing Territory."

Ben chuckled. "I can only do that if you come with me."

I pushed the blanket down to my collarbones, my hair a wild mess with frizzy, blue strands around my shoulders. "I'll come."

Ben had just reached the wardrobe, his hand resting on the handle, but at my words, he froze mid-step and turned. His brows lifted in surprise. "What?"

"I'll come with you. Tonight. If you promise me, we will be back before Monday morning for the archery challenge."

He seemed lost for words for a long while, but eventually stated, *"That's the plan."*

I flopped back onto my stomach on the mattress again. *"If you kidnap me, I'll kill you."*

He sat down next to me, holding out my flight uniform folded neatly in a pile. "Deal."

The time left until class only allowed for me to brush my hair and put it up in a messy bun and apply more make-up to conceal the old.

Ben handed me a water bottle as we jogged out to the field and we arrived just as Camp Leader Nar had begun her speech, and she flashed me a hateful stare as I lined up next to Kate.

Camp Leader Nar was as focused as ever when she instructed what she expected us to accomplish this lesson. "Only one of you will take part in the archery competition. Apparently, it's a new rule to the seventh challenge where you must put faith in the strongest in the team. Because of some commitments I have, the challenge won't be until the fifth of April, so you have a few extra days to practise."

She had commitments? Sure! More like the general had commanded her to postpone the challenge. There was definitely something sinister going on amongst leadership.

"I'll sit this one out. You've got it covered," Ben whispered into my ear, his voice like velvet as he stroked his hand down my arm.

"The winner," Camp Leader Nar continued, "will receive the reward of any gift they desire. Within reason, of course, and one approved by Captain Coraly. The competition is simple. You stand on the mark. You shoot. We leave the arrow closest to the centre stuck in the board until someone does better and so on. Once everyone has had a go, the arrow which is still stuck to the target board wins. Any questions?"

No one put their hand up, so she dismissed the class to continue practising freely. Ben scanned his eyes along the field as we walked to the far end where we normally liked to practise, where no arrows could hit us from either direction.

"Looking for Cadet Gravelhorn?" I asked.

"Yes." He ripped out a bow from the bow rack and passed it to me. "I'll keep guard while you practise."

I pulled an arrow from a quiver resting against the bow rack and walked towards the mark. "You're not even going to let a few arrows off for fun?"

"We have to win this one, so aim!" he barked, and flicked his finger in the air between the target board and me.

I squinted and looked farther down the lanes. "I'm not worried. Unless the Archery Team is better. Who's taking the shots?"

Ben leaned back against the bow rack and crossed his legs by his ankles. "Ashton. And it doesn't seem like he misses, either. He'll be your strongest opponent."

"I thought as much. If he wasn't such a lovely person, I'd ask Valentina to break some of his bones before the challenge."

Ben's head snapped around, his eyes wide with disbelief as they locked on me. They glanced over me as if he questioned whether he knew the person in front of him, as if I had delivered a blow he had not seen coming.

"Just kidding." I smirked, stepping up to the mark, the bow steady in my hand.

I drew back the string, the familiar tension pressing into my fingers and let the arrow fly. Then I let lose a few more, not missing the bullseye once.

When the centre got clustered with arrows, I strode to the board, yanking them free with sharp tugs before sliding them back into my quiver. My muscles burned from the repetition, but it was the perfect distraction against all my thoughts that were grating the walls of my mind. *Ben's secrets. The betrothal. The trust between us. Surviving the academy.* All of it was too much.

When the lesson time ended, Ben and I headed towards the front of the building, where a heated discussion was in full motion. Emroyce, Brian, Treylieh and Zoe stood in a tight circle, their voices low but edged with tension.

"What's going on?" I asked, stopping just short of them.

Ben's presence loomed close behind me like a shadow.

Emroyce turned towards me, his expression grim. "Mewer has just told Valentina that he isn't allowing her to attend the horse race. Says it'll be too strenuous on her bones, and she must rest to recover.

Zoe folded her arms, shaking her head. "Mewer has drained himself and isn't healing anyone anymore unless absolutely necessary until he has rested himself to regain his strength."

That wasn't good.

If Mewer isn't healing, the outpost is vulnerable.

Valentina frightened me more than a black-wing attack, though. She didn't take it well when she had to miss challenges. She was obsessed with doing them. "Valentina must be so pissed off."

"Yep," Emroyce scoffed. "So, who wants to go comfort her in the infirmary on the first shift before she has calmed down?"

Everyone shook their heads in horror, even me, stepping on Ben's feet as I tried to take a step back from volunteering. "We should send in the Emotions Manipulator. What's her name, in the Agility Team?"

"Cadet Starly? I really doubt she wants to calm Valentina with her magic," Brian answered. "That woman wouldn't even know how to give a hug. Have you spoken to her? She's like barbed wire."

"Rock, paper, scissors to decide who will hug the viper?" Emroyce asked.

"Fine," I muttered, taking a step towards them and holding out my hand. "That's only fair."

"Is the king in too?" Emroyce nodded for Ben.

"Sure," Ben answered, and I gawked at him.

He shrugged his shoulders. "Guarding Cadet Karson when she's extremely angry. Sounds fun."

"Not guarding. Hugging," I corrected to deter him.

"I'm a good hugger. Are you jealous?" he challenged, lifting his brows at me.

"Fine, the king is in," I muttered, and frankly, I'd love to see Valentina's reaction if Ben attempted to hug her.

She'd break one of his bones for sure.

As Emroyce arranged the matches, Ben leaned in close, his breath warm against my ear. "I want to make an effort to get to know your friends. Since we're to be a couple forever."

His strong arms slid around me until my fingers brushed against the cool metal of his forever ring. My heart skipped. Warmth and terror hit me like a bucket of icy water at the finality of his words. Forever. A promise as heavy as the blade at my hip.

The first round began, and I squared off against Kate. A flick of my wrist revealed scissors, slicing clean through her paper. Easy win. I stepped back, pulse steady, but my gaze flicked to Ben as he faced Treylieh. A tie. That meant he'd have to go against Brian next.

Ben held up a rock. Solid. Unshakable. I turned to Brian just in time to see his fingers flash open. Paper. *Damn it.*

Ben clenched his jaw before turning his attention to the next match. Zoe and Treylieh squared off, and Ben's expression twisted, like he already regretted joining the game. Treylieh lost, and Zoe strutted away, grinning as she threw her victory fingers into the air.

Then Emroyce turned to Ben. My stomach knotted so tightly it hurt. If Ben lost and had to hug Valentina…I'd have to guard Ben, so he didn't let black death magic seep into the air like a suffocating mist and kill everyone in the infirmary.

Valentina would undoubtedly say something that would poke at Ben's patience, her usual shallow opinions on war pushing him toward the edge of his composure. I could already see it unfolding in my mind.

Ben and Emroyce lifted their hands in unison, the moment stretching, heavy with anticipation. I held my breath.

Emroyce – rock.

Ben – paper.

Relief hit me so hard my knees nearly buckled.

Phew!

"Crap!" Emroyce cursed and turned to face Treylieh. "Just between you and me now."

"On three. No cheating, Emroyce!"

They counted to three and showed their hands. Emroyce held up scissors, but Treylieh had paper, losing the game.

"Emroyce," Treylieh said in a sweet caress, clearly using his persuasion magic. "I think you want to be a good friend to me and visit Valentina in my stead."

"Yeah sure. No problem. What are friends for," Emroyce said, as if it had been a rehearsed line and he walked straight towards the infirmary.

I couldn't believe Treylieh feared Valentina to the extent that he had used his persuasive magic on Emroyce. Treylieh almost never used his magic unless it was crucial. I guessed this was one of those crucial moments. "No, cheating, hey?" I mocked Treylieh.

Treylieh smirked. "How was that cheating? Emroyce is such a good friend."

"Yeah," I scoffed and playfully patted his shoulder. "When you use your persuasive magic on him."

Treylieh watched Emroyce enter the infirmary, looking a tad bit guilty about what he had done. "He never specified magic was prohibited when he told us the rules. And being Valentina's teammate, I'll see her soon enough. Better she lashes out her anger on Emroyce than also feeling guilty, thinking she has let me down."

"I don't think Valentina believes she has let you down. If you've a beef with anyone, you'd probably have to speak to her horse."

We laughed before heading to the canteen for lunch.

Zayd sat alone at a table in the back corner, so I excused myself from Ben as I saw him aim for the black-wings near the middle. Ben halted and frowned at me, but didn't say a word. He watched me carefully as I slithered between the tables before he took his seat, a grim expression was plastered on his face.

Awkwardly, I stopped by Zayd's table with my tray in hand. I watched him for a moment as he hadn't seen me. He sat slumped over the table, his shoulders folded inward and his fingers traced mindless patterns on the wooden surface. His food was untouched and had probably cooled too much for him to eat.

"Hi Zayd, you're back from the king's counsel meeting. Are you okay?

You seem upset?"

He looked up at me with those clear-blue eyes that lately seemed nothing but distraught. "Hi Angie. Yes, I got back this morning. Nothing new apart from the usual."

So much for trust and secrets.

I put my tray down on the table and sat down opposite him. "You know the time when you were angry and wouldn't talk to me for five days because I had braided pink ribbons into Crusher's mane, and you didn't have time to remove them before your horse race challenge?"

"Yes, that was evil. The guys still refer to my mustang as Pink Ribbons when they see me take him out."

At least I had drawn a subtle smile to his lips.

"Remember that summer when we were camping south of our summer cottage to be near the lake because you wanted to catch the best salmon, and I painted your lips red with my lipstick before you woke up in the morning?"

He nodded. "Yes, but only Harvey and Mazdon saw that, so at least I could contain that gossip." He picked at his pasta. "Fun times."

I twirled my fork in the spaghetti. "Yes…but you didn't think so then…my point is, you've that same sour look on your face. What's wrong?"

He sighed, pushing another meatball into his mouth. "Look around, Angie. This is my life, always stagnant in the camp leader role. They seem to only give the general title and higher promotions to family members to enhance loyalty because the king probably has a hold on them. Harvey might not be as innocent as you want to believe."

"True. I never claimed my brother was innocent. I know he's withholding a lot of secrets from me. Like everyone else." I raised my brows at Zayd.

Zayd's fingers tightened around his fork and then stabbed at the food on his plate. His voice was raw as he finally spoke. "I used to be content with the thought that I could only ever rise to become a camp leader because…because…" His breath hitched, his throat working to expel the words. "Because I had you. You were my world, so nothing else mattered." His fork clattered as he tossed it onto the tray before his hands curled into fists. "And when you left, I still had hope. Hope that you'd come back to me one day and things would be as they were. That I'd be happy again."

His jaw clenched, barely managing to keep a lid on his emotions, as he finally lifted his sapphire-blue eyes to mine. "But then you came back." He jerked his chin over his shoulder in Ben's direction, though he refused to turn and look, "with him." His lips pressed into a tight line once more, his entire frame tensed. "What hope is there for me now?"

A pang of guilt reverberated through me, but I refused to let it take hold. I reached out, sliding my hand over his clenched fist on the table, feeling the rigid tension in his fingers beneath my touch. "Zayd…" I said gently, trying to pull him back from whatever dark place he had locked himself inside of. "What we shared was special. The memories we made I'll cherish forever." I gave his hand a gentle squeeze, trying to offer comfort, but his fingers didn't even twitch in response. "But we were young," I continued. "You'll meet someone else. A woman who sees you for the incredible man you are now." I offered him a small smile.

His shoulders stiffened at my words, his expression easing as he stared down at our hands. The silence stretched, filled with his request for a better explanation. I gestured at him, trying to lighten the moment. "Look at you, Zayd. You're strong, smart, kind, undeniably handsome and–"

"Ow, please put your shield up. I don't want to hear this."

"Oh, sorry, Ben."

I locked the shield into place and focused back on Zayd. "The guys tell me there are a lot of nice and pretty women in the General Operations Unit."

"Yeah, if you prefer women who volunteered to become warriors and have thicker arms than I have legs."

I picked at my food, not sure what else I could tell him so not to sound patronising or insinuate that he should simply man up and walk it off.

"That has my vote. Tell him to walk it off."

"Shit! The shield!" It was like a bloody heavy weapon I had to drag around with me wherever I went.

"If you lose the connection to your shield this easily, your mind is a free for all. Practise keeping it up!"

I threw a mind-your-own-business stare at Ben over Zayd's shoulder, and I saw his shoulders bounce as he chuckled to himself, but he averted his gaze to carry on with his conversation with Murben.

Zayd's fingers laced with mine instead of keeping my hand on top of his. I swallowed. This wasn't good. "The black-wing spring festival is going ahead as planned," Zayd muttered.

I lowered my fork with the meatball still attached to the plate again. Why had he said that? What did he know about the black-wing spring festival? Was that what the king's counsel meeting had been about? To test me?

"Ah, so you knew that, too," he muttered, rolling his eyes and pulling his hand back to the edge of his tray.

Not only was my bonded soul an open book, but apparently, my face was just as easy to read. *Dammit!*

"You knew, I'd know." I leaned in slightly, lowering my voice as if sharing a secret "Ben and I are leaving tonight, taking the route over the west mountain ridge by the slalom flight practice fields," I lied. "We'll be back Monday morning. No one will know we left the outpost premises."

His grip on the fork tightened. He stared at me with what looked like resentment before muttering under his breath. "I hope he brings you back."

The words hit me harder than I could ever admit. He stabbed his fork into another meatball with unnecessary force.

My chest had constricted, and my pulse was erratic now. But I forced a smile even if I knew it wouldn't reach my eyes. "Me too. If not, take care of yourself."

Zayd's fork froze halfway to his mouth, and he stabbed a hard stare into me, questioning my life's choices. But I ignored him, pushing back my chair so hard the legs scraped against the floor in a sharp screech. I stood up, grabbing my tray and wove between the maze of tables. I'd had enough of his gloominess. My appetite was gone, and I needed Kate and Fern's company to drown out the tension haunting the air behind me.

After lunch, Kate and I walked together to the last lesson of the day where Camp Leader Nar taught how an arrow moved in different types of wind pressure. The lesson dragged on and my mind drifted off to think about any potential pitfall of going to the Black Wing Territory. I hadn't noticed that Camp Leader Nar had dismissed the class and walked out when Ben cupped his hand at the back of my neck possessively. "Time to go."

I realised Ben wasn't referring to us leaving this classroom when he nodded at the black-wings gathered by the door, and a knot tightened in my stomach as I nodded.

Not unexpectedly, all the black-wings followed us to our room, and while we walked, Ben instructed them of their tasks and what they needed to pay attention to during our absence.

From the wardrobe, I got out my flight leathers, put them on and loaded myself with my weapons. "I told Zayd we'd take the route over the west mountain ridge. I want to find out what Zayd will do with that information. Can Nesso patrol the area tonight once we leave to scout if there are any movements?"

Ben embraced me from behind, his hands stroking over the hilts of my many daggers. "You're a brilliant woman, you know that?"

Ben twirled me around and saw me roll my eyes at him with a playful smile.

"I'll instruct him as you wish, my queen." He scratched his cheek as he inspected me and all my weapons. "You know that I'm the king in the Black Wing Territory?"

I curved my fingers into his black shirt. "Yes. You've mentioned it once or twice."

"And I have an army and castle guards…There is no need for you to arm yourself to your teeth. You'll be safer there than you are here."

I let go of his shirt and got a backpack from the wardrobe. "That's nothing you can promise."

He gestured for my backpack. "Well, at least don't insult me by bringing luggage. I've gowns and other clothes and food and everything you need in the castle. And if I don't have it, I'll send the servants out to get it for you."

I tossed the backpack onto the wardrobe floor. "Tell me again why we're not living there instead of here."

He shrugged his shoulders as if to say it wasn't his choice, but then he said, "To reinstate the glory of your family name. Never forget how much that means to you."

A hearing portal appeared beside me, startling me to jump a step towards Ben.

"Are you guys on your way? I wanted to say goodbye, as Angie won't," Zoe chirped.

"We're leaving in a minute. Just packing up the last items," I answered.

"Angelica is referring to all the daggers she's planning to stab me with if I don't bring her back," Ben added.

Zoe laughed. "Well, have fun you two. I'll take care of the boys here."

Ben leaned closer to the blue swirling portal. "And how exactly will you take care of–"

I smacked my hand over Ben's mouth. "Don't ask!"

"I'm fucking Murben as we speak, honey," she said shamelessly.

"She has no filter," I moaned.

Ben cleared his throat. "Guess we're leaving them in expert hands, then."

"You don't have any complaints about my hands, do you, honey?" I heard Zoe ask Murben, her distant voice emitting through the portal.

"Spirits, Ben! Stop feeding the fire!" I waved for the portal to go away. "Zoe, don't answer that and take this thing down."

The hearing portal vanished, and I sighed with relief.

Ben stepped closer to my back and snaked his arms around my waist. "Don't worry, Murben will turn Zoe into a lady in no time."

"Or she'll rub off him and make him curse and beg her not to leave his bed." A tremor went through me. Horrible thought. "Maybe we should rescue Murben and take him back to the Black Wing Territory."

"He'll be fine. Ready to go?"

I pocketed the light crystal and the oath bracelet, which I had put in a small purple box adorned with a black ribbon.

Ben craned around me. "What was that?" He pointed to my pocket.

I cocked my head up and our lips almost met, his breath expelling onto my mouth, "It's a secret," I whispered. The heat from the attraction between us tickled my stomach.

I didn't move a muscle, and just waited to see what he would do next.

His gaze dipped to my mouth, the tip of his tongue cautiously wetting his lips. "If I start something, I don't think we'll make it to the Black Wing Territory tonight."

"Promise you'll hold that thought until after we have arrived there?"

He smiled his charming challenge-smile. "Promise."

56

The carriage's wheels tore so violently over the cobblestones that I had to grab hold of the leather seat to keep myself from falling flat on my face. It was amazing that the wheels were still attached to this damned box.

The moment I spotted the black castle ahead, my stomach knotted mercilessly. Black Castle had become a tangible curse. No matter if I was a civilian, a teammate or a mission agent, I could never escape it. The black stone structure devoured the little remaining daylight before the sun set below the horizon.

This castle had once been a place I had stalked like a predator and where I had created memories that I cherished from the few moments spent in the presence of a king. That was before everything had become so complicated. Now, I expected it to be a treacherous place. A prison disguised as my boyfriend's home, or a king's castle, if Ben changed his mind. If he decided not to let me return to the Bensguard Outpost, I might never leave this place again.

A shudder ran through me as I recognised the groan of iron that filled the air from the winged gates. They were creaking open, granting passage toward my fate. The horses whickered as the carriage crossed the threshold and trumpets blew out the royal fanfare. Their keen sense and protest making me reflexively inhale a sharp breath.

The carriage came to a halt outside the back entrance, and as I stepped outside, frosty air swept across my skin. Unwillingly, I carried on, my boots meeting the stone ground with finality as if I were walking towards the gallows.

The castle was exactly how I remembered it with sky-high towers poking at the clouds and monstrous gargoyles baring their fangs as if ready to swallow anyone foolish enough to enter. Water, dyed crimson spilled from their mouths, pouring like blood down the spouts and into the moat at the base.

Once, the eerie display had frightened me. Now, it was nothing compared to the fear curling in my gut. Last time I had entered the castle, I had been undercover, a nobody. Today, I'd walk through those doors as the king's peasant girlfriend – or more accurately, as his mistress, since he was betroth. All eyes from every corner and every shadow would judge me as unworthy.

I tightened the power around my mental shield to ensure Ben couldn't hear my thoughts. It was best to keep them to myself because as soon as we walked inside, past those heavy black doors, Ben had to resume being the king he had to be in the Black Wing Territory. A man who ruled this fortress and who could decide with a single word that I'd never leave again.

Servants thronged to him like ants hailing their queen, pushing me further away from the priority list.

"Maid Bernadette, take care of my guest!" Ben called from across the great hall.

Guest?

That was positively worse than a status as *girlfriend*. I almost preferred toy to being called a *guest*. It sounded so detached At least a toy suggested he liked to play with it.

Ben looked at me. "I have a few things I must tend to urgently." Then he disappeared through a side door.

I glanced around, recalling the balls I had attended in this very room. There was an instant flutter in my stomach when my mind flashed memories of me dancing with the king.

I tried to kill the smile forming on my lips and watched the flames of hundreds of candles lighting up the space. The dark-blue curtains with golden tassels covered parts of the enormous windows. Black stone walls. The room was exactly as I remembered from last year. On a podium at the far back of the room were two thrones chiselled out from black rock; their backs depicting stretched-out black wings.

Maid Bernadette curtsied in front of me. "This way, my lady." She led me out of the great hall and through a labyrinth of corridors. I followed her closely, taking note of every turn so that I could have a chance at finding my way back out.

She stopped abruptly outside a tall, intricate iron door, the flowery artwork a clear mark of the talented blacksmiths employed. Its detailed leaves and petals looked so realistic I almost leaned in to see if the sweet scent of flowers would tickle my nose.

There was a guard outside the door garbed in full armour a shade darker than usual for iron and he held a sword at his side

"This is your guest room. If you need anything, please let Guard

Jackoloy know and he'll arrange for you every need."

A guest room! If Ben believed I'd be happy in a guest room, he'd have more than an earful of complaints. However, that was an issue between Ben and me, so I smiled at the maid and entered.

A fire raged in the fireplace, its flames crackling and casting long shadows across the room. The maid left and I took a few more steps into the space. Two armchairs faced the stone hearth, perched atop sprawled animal furs, and between them stood a wooden burgundy table.

The room had dark, panelled walls lined with portraits in gold frames. Their subjects stared back at me with keen eyes, as if they knew all the secrets Ben never told me. Two enormous windows on one side of the room were partly covered by navy-blue curtains, but they still let the moonlight leak in and pool on the floor. The towering four-poster bed frame draped in velvet had its headboard pushed against the wall.

I rubbed my arm nervously, and crept deeper into the bed chamber, observing every detail down to the fine carvings of the furniture to the ornate candelabras.

I stopped by the wardrobe, hesitating before I pulled open two double doors. Dresses hung in neat rows, each tailored in extravagant fabrics and in various colours. My breath caught in my chest. I reached for one of the shoes beneath them, lifting it into the light. Low-heeled. My size.

My panic grew. Rooted.

Had Ben arranged this for me before we even arrived? That was more ominous than I could process right now. This wasn't just a guest room – it was a cage.

Why wasn't I in *his room*? Had he been so sure I'd come willingly? Or a worse thought; if I had refused, would he have taken me anyway? The dread burrowed deep. But it was nonetheless a concern I'd never know the outcome of before it was too late.

But beyond all of that, the real question burned hotter in my mind. Did he think dressing me in fancy dresses could change who I was? That he could smooth away the rough edges, strip me of my armour, and mould me into a queen I was never meant to be?

I clenched the fabric of my sleeve, my breath turning shallow. I didn't fit in here… My pulse raced and my palms grew sweaty. I didn't belong here… I never had. I was a warrior, raised by a warrior. My place was on the battlefield, not behind castle walls. The walls seemed to draw closer. The firelight flickered across my face, making my reflection in the glass of the wardrobe door look like a trapped spirit.

I have to get out of here.

I needed Ben. I tried searching for him through the bond, but my mental shoulder almost dislocated as I slammed against his rock-hard mind shield.

He had blocked me out.

I ventured out into the corridor, finding Guard Jackoloy staring at me through the slit of his helmet.

"My lady," he said, bowing curtly. "How can I be of service?"

I crossed my arms over my chest, feeling so foreign, almost like a captive. "I want to find King Blackbone."

"He's otherwise engaged at the moment." His voice was deep, suggesting a mature man behind all the iron.

Turning my head to observe either ends of the corridor, I noticed how silent this place was, as if I was high up in a tower, safely tucked away from harm… or hidden away from his betrothed. *Screw that.*

"I guess I'll just entertain myself by snooping around."

He held his hand out to stop me. "You've not been given permission to wander around in the castle, my lady."

Captive!

My mind pivoted from being a guest to an undercover agent. What would a captive agent do to get out of this?

"Why don't you alert the king about it," I snapped at him and had my hand hovering over the hilt of the dagger at my side.

He said no more before I explored the corridor to my right, but I could hear the clunking metal as his armour hit the iron plates against each other as he followed me.

Deep in the castle, I noted that this particular corridor had picture frames coated with a thick layer of dust.

"We shouldn't be in this wing, my lady. I strongly recommend that we turn around," the guard said, walking no more than a step behind me.

"Afraid of ghosts, Guard Jackoloy?"

"If I believed in them, I'd be particularly concerned about this section of the wing, my lady."

He wasn't holding his hand over his sword hilt, so whatever he was afraid of wasn't something one could murder.

"What is hidden away in this wing that is so forbidden?" I paused to look at a portrait of a stoic man just beside a lone door.

The man's resemblance to Ben was uncanny. Black hair, red eyes and a muscular build. The artist had painted the portrait of the man sitting, wearing a dark-blue cape and a golden crown. The painting's careful strokes and shadows were admirable.

Guard Jackoloy's head tilted up slowly, as if scared to look the man in the portrait straight in the eye. "His ghost," he answered, and then snapped his head down to stare at the stone floor.

I stared closer. "Who is that?"

"It was the late king."

"King Blackbone's father?"

The guard nodded, and swallowed, his Adam's apple moving up and down again.

The handle to the door next to the painting also had a layer of dust on it. No one had been here for years. Why? I stretched for the handle.

"I wouldn't go in there."

Hesitating, I looked at him. "Why not?"

"King Blackbone doesn't want anyone to go in there."

Well, I didn't want to be stuck in a guest room either, considering what he had promised me upon arrival, so clearly none of us would get what we wanted. I tugged down the handle and I gave the swollen door a shove with my hip. Guard Jackoloy stayed outside as I walked inside.

The office on the other side of the door was made for a king. The air smelling unmistakably of aged parchment. The thin layer of dust coating the furniture told me that the knowledge held in this room had been for noblemen only, but also undisturbed for many years.

Floor-to-ceiling bookcases lined all four walls, their wooden frames bent by the weight of tomes. Two narrow windows cut through the shelves like watchful eyes, allowing only slivers of light into the room, causing the shadows to cling to the corners and pool beneath furniture as if they had died there when the room stopped being used.

A massive desk, three times the size of Ben's, stood in the centre of the room. On its dark wood surface, a half-burned taper candle sat in a brass holder, the melted wax hardened in rivulets down its side. A book about the treaty of Uppland lay sprawled open, as if the reader had abandoned it in a hurry.

Curious, I approached the desk, my fingers trailing over the items before reaching for the drawers. The top one slid open with a faint creak, its inside disappointingly ordinary, containing sheets of parchment, a wooden ruler, ink vials, the king's sigils. Then I saw the extraordinary item. Nestled among the mundane, my eyes landed on an item far more interesting. It was small, black and in the shape of an iron cube.

My heart gave off one rebellious thud. Black iron had its uses. I could melt it down, forge another black blade for myself, something deadly and sharp. But as soon as I lifted the cube, its weight unexpectedly shifted. A barely audible click echoed through the silence, and the object split cleanly in half.

Cradled inside of the iron shell was a perfect black pyramid. Its surface shimmered with an unnatural polish, and as it caught light it gave off eerie glints. It's three sides bore the same symbol of an eternity mark. The carved lines were precise, as if burned into the iron rather than etched. The metal was cool in my palm, but there was something unsettling about holding it.

As it touched my skin, it sent shivers crawling up my arm and down my spine. This wasn't an object Ben would want me tampering with, let alone melting down.

Snapping the cube shut around the pyramid, I placed it back in the drawer, but now my gaze fell on a folded letter tucked just beneath it. I hesitated, splaying my fingers at its edges before reaching for it. Whatever this was, I had the feeling I wasn't supposed to see it.

But that had never stopped me before.

Dear Guardian,

Our alliance is most crucial in these perilous times and my support for your house does not waiver. When the time comes, I will speak with my son about your lovely daughter and his duties so that their soulmate bond can latch and

And what? The letter was unfinished. Why had he stopped writing the letter?

Ben and his father didn't seem to have been in an agreement about their alliance. Was Ben's father referring to the woman with whom Ben was betrothed? They were soulmates?

Ben had lied.

All those words about breaking it off with her were nothing but empty promises. A deception wrapped in false hope.

My jaw locked down so hard I thought I'd break my teeth. My nails had buried inside flesh as I dug them deep into my palms. But I stood there just staring at the damning truth curved by ink on parchment.

Breaking their bond had never been an option. It wasn't just a matter of choice, it was the will of the Spirits themselves. Not even Ben with all his power, could defy them.

My heart plummeted, but the sinking helplessness was quickly overtaken by wrath.

I shoved the letter back into the drawer and I noted how violently my fingers trembled with fury as I set down the black iron box. Then I slammed the drawer shut, before beginning to pace the room to find more clues about Ben's life.

It felt as though this office had been sealed shut the day Ben's father died and his presence haunted it like a ghost refusing to leave. Dust might still coat the shelves, but the evidence of his brutal rule remained untouched.

By the window, a round table displayed three worn belts, their leather darkened by age. My stomach twisted as I stepped closer, making guesses on what they had been used for.

Each belt had a different buckle. One plain with only a frame, another with a solid iron plate, and the third dotted with sharp studs. The variations weren't for fashion. They had a purpose.

Beside the table stood a tall wooden torture cross and as I looked at its worn use, my breath hitched with terror.

Iron shackles dangled from chains meant to lock his enemy in place with their arms and ankles spread wide and bound. Deep grooves marred the wood, and within them were old bloodstains that had seeped into the grain like a grotesque signature of pain.

The terror I felt warped and instead fuelled my anger. This was the legacy Ben had inherited, the backbone of the throne he sat upon.

And he still thought I belonged here?

I swallowed down the nausea. This wasn't just a room. It was a reminder of what kind of man had ruled before Ben, and a warning of what kind of man Ben might become in the future – or was already.

If he thought he could lie to me and keep me here, he was sorely mistaken.

I sneaked out again and found Guard Jackoloy pacing the corridor outside.

"Any sighting of King Blackbone yet?" I asked, teasing him, seeing him tap his thumb on the pommel of his sword, seeming nervous about getting caught.

"He won't be down this corridor," he answered, but still turned his head around to double check.

"Then why are you worrying so much? Relax," I told him, but even I felt it was easier said than done. "I'm tired," I lied, already plotting an emergency escape route. "You can take me back to my room now."

"Good. This way." He opened the guest room door for me when we arrived. "There will be another guard here for the night shift, but I'll return in the morning. Good night, my lady."

I made a curt bow in thanks, mirroring his.

Behind closed doors, I undressed until I was completely naked and waited in bed for Ben to come to me.

The cold air prickled against my exposed body as I lay there waiting. The silence in the room stretched with time, making my lust-filled heartbeats twist into bitterness.

So much for his promise.

I swallowed the lump of disappointment, but it did nothing to stop the humiliation. I curled my fingers into the sheets, as if holding on to a shred of hope.

Had I misread everything? Had I been foolish to believe his words?

The longer I lay there untouched, the higher I built my wall of resentment. But only shame broke through the walls. The sickening realisation dawned on me that I had let myself be the vulnerable little girl Harvey had tried so hard to train out of me.

I turned onto my side, imagining that mental wall I built, as if it could shield me from the sting of rejection. But what was the point of shielding a bleeding wound when the damage was already done?

The following morning all my weapons were gone from the room and there was a note on the round table between the armchairs.

My naked beauty,

Believe me when I say I'm more than gutted about arriving too late to your room last night and finding you already asleep. My sincerest apologies for having left you on your own while I tended to a few urgent matters. I still have a few meetings in the morning and will try to find you as soon as I have a moment to spare.

Faithfully yours,
King Blackbone

Is he freaking kidding me? The letter was overly formal compared to our usual internal banter. I hated it. I crumpled it and wrung it like I wanted to wring his neck. Then I tossed it into the fireplace to burn.

Time to spare?

Sure.

I'm here when you need me.

Waiting.

Nah!

I glanced at the dresses and immediately repelled any doubts.

I scoffed, shaking my head. Nope. Not in this lifetime.

The irritation simmering beneath my skin needed an outlet. I yanked on my flight leathers, the familiar scent of worn leather grounding me. The snug fit, the weight of the buckles and the feeling of being prepared for more than just standing around like a decoration were exactly what I needed.

Time to find some trouble.

"Good morning," Guard Jackoloy greeted with a curt bow, as I opened the door, and I doubted he could bow any deeper with all that iron around his body.

A display armour at the opposite wall held an enormous sword, and since Ben had taken all my weapons from me, I had no other option than to steal this poor fella's. Then I barged down the corridor, knowing the guard would follow me. "Why did King Blackbone choose you to guard me?"

He wasn't a ferocious man who tried to stop me from walking around as I pleased. It puzzled me. Was I a prisoner or not? I guessed I was a *guest* until I did something Ben didn't agree with.

"Because my family has worked for the royal family for generations and His Majesty trusts me. Or he used to, but I fear that will end with you, Miss Stone."

Miss Stone? Of course! They all thought I was the same old toy that Murben had once declared me to be – and I got it now. If Ben was betrothed to another woman, I was no more than something the king played with until he got bored or had to fulfil his marital duties.

"I like your banter, Guard Jackoloy. I think I'll keep you. Which way is it to the counsel chamber?"

"I don't believe you're meant to be seen around that area, Miss Stone."

"Always brilliant at advising. Which way?" I repeated my question to let him know I'd ignore his advice this time as well.

He pointed me in the right direction at every turn until I saw a golden plated door that was accessed through an outdoor landing. Every step closer to that golden-plated door sent a pulse of restless energy through me. It was ridiculous, really. I wanted to strangle him, shake him, scream at him…and yet, I ached to see him, to touch him, to kiss him – anything, as long as it was with him.

Ben had a way of driving me to madness, but even when I wanted to break his neck, I still longed for him. A few hours apart, and it already felt like days.

I wanted to burst in through the ajar door, demand his attention and make him look at me the way I needed him to. But instead, I hovered outside his counsel chamber, hanging onto his voice like it was the only thing tethering me to reality.

"This is eavesdropping, my lady," Guard Jackoloy muttered beside me.

"Yeah," I whispered back, barely paying attention. "I'm very good at it when no one else is around still talking. Shush."

My chest tightened at the sound of Ben's smooth yet commanding voice as it slithered out through the doorway.

"No, you can't see her now. There are still secrets I'll need to tell her and if she unravels too many at one time, she'll run scared. I cannot afford that happening. Leave. Take the secret passage," Ben instructed.

My body reacted before my mind could catch up, my toes curling inside my boots. I turned to look at Guard Jackoloy, standing behind my back where I had pushed him out of sight from anyone exiting the counsel chamber. "I wonder what that was about."

"Perhaps it concerned Lady Nassara Finningham."

Was that his betrothed? The name gave me an ulcer.

I froze to the spot, my heart wanting to stop beating, as Duke Hartmore passed by, dressed impeccably in a brown tailcoat and top hat the same as last time I had seen him. He entered the counsel room. Was he absolutely suicidal?

"What are you doing here?" Ben roared, a waft of black essence creeping out through the gap in the open door.

"I'm here for the annual spring celebrations, and I heard you had returned to attend them alongside your people and your betrothed. Where is she? I'd like to greet her."

The words hit me like a punch to the gut. Lady Nassara Finningham. Ben's betrothed. Here? In this castle? My world tilted, my stomach wanted to turn inside out as if I'd been poisoned. The mere thought of her existence and of her being anywhere near Ben made bile rise in my throat. Spirits, I felt like vomiting, the sickness clawing at my insides.

"Get out!" Ben's voice exploded through the space, raw with fury. "Or I'll worry what my magic will do to you when I lose control of it."

Duke Hartmore's amused sneer only made it worse. "That's surely no way to treat a duke of your kingdom." His arrogance dripped like he was untouchable. Did he not know of Ben's ill temper?

How dare he come here, parading the truth I was trying to pretend didn't exist? It must mean our lives were tethered with the oath and Ben couldn't kill him without both of us dying, too.

I could hear it in Ben's voice that his anger was barely contained beneath a forced calm. "I'd ask if you'd want a drink, but I don't want you to stay that long. Leave the castle at once!"

"I'll only stay until Monday, I assure you." Hartmore's voice was sickly sweet, deliberate, mocking. Then came the final blow. The words that sent ice spearing through my veins. "By the way, have you seen my bride around anywhere? My spies tell me you brought her here."

My breath stilled in my lungs.

His bride.

He had called me his bride in front of Ben.

I wanted to rip out my heart and bury it under layers of soil if that was the only way I could escape my fate. But maybe I didn't have to if Ben lost control and killed us all.

57

Duke Hartmore rushed out of the counsel chamber the next moment, a thick black cloud at his back followed him like a venomous snake down the stairs to the lower levels.

Guard Jackoloy let out a sharp breath beside me, still rattled from what we'd just witnessed. "That was close," Guard Jackoloy huffed at my side. "I was sure King Blackbone would lose control. Rumour has it that Duke Hartmore has stolen a woman; a Miss Coraly, who King Blackbone wanted as his bride. By love, not by duty." His brow twitched, lips pressing into a thin line as he let out a short, disbelieving laugh. "I thought I'd never see the day when King Blackbone would be besotted by a woman. She must really be something."

I looked over my shoulder and made a show of narrowing my eyes at him. "Guard Jackoloy? You, gossip?"

He gave a half-hearted shrug. "You hear a lot on guard duty."

I snorted, shifting my weight as I glanced back toward the door, hoping Ben would step out at any moment. "Then I'm surprised to learn that you didn't know I'm Miss Coraly."

Silence.

The air went stagnant, and I could practically hear the moment Jackoloy's breath stopped. He stiffened behind me, and even after I had turned around to face forward, I could still feel his stunned gaze burning into the back of my neck.

"You're joking," he scoffed, shaking his head.

But when he saw the seriousness in the glance I flashed him over my shoulder, the amusement drained from his face.

"No," he said flatly. "That's not possible." Even as the words left his mouth, I could see doubt was already creeping into his mind, poisoning his certainty.

"Why? Haven't I showed myself charming enough today?" My words dripped with sarcasm.

"Sure. You're oodles of fun, and a healthy dose of defiance, but..." He trailed off, searching for the right words.

"But what?"

His brows rose, his jade eyes wide and apologetic. "You don't fit the profile."

That was a slap in my face I hadn't expected. *Profile? What profile? A mutt? A traitor?*

I glanced around the landing, pretending I wasn't seething at all. "I think the coast is clear. I want to find this Lady Nassara Finningham."

Still, no response from Jackoloy. Just the crackling energy of his completely shattered understanding of the situation.

"That, too, is a bad idea. She isn't very nice." Guard Jackoloy was still looking me up and down as if he was seeing a ghost, clearly finding it unbelievable that he was looking at the woman who his king was besotted with.

"Good. If Ben thinks that he can only give me his spare time, then bad ideas are what I'm aiming for. Lead the way."

He started walking down the stairs inside a small turret to our left. "You're so going to get me fired...or beheaded."

"It's not like anyone would miss your head. No one can see it," I mocked playfully, descending the stone stairs behind him.

He removed his helmet and there was a handsome man underneath. High ebony hairline and a beard framed those jade eyes I had been seeing a lot of. Maybe he was in his thirties. Square, strong jaw. A perfectly shaped nose.

"Okay, it'd be a shame to chop that head off. It's nice."

"Thank you," he said, and donned the helmet again as we exited the turret, stepping into the light of day.

"Do you want to stay behind? I don't expect you to come with me. My greeting with Lady Nassara won't be pretty. Make a guard shift if you're scared of losing your handsome head. Do you have any enemies in the guard you want to get rid of?"

"Even if I did, I wouldn't want to unleash you on any of them. I heard you're a handful and have pockets heavy with mischief."

I rushed forwards to fall into step beside him. "Who told you that?"

"King Blackbone. Is it not true?" His question was sarcastic. He obviously didn't doubt it was true. I had given him no reason to doubt it, either.

"Um," I hadn't been ready for the question and twisted. "I'll neither agree nor deny."

We chuckled.

"So," I said, looking around the courtyard. "Where can I find the King's bride?"

He signed heavily out through his nose. "She's in the royal wing." He both frowned and cringed as he looked at me.

"Royal wing! And what do you call the wing where the king has stuck me?"

"The duty area, where the offices and strategizing rooms are. It's where higher-ranking generals and unit leaders stay when they visit the castle. It's better than the servants' quarters, I'd say." I think he saw my face turning grimmer because he kept adding things to talk up his king. "I heard he's obsessed with you, so he must have his reasons, wanting to keep you safe."

"King Blackbone said Black Castle was the safest place to be in. I guess that is true if I'm in the service office wing. Take me to this Nassara now!"

Guard Jackoloy moved swiftly through the castle before he led me across the expansive courtyard. We passed beneath shadowed archways and empty halls where secrets had since long been spoken and buried.

It felt like we'd been walking for an eternity when we finally traversed the castle's hidden heart, that was the larger royal courtyard.

Many would pay a fortune to see it. Fools. It was nothing special. It only held a touch of coldness, betrayal and death. With its perfectly manicured grass, the courtyard was a world within a world; an isolated place, a lure to the Underworld.

At the centre of the courtyard, a company of noble ladies sat around a large table. They held onto plates of food and pretty umbrellas to shield themselves from the sun. Their hushed conversations drifted my way as I walked closer.

Heavily armed guards stood to one side with their sheathed weapons gleaming under the sunlight.

The maids seemed to shuffle nervously as they worked.

At the centre of it all, on a throne-like chair made of wrought white iron, sat a woman whose presence commanded every ounce of attention in the courtyard.

Well, that's unnerving.

I inspected her where she sat with a perfect posture; one hand resting elegantly on the armrest, the other holding a delicate fan that she fluttered idly in front of her face.

She was probably one or two years older than me. Her skin was dark-brown and smooth, like chocolate had melted down her body. By impulse, I licked my lips. Her hair was a black river of velvet that cascaded down around her shoulders, and her big lips were the colour of ripe cherries.

Spirits, she's beautiful.

Her curves were in all the right places on her tall, slender body.

Well, that irritated me even more today.

She was dressed in fine silks, the fabric shimmering with her every graceful movement. The way she carried herself with practised kindness and calculating gaze told me she had been raised with the knowledge that one day, all of this – the power, the wealth – would be hers.

I felt the threat of her stare the moment it settled on me, and during that moment everything else seemed to blur.

It was clear who she was without needing an introduction. This was a woman whose future held a crown, and whose destiny had already been written as it had crossed out mine. The woman who was going to stand between Ben and me. *His soulmate.*

She too instantly understood who I was. Not that it was hard to guess when I was wearing my flight leathers, which Guard Jackoloy had failed to convince me to change out of. To be fair, he hadn't put much effort into it since he'd thought I was an army servant. In hindsight, wearing a dress might have been smarter when snooping around. *Although not as much fun.*

Lady Nassara waved a delicate hand to clear her servants from her side and hopped off her seat to approach me. Two of her ladies-in-waiting were on her flanks, accompanied by two armoured guards who wore purple uniforms instead of the dark-blue of the Black Castle guards.

She swayed herself forwards like a white snow fox with long slender legs. Her dress; a shade between silver and white, covered her private areas, but otherwise was mostly strips of translucent fabric that flowed behind her as she walked. Very sensual, but too cold for April, even if today was an uncharacteristically warm spring day.

Seemed the Spirits were on her side.

I swallowed, imagining her in bed with Ben. The thought made my stomach churn and want to run back to Bensguard.

She stopped a short distance away from me. "So, you're the woman who is trying to steal my man?" She looked me up and down with a disgusted grimace on her face, as if I was a peasant who might be carrying a plague.

The thought that Ben was hers, that he was her promised groom, hit me like a slap to the face. It hadn't even crossed my mind until that moment. Ben and Nassara had been betrothed for years, a fact I gathered from the cold, formal letter Ben's father had written. And now, here I was – *the other woman.* The one who had no place in this world, standing in the shadow of her claim on him.

I was the mistress.

The homewrecker.

I was the one who was here to break her world apart.

Her words stung in ways I couldn't have anticipated. She spoke with that casual, smug confidence, like she had already won. Her arrogance made my blood boil with pure rage. I could feel the heat steaming in my veins and practically sizzling with fury. I tried to stop it, but each beat of my heart began thumping louder than the last. It was a struggle not to lash out, not to run her through with my sword and watch her arrogance crumble.

My fingers twitched toward the pommel of the sword at my side. The one I had stolen from the guard's display this morning. The hilt dug into my palm. It was way too heavy for me to wield, weighing me down with each step, a constant reminder of my uninvited presence here. The sword's length dragged behind me as I took a step closer to my opponent, scraping the ground, as it had done for the last few minutes since my belt had sagged low on my hip. I couldn't help but feel the sharp, unbearable tension it brought with it. The sword was more than a physical burden. It was a metaphor for the weight of hardship I was carrying; the anger, the shame, the fear, the betrayals.

I felt my mouth dry, the words I needed were all glued to the roof of my mouth. I could barely string together a coherent sentence as her superiority pressed in on me.

"So, you're the woman," I started, but my voice faltered. *Who is gorgeous and Ben never told me about!* She was stunning, no doubt about it. But Ben had never once mentioned her. Not once. What did that mean for me? "Who wants to marry a man who doesn't love her?"

It wasn't a perfect comeback, but it was all I could muster, the words feeling too small and too weak in comparison to the storm of emotions swirling inside me. But she didn't seem bothered by my remark. Instead, she curved a cold smile on her perfect lips.

"My father's estate is in the north of Cathdear, close to the northern province of Dormondar…" she began, as though she was narrating some grand tale.

Her voice was sweet, but her tone laced with cruelty. The more she spoke, the more my confidence shattered.

"I'm aware of the landscape," I barked. "We have geography lessons in the Bensguard Outpost."

She turned, a mock gasp leaving her lips, her hand flying to her chest in exaggerated surprise. "Oh, I can't believe it," she said, her voice dripping with condescension as she turned to her ladies-in-waiting. "The brute believes she is educated. How adorable."

The way she spoke dismissed me after every word as a reminder of how little I mattered in her world. That was how certain she was of her place in Ben's life. I was nothing more than a passing inconvenience. It made me truly believe I was the abomination.

I couldn't hold back anymore. I wanted to lash out, to rip her apart with more than words, but all I could do was stand there, seething with rage and humiliation.

My grip on the sword tightened, but I held myself back – for now.

"I'm not a brute. But maybe only drinking wine and tumbling around in silk sheets every day have deformed your view of the world."

She glanced at the obscene sword at my hip, and backed up to look me in the eye with her black and gold globes. "Oh, I know what dangers there are in the world, brute. I've fought them myself. But I heard you can fight, too. I wonder whether that information is only a rumour."

"Feel like finding out? I've time to kill, might as well kill you, too."

Guard Jackoloy rattled behind me as he took a step closer, so I turned to face him. "The king wouldn't approve of this," he whispered.

"No, he would not," I replied before turning back to face Lady Nassara. "What are the rules? Fists only?"

"How brute," she mocked again on purpose. "No, the art of blades is better suited to my station."

I prepared myself for the weight of the sword as I pulled it from the belt. "Sword it is then."

"That wouldn't be a fair match. You can barely lift that thing," she delicately giggled into her hand like the daughter of a duke.

"Yes, I can," I barked and held it up for a few seconds before I rested it on the ground again.

In fairness, it was incredibly heavy. I'd guess this sword had never been used in actual combat, but only as a display piece.

She snorted. "We can get the guard to fetch you a dagger like mine."

She beckoned to the guard standing behind the two ladies, who handed her a long oval object. It was made of silver with oval-shaped gems in a variety of colours. She clearly wanted to demonstrate to me how rich and classy she was. Let's see how that matched with a few bruises and if she swelled up, I doubted she'd fit into most of her dresses.

Nassara angled the piece of art downwards and pulled at either end to separate it along the middle, drawing out a flawlessly shiny silver blade. "This blade is so sharp, it can cut air."

I gaped. Was she that stupid? Everything cut air, unless she meant cleaving the air to open a portal to the Underworld, or something.

"You do that. I'm planning on cutting you. My sword is so blunt, I imagine I have to hack at you a few times before pieces of you come off."

I heard Guard Jackoloy chuckle lowly behind me, but he quietened as Nassara's two guards stared at him.

Nassara swept her arm out to have everyone clear a space for us between them, and she took off her high-heeled silver shoes Then she made a quick shrug, folding open her large black wings.

"Here we fight with our wings out."

Shit! Had she heard that I hated to have my wings out? They absolutely destroyed my balance, and a blow to the arm or leg I could handle, but wings were very sensitive. If she jabbed her blade into them, it'd fucking hurt. But to deny the set condition would make me look weak, so what choice did I have?

"Okay," I muttered. "Hold on a moment."

I stretched my back and pushed my shoulder blades one way and then the other to nestle my black wings out. It took longer because I had used the white wings the last time I flew. Although, using the white wings and pissing her off even more was a tempting thought.

But I worried that I'd taken my jealousy too far already. She wore practically nothing and was now barefoot while I wore my flight leathers and solid black hiking boots. Although, I did want to crack open that chocolate facade to see if blood ran inside her veins just like mine.

She began circling me over the cobblestones of the courtyard, and I moved an equal distance away from her, dragging my heavy sword behind me. Perhaps it hadn't been the best choice of weapon, as it was true I could barely lift it.

"Do you know what King Blackbone likes?" she asked.

For starters, he doesn't like when I call him King Blackbone. "Not your voice for sure. It's very high-pitched."

There was the widest grin on her face. "I'll show you what he likes to do with me."

An image appeared in my head. *Shit!* She had magic. *What the fuck was she doing in my head?* Panic shot through me. I tried to slam my shield in place, but it didn't block her, only Ben. That terrifying reality slammed into me like a physical blow. This was her way of weakening me. *The cheat!*

The vision unfolded before me like a nightmare I couldn't escape. A bedchamber. Massive, with dark-blue decor trimmed in gold, the canopy above the bed, five floor-to-ceiling windows framed with the same dark-blue drapes with golden hems looked out over the castle garden. Beyond, the mountains stood cold and distant. The left side of the room held a fireplace, its stone carving depicting wings that flared outwards.

The image rushed forward, spinning past the room until it froze on an enormous dining table. The table's surface was a huge mirror. I couldn't tear my eyes away, even as the dread coiled tighter in my chest. It wasn't its beauty my eyes stuck on, it was *what* lay on that table that shattered me. Ben. Naked, and so was she, sitting on his face. Ben cupped her arse and feasted on her while she arched into him, moaning sweetly, whimpering with pleasure; her arms stirring around in her velvet black hair.

No. No. My stomach churned, bile rising as the image burned itself into my mind.

I couldn't breathe. I couldn't think. The image broke me; all my dreams and hopes felt like ash in my mouth.

This was what she had wanted. To cripple me. To see me lose before the fight had even begun. I buckled to my knees, feeling the twinge of sharp pain as they hit the cobblestones.

Nassara brought me out from the vision. I was shaking, panting heavily, gagging. But nothing came up.

Guard Jackoloy pushed at my elbow to help me up. "She can put images into your head."

I turned towards him, still shaking. "Thank you. I realised," I snapped, seething.

"They might not be true," he whispered. "She can put anything she wants into your head."

Bitch! "I'll return the favour by putting my sword into hers."

I launched myself at her, but the sword dragged behind me and it barely lifted off the ground. *Using this sword had not been a brilliant plan.*

While I was bending my knees to get more power behind my lift, she closed in on me, shoving her knee into my nose, the force of which making my eyes water. I was knocked back and needed to shake my head to clear it.

"May I ask what you are doing?" Even in my mind, Ben sounded annoyed. *"I felt a phantom punch to my nose. I'm in a counsel meeting with my most esteemed subjects. Now isn't the time to distract me."*

Shit! I needed to enhance my shield. I doubted Ben would agree with me engaging in a fight with his betrothed.

"Apologies, Your Highness. I lost balance and fell against the bedpost. I'll be more careful."

I wouldn't want to interrupt you when it isn't your spare time!

The crackling in my ears stopped. He had bought it. Or most likely not, but he hadn't had time for more rebukes.

Nassara got a few more punches in on me and I had to admit, she was fast as a viper. On top of that, I was extra slow with my lump of iron dragging behind me. I needed to think of a way to beat her without using the sword.

The moment her bejewelled blade sliced across my hand, a sharp sting shot through me, and a sickening smile spread across her face as my blood spilled. The sight of it, the feel of it, was enough to push my anger to boiling point. I clenched my jaw and could feel it hurting my mouth. *This wasn't just a fight anymore.*

As she moved in again, her blade gleaming, I quickly shifted my grip, swapping the sword to my left hand. With my right, I threw a punch, aiming for her face, but hit her shoulder, as she was much taller than I. At best I was hoping the hit would throw her off balance. With a brutal, practised motion, she countered, her fists landing hard against my face.

The first punch hit my jaw, then a second collided with my cheek. I could feel the pressure of my skin tearing, the flesh beneath bruising instantly, but it was the third strike right to my nose that set everything on fire. Pain shot through my skull as blood exploded from my nostrils, a hot, sickening river pouring down my face. My body lurched back, my vision blurred with both blood and fury.

I didn't retreat, though. My pulse hammered in my ears, blood dripping from my chin, my hand still clenched tight around the hilt of the sword, even as I tasted copper in my mouth. The fight was far from over, and now I had even more reason to make her regret it.

I couldn't win fighting her like this, but I was too proud to let go of the sword I had told her I could handle. I barely jumped out of the way as she *stabbed at my abdomen.*

I'm a Bensguard warrior. I can do this.

A plan formed in my head, and I stabbed the tip of the sword between the cobblestones, spun around it to gain momentum and used it as a rod to lever myself into the air, kicking high at her back.

She stumbled forward and lost balance, and the force, as she hit the ground, dragged her on her front across the stone.

"My dress!" she roared. "You've ruined my dress! Do you know how expensive this was?" She held up the torn parts for me to see the damage.

She had almost gutted me through my flight leathers! It was combat. *Shit like that happen!*

The ladies behind her gasped and chatted amongst themselves about the disgrace. I rolled my eyes. "Not sure you could call it a dress before. Just strips of fabric. I think I've improved the design," I sneered.

"You brute buffoon!" she screamed and bent down to pick up her high-heels and dart away across the courtyard with her guards and ladies trailing her.

The abrupt end to the fight felt disjointed and my shoulders lowered. I turned to Guard Jackoloy. "I couldn't really see a difference to the dress, could you?"

"It was an improvement, certainly," he agreed with me and chuckled.

"That's what I thought." I scratched my cheek. "I guess I won?"

"Indeed, Miss Coraly. Well done. You've won the battle. Now prepare for the war you've started with King Blackbone."

58

The door flew open, slamming against the wall with a mighty whack as Ben strode inside.

I guess kings didn't have to knock.

I didn't flinch but instead inhaled deeply and stayed where I was stretched out on my stomach on the bed. My fruits and wine were untouched on a silver platter in front of me but their aromas of sweet and vinegar wafted on the wave of wind from the door's movement. I focused even harder on the romance novel lying open to my right, pinching my fingers over the next page.

In my peripheral view I could see Ben's dark-blue king's attire filling up the space between the bedposts, as he stopped just beside the bed, his dark-blue cape billowing behind him.

I slowly turned my head to look at him, as if he'd have to wait until I had reached a good point in the story. Then I observed him. He was handsome in his blue doublet with black trousers tucked into tall boots. His powerful wings remained folded tightly against his sides, as if holding back his simmering fury. A silver band adorned with blue gemstones pressed his onyx hair against his forehead. He'd have looked regal, if not for the scowl darkening his features.

"Why is it," he exhaled something of a roar, "that whenever I receive reports about disturbances in the Black Wing Territory, you are always at the centre of them?" His voice was more irritated than usual. "Normally, I'd be intrigued by your mischief, but today wasn't a day for games. And the mess you made was tedious to resolve."

I tilted my chin up at him with feigned innocence. "*You're* saying…I'm tedious?"

How *dare* he make time in his precious schedule just to scold me?

"Miss Stone!" he warned, his tone edged with barely contained frustration.

Ouch! I imagined he hated when I called him King Blackbone as much as it stung that he called me Miss Stone now.

I kept my gaze trained downward, pretending to be utterly absorbed in the book spread before me. "I believe the exact words were that I am 'a handful and have pockets heavy with mischief.'"

Ben's frown deepened, his jaw flexing. "I think *fighting* with the daughter of one of my dukes, who I'm depending on in the north, goes beyond *a bit* of mischief. Although it's hard to tell, since your mischiefs are normally so severe as to push a black blade at my heart."

"You're never going to let that go, are you?" I turned a paged on the romance novel even though I hadn't fully read the page, just to give the appearance that his shouting wasn't getting to me.

"I wanted you as far away from Nassara as possible!"

Yeah, putting me in the servant's quarters ought to do it.

I popped a strawberry into my mouth from the pudding plate. "Did I get too close?" I kept my expression carefully blank, my fingers curled just slightly against the page to busy them.

"I had to deal with her rage as she showed me her torn dress, which I had to offer to pay for to pacify her anger."

"Did she genuinely think she could challenge me to a duel and get away without a scratch on her dress?"

"It was a friendly fight."

"Friendly!" I sat up with crossed legs. "Her dagger would have impaled my gut had I not jumped to the side." I pointed towards my side where she had almost stabbed me.

"Your gut, yes, but she didn't stab at your heart. We have excellent healers here. But that's not the point. Look at you. You're bruised everywhere, and can I assume that is your own blood on the leathers? And it could have gone a lot worse. She is highly skilled at combat."

I scoffed. "Hardly. I was never in any danger. I was armed. Since you had taken my weapons, I borrowed the tin man's sword from across the corridor."

"You fought her with a five-hundred-year-old display sword blunt as a spoon just to prove a point?"

He was staring at me with a king's resolve, so I stared back at him. "You had taken all my own weapons away."

"Yes, because you had so much iron on you that you'd have sunk to the bottom of my shallow garden pond before you could remove all the things you were wearing. I feared you'd have drowned if you fell in. And since you're known around here to be waving a black blade around, my servants grew anxious. But I'll return your weight worth in iron to you if you're adamant to carry weapons in my home. You may as well use something you can wield to defend yourself with. That one is too big for that purpose." He pointed at the sword I had leaned on the wall beside the door.

I crossed my arms over my chest. "Since I meant for it to piss you off, I think it has served its purpose perfectly."

He sighed, massaging his temples. "Why are you angry with me this time?"

"You have the nerve to tell me I can only see you during your spare time, and then you stick me into a servant's guest room instead of sharing your own, but perhaps it's not proper of a king to keep servants in his bed?"

"Angelica," he purred with restrained patience, and he crouched by the foot of the bed to look deep into my eyes. "I have placed all my efforts into you the last seven months, so it was only natural that my duties here have fallen behind and my schedule has been packed in order to clear as much of it as possible until we must return to the Bensguard Outpost after tomorrow."

"You believe that if I stayed in your private bedchamber, it'd distract you from your duties? I have barely seen you since we arrived here. Or is it because Nassara is already warming your bed and that's why there is no space in it for me?"

"She's not in my bed!"

"Ah, that's true. You guys prefer the dining table." I opened my shield and shared the image Nassara had forced into my head.

Ben rose, flinging his arms around his head as if he could swat it away, so I broke the connection, putting my shield up.

When he looked at me again, his eyes had changed. They were tender. "That never happened. I've never seen her naked. She has never seen me naked. We have never shared a bed…or a table. And I'm disappointed you could think so when you're one of the few people who knows the reason I never get close to women, apart from the other fact that none ever interested me."

"It could have happened before you met me, or before you got your magic."

"It never happened!" he shouted at me before he panted out his anger, walking a full circle on the spot before turning to look at me again. "You and I could only make love because you used some sort of blocking magic."

"I have no magic."

He closed his eyes and gathered patience. "The reason I put you in this room was because I wanted people to think you were a nobody and simply one of my protection details, so that no one would target you. Nassara will do anything to keep our engagement on, even lower herself to sending assassins. But now, thanks to your introduction and the ripping apart of her dress, the entire castle household knows who you are and what you mean to me. Hence, tonight you must sleep in my bed so I can protect you."

Great! That's what I wanted. My mischiefs hadn't been in vain after all. I did my utmost to keep from smiling in victory.

"What if Nassara finds out?"

"I couldn't care less what she thinks about us. I made no vow to her to be faithful. She can taunt herself with that image of us in her head."

"You promised me things in our room in Bensguard before we left."

He sat down on the bedside to get closer to me. "That I did."

Finally, he lifted a smile.

"Which were not delivered," I challenged.

"I'll deliver tonight. With interest." He held out his hand. "Come with me to my room, please."

I got off the bed and retrieved my light crystal and the purple box from the drawer in the bedside table before taking his warm hand.

"Hmm," he mused. "That mysterious purple packet."

I waited to comment until we were alone in the corridor after Ben had dismissed Guard Jackoloy. "You can have the gift in the morning, unless you've pissed me off again. Then it might be counterproductive to what I want to do to you."

"Cryptic. I can't wait to find out what you have in store for me."

"A thoughtful birthday gift from someone who loves you."

"You know it's my birthday tomorrow?"

We began to ascend the grand stairs in the royal wing that were so wide they could hold twenty soldiers abreast. "You think you're the only one who has spies?"

He smiled. "You love me?"

There was a flutter in my stomach, but I held it at bay. "I used to before you started paying for other women's dresses."

At the top of the stairs, he swirled me around so that I ended up with my back curved along his chest and he wrapped his arms around my waist, resting his chin on my shoulder. "Let's see if I can remedy that tonight and be forgiven. If I'm lucky, maybe we can exchange you for Nassara in that image of hers and send it back to her."

I giggled at the thought as Ben opened the door to his bedroom and swept an arm out to grant me access.

The sight of it was unsettling as the bedroom looked exactly like the vision Nassara had projected in my mind. That meant she must have been in this room before. Jealousy shot through me like lightning. Why had she been in the king's private chamber? Did I want to know? No, I didn't.

The room was majestic with the enormous windows and the huge bed wrapped in dark-blue and golden fabric, embroidered with his double B emblem. There was the winged fireplace next to the traitorous dining table with the mirrored tabletop. I wanted to gag.

"What do you think of my bedroom?"

"If I'm going to stay here tonight, I'd say that either you'll have to feast on me atop that dining table until I've learned to love it, or you'll have to get rid of it."

"I've not had dinner yet, so feasting on you, it is."

He slowly, teasingly, unbuttoned his jacket and dropped it onto the dark-blue bedding before he continued with his shirt in the same way. I felt myself instantly going wet when he had bared his chest, his shelf of muscles jumping as he moved his arms down to unbutton his trousers. He tugged his boots off one after the other, slowly. With his trouser button open to display the v of abdomen dipping low, and his feet and chest naked, he strode up to me, pushing his fingers into my hair.

He looked down at me as his palms cupped my face and his thumbs stroked either side of my cheeks. He pushed me backwards until the small of my back hit the edge of the mirrored dining table, where he hooked his hands under my thighs instead and lifted me up to sit on it.

I had expected the mirror to be of an icy temperature, but it was surprisingly tepid from the warmth of the fireplace. There was still a temperature difference though, that increased the sensitivity to my nerve-endings. It was as if my skin had awoken and was alert to every touch.

When Ben had separated my knees and pushed himself closer, he unbuttoned my flight jacket at the same time as he trailed kisses down my neck.

I surrendered to the pleasure that shot through me at his every touch. They were loaded with power. Assertiveness. Desire.

His eyes gleamed as he looked into mine, only a few centimetres apart, and he pushed the jacket off my shoulders and pulled me out of my sleeves.

"Do that trick when you rip all the buttons," I moaned. *"It drives me insane."*

He leered impishly and gripped between two buttons at the middle of my Bensguard shirt, and then he ripped it open, buttons scattering across the floor.

I moaned into his mouth that was pressing around mine, and it sent my arousal level to new heights. One by one, he lowered the shoulder straps of my bra and kissed the swell of my breasts.

"Am I forgiven?" he purred into my ear.

I stretched my neck, tipping my chin up even more. "Not by far! Carry on!"

He took a step aside, along the table, leaned back towards me and gripped under my armpits, sweeping my entire body over the tabletop towards the centre of the table. I leaned up, hesitating, but he put his hand on my chest to keep me down. I panted and felt my nipples going stiff from being on display in front of the enormous windows with the garden below.

"Can anyone see us?"

"Let them watch. You're beautiful." Then he grinned. *"No one can see us this high up. Powerful men don't share their toys, remember?"*

"That sounds more like you. You don't like sharing."

"Not when it comes to you."

I let my head lull to the side, and I saw the reflection of my bare skin in the mirror beneath me and the rise and fall of my chest against his as he leaned down. His lips brushed over my nipple in a teasing touch that sent a lust rippling through me. Slowly, he trailed kisses lower, his warmth leaving a path of fire down my stomach.

With measured patience, he gripped my hips, lifting me just enough to slide my trousers down, the fabric gliding over my skin, agonising in its slowness. He peeled them from my legs, discarding them without care, and when he returned, I lay bare before him, clad only in the thin lace of my knickers.

His gaze roamed over me, taking in the curves of my waist, the quickened pace of my breath and the way I trembled beneath his attention.

"You're breathtaking." His voice was thick with hunger.

He traced two fingers over the sensitive bundle of nerves, teasing my clit through the lace that sent pulses of pleasure shooting through me. "And this mirror…I hadn't realised when I purchased it what a treasure it'd be, seeing you like this, twice over."

He pressed a warm hand between my breasts, holding me possessively, before sliding the lace aside. The first stroke of his fingers inside me sent my back arching, and a desperate moan caught in my throat. "To watch the two of you come undone."

My body was a taut wire, stretched between torment and ecstasy. The pleasure built in aching waves, an unbearable need coiling tighter. It was confusing me whether I wanted to beg him to stop or beg him for more.

And then he shed the last barrier between us, his boxer shorts falling away. My breath faltered at the sight of him, every bit of my skin igniting with raw desire. I watched his impressive length, and the lust heated inside me like I was lying too close to a roaring fire.

With his warm fingers trailing down my waist, down to my hip, he gripped the lace and swept my knickers all the way off. Ben was working me into insanity. His gaze darkened, his hunger almost predatory, his movements slow and torturous. He was unravelling me, breaking me apart with every lingering glance, every deliberate touch, until all that remained was my body trembling beneath him and praying to be claimed.

"You're gorgeous. All of you." He looked at my naked body, bracing his palms flat onto the mirror before he folded his knee onto the short side of the table to get up, climbing higher between my legs like a prowling predator ready to pounce at its prey. His eyes were locked on mine as he lowered between my legs, his hands clenching my buttcheeks. He planted a single, slow kiss on my clit. The tingles coiled in my stomach, sending tendrils of burning desire to my chest. I inhaled sharply.

"More, I wanted more. Faster."

"I love it when you beg for more of me." He stroked his tongue across my clit. Soft. Warm. Moist.

I moaned, crazed for more.

He grinned. "You need to beg better if you want more."

"Finish me off, or I'll fucking get a black blade and finish you off, right now!" The wait for more made my heart race. I gripped onto his hair, pushing his head down as a gentle hint to dive into me.

He clicked his tongue in rebuke. "Tell me you're mine."

"Forever," I moaned. "Please. Give me more."

"That was better. Are you ready for your reward?"

"Yes!" I shouted so loudly I was certain the door guard had heard me.

He smiled that satisfied cheeky grin, and I knew I was in for it. At the first touch of his tongue, I whimpered and the hard breaths from his own arousal brushed at my sensitive skin. Right after my pleasure cry, Ben was torn into a frenzy, and he used the hold on my arse to control the way he moved me to suit his mouth. We both ignored the sting of the oath. Going deeper, my clit got wetter, and it tightened with a painful bliss that wouldn't keep for long if he carried on like that. My back arched off the table and my moans escaped my mouth as fast as my breathing, the rapid stints fuelling my drumming heart.

I loved this man to the point I worried it bordered on madness.

He licked and dipped his tongue into me and my clit tightened even harder; the tingles surging like a second pulse.

"You're mine. All this is mine. The only thing that is mine that I care about keeping private. My own personal pleasure. For me. You're amazing. Stunning. I love you so damned much!" His thoughts repeated in my mind, and I was unsure if he realised that I'd heard them.

"Faster. Faster."

A guttural growl from the pit of his stomach reverberated through me. His black death magic began making an appearance, swirling out from his skin and hovering around us.

Damn. He was losing control of his emotions, and his face looked conflicted as if he was enjoying himself too much to stop, but if he lost too much control, the essence would kill me. If he stopped the coming orgasm, Spirits, that'd kill me, too!

"Don't stop. I'm close." I moved my hands from his hair to claw at his shoulders.

He went faster, making his tongue wider, feasting on me as if he had been starved of love for a lifetime. He was too engaged with pleasure to stop. I'd have to trust that he knew his limits and could keep the magic balanced, as there was no way I could call it off. My build intensified and got stronger and stronger.

"Almost there."

"Cum for me, my love!"

I inhaled as much as my lungs could stretch and only allowed shallow breaths as the last peak of the climax built up, tightening the tension more and more until everything inside me released. My back spasmed into arches with my whimpers. I clawed at Ben's back as if it was the only lifeline I had, not to be ripped apart. Where my nails dug into his skin, black smoke leaked out from him and circled my hands. But it didn't hurt me. It swirled gently along his skin as if it was calming down.

Ben pressed down his fingers onto my clit to soothe the throbbing and edged himself higher to tease with his cock at the entrance. He knew the oath forbade him to penetrate me, but the suggestive thrust made me want to go again. I wanted more of him.

He swung his legs off the table and pulled me towards him, locking my legs around him and I leaned into his chest, feeling my throbbing clit massage against his stomach as he carried me to his bed. I was so proud of his performance and that he had held himself together during the entirety of it, leaving the smoke behind to linger over the dining table as we crossed the room. He held me up with one hand as he used the other to pull off the bed covers before he laid us down and his naked form nestled around mine.

He played with strands of my hair as he looked at me with a worshipping gleam in his eyes.

"Like my table a bit better now?"

I swiped my hand down his sweaty chest. "Oh yeah. We're keeping it."

"Maybe if I'm lucky, next time you can use that blocking magic, so I can have even more fun."

I froze. This was always a topic I was uncomfortable talking about and I couldn't just do magic on command like that. "I have no magic," I answered, with no smile to offer him.

He looked at me in silence for a while, stroking his thumb over my breast. "You're just full of mischief." His features shifted in an instance and the playful glint in his eyes dimmed making way for the subtle creases on his forehead. His jaw tightening as his lips pressed into a firm line. "I heard you sneaked into my father's office even when the guard specifically told you it was off limits and that no one goes in there."

I rested my arm between us, not touching any part of his naked body.

"Do you want me to remind you about sticking me into the servants' quarters and not seeing me all day? What would one do in a castle, bored all day?"

"Fair point. But that room is closed. Don't go there again."

"Why?" I tipped my head up to look at him, almost holding my breath for the answer.

He didn't respond for a span of time, even though it looked as if he was working on an answer.

I lowered my gaze, pulling the blanket up between us to conceal my body. "If you want me to let you into my life, you're going to have to do the same. Or is this yet another secret? How many secrets do you feel is fair that I accept you keep without questioning you? Five? Fifty? A hundred?"

His breathing sped up, so I looked into his eyes again.

"I was called into his office when he was discontent with me." He inhaled a ragged breath. "Father forced me to align to the wooden cross with my back towards him, as he strapped me in by the leather cuffs." Ben took a few more calm breaths before he continued, his eyes filled with grief; too ashamed to meet mine, so they strayed to my fingers that curled around the edge of the blanket. "If my disobedience had been minor, he used the belt to the left with only an iron framed buckle as he whipped it across my back. When he was more annoyed with my performance or if he'd had a bad day, he used the belt in the middle with the wide buckle and he normally struck higher on my shoulder. Sometimes it hit my face. The times I had shamed him in public, he used the belt to the right with the studded buckle."

The hair rose on my arms as I recalled the belts and the wooden cross that I had thought the late king had used for enemy interrogations. But he had used for his son.

"To this day, I find it discomforting to have my wrists in shackles," he confessed. "You're the only thing that doesn't feel like a shackle to my life."

Oh, my Spirits! I couldn't bear hearing this. Poor Ben. My poor king. How could a father beat his son like that? Beat my Ben? Beaten him like an enemy, like a criminal, like a traitor…a punishment meant for someone like me. With the rage that built up in me, I was glad his father was already dead, or I feared I'd have killed him myself.

I squeezed myself closer to him, tucking my face into the fold of his neck, and pushed my leg between his so we were as close to each other as we possibly could. Ben folded the blanket over us and tucked his arm tightly to my back. No one said another word as we fell asleep.

59

I woke up still wrapped into Ben's body. His bulging arms locked around me in a protective hold, not wanting to let me go even in sleep. Ben's face was soft, as if he could relax now when he was home, not exhausted as he normally was in Bensguard. His breaths were slow, but there was a weariness in the slight furrow of his brows, as if even in his dreams he couldn't escape from the duties of his crown.

Careful not to disturb him, I untangled myself from his grasp bit by bit until I was free. He didn't stir. Holding my breath, I tiptoed to the door and carefully opened it before peering into the hallway. The guard outside straightened as I leaned out just enough to whisper an order to bring a breakfast grand enough for a king's birthday. Ben would never request luxuries for himself, but today, and after all he had endured protecting his kingdom, he deserved to be spoiled.

Slipping back inside, I retrieved the small purple box from the bedside table's drawer, as the servants sneaked in to arrange the breakfast on the table.

I tensed each time Ben shifted in his sleep, my heartbeat skipping a beat when I thought he might wake too soon and ruin the surprise. The scent of fresh bread, warm crepes, and fruit was gorgeous. A new fire had been brought back to life in the hearth and together with the lit candles, they cast a golden glow over the room. Perfect.

Once everything was in place, I dismissed the servants with a silent wave. Clutching the small gift, I climbed onto the bed. Leaning down, I brushed my lips against Ben's in a feather-light kiss, enjoying the quiet moment fully before he woke.

"Good morning, birthday boy," I whispered.

His smile widened immediately. "Is it morning already?"

"Yes. There is breakfast-in-bed. Well, on the table. It's ready for you."

He pried his eyes open and leaned up on his elbows, looking at the table.

"You did that for me?"

I held out my gift towards him. "Now, you can open your present. It's nothing special. Just something silly."

"The gifts you've given people so far have been second to none when it comes to the thought you put into them. I'm intrigued by what a 'silly little thing' could mean."

He tugged away the black string and opened the lid of the purple box, looking at the leather band for a while. "What is it?"

I folded up to sit on my knees and pointed at it. "It's an oath band. It's infused with magic disabling me from ever stabbing you with a black blade."

"Seriously?" He looked at the band again with new fascination. "That's big of you. You love threatening me with black blades."

I glowered at him playfully, and he chuckled, his pectorals jumping with their rhythm.

"Yep. No more looking over your shoulder." I observed his face to try to gauge his reaction.

He raised his eyes, looking at me. "To be fair, you've always pointed the blades against my front." He pinched it with his fingers and picked it up to inspect it more closely. "But I don't need your oath. I know you won't stab me." He leaned over, giving me a kiss.

Savouring the kiss before it broke, I inhaled a large breath. "You still have many secrets to reveal to me, so you don't know that."

He pulled back from me. "Yes, hmm. Perhaps best to put it on." We both laughed.

"The man who cast the oath on the band said to put it on your left wrist." I took the band from his fingers and stretched the leather to a wide circle.

Ben held his hand out so I could thread the bracelet over his left wrist. Then I let go, and it snapped into place and vanished, leaving a black tattooed band in its stead. A whirl of black tattoos grew from the band up his arm. My eyes followed the swirls as they curled over his shoulder and down around his heart where the effect stopped. We locked eyes, and I cleared my throat. "I did not know it was going to do that."

He twisted his arm around to look at the black tattoos. "They look manly. This is amazing. Thank you for this 'silly little gift' that will save my life."

"You're welcome," I chirped, and jumped off the bed, approaching the table. "Shall we have breakfast?"

Ben got off the bed too, and came to stand next to me with an arm hooking around my waist, eyeing at the laid out dishes. "I prefer the feast I ate on the table yesterday." He popped a strawberry into his mouth and grabbed a bread roll before he left my side, fetching his clothes that had ended up on the floor, and got dressed. "I'm afraid I can't stay."

I watched him dress as my brain processed what he had told me. "What? You don't have the time to eat a birthday breakfast with me?"

"No." He avoided looking at me. "And tonight, don't wait up for me. I'll arrive back late. Please, stay in here so that I can be sure you're keeping out of trouble. Tomorrow morning, we'll travel back to Bensguard. We must leave here at five in the morning to ensure we get to class on time."

I blinked. Gobsmacked at what he was instructing me to do. I couldn't stay inside the same room all day! I'd die of boredom.

I rested the small of my back against the tabletop and crossed my arms over my naked breasts that he was passing up on, attending to his other duties. "All my life, I've been told where to be and what mission to carry out, confined to what the military needed from me. I've hated that I was never free to choose my own life, my own profession or my own hobbies outside the outpost. But never has anyone confined me to one room like a captive. Can I at least go to the library or the common rooms in the wing?"

"No!" He saw me startle when he barked and sighed, calming down. "I can't think straight when I worry that there is a possibility you're in danger. Stay here so I know you're safe."

I gawked, and my jaw literally dropped. "Is this how you plan to treat your future queen? Because if it is, it won't be me."

His anger ignited, gleaming in his eyes, as he buttoned his blue coat at the side of his chest. With irate shoves, he tucked his feet into his high boots. Then he combed his fingers through his hair to make it lay in some sort of order and pressed the silver band down to sit over his forehead. "I don't have time for this. What if I come back here to eat a quick dinner with you? How does that sound?"

I nonchalantly grabbed a handful of almonds from a bowl at my side and put one nut into my mouth, chewing slowly. "Fine. I guess I'm back to sharing your spare time with your servants, but whatever." I turned around to keep my back against him and looked out at the view of the castle garden and the mountains beyond.

"I apologise for being distant." Frustration laced every syllable.

It didn't sound like an earnest apology. It sounded like an excuse. So, I didn't bother looking at him.

"I've had to execute and punish more people than I can count in just two days," he continued with a strained tone. "And after what I told you about my father, you should understand that I'm not exactly enjoying my time here."

I ate another almond from my hand. Then I turned to face him. "It may come as a surprise, but my time here hasn't exactly been peachy, either." My words were sharp because I was done pretending his burdens were the only ones that mattered.

He took a step closer, then another, but as his gaze dragged over my bare skin, whatever argument he had been forming slipped away. For a brief moment, he appeared lost, struggling between guilt and desire. His callous hands slid down my arms, leaving a fleeting warmth in their wake before his fingers curled around my wrists. When his eyes finally locked onto mine, something in them had softened.

"I'll do better," he whispered. "I'll make it up to you. I swear it."

At least now, he sounded like he meant it.

I exhaled slowly, my pulse in uproar but my resolve unshaken. "You have so much to make up for from past mistakes, and from whatever damage you'll undoubtedly cause in the future, that I don't even know if 'forever' will be enough time for you to make it up to me."

He cupped my cheeks with his palms, wincing mildly at what Nassara's punches had done to my face yesterday before he gazed even deeper into my eyes. "Then we'll keep our souls bonded and I'll keep making it up to you in the life after this and the next and for as long as it takes until I'm forgiven."

That stupid attraction between us, which I had fought so many times and lost, gripped at my heart and held on tightly once more. "Stop being so romantic when I'm trying to be pissed-off with you."

He kissed my forehead. "We'll speak more during dinner, and if not then, in the morning." Then he let go of my face, turned away from me and left the room, leaving me to my lonesome again.

In the morning? It was morning now! That was a whole day away! My doubts about staying here and my insecurities about his love would drive me crazy by then.

All that I had prepared for him this morning seemed a waste. "I guess I'll be eating my breakfast alone," I muttered.

I donned my flight leathers, got my romantic novel from the bedside table and opened it into my lap after I'd curled up into the throne-like armchair.

Picking at the breakfast as I read the book, the sun rose higher and higher in the sky. Then the servants entered with lunch, and I waited until it was cold, but Ben never showed. Hours after, the servants served dinner and left promptly and there still weren't any sign of Ben. I noticed the sun lowering in the sky. I sighed as I finished the last page of the novel. This had been the most boring day of my life. I should get a medal for obeying the black-wing king's wishes to stay a captive in this room.

When evening fell over the castle and the stars shone brighter in the sky, I noted noises coming from outside the windows. I got off the bed and walked up to one of them and peered out to observe the castle garden.

Guest and servants filled every corner of it to enjoy the spring festival.

I opened the window, and I hung out over the sill to listen to the festivities, feeling the warmth of the setting spring sun on my face. There was a pleasant violin orchestra playing and I heard polite laughter that I couldn't tell whether it was genuine or to keep up appearances. I rested my cheeks in my palms, elbows supported on the sill and swayed gently to the music. Well-dressed black-wing people mingle and dance, and I wished I was down there enjoying the ambiance with them.

The rich aroma of garlic and thyme coming from one of the many food tents teased my nostrils. My stomach clenched in protest, a sharp reminder of everything I was missing. Laughter drifted up from the garden party, mingling with the clinking of glasses and soft conversation. A world full of life and indulgence was unfolding just beyond these walls, yet I was here, safely locked away in his room.

This wasn't how my life with Ben was supposed to be. It couldn't be. I didn't choose this.

A spark of defiance flared inside me. I had agreed to stay put, but I decided that demand was no longer reasonable, especially since he hadn't held up his end of the bargain. I'd go down there only for a brief moment. Not being completely reckless I could agree to wear something that blended in, something that wasn't the flight leathers. I wasn't above compromising.

I slipped into a simple white and blue dress and inspected myself in the wall mirror.

This is so not me.

Even the clothes felt like a second cage instead of an ally. Releasing a deep sigh, I draped a dark blue cloak over my shoulders, pulling the hood low to conceal the bruises from my recent fistfight. It was a reminder of my mischief, but I didn't let it stop me. They felt more comfortable and familiar on me than the dress.

As a final precaution, I tucked the light crystal into my bra to serve as a lifeline. Immediately, it throbbed against my skin, pulsing with traces of Mewer's healing magic. If things went south, I'd at least have that for my protection.

Now, I needed a distraction for the door guard. The wine bottle and glass that the servants had left for me after dinner went to the floor with a clatter and I yelped extra loudly. The door guard swung the door open immediately, scanning the room for dangers, sword already drawn and raised.

"I'm so clumsy. Can you call for the maid to help me clean this up?"

He sheathed his sword and left the room. Once he took the corner of the corridor, I rushed the other way, taking the turns of each corridor from what I had memorised, and descended the stairs to the ground floor where

I could follow the noise outside. I'd give it twenty minutes for the guard to realise I was missing from my room and another ten to alert Ben, but that would be enough time for me to have a taste of the party.

I marvelled at the beautiful clothing and the rich bejewelled court folk, soaking in the joyous atmosphere as I listened to the music and watched people dancing. This was how the black-wings conducted their diplomatic affairs, not as a harsh discussion around a counsel table like the white-wings did. Here, Ben ruled, and took counsel from whoever he wished, so if the nobility wanted something said, here was where they could slip it into a casual conversation.

Observing everyone mingling, my eyes kept glancing back at the food presented in the stalls, as I was mostly excited about trying new flavours. Identifying the stall that served whatever I had smelt from the window, I held my hands out for a serving, and as I turned around to leave, I almost had the apple-flap-looking pastry fly into the chest of…I looked higher on the fine black tailcoat… No!

Duke Hartmore scanned my face quickly, pulling a horrified grimace. "What in this world have you done to my bride?" he asked in Ben's general direction, who I hadn't seen standing a short distance away from me.

I'd have been concerned by the way the duke was making a scene, if I wasn't distracted, almost choking, at the sight of Ben and Nassara and two dozen guards surrounding them.

Ben had a small paper gift box in one hand and Lady Nassara's hand in the other, their fingers laced together. My promise ring was not on Ben's finger.

He had taken it off!

The sorrow hit so potently I could barely breathe. My heart lurched as if gripped by an invisible fist, squeezing so tight it struggled to beat. My blood drained from my face, leaving me light-headed.

They were fucking holding hands!

Was this real?

Had I missed the signs, or had I simply refused to see them?

A sick, twisting ache coiled in my stomach as betrayal sank its claws deep into me. Betrayal. My biggest fear.

The warmth of his hand, that had belonged to me alone, now belonged to another. The world blurred at the edges, but that image, the way he held her hand in an easy grip, burned into my mind like a brand impossible to erase.

Ben's eyes flared with annoyance and a hint of fear, as he recognised me beneath the scabs and bruises inside the cowl, and he ripped his hand away from Nassara's.

It is too damn late Ben! I saw it!

He must have seen the hurt caused by his betrayal on my face because he didn't hesitate to barge towards me, and the sea of people between us parted for him; the men and women around him bowing and curtsying, so I mirrored their movement to blend in. But it was too late. Ben was causing a scene, and the noble folk began gasping and gossiping around us.

Although, I couldn't tell why he was coming my way. He was supposed to pretend he didn't know me. Was he approaching to order my imprisonment now when I had caught him out on his lie? I should never have come here. Never have trusted him.

I had moments to form an escape plan if I was to survive this.

Theatrically, I fell onto one knee as he arrived before me, and I stole his hand from his side to pretend to kiss the king with a peasant's adoration, but instead I used every sliver of Mewer's healing magic I had left in me and the light magic in the crystal to break the soul bond between us.

The moment I reached into the depths of the light crystal, a force unlike anything I had ever known seized hold of me. It was raw magic, an unbalanced pure power, a relentless pull that felt as though the crystal itself was clawing to get into my soul, demanding more of me, demanding everything. Zayd's warnings hadn't been exaggerated; if anything, he hadn't done justice to the agony of being possessed and drained of soul from within. It was an all-consuming force that tore through my flesh like slices from a hundred blades.

But I couldn't stop. Not turn off the pain. Not yet.

I clung to the last shreds of my strength, knowing that the soul bond tethering Ben to me had to be severed. If it didn't break, I couldn't leave. He didn't deserve to be bound to me, not after I had seen where his true loyalty lay. Nassara. His soulmate.

His choices had spoken louder than any words ever could, and I had been too naïve, too blind, to see the truth until now. I was nothing more than his toy, a pawn to be played with and discarded. If I didn't leave, I wouldn't just be trapped here, I would be destroyed.

The pain in my chest exploded as the bond snapped like a rope stretched too thin. A sharp cry tore from my throat as the force slung me backwards and onto my arse on the grass. In front of me, Ben gasped as he stumbled back a step, his eyes wide open in terror. He must have felt the unbearable ripping sensation, too. The hum in my ears vanishing into an eerie silence, and it felt like I was dying – from the separation, from the heartache.

When Duke Hartmore pushed me backwards to speak with Ben, I wobbled to my feet and darted between the guests to get away from all this. I couldn't stand it for another second. The charades. The betrayals. The hurt.

My legs didn't carry me as fast as I wanted them to, but I was doing well.

Ben hadn't caught up with me, being occupied with the duke and the other guests. When I reached the stable, I saw a guard's saddled horse, its rider was speaking to the stable master in the tack room. I mounted the black charger and kicked its flanks to ride out into the night, through the city and over the plains towards the mountain pass and Bensguard.

I rode along the edge of the border when my eyes started to tear up and I didn't care to hold them in anymore. I let them seep down my cheeks as I cried out my grief. Nassara's leer at me when I had seen their laced hands played on repeat in my mind. In the end, she had won.

It was a little over three o'clock in the morning when I finally arrived in front of the watch tower, where Ben had organised for Brian to be on watch alone to open the gates for us.

At the stable, I slung down from the horse and rummaged through the tack room for four horseshoe nails and a hammer before going to my dorm room. The adrenaline helped as I dragged Ben's bed away from mine, and after I had separated them, I walked around to push his bed towards the other wall, using my leg muscles. Getting up into his bed, I removed the bedding to get access to the wooden bed frame and hammered the long horseshoe nails in, securing the bed to the wall in four places. Then I chucked the hammer on the floor as I spat cusses, thinking of the cheating bastard.

To be honest, I wasn't sure why I had nailed his bed to the wall, as I doubted he was so stupid as to return to the White Wing Territory now when I had caught him red handed, and he was free from the bond. But I had known him to do maddening things before. Besides, if he did come back, I wouldn't share a room with him ever again! So, I guessed the nails were symbolic, to deal with my grief.

I found a duffle bag at the bottom of the wardrobe and shoved down a couple of uniforms, my makeup, toothbrush and hairbrush before making my way to the second floor.

I froze for a second as I found Harvey crouching, painting his door white. Turning my wrist over, I noted it was four o'clock in the morning.

"What are you doing?"

"Spirits!" he yelped, as I had startled him, and he twisted his head to look at me, pointing at the paintbrush he pressed against the door. "I'm finishing off the door. There was another attack."

I shook my head at the madness. "Have you raised it in a leadership meeting?"

He rose to his feet and faced me. "There is no use. It's never the same people attacking twice. I make sure of that." Harvey glanced at my duffle bag and then again at my face. "Dare I ask why you're on the leadership floor with a duffle bag and a face full of bruises and dried tears?"

I walked closer. "I'm staying in your bed tonight."

Harvey put the paintbrush down into the cleaning pot and dried his hands with a cloth he had over his shoulder. "King Blackbone and you had another fight?"

My breath hiccuped. "Yes. The last one."

He pointed at my face. "Did he do that?" his voice clipped.

"No," I said curtly, not offering an explanation.

He frowned and sighed out a large breath from his nose. "If this is going to be a reoccurring thing, should I reinstate your bedroom?" Harvey grabbed the two pots from the floor and walked into his apartment. "Come on!"

I followed him and crawled straight into his bed, too exhausted to change.

Harvey tucked himself in beside me. "Things will look brighter in the morning."

I pulled the blanket to my chest and folded my arms around the hem. "Only because the sun is up. I think I'll live the rest of my life in the shadows where one can't be betrayed."

In my peripheral view, Harvey turned his head towards me, but I kept looking at the ceiling. "Considering it, sister, had you not expected that the black-wing king would eventually break your heart?"

I thought about it. Had I been so gullible? "He has gone through so much effort to show me love that I guess I've forgotten he is my enemy. He gave me this peanut butter cake last week, and I almost came to your door so you could taste it. He didn't tell me where he had bought it, but it tasted exactly like Mother's."

"I didn't know you were getting that serious. Zayd will help me this weekend to put your room back to how it was when you lived here. You'll not stay in the same room as him."

Harvey obviously didn't know that Ben no longer was at Bensguard and only the Spirits knew what leadership would do to us when they found out what I'd done setting him free.

"We're teammates," I said, keeping the lie about us alive.

"Not unless chaperoned. And you'll come with me to the Abarath Outpost after the archery challenge. I want you in my sight." Harvey put his hands to rest on his stomach and closed his eyes. "Well, enough about black-wings. We should get some sleep."

"You never speak about her, you know?" I felt my heart beat harder as I asked.

"Who?"

"Mother." I swallowed hard, feeling my pulse hammer against my ribs. "You never told me about the time you killed her."

Harvey lay on his back, seemingly undisturbed, eyes closed as if he could will away the past I was about to dig up. "Not a memory I'm fond of." He still lay relaxed with no sign of distress or raced heartbeat from my question.

My hands curled into fists against the sheets. "Did you make her suffer?" I hoped he had made her suffer, if she had felt the pain of her own sins, then maybe it'd be easier to accept that she was gone.

He exhaled, as if trying to recall an old assignment. "No. I chased her to the black-wing border and caught her by the east foot of the plain between the mountain pass. For one second, I hesitated, but when I thought about all the friends she had cut down at the Bensguard Outpost, I drove the sword into her gut. She spat blood, and the words that she had always loved us, and then she fell off my blade, her eyes vacant. I bent down to close them and that was that," he murmured, still so indifferent, as if he were discussing the weather and not the moment he had ended our mother's life.

A thousand emotions were warring inside me.

He had stood over her as the light left her eyes. He had closed them with his own hands. Had his fingers trembled? Had he felt sadness for what he'd done?

I clenched my teeth. A sharp breath left me. "You didn't bury her?" I turned my head, searching his face for a crack in its cold exterior.

"Bury? Uh. I took her body to Lake Pharoon, tied rocks around the corpse and sank her to the bottom."

"Lake Pharoon?" My voice wavered. "But we swim the last challenge of the year in that lake."

"It was five years ago." He finally opened his eyes, but there was no remorse. Not one flicker of guilt. Just a statement of fact. "There's nothing left of her body but clean bones."

I felt sick. My fingers dug into the sheets to ground myself from agony. "Ew! Disgusting!"

The words left my lips in a horrified whisper. But the truth was, it wasn't just the thought of her bones resting beneath the lake that made me sick, it was the sheer finality of it. That was one way to die. Forgotten. Sunk into the depths where no one could mourn you.

Suddenly there was a new look in his eyes – regret? Pain? It passed over his face, but it was gone before I could be sure it had been there. "Angie, get some sleep."

Sleep? How could I sleep when the thought of my mother's death wrapped itself around everything inside my mind like a choking vine?

The sorrow pressed against my ribs, making my heart feel like it was beating in a cage too small to hold it. A dull ache pulsed behind my eyes, but no amount of blinking could rid me of the image seared into my mind: my mother falling from his blade, bloodied lips whispering her final, damning words. *She had always loved us.* What a cruel, useless confession to make in her dying breath. I hated myself for thinking it, hated Harvey for what he'd done, for how easily he seemed to live with it. A deeper, more insidious pain coiled inside me.

But she had deserved death and so did Ben. I considered how I could kill Ben for his betrayal, now that I no longer had the option to finish my initial mission to run the Black Blade through him, watching his eyes widen in surprise as the Black Blade sank into his chest, feeling his blood coat my hands, stealing from him the life he had stolen from me. Because I felt lifeless without him. I tried to tell myself it'd be justice to end his life. That after all his betrayals, after all the ways he had twisted and shattered my heart, I'd be in my right to do it. And yet…

I had been a fool. A fool who had protected him instead, providing him with an oath that ensured I couldn't stab him with a black blade. I snorted to myself as I realised that even knowing the truth about Nassara, I could never kill Ben. Because for all my rage, for all my stubbornness, my heart was a pathetic, treacherous thing.

It would have been easier if I could hate him entirely, if I could carve out every ounce of love from my heart the way he had torn through my trust. But it remained, rotting inside me, poisoning me with the knowledge that I'd never be free. I was shackled to him, not by magic or duty, but by something far worse – by the very thing that made me weak. Love.

No matter how much he had hurt me, no matter how many times I swore I hated him, no matter how much I wanted to forget him, and no matter how much I wanted to sever the bond between us, the love had already burrowed too deep. It was an undeniable truth I could never outrun. Ben would always be the only man I would ever truly love.

It was an endless, unbearable agony, knowing that even after everything…I was still his.

And that, more than anything, was what truly broke me.

60

I pounded my fist on Zoe's door hard enough to wake the dead. Probably the Spirits lost their sleep-in, too. I was determined she'd be my punch cushion today, so if she didn't wake up, I'd kick the damned door down. Wrath still surged through me so potently I felt my pulse roar in my ears and my breaths came out ragged from sprinting to Zoe's room.

My thoughts were wiring in my mind.

Betrayal. Betrothal. Betrayal. Hurt.

I couldn't shake the memory of Ben's betrayal. It was burning through me like poison, scorching every rational thought.

The door creaked open, and Zoe's sleepy face barely had time to register my presence before I snapped, "Get dressed! We're training!"

She flinched at my tone, but I didn't care. I was beyond empathy for her beauty sleep. My skin was too tight, my blood too hot, and if I didn't busy myself with something, I was going to explode. I had already been twisting and turning in bed to wait this long before I decided to drag her out of bed.

Murben's head poked up from the bed, and I cussed. I didn't want to see Murben and be reminded of Ben, but I realised it was that or nothing, as they seemed to be a package deal now.

Dressed in flight leathers, we headed out to the archery field, the golden gleam striking my eyes as the sun barrelled over the mountains. There'd be little chance of flying, considering the thick, brooding storm clouds overhead. Good. Let the storm come. Let it rage. Maybe then I wouldn't feel like the only thing ready to tear itself apart, like the air was a too heavy burden to bear. Fitting. My chest felt the same, like I was unable to breath fully because a fist was wrapped around my lungs, squeezing it tight every time I thought of Ben with Nassara.

We stalked across the field, boots crunching against damp grass, straight to the farthest target board. No wasted time, no idle chatter. Just arrows, bows and violence waiting to be unleashed with my need to hit something – hard.

I snatched an arrow from the quiver and nocked it in one fluid motion. My fingers ached from gripping the bowstring too hard, but I welcomed the sting. That pain was better than the hurt of betrayal.

One after another, we fired. *Twang. Snap. Thud.* The rhythm of bowstrings whipping against the air should have been soothing. It wasn't. The thoughts in my head were louder, crashing over each other in echoing cries.

Murben anchored an arrow beside me, his eyes scanning in my direction, and he finally dared the question he had been dying to ask all morning. "Where's King Blackbone?"

My entire body stiffened. My fingers dug into the grip of the bow and my nails pressed into the worn wood and leather. I didn't look at him. Didn't trust myself to. My grip tightened around feather and string. "Not my concern." The words came out in a snarl, acidic, like rancid milk on my tongue.

I released the arrow. *Twang. Snap. Thud.* The wooden frame trembled from the force, but it wasn't enough to pacify any of my fury. I yanked another from the quiver so fast the fletching burned against my fingers.

Murben, as always, remained infuriatingly calm. He took aim, speaking in that steady, unreadable voice. "May you be so kind as to tell his bodyguard where you saw him last?" His arrow flew, striking just shy of the bullseye. He stepped aside, making space for me.

I stepped forward, taking my place at the mark. My muscles coiled, every fibre of mine wound too tightly. I lifted my bow. Aimed. The world narrowed to the target in front of me, but all I saw was Ben; his face, his lies, the betrayal that had ripped me open from the inside out.

I pulled the bowstring back, my knuckles brushing my cheek. "The garden party at Black Castle. Last night."

Then I let the arrow fly. It slammed into the target with a violent, shuddering thud, dead centre. I wished it had been Ben's heart instead.

Murben exhaled slowly. "What has the king done now?"

I pulled the string with a tight grip on the feathers of another arrow and aimed. My arms burned from the force, from holding back the fury I was barely keeping contained. "He has pissed me off."

Murben let out a dry chuckle. "I worked that much out myself but–" He stopped mid-sentence, eyes shifting past me. I caught the slight tilt of his chin, the nod toward something behind my back. "But I guess I'll ask him myself."

Dread crawled through my insides. I lowered the bow just enough to turn.

Ben.

Ben casually strolled the length of the field towards us, as if he had every right to be here. Ignoring the truth that he deserved to be swallowed whole by the ground beneath his feet for what he'd done.

What in this damned world is he doing here? How dare he come near me?

My fear turned a blinding colour of red. "Zoe, can you open a hearing portal between us?"

Zoe hesitated. "Not sure I want to get between–"

"Zoe!"

She huffed. "Fine."

Her hands traced small circles in the air to widen a portal beside me. The second opening materialised just beside Ben's head, following him like a curse.

"I don't want to talk to you." My voice was ice. "Take another step this way and I'll shoot you."

I pulled the bowstring and aimed the arrow straight for him.

He didn't stop, so I let the arrow fly over his shoulder, just snagging the black leather of his uniform.

He flinched.

"Oops. I missed."

He grunted. "I doubt you did. A warning?"

I walked to the bow rack and brought out two more arrows from the quiver resting on the ground. "You feel like testing that theory?"

"You can't mean to kill me here, in plain sight."

"Oh, I wanted to kill you yesterday in a Black Wing Territory party, so your death is already overdue. Turn around and leave me alone."

"I can't do that."

"Why not?"

"Because I love you more than my will to live." He continued towards me.

Spirits!

"The next one will hit on your left thigh, very close to your balls…I hope."

"What have you done, King Blackbone?" Murben roared and placed himself between us, so I couldn't take the shot.

I couldn't get around him. "Move Murben or tell your betrayer of a king to return to his territory."

"I'm sorry about yesterday!" Ben said through the portal, walking much slower towards me now. "If you knew the big picture, you'd understand."

I darted around Murben, my heart hammering like a war drum. The wet grass soaked my knee as I dropped low, the scent of damp earth distracting. Without hesitation, I clenched one arrow between my teeth, the cool shaft pressing against my tongue. The other arrow I anchored against the bowstring.

Ben came closer, his presence burning against my vision. He didn't stop. He thought I wouldn't do it. That I'd forgive him.

Like fuck I would.

I pulled the bowstring, not enough to kill, but enough to make him feel it. "If you told me the truth, maybe I'd forgive you."

Then I released the arrow.

The arrowhead sliced the air with speed dampened by my restraint, but swift enough to bite into the side of his arm. The impact was sharp but had barely nipped his flesh before it passed him.

Ben growled, his teeth grinding together as he applied pressure to the wound. A dark stain bloomed over his black uniform sleeve beneath his hand.

"Cadet Coraly!" Murben's bark was sharp as a whip, as his hand clamped down on my shoulder.

I barely felt it. Barely cared.

Ben let out a rough, pained groan, his face twisting and sucked in a breath, his jaw tight.

"It's okay, Murben," he ground out, voice strained but steady. "I deserved that." He exhaled, shaking his head, and a wry smirk ghosted his lips. "At least it wasn't my balls."

I didn't laugh.

I shrugged Murben's hand off my shoulder, pushing to my feet. The anger still clamped around my heart. Without breaking my stare from Ben, I snatched the last arrow from between my lips before I anchored it into the bow. This time I took aim with deadly precision.

"You can put the Forever ring down on the bow rack beside you before you leave," I said coldly with no trace of forgiveness. "Since it seems you replaced it with Nassara's fingers."

Murben's head snapped toward the portal, his brows knitting together, his expression shifting from authority to something closer to shock and reluctant agreement, as if he had swapped to support my side. His voice was like flint when he spoke. "You took the ring off?"

Ben had stopped walking. His boots halted mid-stride, tension locking his frame in place.

His eyes, however, never left mine.

"No." He barked as if he'd die before he gave it back, and even then, someone would have to pry it off his finger. "I'm keeping the ring. Yes, I took it off," Ben admitted, lifting his free hand slightly as if trying to steady the air between us. "But not for the reason you think." His gaze darkened, words clipped and urgent now. "I did it to avoid angering Duke

Finningham. I depend on his troops in the north, and a large portion of my army is stationed on his land. If I showed up wearing your ring, it would have put everything at risk."

Some logic from that settled, but I refused to let it show. *Excuses. Just excuses.*

Ben exhaled sharply. "But I wasn't walking around holding Nassara's hand."

I scoffed. *I had seen it with my own eyes.*

He dared to take a step closer. "She must have nestled her fingers into mine the second she saw you. I was too busy speaking with my guests to notice." His throat bobbed, swallowing frustration. "When I saw you, and wanted to reach out to you, that's when I realised my hand was stuck to hers. And I tore it away."

He lifted his injured arm slightly, the wound still seeping red, a silent challenge in his gaze.

I didn't lower my bow. "Delightful story. Did you think that up while you were dancing at the ball last night?"

"I didn't attend the ball. I ran after you, but you'd stolen my patrol guard's horse, and it took me too long to saddle another one. By the time I perused you, you were already long gone. When I got to our room, you had already nailed my bed to the other side of the wall and you weren't there. I couldn't find you. I waited. I slept. But you didn't return."

Had he really left the ball and his guests to come after me? Whatever end he was using me for, how could it be more important than the party, having dishonoured himself by leaving his guests? Was he telling the truth?

"Don't give up on our forever, Angelica. If it's what it takes, I'll tell you everything." Ben's voice had a plea to it, but it was a desperation that came too late.

His eyes locked onto mine, dark with emotion, but I barely heard his words through the roaring blood in my ears.

Lies. Lies wrapped in pretty words.

"You can't tell Cadet Coraly anything!" Murben shouted in warning, his jaw set hard like stone. "Think of how you've suffered after Banessa!"

Banessa? Another lover he'd screwed?

With the breath punched out of me, I could feel the ground tilting beneath my feet. Had I been a fool all this time? Just another name in a long line of discarded lovers? Rage surged through me. A wildfire in my veins.

I threw the bow to the ground, the sound when it hit the dirt barely registering, and I bolted. My wings erupted from my back, flaring wide as I launched into the sky with powerful beats. The wind rushed past my ears, but I couldn't fly fast enough to outrun the grief inside me.

Then – agony.

A white-hot explosion of pain ripped through my right wing. I screamed, as something needle-sharp speared through my nerves. An arrow.

I twisted mid-air, eyes snapping downward, and found Cadet Gravelhorn. The bastard was already nocking another arrow. His stance was firm, and his eyes gleamed with satisfaction.

He meant to bring me down.

Ben's roar shattered through the chaos. "Gravelhorn, stand down!"

But Gravelhorn never got the chance to release the second shot because Ben threw himself at him. They hit the ground hard, wrestling in a flurry of limbs and snarled curses. But it was a losing fight as Gravelhorn was built for strength, his magic making him nearly unstoppable.

But none of that mattered to Ben. He was fearless.

The burn in my wing tore through me like wildfire. My balance switched heavily to my left, as it hurt like death to flap with my right. The wound was bleeding too much, pouring out around the penetrated shaft, the crimson staining my white feathers in a grotesque bloom.

Too heavy to stay in the air with the damaged wing, I plummeted to the ground.

The impact was brutal. My wing slammed into the earth first, sending a fresh bolt of searing pain through me. The momentum had me tumbling uncontrollably, making my good wing scrape against the ground in a desperate attempt to slow to a stop.

Then – stillness.

I came to a stop on my back, my vision swimming as I stared blankly at the sky above, the angry, grey clouds a visualisation of the agony pulsing through every part of me. My wing throbbed with a vicious ache that radiated from the wound.

I strangled a cry. Show no weakness! My brother would tell me if he saw me now.

Zoe was at my side in an instant, her hands urgently inspecting my wing. "Hold still!"

Her words were barely muffled sounds through the haze of pain. I dug my fingers into the grass, nails biting into the dirt as I tried to breathe through it. But when she lifted my wing to assess the damage, a fresh wave of unfathomable pain exploded through me. I choked on a gasp, arching against the pain, every muscle locking tight.

"I need to pull the shaft more my way so I can get a grip around it and break it off," Zoe shouted.

She didn't ask for permission. She just did it.

The second she tugged at it, a fiery sensation shot from the mouth of the wound and forked through my entire wing. It was impossible to hold back the cry that tore from my throat. My vision blurred, but I felt the snap of the arrow breaking behind my plumes.

Zoe moved fast, folding my wing forward, gripping the shaft tight. With one last merciless yank, she pulled the rest of it free.

I gasped, the pain still brutal, but no longer a poisonous knife twisting deeper into me.

But my fury was still very much alive.

I would kill Gravelhorn for this.

Zoe's fingers waved in the air, her magic sparking as she opened a new hearing portal. Her voice urgent. "Mewer! I'm coming in with Angie. Gravelhorn shot her wing with an arrow."

Darkness threatened to take me over, but one thing was crystal clear. Gravelhorn better start running. Because when I got back on my feet, I was going to destroy him.

"I'll prepare her normal bed in the corner," Mewer answered, sounding rushed as if he was working on it already.

With yellow splotches in front of my eyes, I stood up, wobbling from the uneven control of moving simultaneously with both wings. I unsheathed my black blade knife from my boot. Gravelhorn would pay for this. "Where is he?" I growled, looking around, but saw him running for his life across the other end of the field with Ben and Murben on his heels.

Angrily, I shoved the blade back into its place. Gravelhorn was as good as dead already.

Zoe stripped off her bra without removing her shirt entirely in a rather impressive display. She cut the fabric that joined the two cups in half with her dagger before pressing the padding against the wound on either side of my wing to stop the blood from spewing out. She walked by my side to the infirmary and pinned my wings to the middle of my back so I wouldn't knock down the other patients' belongings from their side-tables as I passed.

We reached the bed in the corner where Mewer stood waiting. "An improvement, Cadet Coraly. This time, you're at least conscious."

I grimaced at him and hopped up to sit on the bed. "Heal my wing first and joke later. It hurts like a bitch."

Mewer buttoned his brown coat over his navy-blue uniform so as not to dirty it with my blood and inspected the wound, prodding a finger on it. "Yes. The wings are sensitive just around the spot where the arrow hit."

I winced at the sting his finger caused. "Thank you for the anatomy lesson, Mewer. I'm pretty sure I already learnt that from experience. Please, fix it."

He gestured for the pillow. "Lie down on the bed, and tuck the wings in, and I'll get the ointment."

"Ointment?" I moaned. "There is no need for all that. Can't you just heal me?"

Mewer smiled warmly at me and pushed back his golden hair. "I'm afraid I've exhausted my healing magic for the moment. Healing serious flesh wounds on soldiers and bonding souls are draining work." He looked at me with meaning in his kind green eyes and I blushed.

"Fine, get the ointment," I muttered.

Zoe's hands trembled as she helped me ease down, still pressing the blood-soaked remnants of her bra against my wing. The makeshift bandage was warm against my skin, but the pain refused to ebb.

Fern approached with quiet urgency, and with two fingers already dipped into a tub of green cream. The scent was earthy and medicinal, filling the air as she pulled up a chair beside the bed. Without a word, she gestured for Zoe to move back. With a reluctant hesitation, Zoe lifted her hands off my wound. Cold air kissed the exposed flesh, making me hiss as the pain flared back to life.

"What happened?" Fern asked, her voice calm but edged with concern.

She didn't wait for an answer before she started smoothing a generous layer of ointment over the torn flesh of my wing with practised hands. The salve was cool at first before the sensation settled into a soothing numbness.

That they were using the green cream on me at all was generous. It wasn't exactly something given out lightly. But I supposed that a bloody hole straight through my wing warranted the exception.

I swallowed down my suffering, but the words still came out sharp. "I flew across the archery field, and Cadet Gravelhorn happened to miss his target board by ten metres."

Fern sucked in a sharp breath, her fingers faltering for just a moment. "You're lucky he only hit your wing."

I let out a short, bitter laugh. "Yeah, well, can't say I feel lucky." I exhaled, as my muscles shifted, and I tightened my fingers into the bedsheets as she touched my sore flesh. "But he'll be lucky if he still has arms left to shoot another arrow. Ben and Murben chased after him."

Her lips twitched slightly, not quite a smile, more like a quiet understanding. She probably already knew there would be more work coming her way as soon as Ben and Murben caught Gravelhorn and left him with more than just a bruised ego.

As she worked, I noticed the gentle curve of her belly that was slightly more pronounced since the last time I'd seen her. It wasn't obvious yet. At least not to anyone who didn't already know, but it was there.

"How are you feeling?" I asked, my voice softer this time.

Fern stood up, carefully folding my wing across my stomach to reach the other side of the wound. "I'm good. Thanks to you." A warmth touched her voice. "Robin is excelling under his tutors. Emroyce has been so supportive."

A small warmth pushed through the haze of pain." I tilted my head, watching her. "That's great. And the morning sickness?"

She had been using her speed magic, hands moving quickly as she applied the cream, but at my words, she suddenly froze. Distinct creases formed between her brows. Her fingers tightened around the ointment jar. For the first time, uncertainty flickered across her face.

Zoe, of course, wasted no time. She plopped onto the mattress at the foot of my bed, smirking. "You didn't think your best friends wouldn't figure it out, honey?"

Fern's head snapped up and the colour drained from her face. Her dark eyes darted between us with fear. She opened her mouth, then shut it again. Swallowed hard. The terrified look on her face told me we weren't meant to know about the pregnancy.

"Please don't tell anyone about it," she whispered. Her fingers had sunk deeper into the ointment pot.

"Why?" I asked. "Is Brian not taking it too well?"

She shushed me and the pressure on my wound became more forceful as she slabbed on another blob of cream. After a moment, she looked at me. "Brian told me you made that deal." She nodded for my wrist, even though the tattoo wasn't visible from beneath the sleeve. "To save his life. That's twice you've sacrificed yourself for me. Thank you."

"You don't need to thank me, Fern. That's what friends are for."

"Hold on a minute! What are you two talking about?" Zoe barked.

I gazed up at the vaulted ceiling deciding what to tell Zoe, but I found no reason I should hide the truth from her. "You remember my mission, and that I told you I had to marry Duke Hartmore?"

"Yeah."

"He blackmailed me to take an oath to marry him or he'd cut Brian's throat."

"Wow!" Zoe huffed, pushing her purple hair back. "And, can't King Blackbone do anything about that? Demand the duke breaks the oath?"

I pumped my left hand, as it felt numb. "I doubt he genuinely cares, as he seems to have lots of other women to court as soon as I turn to look the other way."

"What? Is that what that was about outside?" Zoe looked confused and angry at the same time.

"Never mind. I have lots of good friends here." I smiled at Fern.

Zoe crossed her legs and her arms and pouted. "If he cheated on you, I'll cut his balls off."

"Zoe, honey," I answered sarcastically. "If I feel his balls must come off, I'll do it myself. I don't want to talk about it. I want to know how Brian is treating Fern."

Fern smiled. "Brian is fantastic. A true gentleman. The baby wasn't an accident. Well, we hadn't planned it, but we've been seeing each other for two years. The academy training has kept us both together and apart, as I see him more when he has been injured than not. I'm constantly worried about him during the challenges, but he worries more about what will happen after he graduates. He could get stationed anywhere. There is a lot happening in the north." She trembled at the thought and got a tissue from the side-table to wipe the ointment off her fingers.

"Where is Brian now?" I asked.

"He and Winter won the sleep deprivation challenge, then he took a night shift in the guard tower last night on top of that for some reason, so I'd bet anything on that he's sleeping in Captain La Roy's apartment. And probably for a few days."

We laughed. But guilt passed through me momentarily for being the reason Brian had been pushed another twelve hours with no sleep.

"You should get some rest." Fern instructed, throwing a meaningful stare at Zoe.

"Tell that to them, too," I muttered, as Ben and Murben walked in and glanced around the room.

"Will you hate me if I won't?" Fern asked, patting my shoulder. "You two need to work out your issues by listening and reasoning. And you'd look lovely in a tiara and a dress."

I snorted. "Forget that! If I ever become queen, I'll keep dressing in my combat leathers. One never knows when I'll have to kick his butt."

Zoe and Fern laughed as they left my bedside, Zoe heading to the inner corridors avoiding to cross path with the approaching black-wings.

Murben followed her with his gaze, but Ben's eyes were set on me. He stopped at my side with Murben right behind him. "So, it's not just in the Black Wing Territory where the drama revolves around you."

I turned my head to look the other way, and crossed my arms over my chest, but he couldn't see it as my wing concealed my front. "Not sure if I can take all the credit for this one, though."

"I guess Cadet Gravelhorn bears most of the blame."

I stared at him. "Wow. Really? None of it is your fault?"

He was about to utter something, but snapped his teeth together, clearly thinking better of it. Smart man!

"What do you want, King Blackbone?"

"King Blackbone," he muttered, the foul-tasting words he hated me calling him. "The soul bond broke between us, and you ran away in the middle of the night. And Cadet Gravelhorn shot you down whilst flying. Naturally, I have had more than one panic attack."

I didn't respond so he continued.

"Having arrived in our room with my bed nailed to the wall and you nowhere to be found, my imagination ran wild, thinking of the worst possible scenarios."

"And what would those scenarios be?" I muttered, still looking at the wall. "That someone had killed me? Or even worse. That I was in love with another man and was in Bensguard City on a nightly stroll, my fingers laced with his?"

"No. I know you love me and would never cheat on me. I feared that you'd left the outpost, and I'd never see you again. Never able to find you without the bond. Or that you suddenly thought it was a brilliant idea to join the war in the north. Or my most antagonising thought, that you had killed yourself to release the grief."

I cringed and turned my head to stare at him. "Oh, please! Get over yourself!"

Although, going north to see what was happening up there hadn't been a bad idea. Why hadn't I thought of that before? I guessed there was too little time between lessons, and I'd be punished as a deserter, beheaded probably, if I was gone for too long and caught.

Ben planted his hands on the mattress, leaning over me, his face close to mine. His eyes filled with something consuming him; hurt. "You know I feel like half a person without the soul bond connecting us. How could you break it? Was that your magic?"

A hollow, bitter laugh escaped me. "I have no magic." My voice was low, laced with the same hurt as he carried. My fingers curled into the bedsheets, the ache in my wing forgotten beneath the potent ache in my chest. "Maybe when you broke my heart, the soul bond shattered, too."

Ben flinched, clearly the words hit him hard. I had never seen him look this defeated before. His breaths were shallow, his body stiffening like I had run a blade through him. *Good. Let him feel it.*

He straightened slowly. Exhaling hard, it seemed like the wind had been knocked out of him. With hands on his hips, he shifted his weight back onto his heels, his gaze dropping to the floor. *Coward.*

"I have to keep up appearances," he muttered, his voice bleak compared to before. "It didn't mean anythi–"

"Fern advises I should rest," I growled.

Silence.

He held my gaze a moment longer before he gave a sharp nod. A soldier's bow. Accepting a received order. An ending.

He ordered Murben to stay and guard me, and without another word to me, he turned around and left. His shoulders were still stiff as he walked away like a beaten dog with its tail tucked between its legs.

I barely waited for him to disappear before I shoved the blankets off. My wings were filthy, and I hated the feel of stale blood on my feathers.

Rules or not, Mewer could be angry that I left without being dismissed if he wanted, but I wasn't going to sit here covered in my own blood.

The bathing chambers were off-limits for washing off filth like this, and the cadets usually used the showers in the changing rooms, but the last time I stepped foot in there, Courtney and Darling had almost killed me, so I had no intention of returning there alone. I didn't have a death wish – not yet. Nor did I want Murben awkwardly trailing me into the women's changing rooms. My shower in the dorm was too small to fit my wings, even if I tried to fold them in. Which left only one option – the lake pool by the caves.

I pushed off the bed.

"Cadet Coraly!" Murben's voice snapped through the air. He was on his feet in an instant, eyes narrowed as I rushed past him. "You shouldn't be up before Camp Leader Mewer discharges you."

Footsteps pounded behind me as his presence became a shadow at my back. I ignored him, but he was in my footsteps before I had time to step out of them myself.

I huffed. "I have to wash my wings before the challenge, don't I?"

The infirmary storeroom had a sponge, soap and a large towel that I shoved down into a medical shoulder bag before leaving towards the lake.

"You were shot and you're still going to do the challenge?" Murben asked as he followed me beyond the tree line and under the canopy of treetops.

"I was shot in the wing, not my arm."

Murben kept interrogating me, even when I gave him no answers, as I trekked through the woods. The air and quiet I needed to think was overpowered by his concerns. The pain reminded me I had just been shot and the agony from it ate up all my patience, replacing it with ever-increasing levels of irritation.

My sudden stop almost caused a collision as I jerked around. "Ask me one question and I'll answer it truthfully if you agree to keep quiet after that."

"I don't need to ask you any questions. I need to remind you that all the king does, he does to protect you because he loves you. You don't understand how rare that is and how new he is at showing his emotions. So yes, he might be clumsy–"

"Stop, Murben. What he has done to show everyone his standpoint with Nassara is unforgivable. At some point, a man must choose to fight an unavoidable battle because it's what he stands for. If he loves me, he should have chosen to fight for me."

"He is fighting for you! Listen to what I'm telling you. King Blackbone has everything he could ever want, and he can get what he doesn't already have with the flick of a finger. But he doesn't care for any of that or power. He doesn't want to be king. He hates to be responsible for people he always fears he cannot protect. People's deaths and his death magic have haunted him for years, as has the agony of the harm he has caused many innocents."

I looked up at Murben, my gaze trailing over the bodyguard pin I had given him. A bitter reminder. It wasn't just a badge, it was a mark of loyalty, but not to me. To Ben.

Murben was an advocate for the black-wing king, a shadow at his back, bound by duty. He'd always have an excuse for him, always twist the truth in his favour, always justify his actions, even when those actions shattered me.

His deep, brown eyes met mine with an unwavering glare. His tawny skin and jet-black hair cast him as a dark silhouette, looking very much like a reflection of the very enemy I wanted to hate, but desperately wished I could still call a friend.

"If he hated it that much, he could have given it away," I said, resigned.

Murben scoffed. "And who should he have given it to?" His voice came out harsher than usual. "It's not easy to get rid of death magic. Not to someone who won't use it to kill in order to hoard power." Murben's expression didn't change. Steady. Patient. Unshaken. "You asked him why the Spirits gave him death magic, as if that alone made him evil. But did it ever occur to you that the Spirits chose him because they believed he could wield it fairly?"

I clenched my jaw. I didn't want to agree with him. But I couldn't deny he might be right. Ben had been inflicted with magic that could only destroy. A power that could only take. How he must have suffered. Every single day, living with the constant fear of losing control. Of hurting the people he loved. With a power like that, Ben was unstoppable. Yet, he had never used it to conquer territories, never killed just because he could.

I turned away, unable to face Murben as much as I was unable to face the thoughts unravelling in my mind. As I walked, my boots sunk into the damp grass and my shoulders became tight with truths I didn't want to admit.

But Murben wasn't done.

"Despite everything; the burdens, the struggles, the duty, he still found something he wanted for himself." His breaths came out more exasperated, as if he so badly wanted to see Ben find happiness, believing he deserved it. "It took him a decade," Murben continued, his words deliberate. "And then you walked into his life at the spring festival ball two years ago."

I froze.

Murben exhaled softly, almost as if the memory had settled on his shoulders, too. "I remember his words that night."

My breath caught.

Murben cleared his throat, hesitating, probably wondering whether he was crossing a line by revealing the king's private thoughts. But he was hell-bent on setting things straight. "Ben leaned into me, and he genuinely smiled. There was this gleam in his eyes when he said, 'The Spirits seem to have sent me a birthday gift this year'."

A sharp ache speared through my chest, gripping it again, hard enough that I could faint. I couldn't breathe. Ben had called me his gift. A cruel gift by the Spirits who had done nothing but tear us apart as well as they could – *enemies – betrayals – jealousy.* My cheeks blushed thinking of Ben, remembering the moment Murben had spoken about. "Did Ben really say that?"

"Word for word. Then he found out that you were…"

He went quiet, so I looked over my shoulder after having stepped over a branch laying across the path. "I was what?"

Murben's lips were pinned in a straight hard, line. "A spy."

61

Murben had hesitated, rephrased himself. I stared at him with strong accusation. "That wasn't what you were going to say." I stepped over a stone that protruded in the middle of the hiking trail.

The wind howled through the treetops, rustling the leaves ominously.

"No, but it's just…he realised a relationship with you would be complicated. He tried to give you up. Forget about you. But after a year of fighting his own impulses, of fighting the urge to host extra balls just to see you, he knew he couldn't. So now, he's fighting through the complications instead." Murben's words pressed against me the same as the humid air.

I kept walking having lost focus on scanning my surrounding for dangers, knowing Murben had that covered. The towering trees could hide anyone as well as they swallowed the sunlight, but Murben would notice them. I wanted to keep my focus on the narrow bridleway before me, or anything but the conversation Murben was forcing me to have.

He didn't stop. "The problem is that you aren't allowed to see the demons he's battling to be with you. And because of the betrayals you've faced in your life, you don't trust what you can't see."

I stopped abruptly. "I don't know if you're right this time, Murben." I exhaled sharply, insecurity coiling tighter inside me. "I don't trust him for the things *I have* seen."

The wind stirred again, carrying the scent of pine and damp stone. Murben let a beat of silence pass before he spoke again. "Okay, think about this, then. If he only wanted to toy with you, why keep being this persistent? Why hasn't he used his trust magic to keep you at his side? He could have. But he doesn't. Because he wants you for real. You. Not some manipulated version of you."

I pushed my shoulder bag farther back and lifted my tangled hair from where it clung to my neck, the sweat making my skin feel stifling. "I believe his feelings are genuine," I admitted, voice tight. "It's his loyalty and commitment that I question."

Murben sighed, but there was no impatience in it, just a quiet understanding. "And he's working on those. Forgive him on this instance and give him time to prove himself."

I let out a bitter laugh. "Spirits!" I turned my head and snorted at him. "Have you opened that matchmaking business yet?"

Murben smirked, unfazed. "I care for my king." He nodded ahead, urging me forward. "Now watch where you're going."

I shook my head but didn't argue. "You're a good friend to Ben."

"I'm a good servant." His response was immediate.

I didn't correct him. The distinction between the two was blurred, and I wasn't sure which one he believed was more true.

The trees thinned as we reached the lake pool. The water stretched before us, smooth as glass, reflecting the storm-heavy sky. The stillness was a lie. Beneath that surface, currents churned, unseen.

Just like my thoughts.

I strode straight to the bank. Behind me, Murben let out a long-suffering groan and turned away, assuming I was about to undress. But it was also making it harder for him to guard me without looking, not knowing exactly where I was.

A humourless smile ghosted over my lips. At least some things were predictable. The perfect gentleman would rather risk a few seconds disadvantage if we were attacked than violate a lady. Maybe I was wrong. Maybe he cared more about keeping his head than keeping his honour if Ben found out he had been staring at my naked body – the king's girlfriend's body – if that was still what he believed I was.

Nesso flew overhead, and Murben whistled for his attention. A moment after, Nesso landed, smirking at me like he always did, and I could assume he hadn't been briefed about recent events.

He and Murben exchanged whispers, and Nesso's face dropped more and more, his eyes darting between mine and Murben's. Nesso twisted in his step and tore his fingers through his hair a lot of times, looking increasingly stressed.

Murben beckoned his hand at Nesso as if he wanted Nesso to give him something, but Nesso shook his head. Murben's face darkened, and he beckoned towards Nesso once more, his whole body tensing and seemingly becoming double in size.

Nesso shrugged back and muttered something I couldn't hear from where I was. If I had to guess, the words were probably curses. Nesso shoved his hand down into his shoulder bag and took out a rolled-up parchment, hitting it down onto Murben's palm before pointing a finger at him, clearly indicating that Murben's actions would be on him.

Nesso took off to the sky, and I'd hoped Murben would leave me alone, and go with him, but surprise, surprise, he stayed.

Murben came closer. Slowly. Not a confident stride but insecurely edging closer.

"If I let you exercise your lungs and tell me what's on your mind, can you leave me alone afterwards?" I asked.

"No. But I can agree to sit over there," he said, pointing at a boulder further away from the lake. "And I can be quiet if you stop running away from me."

My attention kept swaying to the parchment he held in his other hand. I nodded for it. "What is that? More secrets? Love letter? Spy orders?"

He held it up, looking at it, as if being in possession of it would cause him a lot of pain, but the decision was made that it was worth it.

"Technically, it's something I've stolen from my king. Which I don't think will go down well. And it's not a love letter to Nassara."

I crossed my arms and faced the lake. "So, you don't believe me when I said that the king was romantic with Nassara?"

"I believe you, but you saw things out of context, and he won't blame you for being angry."

"And what other context would you tell me to be the truth? Please, clarify a situation where Ben had taken his ring off and had his fingers interlaced with a duke's daughter, who he's betrothed to, walking among his subject on a joyous festival put on for his people and," I emphasised the 'and' as Murben was about to object, "which betrothal he told me he wanted to break off."

Murben held up his finger. "Firstly, thank you for not telling the king that I misspoke about that. I'm quite fond of my fingers…and my entire arm, frankly." He flipped up another finger. "Secondly…well, I will not tell the king what methods to use to deal with the women in his life." He flicked up another counting finger. "And thirdly, I do know that in all this, the only feeling that he has that is true, and the only thing in the world he's passionate about, is you." He held up the parchment. "Nesso told me the king has had this drawn up for you and was going to give it to you tonight after he had arranged a romantic dinner, but I don't think you're ready for that emotionally. I'll risk my life making the judgement that it's better if you hear it from me."

He held the parchment out towards me. I hesitated before gripping it and again before pulling it towards me. It had the royal double B wax seal intact, showing no one had read it. I inhaled a shaky breath, pulling the leather cord off, breaking the seal, and unfurling the paper.

"It's a deed," I commented, and Murben stood silently next to me as I read it. I frowned. "Ben has signed the ownership of Black Castle over to me?"

"Yes," Murben answered curtly.

I frowned. "Why?"

"Because his first choice to show you how serious he is about his love for you was to marry you, but since your oath forbids that, he has given you the thing that matters the most to him. His home."

A burning warmth shot through me and my heart felt too big for my chest. I saw Ben's neat handwriting at the bottom, approving the document as valid. This was more than a token of love. This was pure love – his home. He couldn't do this. No one should ever ask him to give his home away. I'd never accept it. My eyes were watering, but I held the tears back.

"He didn't think it had been easier just to tell Nassara that their betrothal was off? Then he need not gift me his whole world. Honestly, men are so stupid. I don't want a castle." I pointed at the boulder he had mentioned earlier. "Now, go and sit over there." I had to get him away from me before I broke. My pride still held too tight a grip around my heart to show mercy.

His shoulders sank, having lost the battle, and he sauntered away.

I shoved the parchment into the bag as I took out the sponge, soap and towel, wrapping the towel around me as I stripped off my clothes by the bank; all except a dagger that I brought with me.

The water was icy around my toes the moment I stepped down onto the pebbled bed, immediately shifting the attention away from whether Murben was watching my naked arse with my towel discarded behind me on the grass.

"At least could you stay in your own room tonight so you can talk to him?" Murben muttered from a distance behind me.

Ignoring him, I cussed to myself then, remembering that I could have used the bathroom in my brother's apartment to clean my wing as it was big enough. But I was already here and knee-deep in water, so I might as well get this over and done with.

One more step, my leg went in deeper, and the biting frigid water went above my knees. There wasn't a Spirit of Fire, or I'd have prayed to him right now. But I guessed there was always the Spirit of the Sea.

A gust of wind swept around my shoulders and the hair rose on my arms, running an icy chill down to my wrist. Still with the sponge, soap and dagger in hand, I hugged myself, but little did it do to protect against the cold. I strode further out; the ripples pushing out from my legs and my wings dragged across the surface, sinking deeper and deeper with their weight as they soaked, until the water level reached halfway up my thigh.

I pinned the dagger under the surface between my knees, soaped up the sponge, and tossed the soap onto the shore before I wrapped my hand around my shoulder, trying to reach the bloodstained spot on my wing, but my arm wasn't long enough. Frustrated, I sighed. As I stretched harder, my wing moved with my back as I twisted, and I was incapable of reaching the red feathers. With my left hand, I gripped the edge of my wing; my fingers pinching at the membrane to pull it closer, the grip agonising because the wings were so sensitive. Now, my right hand got closer to the wound, but my wing pushed down my arm to the point it was impossible to twist the sponge around in my hand to get a good angle to clean. *Dammit.*

It'd be degrading, but my only option was to ask Murben for help, and preferably before I turned into an icicle. Turning around, I startled, seeing Ben squatting at the bank, watching me. He looked even more enormous than normal with his wings out as a shield behind him and his broad shoulders squaring him in as he reached down to touch the water. His hair had been groomed for the festival and was wafting in the breeze, and his burning-red eyes studied me with interest.

I frowned, trying to look around him. "Where is Murben?" Then I turned around to have our conversation over my shoulder as I realised that I was naked.

"I sent him back to the outpost." His voice was level and calm.

I peered around my wing. "Do you mind? I'm naked here."

"I saw you naked no more than fifteen hours ago, and you're still as beautiful now."

"Don't try your charm on me. That was different. It's highly inappropriate to stare at a naked lady when you're betrothed to another. Please leave."

"Lady…hmm…" he mused. "Ladies aren't normally as lethal as you."

"Then let me remind you that it's even more inappropriate to look at a teammate from the same Special Missions Unit when she's naked. Inappropriate, and against the rules. Although, those rules don't apply to us anymore, as we're no longer a team, and you're to leave the White Wing Territory at once."

"The way you look like a puppy chasing its tail, I can't leave before offering my assistance. Please, let me help you clean the blood off your wing."

Not removing his black uniform or boots, he retracted his wings to the inside of his back, and lowered his legs into the water, pushing forwards to get to me. He crossed the short distance between us so fast I didn't have time to think or object.

With my free left hand, I gripped the hilt of the dagger that was clenched between my knees below the surface and shoved it up against Ben's pectoral by his heart. "Do not come closer!"

He looked surprised that I was armed but quickly found his smirk. "Our normal dance. And you do like to lead," he chuckled. "So, you vow not to stab me with black blades, and then you pull a normal one at me instead?" He kept an eye on me and the blade, as he slowly reached for the sponge in my right hand. His movement and shallow breathing reminded me of the first time I held the Black Blade sword against his heart.

I let go of the sponge as he tugged at it, but didn't lower the dagger. He moved around the blade and gently gripped over the edge of the wing. Slowly, he caressed the sponge against the outside of my plumes. Carefully, he stroked downwards along the feathers in the same direction they grew, and I don't know if I imagined his heart was racing as much as mine did with the tension. The sensual strokes travelled higher up as he cleaned off the blood and he made a subtle move to rinse the blood off the sponge in the lake before continuing.

It was so serene as we both stood in the water with the pool rippling against the shore and around the base of the mountain below the cave opening. The same cave where General Denor had held me captive throughout December. The treetops pulled to the east in the wind with a swooshing sound and the sky was grey but not hinting at rain.

This was so confusing. The way Ben had come here and clearly cared for me, risking his life to come close. His eyes told me he was in an emotional place of needing me. He craved my forgiveness and closeness. He was here. Caring for me. *'He tried to give you up. Forget about you. But he couldn't, so he is fighting for you instead.'* Murben's words called through my head.

After a while, Ben folded my wing around and took a step closer to me so that he got a good angle to clean the inside, starting with the lowest bloodstained feather furthest away from the wound. When he had worked the sponge higher, he was extra gentle around the wound, and not once did his eyes stray to look at my naked breasts, even when I had seen the bulge that had grown inside his trousers. Washing the inside of my wing was even more intimate than the outside, and his closeness made my sex tighten involuntarily. *Damn you, sexy man!*

We had been quiet for a long while, only listening to each other's breathing, the tension so palpable that both of us would flinch at the smallest of sounds.

I had no doubt he was keeping an eye on me in his peripheral view but made no move to gain eye-contact. I wanted to moan at the touch of his warm hands. They were so strong yet careful and comforting when he had them on my body and my wings were especially sensitive to his touch, feeling every punctuation of his fingertips.

"I wish that you'd tell me if you leave the premises of the outpost," he whispered eventually.

"Why? So, you can lock me up in our room like you did in Black Castle?" I muttered lowly.

"No," he shook his head and rinsed the sponge in the water again, which had turned from white to red. "So, I can come with you to protect you. It was wrong of me to keep you hidden in my room at the festival. You're right. I should have shown you to the world and died defending you if need be, but the fear of losing you got the better of me. I'll do it differently next time I take you to my castle."

"You mean, my castle?" I teased, trying to hide a subtle smile.

"Yes. True." He glanced over me quickly with an amused smile on his lips. "Your castle."

"You won't punish Murben for giving me the document, will you?"

"Thieves lose their arms. That is the law in the Black Wing Territory."

"We're not in the Black Wing Territory, and if Murben misses an arm, he won't be able to please my best friend as well."

"Murben knew the consequences of stealing from me, and what I always must do to keep my reputation of being a powerful king. He knows I always follow through with the punishments."

"If you harm Murben like that because he tried to help us make up, I'll definitely never speak to you again."

"I give you a castle and you're ruling my kingdom like a queen already," he said, and grinned. "You're just full of mischief."

"You know I'll burn the document. I don't want your castle. Why would you give it away? You love that castle."

He snorted. "No. I've only ever loved two things in this world. The other was my mother."

There was a hard blow to my heart as I thought about Ben having lost his mother when she had been in a battle a decade ago. No one should be that young and lose their mother. No one should have to find out that their mother has betrayed an entire nation when she is fifteen, either. "And the other?" I asked.

He stopped stroking my wing and tipped his head down to look at me as if I had asked something that was obvious. "You." He cupped the back of my neck and stroked his thumb down the side of my throat. My nerve-endings flared with a passion so deeply addictive I couldn't see how I could stop him if he continued touching me.

He stroked his hand up my neck, so his thumb reached my lip and he pushed it gently across it, looking at my mouth. He swallowed hard and frowned. What was that in his eyes? Wanting? Longing? Need? Maybe it was even restraint.

Secrets. Betrayals. Lies. The words kept spinning. Enemy. That word cut the deepest. I wasn't ready to forgive him, not for the wounds he had carved into me, and not for the trust he had shattered.

And yet…I ached for his touch.

It was maddening, the way my body betrayed me while my heart screamed in protest. My skin purred at the warmth of his hand, making me forget the icy waters that lapped around me. I was drowning in the contradiction. Desire or fury.

If neither of us could walk away, this would only end in regret. In ruin.

I forced my legs to move even when my knees were numb from the cold. The pebbled lakebed bit into my feet as I stepped away from him. I needed to get away from the temptation that was him. Every step backwards felt like tearing away a piece of myself, like breaking a puzzle that would never be built again. Pieces lost. Edges damaged.

"Thank you for helping to clean my wing. I must get back to complete the archery challenge."

The moment the words left my lips, I saw the way his expression shattered. The fire in his eyes dulled.

The last part of the puzzle fractured at the sight. But it was his turn to pick up the broken pieces, if he still wanted them. If he thought it was worth his time to piece them back together.

I didn't have the strength to do it anymore.

I turned before the torment in him would make me yield. Because every muscle in my body screamed at me to stop and to stay. They whispered to me to let him close the distance between us, and to let his arms wrap around me the way they had before.

But I couldn't.

I wouldn't.

The rocky shore felt unsteady beneath my feet, or maybe it was just me being shaken, all emotions jumbled up. The cold air bit at my damp skin, but it was nothing compared to the feel of ice frosting over my ribs.

Why did he still have this power over me?

After everything, after the betrayals, the half-truths, the wounds that still bled internally, why did a single look from him make me feel as if the world was tilting beneath my feet? I hated him for it. *But even more, I hated myself for it.*

The water behind me rippled as he took a step forward. *Too close. Too dangerous.*

I quickened my pace to climb onto the bank, forcing my legs to keep moving. Each step away from him felt like pressing on a fresh bruise. I had to go. If I turned back now, I'd lose my own battle.

I reached for my flight leathers and my boots, pulling them on with hands that barely felt like my own. My wings ached and felt stiff from the wound, but I forced them to fold neatly behind me as I straightened. I wouldn't let him see my weakness. Not in this moment. Right now, I was an agent at work. A soldier. Cadet Coraly.

I steeled myself because I was determined to leave my thoughts unsaid. Then I walked away, leaving behind the only person who had ever made me feel like I had a purpose in this world.

62

The wind was a relentless force across the archery field. It had already wiped out most of my competitors over the past three hours. I thanked the Spirit of the World that the wind had worked in my favour. While others struggled to keep their shots straight, I had spent years training in conditions just like this.

Camp Leader Nar stood at the target board, arms crossed, scrutinising the arrows lodged into the bullseye. The silence stretched as she assessed the final shots, but even from here, I could tell it was too close to call between Ashton and me.

She turned and walked back to us. "We'll conduct a sudden-death final."

A murmur rippled through the onlooking cadets. I barely heard it. My gaze flicked over the crowd, searching. Where was Ben? Of all the times to vanish, I thought he'd at least be here to watch me fight for a win.

Zoe's hand slapped against my back. "I knew you could do it. Just you against Cadet Hall now."

No surprise there. Emroyce hadn't named Ashton's team the Archery Team for nothing.

From the bow rack, Brian smirked. "Pressure's on, Angie. Winter and I won it two years ago."

I didn't hesitate to jump at the banter. "Yeah? And you had to be two people to manage a win. I'm winning this all on my own."

Emroyce whistled at the sharp comeback.

Ashton stepped up beside me, his long, black hair tied back like mine to keep it from messing with his aim. "Go easy on her, Brian," he said with a teasing lilt. "She's up against me."

I rolled my eyes. "You're not gonna possess me, are you?"

The last thing I needed was his magic trying to hijack my body mid-shot. If he did, he'd have to suit himself for enduring the throbbing pain in my wing that was even worse when nestled tightly into my back.

Ashton chuckled. "No. Not after what happened in the last challenge. Didn't exactly enjoy the searing pain of getting stabbed in the leg. And knowing you, you'd probably drive the arrow straight into my gut this time."

"Damn right, I would." I twirled an arrow between my fingers.

His laughter faded the next moment, and his blue eyes softened with something I couldn't quite name. "I don't like people getting hurt. Not even black-wings."

The honesty in his voice was unmistakable. Hall was the kind of person who helped others without expecting anything in return. Always fair. Always amiable. And here I was, fully prepared to beat him without hesitation.

I almost felt bad. Almost.

But I wasn't here to lose.

"So, you're giving the win away then," I extended the banter.

I put the quiver strap around my head, as I wore mine on my back. Not like Ashton who used a leg quiver that was strapped around his waist and thigh so that his arrows were at his side for quicker reach. I needed to get me one of those.

"I was born with a bow and arrow in my hands," he retaliated playfully.

"Your poor mother. No wonder you're an only child," Brian retorted.

We all laughed, and Zoe handed me one of the newer looking bows from the bow rack with a tight string that I approved of.

Emroyce, who stood next to Brian, leaned over him and put a hand on his shoulder. "I was born with my cock in my hand as I had to hold it up. It's that heavy."

"Emroyce!" Zoe, Kate and I shouted in unison, but then we all laughed.

"I had to tie mine to my stomach with the umbilical cord, so I could get out of my mother," Mazdon said with a hidden smile on his face.

The women gasped, and there was a brief silence. "Maz!" Kate blared, but she was lost for words at her brother's uncharacteristic claim.

The hysterical laughter that followed brought tears to my eyes. "How am I going to aim now?" I dried them off. "I'm going to have to depend on the wind that the Spirit of the World has generously sent me."

"I shoot well even in the hurricane seasons we get in Abarnack," Ashton countered.

Abarnack was a smaller village north of Abarath, and I had heard of their storms, which were said to be the worst in the White Wing Territory. Gone was that advantage.

"Focus, boy," his father said sharply and pointed for Camp Leader Nar, who prepared for the final, cornering the area off so the spectators wouldn't stand too close; both for their protection and to allow us to concentrate.

I twisted around, looking for Ben, but I couldn't see him anywhere. It was strange that he wasn't here to support me during a challenge, no matter what we had argued about.

"He isn't here!" Zoe barked at me. "Focus on your challenge."

"Where is he?"

"You told him to stay away from you, so he's staying away from you."

"Okay, but where is he staying away from me?"

"Murben and Davis are distracting him and probably keeping him away against his will."

I doubted that. But I got the point.

"Murben and Davis? Isn't that weird?"

"Zero weirdness, honey. Davis and I have really found the sibling bond between us. We're alike in so many ways. We can work together and make a hearing portal all the way to the Ivory Castle to spy on King Emille. It's super cool. Not that your brother has asked us to spy on King Emille, of course."

"Two of you? Spirits. Is the world really ready for that?"

"Very funny." Zoe spat, glowering at me. "Focus on your challenge."

"You've become a real sourpuss after Harvey assigned you to chaperone me."

Harvey had assigned Zoe the special mission of chaperoning me, which I had thought would be futile considering she was my best friend, and she was sleeping with a black-wing, but she was no turncoat, carrying out her duty as instructed.

"I don't find my duty peachy at the moment either, honey."

"Has it come between you and Murben?"

"No. The strain has made us more hot for one another. He's an animal in the sack."

"Next time, remind me I need to be more specific when asking my question. That was not an answer I wanted to hear."

"You asked if you had come between us, but the only thing between us is his twenty centimetre–"

I called out a long tune to drown out her words. "Oversharing, Zoe!"

"Cadet Coraly! Cadet Hall! Get into position!" Camp Leader Nar shouted, and I thanked the Spirit of Luck for the perfect timing.

"Wait!" Zoe pulled the leather band off her short violet hair and quickly braided my ponytail down my back. "May the Spirit of Luck be with you!"

"Luck?"

"You know what I mean. Thrash him!"

I stepped forward to where Camp Leader Nar stood beside Ashton, her expression as rigid as the iron plating strapped over her navy-blue uniform.

She barely spared me a glance. Typical.

Nar made no secret of her disdain for me, and I didn't expect that to change anytime soon. My connection to Ben and General Denor had sealed my fate in her eyes from the beginning of the year.

She was a woman built for war, not diplomacy. Her body was lean and sharp as a drawn blade, her long ebony hair flowing with her wind magic around her shoulders. She had the raw but beautiful appeal about her, fitting equally well in battle gear as a ball gown without looking misplaced. I didn't know about the rest of her body, but her face showed no scars, only rosy cheeks on smooth skin. Rumour had it she had once single-handedly cut through an entire battalion like a scythe through wheat.

Now, she spent her days split between the war in the north and training cadets like me, though she made it clear who were worth her time when she was at the outpost. I was not among them.

Her armoured hand rested on the pommel of her sword as she rattled off the competition rules so fast it was nearly impossible to catch every word. Not that it mattered. I knew them by heart.

When she finished, she waved a dismissive hand. "Ladies first!" Her tone made it sound like a punishment, like she couldn't wait to see me fail.

Then, without another word, she pointed to the white-painted mark on the grass, signalling me to step up.

I needed to cheat the wind and place my arrow in the dead centre of the bullseye to beat Ashton. Because he wouldn't miss.

Before I anchored the arrow, I took a last look around but couldn't see Ben. Fine. I could do this on my own, and I'd never admit to him that I missed the ability to communicate with him through the soul bond.

The grey sky loomed eerily above, portraying perfectly how I felt inside without Ben by my side. Like the wind across the field that found nothing to grasp at but emptiness. Where was he? He should be here watching me, giving me support and advice. Another gust of wind tugged at my bow, its icy fingers clawing at my arms, daring me to falter.

I shook my head, forcing the doubt away. This wouldn't be an easy shot. *But when is life ever easy?* My heartbeat drummed against my ribs, reminding me that hesitation was my enemy.

I sucked in a deep breath so hard the cold air burned my lungs. My fingers curled around the bowstring by memory before my muscles tensed. I placed the arrow against the string, feeling at least in control of the shot when the world often denied me any otherwise. One deep breath. One steady pull.

I narrowed my eyes. Four seconds passed as I listened to the wind's rhythm until I heard its familiar song. Then, I released.

The arrow sliced through the air like a whisper of movement against the brutal wind. For a heartbeat, I didn't breathe.

Until–

A solid, resounding thud.

Dead centre.

An electric surge of triumph pulsed through me. The wind had fought me, the sky had loomed over me, but I had beat them both.

I breathed out and moved to the side, knowing a cocky smile was premature.

All my friends gave me a thumbs up from where they were leaning against the bow rack to watch.

Ashton stepped onto to the painted mark and looked towards the treetops, assessing the wind with quiet calculation. Not a flicker of hesitation. Not a breath of uncertainty. Then, in a flash of motion, he drew and released his arrow so seamlessly it was like watching a river flow. It was so natural and effortless. The bowstring barely had time to quiver before the arrow was loose in a matter of a second.

A thump echoed across the field louder than mine had.

The crowd erupted in cheers.

His arrow had landed exactly where mine had.

"Tie!" Camp Leader Nar's voice rang out, cutting through the commotion.

She strode across the field to the target board, ripping the arrow free like it had offended her. Maybe it was mocking her because I hadn't suffered a humiliating loss, because it hadn't beaten mine. But it couldn't. Mine had been in the dead centre.

A tie. Not bad. Not good. At least it kept me in the running, still within reach of the 'any gift' prize.

Efficiently, she replaced the punctured paper with a fresh target before returning and flicking a hand toward me.

My turn.

I inhaled a deep breath and let it out slowly through my nose. Patience. Focus. I couldn't risk the competition by rushing my next shot. My skills weren't as honed as Ashton's. I needed control, not speed.

As I passed him, Ashton leaned ever so slightly toward me, his voice barely a whisper over his shoulder. "It's getting more humid by the second from the gathering rain clouds. Aim higher with the next arrow."

I froze for half a second. A trick? A distraction? My instincts screamed to be wary, but as I inhaled again, I noticed it. The air was heavier. Thicker. The moisture clung to me like an enemy trying to restrain my efforts. He hadn't been lying.

But why has he helped me?

To aim was harder this time. There were so many conditions to factor in. I had to lower the bow without taking the shot, as acid was building up in my muscles. I breathed a few times and brought the bow up again, resting my thumb over my cheek and closed both eyes to feel the Spirits as they wielded the wind and water around me. Then I opened one eye, swiped my bow up a bit higher, and took the shot.

Bullseye!

Ashton went to the mark and took his shot so fast, I had almost not finished breathing the same breath. His arrow cleaved mine, and it was a tie once more.

Ashton stood himself next to me as Camp Leader Nar walked out on the track to swap the target.

"I enjoy games with a worthy opponent. But I think you'll win," he said with a wink.

What? What in the world did that mean?

Before I had a chance to ask him, Camp Leader Nar called my name impatiently. On the mark, Ashton's wink played in my mind. The wind pushed me a step to the left, and I lost balance, having to right myself on the mark to start again. The weather was angrier by the minute and the rain threatened to come down at any moment. This would have to be a fast shot, or I'd start doubting myself. In one swoop, I brought the arrow out of the quiver, tightened it over the string, and aimed for only three seconds before I released the grip over the feathered end of the shaft.

The wind must have caught the arrow at the last second because it didn't hit the centre of the bullseye. *Damn!* Ashton wouldn't miss his shot. No one would see me being a sore loser, though, so I moved aside and stood with my back straight.

Ashton glanced at his father for one second before he focused on the target. He got an arrow out of the quiver by his leg and anchored it slowly.

What was he thinking? He could take this shot so easily but he was hesitating. What was he waiting for?

Drops fell onto my forehead. Rain. Was Ashton waiting for the rain to hit? *Why? To show off?*

Ashton raised his bow with a steady grip, his eyes locked onto the target. But something was off. I could see that his aim was too high by a few millimetres. A fraction of a miscalculation, but enough to cost him the victory.

He hesitated. Lowered his bow slightly. For a second, I thought he'd caught the mistake.

Then, with his normal fluid sweep, he lifted the bow again to nock the arrow back and released the bowstring.

The arrow lodged into the board just above mine.

What?

With both arrows too close to the centre to call from this distance, I already knew he had thrown the game. My pulse quickened, a storm of confusion brewing inside me, mirroring the downpour that now drenched the field.

Camp Leader Nar, her armour slick with rain, jogged toward the target board. The dagger flashed in her hand as she measured the difference. When she turned back, finding me with her piercing eyes, her voice rang clear through the storm.

"Cadet Coraly wins!"

I barely registered the words before Zoe and the others tackled me, their cheers ringing in my ears. Ashton patted me on the shoulder, a small, knowing smile playing at his lips.

But I stood there, motionless. Stunned.

He had lost on purpose.

Why?

The rain poured harder, sending cadets rushing for cover, but I barely noticed.

Nothing made sense.

Was it a plot to make more cadets hate me, to eliminate the harder competition? No, not Ashton. I couldn't imagine his kindness only being a façade. Thoughts tumbled over each other in my mind. I couldn't work out what this meant. Not alone. I needed someone to brainstorm with. Could I admit the truth to myself or was my pride still a thick wall around my heart. Because all I wanted to do was talk to Ben. He was intelligent and could help me make sense of all of this.

And then, as if the storm outside had cracked something open inside me, I understood.

Now I knew what Ben had meant when he said he only felt like half a person when our souls weren't bound.

The thought sent a tremor through me. Would I dare to finally let down the thick wall around my heart and admit to myself that I missed him? That I was running from the best thing that had ever happened to me. Not because of anything he had done, but because of my own fear.

Because deep down, I was terrified he would betray me the way my mother had.

The harsh truth settled on my chest like a bag of rocks.

It wasn't Ben ruining this.

It was me.

For twenty-two long days, I did everything in my power to avoid Ben.

In combat training, I paired up with Kate, keeping my movements swift and my focus sharp. In classes, I sat beside Emroyce, who seemed to sense my need for a barrier. He didn't ask questions, simply made sure Ben never had a chance to sit next to me.

The closest thing to a confrontation was before me now – Zayd. He had tried to intercept me on the west route before I crossed into Black Wing Territory. I was ready for a fight, and to unleash every ounce of anger I felt for his betrayal.

"Explain," I had demanded.

Zayd sighed, shaking his head. "I wasn't stopping you. I was making sure you weren't being forced. You think I'd let you be taken against your will?"

I searched his face, looking for lies, but there were none. He had even taken our most trusted friends with him on patrol to keep it quiet. No one else knew. Not Harvey and not leadership. I had misjudged him.

After that, I spent more time with Zayd, throwing myself into the obstacle course. We pushed each other to train harder and to go faster, but neither of us could break Ben's record.

At night, I retreated to my childhood bedroom, which Harvey had somehow restored to look exactly like it had before he had sent me on my two-year mission.

Zoe, ever the guardian, ensured we sat with white-wings in the canteen and kept a strict watch so Ben wouldn't approach me. If he got too close, one warning glance from her was enough to make him step back.

He still stayed in the background and was always watching me. There were moments when I almost forgot he was there, until I caught his gaze from across the training grounds.

But today I realised I hadn't seen him for days.

Had he finally given up? Had he left for Black Wing Territory for good?

That uncertainty gnawed at me more and more with each passing day. I hadn't told Harvey about the broken bond. Ben could be anywhere he wanted as he was completely undetectable.

Considering we were approaching the day of the climbing challenge, I worried that we hadn't practised at all together. To keep us both alive, I'd better find him and discuss whether we should change teammates or come to some arrangement and truce.

I went to the sparring hall but found it empty. Ben wasn't in our dorm room, either. Nor in the canteen where most cadets were having their lunch. Ben had a free period as we had War Updates in the assembly straight after, so I didn't expect him to be close by.

It dawned on me that I was better off focusing on my own agenda.

Harvey was going to talk to the assembly about the reinforcements needed in the Abarath Outpost, which he should have visited this month but had postponed until a few days after the summer break, as he was forcing me to accompany him. Forced or not, finally, I'd get some excitement away from the outpost and a glimpse of what was up north.

The library was nearly silent, save for the occasional scratch of a quill or the rustling of parchment. The room smelled of ancient books and candle wax, which were comforting scents that usually put me at ease. But today, tension raked at my heart like nails scraping down a chalkboard.

After studying climbing techniques in Zayd's class, I had decided to visit the library to pick up a few books. Instead, I found Mazdon sitting alone at one of the study tables. No books were spread before him. No notes. Just him, sitting completely still with his head slightly tilted, as if listening to something only he could hear.

I approached cautiously. "Hey, Maz. What are you doing?"

"Shush!" He barely acknowledged me, his brow furrowing in concentration on his pale face, looking olive green from magic exertion. "I'm listening. Zayd just got back from a counsel meeting in the capital. He's in Harvey's office."

Another counsel meeting? My stomach churned. "That's the third one this month," I murmured. "Something's happening, isn't it?"

Mazdon's lips pressed together. "Something is stirring in the capital. And Zayd is about to deliver the king's answer."

I watched Mazdon as he exhaled sharply and shook his head. "Damn magic. Harvey must have Christopher Charney in there. He's blocking me out. I can't hear a thing. Just muffled voices, like they're speaking under water."

Secrets then. "What did Zayd ask of the king?"

Mazdon's gaze flickered to me. "It wasn't Zayd. It was Ben."

My breath hitched. "Ben?"

He nodded. "Ben wanted to negotiate with King Emille, offering soldiers in exchange for Kristine Bostee."

I frowned. "Bostee? The woman with ward magic who can charge the light crystals? Why?" It didn't make sense.

"That's what I'm trying to figure out." Mazdon's voice dropped lower, as if he couldn't speak and listen at the same time. "After her teammate Tony Wix died, King Emille demanded she serve in the castle. Harvey's furious about it."

"Why would my brother be furious about that?"

Mazdon shook his head. "No idea. But Harvey's being careful. He won't say much unless Charney is around. I'd bet my best boots they have him waiting out in the corridor right now."

If Charney was there, blocking magic, there was little Maz could do to eavesdrop on leadership's secrets. This was my cue. I pressed both hands against the table, my pulse quickening. "Can you help me with something?"

Mazdon blinked, severing his focus like a snapped thread of magic. His strawberry-blonde hair bounced slightly as he turned his big-brotherly attention to me. "Sure. What's up, Angie?"

I hesitated, but only for a second. "I can't find Ben. Can you hear where he is?"

Mazdon closed his soft, green eyes and his head jerked one way and then the other, as he searched through the voices. Abruptly, he opened his eyes and looked at me. "He's in Tomason's apartment."

"Oh." The image of the golden beauty appeared in my head.

Jealousy twisted my gut. They'd be a good match. Tomason was battle hardened from growing up in the Candir Outpost where her father was the captain. That woman took bullshit from no one. Ben had spoken to her on many occasions and never told me about it. *Hiding it. Secrets. Betrayals.* The words echoed in my mind.

My stomach twisted with something sharp and ugly.

Mazdon shifted beside me. "Perhaps he needed some advice from the Camp Leader?"

I scoffed, wrenching my fingers in front of me. "The General Operations Infantry Unit camp leader?" I arched a brow, daring him to justify it.

"I'm sure that there is a reasonable explanation."

"Yeah, I bet." My hand reflexively went to the hilt of my dagger, the cool iron grounding me.

Mazdon exhaled, rubbing the back of his neck. "Angie, from what I've heard of him…he seems to be a good man. You're being too hard on him."

My head snapped toward him. "I'm being hard on him?" A bitter laugh escaped my lips. "He's the one who–" I cut myself off, shaking my head. "You know what? I don't have time for this. We have War Update in five minutes. Are you coming?"

Mazdon hesitated before nodding toward the hall. "I'll be there soon. I'm going to keep listening to your brother's conversation."

I strode through the corridors, passing through the building's main doors, and entered the inner courtyard to head toward the east wing and the assembly hall. My mind churned with the suspicion that something wasn't right.

Just as I reached the entrance, a strong hand grabbed my arm and yanked me aside. My back hit the stone wall.

Ben.

His red eyes, darker than I remembered, searching mine with an urgency that was frightening.

"Please, Angelica," he murmured. "Can we talk? I know I should keep my distance, but…I miss you. Terribly."

My heart bled at his plea but also for my own agony. "What is there to talk about?" My voice was colder than I felt. "I know you just came from Camp Leader Tomason's apartment. Do you want to talk about that?"

Ben frowned, his grip loosening slightly. "You're spying on me?"

I laughed, but there was no humour in it. "Are you really in a position to ask that?" I glanced at the door to the assembly hall, which I didn't want my brother to close before I was on the other side. "No. I wasn't spying. Stupidly, I was looking for you. We haven't spoken since I won the archery challenge for us, and you weren't there."

I didn't struggle to get out of his hold. It was as if my body marvelled at his touch like an energy source.

"You were looking for me?" A smile rose on his lips.

"But you seem to chase after anything with breasts. Kristine Bostee, Darling, Nassara, Camp Leader Tomason, me…" *Banessa*! "Are you a collector of women for a specific purpose?"

Ben's gaze burned into me, intense but frail. "Of sorts," he murmured, his voice barely above a whisper. "You're the woman I collect to complete my heart. To make me happy. Though right now, you're making me suffer."

I narrowed my eyes at him, snorting. "I have to go to War Update." I folded my arms across my chest like an extra shield to the one I put up mentally.

"Agree to come with me to a restaurant tonight," he said, stepping closer, "and I'll tell you a few of my secrets."

I gave the proposal some thought. Was he really that desperate to bridge the gap between us? So desperate that he'd trade his secrets. The secrets Murben had warned him not to share solely to get me back? It really didn't look like he could stand being apart. The thought sent a thrill through me, but I shoved it down. I couldn't let him see how much I ached for him. It had been over three weeks since I'd touched him, kissed him, felt his warmth against my body. And damn it, I missed him. But he couldn't know that. He couldn't know what kind of hold he still had on my heart.

"It's raining heavily," I said, deflecting an answer.

Ben tilted his head slightly, considering it. "Is it raining?" A slow, knowing smile tugged at his lips. "I hadn't noticed. My heart burns for you as hot as the sun."

I glared at him, fighting the involuntary warmth that bloomed from my heart and spread to the rest of my body. "Now you're being more cheesy than even Emroyce."

He chuckled, unfazed. "Fine. Have dinner with me in our room?"

Before I could answer, a sharp voice cut through the moment.

"King Blackbone–"

Murben.

Ben turned to face him, jaw tightening. "Not now!"

Murben ignored his king's warning. "I can certainly see my news doesn't come at an ideal moment, but its nature is a matter of urgency."

"What is it?" Ben roared, turning around, the impatience frightening me even when I wasn't the one in the crossfire.

"Duke Finningham has retreated his troops from the north."

"Damn!" Ben's eyes became vacant, as if he was thinking hard about a strategic next move.

I pulled away from Ben, fearing I'd be late for the assembly. "I'll leave you two to talk about all your dark little secrets."

"No! Can you stop running away from me for one second, so I can think? You take priority. I'd rather let Dorondmir burn to the ground before I let you go. I'd rather burn. So, what do I care if the world burns with me?" He put his palm over my chest, guiding me two steps backwards to stand with my back against the wall again as he turned to Murben, and I guessed that holding his hand on my chest comforted him. "We need to inform Lord Malinger to evacuate Dorondmir."

Murben looked at me nervously as I frowned. "Why would you need to evacuate your own city if Duke Finningham has retreated?" I asked.

Murben glanced at Ben sharing an understanding, as if Ben had said too much in front of me.

"Actually, I don't care." I slapped his hand away and headed for the assembly hall doors.

Ben swished by me and caught my hand, dragging me inside the assembly hall, but instead of turning right to climb the steps to the staggered seating, he strode up onto the lecture podium. The noise in the hall died instantly. "I'm sorry, I have to do this because I don't know if I need to leave Bensguard momentarily." He bent over me, hungrily devouring my mouth in front of everyone.

The fear in my stomach burned as fiercely as the igniting lust. The rules forbade the display Ben had put on, and it was punishable by five lashes each. He broke the kiss when Harvey and Zayd walked in.

Ben kept staring at me as if we were the only two people in the room. "That was my 'any gift' that you won us in the archery challenge. You can tell Watson what gift you want, but no kissing, though."

Ben let go of me to walk towards Harvey and Zayd. "The 'any gift'," he barked at them both before he turned to point at me as Harvey led him away. "I love you!"

Then they were gone. What had just happened?

Zayd escorted me away from the podium to seat me in the front row before he took to the stage again. He began talking about the war updates and the development in the north, saying that leadership had sent more soldiers from our outpost to the Abarath Outpost because of the frequent attacks. I didn't understand how that could be. Duke Finningham had retreated his forces. Or had he simply moved them east to attack the white-wings?

Captain La Roy had released his report on the soldiers he had sent north. Camp Leader Nar had already left with ten units of her Air Force soldiers and Camp Leader Ward with five hundred cavalry soldiers and horses. Camp Leader Tomason was leaving today with three thousand infantry soldiers. Harvey had sent two hundred soldiers from the Special Missions Unit.

When I got out of War Updates, I was more confused than when I had entered. Murben was waiting for me in the hallway. "I want to kill your brother!" he said darkly, with no hint of it being a joke. "He has sent Zoe north again, and he has punished King Blackbone to an isolation cell for five hours after beating him up."

63

Every other second was punctuated by the hammering thunder outside. Inside the sparring hall, I hurled my daggers at the target board, but not impressively as my focus constantly drifted to the relentless downpour on the other side of the window.

Davis stood a few metres away from me, throwing his own daggers, his silence more ominous than the storm outside. He'd only spoken once since arriving.

But he was clearly about to. "I can't believe your brother sent my sister to the heart of the war." His voice was edged with restrained anger.

I couldn't tell if he was here to burn off frustration or if he was guarding me. Maybe both.

Then, finally, Murben appeared in the doorway. Relief should have flooded me, but his expression killed that hope instantly.

"Harvey has released King Blackbone," he said. "He's in your room. He's waiting for you…with dinner," Murben said and attempted a smile that didn't touch his eyes.

My heart suddenly raced as if I was going on a first date. Excitement? Dread? Both tangled together so tightly I couldn't tell them apart.

Murben walked me to the door, then stopped short. "Please behave, Cadet Coraly." Then, as if the tension in the corridor was loaded with awkward emotions he didn't want to face, he disappeared down the hall.

I raised my fist. Hesitated. Then knocked. Every second I waited made me incredibly nervous. I wrung my fingers and focused on steadying my breathing.

The door swung open, and the scent of masculine cologne made me inhale a deep breath.

Ben stood before me, dressed in a deep purple shirt embroidered with gold that was regal against his black trousers. His dark hair was slicked back, shining with oil. He looked like a king, if ignoring all the bruises.

My heart lurched at seeing his black-eye.

I barely registered stepping inside as he opened the door wider. He moved too stiffly, the kind of movement warped from pain. Lashes splitting the flesh on his back, kind of stiff.

"Ben…" I stopped in the doorway. "What happened to you? You used the 'any gift' to be cleared from this."

Ben didn't answer at first, having his eyes on the door as he closed it behind me, not wanting me to pity his pain. "It cleared my own lashes but not…" His voice drifted off.

"But not mine?"

"No."

The way he held himself, despite the pain, evidenced he had been lashed before and knew how to live with it. This was nothing new to him, but Spirits, did I want to kill my brother for doing this to him.

"And this?" I gently stroked my thumb below the blackened skin of his eye.

"Your brother doesn't like that I treat you to cake," he finally muttered.

"He gave you a black-eye because you offered me cake?"

"Never mind. At least he didn't keep any demons in the isolation cell. The demons like it pitch dark, so I worried I wouldn't be alone. But don't worry about me now. Come inside."

The room looked so romantic with the roses growing on vines along the walls and the roughly fifty candles he had lit around the room. In the centre, between the beds, there was a round table. He had covered it with a white tablecloth and set dishes for two people and a vase with a single red rose in the middle.

Ben put his palm on the small of my back and pushed me forward. "Please, sit down."

On the plates lay a steak, fries, peppered sauce, and a mix of vegetables and the wine glass was half topped up with red wine.

I lowered onto the seat. "You've really made an effort tonight. It's even more admirable when considering your condition. What are you aiming for here?"

"I have no ulterior motive, but it would be nice to get my soul back."

I rolled my eyes. No small order. He hadn't asked me again how I had removed the connection, which I was thankful for. He only wanted it connected once more. Romantic. I'd give him a point for that.

"Please, start, before it gets cold," Ben said, as he cut his meat.

I cut off a piece of the steak and dipped it in the sauce before bringing it into my mouth and moaned at the perfect flavour. "This is really nice."

"Thank you." His soft and almost boyish smile caught me off guard.

It was the kind of smile that didn't belong to a man feared across battlefields. It wasn't made by a king whose name alone sent shivers through his enemies. Yet, he gave this smile to me. A glimpse of a man no one else in the world would ever see but me.

I glanced around the room before my eyes landed on the plate of food. "You…made this?"

Ben tilted his head to look at it too, and amusement flickered across his face. "No." He smirked. "I made the servants make it."

I cringed, feeling the tension still trapped in my lungs. "They're not servants. They're workers."

He blinked, then exhaled, seeming to feel the same tension as I. "Oh, right. Sorry," he apologised, toning down his arrogance.

It was a short moment of submissiveness, but it reminded me he wasn't purely the ruthless king people feared. He was still *learning* how to be something else – Ben.

An awkward silence stretched between us as we ate, and I listened to the clinking of our cutlery against the porcelain. I shifted in my chair, trying to think of a new topic.

"The eighth challenge next week is climbing. Will you show up for that?"

It wasn't just casual conversation. It was a pointed jab. A low blow, maybe, but I couldn't help myself. He hadn't been there for the seventh challenge.

Ben's hand twitched slightly as he placed a serviette in his lap, his fingers smoothing over the fabric with unnecessary care. "Yes. Of course," he said a little too eagerly. "I only gave you space for the archery challenge because of our…you know…the situation."

I arched a brow. "It still surprised me not to see you there. Or Murben, for that matter."

His gaze flickered. "It was Murben's birthday. I gave him the rest of the day off."

I blinked. "It was Murben's birthday?" He didn't say anything more about it, so I pushed on. "How old is he?"

"Thirty-five."

I almost choked on my bite of food. Thirty-five? He didn't look thirty-five. That was a *huge* age gap between him and Zoe, but it wasn't my place to judge. Still…

"So, are we throwing him a birthday party?" I asked, watching his reaction closely.

Ben's expression tightened before he answered. "No." The word was curt and final.

I leaned forward, resting my forearms on the table. "He doesn't get a party?"

"No," he repeated, firmer this time.

I frowned. "So, what *do* we do for him?"

"I gave him the day off."

I scoffed. "Seriously? You're not giving him a gift? Not even a cake?"

His gaze narrowed at me. "I reiterate. I gave him the day off."

I stared at him. "He's your bodyguard, your best friend, your shadow, for Spirits' sake."

Ben grunted, his fingers tightening around his fork. "No. He's my *servant.*"

I felt stabbed with disbelief. I tilted my head and used my voice as a pointed finger at him. "And what exactly is the difference between a servant and a friend, in your opinion?"

"Friends, you keep away from wars and you want to protect at all costs. Servants might have to follow you into war and fight by your side and you cannot get emotionally attached because you know that it's likely they'll die."

"Sounds like I want to be the second type of friend and not the one locked away just so I won't get hurt."

Ben looked maddeningly calm, his breaths controlled, his expression unreadable. "You're neither of those two," he said evenly. His voice had a weight to it, something deliberate. "You're my queen."

I narrowed my eyes, leaning forward just slightly. "And do *queens* get locked up or not?"

He took a deep breath and let it out slowly, like he was already regretting this conversation. He set down his cutlery carefully before folding his arms on the table. His fingers began drumming lightly against his forearm.

There was a reverence in his eyes when he looked at me then, like I was some untouchable Spirit he worshipped from afar. "She's the one who I fall to my knees in front of," he purred. "The one who can bring me to submission."

I tilted my head up, pretending to consider a proposal. "That does sound pretty tempting," I admitted. "But I'm still getting Murben a gift."

Ben groaned, rubbing a hand down his face. "Angelica…" The way he said my name sent a flurry of butterflies into my stomach. "If you give him anything else, his ego will become unbearable. He still wears that bodyguard pin you gave him *every single day.* Even during tasks it's completely impractical for. I swear, he'd sleep in the damn thing if he could."

I grinned. "Hey! I put a lot of thought into that *damn thing.*"

Ben's lips curled upwards, and *Spirits,* he looked so handsome when he smiled. I had to remind myself why I was keeping him at a distance in the first place.

Still, I pushed on. "It's good that he has confidence. We've almost finished an *entire* year, with only three challenges left, and not one of the Black-Wing teams has won a single challenge."

Ben's smile turned sharp, something dangerous hiding in his eyes. "Oh, don't worry, *my queen*," he said smoothly. "I told them to keep a low profile."

"Good plan." I nodded in agreement but sarcastically hinted that it wasn't. "Except, at least one black-wing has to do the Spirits' Trek after graduation, and I'm no longer certain I fancy going if it puts you at risk."

He picked up his glass and swirled the wine around. "Glad to hear you no longer wish to settle the overdue score of my death. The romance is working, then?" He sipped the wine, amused.

I looked around the candlelit and rose-filled room. It was true that the atmosphere had put me in a good mood. "I don't know. Why were you in Tomason's room?"

He took a larger sip before putting the glass down onto the table and he cleared his throat as if he was ready for my interrogation. "She's my spy in the White Wing Territory and she's the one who sources the things we need from the Black Wing Territory, such as family portraits and peanut butter cakes."

I dropped my jaw. Wow! He had answered me. Told me one of his secrets. "How.... how..." was the only words I could stammer out.

"Guard Jackoloy is her fiancé, who I stationed outside your door to protect you in...*your castle*."

"What is happening in the north?" I almost shouted out, hoping he might finally answer.

Ben leaned back in his chair, looking far too relaxed for a king who'd drop forbidden information like casual gossip. "Nope. We're not quite there yet," he said, his smirk playing at the edge of his lips. "I *did* tell you that it's not the Black-Wings attacking Pharanir I can also tell you that General Denor is very interested in you. Specifically, in your magic. He thinks it could be useful in the, uh...let's call it the *problem area* above Doromir." He made little air quotes, as if it was some minor inconvenience instead of an impending disaster. "That's why everyone has been keeping an eye on you and why leadership, Harvey included, has strictly forbidden anyone, including me, from telling you a damn thing about it."

I frowned. "Harvey has told you specifically that you're not allowed to tell me anything?"

"Correct. Not just told me but threatened a few of my people with death and 'excruciating pain' if we get too close to you. Although, I think I've already crossed that line." He pointed for his black-eye, amusedly.

"Shouldn't you be there to help evacuate Doromir? It sounds serious. You're not forced to stay here anymore with our soul bond severed."

His smirk softened into something more sincere. "I'm where I should be. With you."

I groaned. "Ben." I folded my arms. "If you knew that I would be here when you got back, *should* you have been there…in the north…now?"

He tilted his head, considering. "Probably. I had hoped that we would have married and that you were content living in Black Castle by now. I could have nipped away to the north and sorted a few things out, but life has a funny way of throwing your soul on a detour, no matter if you pray to two Spirits or nine. So, I sent the general of my forces to the war in my stead."

"The nine Spirits don't seem to favour our relationship." That thought stung in my heart. "You should go."

"No. Not until you're satisfied with all the answers to the questions you have. I told you we should get as many secrets out in the open as we can. I can't do this anymore, having my heart dragged into the pit of chaos, worrying whether I'll lose you at every turn I take. And I'm not scared of defying the Spirits. So next question!"

I rolled my eyes. "You're a menace."

He grinned. "And yet, you *love me*." He leaned over the table, challenging, staring straight at me. "Come on. Next question. Hit me."

"I don't know," I muttered, tucking a strand of blue hair behind my ear. "They all feel small now."

He reached over the table to take my hand and caress it. "What else? Uh…Let's see…" he said thoughtfully, prepared to deliver answers to questions I had not asked. "I think there is something special going on with your two pairs of wings. But I don't yet know the answer to that myself. You know my father beat me as a child. Regarding my betrothal to Nassara; as soon as her father broke our treaty about the troops in the north, I sent a letter officially breaking the engagement. So that's done. And I have two people assigned day and night, seeking a solution to your marriage oath to Duke Hartmore."

"You're very generous with information today." I lifted the wine glass to my lips and hid a smile behind it before I sipped.

He had broken off his betrothal with Nassara! How could he do that and go against their soulmate bond? Maybe I had misunderstood the letter in his father's drawer. I was so confused. Was there another woman involved? But Ben didn't have the soulmate mark on his neck, so he couldn't be mated, unless someone had concealed it with a glamour. Nonetheless, I wished I could have seen the bitch's face when she read that letter. A tingle coiled in my sex. "You said you sent your general to Doromir. What is the difference between the general and the commander?"

"Commander Daffron is in charge of my guards who patrol around the castle and the nearby cities. The general works on a national scale with the army. And speaking of army patrols, and not a secret perhaps, but Nesso reported that Watson had sent a patrol to the mountain ridge and the route you had told him we were taking." He waited for my reaction.

"I know. I confronted him about it. Still hurt, though. I didn't believe he would."

"If it's any consolation. I think he did it to protect you, not to get you punished. He does love you, too. Even if he lost to me." The impish smile was back on his lips as he leaned back in his seat and crossed his legs under the table and took another sip of wine.

"That information wasn't as hard to tell as your other secrets, I assume."

"No, I tossed that one in there for free."

"Free? What are you charging me for the other ones?"

"A lifetime with me."

"That's steep. Although, my lifetime might be very short, considering our next challenge. Why do we have to climb? We have wings."

I had climbed the rock face with Zayd a thousand times since we were young, using double safety ropes and with him helping me every step of the way, but that wasn't the same. In the challenge, I'd have to make it to the top on my own and without safety ropes.

"What if your wings come off your back, get damaged or you're poisoned so you can't use them or bring them out?" Ben quizzed.

"Sounds unlikely. I'll take the risk if I can avoid climbing."

He leaned forward again to stare at me. "But you don't like flying, either."

I gestured for the floor. "What's wrong with being on the ground?"

He scoffed a laugh. "You can just hang off me whilst I climb if you want."

"Show off. No, thank you. I'll make it, and if you don't win me the prize, which is a bigger bedroom, so help me, I'll pray to the Spirit of fucking Death to come get you."

He chuckled, stealing one of my chips, dipping it in the sauce with the comfort of a married couple, before tossing it into his mouth. "Does that mean you'll come back to sleep here and not with your brother?" Chewing leisurely, he shot me a knowing look.

"Let's see if you win me that bigger bedroom first, and then we'll talk."

"In the meantime." He tapped a finger on the table. "I believe you owe me a dance, since I didn't get to go to my own spring ball."

"Really? You want to push that button so soon?"

He stood up and held out his hand. "Please, would you do me the honour of this dance?"

I looked around the small room. "There is no music."

"Then just sway with me."

I stood up, and he slotted his body into mine like a glove made to measure. One of his hands gripped mine, lacing his fingers between mine. The other hand he curled possessively around my waist, pulling me flush against him.

We swayed in silence for a while.

"How has your flying training with Murben been progressing?" he asked.

"Fantastically." I smirked through my mock voice. "I've perfected the art of colliding with trees."

A deep grunt rumbled through his chest, vibrating against mine. "And how much weight can you carry while flying?"

I recognised the careful evaluation in his tone. He was already calculating my odds for the second-year's eighth challenge. It wasn't surprising if he was worried about it. "We haven't started training with weights yet."

Another grunt. His arms tightened around me, his gaze burning into mine with an intensity that made my breath pause. It was that same look as before, like I was something sacred. As important as a piece of his own soul that he'd die for, protecting. "You're complaining about my nine Spirits, but the way you're looking at me, I'm wondering whether you're about to add a third to yours, my king."

That devastatingly charming smile was on his lips; the one I could barely resist.

But at this point, I had forgotten why I was denying myself the pleasure of him. He made me feel alive, like a fire burning at full blaze. Without him, my life was nothing but cold ashes. Did I want to live in the ashes, or did I want to live even if my life risked being set alight? Because without him, my life was purely that – ashes, betrayals and death.

When I tried to pull my hand free, his grip tightened, clearly unwilling to let go. His gaze dropped to the floor, taking on a sadness that told me more than I needed to know. He thought I was about to reject him again.

I wasn't.

When I wrenched my hand free from his, he looked up at me. His eyes searched mine, grasping at everything he was about to lose, pleading me to tell him this wasn't the end. When I saw the tears welling in his eyes, silence ate my words.

His lips parted, wanting to say something, but not finding the strength. A battle waged between pride and pain.

He blinked, refusing to let his tears fall, as if that would keep the moment from breaking. His breath shuddered before finally he whispered.

"Please…don't leave." His words held in his devastation admirably.

I looped one arm over his shoulders while the other slid up his neck, my fingers threading through his dark hair. Then, I kissed him, ignoring the oath's warning.

He groaned out with relief and satisfaction. A frenzy erupted between us with passionate kisses, and our tongues danced around one another like an obsession. His hands pressed around my back to the point it wasn't possible to be any closer to him.

He forcefully kissed down my neck and up again to claim my mouth. "I want you! Spirits, I need you. Please, don't give up on me."

"Stop making me so damn jealous, and I won't."

"You have no reason to be jealous. There is only you. Exclusively. Forever."

"Take my shirt off the way I like it!" I ordered him.

He ripped the buttons off his own shirt first, leaving his muscular pectorals exposed, and I rubbed my palms up them, tracing the swirling pattern of the black tattoos of my oath on his left shoulder. He closed his eyes, clearly taking in the pleasure of my touch as he tipped his head back. Then he focused on me, gripping my shirt and tearing it open, folding it off my shoulders and tugging my sleeves down to discard the fabric on the floor. He cupped my breasts, kissing them, and undid my bra, running his hand up my back to take it off my shoulders. He nestled his hands into my hair to cup the sides of my head and kissed me with an eagerness I though could never be sedated, his tongue entering my mouth to deepen our connection.

The table kept bumping into my butt, and at one time, I was almost sitting on top of it. "I wish your bed wasn't nailed to the wall…or that we had a mirrored table."

He smiled against my lips. "And whose fault is that?"

"I accept your apology."

"Hmm," he mused. "I'm not finished with the apology yet."

He undid the button of my trousers at the same time as I undid his, and then we both stripped entirely naked. Ben wrestled me to the bed, stroking his hands down my side as we let our tongues roll around one another's. The constant sting of the oath was there, warning us that what we were doing was forbidden.

Ben's skin was so firm and smooth as I pushed my palms all over him, but I was careful not to touch the lash wounds on his back.

He gasped for air between our mouths as I grabbed my hand around his cock, and I saw the fire that burned in his red eyes. It made me insanely aroused. He lowered towards me, tracing his tongue downward and around the dark edges of my areola before he went lower and lower…and…lower.

"Is this…" I gasped. His tongue entered me, and the pleasure was instant, "wise? My brother will kill you."

"If you start questioning my sins, and that we're natural enemies, this all falls apart."

"I want to fall apart under you from your sins. Don't stop! Tear me apart!"

His hands clamped onto either side of my hip and the moist tip of his tongue swivelled around my clit before he pushed harder to get his tongue deeper into me. He grunted and moaned, as he rolled his tongue around my clit, and I whimpered. I whimpered like his name was a prayer to a tenths Spirit.

The orgasm hit in waves crashing against the shore and I arched my back in spasms, crying out the insanely elevated sensation that struck repeatedly. Ben nuzzled his face into the crook of my neck and put his palm on my cheek, kissing me as the pleasure ebbed off. Then I took his hand, and I led the still hungry beast into the shower room.

"Turn around! Hands on the wall!" I told him, as I turned the shower on.

The water cascaded over his enormous body, and he hissed as it touched his damaged back. I wanted to cry, seeing the deep wounds where the whip had torn open his skin. I curved around his side to pump his shaft.

He moaned, throwing his head back, his chest heaving. He was clearly close to coming when he gripped my forearm to slow it. "Hands on the wall!" I commanded.

He grunted and braced both palms firmly against the stone, the water that had soaked his hair running like a waterfall down either side of his head as he cocked it low. At this angle, I could see the immense pleasure on his face as he focused on the sensation with closed eyes. I went faster, and he breathed harder, his cock growing thicker until the tension seemed painful. He let out a shuddering roar as he had his release. I softened my movements, drawing out his pleasure as his breaths came in slow waves. After a final tremble, he turned to me, wrapping me in his arms, and pulling me close beneath the cascading water.

The steam of the shower nothing compared to the heat between us. His lips pressed gently against the top of my head, lingering as if trying to seal this moment into eternity.

"You're amazing," he murmured, his voice rough with emotion. "I love you so damned much."

His arms crossed over my back, his hands hooking over my shoulders in a grip that felt unbreakable. I closed my eyes, listening to the steady rhythm of his heart against my ear, knowing that, at least for now, neither of us was letting go.

64

The four horseshoe nails gave way with a crack, barely putting up a fight, as Ben gave one solid tug on the bed frame. Despite how hard I had hammered them into the wall, he ripped them free with startling ease.

When he looked at me, his eyes burned hotter than I had ever seen them, a wildfire of intensity that was sure to set me on fire. I held up the blindfold in front of him, wordlessly daring him. The second he scanned my face, seeing the lust there, everything between us ignited.

Morning came too soon, and reality pressed back in.

Zayd was holding another climbing training for challenge eight. The session had to be early in the morning, as the second-year cadets were practising for their challenge to fly between the two steep cliff faces of the gorge whilst carrying rocks. One mistake, one slip, and those stones could become deadly projectiles for the climbers below. During the real challenge they needed to tie a rope around their teammate and fly them over the gorge. It was the challenge with the highest death toll out of all thirty trials across the three years.

I pulled on my flight leathers, the thick material offering more protection than the standard uniforms and perched on the bedside to lace up my black hiking boots.

Ben was already dressed in the same gear and was finishing polishing his boots. Then he lowered himself to one knee. Without a word, he reached for my laces, his fingers deftly tying my boots as if it was as natural to him as breathing. He had started with my right foot, tying the lace tightly to support my ankle and then he placed my boot steady on his thigh and began polishing it in mindless strokes as if it calmed his nerves.

He put my boot back on the floor and picked up my other foot which didn't don a boot yet. "Is a king supposed to polish servants' boots?" I smirked at him when he cast a quick glance at me before carrying on.

"I thought we covered this topic yesterday. You're not my servant."

He massaged my foot. His strong hands wrapped around my foot and his fingers pressed into the sore muscles with just the right amount of pressure. He worked up my leg, his thumbs kneading into the ache, coaxing out the tension that had built up from hours of training this week. His touch was firm yet careful, moving in slow circles, sending little shivers of relief through me.

"And, I like taking care of my teammate."

I purred while he traced his fingers along the ball of my foot, then moved to my heel, pressing deeply into the aching spot that had been bothering me for days. Every press of his hand felt like a silent promise that he'd always take care of me. That he'd work hard to soothe away my every ache and pain. My toes curled slightly as he grazed over a particularly sensitive spot, and I bit my lip to keep from making a sound.

"You're tense," he murmured, as he glanced up at me.

I barely managed a nod, melting under his touch, completely undone by the intoxicating pleasure of his hands on me.

I stroked my hands through his hair that was close to my middle area and wished I was naked and that we didn't have to go out training.

He glanced up at me. "You've got that mischievous look on your face. We don't have time for any of your kinky ideas but save them until tonight."

My lip curved at one side. Ben certainly had learned how to read me. "I can skip breakfast."

He scoffed and shook his head as he put my foot into the boot, tying it tighter than the other. "I won't allow you to climb on an empty stomach."

I'd save it for tonight then, but I craved to have him inside me, too. Not purely his tongue. "Any news on the oath breaking front?"

His charming smile lowered. "Not yet." He finished polishing my boots and put the shoe wax and brush away.

We left the room and walked to the canteen, and I filled a tray with a plate of scrambled eggs, beans, toast and a glass of orange juice. I ignored the sausages and bacon since I had stopped eating pork after Cadet Hefany had served Flora on the menu. Ben did the same, but his mountain of food was bigger.

The doors to the hall swung open and shut in a constant rhythm as cadets flooded in, the air buzzing with conversation and the clatter of trays. The usual divide between black-wings and white-wings seemed to blur this morning as our friends finally gravitated toward our table. After weeks of sitting on opposite ends of the hall, the sight of them merging felt almost surreal.

"You made up!" Emroyce cheered as he reached us, his grin infectious. "We can finally sit with all our friends again." He tapped on Nesso's shoulder, a firm, familiar pat that lingered just long enough for a friend.

Hovering over my plate from across the table, Emroyce squinted at my breakfast with mock scrutiny. "How's your breakfast? No pork, hey?"

"It's lovely, but the sarcasm is a bit stale," I muttered, glowering at him.

His eyes twinkled with amusement as he slid into the seat next to Nesso. "Was that sarcasm in my happy good morning greeting?"

"No," I drawled, stirring my food lazily with my fork. "It was thinly veiled contempt."

"So…sarcasm?" he chirped, stabbing his entire sausage without cutting it and bit into it from one side.

I rolled my eyes at him.

Kate sat down next to me and Mazdon next to her, followed by Maruto and Penya. On the opposite side of us, Kenyard sat next to Emroyce, followed by Brian, Fern and Winter. To Ben's side, Murben sat down and closest to the wall, as usual, Commander Daffron.

Maruto, Penya and Emroyce looked like a unified military force today. They all wore their black flight leathers with their long, black hair slicked back into a tight ponytail, ready for intense climbing.

Davis and Nesso were already seated when we had arrived, but they were swaying a lot from side to side, their eyes glazed and looking dizzy.

I shared a glance with Ben before looking back at them. "Are you guys all right? You look weird."

"Shush!" Nesso hissed, with a finger over his lips. "We raided Camp Leader Mewer's herb cupboard when we visited Valentina."

They had dared visiting Valentina? No wonder they had drugged themselves, although they seemed to have gone over the top. "And what? Consumed it all?"

"No!" Nesso drawled. "I don't think so. Did we, Davis?"

"Not all, surely," he said, seeming uncertain and sounding drunk. "The third-year cadets are doing the hallucinations challenge this month. It's so cool. I see stuff. Stuff I hope isn't real." He held his hand out as if he was trying to touch something that wasn't there.

"How are you supposed to practise climbing like that?" I flung a hand gesture his way to indicate his disorderly state.

"We're fine," Nesso said, grabbing his fork and stabbing into his sausage, or at least he thought he was, but he missed it by a long-shot. Frowning, he tried again, but it was another miss. His brows furrowed in confusion. "Davis, did you see my sausage move? The pig is still alive," he whispered, or he thought he did, but everyone could hear him. His wide-eyed stare flicked between his plate and Davis, as if the sausage might make a run for it.

Across the table, Brian groaned, rubbing his temples. "Oh Spirits," he muttered to Cadet Winter. "That's what we'll face after lunch?"

Brian's teammate pressed a hand over her mouth, stifling a giggle. "I'll let my astral projection persona consume whatever he has, but you have fun."

"Camp Leader Mewer is too clever to fall for that. He'll know the difference between you and your magical ghost. You're going to be high as a kite with me. Fun," he sneered at her.

Emroyce, grinning mischievously, kept nudging his elbow into Nesso's side. Every time Nesso was about to spear a piece of food with his fork, Emroyce's well-timed jabs sent his utensil clattering against the plate, missing its target entirely. Nesso seemed too drugged up to realise Emroyce was doing it on purpose. He stopped abruptly and looked at everyone around the table. "Karson and Treylieh are doing the 'you know which one' challenge this month. If anyone has any last words to them, now is a good time to visit them."

Everyone around the table went quiet, as if they were doing a minute's silence for their deaths already.

"Hopefully, Camp Leader Mewer will keep Valentina under observation in the infirmary for the entire month," I muttered.

"Do you think that is what he's doing? Protecting her?" Fern asked.

I contemplated it for a second. "She isn't that injured, so I doubt he can get away with keeping her there for much longer. Valentina herself would become furious. I don't think she'd be happy missing the challenge."

"Treylieh should use his persuasion magic on her and tell her to make it over the gorge," Davis said in his drunken voice, and everyone joined in with unserious suggestions and banter.

I tuned out of their drunken discussion, looking at the set of friends I had made this year, and it warmed my heart, especially considering we had established some sort of peace to a group mixed with black-wings and white-wings. The only one who was missing was Zoe, who my lovely brother had sent on a mission north. It'd have been nice to have had Zayd at our table as well, but he had made it a new habit to sit next to Captain La Roy, Camp Leader Neville and the others at the leadership table. I didn't blame him, not when *some of us* were incredibly disorderly.

After Ben had conversed with Murben for a while, he leaned over me. "I might have to leave to pacify the situation in Doromir. Duke Malinger has written a letter calling for help."

I pricked at my scrambled eggs with my fork. "I'll come with you."

"No. It's too dangerous and you need to be seen here."

Tearing off a piece of bread, I hovered it in the air in front of my mouth. "I reiterate. I'll come with you. It's not your choice."

"You're stretching my patience today, Miss Stone." His face showed no sign of compromising.

"You didn't complain this much last night when I stretched other parts of you." I winked and put the bread into my mouth slowly.

The guys had clearly heard my last comment and Emroyce was hooting and cheering, with Kenyard backing him up. Even Brian was slapping his hand on the table, amused.

Ben tried to avoid our railed-up friends by lowering his voice. "Then you aren't in the line of fire."

I turned away from his gaze towards my friends, lifting my eyebrows, hoping they'd catch the drift of what was ironic with Ben's statement. They did, bawling even louder.

Ben realised the double meaning in his statement, and grinned. But didn't encourage anyone by looking at them and focused on his plate of food instead. "You keep eluding me."

Emroyce pointed at Ben's black-eye with his fork. "Damn, Angie must be rough in the sack if she left you that."

Ben tensed beside me, not liking the comment, so I put my hand on his lap. "A king should be kept on his toes…or back, depending on what I want."

He relaxed and looked intently at me. "Well, last night, I won."

"You won? Because of…" I drawled, and he kept waiting for my question. "…the shower?" I whispered, looking around to verify that no one had heard me.

Ben cocked his head sideways to look at me, playing with his tongue along the back of his teeth. "Yep."

I snorted. "No, you didn't. If you had, I'd had also given you a blowjob."

"I would have been satisfied with a cuddle from my efforts last night. I say I got more than I bargained for. A win."

Not finding a comeback for that, he wiggled his eyebrows at me and drank his entire glass of milk in one go.

I had just finished my breakfast as I saw Harvey enter the canteen in his yellow captain's uniform, so I got off the bench and I walked straight up to him. "Couldn't you have turned your emotions off this once, instead of beating up my boyfriend?" I hissed, not to make a scene. "He has a black-eye for Spirits' sake.

Harvey's expression darkened, his gaze sharpening into the kind of anger I usually knew better than to challenge. His jaw tensed, and his voice dropped to a dangerous edge. "Your *boyfriend*? You know the rules, Angie." His eyes locked onto mine, daring me to test him. "Do you want me to drag you down to the dungeon and make sure you'll receive your own lashes in the torture room?"

A shadow loomed behind me. Ben had stopped in his tracks, his posture rigid, his chest rising high as he squared his shoulders. Though he didn't speak, his presence was a warning in itself. His gaze drilled into Harvey, silent but solid like rock, having caught every word of the threat.

Harvey's lip curled slightly, not fearing Ben but not oblivious to the damage a collision could make. He leaned in just enough that only I could hear. "I'll see you tonight in the apartment. Honour your family name, Cadet Coraly," he muttered, then turned on his heel, striding toward the meal trays without another glance back.

Murben joined our side as the tension settled and we went to pick up the pre-packed rock climbing backpacks that Zayd had stacked against the front façade of the building. I crouched to lift mine, the weight heavier than I expected, and far heavier than when Zayd and I usually trained. Before I could fully shoulder it, Ben reached out, holding the weight up with a firm grip while I adjusted the straps around my arms.

Without another word, we fell into step with the others, hiking toward the bottom of the gorge. The group was smaller than before. The gruelling first-year challenges had already thinned the ranks, reducing what had once been two hundred cadets to a mere hundred and thirty-two.

The sun wasn't hitting us in a favourable angle this morning, straight through the gorge between the twenty-metre narrow space of two towering cliff faces.

The weight of the backpack pressed into my shoulders, each strap digging in as I scanned the gathered cadets. My breath felt tight, my pulse thrumming with unease.

Cadet Gravelhorn was here. My stomach clenched at the sight of him, and hating he was unharmed. His limbs were intact, with no visible injuries. That was disappointing. Standing beside him, Cadet Malloopa looked like a ghost of himself, his usually sharp features drained of colour, his dark hair framing a face that seemed to have seen far worse than he was willing to speak of.

The familiar teams had arrived; the Horse Girls Team, the Archery Team with Ashton and his father, and the Healing Team with Penya and Maruto standing together, their expressions unreadable. But there were new faces too, teams I hadn't noticed before. My eyes darted across them, a strange tension settling in my chest.

Emroyce, always quicker to pick up on social dynamics, leaned in slightly, his voice low. "See them?" he murmured, his gaze flicking to the unfamiliar teams pointing them out. "That's the Twin Team. Cadet Jeff and Cadet Giles Flinch, originally from Gaithbry. Their magic is to scry to track people. They're great guys. Model-gorgeous to be sure, and to the point I'm freaking jealous. They're super muscly, but they won't hurt anyone unless it's called for."

I swayed so that my shoulder bumped into his. "You're handsome, too."

"Thank you for noticing, Cadet Coraly." He pointed at two elderly men whose hair was thin and white. "I call them the Elderly Team. Cadet Callum Maghan can become transparent, and no one can touch him. Pretty cool, huh?"

"Yeah, that could come in handy," I said, glancing at Gravelhorn to ensure he wasn't aiming any arrows at me.

"His teammate, Cadet Edgar Dommen's magic enables him to stay awake. He can't fall asleep. You should recognise Cadet Dommen, as he lives by your cottage near the east lake, and he used to deliver firewood to your parents."

As I recalled him, his gaze swept past and stopped on me with a smile. I waved, and he nodded before he carried on speaking to his teammate.

I observed them for a moment. "How come they're at the academy being so old? Dommen should have been allowed to retire. Will he even live until graduation?" I asked Emroyce, and with all the gossip he could provide, I could understand why he got along so well with Nesso.

Emroyce would be a good spy master as well.

"Cadet Maghan spent his entire life in the world below, where the people have no wings. King Emille's spies caught him visiting his nephew after his brother had died last year. I know he still has family in the world below, but he doesn't want to talk about it, as you know it's forbidden to go down there."

"Oh, my Spirits. What a rebel."

"In your league, I would say."

"Hey!" I slapped his shoulder.

Emroyce twisted, looking further to our left. "And I believe you know the Earth Kissing Team. The wind whisperer and the guy who can set his body to the clock."

"Yeah, but I hardly recognised Cadet Quill without his lute. They won't be any competition, but," I said, pointing to the Agility Team, "Cadet Starly and Cadet Darse will."

"Yep. Them and the Prank Team. Cadet Oscarson can climb walls with his bare hands because they stick to them."

I followed Emroyce's glances to the larger group with cadets sitting on the sand and gravelly ground where Cadet Oscarson sat with his teammate Cadet Lerren who had a breath that made you faint. I searched the rest of the groups of cadets, both sitting and standing.

"I can't see Kate and Maz."

"No, they're in the other group who will train tomorrow morning." Emroyce tapped the back of his hand on Kenyard's chest, who had just come to stand next to him. "Then there is Kenyard and me. We will obviously win."

"The Perfection Team. Nice team name for yourself."

"What can I say? The name speaks for itself, so good luck. Break a leg."

"Maybe I'll ask Valentina to break some of your bones."

"That's cheating," Emroyce called over his shoulder, as he jogged closer to the group as Zayd arrived and was gathering everyone for the lesson.

Ben was distracted, staring at Nesso and Davis, who were placing their training swords against each other's. "What are you guys doing?"

Nesso looked up at Ben with his drunken gaze and then back at the sword again. "Measuring who had the largest blade."

Ben looked at them like a disappointed teacher. "Isn't knowing how to use it of greater value than its length?"

"Oh," Nesso scoffed. "You just took the fun out of this." He looked at Commander Daffron, who leered, but kept quiet, as everyone obviously knew he was the most skilled of the three of them. We had all seen it in the combat challenge.

"Quiz!" Nesso spat, the eighteen-year-old wobbled to his left, putting the sword tip on the ground like a cane to steady himself. "Can you put these in order of greatness of warriors? Commander Daffron, King Blackbone or Murben?"

Commander Daffron didn't join in the game, sighing instead.

"I'll give you a hint," Nesso blurted. "King Blackbone and Murben are tied in first place."

Commander Daffron sighed again and glanced towards his king, as if pleading for permission to step away from these idiots.

Ben and I peeled away from Nesso and Davis, leaving them at a distance from the cluster of white-wing cadets. We headed towards Zayd, Commander Daffron's and Murben's shadows looming over us from behind.

"We should have tucked them two into bed and told leadership they were ill today," I muttered.

"Yes," Ben drawled, shooting another glance over his shoulder. His jaw tightened. "I'm quite worried. Both that they'll get caught having stolen herbs from a Camp Leader and also that they risk falling down the cliff." His voice dropped lower. "I'll keep an eye on them."

The tension among the cadets in black uniforms was palpable as we gathered around Zayd. His navy-blue uniform stood out against the sea of darkness, a beacon of authority. Today, he hadn't bothered to gel his auburn hair. It had grown too long, falling messily over his forehead. In the sunlight, the scar Ben had left on Zayd's nose stood out, a reminder of their power battle, and today promised to bring more.

My fingers tightening around the straps of my pack. Whatever was coming next, wouldn't be easy.

"I need a volunteer!" Zayd shouted over the group, but no one offered their assistance, as they scanned the vertical wall. He waved me forward. "Ang…Cadet Coraly?"

Zayd and I had done this many times before for fun with safety harnesses and ropes. I had been so secure, knowing Zayd would never have let me fall. Today, he needed to treat me like any other cadet. Or so I had wrongly assumed, as he helped me get the harness on with his usual familiarity, working his hands all over my body.

"You don't give up, do you?" I whispered, having turned my lips away from the crowd.

"You should know me better than that," he purred into my ear.

I heard Ben grunt behind Commander Daffron and Murben who stood guard against any attempt Ben might make to interfere with the camp leader.

"We will show them just like we used to climb, using two safety ropes," Zayd told me.

He picked up a crossbow from the ground that he had loaded with a grappling hook and aimed it for the top of the cliff before shooting. The hook caught on an outcrop on his first shot. Zayd yanked at the rope to test that the hook wouldn't break loose, and then he secured it in a carabineer on my harness and into his own. He rummaged through his backpack and took out a tub of chalk and I held out my hands for him to dust some over them.

"Just like we used to," Zayd reminded me – and Ben. "Ready?"

He shoved a handful of cams down my leg pocket and jumped up onto the wall to reach a solid first grip, hung off it with one hand and held the other one out for me.

"Yes, just like we used to do together," I repeated. "Maybe you need to say it louder to everyone." I took his hand, and he lifted me up to a good starting point where I had a firm grip around a groove in the rock wall.

"No, I think Ben heard me," Zayd said, climbing higher.

"I did!" Ben called from where he stood with the group of cadets watching us from the ground.

Ben squeezed through between Murben and Commander Daffron's shoulders and picked up the tub of chalk, rubbing some powder over his hands before he too jumped up onto the wall beside me.

"King Blackbone, what are you doing?" I asked, the panic seeping through into my voice. "You're not wearing any safety gear."

"I don't need any. I can climb this cliff without it, and much quicker than our camp leader."

"I'll take that challenge, King Blackbone." Zayd climbed down and lifted me off the wall to put me on the ground.

The cadets began whispering amongst themselves and the chatter was getting louder around us. I could hear Gravelhorn laughing and the Prank Team taking bets.

I began unscrewing the carabineers to remove the rope attaching me to Zayd. "Then I'm in, too."

Ben and Zayd stared at me with wide eyes. "No, you're not," Zayd said, as he removed his harness.

"If you guys are going to be stupid, then I can be stupid, too." I lined up by the wall with my hands at the ready.

"I'm your camp leader, and I say you're not competing in this challenge," Zayd said more firmly.

"Try to stop me."

"Pockets full of mischief," Ben muttered and shook his head. "Then I'm not climbing."

"If you don't do it, you forfeit and I win," Zayd mocked.

"Of course!" Ben barked. "I won't gamble with Cadet Coraly's life!"

It was getting awkward, and all the cadets were watching us intensely.

"No, we're settling this!" Zayd shouted, looking for Emroyce. "Cadet Bengrey, keep Cadet Coraly on the ground."

Emroyce hesitated, looking at me.

"Don't you fucking dare!" I barked.

"Emroyce, don't touch her," Ben warned. "That's not how we do it. Cadet Coraly has a say in our matters."

"In your matters?" Zayd asked sarcastically. "You two aren't an item, King Blackbone. She's soul bound to you to guard you, that's all. When you complete the Spirits' Trek, if you get to go, you'll be separated and you'll be sent back to your territory never to see each other again. And I'll be here to pick up any pieces of her you destroy along the way."

Ben's face turned a tone of darker red with anger and I worried he'd lose control, but yet I hadn't seen any black essence leak out of him. Ben turned my way and ushered me backwards towards the rock wall for more privacy. He rubbed his hands down my arms and was clearly thinking hard about something before he cocked his head down to look me in the eye.

"If we're going to have any chance of being together, I must show these people that I'm superior; a leader they can trust to follow," he whispered.

"Can't you just use your trust magic on all of them?" I hissed back.

"It doesn't work that way. And no, I don't use it on anyone unless I have to save someone's life. Please, let me do this."

I sighed. This was making me irritated. "What does climbing and falling to your death prove?"

"Miss Stone, you're being unreasonable again." His voice was clipped.

My irritation flared to new heights. "And, you think you can change the rules to suit your needs because you're a king."

"You think I can't win, is that it? That I can't climb this?" He didn't even take his eyes off mine for one second to assess the cliff again.

"Oh, you're good at this emotional manipulation game." I crossed my arms over my chest and tapped my fingers on my arm. "Will you be able to fold out your wings and sail down if you fall?"

Now, he looked up at the height of the cliff. "It'll take me about three to four seconds to fold them out, and falling the forty metres of the cliff takes less than three seconds. So no, I won't get any use of them before I hit the ground."

"Will a fall from forty metres kill a person?" I looked up at the height, inspecting the overhang of the cliff where it leant out with a steeper angle.

"A fall would kill me, yes." His gaze traced the jagged rocks, calculating the impossible. "I could survive a fall from below twenty-five metres, but after that…" He cut off, shaking his head.

His teeth clenched, biting back a thought he didn't want to acknowledge. His fingers twitched, brushing against mine, as if he was debating if he could afford dying and leave me in Zayd's care.

My nerves were crawling inside me, and I craned my head to look around Ben to see Zayd waiting for us to finish our discussion. By reflex, my foot tapped on the ground. "Wings must be out during the entire climb."

"Agreed."

"If he needs your help at any stage, you will give it?"

"Agreed."

"And you'll owe me a massage tonight to smoothen out my knotted nerves…with oils!"

"Okay, that's perfectly acceptable," he said, flashing me an impish smile. "Although, I don't accept responsibility for what happens after the massage."

I nodded, agreeing with this chauvinistic stupidity.

Ben set course for Zayd. "Terms. Cadet Bengrey counts us down and we start on the word 'go'. The first one to stand on the ground at the top wins. We'll do the climb with our wings out. Anything to add?"

"No wings. The rest is fine by me." Zayd cracked a bone in his neck while stretching it around his shoulders.

"Cadet Coraly's term was that the wings have to be out during the climb."

"And is Cadet Coraly the one dictating your life now?" Zayd challenged.

Ben didn't accept defeat, retaliating hard. "As my future wife, we make these decisions together. If you disregarded her in the decision-making, maybe that was why your relationship failed."

A cacophony of gasps and wolf whistles sounded from the group of cadets, and I felt like sinking through the ground. I couldn't believe Ben had just said he planned to marry me in front of everyone. My cheeks heated and reddened even worse when Zayd looked at me for confirmation.

When I didn't object, he frowned and barked. "No wings!"

Why was he so stubborn? Was he planning on ensuring the black-wing king didn't survive, so we couldn't wed? Worse. Did that fact make him hate me so much that he didn't care whether I died? He believed Ben and I were bonded so if he died, I died. Unless...Zayd already knew we hadn't been bonded ever since coming back from the diabolical spring festival. That meant Harvey knew, too. But why had he let it go unpunished?

"Wings out!" I barked at Zayd.

"If the king of the entire Black Wing Territory isn't brave enough to climb a cliff without his wings out, then what kind of king is he? What kind of protector of his family will he be?"

Emroyce took a step forward. "Come on, Camp Leader Watson, climb with the wings out if it makes it easier on Cadet Coraly."

Gravelhorn was at the forefront of the throng of cadets. "No wings! I agree with Camp Leader Watson. King Blackbone is a king, and the camp leader is braver than him!"

Ben looked at me pleadingly, crumbling from all the verbal abuse.

I shook my head. "No."

"I'm sorry, Miss Stone. I'm going to have to make a judgement call on this one." Ben turned to Zayd. "I accept your terms."

"What? No!" I walked over to Zayd to push at his shoulder. "I don't want to lose you, either. Stop this. You're being childish."

"Apologies for your grievances, Cadet Coraly. I know you were an agent for a long time, but we're soldiers. This is our job."

"You kidnapped the black-wings, or they wouldn't be here!"

"I gave the king a choice to forfeit the challenge." Zayd pushed past me to line up next to Ben at the starting line with bent knees to be ready to push away.

They stood with readied arms at their side, and their eyes focused on the target.

Emroyce walked forth to stand beside them, lifting his pocket watch to look at the time. "Ready in Five–"

"Emroyce, stop counting!" I shouted. "This isn't appropriate training for anyone." I swiped my arm towards the group of cadets, who looked on in amusement.

"Count!" Zayd called to Emroyce.

"Four...three–"

"I'm going to tell Captain Coraly about this!" I barked, fuming.

Emroyce looked at Zayd, but Zayd simply nodded at him.

Spirits!

"Two…one…go!"

They were off with incredible speed, both jumping up to the foot of the cliff and then grabbing for new grips as they pulled themselves up.

I lunged for the wall, my fingers barely brushing the rough surface before strong arms wrapped around my waist, yanking me backward. My body hit the ground hard, and before I could scramble up again, Emroyce pinned me down, his grip like iron bands around my torso. I thrashed against him, kicking at his shins, slamming my fists against his arms, but he held firm.

"Emroyce, let me go!" My voice was raw with fury, breaths coming in short gasps.

"Apologies, Cadet Coraly," he grunted, tightening his grip as I bucked against him. "But I'm following the camp leader's orders."

I craned my neck, my heart hammering as I looked up. Ben and Zayd were already high above the ground, their bodies a blur of motion as they scaled the vertical rock face. They were advancing at terrifying speed as their muscular legs pushed them up fast.

Fear burned in my chest.

Ben was fast, stronger, maybe. They were both twenty-six-years-old with the same body build, although Ben was slightly larger, and both were stubborn, used to working hard and never giving up. *Apparently not even if it was likely to kill them.*

But this wasn't a fair challenge. Zayd had climbed this wall a thousand times before, so his hands knew exactly where each groove and ledge was. Ben, on the other hand, had to rely on instinct and sheer determination. The muscles in his arms flexed as he reached for another handhold, and I saw his boots scraping for purchase.

But this wasn't just a challenge. It was a death race.

And I was stuck on the ground, powerless to stop it.

My eyes locked onto Ben. He dangled over the sheer drop, clinging to the wall with just one hand, his fingers straining against the rough stone. My breath caught in my throat as he reached for another outcrop. One wrong move and he'd fall straight to his death. I couldn't watch. I turned my gaze to Zayd instead, not because I wanted him to win, but because I couldn't bear to see either of them lose. None of them would lose before they were dead.

"Have they hit twenty-five meters yet?"

"Not yet," Emroyce muttered, glancing at his pocket watch, but still keeping his firm grip on me.

I swallowed hard and looked back up. Ben never ceased to amaze me. He was matching Zayd, move for move. A miracle. No, not a miracle. A lifetime of brutal training. He hadn't grown strong by chance. He'd had no choice. I could almost hear the crack of a studded belt, see the torture cross in his father's office. Failure wasn't an option. Not then. Not now.

But the rock didn't care about past scars. One slip, one miscalculation, and it would claim him anyway.

Ben's huge hands cupped the outcrops expertly and sometimes he didn't even wait to get a foothold before he heaved himself up solely with the use of his biceps. Zayd's efforts were impressive, too, but I had seen them before. He was the best cadet the Bensguard Outpost had ever had, save for my brother. But I bet Harvey cheated and always used some magic.

I looked at Emroyce again, who checked their height and nodded to confirm they were high enough now that a fall would kill them.

My heart was in my throat. There was so much acid building up in my gut I wanted to vomit. Rocks tore loose from the wall and Zayd's foot slid off its hold and Ben immediately reached out for him, as he had promised me. But Zayd ignored him, holding on to a particularly protruding outcrop. Without finding a stable foothold, there weren't many places he could go.

Ben hung back, waiting to see how Zayd would do, and if Zayd could afford to let go with one hand, I was sure he would have flashed Ben his finger. Zayd scrambled his feet against the wall again, but nothing stuck.

"Come on, camp leader! You're embarrassing us!" Gravelhorn shouted from the ground.

"Shut up, Gravelhorn! Respect your leader! Or I hope he puts you in the isolation cell!" I shouted at him.

He smirked at me. "Does falling and hitting the ground hurt like having an arrow shot through your wing?"

"Fuck you, Gravelhorn!"

"Sure, but I'll warn you. I'm rougher in bed than a royal fuck. You might find King Blackbone mediocre after that."

Ew! I ignored him and looked up.

Zayd was panting hard now, holding onto the same outcrop. "Shut up, Cadet Gravelhorn. Or I'll kick your arse on the sparring mat later with Cadet Charney present, so you can't use your magic," Zayd warned.

I couldn't care less what Gravelhorn muttered about to the cadets around him. My focus was on Zayd.

Ben climbed down a few steps. "Do you want some help there, camp leader? It looks like you took a wrong turn below the indenture coming up on your left."

Zayd didn't respond, his focus locked on the rock face. The rope from his grapple hook scraped against his back, but he ignored it, shifting his weight. Forcefully, he swung his legs sideways and managed to get them steady onto a small ledge. His muscles strained as he pulled himself higher. He jerked himself upwards to launch one hand for a new grip to his right. His fingers stretched for a darker section of stone, just within reach and shifted his weight across.

For a heartbeat, he had it.

Then the rock crumbled.

A sickening crack echoed through the gorge as the brittle stone gave way beneath his fingertips. Zayd's grip shattered along with the rock. No longer holding onto anything, his feet slid off the wall.

His body jerked violently, his feet scraping against the wall for any hold, any chance to stop what was coming.

But there was nothing.

Then Zayd fell.

65

My heart fell to the pit of my stomach, watching Zayd fall.

"No! Zayd!" I screamed, my voice breaking as the panic gripped tightly around my throat.

He was plummeting through the air, fast towards the ground.

He could never survive this.

The moment he hit, there would be nothing left but shattered bones and a pool of blood.

I was sure I'd soon faint.

"Grab the rope, Watson!" Ben's voice boomed over the roaring wind.

Zayd flung his hand around in the air, but he couldn't get a grip on the rope.

Miss. Miss. Miss.

I can't watch this!

Then – a grip.

His hand found the rope, his body jerking as the speed of his descent slowed, but at a terrible cost. He roared in agony, the rope tearing deep into his palms, splitting his skin open. Blood poured from his fists, soaking the cuffs of his sleeves as he slid lower and lower toward the ground.

With one final jarring thud, his feet landed impossibly steady, like a rehearsed move he had meant to do all along.

Ben was still on his way climbing down and I barely had time to breathe before Zayd barked orders, directing cadets to space themselves along the wall, distributing crossbows as if he hadn't just *almost died.*

Rage and relief crashed together inside me. I stormed up to him and slammed a fist into his shoulder. "You could have died!"

He held his hands out to look at them and they were shaking, covered in torn flesh and blood.

"Have Penya heal that," I told him.

He stepped in close, his sky-blue eyes burrowing into mine, not with scorn, but with something far worse. *Desperation.*

"You can't marry him." His voice was shaking with barely contained fury. It was a plea pulled from the depth of his core. "He's not just some man, Angie. He's the king of our enemy. The one sitting on a throne built from the bones of those we've lost. People, our people, are dying because of him. Our friends, our families, are torn apart while he gives the orders. And you want to stand beside him?" His breath was ragged. "Tell me how the fuck I am supposed to stand by and watch that?"

Ben had assured me that he wasn't the one attacking the white-wings, but I couldn't tell Zayd that.

"Do you think it's an act when he says he loves me? He just risked his life for me. Or do you believe no king could love a traitor like me?"

"Angie," he breathed. "Spirits or kings or generals, it doesn't matter. Anyone who knows you, and lets you go is a fool. I was a fool for not paying attention when Harvey sent you away. If I had known, I'd have stopped it and we'd still be together. I'm still fighting to get you back, Angie."

"By killing off my boyfriend?"

"It'd have helped," he said with a playful smile, trying to get me to cheer up. I stared hard at him, and he rolled his eyes. "At least, it'd have been nice to know that if I was about to fall to my death that you'd actually use your magic to save me, no matter if anyone saw it."

I shook my head, looking around at the cadets watching; water wielder, possession, speed, strength, cloner, aurora stripping, healing, reflexes, speaking to animals, sensuality, slow motion, emotional manipulator and a few more magical abilities, which were totally useless to help someone falling through the sky to their death.

"There is no one here who has the magic to do anything that could have helped you, Zayd."

"Cadet Darse can slow time," he said, his tone icy.

"I didn't think of that. I panicked."

Zayd didn't take his eyes off me. He was clearly very disappointed but finally sighed. "Next time you panic, I might die. You should work on that."

Ben came walking our way after having climbed down from the cliff, Murben tailing him. "On aiding your death, or not panicking?" Ben asked for clarification, hiding his mockery well.

"Get practising, Cadet Coraly," Zayd barked, walking towards his backpack, probably looking for something to tend to his hands with.

"Is he okay?" Ben asked, looking Zayd's way.

"Yes, he's shaken but alive."

Ben twisted, glancing around the area. "The cadets have started using their crossbows, so I don't want you in the open. Let's move over there next to Emroyce and Kenyard." He glanced around to see Nesso and Davis still playing around with their borrowed swords at a distance, having missed all the action. "We should bring them with us." He gestured for Murben to fetch them as we made our way to the cliff face.

Ben let me use the crossbow, so as not to upset leadership by using a weapon. He didn't want to betray their trust now when leadership had entrusted him to carry a sword during training away from the outpost. Although, whether it was a great idea giving Davis and Nesso a sword each when they were still high on herbs, could be debated.

Ben commanded Nesso and Davis to stay grounded when they had arrived with Murben, although I doubted they knew what was up or down.

We strapped ourselves to the harnesses and followed the appropriate climbing procedure with no further displays of bravery, using the cams to hammer into the grooves in the rock face and fastening ourselves with the safety rope. It took us a little over an hour to reach the top, and Ben pushed his hand on my arse to help me crawl over the ledge. It was heavenly to stand on the ground once more as heights, no matter whether climbing or flying, had never been one of my virtues.

Murben and Commander Daffron, Emroyce and Kenyard were soon by our side, as well as Maruto and Penya, the Elderly Team, the Earth Kissing Team and the Twin Team whilst the other teams had climbed the cliff on the other side of the gorge. We took the back route down the mountain to return to Davis and Nesso just in time to hear Zayd dismiss us so we could hike back to the military building for lunch.

As we arrived at the outpost, a gnawing unease settled in my gut. It wasn't solely Nesso and Davis who looked drugged. A strange haze clung to most of the third-year cadets like a shadow. Their eyes were unfocused and their movements sluggish, as if they were fighting a battle inside their own heads. Brian stood with his arms crossed and his jaw clenched so tightly I thought his teeth might crack. Winter was no better, her fingers twitched at her sides and her usually sharp gaze was glassy and distant. They weren't only distracted. They were seeing things.

Mewer had discharged Valentina from the infirmary, and she joined us for lunch alongside Treylieh. The tension between them was like a string pulled too tight, seconds from snapping. Valentina barely touched her food, instead her fingers drummed restlessly against the table and her leg bounced beneath the table. Treylieh kept stealing careful glances at her, his lips twitching, as if debating whether to say something or keep his silence.

After the afternoon's mathematics lesson, Ben took me out to the field to train bringing out my wings. I reduced the time to seven seconds and sometimes even six, but Ben was still not pleased with that. He wouldn't settle for anything above five seconds and threatened to take me out more often.

We made it in good time for the history lesson after changing into normal black uniforms without getting too distracted by our naked bodies.

I settled between Ben and Kate in the tiered seating of the battle classroom, my gaze locking onto the massive map Zayd had pinned to the front wall. It wasn't any map. Unlike the usual lesson layouts, which focused solely on the landscape of Skyberg, this one was different. It displayed the entirety of the Black Wing Territory and not only the narrow strip along our borders. A ripple of intrigue spread through the room. Whispers hummed like static, as cadets exchanged wary glances.

What was Zayd up to? Why was he showing these details to the class?

I sighed.

A hint for me?

He was relentless.

Some stared at the map as if Zayd had just revealed a long-buried secret.

But I wasn't one of them. I had already seen a better version of it. Zoe had mapped out more details, especially around Cathdear, during our mission in the Black Wing Territory. Still, if felt like an official war order when seeing it here, in an official battle class.

Yet, I was curious to know if the northern and southern parts were accurate. I leaned slightly, keeping my voice low. "Is that a fair representation of the Black Wing Territory?" I whispered, my question aimed at the only person in the room who would truly know. The king himself.

Ben turned his head and raised his brows at me, and when my questioning gaze didn't fall away, he lolled his head from side to side. "More or less," he replied whispering.

I glanced over the map once more. "What strikes you as the biggest difference?"

"With a guy possessing magical super hearing seated three spaces from me, I think this is a private conversation we can have later."

Mazdon smiled at us.

"No offence," Ben offered.

"None taken," Maz replied. "But know that if any secrets would slip, I wouldn't tell leadership about them."

"I appreciate it," Ben thanked.

I inspected the map and the three provinces with Dormondar in the north, Cathdear in the centre, where Black Castle was located near the largest lake, and Banaly in the south, where the iron welding forts stood. My toes curved with fury inside my boots as I saw the Finningham Manor at the north of Cathdear by the border to Dormondar. There was where Nassara resided. Further north, though, was Lord Malinger's Manor, which was the place currently under siege. It was where Ben should be right now, helping, instead of prioritising me.

"I do have smaller cities scattered around the lands. Camp leader Watson has only marked out the more densely populated areas. And I think both leadership and you know where the military base is, considering it's from where you stole the Black Blade."

I smirked at him. "Did you put it back there, so I'll get a chance to steal it again?"

"No. You already had one chance at impaling my heart. Foolish to allow you the same opportunity to do it again. Although…" He rolled up his sleeves halfway up his forearms, displaying the black tattoos swirling across his left arm. "You can't do that again."

I rolled my eyes at him, and it made him chuckle. Then he pointed at the north of Dormondar. "And leadership has clearly not mapped out all the destroyed villages in the far north with much detail. Ask Captain Coraly why. I'd love to see him squirm." Then he shifted his gaze to the white-wing side of the island to the east. "And the Spirits' Trek…is hmm…longer than that and it can't really be mapped out right with the mountains as such, but it's a fair attempt."

"How do you know what the Spirits' Trek looks like?"

"I have hiked it."

Mazdon, Kate, Emroyce and Kenyard leaned forward at the same time to stare at him.

I blinked, trying to find some sense of the information in my head. "What? When?"

"Ten years ago. How did you think I got my powers? My father didn't have any magic."

My head was spinning. Ben had hiked the Spirits' Trek before? Did leadership know this?

"I even gifted my healing magic to someone else."

"The Spirits gave you healing magic and you gave it away?"

"Yes, my general needs it more than I do."

"King Blackbone!" Zayd shouted across the entire room. "Do you have anything to add, or can you shut up?"

Ben craned his neck up. "My apologies, Camp Leader Watson. Please, continue."

Zayd went back to pointing on different landmarks, going over what advantages and disadvantages a curving landscape made to where you placed your soldiers. He also talked about where the best places were to make camp and how natural borders of mountains, forests or rocks helped or were an obstacle to a battle. All the information was in general terms, and he never mentioned any details of where the white-wings had their troops.

During the entire lesson, my mind had drifted off to ponder on how Ben had hiked the Spirits' Trek. If he could do it on his own, he was obviously not at the Bensguard Outpost to get help from other cadets to take him across it to gain more magic. He had been sixteen at the time. Who had he gone with? He must have had a white-wing present, or the Spirits would never have gifted him any magic.

I turned to Ben, and he looked back at me with curiosity. "If you already know how to get through the Spirits' Trek, then why am I wasting three years of my life in the academy when we could go tomorrow?"

He shook his head and observed Zayd, who again seemed to have heard me.

"We need to draw out as much magic as possible into the world of the living. That's all I can say. The rest will remain my secrets for now."

Oh, my Spirits, his secrets were driving me crazy. No matter how much I pondered his hints and clues, I couldn't understand him.

When Zayd dismissed the class, Ben and I visited the stables, and Ben watched me as I stubbornly tried to teach Fiona how to sit, lay down and roll over, but she was no Flora.

After a good hour of being frustrated with the pig and another hour of fooling around with Ben in the hay, Kate popped her head into the stable.

"Take your king by the ear and bring him out to the obstacle course. Emroyce is timing Zayd again."

We walked out to the field, and at the last moment, I pinched Ben's ear and dragged him closer for show. "Okay, I'm here," I called to Kate.

Ben rubbed at his ear as I let go. "Ouch," he grunted. "Why am I here? Is Camp Leader Watson even close to beating my record?"

Kate flicked her red hair back. "I didn't mean you should pull his ear literally."

"Well, it was fun. And probably necessary. He never listens," I defended.

Ben grunted. "Maybe if you didn't damage my ear, I could."

Zayd stood at the starting line, his muscles taut with clogged energy seeking release. His auburn hair was damp with sweat, strands clinging to his forehead from the earlier warm-ups. His sky-blue eyes were sharp as an eagle's, scanning the course like a predator assessing its prey.

He appeared in excellent form, his body honed, his reflexes sharp, and he was furious enough to tear through the course, pushing himself to the absolute limit. He wanted to break Ben's record. I suspected his relentless training wasn't just about proving himself. It was about me. But even if he shattered Ben's record by blazing through every obstacle in record time, it wouldn't change the way I felt.

From the starting line, Zayd looked over his shoulder at me. Ben saw it, and wrapped his arms possessively down my chest from behind me. That egged Zayd on even more, and he snapped his head towards the obstacle course to wait for Emroyce to count down.

"Three…two…one…ready! Go!"

Zayd shot forwards with incredible speed, his body flowing around the obstacles without putting a step out of place. A few cadets who watched held their breaths and the quiet tension was felt in the air, stiffening my spine and making my muscles even more sore than they were after the climbing this morning.

He was already on the balance bar and practically flew between the steppingstones and across the finish line.

Emroyce stared at his watch. "Four minutes and sixteen seconds. A tie with King Blackbone's record."

Ben grunted from behind my back but offered a 'well done' when Zayd walked past us, like Zayd had done to him in good sport.

"Yes, that was impressive," I offered, and Zayd glanced at me as if to say, 'There, I did it. I'm as good as the king'.

Ben was walking quietly next to me as we returned to our room. He went to the bathroom and rummaged through the cabinet above the washbasin. "Rose oil, lavender oil or camomile oil are what we have!" he shouted. "Which one do you want for your massage?"

Ben was keen on massaging me. Could it have anything to do with Zayd's progress? Ben had to put his hands all over me to feel in control and that I was his?

I looked around at the jungle of roses in our room that had already made the room possess their distinct scent. Maybe adding another scent to it would be too much. "Rose oil, please."

He exited the bathroom with the tub in his hand. "Get naked and lie down on your stomach on the bed."

"You aren't massaging me fully dressed in your uniform. An eye for an eye." I began to undress.

He removed his shirt, hanging it across the armrest of the desk chair and I marvelled at the sexy black tattoos on his left side.

"Not sure if that statement means that, but I'm happy to oblige. Do you need help with the buttons?" He wiggled his brows.

"Yes, please," I moaned, pushing my long, blue hair back, and Ben gripped the parting in the front and ripped my shirt wide open and the buttons went flying. The force had an immediate effect on my arousal levels.

"The king is again serving the servant."

"I'd worry how Watson treated you when you make statements like that, but I truly believe he treated you well. I heard what he said during the climb. 'Spirits or kings or generals, it doesn't matter. Anyone who knows you, and lets you go is a fool'. And I agree. Although, I seriously hope that the Spirits don't send a handsome offspring to compete for you because then I'm screwed." Naked, he guided me to stand in front of the bathroom mirror. "Don't simply look but really see yourself in the mirror. You're beautiful, and you're an amazing person."

Conscious of seeing my naked, slender body in the mirror, I tossed in his grip. But he turned me back and clamped one arm across my chest, beneath my breasts, and the other across my stomach. "Look at yourself! It isn't a traitor staring back at you. Because that is what you see, isn't it? I don't see that. You are beautiful."

His hand swiped down my body as he gazed at me in the mirror. His eyes were serene, not filled with lust or hunger or greed, but pure adoration of my beauty. He was seeing the naked body in its most natural form. Me, raw.

"Says the enemy," I muttered, and had no leeway at all to wrestle out of his grip.

He grunted. "It's my belief that you're living with the enemy, not the other way around. If you come with me to the Black Wing Territory to live permanently, I'll tell you all my secrets. It's the white-wing leadership who is forbidding me from talking."

"And I'm still baffled as to why you follow their orders?"

"When they threaten your life, I do, yes. When they even mention anything hinting at harming you, something inside me turns dark and uncontrollable. I fear that there will be another Battle of Bensguard if they push the threat on your life any harder. I have this inexplicable pull towards you that I can't control, little less understand."

"Like soulmates?"

"No, that's something different. Soulmates' souls are bound naturally to one another, and the two mates can hear each other from any distance apart. It isn't one you can remove; not by magic, or by any of the Spirits' marks of blessings. The soulmate connection is even above the will of the Spirits."

"Have you known anyone bonded as soulmates?"

"Not personally, but I have five couples in the Black Wing Territory." Ben's hands moved to caress my breasts, cupping them and then stroking his hands down my curves. "Get into bed before this turn into something other than a massage."

I sneaked out of the bathroom and lay down on the mattress. With my stomach on the bed, I tucked my arms along my body and sighed out a large breath through my nose to relax. Ben climbed up to sit on my arse with his knees hooked, and his legs along mine. He pressed his palms down on me, making rotating movements over my back.

"The muscles at the top of my shoulder blades are particularly sore after all the climbing."

"Here?" Ben pushed the heel of his palm where I'd described.

"Yes. Oh, that's good!"

The door burst open without warning, slamming against the wall as ten infantry soldiers stormed inside. At their front stood Camp Leader Tomason, her face unreadable, her stance rigid with authority.

Ben reacted instantly, yanking the sheet up to shield our bare bodies, his muscles tensing around me.

"Camp Leader Tomason!" Ben's voice thundered through the room.

Tomason didn't flinch. "Apologies for the intrusion, King Blackbone, but I have orders from Captain Coraly to apprehend you."

Ben's grip on the sheet tightened. "On what grounds?" he barked, his voice a dangerous growl.

Tomason's gaze remained steady. "Here, you don't have rank to question orders." She took a measured step forward. "We're to proceed to Camp Leader Mewer in the infirmary immediately to transfer your soul bond. Captain Coraly will no longer be your anchor. That role will temporarily belong to me."

A thick silence followed, broken only by my rapid breaths.

Ben didn't move. His breathing was steady, but the fire in his eyes was unmistakable. He knew what this was. This was bullshit. Harvey knew Ben wasn't bonded to anyone.

Tomason looked at Ben and discretely nodded towards me, so that the soldiers flanking her wouldn't see it, and Ben nodded once in response, as if to inform her that I knew of their association through Guard Jackoloy.

"Everyone out so King Blackbone can get dressed!"

Ben collected his uniform from the backrest of the chair and donned it quickly and held out his hands as Tomason held out shackles. I panicked, knowing what chains and shackles meant to Ben and how uncomfortable they made him.

"The shackles! They aren't necessary, Camp Leader Tomason!"

She ignored me and leaned closer towards Ben and whispered, "Captain Coraly prodded through Nesso's head when he was high on herbs. He discovered that you and Cadet Coraly were no longer bonded and he's not happy with her. I don't know what else he extracted from Nesso's mind, but the captain moved some troops around along the northern borders."

Ben stiffened. "He must know that Duke Finningham has retreated his troops then. Shit."

Tomason dragged Ben out to the corridor and threw a glance at me. "Cadet Coraly, Captain Coraly is expecting you in your family apartment this evening."

"Where is he now?" I growled. "I'd like a word with him."

"In the captain's office, I believe," she answered before leading Ben away.

I pulled on a uniform and stomped up the steps to the second floor and into his office where he sat in his yellow uniform behind his desk, his dark-blonde hair messy as if he had raked his fingers through it a few too many times.

"Harvey, this time you've gone too far. Shackles? You know he hasn't been soul bound to me for a while, and he has still not escaped. You could have escorted him to the infirmary with more dignity and no infantry soldiers!" I was fuming, and I wasn't holding back on my condemnation.

"You have the same determination as when you were five-years-old and refused to eat your vegetables, you have the patience to teach a pig to roll over, the stubbornness to get beaten up on the sparring mat until almost dead just to win, but to be so reckless as to allow the enemy king free reins in our military academy takes the prize. You're supposed to know exactly where King Blackbone is, what he's doing and what he's thinking at all times. And to report any suspicions to me! That's your job! If King Emille finds out what you've done, it'll be catastrophic for you and me! When will you see this? You've put us in further danger. General Denor can look inside our heads and learn of this and then what? He tells King Emille and we'll both be hanged for treason! You cannot be this naïve and let your emotions wipe your intelligence away! Angie, from now on, you aren't allowed to do anything without another white-wing present or go anywhere alone. Mazdon will guard you, so report to him where you will be going. And if you break my rules, I'll put you in the isolation cell where I'll know where I have you."

Wow! Had my brother just threatened to put me in the isolation cell? If he was going to pull rank on me, then there was nothing more to say. "What about out of this room? May I leave?"

"You shouldn't have been here in the first place!" he shouted at me so loudly it was clearly uncalled for in this small room.

I turned on my heel, walked out, and slammed the door shut. I let my frustration rip out of my throat in a scream, but it did nothing to pacify me. "I'm going to the canteen to get lunch!" I shouted to no one, as the second floor was empty, but I knew Mazdon would hear me.

As sure as anything, Mazdon was waiting for me by the doors to the canteen. His kind jade eyes watched me as I approached, and his strawberry-blonde hair was loose around his shoulders. His small mouth was pinned in a restrained smile.

"In trouble again, I hear," Maz said, a playful tug teasing at the side of his mouth.

"And apparently, my brother doesn't think you've anything better to do than babysit me and Kate."

"Like good old times in the cottage," he said, following me.

"Where's Kate?" I pushed open the door and entered the canteen, smelling garlic chicken and we grabbed a serving each.

"Practising fire wielding with Captain La Roy. She wanted to take a test this afternoon to see if she can receive a second circle on her uniform. She has been nervous about it all week."

We sat down at a table by the window with the view of the forest at the back of the building.

"Damn! I hadn't noticed. She hasn't told me."

"She knows that you've a lot on your plate already. And then there is the fact that she's nervous of failing, and also, she hates to tell you when she's with Captain La Roy, as it feels like a betrayal of your brother."

Ben placed himself at the door and scanned the canteen, so I waved for him to see me. He grabbed a tray with lunch and came to sit down. He was shrugging his shoulders a lot, as if he was feeling uncomfortable.

"Is there anything I can do?" I asked carefully.

Ben grunted. "Not unless you let me kill a few people."

I stopped chewing. "Who do you have in mind?"

"Camp Leader Tomason, for starters." He twisted his neck until it cracked. "When I'm bonded to Captain Coraly, the bond is entirely mute. When I'm bonded with you, it's like walking through a summer field enjoying the colours and scents of wildflowers. But, Camp Leader Tomason. Fucking unsettling, like flying as high as the clouds during a thunderstorm trying to avoid the lightning bolts."

Mazdon chuckled. "Yes, she's feisty, that one."

"Have you seen Nesso?" Ben asked me, twisting on the bench to have another look around the canteen.

"No. Why?"

"Him, I do actually really need to kill." His biceps tensed as he leaned his forearms on the table edge.

"What? No!" The garlic chicken that I had swallowed threatened to come back up.

Ben focused on his food. "From being reckless, he leaked information that could jeopardise my territory's safety. Your brother likely knows where I have my troops stationed, how many soldiers I have and the identity of my higher-ranking officers."

"But still…You can't kill Nesso! It's…Nesso!"

"Don't interfere with Black Wing Territory's laws, Cadet Coraly."

I ignored his rude use of my military name, which he otherwise never called me. Getting into an argument about it could cost me Nesso. "Okay. Wait. Let me think." The panic was stacking up like building blocks inside my chest. He couldn't execute Nesso! "I'll make you a deal. Don't execute Nesso, and I'll move with you permanently to Black Castle after graduation."

Mazdon deliberately cleared his throat at me, and I shushed him, staring at Ben.

He grunted. "You can't make that deal. You're marrying Duke Hartmore."

Shit! I had forgotten about that. "Wait. Well… Don't execute Nesso, and I'll come up with a better deal for you. Just give me some time to ponder over it."

"This is all going fucking badly," Ben said and left his seat without having touched his food.

I ran after him into the inner courtyard. "Where are you going?"

"I'm going for a walk. I need to think."

"But don't walk past Nesso and…you know…lash out and kill him. Please, I beg you to hold off until this has calmed down."

"This was what I talked about before when saying that they're servants, not friends. It's a fine line between a king and common folk, and you have to be a king to see it."

I inhaled the outdoor air. "You're saying I'm stupid?"

"No. You're a…" he sighed, pulling his fingers through his hair. He pulled me into his arms, his embrace firm, almost possessive. "You're my Spirit. You see things I don't even see. Like how stupid that comment was."

It was a public compliment slipping from his lips like a rare gift. But instead of reassurance, I felt dread.

This didn't bode well.

I had pacified him too easily. His anger should have lasted longer, burned hotter. But now, beneath his composed exterior, something dangerous dwelled, waiting to strike.

Was he planning on finding Nesso the second I turned my back?

His so-called 'walk' suddenly felt more like a hunt.

And I had just let the predator loose.

66

Mazdon and I sparred for a while after lunch and I kicked his arse, although I knew he had let me. After dinner, we headed out to the field to watch Kate's skills exam. I looked up towards the window of our family apartment and saw Harvey watching too.

"Why is my brother such a coward?" I muttered to Mazdon, as we lined up with the other spectators in a wide circle on the grass field.

Mazdon didn't answer right away. Instead, he exhaled slowly, as if choosing his words carefully. "He is not. You have a higher risk apatite when it comes to losing the people you love. Harvey chooses to see my sister happy with someone else rather than being dead."

We stepped into the circle of spectators, the damp grass wetting my boots. I leaned towards Maz to keep our conversation private. "Kate feels dead without him. You know that."

Mazdon's expression softened, but the sadness in his eyes only made my anger worsen.

The crowd thickened around us. A little too thick. My fingers drifted to the dagger sheathed at my belt and my grip tightened on the rune-carved hilt. Something about the air felt off – too charged.

I didn't trust this many people in one place, and I didn't want a dagger jabbed into my back.

Mazdon noticed. His gaze swept the crowd, and his shoulders tensed beside me. He wasn't quick to temper and to promise a fight like I was, but he wasn't stupid, either. He knew when something wasn't right. In a quiet voice that somehow cut through all the noise, he said, "Maybe Harvey believes he isn't worthy of her."

"He isn't," I spat. "He's an idiot, but I don't question your sister's logic for love."

Mazdon looked around. "And she absolutely hates this much attention. I hope she can focus on the test when there is such a large crowd surrounding her."

Captain La Roy began the test with the first measure of true power. Potency. He squared his shoulders and gave Kate a curt nod. "Straight up," he commanded, stepping back to give her space.

Kate inhaled deeply, then lifted her palm toward the sky. A second later, fire roared to life, a pillar of yellow and orange flame blasting upward, splitting the evening gloom apart. The sheer intensity of it sent a wave of scorching heat rolling over the field, forcing the line of spectators to stumble back and many shielded their faces. Gasps rippled through the crowd. The cadets were awed, but maybe also felt a little afraid.

The fire burned for several long heartbeats before Kate closed her fist, cutting the flames off as suddenly as she had summoned them. Smoke curled upwards from her closed fist, and it was the only lingering evidence of the power she had just unleashed.

Captain La Roy showed no reaction, but he didn't need to, the pride in his face was clear as day. He merely turned to gesture toward the next test. A scarecrow stuffed with straw was bound to a pole that had been hammered deep into the earth a distance away.

"Control," he said simply.

Kate didn't hesitate. She extended her palm, keeping it steady, as a thin, controlled stream of fire coiled through the air like a serpent before striking its mark. The scarecrow ignited instantly, and flames licked hungrily at the dry straw, devouring it from the inside out.

The spectators went rigid. This wasn't just a demonstration. This was a warning. Anyone who had doubted her skill had just received a very clear answer. The crackling fire cast flickering shadows over their stunned faces, and for the first time this year, respect gleamed in their wary eyes. Because now, they knew exactly what Kate could do. And none of them wanted to find out what it felt like to burn.

The last test was to verify her endurance, and she had to hold a flame in her hand for ten minutes. Captain La Roy found Emroyce in the audience, who seemed to have become Bensguard's official timekeeper.

Emroyce took a step forward and took out his pocket watch. "Three…two…one…ready! Go!"

Kate ignited the flame, and at first, it flickered in her palm, but she soon held it steady. After about half the time had passed, she began panting through her nose. "You can do it!" I shouted and saw her smile.

"And time's up!" Emroyce shouted as the ten minutes had passed.

Kate extinguished the flame and raised her hands up in victory, screaming out in glee. Captain La Roy shook her hand and handed over a symbolic second circle patch for her uniform. She didn't have to sew it on since Captain La Roy would inform administration of her advancement, and they'd ensure central depot delivered uniforms to her room with the second circle on it already from now on.

Kate let out a joyful laugh as she sprinted towards me, throwing herself into my arms with enough force to knock me back a step. "I did it!" she shouted, her eyes gleaming with exhilaration.

"We need to celebrate!" I grinned, squeezing her tightly. "I'm sure my brother has a few bottles of wine in the apartment we can steal."

"Well done," Ben said, his voice regal as he stepped up beside me.

I glanced around, my smile faltering. Murben was hovering just behind him, watching closely, probably making sure he didn't take off after Nesso with a knife in hand. My stomach twisted. Nesso was nowhere to be seen. I hadn't spotted him since the climbing lesson this morning, and the knot of unease in my gut only tightened at the realisation.

"We're heading up to the apartment to celebrate," I said, forcing the tension from my voice. "Have you finished walking off your troubles and want to come with us?"

Ben let out a dark grunt, his expression unreadable. "I'm sure your brother doesn't want me there."

I narrowed my eyes. "I wasn't going to ask for his permission. You're not yourself, Ben. You've been in a foul mood all day."

His gaze flicked to Mazdon, then back to me, a warning glinting in his eyes. He clearly thought this wasn't a conversation to have in front of an audience. Not that it mattered, considering Maz could pick up on the faintest whisper.

"That's why I went for a walk," he ground out, his jaw tight.

I scoffed. "Well, obviously, it didn't help."

His stare sharpened, daring me to push him further. His fingers flexed at his sides, controlled but rigged with tension. "I would have been worse if I hadn't."

Something unspoken passed between us in that moment. There was a flicker in his eyes I had trouble putting into words. Anger, frustration, or it could have even been from something darker lurking beneath the surface of his patience. For the first time since Ben had become my teammate, I wondered just how much trouble Ben had walked away from because I had refused to leave Bensguard…and how much he was still holding onto because he had to keep his kingdom from falling into chaos.

Fine, whatever. If he wanted to win, I'd let him have this one. I put my hands on my hips. "Did you kill Nesso?"

"Not yet. I was occupied watching the second-year cadets practise for their challenge. Five cadets died. It was gruesome to see how I'll end up looking in a year's time with my body smashed to the bottom of the gorge."

"I won't drop you. And I'm getting stronger." I circled my palm around my bicep to measure it.

Ben inspected the small rising bulge. "Maybe I need to lose weight."

I slapped at his bulging biceps, and they flexed, making the shirt move like a second skin.

"Only sixty teams left in first-year now. That's a record low." He cocked an eyebrow at me, loaded with a hint. "Still certain that your brother wouldn't jeopardise your life?"

"I never was." I sighed and smiled at Kate, who was eager to pull me away. "Ben, I must stay in the apartment tonight or my brother will make the situation worse for us. See you tomorrow?"

"Bright and early. We need to practise bringing out your wings, flying carrying heavy objects, as well as climbing."

I nodded before Kate, and I rushed up the steps to the second floor with Mazdon on our heels and burst into the apartment.

"I did it!" Kate shouted and jumped into Harvey's arms, who held her in the air.

"I knew you would. I've been training you since you were thirteen."

"Don't make this about you, you arse!" Kate bellowed with laughter.

Harvey put Kate down and retrieved a bottle of white wine and four glasses. He filled Kate's glass first, and after he gave me mine, I threw myself down on the sofa and stared at the flames dancing in the fireplace. We talked for a long while and it felt just like when the four of us had been in the cottage when we grew up, except we were older and were possibly getting more drunk.

When my eyes were about to close, I whispered to myself, knowing only Mazdon would hear me. "I'm going to bed soon, so maybe you should head back first and then I can leave these two to talk."

Mazdon stretched one arm into the air and had his other hand cover a yawn. "I'm tired. See you guys in the morning," he said and left swiftly.

Only minutes after he had left, I excused myself, too, quietly sneaking into my room, but left the door ajar, so I could watch them. But when I saw Kate climbing up onto my brother's lap and began pulling his uniform off, my eyes hurt, and I crawled into bed.

The days rushed past in a blur of training, drills, and stolen moments of peace. For once, my brother seemed lighter. Happy, even. His rare smiles had eased the tension that so often settled in the lines of his face.

But that all changed on the morning of Challenge Eight.

The moment I stepped inside our apartment after returning from breakfast, he was on me like a hawk, his sharp gaze scanning my face as if searching for answers. Answers I didn't have. His boots paced relentlessly across the floor of our apartment, like a signature sound of his agitation.

"Did Kate eat a steady breakfast this morning?" he asked, his voice clipped. He followed me into my room as I strapped on my daggers, his worry practically crackling in the air.

I hesitated, trying to recall the morning's gathering. "I think so."

Harvey exhaled sharply, clearly unimpressed with my vague response. "Make sure she remains focused when climbing," he pressed, as I buckled the last strap of my flight leathers and turned toward the door. "She can climb with her wings out if she needs to. That's allowed. There's no shame in that."

I stopped, fixing him with a look. "You do realise these are things you should be telling Mazdon, right? I can't help their team climb."

Harvey barely blinked. "I already told Mazdon." His expression hardened. "And he can probably hear me now."

A shiver ran down my spine. Not just from the pressure of my brother's concern, but from the unshakable feeling that something was about to go terribly wrong.

I nodded and bore my stares into him. "Anything you'd like to say to me?" I shoved the last dagger into my leg strap and bent low to put my small black blade knife into my boot.

"Yes. Don't make an embarrassment of our family name. And re-tie your right boot. It's too loose for climbing."

I crouched to tighten my boot. "I guess that translates to a 'good luck' in your screwed up language."

"If I told you 'good luck', it wouldn't ignite your stubbornness to prove me wrong."

Okay, fine, I guess my brother knew that much about me. "Sure, but it'd be nice once in a while."

I pushed past him and was about to close the front door when he shouted, "Hey, Angie! May the Spirit of Luck be with you!"

I rolled my eyes. That had made me even more furious and now I wanted to break all the records to prove to him I could do this and that he was an arsehole, which was probably the effect he had aimed for.

I darted down the stairs and reached the front courtyard, seeming to be the last one out to the front of the building. I inhaled a deep breath, and exhaled relief, as I saw Nesso standing next to Ben – alive. All the black-wings were there and my white-wing friends, including Brian, looking more or less cleared from drugs from yesterday's hallucination challenge, which

Cadet Somers and Cadet Crawly in the Boss Team had won.

"Captain La Roy sent you to protect Kate?" I asked Brian.

Brian nodded but then froze mid-step, his entire body tensing as if the ground beneath him had tilted. "I told my brother that Harvey probably had it covered, but he wouldn't let it go. He insisted. I also wanted to check on Valentina and Treylieh. Their challenge is right after yours."

I rolled my shoulders to shake off my own nerves. "Yeah…that one has got me on edge this morning too."

At least the Spirit of the World, for once, seemed to be in a merciful mood. Despite the tension twisting in my gut, the late April morning had come with pre-summer warmth. The ground at the bottom of the gorge between the mountains had grown thick with grass. The wildflower that blossomed at the edges of the cliff face basked in the sun as it shone on them. It smelt of spring and the birds in the surrounding trees were preparing for their offspring, chirping in merry tunes.

The sun kissed my skin as we made our way toward the cliff face, where Zayd stood waiting, already deep in preparation. His sharp camp leader gaze roamed across the gathered cadets as he organised six groups, assigning time slots to each. Ten teams would climb at a time. Five on either side of the gorge.

At the top of the cliffs, Camp Leader Neville and Camp Leader Tomason had positioned a team of third-year cadets to record times, their silhouettes like large birds against the sky. Behind them, Camp Leader Nar worked to set up for the second-year challenge. Mewer and Ward were notably absent. Mewer tied to his duties in the infirmary and Ward out patrolling the perimeter.

Ben and I were in the final climbing group. Maruto and Penya were set to go in the second, while Davis and Murben would climb in the fifth.

The first group contained Mazdon, Kate, Emroyce, Kenyard, Commander Daffron, and Nesso. They stood at the starting marks by the cliff face, wings unfurled, ready for the signal. From where we watched at a distance, I could see the rigid set of Kate's shoulders, and the way Mazdon subtly flexed his fingers at his sides. Every cadet bracing themselves for the challenge.

Zayd walked across the greenery to check on each team to see that they were happy to start. "I'll count backwards from three and then whistle. At the whistle, you start!" he shouted his instructions, as he walked out to stand in the middle of the pass. "Three…two…one…" Then, Zayd put his fingers into his mouth and made a sharp whistle.

The teams rushed to the wall and started climbing. Mazdon and Kate made good headway.

My chest hurt, thinking of the possibility that Kate could fall to her death at any moment.

Ben reached for my hand and held it steady in his. "She'll be fine. Mazdon won't let them fall."

"That's all up to the Spirit of Death." My breath came stuttering out of me. This was so hard to watch.

Ben tipped his head down. The pitiful shine to his eyes made my heart sore. "Don't you have a Spirit of Life, as well?" he asked. There was no sarcasm, counting my Spirits this time.

"Yes, but you pray to him when you're on the verge of dying and want to live, or during child labour, or to wish for a happy life. This is all in the Spirit of Death's hands."

Both of us looked around at the climbers, wondering who of them the Spirit of Death wanted to take.

On average, it took thirty-five minutes to climb the forty metres to the top. The winner could make it just under thirty. As always, there seemed to be fierce competition between Emroyce and Commander Daffron. Kenyard and Nesso weren't far behind, but Emroyce and Commander Daffron didn't seem to remember that they had teammates as they left them behind, racing toward the top.

Kate and Mazdon had been ascending the wall for about fifteen minutes, and I wasn't any less nervous, unable to stand still. Zayd paraded the grounds and walked toward me.

"How are you feeling, Angie?"

I pinched my waist with both hands to hide my trembling. "Top form. How is Kate doing? Is she steady or has she started shaking? Can you see?"

Zayd twisted in his step, looking up at Kate and sharpened his far-sight on her. "She has been climbing for almost twenty minutes. Slightly shaky hands by this point is normal."

"So, she's shaking? She's getting tired?" Spirits, that didn't help my nerves.

"She's fine, Angie. She looks strong." He took my hand from my waist and lifted it up to inspect my palms. "You haven't applied chalk. I have some extra in my backpack if you need."

"I'll prepare her," Ben interjected so sternly I removed my hand from Zayd's hold.

I trampled in my own steps, looking up every few seconds to find Kate still secure on the wall and getting closer to the top. Emroyce and Kenyard had reached the finish line way before anyone else and stood gloating at the top of the cliff.

At least that was one team of friends out of danger.

The burning sensation in my chest vanished into thin air as Kate and Mazdon crawled over the ledge and mounted the top. They weren't the last ones. The Horse Girls Team had finished last, yet it was still an achievement as neither of them had fallen.

Now I just had to sit down on the gravel and endure the excruciating wait whilst watching groups two through five climb. Ben sat down next to me, guarding me like a hawk.

I put my hand on his broad thigh. "You're very quiet today."

"It's challenge day. I'm focused. Killing is permitted today, and I don't want an ambush to end us."

The feeling of being targeted crawled over my arms and I glanced around, finding Gravelhorn leering at me.

"You think Gravelhorn will try something?"

"He's in our climbing group, so I wouldn't put it past him."

The sharp whistle startled me as Zayd started the second group. The Backstabber Team looked strong, but the Elderly Team was struggling. Cadet Dommen was nearly eighty years old. How was he supposed to climb that tall cliff, and why had he not forfeited the challenge?

"If you ever think I'm cruel to my soldiers, remember this," Ben said, pointing at Cadet Dommen.

I nodded, squinting against the sun as I watched them climb.

Halfway up, Cadet Dommen lost his foothold, his front slamming into the rock and he sprawled along the wall. I stood up, too edgy to sit, and held a hand up to shield my eyes from the glare of the sun.

"Shit! He needs to get a new foothold!"

Ben wrapped around me, pulling me to his chest. "He'll fall. Don't look. You'll go into shock before our climb."

"He's a good man. He was always so kind to us at the cottage. This isn't fair."

Ben grunted. "Don't look."

"He'll be fine, right? His wings were out, right?"

"He has no strength left to push away from the wall to get space to use them. Don't look."

I burrowed my face into Ben's flight jacket. A gasp tore through the group, and I knew Dommen fell. There was another gasp, and some cadets covered their mouths with their hands. He was dead. Damn!

"What's happening?" I demanded, my pulse hammering in my ears.

"Cadets are helping to clear the body to one side." His voice was tight, controlled.

My heart was pounding. "How are Maruto and Penya doing?"

Ben cocked his head up. "Maruto and Penya are nearing the top." Ben held me tightly, with no sign of letting me go. Time crawled, stretching unbearably thin. "The third group is ready to go," he muttered after a while.

Zayd whistled again.

My breath stuttered.

Thankfully, everyone in this group made it up safely, and with no foul play. The Party Girl Team had been among them, though, and I can't say I'd have lost sleep over Cadet Darling's death if she had fallen. The Archery Team with Ashton and his father had climbed to the top first, but the Serious Team hadn't been far behind.

Another whistle.

The fourth group took their marks and after another forty minutes had passed, Zayd whistled again, and it was the fifth group's turn. My stomach twisted. This group had Murben and Davis in it, but also the Agility Team, The Twin Team, the Prank Team and the Earth Kissing Team.

I clenched my fists, every muscle in my body tensed as I watched them prepare. This was it. If something was going to go wrong, it would be now.

Cadet Oscarson's magic was to climb walls, and his hands stuck to the rock, so he happily swung around not seeming to have a care in the world whilst his teammate Cadet Lerren, who had a breath that made humans and animals faint, steadily ascended the cliff. Although, Cadet Lerren was diverting from his upward trajectory and was heading into Cadet Wells space in the Earth Kissing Team.

I took my hand off Ben's thigh and pointed up the wall. "What is Cadet Lerren doing? He needs to keep to his path."

Ben grunted. "I'm sensing that you might have to look away again soon."

"What? He's going to kill Cadet Wells?"

Ben didn't answer as he kept watching.

"But…but…" I stammered. "Cadet Wells is like the nerdiest, sweetest man ever. He isn't built muscly like you other guys and is probably suited for intel in the future. Why would he be a threat?"

"Maybe the Spirit of Death needs an intel guy." This time, there was definitely sarcasm.

"That's morbid and not the slightest bit funny." I walked up to Zayd. "Surely, you must disqualify Cadet Lerren. Tell him to move away from Cadet Wells."

Zayd shook his head. "I can't do that. In the challenges, this is allowed. You know the rules, Angie."

Fury surged through me, and before I could stop myself, I lashed out, driving my fist hard into his shoulder. He barely flinched. No sharp intake of breath, no startled reaction. He just deliberately turned his head slowly to meet my glare.

Shit. I shouldn't have done that.

Then the bastard had the audacity to smile. "Steady your emotions," he murmured, voice as smooth as ever. "You'll need them under control when it's your turn to climb."

I spun on my heel, stalking back toward Ben, but as I lifted my gaze back to the cliff, a movement caught my eye. The sight was a flash of chaos. Cadet Lerren threw himself after a fleeing Cadet Wells, getting a hold of his trouser leg and yanked hard. Wells clung hard to the stony wall, not letting go. Cadet Lerren climbed, slithering along his back like a snake, and breathed into his face.

The effect was instant.

Cadet Wells fainted, his body folding like a collapsing building and he fell through the air. The air split with a collective gasp, as his body plummeted, gravity seizing him and pulling him into a deadly spiral.

Cadet Lerren folded his wings out to sail the winds casually, as if he hadn't just murdered someone. He had rather made the effort to kill another cadet than try to win. I couldn't believe it. I stood frozen, disbelief and horror locking my breath in my throat.

Ben turned me towards his chest again. "Don't look." His voice had no hint of shock or empathy, like a trained king in battle.

At least the Prank Team wouldn't win this challenge, even as Cadet Oscarson was clearly the fastest to reach the top out of everyone. But both members of the team had to get to the top for the time to be recorded.

"I'm getting ideas, Black Queen!" Gravelhorn shouted over the sixth group whose members were sitting waiting for their turn.

"Drop dead, Gravelhorn!" Literally please!

He calls me 'Black Queen' now?

I was shaking. Another one dead. There were only fifty-eight teams remaining of first-years.

I was relieved when I saw Murben and Davis climb over the top of the wall, but at the same moment, a completely new anxiety bubbled up inside me.

It was my turn.

Spirit of Death, please don't take me to the Underworld.

This was going to get fucking awkward, but I had to use my black wings, as my white ones were still hurting from being shot with an arrow by Gravelhorn. As I unfurled them from my back, a gasp rode like a wave over the cadets, and one cadet coughed. "Mutt!"

Ben ripped the dagger out from my leg holster and hurled it towards the man, landing the blade straight into his jugular. One second, his eyes shot wide open, the next his back tipped onto the ground as blood pumped out of him. The cadets surrounding him gasped. Then there were screams of panic. Chaos broke out. Cadets pushed each other, so Ben kept an arm in front of me for protection in case a weapon would come hurling our way.

"Anyone else plans to call my queen an uncalled-for nickname?" Ben asked, his voice grim.

Everyone settled. No one said a word as they stared at him. Even Gravelhorn was quiet.

Ben and I picked up our backpacks from the ground.

"You didn't want me to see people falling off a cliff a long distance away from us, so I wouldn't go into shock, but that," I nodded with my head for the dead cadet. "You thought was a good idea?"

"I told you, I lose control when people threaten you."

I rubbed my hands over my face. "Like when you severed Davis's thumb just for making red marks on my wrists?"

"Yes. But you must admit, I've become a lot better since then."

"You just threw a knife into a cadet's jugular because he called me a mutt."

"Okay, so with a few exceptions."

"And I liked that blade. It was my father's."

Ben turned around and looked at the dead guy's teammate, who hadn't moved and was gasping in shock, seemingly unsure about what to do with the body. "Clean that blade and give it back to Cadet Coraly safely, or I'll have another one in your throat by the end of the week."

The man nodded. Tears streaming down his face.

"There. Problem solved," Ben muttered, but his voice was tight, his jaw clenched.

I barely had time to process what had happened before he guided me toward the spot Zayd had assigned us, which was the first slot on the west side. Behind us, the third-year cadets moved in swiftly to drag Cadet Wells' corpse away.

I risked a glance back. *A mistake.*

The corpse dragged limply across the ground, dirt and blood streaking together beneath it. The other two bodies lay stiff and silent in a grotesque row, their faces obscured by a black Bensguard branded cloth.

Ben's hand found my back, pressing me forward. "Don't look," he murmured, his tone leaving no room for argument.

But I already had. And I could never unsee it.

Zayd glowered at me, before he repeated the rules the same way he did for every team before a new start. If he was angry with me, he was barking up the wrong tree. I had done nothing, and it was leadership who had thought it'd be a great idea to kidnap black-wings to keep in the camps. So, this was his own bloody mistake.

I pinned that stare right back into him and I believe he got the hint before he moved on to the next team along, which unfortunately was the Angry team with Cadet Gravelhorn and Cadet Malloopa who, using his magic, learned everything by a mere touch, and was probably an expert at climbing at this point.

The Fistfight Boys Team was also in our group and placed on the other side of the Angry Team. The claw-extension-guy, Cadet Lewis, and Cadet Kwi, who could weaken other's magic, were more focused on the Angry Team than us, though.

Ben took out the tub of chalk from the backpack and waited for me to hold out my hands before he powdered over them and then he did his own, rubbing his hands together. "I won't let you die. You climb close to me. If you fall, push your feet against the wall like we've practised, so you can sail down with your wings. If you can't, fold your wings tightly to your body, so I can get a good hold on you and fly you to the ground."

"I can't do this," I whimpered, my hands shaking so hard the chalk was dusting off them.

Ben grabbed at my wrists and looked deep into my eyes. "Yes, you can. You've done this hundreds of times."

"With a harness and rope."

"And you've never fallen. This is the same, and Watson has done us a solid again."

"What?"

"He has placed Cadet Kwi next to Cadet Gravelhorn. They aren't on friendly terms, and Cadet Kwi will most likely weaken Gravelhorn's strength magic. That will put him off-kilter to how he's normally used to climbing. And you'll climb on my left, so they won't get to you without going through me first. You purely have to focus on your own climbing."

I nodded, forcing a few deep breaths.

Then Zayd whistled.

The sharp sound pierced my ears, and as I reflexively turned towards the sound, I found his eyes locked onto mine like a silent command. A warning. A threat almost.

Don't fall. Don't die.

Whatever fear I had, whatever doubts clawed at the edges of my mind, there was no room for them now.

Not when failure meant more than just losing.

My heart raced, and fear pounded my chest as I darted towards the wall and searched for good grips.

"Take that path a bit more to your left. It has that outcrop and the fissure in the wall that you can hold on to," Ben instructed and pointed.

I saw the marks and headed for them, keeping an eye on the Angry Team beside us. But Ben had been right. Gravelhorn was clearly struggling and was throwing angry stares at Kwi.

Halfway up, the burning in my muscles started to intensify, and I could feel the acid building up in my limbs, each movement more laboured than the last. My hands trembled, and my biceps quivered, threatening to give out at any second.

"Are you okay?" Ben's voice broke through my growing panic, the concern clear in his tone.

"I don't know," I called, struggling to breathe. "I don't normally get this tired. We're not even halfway up."

Ben's brow furrowed, his eyes scanning me quickly. "It's the shock of what you've experienced today," he said, his voice calm but urgent. "And it's been a while since breakfast." Without another word, he climbed towards me. He pulled something from his pocket, pressing it into my mouth before I had time to react.

"Here," he urged.

A rush of sweetness exploded in my mouth, making me momentarily dizzy. "What was that?" I asked, trying to focus, but my thoughts were spinning.

"Glucose tablet," Ben said, his voice clipped but still tense. "It'll help you keep going."

"Spirits, it's too sweet," I muttered, my teeth almost aching from the intensity of it.

"Focus," Ben prompted. "Continue climbing!"

The jagged rock was rough against my fingers, but I kept going, one stretch of my arm at a time. Higher foothold, another grip. Higher foothold, another grip. Ben was right at my flank, and I could feel his hand on the small of my back every now and again. The burning in my chest that had been pumping since I left the ground eased off the closer we got to the top.

I curved my fingers over the ledge and felt grass. I only had to heave myself up to the top and I'd be done. But as I tried, I failed. I was too heavy for the strength I had left, and my wings were dragging me down. I bent my knees to fling them upwards but couldn't get them over the ledge.

I was stuck and my arms burned with exhaustion.

"I can't get up," I panted with no strength left to even turn my head to look at Ben, so I couldn't tell where he was.

My heart pounded in my chest and my muscles screamed in protest, as the tension mounted with every breath. It didn't make a damn bit of difference that I had come this far. Every second was a battle I wasn't sure I could win. My fingers were on fire, hurting like the Underworld against the rough stone. No matter how hard I tried, they kept slipping. Slowly, the grip I had was weakening.

I tipped my head up, panic creeping in as I saw Tomason's face above me, her eyes hard, but there was also a tint of pity glazing them.

"Get yourself together," she hissed.

I couldn't. I was too weak, every part of my body screaming for rest. My wings, heavy and clammy with sweat, were dragging me down. I tried to steady my grip, but it was futile. My fingers kept slipping, bit by bit.

"I'm too weak," I cried out. "My wings are too heavy."

It was bitter-sweet, but it was the truth.

I couldn't fight it.

I was done.

With a torturing realisation, I felt my body tremble as my last grip faltered. "Tell Ben I love him," I shouted, my voice as broken as my hopes. But I desperately wanted to send Ben that message, even if it was the last thing I'd say in this life.

Then, the last shred of strength I had left in my fingers abandoned me, and with a sickening lurch in my gut, I felt my hand slip completely off the rock.

67

The world tilted. I saw the ground far below. My body paralysed by the thought of the terrifying free-fall.

Then, out of nowhere, a hand shot down. Tomason's arm. Her grip wrapped tightly around the leather strap across my back, yanking me upward with a strength I didn't know she had. The shock of the sudden movement knocked the breath out of me, but I didn't care. Her hands were my lifeline.

She had broken the rules. Camp leaders weren't allowed to interfere. She had risked everything to save me; her reputation and her career. On top of that, she would get lashed.

I gasped for air, barely able to form the words. "Thank you, Camp Leader Tomason."

My fingers dug into the rocky surface in disbelief that I was still alive, that I was still here, and not murdered by the hands of gravity. I clawed forwards to where Ben had just heaved himself over the cliff edge. Before I could process the moment, he had sprinted to my side and wrapped his arm around me, lifting me up with a force that left me breathless. I was weightless for a second, my feet leaving the ground as he held me close, his body radiating heat and relief.

"Never do that to me again!" His voice cracked and a thread of panic laced every word. "Next time, you fucking climb!" His words were edged with his fear as he held me.

He was terrified of losing me. That much was clear.

Every part of my body was shaking, reeling from the adrenaline and I realised just how much I needed him to hold me, fiercely, as if my life depended on it. The arms he had curved around my back held me up, refusing to let go of me. Then, one hand slid to cup the back of my head as he pressed his forehead against mine, his breath ragged and hot. "And next time," he growled, "you fucking tell me you love me yourself."

He kissed me as if no one was watching, as if the world around us didn't exist. This moment, this connection, was the only thing that mattered. His lips claimed mine with a hunger I had never felt before, his tongue sweeping into my mouth, as if he needed the taste of me or he'd die.

Ben didn't hold back. He let the fire consume him, consume us. His kiss deepened and his grip tightened, and it seemed that all his fear of nearly losing me melted into pure passion. He entered my mouth with his tongue again and again, and let our wet lips meet. There was no hesitation, no restraint. We were tangled together in the aftermath of chaos.

"That's enough," Tomason growled, and Ben made a conscious effort to pull away from me. "Helping Cadet Coraly, and using my magic to cloak this, will be considered as your 'any gift' from the archery challenge prize, so that it gets me out of trouble. Understood?"

We both nodded. What she had done for us, for me, was something I'd always remember and if I got the chance, I'd repay her. Accepting it as the 'any prize' was the best bet we had to protect her from her demise. "Thank you," I whispered.

Tomason walked off towards the third-year cadets who were helping her time the other first-year cadets.

Ben put his forehead against mine and we stared into each other's eyes for a long while and laughed in nervous fits.

The climbers had all finished, and Gravelhorn gave us a wide berth as he and Malloopa walked down from the mountain.

Ben stroked my hair and kissed the top of my head. "It's time for the second-year cadets' eighth challenge. Tomason says we must descend to the ground again to watch from there."

I snapped my wings into my back. "When did Tomason tell you that?"

Ben tapped a finger on his head. "The soul bond."

Oh, right. Jealousy totally bubbled up inside me. "What else do you two share through the bond?"

"Only active thoughts. She has no power in retrieving more than I want to share. It's the same as if I was standing next to her talking."

"So, the same treatment as with me? I didn't get to learn any other information, either."

"No." He shook his head, correcting me. "You could have had more if you wanted. Not the secrets, but I don't mind sharing my emotions with you or the other senses; touch, smell, hearing, seeing and tasting. But you wanted privacy, so I taught you how to put up a powerful shield. It was your choice."

I cocked my brows at him. "Remember you said that for the next time we're bound."

A grin curved into his challenge-smile. "I take that as a challenge." We moved towards the back route of the mountain. "Should we fly down?" The tone in Ben's voice suggested he already knew my answer.

"No, thank you. I want to keep my feet on the ground."

"If you're going to the First Year Ball, you'll have to train your wing muscles."

"Not today. I've already tucked them back in."

He sighed and snapped his wings into his back before he took my hand as we walked down together. It felt strange to hold his hand in public. I wasn't ashamed, but proud to be his woman. We joined Emroyce, Kenyard, Brian, Kate and Mazdon, who had stayed behind to watch Valentina and Treylieh as they were about to fly across the gorge in the infamously deadly eighth challenge.

"Well done, Angie," Mazdon and Emroyce said as Kate crashed into me in an embrace like usual.

"We survived our eighth challenge!" she chirped before letting go of me.

"I barely did. But Emroyce, Kenyard and you were so fast climbing to the top."

Emroyce tossed our backpacks in front of our feet. "Yep. Camp Leader Nar said we won. Unofficially, of course. They will announce it tomorrow during the assembly."

"Congratulations to my bigger bedroom."

"Your? No, no, no! It already had my plaque on the door before we left this morning," Emroyce teased.

Our laughter faded from my lips. A short distance away, standing rigid among the crowd, was Valentina's mother. A sharp pang twisted in my chest. My heart really hurt. Memories surged forward, flashing brightly in my mind even when I fought to keep them away. Duke Hartmore's guard slitting Sergeant Karson's throat, the life draining from him in an instant.

Oh Spirits, don't let her see her daughter die today.

My feet itched to move, to go to her, to offer some kind of comfort. But how could I? How could I stand beside her when I was the reason her husband was gone?

I swallowed hard and nodded toward her. "Valentina's mother is here."

Ben followed my gaze, his expression grim like he wanted badly to kill the duke. We watched her anxiously as she bit her nails.

Ben exhaled sharply, tipping his head down, pinning his eyes on me. "I could never watch my child go through this…" His jaw clenched, his fingers tightening at his sides. Then he turned to me, his eyes fierce, unyielding. "Our children will not attend this academy. They'll not participate in these insane challenges. I won't allow it."

His words rang between us, a promise, a vow.

He was clearly worked up about it, and I lost my words. It took me about fifteen seconds of hesitation and fifty blinks to get the words out. "Our children?"

He was a king, so of course he needed an heir, but I had never given it a thought. We still had the problem of Duke Hartmore looming over us. Plus the fact that Ben had the tendency to eject death magic that could kill me every time we got too intimate.

"Aren't you planning a little too far ahead?" I muttered and crouched, opening my backpack.

Ben grunted. "Perhaps, but as long as you know that I need at least two sons, we can discuss the details later."

"Spirits! And what if we only have daughters?"

Why was I even entertaining this conversation?

"Then we keep trying."

I brought up a water bottle and a banana from the pack and closed it. "And how would that work exactly with all our issues?"

I took a sip of water and peeled the banana, sliding it into my mouth suggestively.

Ben seemed to lose focus. "Those details can twist our minds another day. Worrying about Karson and Treylieh is enough for today. And you let me worry about Duke Hartmore."

Speaking of my mission squad to Duke Hartmore's Manor, first up was Cadet Crawly and his teammate John Somers. Crawly had the magic ability to perform memory wipes and Somers never needed to eat, so he wouldn't tire, but none of those skills were helpful in this challenge.

Camp Leader Nar stood at the edge of the cliff, commanding the challenge with sharp, decisive gestures. Even from here, I could see her pointing toward the Boss Team as Somers tightened a thick rope around Crawly's torso like a noose preparing for execution.

Zayd stood beside Nar, his expression unreadable, but the moment he whistled, Somers unfurled his wings with a powerful snap, gripping the rope and they sprinted a few steps together before Somers launched into the air. The tension in the rope strained as he lifted Crawly, the wind pushing against them as they soared across the gorge. Somers was one of the strongest second-year cadets, and it showed. He barely faltered, carrying Crawly with ease to the other side.

On the far ledge on the other side, Tomason inspected them with a keen eye but didn't comment. They made the swap seamlessly, Crawly now binding Somers in the same rope. Tomason's sharp eyes scanned every detail for anything that could go wrong. The knot held firm during the flight back, and soon they both stood victorious at the finish line.

Then came the Scare Tactic Team. Cadet Daro Jenson, whose eerie magic could unearth a person's deepest fears and desires, stood poised with his partner, Cadet Christopher Charney. Charney was my brother's most trusted ally, an expert at blocking out the magic of others. It stunned me that leadership had allowed him to compete. His ability was too valuable to risk, but here he was, ready to take on the challenge.

Daro and Charney looked steady as they made their journey across and back, obviously having practised it many times. But the next team wasn't so lucky.

A pair of cadets I didn't recognise stepped forward. The wind had picked up slightly, the tension in the air thick as they began their flight. Halfway across, something went wrong.

The rope.

A snap.

An echo tore through the gorge and the knot unravelled. It was instant and the slimmer cadet tumbled, limbs flailing, a silent scream frozen on his lips as he plummeted.

The height was unforgiving. There was no time to react, no time to spread his wings, no time to save himself.

The teammate who was flying them, tried desperately to grab for his friend but couldn't get a grip and the body plummeted incredibly fast towards the ground. The flying cadet had to abort, so he wouldn't follow the same fate as his teammate.

"Don't look," Ben grunted and folded me into his chest, as the man was about to splatter onto the ground.

"This is madness," I cried into his flight jacket but looked anyway.

"It is," Ben agreed.

The cadet hit the ground with a brutal finality.

A death designed by the academy itself.

Way to go motivation!

I kept myself curled into the curve of Ben's chest as the next team failed. The smaller woman couldn't hold on to her larger male friend and he dropped like a rock, dying instantly at impact with the bottom of the gorge.

"Madness," I muttered once more, but then stiffened as I saw purple hair step out onto the edge of the cliff.

It was Valentina and Treylieh' turn. *Spirits!*

My nail dug into Ben's arms, and I could barely breathe. "Please, Spirit of Death, I'll owe you one."

"No! You'll not owe the Spirit of Death anything. They'll make it. I'll pray to the Spirit of the Living if need be."

I noticed Valentina's mother shifting the balance from one leg to another. Oh, my Spirits, the suspense was killing me. She had to make it. They had to make it. This was the hardest challenge of the academy, with most casualties. But they weren't going to be one of them.

Ben clamped his arms too tightly around me. I pushed my elbows out. "I need more air. I can't breathe. I feel dizzy."

"Breathe slowly but deeply. Come on. In through your nose. There you go. All the way. And out through your mouth," Ben instructed, raising and lowering his hand in the air in front of me.

"Thanks. It's better."

Treylieh began tying the rope around Valentina and it was hard to see from where we stood, but it looked like he was tugging at the rope more times than necessary to check that the knot would hold.

Zayd whistled.

My heart galloped. Stomach clenched. Breathing stopped.

Treylieh lifted off the cliff and took Valentina over the gorge.

"Come on. Come on. Come on," I chanted, nervously bouncing on my legs.

He landed on the other side. *He's across! Valentina is safe!*

Tomason stepped in, double-checking the knot with swift, precise fingers. It was a clear violation of the rules, but did anyone see? Would anyone dare report it? Zayd, with his unnerving far-sight, had likely caught it, but he had never been the type to throw someone to the wolves. But, if he thought Ben would take her lashes, who knew what Zayd planned to do with the information?

A gust of wind rustled through the air as Valentina beat her wings furiously, lifting Treylieh from the ledge. My breath hitched as I watched them take off over the gorge.

Then it happened.

She was losing altitude.

Too fast.

Too damn fast.

My heart slammed against my ribs. Valentina's wings strained, her entire body trembling with effort, but she wasn't built for this. She wasn't strong enough to carry a man of Treylieh's size.

They were falling.

Not a slip, not a struggle. A straight, merciless drop.

Valentina would never let go of him. They were teammates. Teammates were sacred. She would rather die than release him, and at the speed they were plummeting, that was exactly what would happen.

A violent curse tore through my mind.

My eyes darted to Ben, and although he was built like a force of nature, he had as little control over this as I had. Moreover, he was monstrous in size. How the heck was I supposed to carry him over the gorge next year?

My panic built up and grew stronger as Valentina wouldn't let go of Treylieh to save herself.

Ben threw his arm around my shoulders and pulled me towards him. "Don't look."

No! I knew what that meant. Ben knew they wouldn't make it. "No!" I cried. "Not Valentina."

The nerves were dancing along my spine too potently to keep myself locked in Ben's hold. I wrenched myself free, turning just in time to see Valentina desperately beating her wings, straining every muscle in her body to slow their descent.

But she wasn't strong enough.

The ground was nearing. At the last possible second, Valentina made an agonising choice. She let go.

Treylieh plunged the final meters, his body crashing onto the earth with a bone-cracking thud. Valentina, lighter and more agile, managed to catch herself mid-air, hovering for a breath before landing shakily beside him.

We sprinted.

Ben, Mazdon, Emroyce, Kate and Brian raced across the field, but my mind barely registered them. I dropped to my knees beside Treylieh just as a guttural scream ripped through him.

Bones. Exposed. Everywhere.

They were jutting through his skin and piercing the flesh at impossible angles. His arm was twisted unnaturally and his leg bent where no joint should exist. Blood seeped into the dirt beneath him. His agony was unbearable to witness.

I reached for him, but what could I do?

His screams tore through the air, matching the wreckage of his body.

"I'm sorry, mate," Valentina barked irritably. "Just stop bitching about it like a child. You'll live."

She held her hands over his body, bridging his bones together and into their right place one at a time. I could hear the cracks and snaps as they mended.

I wanted to hug her so badly, but she was busy, swearing to herself as she worked.

Brian gave Emroyce a high-five as we all recognised Valentina for who she was. "I'll get a stretcher, so we can carry you to the infirmary, Treylieh," Brian explained and walked off.

"You return with Emroyce and Mazdon," Ben ordered me. "I need to have a word with Tomason before I return."

He marched over the grass and up the path that wound along the back of the mountain. I couldn't help but watch the way Ben's muscles flexed with every step and his broad shoulders rolled out the tension of the day's challenges.

We made our way back with the others, and for the first time in what felt like forever, the tension had eased. No one from our group had died today. A rare victory. The relief left us light-hearted. Laughter echoed through the rocky terrain as we teased and bantered with each other, slipping back into the easy rhythm we had known when growing up together.

That afternoon, Kate, Maruto, and I stood at the edge of the training field, watching as the men tore through the obstacle course. Their bodies moved with disciplined power, kicking up mud beneath their feet as they hurdled walls and climbed ropes.

When evening settled, I slipped away to my room and waited for Ben, knowing he would come.

But I also knew my time was limited. Harvey would expect me back in the apartment, and if I didn't return soon, he'd start another fight about my relationship with Ben.

I was sitting by the desk when Ben returned in the late evening. I had been waiting for him for a good hour, mindlessly doodling on a letter I had received from General Denor who was apologising for not being able to have our non-date this month. He had postponed it until five days before the ball.

Ben groaned as he leaned down to kiss my forehead. "I'm sorry we didn't win the bigger bedroom you wanted, but I have a peace offering." He stretched out the same kind of white small paper box that he had held when I had seen him holding hands with Nassara at the black-wing spring festival.

"You had this at the spring festival. It wasn't a gift to Nassara? It was for me?"

"Yes, I was going to bring it to you after the ball. But this is a new one."

I opened the lid and smiled. Inside, there was a large slice of peanut butter cake. I put the box down on the desk and got a bite into my mouth, breathing out a satisfied moan. "It's just like Mother's. You know…sometimes…I miss my mother. Is that wrong? It feels wrong. She killed many people when she fought at the Battle of Bensguard."

He hunched low by the chair and looked up into my eyes. "A mother is always one's mother, Angelica. Of course, you're allowed to miss her."

"She was a great mother, apart from fooling my father for twenty-five years and breaking his heart…and causing his execution. I never knew that growing up, of course. To me, she was simply my mother. She kissed my scraped knees, brushed my hair, tucked me in at night and sang me lullabies. Just like any normal mother. Then, bam! When I turned fifteen, she turned into this traitorous monster. I should miss my father more, but…" I realised I had become sentimental. I cringed. "Where do you buy these from, did you say?"

"Trade secret."

"Hmm…blackmail." I gently tapped a finger on his nose.

He stood up. "How is that blackmail?"

I pondered it with a soft mutter emitting from my throat. "I'm sure you want something in return for this generosity."

He gathered up my hair and pushed it over one shoulder as he bent down to kiss my neck on the other side. "That I'll only tell you after you've finished and are in my debt."

"Jokes on you, because this cake is so totally worth it." I brought a big chunk to his face and smothered its melted chocolate coat over his mouth, nose and a bit of his cheek. "Oh dear," I huffed and turned around to lick the chocolate off his face. "New improved recipe."

When my tongue passed over his, he moaned sensually. "Best cake I've ever had." He picked me off the chair, folding my legs around his waist. "Maybe I'll collect on that debt right now." He carried me to the bed and lowered me onto my back, ripping the uniform shirt open so the buttons flew everywhere in the room, just the way he knew turned me on.

Suddenly, Ben stopped kissing me and rose upright, staring at nothing in particular. "For fuck's sake, Tomason, now isn't a good time," he muttered.

I tugged the shirt sides together to hide my naked front as if Tomason could see me through Ben's eyes. "What is it?"

"Tomason says that Harvey is searching for you, and that you should get back to the apartment."

I deflated with a growl, but I got off the bed and put on a new uniform shirt and headed for the door.

"I've not collected my debt in full yet, just so you know," Ben reminded me from the edge of the bed.

I twisted my head as I grabbed the door handle. "Good to know. And you still owe me a massage from the last time my brother interrupted us."

He grinned at me. "Good to know."

I winked at him before leaving.

Outside the door, I stopped, fascinated by a shiny object on the floor. I smiled seeing my father's dagger. I picked it up. Every groove of the runes was sparkling clean with no traces of blood to evidence that it had been lodged into someone's throat only hours ago.

I snorted to myself as I shoved it home into the empty leg holster. I could bloody need this when seeing my brother in a moment.

68

Every muscle in my body ached, but Harvey didn't care. He pushed me harder on the sparring mat, his voice a whip without mercy against my exhaustion. There were no breaks. No leniency. No room for weakness.

Sparring with my brother should've felt familiar, almost comforting. Instead, it infuriated me to a point where I wanted to kill him. Maybe that was his intention. He wanted me at my best and not stopping before I had reached my full potential. When I trained with the black-wings or my friends, I had control, and I could stop when I needed to. But Harvey wasn't just training me. He was forging me into something unbreakable, whether I wanted it or not.

Sometimes it felt like there was a deeper meaning behind our sessions. An unspoken message he couldn't tell me but wanted me to understand. Ever since he learned that more than thirty second-year cadets had died in their challenge, his grief had made him ruthless, bringing with it a determination that bled into every training session – and I was the victim of his outlet.

His commands rang in my ears, sharp and relentless, echoing words our father had once drilled into him. Coralys didn't raise weaklings.

We sparred early in the mornings to avoid an audience, and I was grateful for that because during my academy time, I had never tapped out this much. Ben always watched from a distance, grunting when Harvey beat me too roughly. More than once when we were out flying alone and I wobbled in the wind, Harvey had complained that neither Zayd nor my teammate had done me any favours by taking it too easy on me.

When May neared its end, I still didn't feel ready for the ninth challenge; the dreaded altitude flight. On many days it had even been too windy to carry out flight practice. I found it impossible to assess the right speed, the correct angle and start from a ground position to fly to the top of the selected mountaintop, and the prize for winning wasn't motivating enough. A measly letter to be delivered to your family, of which I had none. Not counting Uncle Teddy, who lived in the forest by our lake cottage. Everyone knew he was a bit loopy.

Defying Harvey had been a mistake. I had stayed in my dorm last night, knowing it'd set my brother off, but not caring enough to stop myself. I had rightly guessed it would make today's brutal training even worse. Now, every part of me throbbed with exhaustion, my limbs weighted down as a consequence from my stolen hours in Ben's arms.

Ben was already up and ready for a new day, dressed in his flight leathers, looking infuriatingly sharp. His black hair was brushed back, his jaw freshly shaven, like he hadn't spent the entire night holding me. And not once had he let the darkness slip.

I groaned, burying my face in the pillow. "I can't do the ninth challenge. Might as well stay in bed."

Ben chuckled, low and knowing. We both knew why I was drained. It was from every whispered confession, every slow-burning kiss and every touch that had sent fire through my veins. It was safe to say we had settled every last debt of desire and of longing. Although now, I was paying the price.

"Shake it off and get on your feet, soldier. You look like a dead demon, but I know I haven't stabbed you with black iron."

Spirits, he was perky today. "Is that a new nickname for your cock? Black iron rod?" I pulled the blanket over my head.

"No!" He grabbed the blanket and pulled it down, pinning it on either side of my breasts with his hands nailed to the mattress.

I traced the swirling black oath tattoos on his bulging left pectoral with my fingertips. "Are you gloating because I can't stab you with a black blade?"

"No! I'm saying that I don't care if we lose, but if you don't show up, leadership will have a reason to lash or expel you from the academy and put you directly into service in the General Operations Unit. Although, if you're lucky, you can go back to doing undercover missions as an agent again. But then again, Duke Hartmore will kidnap you and make you wed him, as was your deal. That particular part, I'm not keen on, as I need more time to figure out a solution. If you wed, there is no coming back from that. No one can defy the Spirits, neither my two Spirits, nor your nine."

"You certainly know what motivates me," I muttered, thinking of the horror-picture he had painted, and I pushed his arm aside so I could roll out of bed. I searched through the wardrobe to find my summer flight leathers, which were thinner than the winter ones.

Ben leaned back against the desk, watching me with one foot crossed over the other and his hands in his pockets. "How much do you wish right now that you had taken up my offer to come live with me in Black Castle as my queen?"

I pulled a shirt off a hanger and twisted my head to roll my eyes at him. "Now, that's gloating!"

"Okay, yeah, a little," he sniggered.

What? What type of shirt was this? "What the heck?" I barked, trying to do the first button on the shirt, but realising there was none.

Ben frowned, staring at my fingers, too. "What's wrong?"

"There's no buttons on the shirt." On inspection of another shirt, I found it also without buttons and flicked the hangars to one side in the wardrobe until I found one with its buttons intact.

"Maybe the central depot assumed you don't want buttons as we keep tearing them off."

Leaving the shirt without the buttons on the floor of the wardrobe, I donned the one I had found with buttons. "I've to deal with people like Gravelhorn and now the workers in central depot find it funny to play pranks on me?"

Ben stepped closer, his hands gentle but firm as he tugged my shirt into place and started fastening the buttons.

"Don't let that bother you today. Focus." His fingers trailed down between my breasts with a simple fleeting touch.

I searched his face, my voice raw. "How can you always be so calm? Do you have no fear for today? No worry that I might die?"

Ben's eyes darkened, but his smirk was maddeningly intact. "If you were to die, at least you'd be wearing a shirt with buttons."

Anger and affection tangled inside me. I shoved my palms against his chest and fumbled to finish the last two buttons myself. "Hilarious."

His smirk didn't waver, and damn it, it was distracting.

Then, his voice softened, threading through my defences. "Angelica, I always worry about you. Every damn day. But today shouldn't be that hard unless you insist on using your white wings." His fingers ghosted over my shoulder blade as if he could touch where the arrow wound had healed. "I know your wound is better, but your black wings are stronger now. You've trained with them more. Trust in that."

I swallowed hard when I realised how deep his concern had dug into his soul.

I tucked the shirt into my trousers. "When I use the black wings, everyone looks at me like I'm a traitor."

He raised his brows at me. "When you use your white wings, you risk dying."

"Must you always be so logical?" My weapons lay on the desk, so I went over to them.

Ben turned his head to follow my walk. "No, but it's good when one of us is."

I shoved the first dagger into my leg strap with a sharp snap. "Ha! You're full of jokes this morning."

Before I could grab the second, Ben closed in behind me, his heat pressing against my back as his arms wrapped around my waist. His voice was low, teasing. "I'm in a good mood. I had a beautiful woman in my bed last night."

I snatched the second dagger from the desk, my fingers curling tightly around its hilt. Without hesitation, I pointed the tip behind me and straight at his crotch. "And how frustrating for you that you couldn't give me 'stick' last night the way you do now with your words."

He flipped me around and pushed me up against the wall beside the wardrobe. His face had lost all humour. "Believe me," he growled, "there is nothing I'd rather do than fuck you hard against this wall right now. But you made an oath to marry another man, so I can't."

"Really?" I scoffed in his face. "You can't make love to me because of your death magic and I'm patient and understanding, but as soon as I make an oath to save my friend, you curse me?"

His expression turned playful again. "What can I say? I'm a man. You showed me how sweet sex was, and it only took once for me to get obsessed with being inside you." His possessive grip tightened for a split second before he shoved away, leaving me breathless and trembling.

"Well…" I flicked my finger on his bottom lip. "Your tongue can be inside me whenever it wants."

His hand lowered to the button of my trousers and undid it.

"I didn't mean literally whenever. We have to go."

He made a low shush with my finger still resting on his lower lip, and it was so sensual, it broke my resolve to reject him. One hand slid inside my knickers and two fingers massaged my clit.

Spirits, that's good! I moaned, making shallow whimpering sounds that drove him insane, making his eyes look feral.

Ben tugged hard, lowering my trousers until they caught above the leg straps. Then he fell onto both knees in front of me.

Spirits, he was so hot when he looked this wild, and it was as if my bones would turn into jelly at any moment.

His tongue pushed inside me, and I called out from the peaking arousal. "What you can do to me isn't logical," I cussed.

He kissed below my abdomen. "You aren't the logical one of us, love. Since I met you, licking you is the most logical pleasure I've come to know."

He kissed my sex a few more times and then he stopped.

I glared at him. "Finish!"

"No. You said the prize to win the ninth challenge wasn't motivating enough. If you complete the challenge without dying, I'll finish what I started. How's that for motivation?"

My fingers tugged irritably at the hair at the back of his head. "It's more frustrating than motivating."

"Maybe both those virtues will help you. Let's go before we're late," he said, getting off his knees, as if it had been me delaying our departure.

I pulled my trousers back up, did the button and pushed down my black blade knife into my boot before we left the room.

As had been the custom for the last nine months, our friends waited for us in front of the military building. We hiked together to the designated clearing where there was a long strip of grass between the dense forest on either side. Camp Leader Nar watched as all the cadets gathered in front of her in the clearing, baking under the scrutiny of the sun. Unfortunately, today there wasn't any wind, not even a soft breeze that could help ease the scorching heat.

Camp Leader Nar's air wielding magic flowed around her, tearing at her long black hair where she stood, making her look like a storm Spirit – an angry storm Spirit, who wanted to murder everyone she laid eyes on.

The only one who I had ever seen her face soften for was General Denor, and he hadn't visited the outpost for weeks.

Because of her air wielding magic, Camp Leader Nar was the one who conducted all the flight training, including the altitude tutoring and coordinating of the challenge. As always, the camp leader in charge had to inform us of the rules of the challenge, even though everyone was clear about what to do. It was an official notice, so that no parent could contest their child's death, saying the academy hadn't informed the cadets of the rules or dangers. Because King Emille had insisted on the procedure, too, to prevent an ill reputation, it was how it was done.

"The challenge is to run down the strip of grass so the cadets can gain speed to take off and land on that mountaintop," she said, getting straight to the point, and gestured with her hand towards the mountaintop a short distance away. "As you know, a winged person can only ascend at an angle of forty-five degrees, which leaves little room for error between here," she said, pointing at her boots, "until there." She pointed towards the mountain once more. "If you don't ascend steeply enough, you'll slam into the mountain wall. Camp Leader Watson is standing on the mountaintop to record your time. The fastest team to the top wins and the team members can write a letter to their family. Any questions?" She waited a while, but no one spoke. "Great. Up first…" She looked at a stack of papers clipped to her chart, "Cadet Darling and Cadet Courtney."

When Darling shoved past the group toward the starting line, she made a show of swaying her hip exaggeratedly as she passed Ben, a smirk tugging at her lips. My fingers curled around the hilt of my dagger, my blood thrumming with irritation. Before I could unsheathe it, Ben's palm came down hard over my hand, locking it in place. His grip was firm, warning, but that didn't stop the guttural growl that rumbled in my throat.

The tension ebbed, as both women launched into a sprint down the runway. Their wings unfurled in perfect sync, catching the wind just as their feet left the ground. A minute later, they were nearing the mountaintop, the air around them turbulent with their powerful flaps.

The last few meters were a brutal struggle, and it seemed that their wings were straining and their bodies fighting against gravity. Just as they reached the ledge, a breathless moment past where I prayed that they'd drop dead, but they both rolled onto the rocky ground, just barely avoiding a bone-shattering collision with the mountainside.

"Next!" Camp Leader Nar shouted. "Cadets Jeff and Giles Flinch!"

The Twin Team. They were strong men, so I doubted they'd have any issues. They dashed down the path like a double vision and took off, and as assumed, they landed comfortably a few metres in on the mountaintop. So did the Angry Team, the Perfection Team, the Fistfight Boys Team, and both black-wing teams, but most impressive of them all was The Agility Team. Not surprising, as both women had practically spent their entire life in the air at Darse's parents Flight Practise Academy.

"Cadet Coraly and King Blackbone!"

My composure crumbled and my nerves kicked in the moment my name rang in my ears. A stab of anxiety hit me like a blade to the gut. I had thought I was calm, but now my body betrayed me. I noted that my fingers trembled, and my knees weakened.

Ben stood beside me, arms crossed, his gaze irate as I struggled to rearrange my wings inside my back and push out the black ones. It took longer than it should have and definitely longer than he wanted, but finally I could spread them wide.

A murmur rippled through the crowd behind us at the sight of their colour.

Ben's hands hovered near my daggers in a silent threat to anyone thinking of calling me *Mutt* today. His stance, his very presence, warned them all – dare, and suffer the consequences.

As we strode past Camp Leader Nar, curiosity burned too hot for me to hold back. "Do you know where General Denor is stationed?" My voice was steady, but my pulse pounded. "I'm surprised he hasn't visited the outpost in some time."

Nar's expression hardened. "He's none of your concern. Generals don't answer to cadets."

A dismissive slap of authority, meant to put me in my place.

I nodded once. "Sure. My apologies, Camp Leader Nar." The words felt bitter in my mouth, but I let them go and turned toward the runway.

Ben fell into step beside me, matching my pace as we approached the starting line. He wasn't running at full speed, not yet. He was waiting for me, making sure that when we lifted off, we did it *together*.

Each time my boot pounded the ground, I prayed that I'd lift off the ground gracefully. That wasn't always a given, as most of the times I crashed and skidded across the grass, which would be highly embarrassing in front of the other cadets.

My balance was slightly off as I beat the wings, but I could feel my weight lifting from the ground, and I made a final push to launch myself into the air.

The ground vanished beneath me as I launched into the sky, relief washed over me as I took flight from running. Harvey's rigorous training was to thank for that, and the fact that I watched out for the trees thanks to Murben's flight lessons.

"Push yourself higher up," Ben warned when we had been in the air for twenty seconds.

I flapped harder, forcing my wings to drive me upward, but my ascent was too slow. The best I could manage was a shallow forty-degree angle, and without headwind, even that felt like a battle.

"You must go higher," Ben urged again, his tone tight.

"I'm doing my best!" My muscles burned with the effort, but no matter how hard I strained, I wasn't gaining enough height as the air fought against me.

"You're doing good, but it won't be enough to clear the mountain wall." Ben's voice rang out above me, edged with warning.

From above, Ben's massive black wings carried him effortlessly, his body cutting through the sky with the grace and power of a shooting star. He was built for this. Born to rule a kingdom, both on land and in the sky. He looked absolutely magnificent.

"How is '*not clearing the wall*' considered '*doing good*'?" I barked, panic creeping into my voice.

The jagged wall loomed ahead, growing impossibly tall, a stone giant daring me to fail. *Thirty seconds.* That's all I had before I crashed head-first into the rock if I couldn't get higher. My arms ached and my wings – Spirits, my wings felt like they were made of lead.

"This is going to hurt."

"Angelica!" Ben's voice was sharp now, urgent. "Higher! Now!"

Hovering was impossible. No matter how hard I fought against gravity, my wings weren't strong enough to suspend me mid-air, nor could they carry me straight upwards. The human body was simply too heavy. My only chance to avoid a brutal collision with the rock wall was to zigzag upward.

But that would be humiliating, and I probably didn't even have the space for that manoeuvre.

"Don't wait for me, Ben. Lift!" I shouted.

Ben grunted, banking hard to circle around me before pulling up at my side. "New plan," he called. "Slow down, hit the rock softly, and we climb the last stretch."

I gaped at him. "That's undignified."

"Yes. But it'll keep us alive. I don't need to win. I need to graduate."

His words rattled me. Ben Blackbone, the King of the black-wings, didn't care about winning. My balance faltered for a fraction of a second before I forced myself steady again.

"You want to graduate the white-wing academy?" I asked, breathless.

Ben shot me a sharp look. "Correction. I want you to graduate, so I can take you home with me when you're finished with all this nonsense."

His wings angled upward, his speed breaking. "Slow down, Angelica! Now!"

The cliff face was right in front of us and I had about ten seconds to slow as much as I could, hoping it was enough not to break any bones when smashing into the wall.

I put my wings flat upwards to make a complete break, but the momentum was still too great.

Impact!

I whacked into the wall. Everything hurt. The side of my forehead hit stone and blood seeped down my face. My vision became dazed. "Ben!" I called, not able to see much.

"I'm here! I'm coming. Do you have a grip?"

Luckily, I had got my fingers into a crevice and my feet onto a substantial outcrop, or I'd be falling, considering how faint I felt. I focused on breathing. On keeping my eyes open.

Everything fucking hurt!

I wiped my arm across my face to clear the blood that was bothering my eyes. "I can't promise I'll stay conscious. Are you okay?" My breath came in ragged gasps.

"I'm fine," he murmured. His voice sounded right by my side. "You took a bad hit. You're bleeding." There was tension in his tone, a sharp edge.

I let out a bitter laugh. "Thank you. I know that!" A jagged outcrop was right by my forehead, so I rested my head against it, feeling the rough surface prick against my skin, but at least it kept me from swaying.

"I mean that you're bleeding a lot. Too much. And you're going to have to climb."

I looked down. *Dammit.* I shouldn't have looked down. My eyes narrowed, the world closing with darkness. My cheeks became clammy and hot. "I'm going to faint, Ben."

"No, you're not. Look at me." A hand cupped my cheek and turned my face towards him. "Look at me."

I tried to focus my sight on Ben, as the world swam before my eyes, and found his gorgeous red eyes not far from mine.

"There you are. Good girl. Listen to me," he murmured, his grip tightening just slightly. "I need you to climb. One step at a time. It's not far to the top."

I looked up and saw Emroyce and Murben peering over the ledge at me, their faces taut with worry. "Come on, Angie!" Emroyce shouted. "You can do this!"

Ben's husky voice cut through the fog again, firm, commanding. "There is a protrusion twenty centimetres above your left foot. Lift your leg up and put your foot onto it."

I checked and saw it, lifted my boot to it and pushed upwards.

"That's it. You're doing it. Keep going. Another foothold."

Step by step, I climbed, my body screaming in agony, my muscles trembling under the unbearable strain. My hands burned, slick with sweat and the blood I had wiped off my forehead, making every grip feel precarious, every movement a battle against gravity itself. My lungs felt tight, not letting in the needed gasps. My vision appeared in different shades from light to dark to light, threatening to close in on me completely. But Ben was there, his presence more solid than anything in this world and his voice a steady pulse of reassurance at my side to chase away my fear. His words echoed in my ears, urging me forward with unwavering belief.

When we were at the top, Ben roared to the others. "Lift her up, damn it!"

Hands clamped over my arms, and I was lifted through the air and put down onto the ground. Lying flat on my back, panting, my limbs like a puddle on the ground, I heard Ben roar. "Where is Cadet Penya? Cadet Coraly needs healing. Now!"

I woke up like a crack of thunder, sitting right up in my customary corner bed in the infirmary. Ben was sleeping sprawled out in a chair next to my bedside. It was dark in the hall and only a few candles were lit, so the healers could see while working. I adjusted in bed, relaxing back onto the mattress, my head on the soft pillow. Everything still hurt. Especially my head. I put my hand on my forehead and noticed the bandage wrapped around it. The movement made my head scream with pain. *Ouch!*

A healer spotted my movements and came to check on me, pinning my eyes open with bony fingers, and asking me to look one way and the other. This obviously woke Ben up, who sat upright and waited for the healer to finish.

Ben stood up and leaned over me as soon as the healer had left. "How are you feeling?"

"I've been better. I'm sorry I embarrassed you."

He shook his head at me. "You didn't embarrass me. This academy is embarrassing." He pointed at my head. "You almost died today. You know how I panic when you're in near death situations. Are you ready to come home with me now?"

"No! Ouch!" My head thundered as I shouted. "I have to do this, or I'll have to marry Duke Hartmore immediately," I whispered.

Ben grunted. "It's a shame you weren't concussed and forgot that part."

I held my wrist up with the golden tattoo. "And how would you've explained this to your amnesia-struck girlfriend?"

Ben shrugged his shoulders. "I wouldn't."

I raised my eyebrows. "Great." I sighed and let my memories of the day slowly sink in. "Who won?"

"The Agility Team won."

I pulled myself higher in the bed and moaned from the pain it caused. "Not a surprise."

Ben frowned and fluffed up the pillow before he tugged it down to support my neck. "Only a second ahead of Commander Daffron and Nesso. Both of them are good fliers and I expect they didn't push themselves to their limits."

"Yeah, I've seen Nesso fly. He's quick. And Daffron and Murben, too."

"Yes, Davis is chunkier."

I giggled but stopped as it hurt my head and my lungs. "What about the breathing under water challenge for the second-year cadets. How did it go for Valentina and Treylieh?"

"Camp Leader Mewer didn't let Treylieh compete after what happened to him in challenge eight. I think Treylieh's summer holiday has already started."

"Then you don't know Valentina very well. She'll be pissed off with Mewer for a second challenge missed this year. She won't miss the last one of the year if she gets a say in it. What about the truth reading challenge? How did Brian and Winter do?"

"Cadet Dark and Cadet Dessen won."

Dessen's magic was torture, so I wondered if that had anything to do with the truth reading win. Had he tortured someone to get his way?

I let my fingers mindlessly trace the embroidery of the crown emblem on Ben's shoulder. "And what is the verdict on my head?"

Ben sighed hard, making me worry. "You hit it pretty hard, so I think it works better now than it did before."

I raised my rude finger at him, and he chuckled at me. "Summer break can't come soon enough. I need it to recover from taunting kings!"

Ben grunted. "There is only one challenge left this year before the summer break. Have you thought about how you'll spend the break?"

"Harvey, Mazdon, Kate and I normally go to the summer cottage. That is if Captain La Roy covers for Harvey here, or else he isn't allowed to leave the premises."

Ben looked irritated and supported his palms on the mattress. "How long would you be gone?"

Avoiding his stare, I looked up at the stone ceiling. "Normally the entire summer."

"That's a long time apart," he muttered.

"I'd extend an invitation, but I'd have to clear it with Harvey first."

"I'd love to see your cottage."

"It's nothing special. It's tiny, but it has a sizeable lake around the back."

"Considering our final challenge, do I dare to ask how skilled you're at swimming?"

I looked back at him and cringed. "I'm used to being in water and I know how to swim, but my weight makes me sink like iron armour once I get tired."

"So, whether or not you're armed to your teeth with iron, you'll still sink the same. Like throwing a flat stone that skims the water before sinking. Got it." He smirked, clearly remembering our first ever encounter.

I recalled the fond memory of when we had been skimming stones in the garden lake at a ball in Black Castle. The fact had been as avoidable then as it was now. A stone sinks, even if it can stay afloat for a while whilst skimming the surface. "What about you?"

He grinned. "I'm like a sea monster in water. No need to worry about me. You saw the lake beyond the garden in Black Castle. I spent a lot of time there hiding from Father when he was in a bad mood." Ben leaned across the bed. "What's wrong? You drifted off. Something's bothering you."

I fiddled with my fingers in my lap. "It's nothing. It's silly."

"Okay, then we can laugh about it together. Tell me."

"The challenge is in Lake Pharoon. When my brother killed Mum, he tied rocks to her and sunk her to the bottom of that lake. I don't exactly fancy dipping my toes into it. It kind of creeps me out."

"I see." He looked at me for a while, as if he was trying to find the right words to say. "What Captain Coraly says he has done would have been a long time ago. I'm sure her spirit isn't at the bottom of that lake."

"I know. It's just–"

"Don't worry about that now. You need your rest. Once you're discharged, we can practise for the challenge in the bathing chamber."

When I woke, the chair beside my bed was empty. My pulse kicked up. Why was it empty? Ben was always there. Always.

I turned my head, and my breath almost stopped at seeing the towering figure beside me. My instincts screamed at me to move and to reach for a dagger I didn't have. What the heck was he doing here?

"General Denor," I forced out, my throat dry. "You wrote in your letter that you couldn't visit this month. That you were otherwise engaged."

His sharp gaze never wavered. "It wasn't a lie," he said smoothly. "But when I heard how badly you were injured in challenge nine, I rearranged my priorities." A pause, calculated. "I was told you'd been asking for me." He leered. "Missed me?"

I snorted. Camp Leader Nar was a damn snitch.

"Where is King Blackbone?"

"I dismissed him," Denor said coolly. "Seeing as I'm here."

An icy chill settled in my stomach. "And you're willing to risk your life for me, as the king is? There's more than one cadet in this place who's trying to kill me."

His answer was immediate. Steady.

"Yes."

How would I respond to that? He was my general, so there were limits to how rudely I could treat him. I doubted calling him a liar would go down well.

Moments passed, and I still didn't know what to say. It didn't help that the general looked highly amused. His black hair had grown longer, as if he hadn't had time to tend to himself, but he was cleanly shaven, his red uniform was ironed and his black leather belt polished. I frowned and crossed my arms over my chest, as he kept staring at me blatantly with those unnerving eyes, dark as an abyss.

Harvey walked into the infirmary and strode straight for General Denor without even glancing over at me once.

"General Denor, a word in my office, please."

I tried to glean whether there was any fear in the general's eyes. Ben had told Nesso to find who at this outpost made him skittish, but it didn't seem to be my brother.

"Certainly," the general answered calmly before he leaned down to give me a kiss on my cheek.

I froze with fear at the gesture. A sinister message. My breath caught in my chest as he hovered a centimetre over my skin after the kiss and whispered, "I have prepared a perfect final non-date for us. Get better soon."

Cadets, workers and healers moved out of the way as they barged out. Together, they'd be a powerful duo who could break the world.

As powerful as they were, they weren't very smart, as they had left me unattended. There were no eyes on me now. I hurried to open the drawer of the side-table to find my uniform and daggers and changed before sneaking after my brother, ascending the stairs to the leadership floor. The Captain's Office's door was closed, so I pressed my ear up against it and could hear them arguing. Luckily for me, their discussion was heated and loud.

"I heard you were going to escort Cadet Coraly to the First Year Ball at Gaithorpe. If you're planning on introducing her to King Emille and his counsel, forget it. I forbid it."

"You're a captain. You can't forbid a general from doing anything. You know King Emille has his eye on Mewer, Charney, Randall, Bostee and her."

The words struck like a blade, sharp and deep. *King Emille wants me?* My chest tightened, heat burning beneath my ribs. I wasn't sure if it was fear, or fury. Why would he want me? My magic was nothing compared to others' – not publicly known anyway. I wasn't the strongest, the fastest, or the most ruthless. Yet, my name had been spoken in the same breath as some of the best.

My fists clenched at my sides. *Has General Denor told him about my magic?* He had looked through my mind. He could know the truth.

Then my brother's words hit me even harder.

"The king's counsel agreed she might join the king's inner circle when she was ready. She isn't yet ready. You know very well that the king will assign her to every battle, and she'll have to fight every day of her life. I'm telling you that she isn't ready for that. You'll break her mentally."

My breath caught in my throat. *Not ready?* Harvey thought I wasn't ready? My pulse pounded in my ears, a mix of anger and doubt twisting inside me. He still thought of me as weak. Someone who would break under the brutality of war. I had spent years proving myself, bleeding, pushing past every limit, clawing my way forward – only to be dismissed as *not ready?*

But beneath the fury, fear slithered through me.

Not fear of battle.

Not even fear of death.

Fear that he might be right.

"If the king breaks his toys, I'm there to fix them for him with my mind magic."

I swallowed. This was horrendous. The general thought nothing more of me than a tool that he could tinker with to set straight after it had been damaged.

"She isn't a toy. She's my sister," Harvey roared, the soreness in my heart hurting for a completely different reason. It had sounded as if he genuinely cared for me.

"You forget yourself, Captain. You know who she is as well as I do. I've seen inside her mind and it's remarkable. You're using only a grain of her capacity. The problem is that I think King Blackbone suspects it too, and if he turns her to their side, well, let's just say King Emille won't be merciful to any of us."

What in the world were they talking about? Who was I? Another secret Ben knew about and was keeping from me? The general made it sound like Ben was courting me purely to persuade a powerful weapon to fight his corner. I couldn't breathe at the thought. Perhaps he didn't love me at all, and he was the intelligent man everyone told me he was, only scheming to gain my loyalty.

"Give her at least until graduation," Harvey told Denor.

"I will, but that is only because I need to find a solution to break the oath that she made to Duke Hartmore. We're all fucked if they get the mark of the Spirits' blessing."

"Agreed."

Spirits, this was so overwhelming. Two of the most powerful men in Skyberg were discussing my fate. I swapped my ear around as my right was getting warm from being pressed so hard against the door.

"King Emille is also insisting on royal guards stationed around Cadet Coraly."

What? Guards? No! No! No! I'd never get a lone moment with Ben, and it would make me an even bigger target for other cadets attempting to kill me.

"That will make her suspicious and rebellious."

"Agreed. I'll try to put it off for as long as I can."

Okay, so they seemed to both know me pretty well. Fantastic! In fairness, I would rebel if they put guards on me.

"Good. And General, do me the favour of treating her as a person and not as a weapon whilst you figure everything out."

"Oh, I'm planning on enjoying every aspect of her."

Ew! I don't think so! Prepare to be rejected, General!

"If you screw with her mind, I'll kill you and I don't care what happens to me. Believe what you will, but she's the only family I have."

"You're threatening your general. May I remind you that you're getting away without punishment because of your magic, but others around you might not be so lucky. I heard Cadet Pere earned another skill circle on her uniform for her fire wielding. Impressive work. I know you've trained her personally. I wonder what else you've taught her in private. It'd be interesting to know how good she is in bed if trained by a captain first hand."

Oh, no! Harvey had threatened Denor, and the general had worked out the connection between Kate and my brother. This won't end well.

"Get out!" my brother roared at the general so loudly I startled away from the door.

69

Ben and I walked towards the east wing to get to the bathing chamber. I could smell the scent of minerals and salt as we got closer. A duffle bag hung over each of our shoulders, packed with swimwear and towels.

Ben reached for my hand and laced his fingers through mine. A silent claim. A reassurance. A reminder.

"You've been quiet for weeks," he murmured. "Ever since you slipped out of the infirmary before you were supposed to. Did Camp Leader Mewer give you a hard time for that?"

I kept my gaze ahead not even managing a fake smile. "No. I'm fine."

Fine. A hollow, bitter lie. Everyone saw me as nothing more than a tool, a weapon to be wielded at their convenience. But sure. *I'm fine.*

Ben scoffed under his breath. "Fine? If you hadn't given me the black blade oath, I think I'd be terrified of you right now."

The acid of something wicked seeped into my chest. *Is he afraid of me?* The idea should've been absurd. It was Ben I was considering. But I couldn't shake his words. I thought back to General Denor's conversation with my brother. The warning. The careful restraint that had followed me my entire life.

Had they all been lying to me? Telling me never to use my magic because it was dangerous? Or was it because it made me too powerful?

Was Ben just another player in this game? Someone who'd marry me, not for love, not for loyalty, but for control?

If everyone wanted me for my magic…

Then who could I trust at all?

Ben's brow furrowed and his dark eyes scanned my face. "Seriously, Angelica, you're going to give me another panic attack." He sounded truthful. "What's wrong? I know we leave for the last challenge tomorrow. Are you still uneasy about the lake?"

I hesitated, tightening my fingers around the strap of my duffle bag. "That too," I admitted. "But it's not just that."

Ben's expression darkened, and he was about to push further when I blurted out the question burning inside me.

"If I asked you to bring me to the war in the north, so that I could fight the war under your banner, would you take me?"

His entire body stiffened. "What?" His pace slowed to a near stop, and he turned toward me with eyes narrowed in confusion. He searched my face as if trying to decipher a hidden meaning. "Where is this coming from?"

That was the part I didn't understand. The piece of the puzzle that refused to fit. I was already willing to fight for him. Already willing to risk everything. And yet…he still wasn't taking me there.

"Ben," I pressed, my voice steady despite my inner turmoil. "When can you take me north? I need to see the war with my own eyes."

His jaw clenched down from making any compromise. In that moment, I knew that whatever his answer was, it wasn't going to be the one I wanted.

Maybe he was invading the white-wings, and he didn't believe I'd fight for him, not yet. He was working on turning me against my own people.

"If you take me there, I'll be willing to say an oath to fight for you and kill white-wings who cross into the Black Wing Territory. Tell me your terms. I'll do whatever you want. Just be honest with me."

He tore his fingers through his hair, having let go of my hand. "I told you. I'm not fighting white-wings," he whispered. "And I don't want you anywhere near the north. It's dangerous. Women shouldn't be on the battlefield. Especially not the ones I love."

"If you don't want me to battle, then what do you want with me? What are you planning?"

He stopped three steps down on the stairs and our faces were at the same height. "What's going on with you? Who has messed with your mind? Did General Denor get to you? Shit! I need to get the soul bond connected to you again so I can keep him out of your mind."

"General Denor said that I was a weapon that no one could love. He said you knew who I really was. So, I'm wondering what you've planned to use me for."

"I don't know about your magic. I'm trying to work it out and I can speculate, but I've nothing concrete. Maybe he thinks you've told me about it, but you haven't. With regards to your claim that no one can love you, and I'm incredibly stupid for pointing this out, but do you feel as though Watson never loved you? You're very lovable when you don't poke black blades at my heart."

I glowered at him. "Let that go."

He smiled, putting his hands on my arse and tugged me closer. "I love you."

"You'd say that if you wanted me to be your weapon against the white-wings."

"Okay." He took my hand to continue walking and led me down the stairs. "Let's for argument's sake say that you're the most powerful weapon in the world and there would be a tug of war between black-wings and white-wings about whose side you'd fight for. Wouldn't you think that if you were that powerful, no one could get you to do something you didn't want to do? You'd just kill the person asking something unreasonable of you."

"I guess. I never thought about it that way."

"And, for argument's sake, let's say I'd try to convince you I loved you, even if I didn't, to get you under my control. Don't you think I'd know that as soon as you found out the truth, you'd kill me? Slowly and painfully."

"You have trust magic. Maybe you can keep me from ever finding out."

"I don't know what else to tell you. You've been in control all the time, and we've been equals at this outpost. That's all I've got for now, but I hope you'll allow me to keep proving myself. And I definitely prefer showing you how I feel about you rather than telling you. See you in the pool." He kissed me in the doorway to the women's changing room and carried on down the hall to the men's changing room.

I changed and walked into the dim light of the bathing chamber and saw Ben sitting in the pool by the side with his arms folded over the ledge. It was the first time in the last three weeks that we were completely alone without any other cadets training around us.

Ben turned around to watch me walk down the steps to the water in my black Bensguard bathing suit.

"Spirits, you're so beautiful."

I pushed against the water resistance to get to him. "I don't hold a candle to you." At his side, I pushed my hands over his chest and down his biceps, watching the black swirling tattoos on his left side that carried on down his arm to the end of his wrist.

He wrapped his arms around me and pulled me closer, prying my legs open with his large hand to straddle me over his lap. "Sounds like we must check your eyesight."

His hands cupped my arse and stroked along my curves, pushing his hands along my back and all the way up to cup the back of my head. He drew me into an intense kiss, and I felt his cock grow underneath me.

He smiled against my lips. "How would you explain that, if I didn't love you?"

I wrapped my arms around his neck. "That you're a man? All men get erections when women sit on their laps and kiss them."

His hands fell to rest on my thighs. "I'm more than happy to put another woman in the same position to disprove your theory."

"Touché. The visual of you and Nassara was quite enough. It'll haunt me for the rest of my life."

"No, it won't," he promised. "I'll make you forget she ever existed."

Beneath the surface, his hand found me, cupping around my aching core. He pushed my bathing suit aside and pressed his thumb on my clit. Precisely on the right spot.

A choked moan escaped me, swallowed by his mouth as he claimed me with a fierce kiss. "We–" I gasped, barely able to hold onto my thoughts. "We need to train…swimming."

The tip of his tongue slowly teased over mine, unfurling every last thread of my resistance. "There is enough time for business and pleasure."

I shook my head weakly, but my body betrayed me, arching into his touch. "I don't know. Harvey has been relentless this month. He wants me home by eight and doesn't want me near you outside of training or challenges."

Ben tensed against me. "I know." His fingers pressed deeper, making me whimper. "I hate sneaking around."

But it was worth it. Every stolen moment and every risk was worth every pain my brother put me through. My moan broke the surface as pleasure rippled through me. "I find it quite…exhilarating."

His lips ghosted over my ear and his breath was hot against my skin. "That's because you're so mischievous, Angelica."

A sharp cry threatened to spill from my lips, but he clamped his hand over my mouth. His eyes were dark with amusement as he glanced around. Then, that smirk, the one that always made my knees weak, curved his lips.

His fingers plunged deeper, his palm grinding against my clit with every motion. "Stupid oath," he murmured, his tone irritated. Hungry for more. "I'd really like to fuck you right now."

His lips trailed down my neck, his free hand gripping the small of my back, pressing me closer, tethering me to him." Cum for me, love," he whispered, coaxing, demanding. "Let me feel you unravel."

Pleasure coiled tightly inside me, my body teetering on the edge, but I refused to give in so easily. I forced my eyes open, locking onto his with an impish grin.

"The moment you cum is so beautiful. When I know I've pleased you."

"Beg me, Your Majesty!"

He chuckled. "And you thought I was the one in command of you. Okay, Miss Stone, I beg you, lose control. Cum around my fingers. Please." He worked me faster. "For me. Have an orgasm, you beautiful creature."

My back arched. My nails dug into the skin of his shoulder. I tried my hardest to hold in my culminating release but sounds still came out and Ben dampened them with his hand.

"Lovely. Delicious. Fucking beautiful," he mumbled.

I laughed and kissed him as I enjoyed the throbbing aftermath of his work.

He pushed his hands into my hair at either side of my cheeks. "How could I not love this?" His kiss deepened like he wanted to kiss my soul, and I felt the touch there, deep inside me as if he had succeeded.

I cleared my throat. "So. Swimming?" My pulse thrummed wildly beneath my skin. "I don't want to miss out on my reward this month."

Ben's eyes flickered with confusion. "The prize is a dagger."

I met his gaze, my lips curling with a playful tug at each corner. "And honour. But that's not the reward I meant." I kept my voice low, suggestive, daring him to deny me. "Is the previously offered reward off the table? Admittedly, I didn't complete the last challenge satisfactorily, but I thought you'd give me another chance."

"I don't know," he mused. "I'm not sure you need as much motivation for this challenge."

"Ben!" I smacked his shoulder with a feigned pout on my lips, but he only chuckled.

"Fine," he said, leaning in until his breath was warm against my ear. "I'll tell you what. Win this challenge with me, convince your brother to invite me to your cottage this summer…" His fingers trailed up my arm, his touch barely there, yet it burned along my entire body. "And when we're finally alone, I'll lay you across the dinner table in your cottage and feast on you like you were my last meal." His words were a promise. One, it sounded, he'd rather die before he broke. A promise that carved wicked images into my mind. His too, probably, as his ruby eyes were as intense as a burning flame. "It'll be an aspect of your cottage you've never experienced before." Then, his expression shifted. The teasing glint faded beneath a deep frown. "You haven't with Watson, have you?"

Something cold slithered into his voice, and for the first time tonight, I heard the unspoken jealousy laced beneath the question.

"No! I haven't!" I shrieked. "But I'm looking forward to holding you to your word."

"Good." He flashed me the widest smirk I'd ever seen, his eyes glinting with triumph. Then, without warning, he jerked his chin toward the pool's length, his tone all command. "Now, swim."

"No. It's my turn." Sliding a finger past the waistband of his black swim shorts, I barely grazed skin before his hand gripped my wrist and yanked it away.

Ben's chest was rising and falling as he jerked his gaze away from me, locking onto one of the angel statues watching over the chamber. I could see his muscles rippling beneath his skin as he fought for composure.

"That was close."

He swallowed hard before turning back to me, his control settling into place like a carefully fitted mask. "I want you to get some actual practice in before we leave for Lake Pharoon tomorrow."

I narrowed my eyes at him. "So, you get to play, but I can't touch you?" I tapped a finger against my chin, feigning deep thought. "Highly suspicious when trying to convince me your feelings are genuine, don't you think?"

His grin twisted into something dangerous and full of promise. "Oh, Angelica." His hands slid into my hair, threading through the strands as he tugged my head back, exposing the length of my throat. His lips swept softly over my skin, planting slow kisses along the vulnerable curve of my neck.

Heat coiled low in my stomach as his voice rumbled against my throat. "When we get to the military barracks by the lake, sneak into my quarters, and I'll let you do whatever you want to me in private."

A sharp thrill spiked through me at the thought, but reality yanked me back down. I scowled. "That's assuming I can escape my barrack. Harvey has me assigned to Camp Leader Neville in the camp leader's barracks." My lips pressed into an irritated, hard line. "He doesn't want us together."

Ben chuckled darkly, his fingers still tangled in my hair as he leaned in, lips brushing over mine. "Anything can be accomplished with the right motivation."

"Ah, so that's what you're doing here. Motivating me. Last time, I lost out and I can assure you, there was nothing wrong with the motivation. So, what makes this time any different?"

"Okay, so I'll add more rewards. You can do anything you want to me, and you can tell me to do anything you want to you." He kissed at my cleavage before gripping around my waist and lifting me off his lap. "Ten laps to the other side and back. Go! Before you weaken me to my knees."

I grunted at him and pushed off the wall with my feet, swimming the length with Ben following at my side. He was by far a faster swimmer, but I guessed I could have given him a run for the money if it weren't for the weight of my wings.

Having done the laps, we got showered and changed to head for lunch and arrived at the same time as our white-wing friends. The black-wings seemed to stay away from the common areas when the general was at the outpost.

The canteen was alive with noise, trays clattering, voices rising and falling in power battles. The scent of venison stew curled in the air, as we filed into the queue with the trays in our hands. The serving workers slapped portions onto our plates with their usual efficiency.

I snapped up a bottle of orange juice and followed Emroyce toward an empty table. Ben sat beside me, solid and ever-present, while Kate and Mazdon took their places next to Emroyce. Across from us, Kenyard, Penya, Maruto, Brian, and Winter settled in, their bodies still bearing the bruises from this month's brutal interrogation training.

Yet, despite the purpling welts and swollen knuckles, Brian and Winter were grinning. Laughing even. The final challenge before graduation had clearly left them in high spirits, either from relief or sheer delirium.

I scanned the room, feeling something wasn't right. Where were the second-year cadets? Valentina and Treylieh were nowhere in sight. They should've finished the torture challenge by now. My stomach clenched. It was the final trial before advancing to the third year, and it was said to be the most gruelling of them all, only short of dying. Many cadets had begged for death during the sessions. Although, I should be fearing for Camp Leader Ward's life, as Valentina would break his bones if she thought he wasn't playing fairly.

I pushed at the thick, brown venison stew with my fork, my appetite waning. "Ben, has Murben said anything about how Zoe's doing?"

I barely finished the question before Ben snapped upright, his entire body going rigid. "Wait!" he barked, sniffing at the meat on his food.

I stiffened.

His sharp gaze swept the room. Muscles coiled. A predator sensing a trap.

Then, louder, more urgent. "Stop!" he called across the table. "No one eat the food!"

Every movement around the table froze. A fork hovered close to Kate's mouth. Mazdon reacted first, slapping it from her fingers before she could take a bite. It clattered to the tray, the sound eerily loud in the sudden silence.

"Something's wrong," Ben said, turning in his seat scanning the room, his shoulders taut with warning.

A thud sounded from the end of the table, so I leaned over to find Winter collapsed over her plate. Brian threw himself over her, shaking her shoulders. "Winter! Glenna!" He checked her pulse and shouted for Mewer, who sat at the camp leaders' table.

Ben put his fork down on the plate. "It's poisoned."

I pushed the tray away from me and watched as Mewer came rushing our way and attempted healing Winter, but he couldn't bring her back to life.

"She's dead." He sniffed the meat and inspected the consistency of the sauce. "This could be from Terence's venom. Her death was so quick, I had no chance of healing her."

General Denor walked over to us but greeted only me. He glanced around the room and suddenly a third-year cadet in the corner put his hands around his head and screamed in pain. My adrenaline pumped fast at seeing the brutal scene and the panicked cadet. The next second, he dropped to the floor under his own weight.

Highly worked up, I snapped my head back to General Denor, who shrugged his shoulders. "He was the one adding the poison to your food. We aren't in a challenge, so his penalty was death. I'm an official for the King and authorised to carry out executions."

I dropped my jaw. Denor had sifted through everyone's mind, found the one guilty and killed him within seconds, not moving a muscle but simply using his mind. Worse was that he was allowed by the king to do that! The severity of how dangerous this man was, hit me like a slap in the face. It was no wonder the black-wings stayed away. I could scarcely breathe.

Chaos erupted. Screams tore through the canteen and there was a cacophony of panic and confusion. Cadets shoved back from the tables and their trays were crashing to the floor. Boots pounded against the tiles as people scrambled away from the fallen bodies. Two cadets were motionless – dead!

This damned place!

Winter's face was ashen, her eyes glassy and staring at nothing, her mouth slightly open as if her final breath had been a stolen gasp. She was collapsed forward onto her tray, the venison stew soaking into her brown curly hair, mixing with the foaming at the corner of her lips. The other dead cadet was sprawled across the floor, his fingers still twitching slightly before stilling forever.

A ripple of hysteria surged through the room. Some cadets shouted orders, others barked questions, but most just screamed. Chairs scraped back. Someone retched into their hands. Others dropped to their knees, whispering prayers under their breaths.

Then – "Enough."

Denor's voice cut through the chaos like a blade. It wasn't just loud, it commanded order. The sound rippled out of him like an invisible force. The screams choked off mid-breath. Shouts died in cadets' throats. Even those in blind panic fell silent with their mouths still open as if they had been forcibly muted.

A shiver ran through me. *Magic.*

Denor stood near the bodies, his gaze sweeping over the room like he was gathering strength. His presence was so powerful and inescapable. He had silenced the room, not through fear alone, but with something more potent and unnatural.

And judging by the way some cadets clutched their throats, not all of them had chosen silence willingly.

He could control any aspect of a human with a mere thought. A second shiver loaded with potent fear ran down my spine.

Brian was crying, gripping onto the back of Winter's uniform so hard his knuckles had turned white, and he was calling her name – the reality of her death settling in. His teammate was gone. He had lost a close friend. I walked around the table, prying his hands off Winter's body, and hugged him. He held his arms around me tightly.

"This damned academy," Brian sobbed into my hair. "Our fucking fate to grow up here, Angie." He pulled away and dried his nose with his sleeved forearm. "Get out of here if you get the chance, Angie. Let your family name burn, and live instead."

Denor had walked over to us and pushed Brian in front of him and towards the exit of the canteen. "The perpetrator has been taken care of and I'll take you to the infirmary. Everyone leave the canteen so that the chefs can clean out the food and ensure there are no remains of any poison."

There was so much more comfort I had wanted to give Brian, considering I was leaving tomorrow morning for Lake Pharoon, and was going to be away for a few days. I looked at Winter. Sweet, smiling Glenna.

She is dead.

I glanced at my plate of food.

Were it not for Ben, that could have been me.

Ben folded his arm across my shoulder. "Come. We should leave. There is no benefit to you watching this."

"We. All our friends. Could have died today." My voice stuttered as I mindlessly let Ben lead me through the corridor.

"I know. This is the Bensguard Outpost. You know this. My chefs don't poison my food in Black Castle."

I stared at him. "How can you take advantage of a situation like this by saying that when my friend has just died?"

"Distasteful perhaps. But the truth. I want you to come with me to where I know we'll be safe and can live happily together."

"I need some time alone," I barked, and took faster steps to widen the distance between us.

Ben let me walk away from him without pursuing me, and when I turned the corner to the west wing, I crossed paths with Davis and Murben.

"You're alone," Murben remarked. "Where is your guard or King Blackbone?"

I halted by their side. "I left him around the corner," I said, pointing backwards. "But I'm sure he has gone to find Nesso to order him to spy around…if Nesso is still alive. A third-year cadet poisoned Winter in the canteen and General Denor blinked and killed the guy. It's a mess."

Murben frowned. "Was King Blackbone poisoned?"

"No. Only with stupidity."

"Ah, I see. What has our good king done now?" Murben asked, lacing his brown fingers over his stomach.

"Nothing I'll confide in you, Murben. I wish Zoe was here, though." I looked at Davis. "Any word from your sister?"

Davis leaned his shoulder against the wall. "Sure. She's all right. I talk to her every other night or so."

"What? Why didn't you tell me?"

"We link our portals. The signal is weak, so her voice isn't more than a whisper, but she tells me about her days."

I took an eager step closer to him, staring at those grey eyes under his blonde mop of hair. "Can I speak to her?"

"Sure. Let's do it in our room, though. I need to concentrate a lot." He pushed off from the wall.

I nodded and followed Murben and Davis to their dorm room and sat down on the bed next to Davis. He circled his hands in the air, building up more and more of the blue essence that swirled around. With his palms, he pumped the air away from him.

"The pressure will help her feel that I'm calling her," he said, as a response to my confused expression.

"Couldn't you wait until tonight? I'm having my freaking lunch break!" Zoe shouted through the hearing portal, but it was still not loud enough that anyone outside the room could hear her.

"Don't blame me. Angelica is here to talk to you."

"Angie, honey!"

It was so heavenly to hear her voice, even if it wasn't more than a whisper. Actually, the whispering was a nice touch to her normally loud voice. "Hi, girl! How's life in the north?"

Zoe was quiet for a while. "A fucking holiday!"

"I'm not having a picnic here, either. Winter was just poisoned in the canteen and if Ben hadn't told everyone else not to touch their food, you could have been friendless when you got back."

"Shit! Bloody Spirits!"

"Blasphemy, Zoe!"

"Well, the Spirits bloody deserve it."

"What?" I frowned, sensing she didn't like her mission.

"Never mind. I'm sorry to hear about Winter. How's Brian taking it?"

"Not well, but General Denor was taking him to the infirmary, so who knows what he'll be feeling when he gets discharged?" I nervously fiddled my fingers over the black Bensguard blanket laid over Davis's bed.

"Maybe he can be assigned to a job at the outpost to be close to Fern?"

"I hope so. I'll murder my brother if he sends Brian away when Fern is due to give birth to their child during the summer. With the way things are going around here, I'm contemplating moving to Black Castle."

"No! No…" she drawled. "Don't cross over to the Black Wing Territory."

"Why not? What is up there, Zoe? What have you seen? Tell me." The secrets were killing me, especially those about the north and those about who I was. Everyone in leadership knew, but the king had forbidden them from telling me. Why?

"Nothing. But you've almost finished your first year. Only challenge ten left, right? The lake swim? You're an awesome swimmer. And I guess you're too, King Blackbone?"

There was a brief silence. "He isn't here," I muttered.

"Angie! You guys had another fight?" She sounded resigned. "I thought you said he had just saved your life."

"General Denor believes that King Blackbone is only courting me to access my magic." I glanced at Murben and Davis, but they had straight faces, and didn't seem to be judging me.

"Even if that was the case, take it from your best friend and marry the guy. There are other things to life than love."

My eyes snapped wide open. "What? Like what?"

"Like comfort. The temporary barracks up here are killing me and the woman I bunk with is so annoying. The women don't work with me as well as you do, and they complain about not receiving the backup they ask for."

"Zoe, did you forget to send backup again?"

"No! I'm used to working with you and I just didn't realise that this one woman might actually have needed the backup. She was no you, I'll tell ya. You wouldn't have asked for backup in her situation. Well, she's dead now, so I don't have to hear her bitching about it anymore."

"You're brutal."

"I like to think of it as saving on resources and military funding. Anyway, Camp Leader Nar is shouting for everyone to line up. I must to go."

"Camp Leader Nar is there with you? She was just here to hold the altitude flight challenge."

"Yeah, she came a few days ago."

"How long will leadership keep you up there? When will you be back?" It was so odd speaking into a void when telling your best friend you missed her. I wanted to see her face.

"I don't know. Maybe I'll be stationed here until after the summer."

"They're not giving you leave over the summer? A few of us will go to the summer cottage and I had hoped you'd come with us."

"I'm not a cadet, Angie. There is no summer break for agents. Shit! General Lola Desry is on site, and if you're frightened of Camp Leader Nar, the general of the General Operation's Unit will scare the crap out of you. I need to go. Bye!"

The portal died, and Davis lowered his hands. "Don't you just feel so much better after having spoken to my sister?"

"Oh, shut up! I need to blow off some steam. Sparring anyone?"

Murben tapped at the bodyguard pin I had gifted him. "I need to find the king."

"I'll spar with you," Davis offered and stood up to leave.

I got off the bed looking around the room and saw a shelf of wolf figurines and a shield pin with the word 'Wolfsbane Court', similar to the ones Zoe had. They had really merged like twins, liking the same things. Although, it wasn't as odd that Davis liked wolves compared to Zoe, as the wolves' habitat was in the western part of Cathdear in the Black Wing Territory.

"Are you not going to change into combat leathers?" I asked him.

"Are you that angry?"

"It's up to you how sore you want to feel when I kick your arse."

He scoffed, and I planned to make him regret it.

We walked to the sparring hall, having to zigzag between central deport carts as the workers were doing the last stock-up before summer. Once on the mat, I lent him one of my daggers and we sparred until the sweat poured down our backs and down our chests. As dinnertime approached, Ben entered the sparring hall with Murben in tow.

They stopped at the edge of the mat and watched for a while. Ben grunted every time Davis got a good hit on me, which obviously made Davis nervous.

"When you're hungry, Angelica, I've got us a few things for dinner in our room, so we don't have to eat in the canteen this afternoon," Ben said, and it sounded as if it was a hint for me to finish soon.

There was movement from the main entry door to the hall, and I turned my head to see Harvey on his way to my mat.

"No. Cadet Coraly will have dinner in our family apartment with me. I want to be assured that she stays in her own bed tonight. She has a long day tomorrow."

Ben's expression darkened instantly. "You're giving Cadet Coraly a curfew for the rest of the day?" His voice was sharp, laced with barely restrained anger.

Harvey didn't as much as flinch. "Yes, and until I can hand her off to

Camp Leader Watson to oversee her care during the challenge."

Ben froze. For a moment, he didn't even breathe. "Camp Leader Watson?" Ben almost choked on the words, like he could barely force them past his throat. His hands curled into fists, his entire body going rigid. "He isn't the camp leader hosting the tenth challenge!"

Harvey's gaze remained steady. *Unbothered.* "I had to send Camp Leader Neville to the north, so Cadet Coraly will stay in the barrack with Camp Leader Watson, who takes charge of the challenge."

"Oh, fuck no!" The shout tore from Ben's chest, raw and furious.

He took a step forward, eyes blazing, body tensed like he was ready to rip someone apart – violently.

Harvey finally reacted, his expression hardening. "That isn't your decision to make, *Cadet* Blackbone."

Ben's breathing was ragged. His jaw clenched so tightly, I thought his teeth might crack. "Like hell it isn't."

70

The silence, as I awoke in my childhood room was unnerving. The emptiness I felt was pressing down on me like a solid weight. *No voices. No footsteps. No Ben. Just me. Alone.*

My glances traced the familiar space, recalling the memories that felt like a lifetime ago. This room had been my sanctuary and a place to hide when my parents hosted lavish dinners for high-ranking officers or threw grand Turning of the Year celebrations. I had sat just like this in the bed too, knees pulled to my chest, listening to the muffled laughter and clinking glasses beyond the door.

Harvey and I had been different then. Younger. Our fights had been over trivial things like the time he snapped the head off my doll and, as if that weren't enough, defiled my carved wooden horse with a ridiculous moustache. In retaliation, I had tossed his prized toy soldier into the fire, never once confessing where it had vanished to. Maybe today was the day I'd tell him, just to even the score for locking my boyfriend in a pitch-black isolation cell last night.

The thought levitated my fury. I swung my legs over the bed frame and stood, shaking off the memories. Time to move. I got out of bed and dressed in my black flight leathers, as the four hours' hike to the camp at Lake Pharoon could require some flying.

Harvey was already in the kitchen when I entered. Seated at the table, back straight, his cursed yellow captain's uniform ironed to infuriating perfection.

I said nothing.

Instead, I rummaged through the cupboards. The cereal was exactly where it had always was. I poured a bowl, added milk, and stood at the counter to eat, pointedly avoiding looking at my despicable brother.

Let him sit there. Let him stew. He deserved it.

"Not going to talk to me today?" he asked with a levelled voice.

"Today, next week, maybe never again." I grabbed my bowl from the counter to take it out to the dining table to finish eating there and shouted to him over my shoulder. "By the way, I burnt your toy soldier, Rickety, in our fireplace as revenge for my doll."

For a moment, there was only silence.

Then—a dry laugh.

"You don't think I knew that?" Harvey said, stirring his spoon through his cereal without even glancing up "After its disappearance, I found a cadet at the outpost who could see the past. She told me you burnt it. Why do you think I broke your finger during tackle ball that week?"

I stopped in the doorway and turned around, but he didn't look up. "You broke my finger…on purpose? Only because I burnt your toy?"

Slowly, he turned in his seat, his blue eyes locked onto mine. "Angie," he said, his voice softer now, as if I was being ridiculous. "We were twelve and six years old. And Mother sewed the head back onto Nelly."

As if that justified everything.

"If I wouldn't have been an established cadet with the potential to be a queen one day," I muttered, narrowing my eyes. "I'd fling a spoon of cereal at you right now."

Harvey, annoyingly unfazed, leaned back in his chair and smirked. "If you did, it'd take me longer to get ready and release King Blackbone from the isolation cell. I'd have to change my uniform first. So, go ahead, throw it if you want."

I shoved the spoon that I had prepared to launch at him into my mouth. He grinned victoriously. That smug, satisfied smile was the exact same one he wore every time he won at childhood games, as if the universe itself had handed him the prize. It made my skin itch.

To rub it all in, he added, "And about the queen comment, you'll never get my blessing to marry King Blackbone."

I snorted, my cereal almost going down the wrong way. "I don't care about your blessing." But the bitter truth was, I did. Even if I'd never admit it.

He sighed, pushing cereal around in his bowl with a silver tablespoon. "Why don't you give Zayd another chance? He's no king, but he's a reputable camp leader and has a seat with King Emille's counsel already. Do you really need to aspire for a higher stature than that?"

"Is that what you think I'm doing? Whoring myself with King Blackbone, so that I could become a queen?"

"I'm not really sure what you're doing with him now that I've released you from the soul bond to him."

"King Blackbone is still my teammate, and he genuinely loves me. He doesn't care about being a king. He says that he'd abdicate and live in a cottage in the middle of nowhere if I'd only marry him."

"Yeah, he *would* say that."

Ouch! That stung. The fear had already been brewing inside me, and it didn't help when my brother pointed it out. What if Ben was only using me? "You're a jerk!"

"Are you still doing that thing where you want to prove you can do whatever I tell you that you can't do? Because if that is the case, I'll have to terminate this conversation."

"Terminate? Are you serious? You may be a captain at this outpost, but in this apartment, you're my brother. You can't tell me that you'll terminate our conversation."

"So, confirmed. You're still rebelling against everything I say." He carried on eating his breakfast, ignoring me.

"I'm not rebelling against everything you say. You're asking me to make up with your best friend, which is none of your business!"

"I'm not saying you must marry Zayd. I'm just saying you can be nice to him. None of this is his fault, and he has suffered enough. You know that you're his entire world, and if you'd have spoken to him lately, you'd have known that he feels as though his life doesn't matter. You could say something to cheer him up, so he doesn't lose everything he has worked so hard to build here."

"I am nice!"

"Show him that by being on time. Don't be late to the gathering at the front of the building. He's probably there already."

"I can take care of myself! And by the way, the quality of the central depot is slipping. They've supplied me with shirts without buttons! That's your job to fix. Do something about that!"

"Yeah, they complained to me about it, so I told them simply to stock your uniforms in the same state, as it seemed you had an issue with having buttons on your shirt. And I don't even want an explanation of why that is."

"You did what? Really? Can't they just sew the buttons back on before they re-stock my wardrobe?"

"As I said, I don't want to know why the buttons are off in the first place, but however you send your shirts down to the depot is how you'll have them returned. I think that is fair."

I growled and went to the hallway to sit down on a chair to put on my boots, balancing the bowl of cereal on the armrest of the chair and continued eating while I tied my laces.

Not wanting to return to the kitchen, I left the dirty bowl on the floor, grabbed my backpack, and jogged down the stairs and out to the front courtyard.

Mazdon and Kate approached me immediately. "How can you love that man?" I asked Kate.

"He has only asked you to be nice to Zayd. That's hardly a crime, and it wouldn't hurt if you comforted him a bit."

I glowered at Mazdon, who must have told her about our conversation already. "So typical of you, Kate, to be on his side. Every summer–"

"Girls! Stop bickering," Mazdon interrupted. "Angie. Kate and I are sorry that Harvey locked King Blackbone in the isolation cell overnight."

"He had it coming," Kate muttered, flicking her long red hair back with a sassy twitch.

"Kate!" Mazdon warned.

"He was talking back to Harvey. A captain!"

"It's probably not easy to adjust since he has been a king for a long time," Mazdon defended.

Kate smiled from ear to ear when she saw Harvey escorting Ben outside. Harvey stopped at the door, though, whilst Ben walked to us. Harvey's glance lingered on Kate before he turned and disappeared into the building again.

Emroyce, Kenyard, Penya, Maruto and the black-wings also joined us before Zayd took to the front and began shouting.

"This is your final challenge of the first year, and as you all know, it'll be the hardest! That is why it will start at this very moment, rather than when we arrive at camp!"

What! Shit! Anyone can kill another cadet at any time from now and until the time when the challenge is finished!

A low murmur tore through the crowd of cadets.

"This day just gets better and better," Ben muttered.

"Does that mean we can start to kill everyone?" Nesso asked.

Ben pinned his stares on Nesso. "Keep to your job, Nesso. I don't want to begin a bloodbath at the doorstep of the Bensguard Outpost."

"No, my mother has already done that trick," I bit under my breath.

Zayd carried on as the murmurs died down. "You don't need to travel in the group with me if you can find your own way there, but I'll expect everyone to show up to the challenge the morning after tomorrow; nine o'clock sharp! Dismissed!"

Zayd weaved through the cluster of cadets with deliberate, calculated steps, his eyes locked on me as he made his way closer. The air around him thickened, charged with something volatile. Ben clearly sensed the tension shift and slid closer to me like a protective shield. His hand pressed lightly but possessively against my back.

Zayd came to a halt in front of us, his gaze flicking toward Ben with a challenge simmering in his eyes. "Good morning, King Blackbone," he drawled, the words laced with mockery. "Did you sleep well last night?" The taunt hung in the air with the knowledge of where Ben had been.

Ben raised his chin even higher. "Slept like a baby," he replied calmly, but the edge of his fury was there, thinly veiled. "The curtains in the dorm room don't block out all the sunlight. *We* normally wake up early. Not that I complain." He flashed me a quick glance. "We find things to fill the time as we wait for class to start. Angelica can be very inventive. But considering the long hike, I appreciated the lie-in this morning."

The air between them crackled with unspoken threats, the silence more oppressive than any words. "Hopefully, your barrack will be as comfortable," Zayd finally said, his voice dripping with sarcasm. "I've arranged the largest one for you, where the high-ranking soldiers stay, or even King Emille when he visits. It should be good enough for you when not having to share it with anyone."

Ben didn't flinch, not even a muscle, but the tone in his voice told me he wasn't happy. "That's at the outskirts of the camp and furthest away from the other barracks."

"I'm both concerned and impressed that you know that. Don't worry, you'll have splendid company, as Camp Leader Ward will stay in a barrack near you once he has finished the torture challenge for the second-year cadets. I'll humbly squeeze into one of the more intimate cadet barracks with Cadet Coraly. Not that I'm complaining. As you said, Angelica can be very inventive, so I'm sure we'll make do with the small space."

"Watson, stop tormenting King Blackbone," I hissed.

He smirked as if to tell me that it wasn't going to happen. "Captain Coraly has ordered that I escort you to the camp personally. And the blackwings must come with us, too. Are you guys ready to leave?"

Zayd had invited Ben to come with us? I stared at Ben quizzically.

"Camp Leader Tomason isn't joining this challenge and Captain Coraly no longer wants us to be bound…" He nodded at Zayd.

"No! My brother soul bound you to Zayd?"

My brother was dancing on my last fucking nerve.

Irked, Ben cracked the fingers of his one hand with his thumb. "It's a hoot and a half to learn how much Camp Leader Watson loves you." Then Ben cocked his head to leer back at Zayd. "And to indulge in the jealousy he feels from knowing you chose me."

I rocked back and forth on the heel of my boot and the pads of my feet as I watched our friends standing around us, observing our conversation whilst all the other cadets had left.

Zayd pointed a stern finger at Ben. "You should be very careful to stay clear of my head."

Ben walked into his finger and stared hard at him. "As long as you stay out of mine."

Oh, my Spirits, this was a nightmare. I snapped my head sideways to stare at Kate.

"Well, I didn't know Harvey had done that, did I? It's not like it's my fault." She in turn looked at her brother and Mazdon shook his head as if to tell her she didn't have the right to all his information.

At least one thing was positive about this. The cadets were prohibited from killing Zayd, hence as long as they were bound, no one could kill Ben, either. But Zayd would have to announce it to the cadets, or they'd both be in danger.

Ben took my hand and began dragging me north towards Lake Pharoon, which was located on the border between the provinces of Pharanir and Katagoon to the west by the natural border of the mountain ridge to the Black Wing Territory.

Zayd fell into step next to me and none of us three spoke much for the four hours it took us to reach the camp. I had looked over my shoulder several times along the way, though, finding the black-wings and my white-wing friends were interacting nicely. All except for Commander Daffron, who walked in silence at the rear and scouted the surrounding area for threats.

The camp was in a beautiful location where the mountains towered to the east, and across the lake to the north was the Abarath Outpost. Surrounding the east side of the camp was a dense forest with lots of greenery. The barracks were small wooden houses with thatched roofs and three small paned windows. Four sets of stairs led up to a small porch. Smoke billowed out from each chimney so there would be a fireplace inside, too.

Zayd stopped at an area where the lake extended between a group of five barracks. Lit lanterns at each porch gleamed romantically and cast a glow onto the mirror-calm surface of the lake.

"I have reserved these for us, as they're the nicest ones. Cadet Coraly and I will take that cabin," he said, pointing at the one nearest the lake's bank. "That one is for Kate and Mazdon, the next for Emroyce and Kenyard, the one further along is for Penya and Maruto and the last in the row is for whichever of the Black-wing Teams you prefer, King Blackbone. You, the other Black-wing Team and Camp Leader Ward will stay over there," he explained, pointing at a hillside in the far distance. "Yours is cabin number three and the Black-wing Team's is in number four, so you can go and find it." Zayd quietened to hint that it was a dismissal and waited for Ben to head off.

Ben grunted and his glance swept over me before he beckoned for Murben and Davis to follow. Commander Daffron immediately turned towards his assigned cabin and Nesso scurried after him. The others also turned towards their cabins.

Zayd gestured for me to go into ours.

This is going to be so awkward.

I climbed the porch steps and pushed open the door, glancing around the small room with only a table with two chairs, a bunk bed, a small wardrobe and a fireplace; that didn't leave much floor space.

"Zayd, I'm sorry Harvey put you up to this."

Zayd rested his hands on my shoulder where I stood in the doorway. "Me too. It doesn't really help my case if he tries to force you into my arms. We just have to make the best of the situation. Your brother insisted you take the top bunk, so I could hear if you tried to sneak out to King Blackbone during the night." His brows lowered apologetically when I looked at him over my shoulder.

It surprised me to hear that he hadn't been the one initiating this whole coop.

I entered and thumped the backpack onto one of the chairs. "Fine."

"I brought the tackle ball if you want to play after dinner."

"No, thank you. I want to get a few laps in before the sun lowers and it's still warm."

"You know I have to watch you, right? The challenge has commenced already."

"Sure. Not a problem." I opened my backpack to dig around for my swimwear.

"Really? You're…reasonable today."

I had to be, or my brother would pull more of this kind of shit on me. Harvey had asked me to be nice to Zayd, so I was going to be nice. I smiled at him and nodded, fearing that if I answered verbally, it'd sound sarcastic.

Zayd looked to one side as if he was listening to something. "King Blackbone asks if you're safe."

I pulled up my nightgown from the backpack and put it under my pillow. "Yes, he does that every hour or so."

"Every hour? Spirits! Doesn't he think you can handle yourself?" Zayd put his backpack down on the other chair.

I raised my brows at him, and he held up his hands in apology. "Sorry. None of my business. I didn't mean to start a fight."

I focused my stares into my backpack. "How many daggers did you bring?"

Zayd looked around himself to view all the holsters he had strapped on and counted. "About ten."

"Can I borrow one to keep under my pillow? I only brought two."

"Sure." He pulled one out of his leg holder and tossed it half a turn in his palm before handing it to me hilt first. "Here."

I hid it inside my nightgown and continued to unpack my things in the wardrobe, so I could get to my swimsuit. "Is it okay if I use the lower part of the wardrobe?"

"I'm taller than you, so that would be logical. Feel free to use your magic in here when it's only you and me."

That reminded me of the conversation I had listened to between my brother and Denor, and I wondered what Zayd knew about the king's interest in me and the other cadets. Considering he sat on the king's counsel, he should know more than Harvey.

"I can't remember what magic Cadet Randall possesses in the Backstabber Team. Do you know?" I asked, trying to sound casual.

"His magic tells him what magic other people possess. Why do you ask?"

"I heard a conversation Harvey had with General Denor."

"You mean you eavesdropped?"

I ignored the accusation. "Why would King Emille need a magic reader in his inner circle of soldiers?"

"It could be an asset, I suppose, if he can tell the king what threat a person with magic could be to him."

Zayd was right. I had thought about the magic use in terms of winning a war, but maybe Cadet Randall was for his own personal protection.

I held up my swimsuit. "So, where do I change into this now when I share a cabin with you?"

"I would say that I've seen you naked a thousand times, so there's no need to be shy, but I fear there'll be an argument following that, so I'll just step outside."

"Thank you."

Zayd halted, taking up the entire door frame. "Did you say, 'thank you'? Wow, you're laying it on thick with the niceness today."

I unbuttoned my leather jacket. "Harvey ordered me to be nice to you."

"One of his better orders, I must say."

I smiled and pointed at the door. "Out!"

Zayd grabbed the door handle. "And there is the short-tempered Angie that I expected. Not to worry. I hadn't expected it to last this long. We'll practice the niceness short stints at a time." He winked and shut the door.

I shook my head. Zayd was charming, and it was hard to admit, but it was nice having him around. It felt like home, somehow. He was someone who knew everything about me, so I didn't have to pretend to be someone I wasn't to impress or make a point. It was just so simple with him; except for the fact that he was persistent, wanting me back, and my boyfriend was a dominant king who was used to killing whatever got in his way. Not to mention the awkwardness with my brother having bound their souls.

I donned the bathing suit and slung a towel over my arm before I walked out. Zayd was waiting for me on the porch and made a low whistle when he saw me. "Still got it, Angie."

"Make a comment about my body again, and I'll kick you in the balls."

The damp grass clung to my bare feet, each step sending tiny shivers up my legs. My stomach churned as Zayd led me to the lake's edge, his hands raised in surrender as if that could make this moment any easier. My arms wrapped tightly around myself, which was a poor substitute for armour against the horror clawing at the back of my mind.

I forced myself to look out over the water, but every ripple felt like a whisper of something lurking beneath the surface. The image of my decomposed mother struck me. Bones, pale and smooth, protruding from the lakebed like grotesque roots. Where had Harvey sunk our mother's body? How deep did she rest beneath these dark waters? The nausea curled hot in my stomach as I dipped my toe in. The temperature was well below twenty degrees, but not nearly as icy as the feeling creeping up my spine. Not nearly as paralyzingly frozen as I felt by the idea that I could be swimming over my mother's grave.

"Are you okay?" Zayd's voice pulled me back, his hand steadying my elbow as I wavered on the uneven stones.

I swallowed the bile rising in my throat and forced out the words. "If you were to sink a body in this lake…where would dump it?"

His fingers twitched around my arm. "What?" His voice dipped in alarm. "I'll not let you sink, Angie."

That was reassuring, too. I inhaled a stuttering breath. "Harvey told me…" My stomach warning me that more than words would spill out. I put the back of my hand to my mouth stifling a gag. "Harvey ran Mother through with his sword and then tied rocks to her body before dropping her into this lake." The words felt foreign, like the story they told belonged to someone else. Someone more composed. Not me, not the girl trying not to vomit into these cursed waters. I forced myself to keep staring outward and to push the image away. "I just don't want to swim too close to her."

Zayd hesitated, his grip tightening slightly. "Oh…uh. I mean, I'd probably dump a body farther from the camp."

I cocked my head up to view farther out. His reassurance was barely comforting. It was still the same lake out there as the water that touched my foot here. I had to get over it, and fast. The challenge wouldn't be cancelled just because I didn't want to swim in my mother's remains. I had to grasp at something. Anything. "True. He would, right?"

Zayd shook his head, watching me closely as I lingered, my body stiff with unease. "Angie, if you're uncomfortable with this, I can clear you from the challenge, but you'd have to talk to a healer and be declared fit for duty to continue with your training next year. But therapy doesn't take more than an hour–"

"No." I barked before he could finish that thought.

Harvey would never let me live that down. Coralys were strong and they showed no weaknesses. I forced myself to take the next step onto the jagged stone, my balance shaky.

"I'm fine. I'll do the challenge. I just needed to get my head around it."

I stepped onto the lake floor. My entire body recoiled. My stomach twisted violently, and for a second, I almost vomited. I clenched my teeth to keep it down, unwilling to let Zayd see how deeply this was affecting me.

The water lapped against my thighs, then my waist, then my shoulders. Every step further out was a battle, but I fought the growing panic, fought to keep my mind from spiralling into the abyss of what lay below. By the time I reached the red buoy a hundred meters out, my chest didn't heave from exertion but from the war raging inside me.

I turned back, forcing my strokes to be stronger, faster.

Zayd stared at his watch to note the lap time but raised an unimpressed brow as I pulled myself out of the water. "That was purely a leisurely swim, right? You can go faster than that?"

I rolled my eyes, hiding the way my hands still trembled. "Count me down for the next lap."

Lap after lap. Stroke after stroke. I forced myself through the motions, focusing on the burn in my muscles instead of the Spirit of Death's whispers in my head.

As the afternoon approached, I was exhausted. By late afternoon, I was numb. But at least Zayd was happy with my lap times.

"You've become much faster. I'm pleased that you've put in the training this month in the bathing chamber," he handed me a black Bensguard towel and fell into step next to me as we walked back to the cabin.

I was satisfied with my day. At least I had made it through without breaking.

In the evening, Camp Leader Ward joined us for wine at the cabin when he arrived. He looked worse for wear, having used his magic to amplify Cadet Dessen's torture magic in the last challenge for the second-year cadets. His shoulder-length black hair draped on either side of his thin face that looked greenish-pale this evening. He had taken off his navy-blue uniform shirt and sat on a chair on the porch, basking his incredibly contoured abs in the remaining sunlight, whilst sipping his wine like a gentleman.

"How did the challenge go for Valentina and Treylieh?" I asked, as I sat down on one of the porch steps, having towel dried and dressed in a blue tunic over a pair of black trousers.

I leaned my back against the balustrade, my wet, blue hair slithering around my shoulders, and watched the sunset.

Ward looked at me with his gorgeous, teal-coloured eyes. "I chickened out, and didn't go hard on them. It's Valentina! She threatened to break all my bones, so they won."

I smiled. Yep, that was Valentina. She wouldn't shy away from threatening a camp leader during a challenge. "She's highly competitive."

"Yes, but so are you. Two wins; in challenge three, to classify herbs, and in challenge seven, in archery. And that one was impressive since Cadet Hall is a very good archer."

Yeah, if he hadn't lost on purpose, I wouldn't have won that one.

"We're tied with Emroyce and Kenyard so far, but Cadet Starly and Cadet Darse have three wins, although the slalom flight was tied with Cadet Penya and Cadet Maruto."

"If you win this last challenge, you will be in a very good starting position for next year. And I know you're very good at swimming." Ward looked at Zayd for confirmation, who was sitting on top of the wooden railing and leaning against the facade with one leg propped up on it and the other hanging along the side.

Zayd was also in casual clothes, wearing a white tunic and beige trousers. He had gelled his auburn hair up like usual after having cut it short again. He finished his sip of wine gracefully and swirled the wine around at the bottom of his glass. "Yes, if she can endure the entire track without anyone attacking her. With any more weight, she'll sink like a rock."

"Thank you, Watson, for that clarification. I'm sure I can get the fastest time. And what do you mean by no one attacking me?"

Zayd's eyes widened when he looked at me. "You don't win this challenge by purely having the best time. Everyone starts at the same time, manoeuvres through a labyrinth of nets to get around a buoy at the end and then swims back to shore. During the challenge, you're allowed to push each other down and drown one another. Surely, you knew that after all these years, and are prepared to take the risk, considering you insisted on being a cadet rather than an agent?"

"I've never come here during the challenge. How could I've known?"

"That should've been an important part of your training this month." His head jerked sideways as if he was trying to gain control of his thoughts.

"Don't get angry with me," I chided. "It's not like you die if I die. It's King Blackbone you have to worry about."

"Wait!" Zayd barked, holding up a finger towards me. "I'm checking with King Blackbone, and he didn't seem to know those rules, either. And did you know he can sound furious through the mind, too?"

"Yeah," I snorted. "He's good at most things."

"And neither me nor King Blackbone thought your comment about you dying was funny."

I almost inhaled my wine down my windpipe. "So, you two are teaming up against me now?"

I wanted to scream and go for a long run, having learnt this information. I was most likely going to die the day after tomorrow then, unless I got a head start, and could swim faster than everyone else. Gravelhorn wouldn't miss the opportunity to push me under the surface and keep me there until my last breath, as revenge for his brothers' deaths.

"We aren't teaming up against you, Angie. We're more like your protective family."

"Some healthy family." I twisted my head to the other side of the porch. "What about you, Ward? Is your family still persistent about you becoming a sergeant instead of a camp leader, and hoping you're stationed somewhere closer to home?"

"Yes. They nag me every summer and during every visit. But General Lola Desry would never allow it. She keeps saying that she has seen things in her visions and that I'm a crucial instrument to saving Skyberg. Whatever that means."

General Denor hadn't mentioned Ward's name in the list of people King Emille wanted for his inner circle, so that was odd. But I was too exhausted to try and decipher the many secrets people kept from me.

I finished the last wine in my glass and stood up, not feeling in the mood for more small-talk, and as I had no chance of sneaking away to see Ben in my final hours, I might as well catch up on some sleep.

"I'm off to bed, guys. Good night."

"Good night," they both answered, but remained outside.

"And I forbid you from dying on me tomorrow!" Zayd shouted in his camp leader voice. "It's only a training day. Stay away from the others."

"Good night, Camp Leader Watson!" I barked.

"Good night, Angie."

71

The morning got off to a great start with a murderous look in Ben's eyes. On the shore, Ben stood rigid with his arms crossed over his chest and his expression carved from stone. Whether his anger was aimed at Zayd or at me for agreeing to this insanity, I couldn't tell.

Zayd was relentless. He insisted on combat training in the deepest part of the lake where my feet couldn't reach the bottom, where every movement would be a struggle against the pull of the water.

The way Zayd worked me, I couldn't for the world understand why he had insisted on notifying Ben of our training. Ben's presence alone made it clear that Zayd had doubts about my survival. Maybe he wasn't so sure he could protect me, not after officially declaring the start of the challenge back at the Bensguard Outpost. Maybe he had brought Ben here as an extra guard, a fail-safe.

As I adjusted the shoulder straps on my swimwear, I saw Mazdon at the bank, a knowing look flashing across his face. The one that told me he had eavesdropped on last night's conversation. Saying nothing, he slipped into the water, joining his sister for a final round of training.

The lake rippled with movement as cadets raced to the buoy and back, their arms cutting the surface. Even the black-wings had traded their armour for black Bensguard Outpost bathing shorts. The sight of every cadet's hunger to win pushed over my chest as if I was already suffocating beneath the surface. This wasn't just training. This was a test to see if we could survive the Spirits' Trek. I wasn't so sure I wanted to hike it anymore if these sorts of challenges were to be expected.

Zayd counted to three before he began pushing me under the water. My task was to get back up for air. My punches and kicks through the water didn't do enough damage, so I had to find a way to pry myself free. A few times, Zayd had to dive to bring me to the surface, and when I panted in heaps of air, Ben's expression held a blend of worry and fury.

When we broke for lunch, Ben kissed me as soon as I got out of the water, as if he needed to re-affirm to everyone that I was still his.

Zayd walked out after me, wrapping a towel around himself, his eyes boring into Ben's. "I give you the courtesy to let you know we came here to train, and you throw those emotions in my face."

"I apologise, camp leader, but you watched her after she had fallen asleep last night. A mistake. You seemed confused about who she belongs to. The kiss was necessary to remind you."

Belongs?

He was extremely territorial today!

I cringed and turned to Zayd. "You watched me sleep?"

He picked up his belt, the dagger gleaming in its sheath as he fastened it around his waist "You're so reasonable and peaceful when you sleep."

"That we can agree on," Ben chimed in, flashing me a wicked smile before pulling me against him, his arm settling possessively around my shoulders.

I narrowed my eyes. "When you sleep, the entire kingdom relaxes," I muttered under my breath.

Ben chuckled, his grip tightening slightly as if he found amusement in my irritation. "You might have meant that as an insult, Cadet Coraly, but I'll take it as a compliment."

"It wasn't," I snapped, barging for the cabin and reaching for the door and yanking it open. I stepped inside and pulled the door shut behind me, leaving him standing smugly on the porch.

I quickly stripped out of my damp clothes and changed into my combat uniform. Lunch passed in a blur of clinking trays and idle chatter, but my mind was elsewhere. The moment I saw an opportunity, I slipped away from the canteen, my boots barely making a sound against the worn path leading to the lake.

I hurried to change into my swimwear again and I was ready to dive in and lose myself in the rhythmic strokes of the swim. But that was until I reached the water's edge and froze.

My breath paused in my lungs and then burned with fear at each inhale.

I dropped my jaw, seeing who was standing at the bank, wearing nothing but red swim shorts and an air of absolute confidence.

Of all people, why does he have to be here?

General Denor had his muscular back towards me as he watched the lake, his raven-black hair swaying in the gentle winds.

"What are you doing here?" I scoffed.

He turned around and hesitated for a brief moment, as he looked at me. "Good afternoon, Cadet Coraly. As I expressed in my letter, I'm here to visit you five days before the ball for our non-date. I trust that your head is much better."

Why was he being so unnervingly sweet when it was no secret how cruel and dangerous he was? Although ruthless, he did have a hot body.

"Couldn't our final non-date have waited and been in conjunction with the ball since it's so close? I'm a bit busy with my tenth challenge." I dropped the towel from my arm onto a stone a distance away from the bank.

Denor followed me with his eyes as I approached him. "Awe, is that your way of saying you missed me? I'm afraid I couldn't come sooner. I've spent a great deal of time investigating what I can do with my magic to break the oath you formed with Duke Hartmore. If you allow it, I'd like to access your mind to see if what I've learned can remove the block."

If I allowed him to do that, then nothing in my mind would be safe. Every secret, every thought I had buried deep, could be pulled to the surface, and yet, he was asking for permission. Why? He didn't need it. If he truly wanted to pry, I wouldn't be able to stop him.

I crossed my arms, my gaze narrowing. "Don't you just rummage through people's brains whenever you feel like it?" The wind caught my hair, strands whipping across my face. I tucked one behind my ear, using the small movement to steady myself.

"I could," he admitted, each word drawn out as if he enjoyed the power behind them.

His hands folded neatly behind his back like a gentleman, as he closed the final distance between us. "But in some instances, I respect the person enough to ask."

Respect. That was an interesting choice of words. My pulse quickened as I held his gaze, searching for any cracks in that composed exterior. He was too calm, too controlled. I hated how easily he got under my skin.

I forced a smirk, tilting my chin up. "Let's see what you've planned for our non-date first," I said, my voice laced with defiance. "Then I'll decide how deep I want to let you into my mind."

"That is fair." He gestured with his hand towards the lake. "So, let me see what you've got." He held up a hand like a gentleman to lead me into the water until it was chest-high on us both. "You know, I'm really displeased to see you walking about on your own without any guards. Where are your protectors?"

I thought back to the conversation I had eavesdropped on between him and Harvey and how Denor had mentioned that King Emille had wanted to assign royal guards to me. If King Emille's spies reported to him that I was walking around alone, perhaps that'd make it harder for Denor to argue the case that I didn't need any.

"I can handle myself," I muttered and inhaled sharply at the cold water when I dipped myself, so the surface reached my chin.

He chuckled. "Regardless, I insist on you having a guard. If you don't choose one by yourself, I'll have to permanently stay at your side and guard you myself."

"Fine. I'll let a camp leader know where I go next time." I rose from the lakebed to get ready for whatever he had planned as he came to my side in the water.

"Good," he drawled and watched the droplets run down my cleavage. "Now, come at me with a few kicks and punches."

With pleasure!

"Indeed," he purred.

I gasped, feeling the cold water tickle around my stomach. My anger grew when I realised that he was constantly reading my mind and–

"Yes," he chuckled, standing right next to me. *"It's my greatest amusement, and the thought about me having a hot body was nice to hear."*

Blushing, I launched a fist towards his face, but he hooked his elbow and blocked it with his forearm. My left fist went for his stomach, but under the surface it was slow, and he simply clicked his tongue at me as he let it make impact. "You're better off going for an arm lock in the water and trying to sink the other person. Have you practised holding your breath?"

"I have."

"Good. I'm going to swim for the buoy and your task is to try to pull me under. I won't retaliate."

The water swallowed him up as he dived deep and disappeared. Four minutes passed whilst I waited for him to re-surface. *Where did he go?*

"Come find me," he teased.

How in this world would I find him inside the darkness below the surface?

"That's what you need to figure out, Cadet Coraly. Find a way to fight the darkness."

His head popped up right at the buoy and he flicked his chin sideways to clear his fringe from his eyes. "Cadet Coraly? Why are you still over there?"

"I didn't realise where you went at first and then you had too much of a head-start. I'll come to you, and we can start over from there."

With big strokes, I swam to him, and before he gave the go ahead to start, I wrapped my arms around his neck and my legs around his waist to tug him downwards.

Denor simply swam back to the shore with me clinging onto his back. "You're too lightweight, so you won't be able to drown any muscular man. Take a knife to the battle in the water. Do you still have the black blade knife I gave you?"

He hadn't meant to patronise me, but I took it that way.

"Yes, maybe I'll show it to you up-close one day!"

Angry, I jumped at him and punched at his face and tried to twist his arm around his back. He blocked and bent out of my every attempt until I was too tired to carry on. He threw me high up in the air and I fell into the water with a splash before his hand gripped me just as I went under the surface so he could pick me up.

"Maybe you should try biting," he teased, a wicked gleam in his eyes.

I didn't hesitate. My fist shot out, landing squarely on his shoulder. This time, he didn't bother to block it. He knew he deserved it.

He smirked, rubbing the spot where I'd hit him. "Have you learned anything from our training?"

"Yeah. That you've a death wish," I shot back, shaking the lingering sting from my knuckles. "Thank you. It's been a good training session, honestly," I confessed even though it was hard to admit. "I was half-expecting you to make me do something disgustingly romantic."

His tone was teasing, but when he lifted his brows, there was something else lurking behind his gaze. "You don't think this is romantic?" he asked, gesturing around us. "We've got the mountains towering behind us, the faintly visible stars in the abyss above, the cabins scattered around like something out of a fairytale. And here we are, practically naked in a lake."

I scoffed, crossing my arms over my damp swimwear. "We're training for combat in our uniforms, in near-freezing water, with nothing but primitive supplies to keep us from hypothermia once we get out."

His smirk shifted to something serious, and he took a step closer. "Maybe that's just how you see it. Do you want me to bend your mind? Show you my version of this moment?"

I stiffened.

He tilted his head. "Because yours seems distorted by grief. You're still looking at the world through a bitter lens from your parents' deaths."

The words hit harder than his teasing ever had. He had no right to say that, and yet, the worst part was that I wasn't sure he was wrong.

Before I got the chance to tell him to stay the fuck away from me, he pushed a picture into my mind and there were no traces of the real world around me. The general and I were cuddled up on a grey sofa, tall windows towering around us and in front of us was a beautifully crafted fireplace enveloped in gems and iron artwork. We were wrapped up in black Bensguard Outpost blankets and I could even feel the heat from the flames kissing my cheeks.

"How's your hot chocolate?" he asked, nodding for the mug I held in both my hands to warm them.

I attempted to get off the sofa, but my body didn't obey me, so I searched around for a hole in his mind magic. How the heck could I free myself from this?

"Relax, please," he said, and made a sweet smile I believed he'd never use in real life. "I'll bring you back to the lake in a moment if you play along."

I hesitantly brought my lips to the mug, feeling the hard but smooth surface of the porcelain. I sipped. The taste of hot chocolate was so real it was incredible.

He pushed a strand of my hair behind my ear, and I couldn't move my hand to swat him away. "You're a very beautiful woman, noted by kings, dukes…and generals."

He looked quite handsome when he showed his vulnerable side. Like a gentleman, he sat with his legs crossed; his foot maintaining a casual swing and leaned into me with a slight curve of his torso, wearing black trousers and a dark grey shirt that was unbuttoned halfway down his chest. I looked down and saw I was wearing a grey woolly jumper and comfortable black tracksuit trousers.

Stressed, I looked around again, but I saw no weapons, neither did I see faded edges to this vision that I could break through. He was keeping my mind trapped in his own fantasy.

"Why are you doing this to me?" I asked, finally able to lean away from him.

He gestured wide in the air in front of him and around the high ceiling of the cabin. "I want to impress you."

"Just because your magic is impressive doesn't mean you are," I snapped, and sipped more of the chocolate, although I couldn't understand why I did as the drink wasn't real.

"Isn't magic a large part of who we are? Maybe you don't realise that since you're not using yours to your full potential."

"I have no magic."

He raised his brows at me as if to say I was silly for trying to fool a mind bender.

"Join me. Be loyal to only me. In return, I promise I'll take your mind wherever it wants to go, whenever you want. You can feel like you live in luxury or peace in the blink of an eye."

In the next moment, I was holding a tray with a large turkey on it, walking towards a dinner table. I stopped to look around and saw my parents, Harvey and Kate, and Denor laughing as they entertained four children. Two of the three boys had features that were a mix of the general's and mine. "Happy Turning of the Year!" I shouted, as I placed the turkey on the table and leaned down to kiss Denor.

I struggled against my conscience to get control of myself, slamming my shoulder against the shield he had forged in my mind. "Get me out of here!

Take me back to the lake!"

My vision of the lake reappeared, or at least I hoped it was my own sight, as only the Spirits knew what Denor could do to me, and this could be another trick. I dried the tears that had fallen down my cheeks from the heartache of seeing my parents; my family, happy. The way my life should have been. Denor had rummaged through me and found my deepest desire and used it against me.

I heard the sudden splash of water behind me. My heart stammered in my chest as I turned, seeing Ben striding toward us, the lake rippling violently around him. His combat uniform clung to him, soaked through, but he moved with single-minded determination, barely acknowledging the water slowing him down.

Before I could say a word, his hands were on me; gripping, pulling, shielding. He yanked me away from the general and cupped my face, his palms warm despite the chill of the lake. His thumbs brushed over my damp cheeks, his sharp gaze scanning my face for hurts that would demand answers.

"Are you okay?"

I blinked, having only had seconds to take in the real world around us once more. "Yeah, I'm okay."

His eyes flickered with doubt, but he didn't push. Instead, he turned toward General Denor.

And just like that, the warmth in his touch vanished.

His entire body coiled like a beast ready to strike. His broad shoulders squared, and his muscles became taut beneath the drenched fabric. His expression darkened until his eyes were no longer the warm burgundy I knew, but a deep, furious shade of blood, burning with a clear warning.

"Do not force a war upon the White Wing Territory, General," he growled, his voice thunderous. "Do not push me this far."

The lake, the air, everything around us seemed to register the sincerity of his warning – even the general.

Denor put his hands behind his back in a gentlemanly way and smiled at me. "What man would start a war against innocent people to save one woman?"

Ben didn't answer and pushed me towards the bank where Zayd stood and watched us.

"You wouldn't do that for love," General Denor called after us. "Only for power."

There it was again, the hint that Ben only wanted me for my magic and not for love. The thoughts rushed through my head as Zayd wrapped me in my towel.

I hated that the general could read my mind and know he had made me doubt Ben's love.

"Take her to your cabin," Ben instructed Zayd. "I need to get changed into dry clothes. And keep the general away from her."

Inside the cabin, I was too worked up to remember that I had changed into my dry clothes with Zayd still there, but when I turned around, I saw him facing away from my naked body.

He was pinching his fingers over his temples. "Angie, I tapped into King Blackbone's mind when he panicked and it's not natural how powerful the feelings he has for you are. I'm not sure he's of sane mind. It's like his world begins and ends with you. I'm really worried about you."

My entire mind had just been violated by the general, but it was Ben he was worried about? *Spirits!*

I donned a black tunic over my brown leather trousers. "Maybe you aren't interpreting Ben's emotions correctly as you're not used to being soul bound with someone as strong as the king?"

"Angie, I'm linked to all of the black-wings at the same time and I can still hold my shields up. I've had my training."

"You're linked to all of them?" I pushed my hands into my pockets to arrange them flat against my hips.

Zayd flailed his hands wide. "How else would they be able to be here?"

When I found my small black blade knife, I pushed it into my right boot. "No. Of course. I just hadn't considered it. Harvey should've let me take some of them. Commander Daffron surely doesn't make much noise."

Zayd snorted. "No. He's silent. Nesso is funny to let inside my head at times. He amuses me."

Spirits! Zayd didn't know that Nesso was a highly skilled spy for the black-wing king. Nesso was probably garnering information rather than simply being inside Zayd's head for the entertainment value. Perhaps Nesso was even better than I had realised, because his outgoing personality made him seem so trustworthy. Nesso also had a lot to make up for if he wanted to keep his life and be forgiven by his king.

"Wine?" Zayd asked and picked up a bottle that stood on the small table.

"Yes, please. Red."

He swapped the white wine bottle he held for a red one and opened it, pouring two glasses and handing one to me. "How do you feel your training has gone for this challenge?"

"I've given up. The general's training made me realise that I'm not becoming any better at staying alive in the water, and I've decided my best bet is to swim damned fast."

"Cheers to that," Zayd said, and brought his glass towards me, and I toasted with him before taking a sip, the rich flavour warming me as I swallowed.

Zayd gulped down half his glass and moved closer to me, keeping one hand on my back as he stared at me. "I saw you cry, and that doesn't happen often. I'm sorry for whatever the general did to you." He took more large gulps of wine and leaned in closer.

The door opened and Ben walked in, immediately pushing Zayd away. "You've got the entire White Wing Territory to search for any other woman than Cadet Coraly. She's mine!"

Zayd looked at me as if to remind me of his warning. I took Ben's hand. "Let's go for a walk."

Ben and I distanced ourselves from the others by taking a stroll hand in hand along the lake. It was very romantic with the beautiful landscape surrounding us and the moon shining brightly in the dark sky amid a million stars. It was funny how I hadn't noticed the stunning views when the general had pointed them out.

We both wore casual clothes, matching in a black tunic and brown leather trousers. With no time to shave, Ben's face was stubbly, and his black hair reached below his ears, tossing in the wind.

Ben stretched his free hand into the sky and pointed at a star constellation. "There is the Golden Stallion. That's my favourite."

To me, the eight stars, forming a shape with a neck, back, and front legs connected to its spine, seemed like a stretch of the imagination to resemble a horse. But I knew enough about astronomy to recognise he was right. He shifted his hand to the left, pointing at the next cluster of stars, five brilliant points radiating from a single base. "And there, Miss Stone, is the Spirits' Hand," he said. "Did you know that stars are burning stones far away, forever alight?"

"Yes. Captain La Roy also likes stars and calls Kate his star. He often joined our tutoring lessons growing up when we learned about astronomy. And by the way, 'star' is a much more endearing nickname than 'stone'."

"Yet, both nicknames are such a fair representation of your personalities. Kate has a hot temper, and your resolve is hard as stone." Ben chuckled, putting his hand casually in his pocket as we slowly sauntered forwards. "You remember what I promised you as we came here? Your reward."

"It's been on my mind every damned minute. That, and how angry I am with Harvey for connecting your soul to Zayd's."

He watched me with a soft smile, his eyes filled with something I couldn't quite read. "Are we talking about the same thing here?"

I hesitated, the awkwardness of the conversation catching up with me. "Probably. But I can't be intimate with you, knowing you could use it to tease Zayd. It's…weird."

His smile faltered, but only slightly, before he nodded, his tone becoming more serious. "Okay, that does it. Since your determination is as unyielding as stone, I won't even try to change your mind. The bond can't stay then. Break it."

My eyes darted around in their sockets. "Break it?" My voice wavered, uncertainty creeping in. "What do you mean?"

He leaned in, his gaze sharp and intense as he spoke. "Use your magic like you did at the spring festival. Break the bond."

I looked away, my eyes landing on the calm, placid lake, trying to steady the sudden turmoil inside me. "I have no magic," I muttered, more to myself than to him.

He shouldn't know about my magic and certainly not expect that I'd use it.

"That's disappointing." There was a hint of resignation in his words.

My heart thudded painfully in my chest.

Why? Because I wouldn't be intimate, or because I wouldn't be his weapon!

I jerked my hand out of his, the touch suddenly feeling like a shackle I didn't want to wear. "I can't do this, Ben. You have secrets. I have secrets. We're always fighting about them. I never know what you want from me." My voice broke, and I turned, unable to look at him any longer. I rushed back toward camp, not daring to glance over my shoulder as Ben's voice cut through the air.

"Nothing. I just want you!"

His words echoed in my mind, but I didn't stop. I couldn't.

72

I felt the chill of the morning air crawl under my skin as I stepped onto the shore, my legs heavy like lead. It was nine o'clock sharp, and I stood with all the remaining one hundred and ten cadets of the first year by the lake. Three teams had dropped off already during practice, with one or both teammates dead. My heart was a drumbeat, thumping louder and louder with panic. I had finally comprehended the brutality of this challenge, and I could already feel the weight of the water pressing me down under the surface, suffocating me.

A gut-wrenching anxiety surged within me as the challenge was about to start. I surveyed the cadets around me, all in their swimwear. They were lined up by the bank. Their faces filled with anticipation, some grinning, some nervously shifting their weight. It only made my anxiety surge higher. They were ready for this. But I was definitely not.

Zayd was standing at the shore in his camp leader shorts, waiting for everyone to arrive. He had been up early, preparing for the challenge with Ward.

I stepped closer, flashing him a pitiful smile. "You got little sleep last night." It wasn't just a statement of fact, I still cared about him, and this situation wasn't easy on him, either. He didn't have to swim for his life today, but he might have to watch friends die.

"It wasn't easy to sleep when Ben kept threatening me every hour, saying, '*if you touch her, I'll kill you*', over and over again. Those thoughts aren't easy to shake. If I had any doubts before, they're gone now: Ben's wrath is a force I don't want to test."

I wanted to apologise. It felt as if it was my fault that Ben was on edge. I had left him with an eternal void of uncertainty last night. It seemed the only way to fill the void with something, and to gain some kind of control, was by delivering threats to Zayd.

The way I had left it with Ben was feeding my dread now–right before our challenge.

I caught Zayd's eye briefly before he turned toward the crowd of cadets.

I stepped away from him as he resumed his camp leader role.

Raising his voice, I could hear him clearly from where I stood, but his words were muffled by my reeling thoughts.

Zayd explained the rules of the challenge; basically what we needed to do to survive. But as he spoke of the dangers; the nets that could trap us, and the risk of exhaustion before we even made it back to shore, the fear I already felt settled deeper in my bones.

Then, as if to push that fear over the edge, Zayd got to the part about *'trying not to kill each other',* and that was when I saw Gravelhorn's grin.

The bastard grinned at me; a cruel, twisted grin that made my nerves sting. His hazel eyes gleaming with revenge. He wasn't listening to the rules. He was imagining the chaos that would unfold as soon as Zayd gave the go ahead.

I felt trapped, suffocated by everything; the water, the other cadets, the challenge, and the tension between Ben and me. I wanted to turn around, to run back to the safety of the outpost, but I couldn't. I had to do this. Somehow, I had to survive this day.

In my peripheral view, I saw Ben step up beside me, glancing at me, but neither of us said a word to each other. I rubbed at my tattooed wrist and at least took comfort in the fact that if I died today, Duke Hartmore wouldn't get me as his weapon, either.

"He could have worn his uniform," Ben muttered.

Zayd's body was toned to perfection, similarly to Ben's calibre, so I could see where his jealousy stemmed from. Zayd was only wearing his navy-blue bathing shorts, and surely enough, all the female cadets were eating him up with their eyes. All but Cadet Darling, who still had her eyes on Ben. Everything about her screamed beauty and that made me wish I had my dagger on me so I could slit her throat there and then or at least take her eyes out. But Denor had enforced a new rule on the challenge that no one was allowed weapons.

"Look away, or I'll gut you!" I barked at her, but that made Cadet Darling look even harder, inspecting Ben's black tattoo swirls.

She flicked her slender fingers so gracefully in the air to indicate toward Ben's body. "I can look as much as I want until I see a ring on that finger."

Ben held his hand up with the ring I had given him. My heart bled a bit. He was still wearing my ring, and he clearly took the commitment seriously.

I stared at her hard again and she and Cadet Courtney moved further away from us, and I prayed to the Spirit of Luck that Courtney wouldn't freeze the lake to ice before I had got out from it.

I took Ben's hand as Zayd rambled something about the maze of nets that we had to swim through.

"I'm sorry about yesterday. I freaked out. The summer break can't come soon enough. I need it. Can you forgive me?"

His hand held harder around mine than normal. "I've told you never to doubt my feelings for you." There was an unforgiving tone to his voice even as he said it.

My gaze tipped to rest on the grass. "I know, but considering our circumstances, it's hard."

He cocked my chin up with a knuckle so he could look me in the eye. "What is it that is so hard about loving me?" There was so much pain in the eyes that looked back at me.

I sighed while my heart threatened to burn a hole through my chest. "I don't want to be manipulated into being used as a weapon."

His knuckle fell away, his chest raising with a deep breath. "What weapon? You have no magic?"

I rolled my eyes at him and whispered, "You know I do."

He narrowed his eyes as if a question gnawed on his mind. "Not strong enough to break the bond between Watson and me, or I think you would have, considering the reward I had planned to give you."

I bit my lip. The playfulness that cut through my fear was a blessing. "Confident in your skills there, my king?"

"I freaking am." He wrapped his arms around my back and pulled me tight to his chest, kissing me without caring who was watching us in the myriad of cadets surrounding us. "And I can win my wars on my own. I don't even want you on the battlefield."

"So. I'm forgiven?" I looked up at him with my large, blue, puppy-dog eyes.

"Of course you are. How can I stay mad at you?" He brushed his nose against mine. "You're as mischievous as you were when I first met you."

"No false marketing there."

Zayd's voice cut us off as he shouted. "Go!"

I was confused. I hadn't heard his instructions, or that he had counted down for the start. The cadets were ploughing through the shallow water towards the maze of nets. Ben and I had one quick look at each other before we sprinted into the lake.

"I'm swimming for the buoy underneath the surface, so if I don't come up in two minutes, dive for me!" I shouted to Ben, who got a panicked look on his face, and hesitated to start his crawl, stopping with the water up to his thighs.

"No! Angelica! Keep to the surface where I can see you!"

It was too late. I dived and pushed my arms and legs through the water. The problem was the damn nets that hadn't been here yesterday. It was no longer a straight swim for the buoy. I tore at the nets to try and clear them from my trajectory but couldn't see in which direction to swim. I turned for the surface and took a few strokes towards Ben who was twisting his head around the deeper waters, searching for me.

Gravelhorn saw me and leered. *Shit!*

I risked a glance at Ben who had clearly seen him swimming toward me, his powerful strokes cutting through the water. Panic surged through me as I saw the distance between us vanish in an instant.

Gravelhorn was a giant with strength magic that could drown me with ease. The moment his hands gripped me, it was as if the water itself had turned against me.

I struggled, my limbs thrashing against him, but it was futile. Every punch and kick I landed seemed to bounce off him, like I was trying to fight against a wall of muscle. He pushed me down, the pressure on my chest growing as my body was forced deeper into the murky depths.

No, no, no!

The water swallowed my gasps before I could draw in a breath. His grip on my throat didn't relent, it tightened, cutting off what little air I had left.

I kicked harder, but the more I fought, the tighter and more painful his grip became. My vision began to blur, edges fading into a sickly black.

I need to breathe!

But it was hopeless. The darkness wasn't just around me anymore, it was inside me, creeping into my mind. The coldness, the suffocation, it all blurred together.

I gasped for air, but I only swallowed more water, choking on it, my body jerking in panic.

In the depths of the water, my eyes locked with his as he ducked under the surface. Gravelhorn's furious hazel eyes burned into me, filled with nothing but malice. The hatred in his gaze was palpable, like he was daring me to keep fighting. His grip wasn't going to give, and I saw the twisted satisfaction on his face, the sick pleasure he took in watching me struggle, demanding that I die already – that I stop living.

I was going to die here. I could feel it in my bones. The last of my strength was slipping away with every breathless second. Yet, I couldn't give up. I couldn't let him win. But no matter how I fought him, the darkness crept closer, pulling me under…

I'd have to use my magic and expose my family's secret and put Harvey in danger. *I'm really sorry, Father.*

But I had no time to activate it.

Rapidly, I was brought to the surface, and I gasped for air as soon as Gravelhorn's hands were pulled from my throat. Ben punched him in the face and blood sprayed from it. Cadet Lewis was right behind Ben, flexing his hand in the air to extend his iron claws from his knuckles.

"Behind you, Ben!" I screamed.

Ben jerked left, the movement too slow in water and the claws ripped over his back. He roared in pain, and gripped around Lewis' throat, the black death essence swirling out from his hands, but Lewis didn't die. Ben put more force into his magic, but Lewis lifted his clawed hand to strike again.

"Kill him!" I shouted, not wanting to imagine what would happen if Lewis stabbed his claws into Ben's chest.

I looked around to see what magic was around us and saw Lewis' teammate, Cadet Kwi, focusing on them. He had magic that could lessen other's magic, and he was using it on Ben.

I rushed towards the red-haired, one-eyed beast, throwing, myself around his neck. That was the extent of my ingenious plan, and I knew my life was forfeit when Kwi tore me off him, pushing me deep under the water. He circled his legs under my armpits and held me down while he went up for air.

Grabbing for his cock to inflict damage, I found he was already cupping it with his hand for protection. Unless someone could get to me, how would I get out of this?

Exhaustion held my body in chains, each movement to free myself heavier than the last. My limbs were leaden, and the thought of swimming to the surface, if Kwi was merciful enough to release me, felt like an impossible task. The desperate need for air overpowered everything else. I couldn't even tell how long he'd been holding me; two minutes, five? Time had warped in the void of the water.

The cold liquid pressed against my ears, drowning out all sound. I clawed at Kwi's thigh, my nails digging into the hard muscle, but he didn't flinch. Nothing.

Desperation surged through me, and without thinking, I sank my teeth into his leg. The taste of seaweed was in my mouth as I dug my teeth deeper. Finally, he moved. But it wasn't the release I had hoped for.

His fingers tangled into my hair as he shoved me down further into the water. I gasped, the shock of the deeper, icier, water flooding me. But the more I struggled, the harder he pushed.

This was worse. Deeper. Darker.

This is it.

I was losing myself, spiralling into darkness.

Air! I need air!

I had nothing left to give. Nothing to bargain with the Spirit of Life. No promises. No hope.

I'm going to die here…

At least Ben and I hadn't ended on bad terms when I died.

Kwi's hands took a firm grip of my swimsuit and pulled me to the surface. I gasped for air as soon as I could, and water poured out of my nose.

The look in Kwi's eyes was haunting – his eyes vacant and staring at nothing in particular. He wasn't moving or talking. I looked around and saw all the cadets treading water, even Ben. Emroyce and Kenyard were almost at the bank on their way back and the Agility Team wasn't far behind. But they had stopped. Everything had stopped except the wind rattling the leaves of the nearby trees.

Eerily, Kwi started swimming with his grip still around my swimsuit, pushing me forwards and past everyone who wasn't reacting. No one flinched. They were mindlessly bobbing along with the small waves. Ben followed us in a graceful swim as we passed by him.

On the way back to the bank, I looked up at the shore to see Zayd staring at Emroyce as if he was also frozen in time.

Then I looked further up at the shore and saw General Denor.

"Make haste, Cadet Coraly if you want to win," he said calmly, as if this wasn't strange at all.

I gawked at him, at everything, as Kwi helped me up by the rocks at the bank.

"Run toward, Camp Leader Watson," Denor encouraged, as I stood stunned in shock.

At his command, I stumbled forwards, Ben helping me from behind my back like a mindless servant.

Every movement that was supposed to be happening around me sped up and the challenge was full on once again. I almost walked over the finish line, mindless and baffled. Ben rushed past it and Zayd cheered as if he had expected us to win. None of the other cadets exclaimed that I had cheated or asked what had been going on. Emroyce patted my back and congratulated me, and Mazdon and Kate did the same.

Shocked, I gasped for breath, the suffocation more murderous than it had when I was under water. The truth hit me like a cold wave. Denor's power, his control, stretched far beyond anything I had ever imagined. His mind was capable of things fairytales couldn't even conjure up. The fact that he was also holding back...*that* was even more terrifying. The sheer magnitude of his abilities left me feeling small, vulnerable. He wasn't just a threat. He was something *worse.* The truth was unthinkable, but also the only plausible strategy if I wanted to survive. *This man is far better to keep as an ally than an enemy.*

"I knew you could do it," Zayd said casually, his tone almost too calm, as though there was nothing strange at all about the scene that had just unfolded. "You're a fast swimmer." He handed me the dagger, which was the prize for surviving this twisted challenge.

The cold steel of the blade felt eerie as I took it from his hands. The dark iron gleamed in the light, its blade as sharp as it was beautiful. Intricate gems sparkled along the hilt, braided iron twisting into a smooth handle, while the pommel bore the key insignia of the Bensguard Outpost. It felt heavy, not just in my hand. It was a reminder of what had just happened, and a death I had barely escaped. *Thanks to the general.*

My mind raced, trying to make sense of it all, but all I could focus on was the sight of Kwi, Gravelhorn, and his teammate Malloopa hauling Lewis's lifeless body to shore.

My anger flared, and before I could stop myself, I had stormed up to Denor, the words rushing out of me in a fierce rush of emotion. "What the fuck did you do? You could control all of them? You could just erase their memories like nothing?"

The general smiled an almost cruel curve of his lips. "Not just erase, Cadet. I can alter their memories, make them believe things that never happened, things they never saw. I usually don't like cheating, but Cadet Kwi would've killed you. It was necessary."

I ran my hand over my head, trying to process it all. My mind felt scrambled, like I couldn't hold onto any one thought for too long. "Spirits…"

Denor folded his arms, his red combat uniform stretching across them. His eyes gleamed, a mixture of pride and amusement. "Are you at least a little impressed?" he asked, the arrogance in his voice impossible to ignore.

I swallowed hard, realising that having the general's attention was beyond dangerous. "I'm fucking terrified. Could you do that to everyone?" My voice cracked, the question left my fear exposed.

He didn't hesitate to give a reply. "Everyone, except a select few." His answer had been surprisingly earnest.

Who could those people be with magic more powerful than Denor's?

My head was shaking by reflex as I tried to comprehend the extent of his power. "You could command King Blackbone to start a war or make him stop loving me…or make him love me?" I panicked, thinking about what Zayd had told me about not believing Ben's love for me was natural.

"I could. Yes. I could make you do anything for me…or with me," he said and winked. "Without you knowing it had happened afterwards. But I don't want any of those things."

"You could make every person in this world into your slave."

"That's an intriguing thought and interesting that you'd think of such high aspirations. But what would be the fun in that? A very lonely and fictitious life. And unfortunately, I couldn't do anything for you regarding removing the oath. I'll do some more research and try again at another time. My time here is up, and I've a few things yet to arrange for the First Year Ball before I've a war to attend to."

Ben grabbed a towel for each of us and stepped to my side. The sight of his injuries; four deep claw marks slashed across his chest, each one oozing blood in jagged lines, made me want to cry. My eyes stung as I held back my tears, watching him. Lewis had torn into him, leaving behind wounds that would scar. But the worst was the gash trailing from behind his ear down to his shoulder, an angry red streak that looked particularly raw.

He should've been wincing, his body should've trembled with pain, but Ben didn't flinch. He didn't acknowledge the suffering his own body endured. Instead, his eyes burned with cold hatred as he fixed his gaze on General Denor.

Without a word, he draped the black towel around my shoulders, his fingers barely brushing my skin, but the gesture was enough to remind me that despite everything, he was here. Protecting me.

Yet, we both knew the truth. No amount of strength, no amount of rage, would be enough to overpower the general. Ben understood it. He was powerless against him. We both were. That realisation hurt more than any wound Lewis had left behind.

"I *trust* that you'll take care of Cadet Coraly from here on, and I'll take my leave," he said, looking at Ben.

So, clearly Ben was using his trust magic on the general, and I wondered whether it was a counterattack, having figured out that the general had done something with his magic, too.

Denor bowed towards me. "I'll see you again in five days' time for the ball. I'd like to escort you there, if you wouldn't mind meeting me at Kabry City Harbour on Friday at four o'clock. That should give us sufficient time to get ready, with some time left to relax after the flight, before the ball starts at seven o'clock."

It was Monday today, and it took four days to get to Gaithorpe, so that sounded reasonable. It would be the last encounter from our deal, and then I'd be free of him.

"If you want to be free of me after that night," he said, and winked at me before turning around to walk away.

"Stay out of my head!" I shouted after him.

73

After lunch, I changed into combat uniform and regrouped with everyone at the gates. We hiked the dirt path back to the Bensguard Outpost in a steady rhythm.

By the time we arrived, exhaustion clung to my limbs, but there was no time to rest. We showered quickly, scrubbing away the last traces of the lake and battle, before gathering in the canteen for dinner. The atmosphere was charged with excitement for the end-of-year ceremony.

As night fell, we filed into the grand assembly hall, and the space hummed with tension. It was a moment of recognition and transition, not just for us, but also for the graduating third-year cadets from the Special Missions Unit. Tomorrow would bring the General Operations ceremony and another round of farewells, but I had no connections in those units. By then, I'd already be on my way to Gaithorpe.

The hall fell into hushed anticipation as six camp leaders, along with Captain La Roy and Harvey, ascended the podium. But it was my brother, standing tall in his striking orange uniform, who commanded the room. The insignia on his shoulder gleamed like a bold reminder of his authority as Camp Master. As he stepped behind the speaker's lectern, the room collectively held its breath.

This was it. The moment we had all been waiting for.

"Good afternoon, cadets!"

"Good afternoon, Captain!" all the cadets bellowed in unison.

"This has been an exceptional year. Congratulations to all of you on your achievements and new skills. I also express my condolences to all those with friends or family who fell during the year. I salute their bravery and wish they reincarnate to live a better life." He cleared his throat and took a silent moment. He never liked to talk about the dead, which was probably why his speeches were short and concise. "This assembly marks the end of the year and the start of your summer break, so when it finishes, you're all dismissed and allowed to leave the premises to go home to your families. After the summer, we'll gain a new class to care for here at the Bensguard Outpost. Treat them well and earn friendships, as many of you've already found here. As for our third-year cadets, the time at the academy has ended, and you'll now go out into the field and help our territory in actual battles. May the Spirit of Luck be with you all."

Ben put his hand over mine that was sprawled over the armrest of the seat and we shared a sentimental look before he continued listening to Harvey. My gaze drifted up to the large bandage Mewer had put on Ben's neck after cleaning him up, and then my stomach fluttered as I noted the crown badge on his arm. After the summer I'd have earned two crosses, but he'd still be a king; the highest rank and badge anyone could have. I turned to look at Kate to my right and felt proud of her two circles of magic adeptness on her shoulder. Lost watching Harvey on the podium, Kate didn't notice my glances. We had advanced this year, and we hadn't died, so I guessed that was a successful year.

"I'll call the graduating cadets to come up to the podium one by one to receive their uniforms and letters of instruction regarding where they'll be stationed and when they're expected at their new posts." Harvey turned towards Captain La Roy, who had tied his light-blonde hair into a short ponytail that didn't reach the collar of his yellow uniform.

Harvey signalled for him to pick up the first folded uniform and letter from the table, upon which lay the uniforms in three groups; green for infantry, brown for cavalry and sky-blue for the Air Force.

The hall buzzed with anticipation as Captain La Roy stepped forward, holding a crisp white worker's uniform, which was a rare sight, and only one cadet would be awarded that uniform this year. The room hushed, waiting for the announcement.

"Dungeon Master Apprentice Carl Dessen!" Harvey's voice boomed through the assembly hall. "Stationed at the Ivory Castle in the torture chamber alongside Dungeon Master Dessen!"

A murmur rippled through the crowd. The Ivory Castle. The torture chamber. It was an assignment whispered about in the dark corners of the camp, a place of secrets and shadows.

Cadet Dessen stood, his movements steady as he descended the staggered seating rows, his face unreadable. Applause followed him, though some clapped more hesitantly than others. He stepped onto the podium, shaking Harvey's hand before turning to Captain La Roy, who handed him the white uniform and letter of assignment. Without a word, Zayd guided him to the end of the stage, where the other cadets would soon join him.

Harvey barely paused before calling the next name.

"Sergeant Henry Dark! Stationed at the Dashqaz Outpost in the Air

Force Unit!"

A cheer erupted as Henry Dark, now Sergeant Dark, pushed to his feet. He was known for his deadly precision as he was able to hurl charged orbs of voltage with alarming accuracy. The Air Force Unit had gained a formidable soldier.

Dark strode up to the stage, head held high, confidence radiating from him as he took the sky-blue uniform. The fabric bore the Dashqaz Outpost's sword emblem at the collar, and the insignia of his new rank, three horizontal stripes by a single vertical line, marked him as a Sergeant in the Air Force.

Camp Leader Nar stepped forward, nodding approvingly as she directed Dark to stand beside Dessen, his former teammate. They clasped hands in victory for a brief moment, bumping their shoulders, because it was a true victory if you graduated with your teammate still alive. For three years you had protected your teammate and made an eternal friend, and that was no small feat.

The ceremony was only beginning, but as night approached cadets called to the podium today would leave behind the life they had known, stepping into a future that promised both honour and danger.

Harvey called up a few more names of cadets I hadn't known that well, who were also assigned to the Air Force unit under Camp Leader Nar's command.

I lost focus for a while, but startled when I heard Harvey call out Brian's name.

"Sergeant Brian La Roy!"

I leaned over to whisper in Kate's ear. "But Brian didn't graduate with a teammate. They get their letters in private instead of on the podium."

"When you've a captain as a brother, you get to go up on the stage. Leadership agreed that he could do the last challenge without a teammate if he took it twice," she hissed, clearly annoyed to be interrupted from watching Harvey.

"I can't see the colour of the uniform. Is it brown?" I hissed towards Kate. I was so nervous for him, knowing he wanted to join the Cavalry as he was fond of horses.

"Yes, it's brown. Listen to Harvey," Kate hissed at me again.

"Stationed at Candir Outpost in the Cavalry Unit."

My blood froze. Candir? Why had my brother stationed him there? Brian had to be at Bensguard with Fern and the baby. Anger heated my blood as my knuckles went white, clenching onto the edges of the armrests, unable to applaud as he made his way to the podium.

How dare my brother do this to our friend?

Ben tried to hold my hand, but they were stuck on the armrest, so he put a warm hand on my knee.

Captain La Roy threw his arms around his little brother and patted him on his back. "Well done."

Brian looked confused when Tomason came to hold his elbow, nudging him to line up at the end of the podium with the other Sergeants, holding onto his brown uniform that would have the Candir Outpost Eagle badge.

Ben leaned over me and whispered, "Camp Leader Tomason's father is the captain at the Candir Outpost. Sergeant La Roy will be well taken care of there."

The way Ben had mentioned everyone by their rank angered me even further, realising that no one cared about anyone in this place. They weren't a number in a unit; they were our friends. People I had grown up with and loved. I didn't keep friends like servants, who I could just dispose of when I needed to protect myself.

"His name is Brian. Will you call no one your friend?"

He looked at me as if I had scolded him for nothing. "That's how I was raised to talk in order to show appropriate respect. And no, my parents never allowed me to keep friends, so the only relationships I have are with my servants, which makes it hard to keep the concepts apart. You can understand that calling a white-wing a friend is difficult for me. I meant what I said with good intentions. To console you. His situation could have turned out far worse. He could have been sent to the Abarath Outpost in the north. The Candir Outpost isn't as brutal as the rest, so I think he'll be treated well; as he deserves."

"Yes, but who will take care of Fern and the baby?"

"We will." He nodded as if it was the Spirits' honest truth. "Together with the baby's uncles; Emroyce and Tomas. And I'm sure Valentina, Andress, Zayd and Zoe will help, too."

I rolled my eyes at him for having named all our friends by first name on purpose instead of rank and surname. I twisted my head forwards once more to listen to all the other names my brother called. Camp Leader Ward escorted the new sergeants of the Cavalry Unit to line up.

But I couldn't focus. The thought of Ben growing up alone with no friend to play with was heartbreaking.

"You really don't have any friends?"

Ben didn't answer right away. Instead, he watched me carefully, his expression unreadable, before turning his gaze forward. A storm brewed behind his eyes, an internal battle waging as if he was deciding whether to trust me with a fragile secret. His fingers twitched, then tightened into a fist against his knee. When he finally spoke, his voice was lower, edged with hesitation.

"I keep one friend in secret. No one knows of him. Not even Murben.

I don't want to talk about it. He's very dear to me."

A hidden friend? My curiosity flared instantly. "What? Like a lover?"

Ben snapped his head toward me, his smirk breaking through the tension. "What? Spirits, no!" His grin widened, his ruby eyes speaking directly to my heart. "No need to be jealous. There is only you."

I narrowed my eyes at him, unconvinced. "When will I meet this mysterious man?"

Ben groaned, running a hand down his face. "Miss Stone, please, drop it." He sighed, wanting to share, but obviously fearing he was risking too much. "You still have one more encounter with General Denor, and I don't want anyone learning about my friend. He doesn't have magic, which means he can't protect himself. If our friendship became common knowledge, he wouldn't survive for long."

I frowned and buried my teeth into my bottom lip to stop the flood of questions bubbling inside me from spilling out. Secrets unsettled me. After my mother's betrayal, I had come to loathe them. Information was power, and I had a desperate need to be in control of it.

Ben saw my struggle to keep quiet and let out a low laugh. "You're dying to ask more, aren't you?"

I had practically crawled onto his lap at this point, unable to contain myself. "Just one question. That's all, I promise."

"Miss Stone." His voice was sharp now, his gaze locking onto mine in warning. "Drop it."

I grinned slyly. I couldn't. I was too curious. "Do you think he'll like me?"

Ben blew out his lips in exaggerated thought, but the act didn't last long. A deep chuckle rumbled from his chest, his amusement breaking through his guarded demeanour. "Of course he would. If I ever decided to introduce you, that is. Only a fool wouldn't like you, and he's no fool."

I pursed my lips, unsatisfied. "That's not the specific answer I was hoping for."

"Your question wasn't specific. Are you asking if he'll like your stunning curves?" Ben pushed his hand over my lap and curved his palm around my loins. "Or are you asking if he'll love that witty mouth of yours?" He gently nudged his lips at mine with such a soft touch, I wasn't sure if our lips had actually met. "Or the way you taste?" He made a full kiss, entering his tongue into my mouth.

I jerked my head away. "Ben! We're in the assembly hall, and all the camp leaders and the captains are here. We can be lashed."

"It's worth it. None of the camp leaders beat me as hard as my father ever did. It's more of a tickle."

Kate, Mazdon and Emroyce, who were sitting beside Mazdon, all turned to stare at us.

"What?" Ben scoffed, and he had a playful gleam in the steel of his eyes. "I was checking for poison in her mouth."

Harvey's voice boomed out louder, as if to make a point to quieten the whispers going around in the hall. "And the cadets who have won the most challenges throughout their three years at the Bensguard Outpost Academy, and have selected the team to go with them on the Spirits' Trek this summer..." Harvey paused, as this was the part everyone was most excited about.

The winners obviously knew that Harvey would announce them as they had been briefed in advance.

Harvey glanced over the crowd to hold us in suspense. "Special Mission Agent Tiffany Longton and Special Mission Agent Wilf Pret."

Everyone applauded and cheered as the blonde water breather and the grey-haired calm manipulator took to the stage. If you had assessed them by their magic, they would seem an unlikely team to win, but both their fathers were infantry soldiers at the Dashqaz Outpost, so they had grown up as a team from birth and knew each other like the back of their hands. They had sparred together and been taught military life together, and they were very protective of each other, so to me it came as no surprise.

Their relationship was purely platonic, yet they held hands as they walked up to Harvey to shake his hand, and afterwards, they clasped their hands once more and held them up to show their victory, and everyone cheered again. I hadn't known them to be joyous people, both of them preferred a calm and quiet corner, but today they smiled proudly towards the audience, although timidly.

They wouldn't receive their uniforms at the assembly, as they needed to be prepared for the long trek, so Harvey held up his hands to quieten everyone, holding up the final letter of today.

The anticipation in the hall was invisible yet palpable. My heart pounding against my ribs as Harvey lifted the letter higher, his pause stretching unbearably long. Every cadet in the assembly held their breath, eyes locked on the announcement that would change six lives forever.

Whoever got chosen was as good as dead. The Spirits' Trek wasn't just another mission, it was a test of survival, a gruelling pilgrim that pushed cadets past every limit, physically and mentally. Those who returned came back different, hardened by the experience - if they returned at all. Most didn't.

Harvey finally spoke.

"And the four other members of the team going on the Spirits' Trek are..."

The hall was eerily silent, the tension thick enough to choke on. Even those who longed for the honour of selection were visibly nervous. No one knew who the other two teams were, only that Agent Longton and Agent Pret had made their choices in advance. The secrecy added to the suspense.

Harvey unfolded the paper.

"Sergeant Dominique Bevinski and his teammate, Sergeant Roshan Dalrinjo!"

A deafening roar erupted as Dominique and Roshan's fists punching the air in triumph. Their joy was genuine, and for a moment, I envied them. I envied their confidence, and their belief that they could face whatever awaited them beyond the safety of this hall. They quickly composed themselves and strode forward, stopping at the mark where Zayd gestured.

They were formidable choices. Dominique's magic could illuminate him in the darkest of places, and Roshan could fly, even without his wings. That kind of ability could make a difference in the unknown, treacherous terrain.

But would it be enough?

Harvey continued, his voice unwavering.

"And lastly, Sergeant Darren Jacobs and Sergeant Sarah Minjasko!"

Another wave of cheers rang out as Sergeant Jacobs and Sergeant Minjasko gripped each other's arms before moving toward the others. I couldn't help but notice the way they held their heads high, yet there was something in their eyes…fear. Sergeant Jacob's earth-bending would serve them well, and Sergeant Minjasko's magic enabling her to sense danger before it struck, was invaluable.

And yet, what good was sensing danger if you couldn't escape it?

Rumours whispered through the ranks that they were more than just teammates, that their bond ran deeper. A cruel twist of fate, perhaps. The Spirits' Trek didn't just separate lovers, it often ensured they'd never return together. Maybe this mission wouldn't just mean fighting for survival. Maybe it meant dying in each other's arms instead of at separate outposts, or in war at the opposite end of the kingdom.

Once the six stood in formation, Agent Pret took the letter from Harvey, saluting him.

Then, Harvey paraded in front of the mission squad, and his voice rang out once more. "Do you accept this mission?"

The six sergeants straightened their backs, their voices unwavering.

"Yes!" they all shouted in unison.

The hall erupted into cheers, cadets standing in applause. The end of the academic year had arrived, but for those moving into second-year, including me, it was far from over.

I should've been celebrating. I should've felt relief. Instead, dread curled in my stomach like a coiled serpent.

If the training for the Spirits' Trek was meant to push cadets to their breaking point…what awaited us in second-year? There were ten new and even more deadly challenges, than those I had survived, ready to rip me apart after the summer break. How many deaths would I witness? What friends would I lose? Would I lose Ben?

74

In the morning, Harvey leaned against the door frame of my bedroom, taking up the entire doorway. "Please, don't take too long saying your farewells to King Blackbone. I'll be embarrassed if you let General Denor wait for you."

He was holding a cup of coffee in his hand, and he had dressed in his orange camp master uniform, which he'd be wearing until September now when the term had finished. Leadership were employees of the royal house, not cadets, so they still had to work during the summer.

I hoisted my flight backpack over my shoulders, adjusting the straps to accommodate my wings. The design allowed for flight, but as I tested the weight, my stomach clenched. Too heavy. I'd have to carry this the entire way from Skyberg to Gaithorpe for the First Year Ball, and even on a good day, I struggled to stay in the air for more than fifteen minutes. This flight could take over twenty.

"I hadn't planned on saying goodbye," I muttered, focusing on the backpack instead of the anxiety creeping in. "I'll see him soon enough." A lie. I had been working all morning on plucking up the courage to say….something.

"Well," came the dry response, "I believe King Blackbone is well aware of your tendency to disappear without farewells, especially after what happened with Zayd. Which is why he has been sitting at the top of the stairs since six o'clock this morning, ensuring you don't sneak away."

My head snapped up. *Shit!* I still hadn't worked out what to say to him. He detested the thought of me kissing the general during the ball. One silly, meaningless touch of the lips, yet it bothered him so much.

I exhaled sharply, my frustration doubling. As if the weight of the backpack wasn't enough, now I had to face the king. Reflexively, to call on strength, my hand felt over my chest where I had hidden the light crystal in my bra.

It didn't help my situation much.

Well, first things first. The backpack. It needed to become lighter.

I unpacked the gown I had chosen for the occasion. I'd just have to buy a new one when I arrived in the city. Maybe I didn't need seven daggers. I removed four. The backpack was lighter, but it still wasn't enough. Maybe I could ask Emroyce to take my two water bottles. Mazdon would probably already be overloaded from helping Kate. Penya would be a gentleman to Maruto, too, no doubt. Ashton was also flying with us, as his father had no interest in going.

"You could have let Ben inside the apartment."

"And get the images of my little sister being defiled by a five year older black-wing king in my home? No, thank you."

I was about to shove my oath tattoo in his face, but stopped myself just in time, wondering whether my brother knew about it. Then I wondered if General Denor had anything to do with who knew what around this place.

"Zayd is five years older than me, and he's your best friend. You didn't complain about that when we were dating."

"No. I know Zayd is a good man. And you kept your intimate moments confined to his apartment."

"Ben is a good man, too. Overprotective, but I'd like to see that as commitment. You could at least have let him go with me to the ball to shield my mind from General Denor."

"A black-wing king near King Emille? That's a hard pass." Harvey walked into the room and put the coffee mug down on the bedside table before he lifted my backpack. "This is too heavy for you."

"I know, but I need all the things I've packed. I've already removed the gown and four daggers." I pointed at the items laid on the bed.

"Remove all your casual clothes and jewellery."

I gasped. "I can't go to the ball without jewellery."

"Do you need jewellery in the world below, because that's where you'll end up if you don't make your backpack lighter."

"Mazdon won't let me fall."

"He might not be strong enough to carry both you and that sack of stones you have there."

"Harvey, do you remember that time when you said I couldn't carry my backpack all the way to the summer cottage?"

"Yes. You kept an entire log in it because you were practising wood carving, despite the fact that the cottage is in the woods and there are logs everywhere."

"I had already started on the project!"

"Yes, it became a lovely hill."

"It was an owl! It had eyes and sort of… Anyway! Not the point. Didn't

I carry it all the way there by myself? I can do this."

Or I'd die trying. Either way, I wouldn't have to hear him say 'I told you so'.

With that argument, he finally left me alone in the room. Or so I thought before he came back inside with Ben in tow.

Harvey swept his hand around, gesturing for me. "She's all yours."

"Good morning, love," Ben said softly, and edged forward as if he was approaching someone at flight-risk. "Captain Coraly–"

"Harvey!" I hissed angrily. "His name is Harvey!"

Ben held up his hands, again as if pacifying a crazy person. "Harvey…he tells me you've been packing. A lot." Ben took the last step to get to the bedside and lifted the backpack to check it. "Love, this is too heavy."

"Harvey suggested I'd go with General Denor to the ball without much on, and at the rate he's going I might as well attend naked. Would you say you agree?"

He swallowed as if he had tasted something sour. "How much iron do you have in there?"

"Only three daggers, and none on me." I swiped along my black leather flight uniform to show I had no weapons stuffed in any pockets or holsters.

"Do you need all three? Perhaps remove two more?" He held up two fingers in front of me as if I didn't know how many two were. This was getting a bit too patronising.

"No. I need them in case I've to throw them at someone," I told him slowly, as if he was the dumb one.

"Miss Stone, you're being unreasonable again."

"So, you'll be okay with me going to this event unarmed?"

"No, I'm losing my damn mind thinking about letting you out of my sight, but I believe the threat of you falling to the world below is greater than anyone attacking you at a ball that the white-wing king is attending and has assigned a thousand guards to."

How did he know how many guards King Emille had? I stared at him. "The guards won't allow weapons into the palace. I need my daggers when I'm sleeping at the inn in the city."

"What if I give you some money and you can buy everything new when you get there? How does that sound? You wouldn't have to carry a backpack at all."

"Sounds like you're trying to buy my obedience."

"No," he drawled, taking my hand and rubbing his thumb over the back of it. "More like trying to buy your life from the Spirit of Death."

"It's incredible how much you two lack faith in me." I grabbed the backpack and hoisted it onto my back. "I've to go. My friends are waiting for me at the front courtyard."

"Bye Angie!" Harvey called from the doorway as I left the apartment, and I quickly folded up my rude finger towards him before descending the stairs with Ben on my heels.

Kate, Mazdon, Emroyce, Kenyard, Ashton, Penya and Maruto stood in a circle in the middle of the courtyard, ready to leave, whilst Murben, Nesso and Davis leant against the façade, sunbathing with their chins high in the air. Most likely, they were also keeping guard.

Emroyce was the first one to step out of the circle of friends to greet us. "I know you're mostly doing this for me. To save Robin. I'm really grateful you're coming, risking your life for my family again." This side of Emroyce was rare and knowing him, I knew he meant what he said.

"Not mostly. I'm purely going because of my deal with General Denor to save Robin."

"You won't say that when I swing you around on the dance floor." There he was, back to his normal self. Vulnerability and seriousness gone.

"You, can dance?" I laid on the incredulity thick.

"Like a king."

I looked at Ben, who quizzically cocked his head from side to side. "I'll accept that challenge."

"You can dance?" I asked him, too, not able to imagine his muscular form to be light on his feet.

"Like a king," he said and smirked. Then he put his focus back on Emroyce. "Angelica," he pronounced every syllable to emphasise to me that he was using my first name among our friends, "has packed rocks in her backpack, so make sure she keeps up."

Mazdon barked a laugh. "She does pack odd things. One year when she was about thirteen, she packed a log carved into a hill in her backpack when hiking to the cottage."

I put my hand on my hip. "It was an owl! And it was a summer project for our tutor. What was his name?"

"Professor Karkgo!" Mazdon, Emroyce and Kate bellowed at the same time.

Emroyce nicked the two water bottles from my side pockets and lowered his backpack from his back. "I'll be taking these then." He packed them and then he hesitated to close his bag, looking up at me. "You haven't really packed stones, right?"

"No!" I barked.

"Is there anything else I can take for you?"

I tapped my finger on my lip. "Let's see… You took my dignity, my pride, confidence…no, I think you took just about everything."

Emroyce made a crooked smile. "Sure you haven't got egotism, pretentiousness or recklessness packed in there that I can carry for you?"

"You've got plenty of that in your own backpack."

"Great," he said, smiling. "Sounds like we're ready to leave."

Ben's muscles tensed, and I noted that his breathing became shallow. "I'll distract Gravelhorn, Malloopa, Grim and Randall until you're on your way, so they don't attack you mid-flight."

"That's appreciated," Mazdon said, and he followed Emroyce and the rest of our friends towards the stable where Brian had saddled our horses, leaving me alone with Ben.

Ben folded my arms around his own neck and hugged me, lifting my feet off the ground before putting me back down again. "I'm going to miss you."

"It's only for ten days."

"That's ten days too many that you're going to be away from me. I've noted that you haven't said goodbye to Valentina, Fern, Brian or Zayd."

"Nah. I'll say hello to them when I get back."

"Good answer. Please, be careful. If anything happens to you…" He bit his teeth together, controlling his anger, but I could see the storm in his red eyes. "Nothing can happen to you. Understood?"

I thought about Cadet Randall and the interest King Emille had in his magic of being able to see what magic others had, and I wondered whether the white-wing king would approach him during the ball. If he would approach me!

I felt my hands clammy at the horrible thought, but it'd be stupid to believe I'd go unnoticed, considering General Denor was escorting me to the ball. Placing my faith in him was my only choice, no matter how much I hated it.

The kiss Ben gave me was more than just a goodbye, it was an imprint, a lingering brand I knew I'd carry with me. It stole the breath from my lungs, sent my pulse spiralling, and left my legs trembling beneath me.

I pressed a finger against his chest, feeling the steady thrum of his heart beneath my touch. "Nothing can happen to Nesso while I'm away. You promised me time to think about my negotiation."

Ben's expression darkened, a muscle twitched in his jaw. "He's a servant, Angelica. And he has lived far too long after his mistake. I won't postpone it for much longer."

My stomach clenched. I thought he had let it go. The cold finality in his voice told me otherwise. My teeth sank into my lip, desperately thinking of a way to stall this.

"Give me until I leave for the cottage," I pleaded.

His brows knitted with a thought. Something wasn't quite right. "You mean, when we leave for your cottage?"

"I haven't spoken to Harvey yet. But I will." I swallowed hard. "Promise me, Ben. Nesso stays alive until I return from the ball."

A long pause. Then, finally he answered. "Fine, Miss Stone. You have my promise." But then, his voice switched to firm. "And in return, you'll promise me that you won't drag out the negotiations any further."

I exhaled. "Agreed."

Ben's arms unwound from around me, the warmth of his embrace fading too quickly. My heart twisted as I turned away, forcing my legs to move, to jog after my friends even though every part of me wanted to stay.

"Angelica!" Ben called.

I froze mid-step, turning back.

Ben stood there, an impish smile tugging at his lips, but something softer, something almost vulnerable, lingered in his eyes. "Bye," he coughed out, as if the word itself was forbidden.

A shaky smile pulled at my own lips. "I'll see you soon," I called, though a part of me hated how uncertain that promise felt.

Then I turned, catching up with the others, feeling the hollow ache of something unfinished settling deep in my chest.

We had journeyed for four days. One of the nights, we slept under the stars and the other two in questionable taverns. I had stayed with Maruto those nights. Penya had shared a room with Ashton. During the night around the campfire, we had taken turns to wake each other up for guard duty.

We had found out that Ashton could sing, and he had sung us old folk songs until we fell asleep. I had also learned that Ashton's father hadn't only refused to go to the ball himself but had forbidden Ashton from going. But people from the province of Pharanir weren't easily deterred, which I had experienced during my time with General Denor, so Ashton had gone against his father's wishes and had left with us.

At exactly four o'clock, we reached the edge of Skyberg, near the Kabry City Harbour, where General Denor had ordered me to meet him. The wind howled around the cliff edge of the floating sky island and out across the open expanse. Emroyce strode right up to the last piece of land before the great drop to the world below, his black hair tearing upward as he leaned over the ledge, peering down into the endless void of grey sky.

I couldn't keep still. My boots trampled over the rocky ground as my nerves prickled with impatience. I still had shopping to do before seven, and the ball was looming closer with every passing second.

I exhaled sharply and began unfolding my wings. The familiar tension spread through my back as the bright white feathers fanned out, catching the wind. Penya and Maruto watched, wide-eyed, with the same unnerved expressions everyone wore when they saw me struggling to bring them out; like I had a spider crawling up my back.

Seven long seconds. That's how long it took for them to fully extend. I lifted them high, testing the injured one, wincing slightly as I flapped it. The pain was manageable – *for now.*

"I wish you'd consider using the black ones," Emroyce muttered beside me. His voice barely carrying over the wind. "Have you even tried flying with the white ones since you were shot?"

I clenched my jaw. "Emroyce, I'll not use my black wings this close to an aristocratic society, and certainly not in the province of Gaithbry."

He sipped from his water bottle, then lazily extended mine. "I only saw sky and no land as I looked down, Angie. It's a long fall."

"Then don't look down!" I snapped, snatching the bottle from his hand.

A flicker of red appeared in the distance, cutting through the storm-darkened horizon.

Denor.

The wind pressed against his uniform as he strode over the sand dunes and rolling hills, his presence as commanding as always.

He ignored the others, walking straight toward me. Without hesitation, he took my hand and kissed the back of it, his sharp eyes locking onto mine.

"We meet again," he said smoothly.

I yanked my hand back, my teeth grinding. "You ordered me to be here."

Denor smiled as if amused by my hostility, then spread his wings. They were massive and powerful, stretching wide against the sky.

"Are you all ready to go?" he asked.

My gaze shifted towards the sky, where clouds the colour of ash rolled across the distance ahead and the winds grew stronger and more unpredictable as the storm picked up.

I really missed having Ben's voice in my head, telling me it was going to be all right.

"Everything will be all right. I won't let you fall. I promise," Denor's voice sounded in my mind.

I gasped and widened my eyes at him. "You're already in my head, spying?"

He was listening to all my thoughts. Nothing inside my head was safe.

"Don't worry, I don't always pry. I needed a quick peek to see how stable your mind is for the flight. I'll get out now."

"Wait?"

"Yes?"

"There is actually one image I wouldn't mind you erasing from my memory. It's another mind bender's trick and not a real image." I showed him the image of Nassara sitting on Ben's face.

"Oh," he laughed. *"Juicy. I like this woman's humour."*

I glowered at him and no one in the group seemed to notice our mind communication as they brought out their wings and Mazdon re-tied the laces of his boots.

"What will I get in return if I remove it?"

"What do you want?"

"You can hold my hand as we walk into the ballroom."

"No deal."

"Okay. The kiss of our previous deal. Kiss me like you mean it."

"But I don't mean it."

"Put effort into it."

"You know it will sting because of the oath to Duke Hartmore, right?"

"I can turn the part of my brain off that feels pain, and yours. You'll love it. If you allow yourself to enjoy it."

"Can you not feel how much I love Ben?"

"Yes. But that can change. I can change that."

"No! You fucking wouldn't dare! I'll kill you if you ever hint at it again!"

"I didn't mean I'd change it, forcing your mind. I meant you'll find me charming."

"I'll keep the damn image in my head. It's not worth this shit."

"Suit yourself."

I turned my face up from the ground and found Mazdon and Emroyce frowning at me. "Are you okay?" Emroyce asked. "You've a weird look on your face."

"I'm fine." I handed the water bottle back to Emroyce.

Both Emroyce and Mazdon reflexively put their hands on their hilts after the many times that Ben had joked about me stabbing him following my claim that I was 'fine'.

I narrowed my eyes at them. "Shut up. Let's fly before it starts to–" I held my hands out, feeling the drops on my palm, "rain."

Shit! Rain would soak my wings and make them even heavier, and we had no spare time to delay the flight if we were going to make it to the ball on time. But I would become like one of those flies that I flushed down the drain with my showerhead if the rain got any denser.

I took a few steps back and sprinted for the edge, launching myself out and flapped my wings before the fear of setting off grew too strong. There was no time for hesitation. Denor followed me without having taken up speed first, then Kate and Maruto followed whilst the men waited for us to stabilise through the rough wind currents.

The rain drops seemed to become larger, and they fell faster. My heart raced, thinking about what Ben would do the moment Denor notified him of my death. Emroyce flew up on my left, his large wings beating the air, his arms out for balance. Denor flanked my right, and I had the rest of the group right behind me.

Five minutes into the flight, the rain grew into a relentless downpour, hammering against us with icy water. The water clung to my skin, plastering my hair to my face, while my feathers became heavy, dragging me downward like dead weight. I gave a few sharp shudders, trying to shake off the excess moisture, but it was useless as the sky kept dumping more on me, drenching me to the bone.

It had only been five damned minutes, yet my wings felt as if they'd been soaked in lead and my backpack felt heavier than if it had been full of rocks. Each flap took twice the effort, my muscles burned like I'd been flying flat out for hours. My breaths came fast and ragged, as if I'd been sprinting across a battlefield instead of gliding through the sky.

Behind me, I could hear Maruto and Kate struggling, too. Their laboured panting pushed through the storm. Maruto's dark hair stuck to her forehead, droplets streaming down her face. Kate held her signature fierce determination not seeming to care about what tried to beat her. They both fought against the wind with their brows furrowed and their movements were stiff from exhaustion.

I risked a glance at Emroyce. His expression was stern, his flight steady. His white wings sliced through the storm with practised ease, the rain sliding off him like he belonged in this chaos.

Meanwhile, I could feel my own strength slipping, my wings aching with each desperate beat.

The thought crept into my mind like poison. This isn't sustainable. I won't last.

And yet, stopping wasn't an option. There was nowhere to perch.

"Why don't you ask the water bender to bend the water away from us?"

"Why don't you command her? You're the general."

"I assume it might impress your friends if you think of it first."

This time, the general truly impressed me. The suggestion hadn't required him interfering with his magic, but it had come from his intelligence.

"Yeah, but I've had years of practice already. I'm used to evaluating what useful magic there is around me."

"That was a passive thought not meant for you. Stay out of my head."

"Put your shield up."

"You sound just like Ben."

"We only have to perfect the kiss, and I'm as good as him. Because of the oath, I

know you haven't made love yet."

"Oh, we have." I showed him the image from when we ravaged each other in the dorm room.

He shook his head, losing his balance, banking left. Then there was silence in my head. I was about to smile at my triumph when lightning struck only a short distance away and I wobbled through the sky as the thunder set in.

If I were to survive, I'd have to lower my pride and ask for help. There wasn't much magic around me that was useful other than water bending. Emroyce had speed, Mazdon had his hearing, Kate had fire wielding, Ashton could possess me which I doubted he wanted to do when I fell to my death, Penya had healing and Kenyard had intention-reading from hearing you speak. Although, that could be useful to find out what Denor wanted out of me.

"A crafty little plan you have there, Cadet Coraly. But how'd you know that I hadn't manipulated his answer? Go on. Ask him."

I shook the temptation out of my head, considering the lethal situation at hand that needed to be fixed first.

"Maruto! Can you do anything to keep the rain off us?" I shouted through the roaring storm, my voice barely cutting through the wind.

Maruto turned her head slightly through the sheets of rain and I saw the hesitation in her wide eyes. "I… I can try," she called back, but there was no confidence in her voice. I knew why. She only had one magical circle to her rank, so this was far beyond what she was trained to handle.

But if she failed, I'd fall.

Her breathing stuttered, her wings struggling to keep her airborne as she reached deep inside herself for the magic. Then, trembling fingers stretched forward, and I saw the pull of water shifting unnaturally around us. Slowly, the rain twisted and bent, forming a dome above our heads. It was imperfect, flickering, unstable, but it held like a bridge, redirecting the deluge into a cascading slide behind our backs.

A gasp of relief escaped me as my wings suddenly felt lighter, droplets seeping from my feathers. I could move again. Fly a while longer.

"Well done, Maruto!" I shouted, my voice laced with gratitude.

"Yeah, that's impressive," Penya added, though his own wings trembled with the strain of fighting the wind. He looked worse off than the other men, his flight uneven, his breath harsh.

"Thank you." Maruto let out a shaky exhale, but I could see the strain rippling through her. Her arms trembled, her flight faltering slightly as she tried to hold the spell and keep herself airborne at the same time. Her magic wavered, just a flicker, but it was enough for me to notice how much this was costing her.

"I… I don't think I can hold it the whole way," she admitted, her voice tight with effort. "It's… It's too much."

I clenched my jaw. I wanted to tell her to push through, that we were almost there. But I knew better. There was still over five minutes left of the journey. If she drained herself too much, she wouldn't make it all the way, and then we'd have another problem.

"Stop when you need to," I said firmly. "Don't push past your limit. But for now, this is incredible."

She nodded, swallowing hard. And I swore I saw the determination like a ball of light in her exhausted eyes.

We flew for another four minutes in silence, but after a while, I nodded toward Kenyard. "Hey. Could you do me a favour?"

Kenyard raised groomed eyebrows above his yellow eyes and flicked his head to make the floppy hair on his unshaved side snatch backwards. "What do you need?"

"Can you ask the general what his intentions are with me?"

Kenyard tremored. "I sense some mischief from your tone of voice." He looked at the general.

"Go ahead and ask me your question and use your magic to read me," Denor said, and his voice was so polite I already knew this was a fruitless exercise.

Kenyard hadn't even asked the question yet when his eyes went vacant. "The General is a great man, who only wants peace for all people, and he respects you for your tenacity and bravery."

"Thank you for those kind words, Cadet Kenyard."

I cocked my head back to stare at Denor, who playfully wiggled his eyebrows at me and winked.

"You're terrible, General Denor."

"Terribly adorable. And please, must you insist on calling me general? At least in our heads you can call me Wallan."

"You're trying to brainwash me to become more familiar with you. It won't work. General!"

"It'll work. Unless you use your magic."

"I have no magic."

He snorted, but then a concerned expression materialised on his face. "You're getting tired."

Everyone in the group seemed to have heard him, and Emroyce pulled up on my left. "Are you going to be okay, Angie?"

"I'll make it." But I was losing altitude, and that wasn't a fact I could hide from the others.

I wobbled on a new wave of current, resulting in Denor flying closer to me.

It wasn't shameful. Mazdon also took a grip over Kate's backpack to help her upwards, and Penya did the same to Maruto.

"May I?" Denor asked, nodding at my backpack.

"No, you may not!"

I beat my wings harder, and my legs propelled simultaneously with the movement as I tried to fly higher. But my wing-muscles were so damn sore and the lower part of my right wing with the scar from the arrow cramped frequently.

Denor looked at his watch. "We've got about two minutes left."

The sky island's silhouette showed in the distance. I could make it. I had to.

The bridge of water above our head burst then, and water cascaded over us.

"I'm sorry," Maruto cried. "I can't hold it any longer."

I sunk rapidly through the sky and with this low altitude I wouldn't make it up to the ground level edge of the island. Fuck! I really didn't want to ask for help.

"You've one of two options, Cadet Coraly. Either, I'll forcefully help you, or you'll ask any of your friends for help if you find that less degrading. Because, the way you're going, you won't make it all the way to Gaithorpe. I promised I wouldn't let you die."

"And what did that cost me?"

"Nothing. I threw that one into the deal for free."

"You're so generous, General."

I hadn't even realised how close I was to losing control until my wings completely shut down and I was too tired to move them. Mid-air, they just stopped, and I began dropping through the sky, screaming, praying to the Spirit of Luck, the Spirit of Life, or anyone who wanted to listen.

Air tore all around me and my legs treaded air, my arms trying to grip for anything, but there was nothing to hold on to anywhere remotely close to me.

Please, Spirits, don't let this be the way I die!

"General! Help me!"

75

Denor dived through the air, his form sleek and determined as he barrelled toward me. But with speed magic, Emroyce grabbed my arm before him, and yanked me up against his chest, holding me steady.

"I've got her," Emroyce snapped, his warning sharp.

His gaze locked with the general's, and for a moment, I saw the briefest flash of frustration in Denor's eyes. After that, Denor kept out of Emroyce's way, but remained close by – too close, as if he too sensed the fragile edge I was teetering on.

My breath came in ragged gasps, and I could feel the tremor in my hands as I clutched at his clothes, trying to steady myself. "Thank you, Emroyce," I panted, still feeling vulnerable. I had no stamina left. No wings to carry me in the sky, *and I was still very much in it!*

His grip tightened ever so slightly around me, as if sensing the turmoil racing through me. "Don't worry. You're safe now."

Emroyce was stronger than I thought, flying me the rest of the way through the harsh winds and pelting rain tucked safely in his arms. With one smooth, effortless motion, he gently lowered me to the ground, placing me on the soft grass of Gaithorpe Island.

I tried to steady myself, but the world spun beneath me. My wings, my once strong and reliable wings, were now nothing but a sore, heavy burden. I buried them deep within my back, the ache turning into cotton-soft pressure as they folded against me.

We all collapsed of exhaustion, sitting on the grassy edge of the sky island. The distant hum of Gaithorpe town beckoned, but I was far too shaken to even think about moving. I buried my head between my knees, trying to ground myself. The warmth of Emroyce's touch against my back sent jolts of comfort through my frazzled nerves, but it wasn't enough to stop the overwhelming wave of fear that still surged within me.

I knew what this moment represented. I was reminded what our friendship meant to me. Emroyce wasn't just here to protect me physically, but he understood the kind of danger I'd just faced. This was more than just flight. This was about control. This was about *losing* it in the most visceral way possible.

With a shaky breath, I spoke the words that had been clawing at my chest. "Please, don't tell King Blackbone about this."

I couldn't bear the thought of him knowing. Not yet, at least. The weight of my failure, the fear I still carried, would only make it worse. Ben would panic, and I couldn't have that happening. Not now, when we were so far apart and when everything was on the edge of crumbling.

Denor jerked his head up from where he stood watching us, not looking the least bit tired unlike the rest of us who had heaped on the ground. "Too late. I already showed him the image of you plummeting through the sky, and for my own entertainment, I may have added a bonus scene of you splattering to the ground into a puddle of blood. I'm toing and froing on whether I'll make him believe the image is true or if he should be sceptical as to whether I have been manipulating his mind. Although, I lost contact with his mind a few seconds ago after he went ballistic in the canteen, throwing the food tray and everything on it through the window and tipping over the table. Then it went black, so I assume someone might have tranquillised him."

I shrugged out of my backpack and lay down on the grass, cupping my palms over my forehead as I looked up at the sky. The rain was still falling on me, and my black flight leathers were sticking to my skin. "Why the fuck are you doing this to him, General?"

"I told you. For my entertainment, and I also wanted to find out how he would react. Heads up, he didn't take it too well. It felt like his heart kind of…broke."

I wanted to rebuke Denor and lash out at him to match the extent of anger I felt. But I couldn't. I was close to tears, so if I spoke now, I'd come undone.

Poor Ben.

"That's not cool, man," Emroyce muttered below his breath.

"Don't worry. I only want to see how much alcohol he will consume to try to dull the hurt and then I'll show him the true picture. I've to do it soon anyway if he's to enjoy the new image I want to put in his mind of our kiss."

"Can you add another part to that image when I punch you in the face?"

He simply chuckled; the sound rich with amusement. "We should get to my mansion and dry off before we all end up sick."

I jolted upright, staring at him in disbelief. "You own a mansion on Gaithorpe?"

This island was a rare gem. A small stretch of land where real estate was worth a fortune. A single home here cost ten times more than the most lavish estate in the capital of Skyberg. Only the wealthiest aristocrats could afford to own property in Gaithorpe. And yet, here he was, speaking about it as if it were nothing more than a casual retreat.

"Yes, it's not far from here. We can walk." He pointed at something tall and yellow in the far distance that was surrounded by some greenery right outside the outskirts of the busy city core.

Emroyce held out a hand and helped me up as I clasped it, putting a protective hand at my back as we walked. None of us had been to this sky island before so we didn't know what to expect regarding any surrounding dangers.

The walk was pleasant as my legs were rested. It was only my back that throbbed. The further we hiked, the taller the mansion towered over us. At one point or another, I believed we all gasped at the grandiosity of it.

"That's a large house," Kate scoffed.

"It's not a house. It's a mansion. Just short of a castle. Wouldn't you say, Cadet Coraly?"

He was trying extremely hard to measure up to Ben. Little did he know that Ben didn't own a castle anymore. Technically, it was mine. I doubted Denor would gift me his mansion to top that.

Ten servants lined up to our left in the enormous foyer when we stepped through the door. White pillars stretched from the white marble floor to the tall ceiling in various places and a white curving staircase opened up in front of us that split by the opposite wall and continues upwards both to the left and to the right, linking to the floor above. The windows were enormous and arched at the top, letting in plenty of light to showcase the elegant white statues of forest animals that stood on plinths.

The general took a deep breath with a pondering look on his face. "Uh, Miss Dove," he called to address the first servant girl, who curtsied at hearing her name. "You can take Cadet Maruto to the seventh room on the right. I think that would be a good match for her." The young woman, clad in a simple brown dress, a white apron and a white mobcap with a neat bun below it, beckoned for Maruto to follow her.

This was crazy. We were all going to get our own rooms? How big was this place?

"Mister Brack, escort Cadet Mazdon Pere to room ten–"

"I'm staying in the same room as Kate," Mazdon barked at the general.

"Fine," Denor sighed out. "Mister Brack, can you escort both Cadet Peres to the suite on the second floor?" The servant bowed and beckoned them to follow him.

"Anyone else want to share rooms?"

We exchanged gazes, but no one nodded. "Great. Mister Croner escort Cadet Penya to room five? Mister Grando, take Cadet Kenyard to room six. Mister Kroosh, please take…" Denor hesitated as he made eye-contact with Ashton. Did I see him stiffen? Was I mistaken or was something uncomfortable crawling behind his confident exterior. "Cadet Hall to room nine?" He quickly swiped his gaze to leave Ashton and carry on. "And Mister Forseros can escort Cadet Bengrey to room four." Denor gestured towards them, and the servants led them away. This had left me standing alone with the general and four servants.

"Now. To the star of the show. Where would you like to stay, Cadet Coraly? You've got the choice of staying in a room on the first floor, in a suite on the second floor, or on the entire third floor with me."

"I'll stay in a room close to Emroyce."

The disappointed look in his eyes was puzzling. "Not a room fit for a Spirit like you, but as you wish."

"Fine," I barked, putting a hand on my hip. "I'll stay on your floor, and you can stay in the room close to Emroyce."

He blew out a snort of amusement. "The third floor is big enough to share."

"Not with your big ego taking up all the space."

He stared at me for a while and without breaking eye-contact, he growled lowly, "Miss Balstav, please move my personal belongings from my floor to suite one."

The servant scurried away on light feet and Denor dismissed the others after having instructed them to prepare and deliver refreshments to the rooms.

Once everyone had left the foyer, he pointed towards a door to our right. "That's a bathroom so that you can change into dry clothes as we wait for your floor to be prepared."

I glanced around and shook my head. "Did you steal this place? It must be worth a fortune, and you don't come from a rich family."

"I earned it, although I can't say that I didn't do things along the way which perhaps could be construed as morally grey."

Outside the window, the rain was still pouring down, but I needed a gown for the ball. So, what was the point of getting changed? "I have to go out shopping for a gown. Any pointers on what shop to go to and how to best get there?"

"Tell me your size and what cut and colour you want, and a servant can pick up a few gowns for you to choose from."

I gawked. He was being a pompous arse, trying to impress me. But money wasn't the way to my heart. Trust and honour were. Of which he had none.

He smirked at me. "That's a tad harsh and hurtful, don't you thin–"

"Do you know what? I don't care for this game you're playing, bringing me here to prove some sort of point about controlling me in front of dignitaries and royals. I couldn't care less. You choose the dress. I just want to get this over and done with and get back to Bensguard."

"Very well, that shall be arranged. In the meantime, may I suggest a mug of hot chocolate in front of the fire?" He gestured towards the double doors to my right, and I saw the glimpse of the windows that looked the same as in the vision he had trapped me inside of during the tenth challenge at Pharoon Lake.

The triumphant smile on his face was unmistakable. No wonder he could get the images to be so detailed and feel so real if he had experienced them in reality. If I walked in there, I feared I'd lose the concept of what was reality and what was a fragment of his magic. But I didn't want him to win, thinking I was frightened of him, so I marched into the drawing room and found the expected grey sofa in front of the enormous gem-clad fireplace.

Denor hadn't followed me inside, so I quickly dropped my backpack to the floor and pulled out the driest tunic and black trousers I could find among everything else that was wet and stripped off my flight leathers to change. By the time Denor joined me, I had become comfortable, leaning against the corner of the sofa with a blanket pulled up to my waist, watching the flames in the fireplace. He, too, was in dry clothes; an elegant blue shirt and greyish khaki trousers. He passed me the mug of chocolate but didn't sit down and instead walked to the mantelpiece and leant against it.

"Your friends have settled in nicely and are getting ready for the ball. Your gown and rooms should be available momentarily. The carriage will be outside the front door in an hour to take us to the palace."

The hot chocolate had the same divine flavour as the chocolates I purchased in Emendir, and it tasted heavenly as I sipped it slowly. Obviously, Denor would have known exactly what I liked after rummaging through my mind. "Will you tell me now why you're taking me to this ball? What purpose does it serve you?"

He smirked, still gazing at the fire. "You don't need to know that. But yes, of course it's a power game. Men can't handle when someone else has got their toy."

"You should tell my brother about it. He broke my finger because I burned his wooden soldier," I muttered into the mug.

"So mischievous, Cadet Coraly. Although, saying that, it seems women don't like to share their toys, either. Is that image of Nassara sitting on the king's face still haunting you? Lost your appetite for kings yet and want to try a general?" He only twisted his head to look at me. "You might be pleasantly surprised."

Miss Balstav entered the room and curtsied in an opportune moment, saving me from having to make further conversation with the general.

"Your accommodation is prepared, Cadet Coraly."

I put the mug down on the sofa table and followed her up three flights of stairs and into the jaw-dropping floor. There were crystal chandeliers hanging from the ceiling, large windows, paintings in enormous golden frames with images of landscapes and woven rugs clad the white marble floor. I had never been inside a property this extravagant before.

The bedroom had a separate walk-in closet in which a black and grey dress hung from a stand. On closer inspection, I gawked at the gorgeous fabric in stiff overlapping sections that ended in a high collar at the back with a thinly veiled cape hanging from the neck to the floor.

On a side-table, a matching set of jewellery and shoes were organised neatly in cases.

Miss Balstav brought out a brush from a drawer in the vanity and waited for me to sit without speaking. She brushed my hair gently and braided it into a tight crown on my head and weaved a silver headband through it. When she stepped back, I caught my reflection in the vanity mirror, and my breath hitched. Among the waves of blue, a few rebellious strands of black peeked through. My childhood glamour was fading.

A slow dread settled in my stomach. This was more than just a change in colour; it was a reminder. My mother had put the glamour on me and now she was gone, and soon the glamour would be, too. The illusion I had worn for so long and which had become a mask that kept me from feeling naked, was slipping. How long before others noticed? Before they started asking questions about why I had it in the first place. Questions I didn't know the answers to. I only thought it had been a birthday present, but lately I had started to wonder if there had been more to it. It scared me to death to think about what secret would break free when it finally broke.

I swallowed hard and forced my expression into indifference. Ready in my dress and new makeup, I followed Miss Balstav as she walked down the stairs to the foyer where the others waited. Everyone was so handsome and beautiful in their formal ball wear.

"Newly shaven and all. Scrubbed up well, boys," I teased, inspecting the five of them in turn.

Denor joined us, handing over a stack of letters to the messenger at the door. Had he been working since we got here?

Denor was handsome, too. No matter how much I hated him, I'd give him that. He wore a red general's uniform coat, featuring his rank with a star between two horizontal chevrons on his right shoulder, and he had a black sash across his chest that matched his trousers and boots. He had combed his raven-black hair to one side, and he held his dark eyes pinned on me with a youthful excitement. Sometimes I forgot he was only thirty years of age, considering his high rank.

"Handsome, young and powerful. With those compliments I think we're getting somewhere, even without me using any mind bending."

"Stay out of my head, General. And I didn't say powerful."

"You insinuated it. That's good enough. May I say you look more stunning than a Spirit?"

"You may not."

"I thought so."

He escorted us out to two black carriages drawn by four horses as dark as night each, and I shared the carriage with Denor, Mazdon and Kate whilst Penya, Maruto, Emroyce, Kenyard and Ashton travelled in the second.

When arriving, Denor held up a hand to help me alight the carriage and then he held out his elbow for me to take it, so that he could lead me up the grey carpet to a magnificent white palace. Its white stone was carved in symmetrical rectangular blocks and there were six towers with burgundy domed rooftops. Like the style on this island, the windows were enormous and arched at the top, and there were white statues of animals both scattered on the lawn and courtyard outside as well as in various places inside of the palace. Large abstract portraits of Spirits hung in the hallway and candles gleamed from torches in the sconces and from the chandeliers that hung from the ceilings.

I kept my pace measured, ensuring my friends remained close behind me. But their steps lagged, their gazes darting in every direction, mesmerised by the breathtaking sights around us. Every few strides, they slowed further, pausing in awe, their wonder palpable as they took in the dazzling world unfolding before them.

Denor put his hand over the one I held around his arm. "The way your head twitches around to watch everything is adorable. I'm surprised King Blackbone didn't show you such extravagant things when you were in Black Castle."

"King Blackbone isn't a man who likes flaunting his belongings in order to impress others."

"Perhaps he has the right approach to life. If you have the one thing that matters, you may not need everything else." He squeezed my hand tighter and looked forwards where a man dressed similarly to Denor, but in a yellow coat, approached us.

"Captain Tomason," Denor greeted.

"General. And Cadet Coraly." He gave a curt bow.

For some odd reason, I bent my knees to curtsy towards him. This was

Camp Leader Tomason's father, and the person who could determine the comfort of Brian's stay at the Candir Outpost. It was frightening how alike Tomason he looked, with golden hair and bright blue eyes with a touch of bronze to the tone of their skin.

"How's life at the Bensguard Outpost?" the captain asked me.

"Rella is great!" I barked out, not knowing where it came from since, not only did I sound like an idiot, I had also addressed his daughter incorrectly. "Camp Leader Tomason is highly skilled at her job. You must be proud," I corrected to save my dignity.

Denor stood up straighter and I saw Captain Tomason lean back as if intimidated. "Cadet Coraly and her teammate have tied with the highest number of challenge wins during her first year. Three very impressive wins."

"Not sure they were impressive," I muttered to myself.

The way I recalled them, they weren't impressive at all. Classifying herbs, we had won because I had borrowed Mewer's personal study text and been a second faster than Emroyce to the desk. That didn't ring right in my ears on a second thought. Emroyce had speed magic. I wouldn't have been faster than he. He had thrown the win and given it away to me. Why? I thought about the other challenges. The archery challenge, we had won because Ashton had thrown the game, and Denor had manipulated everyone's mind to let me take the lead in the swimming challenge. None of them were based on my own skills and efforts.,

"You're too humble, Cadet Coraly," Captain Tomason said, bowing as Capitan La Roy joined my side.

However, Captain La Roy was still distracted and kept looking around the room over my head, probably looking for Kate.

By this time, I had lost sight of all my friends, and the last I had seen of them was Mazdon and Kate on the dance floor and Emroyce, Kenyard and Ashton by the food tables.

I hadn't known Capitan La Roy was going to the ball, but it made sense, as every other outpost had a captain represented, and I guessed Captain La Roy hadn't wanted to journey here with us. No one wanted to spend time with General Denor if it could be avoided.

"Ouch, that hurt," the general scoffed in my mind.

"You've yourself to blame when you invade people's minds and put voices and images in their heads."

The general looked forward again to pay attention to the conversation. "I heard that the Bensguard Outpost leadership has assigned your younger brother to the Candir Outpost," Denor told La Roy.

"Sergeant La Roy is a fine contribution to my camp," Tomason replied.

Captain La Roy seemed to stretch taller with pride. "I hope you'll treat him well and not send him too far north."

"His fire wielding magic isn't only to be used to light the hearth, Captain La Roy, but I'll do what I can to keep him at a safe distance from–"

Denor cleared his throat, not allowing Tomason to finish his sentence.

Safe distance from what?

Had he been about to say what was happening in the north? The thought of Brian getting sent there made my stomach churn.

Tomason bowed towards him. "I shouldn't take up more of your time, as I'm sure you've many people to speak to this evening. Please, enjoy the ball."

"What was he going to say?" I asked when Denor turned me around to walk towards a servant holding a tray with glasses of sparkling wine.

"I'm no mind reader, Cadet Coraly."

I rolled my eyes at him, to which he chuckled as he grabbed a wine glass for each of us before we carried on talking to people.

We also talked to Captain Blingster from the Emendroth Outpost and John's father, Captain Somers from the Abarath Outpost.

During all the conversations we had, no one mentioned anything about my parents, but only praised Harvey and me for our commitment to the academy. That didn't sit well with me. My father had been executed but had done nothing wrong other than love a woman who had betrayed him. This party should sing fucking songs about my father's achievements at the Bensguard Outpost. I realised it'd be harder than I had thought to restore his reputation.

I tried to shake it off and relax. There were people in this room who could pick up on fury, and that wouldn't bode well for me. I wasn't going to give them any opportunity to call me a traitor. Although, trying to shake off an injustice done to our family was easier said than done.

"Let's turn this way. That," Denor pointed towards a woman with blonde hair in a tight bun, standing so straight that the back of her dress could hide a long-sword, "is Captain Wix from the Dashqaz outpost. I heard she isn't too pleased with you since you murdered her son."

"I didn't murder him. He tried to suffocate me under a pillow and Zayd threw a dagger into his heart."

"This isn't the time to debate semantics. Let's meet King Emille. Do you know the history behind the king, his wife and his two counsellors? Don't want you to go into the conversation blindfold."

I looked over to where King Emille stood gazing lovingly at his wife, Queen Miriam, by one of the large windows with a crowd of noble people surrounding them. He was tall and strong and apparently he had quite a reasonable temperament. His brown hair was pushed backwards by the hefty silver crown pressed down on his head. His face was smooth, with a bushy set of eyebrows over brown eyes. Although, I didn't like the moustache he had grown on his upper lip. It didn't suit a young king of thirty-four. His wife was like a dream, with white hair that reached to her bottom and shimmered in the tone of gold, matching her white dress with golden details. She was standing next to her sister, General Desry, both daughters of Counsellor Desry, who was one of the king's two trusted advisors. Counsellor Desry, being the one who had destroyed Robin's mind, and was the reason Denor had negotiated to restore it in exchange for me having to endure being here now.

"Let's not go there tonight and spoil the ball."

My nails dug harder into Denor's arm, and I lowered my voice to a whisper. "King Emille's magic is to absorb items into light, and he can bring them out whenever he wants, so he could literally have a thousand daggers at his disposal just a centimetre away from his palm."

"True," Denor praised me like a teacher. "But I was thinking more about history than magic lessons here."

"King Emille is a young king because his and Ben's fathers both died in a duel with one another seven years ago. Although, King Blackbone has done better than him, and he was even younger."

"That's not the important part, either. I'll guide you a bit here. When speaking to King Emille, bear in mind that his wife is sacred to him. They grew up together, and he's extremely protective of her, so don't under any circumstances insult her. That can end badly, even for me. He also has two counsellors that you should know where they are at all times. I believe Counsellor Desry isn't present today and has sent General Desry in his stead. The other one is Counsellor Lucka Pontus, and he could be anywhere, but he's never too far away from King Emille. His magic is–"

A flash zapped in bright blue beside Denor and a young man not much older than me, with shoulder-length, black hair and charcoal-black eyes, appeared from out of nowhere.

"He's a teleporter," Denor finished and bowed. "Good evening, Counsellor Pontus."

"The king is looking for you," he said, and as quickly as he had arrived, he was gone, gifting yellow splotches in front of my eyes from the light blast.

"I guess our king has summoned us," Denor smiled toward me, and we walked up to the white-wing king.

This time, Denor made a bow that was much lower than to the other dignitaries he had introduced me to. "My king," he greeted.

The general turned my way with raised brows. I quickly curtsied and greeted both him and the queen, complimenting the queen on her beauty.

"Clever woman. Fast learner."

"You should've thought of it first."

"The king doesn't like other men complimenting his wife. Told you he's overly protective of her."

"And you brought Cadet Coraly here this evening as you promised," the king mused, looking me up and down, but he didn't compliment my beauty, and I guessed I knew why. "I've wanted my dear sister-in-law to have a look at you, but each time she has visited the Bensguard Outpost, your captain has sent you away on missions."

"So, that was why my brother sent me away." I glanced at Denor. "And you betrayed me by taking me to him instead."

"Betrayal is such a strong word. I executed my king's order."

"You've a busy and skilled workforce, my king," I said with a forced smile, wanting no more than to disappear into a dark corner of the room to lick the wound from the general's betrayal.

"Indeed, so I have. I was told you spent two years on an undercover special mission in the Black Wing Territory. You failed to kill the black-wing king, and you failed to bring back the Black Blade, but you must have gained some experience or intel useful to me."

My fingernails dug into my palm, forming crescents into my flesh as I learned this man's intention was to kill the man I loved.

I avoided looking him in the eye, fearing he'd see straight through me and learn where my loyalty lay. "There are certainly dissimilarities between the two lands, my king."

"How so? How would you describe the Black Wing Territory compared to my lands?"

Not as big of a shithole with so many arseholes in it.

"Be careful what you think around here. There are more people surrounding us who can read minds, one way or another."

"Then protect mine."

"I can. But it's going to cost you."

Nervously, I gripped at the black fabric of my dress with my free hand. *"What do you want now?"*

"Your loyalty, but I think I'm getting there on my own."

My mouth opened and I wasn't the one controlling it, or the words that came out. "I'd say you're a lousy king and should be hanged, so I can be queen," I said out loud – in the face of the fucking king!

But it hadn't been me. The general had made me say it.

I panicked as I saw King Emille's brows furrow in anger. I wanted to apologise and explain that it was the general who toyed with my mind, but my lips were sealed.

My heart raced as King Emille spoke. "You're as big a traitor as your parents. I can't believe my naivety for pardoning you and your brother. I shall hang you both before this month has ended. General Desry, call for the guards."

I couldn't breathe. I couldn't think. Denor had just arranged for my brother and my death sentences. Why had he done that? My chest hurt and my knees began to cave in.

Suddenly, King Emille's, Queen Miriam's and General Desry's eyes went blank before they zoomed back to focus on me again.

"So lovely that you could join us this evening, Cadet Coraly. General Denor has told us so many great things about you and every time we've attempted seeing you in person, Captain Coraly had you working hard on a mission."

I was lost for words. What had just happened? No one seemed to recall the conversation we had a moment ago where I was about to be executed. My heart was still racing, and it was impossible to sort my mind out with what was real and what was Denor's fictional mind game. Glancing around the room, everyone seemed as calm and amused by the party as normal.

Denor leaned over to whisper to the king. "I believe Cadet Coraly has been stunned by stage fright when talking to someone such as yourself."

"Stop playing with people's minds, and my emotions!" My heart still throbbed with the agony of my potential death.

"Why? It's entertaining."

I wanted to cry or at least go out into the gardens to get some air. *"That wasn't entertaining!"*

The king looked at me and probably saw the extreme discomfort on my face. King Emille leaned closer to General Desry to whisper. "Are you sure this is her?"

Desry was every bit the nightmare Zoe had warned me about. Her helm, a menacing piece of iron, covered her head but left her face exposed, with jagged protrusions extending from either side like eerie conduits meant to capture sound and funnel it straight into her mind. The metal was so thick that I couldn't help but wonder if it served as more than mere protection. Perhaps it anchored her magic, trapping her thoughts within its cold embrace. Strands of pitch-black hair slithered from beneath the helm, unlike her sister's ghostly white. Unlike the flowing gowns of other aristocrats, she was clad head to toe in polished armoured plates. Her face was grim, devoid of the slightest hint of a smile on her lips.

"Desry looks more like her mother, whilst the queen takes after her father." Denor explained.

"Yes," Desry finally answered. "She's the same as when I met her as young. She's as we expected. And who knows what is under that strong glamour, conjured by magic from the world below? Powerful magic, indeed."

My breath stopped for four beats.

Magic from the world below?

Why had she mentioned my glamour? It had been placed on me to hide who I was underneath…because of my magic…or had it not?

Denor didn't answer me in my mind but turned to address the king.

"There you have it, King Emille. Let's not bother *my date* any further. She and I have much to discuss and to do this evening. I wish you a pleasant ball, my king."

Denor had emphasised the words 'my date' as if he wanted to let the king know that I was loyal to him. It was unsettling, as my heart belonged to Ben.

"Only momentarily. You'll come around to my charm." He led me towards the dance floor where I could see Kate and Mazdon were still dancing.

"I don't think I'll live that long."

He smiled as he pulled me into a romantic sway on the dance floor. "I think I've come to like you, Cadet Coraly, not only for your magic but for your wit and enjoyable company."

"Let me off the blackmail kiss commitment and we can see how real our relationship can get."

"Tempting offer, but it's too soon to sever my hold on you now. You must get used to me first. Have faith in me."

"Faith," I snorted. "King Emille must have a lot of faith in you not rebelling against him, as he hasn't restrained you."

"No army of his could restrain me. If I had wanted to be the king, I would have."

"Interesting. So, General Denor, for someone with almighty powers, what do you want?" Purposely, I let my hand stray from his shoulder to stroke at his neck; the sheep teasing the wolf.

The arm he held around my back tightened. "I haven't figured that out yet. I'm just enjoying life."

My breath landed on his mouth as I seductively pushed my lips close to his. "That sounds like an empty life."

He seemed to want intimacy with me yet wasn't falling for my false allure. He grinned, looking deep into my eyes. "Maybe I need some children to fill my life with joy."

Our children, who had been in the image he had put in my head at the tenth challenge, surfaced again in my mind and they played in a courtyard with wooden soldiers outside the enormous yellow mansion here on Gaithorpe. The feeling that engulfed me was as if I had lived the life he had created for me for years, and it felt like home and happiness.

This time, he didn't hold me in the dream but let me shake it off.

"If you're so almighty, and have no agenda to busy yourself with, why don't you use your magic to end the war in the north?"

"That's above your pay grade, Cadet," he warned. "If you press me on that, I'm going to have to remove that piece of information from your mind and make you think of chocolate instead." He twirled me a half turn around and picked a handful of chocolate nibbles off a tray from a passing servant.

"You cannot sit idle whilst so many…Oh, look at those gorgeous chocolates." The general pushed a chocolate the shape of a heart into my mouth.

Oh, that's so good. The flavour was rich yet milky with a hint of strawberry.

Denor twirled me to the centre of the dance floor that was rather cramped now, but we found a space next to Kate and Mazdon.

"You're not a shabby dancer," I admitted.

"I keep impressing you. Good." His gaze fell to my lips. "And this is when you make good on our deal."

I sighed. "Please, don't show King Blackbone this."

"Oh shit, I forgot to stop the other vision."

"You forgot? Wallan!" I gawked at him, halting our swaying dance.

"So, that's what I've to do for you to call me by my first name?"

I punched his shoulder, hoping it'd hurt him more than it hurt my hand. "How is Ben doing? Is he hurting?"

He only chuckled and pressed me tighter to him. "I should've thought of showing him when King Emille gave you the death sentence. That would have got him even more worked up. Although, I think I've given Camp Leader Nar enough work using her air bending to push away the death clouds King Blackbone has been spewing out."

"Why are you tormenting him? And don't say it's purely for your own amusement."

He twirled me around under his arm and clasped me firmly around my back once more to be close to him. "Because he has what I want."

"So, if I pledged my loyalty to you, you'd stop bothering him?"

"Definitely."

"Well, I won't ever do that, so out with your lips so we can get this over and done with." My stomach twisted as I thought of kissing him, and my chest heated with agony as I saw the ignited hunger in his eyes.

"If you don't mind, I'd like to lead it, and you just make sure you put in the effort into this little show."

"You remember I said this will hurt, right? Because of the oath I've made to Duke Hartmore."

"Yes. I remember. Do you remember, I said I'd turn my pain channels off?" His tongue flicked out to wet his lips. "I believe everyone is watching us now. Time's up."

He removed his hand from mine and pushed it up my neck, cupping the side of my face with his palm, pressing me towards him until our mouth joined. His tongue licked over my bottom lip, then the top, before it entered my mouth and caressed over my tongue.

The oath stung, warning us of this prohibition, and the magical shocks stunned more potently after each second.

"Dammit!" Denor swore, as he broke the kiss clearly sooner than he'd have wanted. "I couldn't manipulate that type of magic. What oath from the Underworld have they put on you?"

"Upset that you're not in control, General?" I leered at him and took his hand to carry on dancing to avoid more of a scene than we'd already caused.

"Don't be so smug, or I'll make you beg me to fuck you tonight."

But his threat was in vain. This was my victory. "You can't. Ben says it hurts the cock like it's about to fall off."

"We've to find a cure to that oath," he muttered, and I assumed his pride was hurt as he tore himself away from me and left me standing alone on the dance floor. But it wasn't long before Emroyce grabbed hold of me and swept me around gracefully.

"Are you okay, Angie?"

"Yes. Now the score is settled for Robin. But I don't think the general is pleased with the result, so we should get out of here as soon as possible."

76

After ten days away from Ben, I was dying to see him again. Nesso had been scouting overhead among some lingering death-clouds from Ben's outbursts, so when crossing over the front courtyard, it was no surprise that Ben sprinted out of the doors towards me. He was wearing his black combat leathers and looked clammy, so I assumed he had deserted a sparring session.

His arms found their home around me and squeezed so tightly, I couldn't breathe.

He nuzzled his nose into the crook of my neck, his black hair and beard tickling over my cheek. "You're alive." The words were said to settle his own anxiety.

"For now," I wheezed from compressed lungs.

He released me and cupped my cheeks with his large palms; his eyes glazing over with a layer of watery sheen. "I thought… I really thought you'd…died."

I pressed my hand against the one he cupped over my cheek. "Whatever the general showed you, the images were all lies. I'm safe and I love you. Only you."

He grinned his charming challenge-smile and glanced around the courtyard. "I'm allowed to kiss you on our summer break, right?"

The others had already gone inside, so we were alone, although many could be watching.

"Yes, but not on the outpost premises."

"Fuck it. I don't care." His fingers dug further into my hair, and he devoured my mouth with such passion it numbed my legs, and caused a potent tingling sensation to run up my thigh and over my sex. The pleasure was mixed with the warning pain from the oath, but I didn't let it beat me.

"Cadet Coraly!" Harvey shouted from the door.

Ben grunted and broke the kiss. "Your damned brother."

Harvey came to our side. "I'm glad to see you back safely. Summer break has started so Zayd, Kate, Mazdon and I will go with you to our cottages. We leave within the hour so–"

"Within the hour? Harvey, I'm exhausted from the journey. Let me sleep here tonight and we can leave tomorrow morning."

"We should leave as soon as possible, as my time is limited. I can't be away from the outpost for too long. I've promised Captain La Roy to be back within a fortnight, and I insist you must visit Uncle Teddy for the rest of the summer to get away from the outpost for a while."

"You have an Uncle Teddy?" Ben asked me, confused. "I thought you had no other family than your brother." The grip he held around me went slack, so I was completely grounded again.

I cringed. "Yeah, he's...eccentric and lives in the wilderness. Not really soldier material."

Ben was frowning low, and he looked kind of angry about it. "How did I not know about this?"

I shrugged my shoulders. It wasn't as if I was going to leave the Bensguard Outpost to live with my crazy uncle in the middle of nowhere. I was an agent; born and bred.

Ben's arms flung in sharp movements in front of my face as he spoke, clearly enraged. "You could have avoided the outpost and lived with him in safety."

"I told her so," Harvey interjected. "Not that it's any of your business, King Blackbone. Angie, go and pack...and not any rocks. Make sure you eat lunch before we go."

Ben's arm shot out and his hand gripped over Harvey's throat. My eyes flung wide open, adrenaline pumping fast even though I thought I had none left after the long journey.

"I'm coming with you, and you'll restore the soul bond between Angelica and me, and I'll take the consequences with that decision. I'm not separating from her again after the torture of the ball in Gaithorpe." He pulled Harvey closer to his face, who grabbed at Ben's hand, trying to pry it off. Black smoke billowed from his hand. "That is not a request." Then he tossed Harvey backwards.

Harvey didn't look frightened, but he was gasping for air and rubbing at his throat. "I can't have Angie out of my sight or running away to the Black Wing Territory. The best I can do is to link you to her, but you two must be bonded to me as well."

"Make it happen," Ben barked, and took my hand, leading me to the infirmary, where he found Mewer.

The orders Ben shouted at Mewer were no more lenient than how he had spoken to Harvey. I didn't like it. Mewer was the nicest person I knew.

He didn't deserve to be in the middle of my drama.

Mewer seemed unfazed about the black-wing king's outburst and continued brewing himself a cup of coffee and gulping it down before Harvey entered. The healer looked pale and spent, so I sneaked out the light crystal from the backpack and tucked it into my bra to help his magic. Mewer signalled for us to join hands, and he pressed his own around both connections and the humming in my ears began like a second rhythm of my heart. *Home.* After a moment, Mewer let go and looked at us to confirm the links.

I glanced at the man I was prepared to do anything for. *"Ben?"*

His eyes glowed with satisfaction. *"There you are, my love."*

Harvey threw a resigned gesture in the air with his hands. *"Uh, guys. Keep this line quiet when you can. And King Blackbone, if you shield the active thoughts out, I'll exclude Angie from this connection."*

Ben embraced me until I disappeared inside his frame. "I love you so damned much. Finally, I feel whole again."

"When I said you shouldn't think it, I didn't mean I wanted you to express it out loud," Harvey muttered, but both I and Harvey had received the burst of admiration Ben held for me through the bond, and Harvey had been more convinced about Ben's feelings being genuine.

"Mewer," I said, turning towards him. "I've your herb book to return. I'll be back in a second."

"No, I told you that you could keep it for the next two years. You'll need it. Give it back to me when you graduate."

"Thank you."

"My pleasure, Cadet Coraly. Now, please stay out of trouble for the rest of the summer."

"I'll think about it," I chuckled, and winked at him.

We left the infirmary and as we split up, Harvey reminded us of the departure schedule and to meet them at the front of the building within the hour.

When we arrived in the dorm room, I made it a point of walking in after Ben and closed the door, leaning my back against it after having tossed the backpack on the floor.

"Harvey accepted that you join our hike to the cottage, but I haven't agreed."

Ben ceased packing a backpack with his clothes and turned around, looking at me, puzzled. "You don't want me to come? Miss Stone, what's going on? What did the general do to you this time?"

The shield I put up in my mind was the strongest I had ever forged, and I ensured it was fortified at its maximum. There was a lot at stake. I crossed my arms in front of my chest to feel as shielded as possible, as I needed all my strength for this conversation.

"Ah," Ben scoffed. "I see what this is. Negotiation?" He sat the bag down onto the bed disturbingly gently and closed the gap between us with his charming challenge-smirk on his face.

One of his palms thumped to press flat against the door, right above my head, and he moved in closer to frame me in. Stroking my hair that lay across my shoulder, he twirled a blue strand around his finger, playing with it beside my breast. Was this his way of intimidating me in this power-battle-situation? "What are your terms, my queen?" His voice was dark, dangerous.

I tipped my head up, and up, to look into his eyes where his face towered over mine. "You can come with me to the cottage if you spare Nesso's life, otherwise you can stay in the dungeon all summer."

He grunted darkly. "That is a bluff, and you know it, as you've already bothered Camp Leader Mewer to connect our bonds. And I'll just follow you, whether or not you forbid it."

Shit! I had nothing else to bargain with. He had that tough king resolve going on that was rather intimidating. I'd have to learn how to work around that if I was ever supposed to become his…queen. That's it. Queen.

"I claim Nesso as my own personal spy. A queen's personal servant. You can't dismiss or execute your queen's servant. Those are your laws, right? And don't you dare argue that I'm not your queen yet and open a whole new argument between us." I did my darned best to keep a queen's resolve in my stare.

He grunted.

Staring. Thinking.

Ha! He didn't have a comeback to that!

Finally, he sighed. "Okay. As you wish, my queen. Nesso will be your responsibility from now on. You'll have to source his very rare and expensive medicine for wing rot, comfort him when he has nightmares about living on the streets and keep his room free from cockroaches. You'll care for his education, get him out of trouble when his mouth has been too big and his body smaller than his opponent, and you'll ensure he doesn't leak any further information that can jeopardise the safety of the Black Wing Territory. And if he does, and the dukes and lords hear of it and demand his execution, you'll give the order."

My bravery faltered briefly. Being queen didn't sound so peachy after all.

I frowned. "Nesso has wing rot?"

"Uh huh."

"But he's such a fast and excellent flyer."

"He gets medicine, and I've trained him."

Ben couldn't think that these things were an issue. I wasn't hesitating, just being curious. I straightened quickly. "I agree."

"You just got yourself a spy, Queen Blackbone."

The tension was killing me, not to mention my longing for him from the many days apart. I wrapped my arms around his neck. "Let's seal our agreement with a kiss."

Ben's hands were around my arse so fast, my brain wobbled as he picked me up onto his hips, and I hooked my ankles behind his back. He shoved me against the door as he claimed my mouth with ravenous hunger. The oath immediately pricked my lips in warning. One of his hands stayed on my arse whilst the other clasped the back of my neck to push us tighter together and deepen the kiss.

But then Ben growled out in anger. "I want more of you, but this damned oath is in the way!" He let go of my neck and slammed a palm against the door. "Fuck!"

I palmed his cheek and turned it so I could look into his eyes. "What's wrong?"

"I love you so damned much. I can't find anyone who can break the oath. How can I ever be enough for you if I can't please you more than with kisses?"

"It's enough. You're enough. More than enough."

He sighed. "Ten days apart was too long."

"I agree."

"Don't do that to me ever again." He watched my face with that look of worship in his eyes. "Your shield is impressive, by the way. Your brother is asking if we're getting ready."

Ben dropped me to the floor and finished packing, then he took my hand and led me up the stairs to the leadership floor. In the apartment, I showered, changed into flight leathers, ate, and packed the rest that I wanted to bring before we met with Harvey, Zayd, Kate and Mazdon at the front of the building.

I walked up to Nesso where the four black-wings stood leaning against the façade to see us off.

"I negotiated with King Blackbone, and so you know, you're the queen's spy from now on. I expect you to stay out of trouble until I get back. And to spy some juicy gossip for me."

It was the first time I had seen Nesso lost for words before he calmly embraced me, and whispered into my ear, "Thank you for saving my life."

I had never experienced Nesso this cool-headed and serene; not even one distasteful joke, so I guessed my act really must have meant something to him. He let go of me and ceremoniously fell onto one knee. "I'll serve you well, my queen."

There seemed to be so much more weight behind his words than what had simply unfolded today. A deeper meaning to his affection that I couldn't interpret. Like the connection we had made was as strong and sacred as those made between people from the same blood. Loyal and unbreakable.

"Oh," I looked around and saw Ben glower at Nesso, who didn't see Ben, as Nesso was looking at my boots. "Okay," I muttered. "So serious. Just be yourself. Get up. I'm still just me."

Nesso stood up and shook his head. "No. Not just you. You're the most important person in this world. A Spirit."

"Okay, whatever, guys!" I caught everyone's attention, even Commander Daffron's, as I waved at the black-wings, who had all been bonded to Tomason, as we left the outpost. "See you after the summer break. Stay out of trouble!"

We hiked east, through the dense forest and the commonly known hunting area, and as soon as the Bensguard Outpost was out of sight, Ben smiled at me.

"I can't wait to see the cottage you've been talking so much about," Ben whispered into my ear as we sauntered next to one another along the narrow bridleway.

"And you remembered what you promised me? On the table?" I asked, too shy to look at him.

"I do. I rarely forget things. Especially not things as important as that."

"Maybe we should speed up this hike. I can't wait to get there."

"This tempo is fine. You must be exhausted from the day's hardships already."

"I am. And the leisurely stroll is nice."

The weather was pleasant, if not a tad hot.

Ben kept looking up at the sun and around in the trees. "The birds aren't chirping," he said, frowning suspiciously.

Our hands laced together, and I never wanted to let go of him again. I could understand what Ben meant when he said it felt like he was only half a person when we weren't together. I needed to be around him and preferably touching him.

"You're mine," I told him with unwavering resolve.

"And here I thought you were mine."

"No. You're definitely mine and I'm the boss."

"You can be the boss. I love you."

Harvey looked over his shoulder. "Can both of you keep your thoughts to yourselves?"

"If you don't want to hear them, get out of our soul bond," Ben teased, his voice light.

The forest around us was green, the towering trees pressing in like silent watchers. The undergrowth was slick with recent rain, and the scent, a crisp bite of pine. Shadows twisted between the trunks, stretching long despite the midday sun, as if the forest itself held its breath.

Then. A sound.

A gurgling, grotesque noise slithered through the trees, carried on the wind like a whisper from something unseen. It was wet, unnatural, and growing louder. Closer.

Ben reacted instantly, his easy demeanour vanishing in an instant. He ripped the dagger from my leg strap, the silver blade flashing in the fractured light, and shoved me backward. "What the fuck!" His voice was edged with something rare. Fear.

Harvey's head snapped toward the sound. His eyes darkened with recognition, his grip tightening around the hilts of his daggers as he ripped them free from the straps on his orange combat leathers. He rushed to my side, his stance low, and braced for a fight.

Mazdon stepped in front of Kate, his sword unsheathed in one fluid motion, his broad frame shielding her from whatever was about to emerge from the forest. Zayd pulled his twin swords from his baldric, the metal clinking, his expression stone-cold.

The forest trembled, the trees groaning as if something massive was pushing through them. The gurgling grew into a louder, guttural, choking snarl.

Something was coming.

"What are they doing so far south?" Harvey asked no one in particular.

He wasn't expecting an answer, but the question hung in the air between us.

Ben stared at him, as if he had himself to blame. "Do you have any black blades with you?"

Harvey scoffed, his frustration flaring. "Of course not. We send all the black iron north, unless it's stolen!" Harvey turned towards Ben, his glare sharp enough to cut.

Ben didn't hold his glare and twisted his head nervously to monitor the tree line as we backed out into a clearing. "So," Ben murmured, voice tight, "what's your plan, Captain?"

"You're the king. What do you propose?"

Ben let out a humourless laugh, and there was no amusement in his eyes. "Oh, so now I can be the king?"

"Guys!" I shouted at them. "What's going on?"

Ben turned to me then, his gaze locking onto mine with chilling intensity. "Do you remember anything I taught you about demons?"

My stomach twisted. "Demons?"

His voice dropped, deadly serious. "The most important fact is that you can't kill them without black iron, and if they kill you, your soul is dragged straight to the Underworld."

77

I crouched quickly. The anxiety twisted around in my gut as my hand gripped the black blade knife from my boot. Thank the Spirits for the general's gift. It might be that he had once again saved my life.

Kate stopped opposite me, flicking her one thick, red braid over her shoulder. "Demons? Come on, guys. Is this a prank?"

Three dark creatures cloaked by dark-grey robes and hoods wandered aimlessly near the tree line, emitting that eerie sound.

"Let's move, guys," Zayd hissed. "They haven't seen us."

We started walking backwards, going faster and faster as we entered the clearing. I was suffering severe palpitations, my chest tightening with fear. Were these creatures really demons? None of the men appeared to be joking, and I didn't believe Ben would lie about something that involved my safety.

"I think you're still messing with us," Kate snorted, but her hands were trembling over the hilts to her daggers.

"You might as well tell her about the rift, Harvey," Zayd said, ensuring he had an eye on Kate and me.

"Quiet, Zayd," Harvey hissed under his breath.

He took Kate's hand and tried to comfort her to make her stop shaking.

"Tell her the truth, or I'll do it. Angie and Kate deserve to know if we're about to fight them." Zayd could be so familiar with Harvey, questioning his orders like no one else dared, something only years of friendship could build up.

"No, you'll put her in danger when she's near the generals," Ben growled at Harvey.

Making sure I held the black blade up to be ready for an attack, I backed closer to Ben. "The generals know everything, anyway. They both assessed me during the ball."

"Damn," Harvey cursed.

The sun was setting towards the back of the forest and the shadows cast from the trees were reaching the clearing. The demons seemed to keep to the shadows, so I urged Ben to edge himself further towards the end of the clearing where the grass field was still hit by sunlight.

Ben took my free hand to know where he had me, keeping his eyes on the demons. "There is a rift in the north of my lands," Ben started. "It's a portal opened from the Underworld to Skyberg, and demons are crawling out of it, claiming the living as they kill them. The Demon King is building an empire to take over all three realms."

"Spirits! And you don't think that is information I should know?" I glanced at my brother, but no one returned my gazes as they were all focused on the three cloaked creatures mindlessly rummaging over the grass in our direction.

"In the capacity of being king of the black-wings, I've asked for aid from the white-wings, but they refuse to give it, saying that the problem isn't on their land. The leaders of the white-wings believe that if you knew, you'd join our side rather than be loyal to theirs."

Gobsmacked, I blinked as I took in the information. "Winged people are bickering about who does what when demons run amok through the world of the living?"

"Men!" Kate scoffed. "Women should rule the world, I've always said."

The three demons sniffed at the air. Simultaneously, their heads snapped in our direction.

Shit, that was ominous.

Ben tightened his grip on my hand and pulled me forwards.

I stumbled after him, almost falling over rocks, my mind somewhere else. "So, you never ordered your soldiers to attack the white-wings?"

Ben grunted. "Of course not. My black-wing soldiers were never in the White Wing Territory. It was the demons crossing over and attacking those villages in Pharanir. King Emille ordered leadership to blame it on me."

My fear grew at the same rate as my rage. "Harvey! How could you!"

"Angie, we can discuss politics later. The priority right now is to survive."

The wet gurgling sound the demons produced amplified, and they pulled daggers from their belts that sparkled with a blue charge and danced around the blade like a flickering flame. *Great! They have blades, too!*

At first, they crept closer to us, and the air felt so ominous the hair at the back of my neck rose. Then they began jogging towards us, and the panic built up in my chest the closer they got. The men shouted commands and ushered me and Kate along the path when the demons were in a full out run towards us.

"Run!" Ben shouted, pushing me forwards even harder, and I leapt over rocks and stones in my way, struggling not to fall.

"Run? Where?" The knife slipped from my grasp, and I skid to a stop, scrambling to pick it up.

Ben came back for me, hauling me forwards by clamping both hands onto my waist. "Let's go!"

In shock, I paused for a moment and saw their grotesque faces inside their hoods, like rotting fabric falling off them in pieces. Their white eyes were staring at you, but not really seeing you.

"What happens if you stab them with a normal blade?" Kate asked.

"Nothing," Mazdon answered. "They don't feel it and just keep going."

Kate was falling behind. "Surely, if you sever their heads, they must be incapacitated?"

"No, their head sort of stays attached to their shoulders by magic and settles back on their bodies. I've tried," Mazdon explained as he sprinted forwards while Harvey waited for Kate to run alongside her.

"You've fought these creatures before?" Kate gasped at her brother.

"I served in the Air Force for a year before going back to the academy, Kate. I fought in the north. Remember?"

"Maybe Kate can flash them her rude finger," Ben whispered to me, but I had no capacity to spare a smile at the internal joke now.

"A little less talking and a bit more running," Harvey shouted, as we darted along the bridleway, crossing over the clearing with the demons perusing us.

"I have a stitch, okay?" Kate spat at him but kept running.

"We can't turn up to the Pharoon City and lead the demons there. We can't keep running forever, either," I bellowed to my brother. "There must be a way of scaring them off."

"They're persistent bastards," he replied without stopping. "Can you fly? They can't reach us in the air."

"I've got her readiness down to seven seconds," Ben replied. "But she can't bring her wings out whilst running, and if we stop for that long, the demons will be upon us. Bringing them out only gives the demons a chance to hack them off."

Ben shot me a look, implying that this was a good example as to why I should've practised more. I shook the rebuke off. I had thought there were two more years to practise before I went to war. He should've told me about the demons sooner. I couldn't have known I'd have to face them today, could I!

"Even if we could hold off the demons to get her airborne," Mazdon added. "After this morning's long flight, I doubt she and Kate could be in the air for very long before their wings cramp. The demons will just find us further down the road. As you said, they're persistent bastards."

"Stop squabbling and keep fucking running!" Zayd shouted.

I pushed my legs harder, but I was still so baffled by all this.

Demons were real?

No! It couldn't be true. They were fairytales to scare children into obedience.

"Were all the things you told me about demons true then?" I asked Ben, looking over my shoulder, seeing the demons gaining on us. They were bloody fast and sweat beads formed at my hairline and at my neck from the exertion. The bloody sun beaming down on us didn't help, either.

"Yes. General Denor forbade me from telling you about them. If I did, King Emille would come for you and send you to the war, so I tried to teach you about them without telling you they existed."

"I could have kept it secret."

"From General Denor?"

Perhaps not.

Shit.

"Can you run faster, love? The demons are on our heels," Ben breathed.

But where were we running to? Today wasn't even a murky day where we might get away with hiding in the shadows under the trees. There was only forest ahead for another half a day's hike before we reached the City of Kansgo. That's where we usually stopped to sleep the first night when hiking to the cottage in the summer. How in the world would we shake three death-eating demons before we reached the city?

I tried to go over all the information Ben had ever told me.

Demons are not merciful.

Demons infect you by mere touch.

What did that mean? Infect you with death?

Demons have no wings.

Demons swing hard, but before thinking or aiming.

Demons' saliva is poisonous.

Again. What did that mean? Was it deadly to touch?

Demons don't like the cold.

Demons like it pitch dark and can't stand the light.

A light crystal, when charged, repels demons or other evil magic within two metres of it.

That was it! I had a light crystal in my bra, although I hadn't had the opportunity to charge it fully. I also had a black blade knife. I had to turn around and fight them, or my friends would die. I skidded to a halt in the grass and colourful wildflowers. The beauty of the scenery was about to be destroyed by the death and darkness of demons.

"What are you doing?" Ben shouted and returned to my side.

I kept a hand on his chest to steady myself. "Does your death magic work on them?"

"No!" He pushed at the small of my back. "Because they're already dead."

I nodded, sensing this was goodbye, but I still couldn't say it. "Then I suggest you run! I'll fight them off."

"I'm not leaving you." He tugged hard at my arm, but I snatched it free.

I was so scared, I trembled as I brought out the crystal from my bra and squeezed it in my hand. "I have a light crystal and a black blade. I'm our best bet."

"Then give the items to me, and I'll fight them off while you run."

I frowned angrily at him. "No! Run!"

"Miss Stone, you're being unreasonable."

"And you make up your own rules. But in this situation, you can't make up your own rules as king. Law always dictates that the king needs to be protected from harm by his soldiers, and that isn't going to change today."

"Law also dictates that you must protect your wife and your family at all costs. You just negotiated with me from a standpoint of being my queen."

The gurgling sound from the demons' throats grew louder.

"Stop arguing. I can't lose you. Your kingdom can't lose you. The demons are getting too close. Please! Run!"

"No!"

The blood inside my veins raced around my body so fast, I felt the flush of heat and panic. Hysteria gripped over my lungs and tightened it so hard I couldn't breathe. "You told me I could be the boss. The boss says run!"

"Your boss privileges have just been revoked."

Harvey joined our side. "What are you guys doing?"

"Apparently, we're all staying and fighting," I spat.

We all discarded our packs and got ready to fight.

Kate held her hands up and a blast of fire ejected from her palms towards the first demon.

"No!" Ben screamed, but it was too late. The robe and the fabric-looking skin disintegrated from the fire until the demon looked like walking blue bones and veins of black death that slithered around them to fade at the edges as they moved forward. "They're not affected by the fire, and it'll only become more angered."

And more fucking terrifying-looking! I held up my black blade knife, and as the first demon charged at us, we split up, and I focused on the first scary-as-hell-looking demon. Harvey and Ben engaged in combat with a demon each.

My demon hesitated at first, clearly finding it hard to come close to me, and I assumed I had the light crystal to thank for that.

The crystal's glow flickered, its energy sputtering like a dying flame. The ward trembled under the demon's sheer force, making cracks of dull light splinter across its surface as it failed to hold him back. With a guttural snarl, he tore through the ward, his form a shifting mass of shadows wrapped around a skeletal frame. His blade, shimmering with an eerie blue essence, cut through the air in a deadly arc, aiming straight for my neck.

I dropped low just in time, the wind from the strike whipping past my head. I drove my black blade into the demon's back with a brutal thrust. The moment the iron pierced him, his body convulsed, and he released an unearthly screech. I wrenched the blade free, bracing for another attack, but there was none.

The demon's form crumbled. His bones cracking apart like shattered glass, and his essence unravelling into dark wisps. The shadows writhed, curling in on themselves before disintegrating into ash, swirling briefly before settling like soot on my boots.

That's utterly disgusting.

An acrid stench rose with the smoke, smelling of a pungent mix of decay, like a graveyard left open to the elements. It clung to the air, making my stomach turn. This was the scent of death. The kind that lingered long after the body was gone.

I looked up. The fight wasn't over. "Move Harvey! Help Ben!" I pushed at my brother's shoulder, who reluctantly took a few steps to the side.

The demon lunged, slicing its dagger toward my stomach. I twisted in time, the cold iron barely missing me, slicing through the fabric of my leather jacket. But before I could react, the creature wrenched its arm back and swung a brutal, iron-clad forearm against my brow. Stars exploded in my vision. Pain cracked through my skull. My knees buckled, and the ground lurched up to meet me.

"Don't let his skin touch yours!" Ben's voice cut through the chaos, as he slashed at his own demon, my dagger flashing in his grip.

I had no time to process the warning before a boot slammed into my ribs. The impact sent me rolling, and the air fleeing my lungs. I clawed at the dirt, trying to right myself, but another vicious kick cracked against my temple. My head snapped sideways, white-hot agony flaring through my skull. My lip split open, the taste of iron flooding my mouth.

Blood dripped onto the trampled grass as I forced myself up, staggering away from the demon stalking towards me. That guttural, wet gurgle rose from its throat. Desperate, I crouched low, kicking out at the back of its knees. The creature buckled with a snarl, but its clawed hands shot out, latching onto my legs. I crashed down on top of it.

"Captain!" Ben bellowed, still locked in his fight. "Angelica needs help!"

The demon thrashed beneath me, its strength overwhelming. I grabbed onto its tattered clothing and drove my knife between its ribs. The black blade sank deep. The creature let out a strangled cry before its body crumbled into a pile of foul-smelling ash.

Yuck.

"Ben!" I shouted, and he glanced at me quickly. I threw the black blade in his direction. "Here!"

Ben rolled over the grass to fetch the knife from where it had landed and was ready to face the demon, but it turned, leaving Ben and coming for me instead. I barely had time to catch my breath, seeing empty black eyes locking onto mine, then charging, its massive frame barrelling forward like a maddened bull.

I had no black blade, no magic, only my father's dagger strapped to my leg. My pulse roared in my ears.

I was out of time.

Dammit.

The force of the impact sent me sprawling and my back slammed against the ground. Then the demon's weight crushed down on me, pinning me like a carcass beneath a starving beast. Its rancid breath beat my face, thick with the scent of something otherworldly, festering and utterly rotten.

Then came the saliva.

A large drop splattered onto my cheek, and instantly the skin beneath it ignited with a searing pain beyond anything I had ever felt. There was a sharp sizzle and then I smelled the acrid stench of burning flesh – my flesh.

My skin bubbled and peeled away beneath the corrosive spit.

I screamed, thrashing beneath the creature, trying to kick him away to get free but it was useless as he was all over me.

The demon snarled, its grotesque maw twisted into something that might have been a grin, and jagged teeth dripped with more of that infectious saliva. Then, before I could react, it struck.

A flash of cold iron.

The demon ran me through with his blue blade, plunging it deep into my abdomen, and I felt the pain as it sliced through muscle and sinew like wet paper. My body arched violently as fire erupted in my gut, the agony so absolute that my vision flickered in and out of focus. The slick warmth of my own blood spilled down my sides and pooled beneath me in the dirt.

The demon didn't stop.

With a guttural growl, it wrenched the blade upward, sawing through my insides. He continued to ruthlessly carve a path through my body. I felt the hard iron tear through me, splitting my flesh and scraping against bone. The pain so overwhelming that my body spasmed violently, sending my limbs twitching in helpless protest.

The world blurred. Colours bled into one another at the sensation of my own body being torn apart.

This was it.

The Spirit of Death would come for me now.

A shadow loomed at the edges of my mind, dark and infinite. The veil between life, and whatever lay beyond it, was thinning.

But something inside me refused to let go. I drew my father's blade, feeling the familiarity of the runes on the hilt and stabbed its blade deep into the demon.

The weight of the demon vanished, and possibly the weight of my own body, too. I saw darkness hovering over my face, but they were nothing more than shadows. Had the Demon King come to claim my soul? Was I dead? I felt darkness like a venomous snake slithering inside me, infecting all of my organs. I couldn't survive this. The infection painfully ate at my insides and although I wanted to cry out, there was no sound. I had no control over my body.

Two shadow silhouettes appeared above my head.

"Captain. You know who is the only magic healer powerful enough to have a chance at healing this. It's not only the blood loss. She's infected," Ben said, the panic was there in his voice, ready to consume him.

"No," Harvey snapped.

"She will die otherwise. I'm not really asking for your permission. Her dying, isn't an option for me." Two muscular arms nestled underneath me and lifted me up, my legs and head dangling down.

"I'll have to come with you as we're bonded," Harvey muttered.

"Since it's saving your sister's life, I thought the choice would be easy."

"Nothing is easy. She'll hate us both forever. No matter what happens, we'll lose her."

I couldn't open my eyes yet, but I was conscious. The weakness in my body hindered me from making any movements. This made it difficult to determine whether I was dead or alive.

"You detest me, and you'll do everything in your power to distance yourself from the black-wings. You've made that point very clear." Ben roared a short distance away from me. "Captain, you need to understand that my feelings for Angelica are genuine."

In the blurred visions of shadows and dark silhouettes, I made my best effort to pry my eyes open. I could make out something like an arm flailing out toward me. "If she dies–"

"I paired you with my sister at the outpost because you're the strongest person in the camp and can keep her alive. But there is where your usefulness ends. Cut your fucking emotions off!" Harvey roared back with the same calibre.

"I'm not you!" Ben shouted, the voice guttural and dark. "I can't just shut off my love for her. Or I bloody would have done it the day I knew I had fallen for her."

"If I hear that you get any closer to her, I'll pair her up with someone else, who won't be as good as you to protect her. Am I making myself clear?"

My head hurt as chair legs scraped over the floor. A warm hand took mine. I recognised it. Callous, muscular, large…mine. Ben held my hand, stroking his thumb over the back of it. I relaxed on the pillow and took a deep breath. I was alive.

"Where am I?" Not that it mattered. Ben was right here next to me.

"You're in the infirmary in Black Castle."

"Kate…Maz…Zay–"

"Everyone is okay. The others continued to your summer cottage and your brother is here. Only you, my brave warrior, got the brunt of it."

A nurse poked with her fingers over my stomach where the demon blade had cut me open, and it was sore still. But I was alive.

"How bad is it?"

"You'll live and are as beautiful as ever, my love."

"Stop that bullshit!" Harvey bellowed. "She's infected by a demon's touch, and we still don't know if she'll survive this! She's a soldier. Not a damsel in distress."

"She's my everything, Captain Coraly!"

"Talk like that, and I'll leave you here and not allow you into the White Wing Territory again."

The nurse's hand cupped my cheek, her palm warm against my fevered skin, then moved to my forehead, checking my temperature with a touch so achingly familiar it sent a shiver through me. When her gentle fingers strayed over my cut brow, I flinched slightly, but it wasn't from pain, it was from something else entirely. A feeling creeping into my bones, one that whispered something impossible.

Then she spoke.

"Boys, if you're going to fight, take it outside. Angelica deserves the rest."

The voice hit me like a hammer to the chest.

My blood turned to ice. My lungs seized mid-breath. No. It couldn't be. It wasn't possible. The world tilted, the air around me growing suddenly too thick to breathe. That voice… I knew that voice. I had known it my entire life, had clung to its warmth as a child, had dreamt of it through nights of grief-ridden sleep.

But she was dead.

Harvey had killed her. I had felt the loss clawing through me for five long, agonising years.

I pried my eyes open with an iron will, my pulse thundering in my ears as I forced my vision to clear. My body felt frozen in time, every muscle locked in terrified anticipation as my gaze slowly lifted until I met her eyes.

Blue.

I saw the same shade of blue I remembered staring into as a child. It was the same soft gaze that had soothed my nightmares and bandaged my wounds.

Wrinkles lined the corners of her eyes, and strands of grey threaded through the dark hair that draped down her shoulders. She had aged, changed…but there was no mistaking her.

She smiled at me, just as she used to when she comforted me in the dark after having checked for monsters under my bed.

A sob wrenched through my chest. My heart pounded so hard it hurt. My fingers trembled, curling around the sheet, as if trying to grip onto reality.

This wasn't a dream.

This wasn't a ghost.

She was here. She was real.

Tears blurred my vision, but I didn't blink them away. I couldn't move, couldn't breathe, couldn't believe what was right in front of me. The grief I had carried for years, the pain of her loss, and the sleepless nights I had spent whispering to the void hurt twice over.

Had all of it been for nothing?

Had she been alive all this time?

Was it really her?

All my insides trembled, and it felt as if my very soul was shaking, witnessing the impossible. My voice cracked, barely more than a whisper, as I forced the word past my lips.

"Mum?"

ABOUT THE AUTHOR

MBA graduate and ACCA member T. M. Caruana lives in Gibraltar, where she consumes too much coffee and chocolate, but finds it to be just the fuel she needs to pursue her passions. T. M. Caruana is best known for her paranormal romance and romantic fantasy quests filled with dragons and wolf shifters, but also many more otherworldly creatures. If you like to travel through portals to other worlds, imagine casting spells, or retrieve magical artefacts among the pages of fiction, then you'll love T. M. Caruana's imaginative stories. You will fall in love with her witty and bantering characters, where enemies to lovers struggle to overcome forbidden love in lands where the sky is not the limit, and magic will make you question what is real.

Your life is your dream,
-if you can dream it, you can live it-

Dear Sophia,

I hope you enjoy the story!

your life is your dream,
if you can dream it,
you can live it!

[illegible]

Printed by Amazon Italia Logistica S.r.l.
Torrazza Piemonte (TO), Italy

76015291R00459